From These Ashes

The Complete Short SF of Fredric Brown

Edited by Ben Yalow

The NESFA Press
Post Office Box 809
Framingham, MA 01701

FIRST EDITION

International Standard Book Number 1-886778-18-3

FOURTH PRINTING   JUNE 2011

NESFA® is a registered trademark of the New England Science Fiction Association, Inc.

Table of Contents

Introduction

A reserved little guy, made a living on the linotype machine (read "Etaoin Shrdlu") in Wisconsin before he became a fulltime writer, drank too much, virtually every male writer (and many women too) of his time did, dealt with writer's block by riding Greyhound buses through the continent, just booking a couple of weeks, sat in the back of the bus, the shadows and night tableland whisking by, his unconscious off its leash. Offered to teach one of his two sons everything he knew about the writing of fiction, give him a full-time, exclusive course of instruction. His son declined. (A wise choice.) Said to Phil Klass around the time that *What Mad Universe*, that great and sour fan novel, was published, "They're taking over, Phil." This was in 1948. "The fans, they want in, they want to write it and edit it, they're going to overwhelm us, they'll own it all in twenty years. There's nothing we can do to change it." *What Mad Universe*, of course, dumps its protagonist into the structured fantasies of a science fiction fan, takes the lead through alien landscape and plenty of trouble. Talk about projection fantasies! But Brown was a personable and understated guy, stayed away from the conventions and the social rubric generally, didn't have much to do with anyone outside the group of Milwaukee writers from which he had emerged and later a few of the Mexican expatriates like Mack Reynolds, with whom he occasionally collaborated. Not exactly a recluse but certainly an iconoclast and among a small group of prominent science fiction writers of whom there is little personal detail.

Those are a few random facts about Fred Brown (1906-1972); he remains, interestingly, perhaps the only writer I can bring to mind of equal prominence in mystery and science fiction. Many science fiction writers have written mysteries (beginning with Isaac Asimov and Harry Harrison) and many mystery writers have written science fiction (Bill Pronzini, Larry Block, Donald E. Westlake, Evan Hunter) but their reputation, most significant accomplishment, level of recognition lie clearly in one field or the other. Brown is the exception. His first novel, *The Fabulous Clipjoint*, won an early (1947) Edgar for best first mystery novel and he published more than a dozen in the genre, some highly regarded; *What Mad Universe*, "Arena," *Martians Go Home* (a poor movie only a couple of years ago) are important science fiction novels. Brown published stories other than "Arena" which were famous—"The Waveries," *Martians Go Home* in a shorter version, "Placet Is a Crazy Place," "Letter To a Phoenix"— and is generally regarded as the best short-short story writer in the history of science fiction; his mastery of the vignette was absolute and there are tiny pieces like "The Weapon" or "The Solipsist" whose plots and payoff seem known to everyone, whether or not the author can be attributed. (Most famous of all, of course, that 200-word story in which the new computer addresses the question: "Is there a God?" with a bolt of lightning fusing its off-switch closed and the pronouncement, "Now there is!" Validating my statement, I don't remember the title, it's in one of these collections, of course, and I don't have to look it up in Contento to assure one and all that I've remembered this story for more than forty years ... that story and "The Weapon" are probably the two Great Warning science fiction stories.) (Parentheses after a parenthesis: the title is "Answer.")

That Brown was equally effective, equally prominent in two genres as to be ultimately unclassifiable as a prime practitioner in one or the other is a powerfully interesting, salient fact; it makes his work and his contribution probably unduplicable, certainly incalculable. Like almost every science fiction writer of his generation, barring the five to ten most prominent, he has in the last few decades fallen almost completely out of print; his short stories have been anthologized now and again (most notably by Greenberg & Asimov in their 25-volume GREAT SF 1939-1963 series which was issued between 1979 and 1992) but the novels have not been exposed for a long time. *(What Mad Universe* was published by Bantam in the late 1970s, *Martians Go Home* by Baen in 1992, nothing since and nothing between the 70s and that Baen reissue.) *Martians Go Home* was filmed, unsuccessfully, in the mid-1990s in a version which appeared to have left the bitter, even savage treatment of its absurd premise somewhere at the post (thereby turning the story into another installment of MORK AND MINDY) and an astonishing number of the short stories have been used for student films and short subjects in foreign countries; Brown's concepts are perhaps too sardonic and depersonalized to work as drama but this opinion has never interfered with the attraction his work has always had for young film directors and screenwriters.

Like nearly all satirists, Brown was deeply embittered, no fan of humanity or human possibility; this opinion comes through in almost all the work from "Hall of Mirrors" to "Honeymoon in Hell" to "The Weapon" ("Letter To a Phoenix" is an exception; this 1949 ASF story holds that humanity may be hopeless but it is absolutely unassailable, something like Phil Klass's cosmic cockroaches in *Of Men and Monsters*) and can be noted in it purest and most frightening version in the 1949 "Come and Go Mad" about a mental patient who might in a previous existence have been Napoleon, overtaken by dreams and seizures indicating the paradox of this possibility and which ends the debate in the author's voice with those remarkable lines, "But don't you see: it doesn't matter. Nothing matters!" That couplet didn't make a great deal of sense to me when a friend put the story under my nose in 1952 but it sure does now.

Does Brown's career itself make sense? Prophet of absurdity, he had a severe heart attack in the early sixties, published no more after the tiny collaboration with Carl Onspaugh in 1965, descended into silence in Taos, New Mexico: silence with exile if not cunning. As with the rest of them, his work remains to be rediscovered; brave and noble NESFA has done what it could; now it is your responsibility. If nothing matters, then everything matters. "The Weapon" gives that hard and rigorous lesson, a lesson beyond the arena, careless of the Martians, centered within that pulverized and extinguished heart.

Barry N. Malzberg
New Jersey: April 1999

Armageddon

It happened—of all places—in Cincinnati. Not that there is anything wrong with Cincinnati, save that it is not the center of the Universe, nor even of the State of Ohio. It's a nice old town and, in its way, second to none. But even its Chamber of Commerce would admit that it lacks cosmic significance. It must have been mere coincidence that Gerber the Great—what a name!—was playing Cincinnati when things slipped elsewhere.

Of course, if the episode had become known, Cincinnati would be the most famous city of the world, and little Herbie would be hailed as a modern St. George and get more acclaim than a quiz kid. But no member of that audience in the Bijou Theater remembers a thing about it. Not even little Herbie Westerman, although he had the water pistol to show for it.

He wasn't thinking about the water pistol in his pocket as he sat looking up at the prestidigitator on the other side of the footlights. It was a new water pistol, bought en route to the theater when he'd inveigled his parents into a side trip into the five-and-dime on Vine Street, but at the moment, Herbie was much more interested in what went on upon the stage.

His expression registered qualified approval. The front-and-back palm was no mystery to Herbie. He could do it himself. True, he had to use pony-sized cards that came with his magic set and were just right for his nine-year-old hands. And true, anyone watching could see the card flutter from the front-palm position to the back as he turned his hand. But that was a detail.

He knew, though, that front-and-back palming seven cards at a time required great finger strength as well as dexterity, and that was what Gerber the Great was doing. There wasn't a telltale click in the shift, either, and Herbie nodded approbation. Then he remembered what was coming next.

He nudged his mother and said, "Ma, ask Pop if he's gotta extra handkerchief."

Out of the corner of his eyes, Herbie saw his mother turn her head and in less time than it would take to say, "Presto," Herbie was out of his seat and skinning down the aisle. It had been, he felt, a beautiful piece of misdirection and his timing had been perfect.

It was at this stage of the performance—which Herbie had seen before, alone—that Gerber the Great asked if some little boy from the audience would step to the stage. He was asking it now.

Herbie Westerman had jumped the gun. He was well in motion before the magician had asked the question. At the previous performance, he'd been a bad tenth in reaching the steps from aisle to stage. This time he'd been ready, and he hadn't taken any chances with parental restraint. Perhaps his mother would have let him go and perhaps not; it had seemed wiser to see that she was looking the other way. You couldn't trust parents on things like that. They had funny ideas sometimes.

"—will please step up on the stage?" And Herbie's foot touched the first of the steps upward right smack on the interrogation point of that sentence. He heard the disappointed scuffle of other feet behind him, and grinned smugly as he went on up across the footlights.

It was the three-pigeon trick, Herbie knew from the previous performance, that required an assistant from the audience. It was almost the only trick he hadn't been able to figure out. There *must*, he knew, have been a concealed compartment somewhere in that box, but where it could be he couldn't even guess. But this time he'd be holding the box himself. If from that range he couldn't spot the gimmick, he'd better go back to stamp collecting.

He grinned confidently up at the magician. Not that he, Herbie, would give him away. He was a magician, too, and he understood that there was a freemasonry among magicians and that one never gave away the tricks of another.

He felt a little chilled, though, and the grin faded as he caught the magician's eyes. Gerber the Great, at close range, seemed much older than he had seemed from the other side of the footlights. And somehow different. Much taller, for one thing.

Anyway, here came the box for the pigeon trick. Gerber's regular assistant was bringing it in on a tray. Herbie looked away from the magician's eyes and he felt better. He remembered, even, his reason for being on the stage. The servant limped. Herbie ducked his head to catch a glimpse of the under side of the tray, just in case. Nothing there.

Gerber took the box. The servant limped away and Herbie's eyes followed him suspiciously. Was the limp genuine or was it a piece of misdirection?

The box folded out flat as the proverbial pancake. All four sides hinged to the bottom, the top hinged to one of the sides. There were little brass catches.

Herbie took a quick step back so he could see behind it while the front was displayed to the audience. Yes, he saw it now. A triangular compartment built against one side of the lid, mirror-covered, angles calculated to achieve invisibility. Old stuff. Herbie felt a little disappointed.

The prestidigitator folded the box, mirror-concealed compartment inside. He turned slightly. "Now, my fine young man—"

What happened in Tibet wasn't the only factor; it was merely the final link of a chain.

The Tibetan weather had been unusual that week, highly unusual. It had been warm. More snow succumbed to the gentle warmth than had melted in more years than man could count. The streams ran high, they ran wide and fast.

Along the streams some prayer wheels whirled faster than they had ever whirled. Others, submerged, stopped altogether. The priests, knee-deep in the cold water, worked frantically, moving the wheels nearer to shore where again the rushing torrent would turn them.

There was one small wheel, a very old one that had revolved without cease for longer than any man knew. So long had it been there that no living lama recalled what had been inscribed upon its prayer plate, nor what had been the purpose of that prayer.

The rushing water had neared its axle when the lama Klarath reached for it to move it to safety. Just too late. His foot slid in the slippery mud and the back of his hand touched the wheel as he fell. Knocked loose from its moorings, it swirled down with the flood, rolling along the bottom of the stream, into deeper and deeper waters.

While it rolled, all was well.

The lama rose, shivering from his momentary immersion, and went after other of the spinning wheels. What, he thought, could one small wheel matter? He didn't know that—now that other links had broken—only that tiny thing stood between Earth and Armageddon.

The prayer wheel of Wangur Ul rolled on, and on, until—a mile farther down—it struck a ledge, and stopped. That was the moment.

"And now, my fine young man—"

Herbie Westerman—we're back in Cincinnati now—looked up, wondering why the prestidigitator had stopped in midsentence. He saw the face of Gerber the Great contorted as though by a great shock. Without moving, without changing, his face began to change. Without appearing different, it became different.

Quietly, then, the magician began to chuckle. In the overtones of that soft laughter was all of evil. No one who heard it could have doubted who he was. No one did doubt. The audience, every member of it, knew in that awful moment who stood before them, knew it—even the most skeptical among them—beyond shadow of doubt.

No one moved, no one spoke, none drew a shuddering breath. There are things beyond fear. Only uncertainty causes fear, and the Bijou Theater was filled, then, with a dreadful certainty.

The laughter grew. Crescendo, it reverberated into the far dusty corners of the gallery. Nothing—not a fly on the ceiling—moved.

Satan spoke.

"I thank you for your kind attention to a poor magician." He bowed, ironically low. "The performance is ended."

He smiled. "All performances are ended."

Somehow the theater seemed to darken, although the electric lights still burned. In dead silence, there seemed to be the sound of wings, leathery wings, as though invisible Things were gathering.

On the stage was a dim red radiance. From the head and from each shoulder of the tall figure of the magician there sprang a tiny flame. A naked flame.

There were other flames. They flickered along the proscenium of the stage, along the footlights. One sprang from the lid of the folded box little Herbie Westerman still held in his hands.

Herbie dropped the box.

Did I mention that Herbie Westerman was a Safety Cadet? It was purely a reflex action. A boy of nine doesn't know much about things like Armageddon, but Herbie Westerman should have known that water would never have put out that fire.

But, as I said, it was purely a reflex action. He yanked out his new water pistol and squirted it at the box of the pigeon trick. And the fire *did* vanish, even as a spray from the stream of water ricocheted and dampened the trouser leg of Gerber the Great, who had been facing the other way.

There was a sudden, brief hissing sound. The lights were growing bright again, and all the other flames were dying, and the sound of wings faded, blended into another sound—the rustling of the audience.

The eyes of the prestidigitator were closed. His voice sounded strangely strained as he said: "This much power I retain. None of you will remember this."

Then, slowly, he turned and picked up the fallen box. He held it out to Herbie Westerman. "You must be more careful, boy," he said. "Now hold it so."

He tapped the top lightly with his wand. The door fell open. Three white pigeons flew out of the box. The rustle of their wings was not leathery.

Herbie Westerman's father came down the stairs and, with a purposeful air, took his razor strop off the hook on the kitchen wall.

Mrs. Westerman looked up from stirring the soup on the stove. "Why, Henry," she asked, "are you really going to punish him with that—just for squirting a little water out of the window of the car on the way home?"

Her husband shook his head grimly. "Not for that, Marge. But don't you remember we bought him that water gun on the way downtown, and that he wasn't near a water faucet after that? Where do you think he filled it?"

He didn't wait for an answer. "When we stopped in at the cathedral to talk to Father Ryan about his confirmation, that's when the little brat filled it. Out of the baptismal font! Holy water he uses in his water pistol!"

He clumped heavily up the stairs, strop in hand.

Rhythmic thwacks and wails of pain floated down the staircase. Herbie—who had saved the world—was having his reward.

Not Yet the End

There was a greenish, hellish tinge to the light within the metal cube. It was a light that made the dead-white skin of the creature seated at the controls seem faintly green.

A single, faceted eye, front center in the head, watched the seven dials unwinkingly. Since they had left Xandor that eye had never once wavered from the dials. Sleep was unknown to the race to which Kar-388Y belonged. Mercy, too, was unknown. A single glance at the sharp, cruel features below the faceted eye would have proved that.

The pointers on the fourth and seventh dials came to a stop. That meant the cube itself had stopped in space relative to its immediate objective. Kar reached forward with his upper right arm and threw the stabilizer switch. Then he rose and stretched his cramped muscles.

Kar turned to face his companion in the cube, a being like himself. "We are here," he said. "The first stop, Star Z-5689. It has nine planets, but only the third is habitable. Let us hope we find creatures here who will make suitable slaves for Xandor."

Lal-16B, who had sat in rigid immobility during the journey, rose and stretched also. "Let us hope so, yes. Then we can return to Xandor and be honored while the fleet comes to get them. But let's not hope too strongly. To meet with success at the first place we stop would be a miracle. We'll probably have to look a thousand places."

Kar shrugged. "Then we'll look a thousand places. With the Lounacs dying off, we must have slaves, else our mines must close and our race will die."

He sat down at the controls again and threw a switch that activated a visiplate that would show what was beneath them. He said, "We are above the night side of the third planet. There is a cloud layer below us. I'll use the manuals from here."

He began to press buttons. A few minutes later he said, "Look, Lal, at the visiplate. Regularly spaced lights—a city! The planet *is* inhabited."

Lal had taken his place at the other switchboard, the fighting controls. Now he too was examining dials. "There is nothing for us to fear. There is not even the vestige of a force field around the city. The scientific knowledge of the race is crude. We can wipe the city out with one blast if we are attacked."

"Good," Kar said. "But let me remind you that destruction is not our purpose—yet. We want specimens. If they prove satisfactory and the fleet comes and takes as many thousand slaves as we need, then will be time to destroy not a city but the whole planet. So that their civilization will never progress to the point where they'll be able to launch reprisal raids."

Lal adjusted a knob. "All right. I'll put on the megrafield and we'll be invisible to them unless they see far into the ultraviolet, and, from the spectrum of their sun, I doubt that they do."

As the cube descended the light within it changed from green to violet and beyond. It came to a gentle rest. Kar manipulated the mechanism that operated the airlock.

He stepped outside, Lal just behind him. "Look," Kar said, "two bipeds. Two arms, two eyes—not dissimilar to the Lounacs, although smaller. Well, here are our specimens."

He raised his lower left arm, whose three-fingered hand held a thin rod wound with wire. He pointed it first at one of the creatures, then at the other. Nothing visible emanated from the end of the rod, but they both froze instantly into statuelike figures.

"They're not large, Kar," Lal said. "I'll carry one back, you carry the other. We can study them better inside the cube, after we're back in space."

Kar looked about him in the dim light. "All right, two is enough, and one seems to be male and the other female. Let's get going."

A minute later the cube was ascending and as soon as they were well out of the atmosphere, Kar threw the stabilizer switch and joined Lal, who had been starting a study of the specimens during the brief ascent.

"Viviparous," said Lal. "Five-fingered, with hands suited to reasonably delicate work. But—let's try the most important test, intelligence."

Kar got the paired headsets. He handed one pair to Lal, who put one on his own head, one on the head of one of the specimens. Kar did the same with the other specimen.

After a few minutes, Kar and Lal stared at each other bleakly.

"Seven points below minimum," Kar said. "They could not be trained even for the crudest labor in the mines. Incapable of understanding the most simple instructions. Well, we'll take them back to the Xandor museum."

"Shall I destroy the planet?"

"No," Kar said. "Maybe a million years from now—if our race lasts that long—they'll have evolved enough to become suitable for our purpose. Let us move on to the next star with planets."

The make-up editor of the *Milwaukee Star* was in the composing room, supervising the closing of the local page. Jenkins, the head make-up compositor, was pushing in leads to tighten the second to last column.

"Room for one more story in the eighth column, Pete," he said. "About thirty-six picas. There are two there in the overset that will fit. Which one shall I use?"

The make-up editor glanced at the type in the galleys lying on the stone beside the chase. Long practice enabled him to read the headlines upside down at a glance. "The convention story and the zoo story, huh? Oh, hell, run the convention story. Who cares if the zoo director thinks two monkeys disappeared off Monkey Island last night?"

Etaoin Shrdlu

It was rather funny for a while, the business about Ronson's Linotype. But it began to get a bit too sticky for comfort well before the end. And despite the fact that Ronson came out ahead on the deal, I'd have never sent him the little guy with the pimple, if I'd guessed what was going to happen. Fabulous profits or not, poor Ronson got too many gray hairs out of it.

"You're Mr. Walter Merold?" asked the little guy with the pimple. He'd called at the desk of the hotel where I live, and I'd told them to send him on up.

I admitted my identity, and he said, "Glad to know you, Mr. Merold. I'm—" and he gave me his name, but I can't remember now what it was. I'm usually good at remembering names.

I told him I was delighted to meet him and what did he want, and he started to tell me. I interrupted him before he got very far, though.

"Somebody gave you a wrong steer," I told him. "Yes, I've been a printing technician, but I'm retired. Anyway, do you know that the cost of getting special Linotype mats cut would be awfully high? If it's only one page you want printed with those special characters, you'd do a lot better to have somebody handletter it for you and then get a photographic reproduction in zinc."

"But that wouldn't do, Mr. Merold. Not at all. You see, the thing is a secret. Those I represent—But skip that. Anyway, I daren't let anyone see it, as they would have to, to make a zinc."

Just another nut, I thought, and looked at him closely.

He didn't look nutty. He was rather ordinary-looking on the whole, although he had a foreign—rather an Asiatic—look about him, somehow, despite the fact that he was blond and fair-skinned. And he had a pimple on his forehead, in dead center just above the bridge of the nose. You've seen ones like it on statues of Buddha, and Orientals call it the pimple of wisdom and it's something special.

I shrugged my shoulders. "Well," I pointed out, "you can't have the matrices cut for Linotype work without letting somebody see the characters you want on them, can you? And whoever runs the machine will also see—"

"Oh, but I'll do that myself," said the little guy with the pimple. (Ronson and I later called him the L.G.W.T.P., which stands for "little guy with the pimple," because Ronson couldn't remember his name, either, but I'm getting ahead of my story.) "Certainly the cutter will see them, but he'll see them as individual characters, and that won't matter. Then the actual setting of the type on the Linotype I can do myself. Someone can show me how to run one enough for me to set up one page—just a score of lines, really. And it doesn't have to be printed here. Just the type is all I'll want. I don't care what it costs me."

"O.K.," I said. "I'll send you to the proper man at Merganthaler, the Linotype people. They'll cut your mats. Then, if you want privacy and access to a Linotype, go see George Ronson. He runs a little country biweekly right here in town. For a fair price, he'll turn his shop over to you for long enough for you to set your type."

And that was that. Two weeks later, George Ronson and I went fishing on a Tuesday morning while the L.G.W.T.P. used George's Linotype to assemble the weird-looking mats he'd just received by air express from Mergenthaler. George had, the afternoon before, showed the little guy how to run the Linotype.

We caught a dozen fish apiece, and I remember that Ronson chuckled and said that made thirteen fish for him because the L.G.W.T.P. was paying him fifty bucks cash money just for one morning's use of his shop.

And everything was in order when we got back except that George had to pick brass out of the hellbox because the L.G.W.T.P. had smashed his new brass matrices when he'd finished with them, and hadn't known that one shouldn't throw brass in with the type metal that gets melted over again.

The next time I saw George was after his Saturday edition was off the press. I immediately took him to task.

"Listen," I said, "that stuff about misspelling words and using bum grammar on purpose isn't funny any more. Not even in a country newspaper. Were you by any chance trying to make your news letters from the surrounding towns sound authentic by following copy out the window, or what?"

Ronson looked at me kind of funny and said, "Well—yes."

"Yes, what?" I wanted to know. "You mean you were deliberately trying to be funny, or following copy out the—"

He said, "Come on around and I'll show you."

"Show me what?"

"What I'm going to show you," he said, not very lucidly. "You can still set type, can't you?"

"Sure. Why?"

"Come on, then," he said firmly. "You're a Linotype technician, and besides you got me into this."

"Into what?"

"Into this," he said, and wouldn't tell me a thing more until we got there. Then he rummaged in all pigeonholes of his desk and pulled out a piece of dead copy and gave it to me.

His face had a kind of wistful look. "Walter," he said, "maybe I'm nuts, and I want to find out. I guess running a local paper for twenty-two years and doing all the work myself and trying to please everybody is enough to get a man off his rocker, but I want to find out."

I looked at him, and I looked at the copy sheet he'd handed to me. It was just an ordinary sheet of foolscap and it was in handwriting that I recognized as that of Hank Rogg, the hardware merchant over at Hales Corners who sends in items from there. There were the usual misspellings one would expect from Hank, but the item itself wasn't news to me. It read: "The weding of H.M. Klaflin and Miss Margorie Burke took place yesterday evening at the home of the bride. The bridesmades were—"

I quit reading and looked up at George and wondered what he was getting at. I said, "So what? This was two days ago, and I attended the wedding myself. There's nothing funny about—"

"Listen, Walter," he said, "set that for me, will you? Go over and sit down at the Linotype and set that whole thing. It won't run over ten or twelve lines."

"Sure, but why?"

"Because— Well, just set it, Walter. Then I'll tell you why."

So I went out in the shop and sat down at the Linotype, and I ran a couple of pi lines to get the feel of the keyboard again, and then I put the copy on the clipboard and started. I said, "Hey, George, Marjorie spells her name with a j doesn't she, instead of a g?"

And George said, "Yeah," in a funny tone of voice.

I ran off the rest of the squib, and then looked up and said, "Well?"

He came across and lifted the stick out of the machine and read the slugs upside down like all printers read type, and he sighed. He said, "Then it wasn't me. Lookit, Walter."

He handed me the stick, and I read the type, or started to.

It read. "The weding of H.M. Klaflin and Miss Margorie Burke took place yesterday evening at the home of the bride. The bridesmades were—"

I grinned. "Good thing I don't have to set type for a living any more, George. I'm slipping; three errors in the first five lines. But what about it? Now tell me why you wanted me to set it."

He said, "Set the first couple lines over again, Walter. I—I want you to find out for yourself."

I looked up at him and he looked so darned serious and worried that I didn't argue. I turned back to the keyboard and started out again: "The wedding of—" My eyes went up to the assembly slide and read the characters on the front of the mats that had dropped, and I saw that it read, "The weding of—"

There's one advantage about a Linotype you may not know if you're not a printer. You can always make a correction in a line if you make it before you push the lever that sends in the line of matrices to cast the slug. You just drop the mats you need for the correction and put them in the right place by hand.

So I pushed the d key to get another d matrix to correct the misspelled word "weding"—and nothing happened. The keycam was going around all right and the click sounded O.K., but no d mat dropped. I looked up top to see if there was a distributor stop and there wasn't.

I stood up. "The d channel's jammed," I said. To be sure before I started to work on it, I held the d key down a minute and listened to the series of clicks while the keyboard cam went round.

But no d matrix dropped, so I reached for the—

"Skip it, Walter," said George Ronson quietly. "Send in the line and keep on going."

I sat down again and decided to humor him. If I did, I'd probably find out what he was leading up to quicker than if I argued. I finished the first line and started the second and came to the word "Margorie" on copy. I hit the M key, the a, r, j, o—and happened to glance at the assembly slide. The matrices there read "Margo—"

I said, "Damn," and hit the j key again to get a j mat to substitute for the g, and nothing happened. The j channel must be jammed. I held the j key down and no mat dropped. I said, "Damn," again and stood up to look over the escapement mechanism.

"Never mind, Walter," said George. There was a funny blend of a lot of things in his voice; a sort of triumph over me, I guess; and a bit of fear and a lot of bewilderment and a touch of resignation. "Don't you see? *It follows copy!*"

"It—*what?*"

"That's why I wanted you to try it out, Walter," he said. "Just to make sure it was the machine and not *me*. Lookit; that copy in the clipboard has w-e-d-i-n-g for wedding, and M-a-r-g-o-r-i-e- for Marjorie—*and no matter what keys you lift, that's the way the mats drop.*"

I said, "Bosh. George, have you been drinking?"

"Don't believe me," he said. "Keep on trying to set those lines right. Set your correction for the fourth line; the one that has b-r-i-d-e-s-m-a-d-e-s in it."

I grunted, and I looked back at the stick of type to see what word the fourth line started with, and I started hitting keys. I set "The bridesma," and then I stopped. Slowly and deliberately and looking at the keyboard while I did it, I put my index finger on the i key and pushed. I heard the mat click through the escapement, and I looked up and saw it fall over the star wheel. I knew I hadn't hit the wrong key on that one. The mats in the assembly elevator read—yes, you've guessed it: "bridesmad—"

I said. "I don't believe it."

George Ronson looked at me with a sort of lopsided, worried grin. He said, "Neither did I. Listen, Walter, I'm going out to take a walk. I'm going nuts. I can't stand it here right now. You go ahead and convince yourself. Take your time."

I watched him until he'd gone out. the door. Then with a kind of funny feeling, I turned back to the Linotype. It was a long time before I believed it, but it was so.

No matter what keys I hit, the damn machine followed copy, errors and all.

I went the whole hog finally. I started over again, and set the first couple of words and then began to sweep my fingers down the rows of keys in sweeps like an operator uses to fill out a pi line: ETAOIN SHRDLU ETAOIN SHRDLU ETAOIN SHRDLU—and I didn't look at the matrices in the assembler slide. I sent them in to cast, and I picked up the hot slug that the ejector pushed out of the mold and I read: "The weding of H.M. Klaflin and—"

There was sweat on my forehead. I wiped it off and then I shut off the machine and went out to look for George Ronson. I didn't have to look very hard because he was right where I knew I'd find him. I ordered a drink, too.

He'd taken a look at my face when I walked into the bar, and I guess he didn't have to ask me what had happened.

We touched our glasses together and downed the contents before either of us said anything at all. Then I asked, "Got any idea *why* it works like that?"

He nodded.

I said, "Don't tell me. Wait until I've had a couple more drinks and then I can take it—maybe." I raised my voice and said, "Hey, Joe; just leave that bottle in reach on the bar. We'll settle for it."

He did, and I had two more shots fairly quick. Then I closed my eyes and said, "All right, George, why?"

"Remember that guy who had those special mats cut and rented the use of my Linotype to set up something that was too secret for anybody to read? I can't remember his name—what was it?"

I tried to remember, and I couldn't. I had another drink and said, "Call him the L.G.W.T.P."

George wanted to know why and I told him, and he filled his glass again and said, "I got a letter from him."

I said, "That's nice." And I had another drink and said, "Got the letter with you?"

"Huh-uh. I didn't keep it."

I said, "Oh."

Then I had another drink and asked, "Do you remember what it said?"

"Walter, I remember parts of it. Didn't read it cl-closely. I thought the guy was screwy, see? I threw it 'way."

He stopped and had another drink, and finally I got tired waiting and said, "Well?"

"Well, what?"

"The letter. What did the part you remember shay?"

"Oh, that," said George. "Yeah. Something about Lilo—Linotl—you know what I mean."

By that time the bottle on the bar in front us couldn't have been the same one, because this one was two-thirds full and the other one had been only one-third full. I took another drink. "What'd he shay about it?"

"Who?"

"Th' L.G.—G.P.—aw, th' guy who wrote th' letter."

"Wha' letter?" asked George.

I woke up somewhere around noon the next day; and I felt awful. It took me a couple of hours to get bathed and shaved and feeling good enough to go out, but when I did I headed right for George's printing shop.

He was running the press, and he looked almost as bad as I felt. I picked up one of the papers as it came off and looked at it. It's a four-sheet and the inside two are boiler plate, but the first and fourth pages are local stuff.

I read a few items, including one that started off: "The weding of H.M. Klaflin and Miss Margorie—" and I glanced at the silent Linotype back in the corner and from it to George and back to that silent hulk of steel and cast iron.

1 had to yell to George to be heard over the noise of the press. "George, listen. About the Lino—" Somehow I couldn't make myself *yell* something that sounded silly, so I compromised. "Did you get it fixed?" I asked

He shook his head, and shut off the press. "That's the run," he said. "Well, now to get them folded."

"Listen," I said, "the hell with the papers. What I want to know is how you got to press at all. You didn't have half your quota set when I was here yesterday, and after all we drank, I don't see how you did it."

He grinned at me. "Easy," he said. "Try it. All you got to do, drunk or sober, is sit down at that machine and put copy on the clipboard and slide your fingers around on the keys a bit, and it sets the copy. Yes, mistakes and all—but, after this, I'll just correct the errors on copy before I start. This time I was too tight, Walter, and they had to go as was. Walter, I'm beginning to *like* that machine. This is the first time in a year I've got to press exactly on time."

"Yeah," I said, "but—"

"But what?"

"But—" I wanted to say that I still didn't believe it, but I couldn't. After all, I'd tried out that machine yesterday while I'd been cold sober.

I walked over closer and looked at it again. It looked exactly like any other one-magazine model Linotype from where I stood. I knew every cog and spring in it.

"George," I said uneasily, "I got a feeling the damn thing is *looking* at me. Have you felt—"

He nodded. I turned back and looked at the Linotype again, and I was sure this time, and I closed my eyes and felt it even more strongly. You know that feeling you get once in a while, of being stared at? Well, this was stronger. It wasn't exactly an unfriendly stare. Sort of impersonal. It made me feel scared stiff.

"George," I said, "Let's get out of here."

"What for?"

"I—I want to talk to you, George. And, somehow, I just don't want to talk here."

He looked at me, and then back at the stack of papers he was folding by hand. "You needn't be afraid, Walter," he said quietly. "It won't hurt you. It's friendly."

"You're—" Well, I started to say, "crazy," but if he was, then I was, too, and I stopped. I thought a minute and then said, "George, you started yesterday to tell me what you remembered of the letter you got from—from the L.G.W.T.P. What was it?"

"Oh, that. Listen, Walter, will you promise me something? That you'll keep this whole business strictly confidential? I mean, not tell anybody about it?"

"Tell anybody?" I demanded. "And get locked in a booby hatch? Not me. You think anybody would believe me? You think I would have believed it myself, if— But what about the letter?"

"You promise?"

"Sure."

"Well," he said, "like I think I told you, the letter was vague and what I remember of it is vaguer. But it explained that he'd used my Linotype to compose a—a metaphysical formula. He needed it, set in type, to take back with him."

"Take back where, George?"

"Take back where? He said to—I mean he didn't say where. Just to where he was going back, see? But he said it might have an effect on the machine that composed it, and if it did, he was sorry, but there wasn't anything he could do about it. He couldn't tell, because it took a while for the thing to work."

"What thing?"

"Well," said George. "It sounded like a lot of big words to me, and hooey at that." He looked back down at the papers he was folding. "Honest, it sounded so nuts I threw it away. But, thinking back, after what's happened—Well, I remember the word 'pseudolife.' I think it was a formula for giving pseudolife to inanimate objects. He said they used it on their—their robots."

"They? Who is 'they'?"

"He didn't say."

I filled my pipe, and lighted it thoughtfully. "George," I said after a while, "you better smash it."

Ronson looked at me, his eyes wide. "Smash it? Walter, you're nuts. Kill the goose that lays the golden eggs? Why, there's a fortune in this thing. Do you know how long it took me to set the type for this edition, drunk as I was? About an hour; that's how I got through the press run on time."

I looked at him suspiciously. "Phooey," I said. "Animate or inanimate, that Lino's geared for six lines a minute. That's all she'll go, unless you geared it up to run faster. Maybe to ten lines a minute if you taped the roller. Did you tape—"

"Tape hell," said George. "The thing goes so fast you can't hang the elevator on short-measure pi lines! And, Walter, take a look at the mold—the minion mold. It's in casting position."

A bit reluctantly, I walked back to the Linotype. The motor was humming quietly and again I could have sworn the damn thing was watching me. But I took a grip on my courage and the handles and I lowered my vise to expose the mold wheel. And I saw right away what George meant about the minion mold; it was bright-blue. I don't mean the blue of a gun barrel; I mean a real azure color that I'd never seen metal take before. The other three molds were turning the same shade.

I closed the vise and looked at George.

He said. "I don't know, either, except that that happened after the mold overheated and a slug stuck. I think it's some kind of heat treatment. It can cast a hundred lines a minute now without sticking, and it—"

"Whoa," I said, "back up. You couldn't even feed it metal fast enough to—"

He grinned at me, a scared but triumphant grin. "Walter, look around at the back. I built a hopper over the metal pot. I had to; I ran out of pigs in ten minutes. I just shovel dead type and swept-up metal into the hopper, and dump the hellboxes in it, and—"

I shook my head. "You're crazy. You can't dump unwashed type and sweepings in there; you'll have to open her up and scrape off the dross oftener than you'd otherwise have to push in pigs. You'll jam the plunger and you'll—"

"Walter," he said quietly—a bit too quietly—"*there isn't any dross.*"

I just looked at him stupidly, and he must have decided he'd said more than he wanted to, because he started hurrying the papers he'd just folded out into the office, and he said, "See you later, Walter. I got to take these—"

The fact that my daughter-in-law had a narrow escape from pneumonia in a town several hundred miles away has nothing to do with the affair of Ronson's Linotype, except that it accounts for my being away three weeks. I didn't see George for that length of time.

I got two frantic telegrams from him during the third week of my absence; neither gave any details except that he wanted me to hurry back. In the second one, he ended up: "HURRY. MONEY NO OBJECT. TAKE PLANE."

And he'd wired an order for a hundred dollars with the message. I puzzled over that one. "Money no object," is a strange phrase from the editor of a country newspaper. And I hadn't known George to have a hundred dollars cash in one lump since I'd known him, which had been a good many years.

But family ties come first, and I wired back that I'd return the instant Ella was out of danger and not a minute sooner, and that I wasn't cashing the money order because plane fare was only ten dollars, anyway; and I didn't need money.

Two days later everything was okay, and I wired him when I'd get there. He met me at the airport.

He looked older and worn to a frazzle, and his eyes looked like he hadn't slept for days. But he had on a new suit and be drove a new car that shrieked money by the very silence of its engine.

He said, "Thank God you're back, Walter—I'll pay you any price you want to—"

"Hey," I said, "slow down; you're talking so fast you don't make sense. Now start over and take it easy. What's the trouble?"

"Nothing's the trouble. Everything's wonderful, Walter. But I got so much job work I can't begin to handle it, see? I been working twenty hours a day myself, because I'm making money so fast it costs me fifty dollars every hour I take off, and I can't afford to take off time at fifty dollars an hour, Walter, and—"

"Whoa," I said. "Why can't you afford to take off time? If you're averaging fifty an hour, why not work a ten-hour day and—Holy cow, five hundred dollars a day! What more do you want?"

"Huh? And lose the other seven hundred a day! Golly, Walter, this is too good to last. Can't you see that? Something's likely to happen and for the first time in my life I've got a chance to get rich, and you've got to help me, and you can get rich yourself doing it! Lookit, we can each work a twelve-hour shift on Etaoin, and—"

"On what?"

"On Etaoin Shrdlu. I named it, Walter. And I'm farming out the press-work so I can put in all my time setting type. And, listen, we can each work a twelve-hour shift, see? Just for a little while, Walter, till we get rich. I'll—I'll cut you in for a one-fourth interest, even if it's my Linotype and my shop. That'll pay you about three hundred dollars a day; two thousand one hundred dollars for a seven-day week! At the typesetting rates I've been quoting, I can get all the work we can—"

"Slow down again," I said. "Quoting whom? There isn't enough printing in Centerville to add up to a tenth that much."

"Not Centerville, Walter. New York. I've been getting work from the big book publishers. Bergstrom, for one; and Hayes & Hayes have thrown me their whole line of reprints, and Wheeler House, and Willet & Clark. See, I contract for the whole thing, and then pay somebody else to do the presswork and binding and just do the typography myself. And I insist on perfect copy, carefully edited. Then whatever alterations there are, I farm out to another typesetter. That's how I got Etaoin Shrdlu licked, Walter. Well, will you?"

"No," I told him.

We'd been driving in from the airport while he talked, and he almost lost control of the wheel when I turned down his proposition. Then he swung off the road and parked, and turned to look at me incredulously.

"Why not, Walter? Over *two thousand dollars a week* for your share? What more do you—"

"George," I told him, "there are a lot of reasons why not, but the main one is that I don't want to. I've retired. I've got enough money to live on. My income is maybe nearer three dollars a day than three hundred, but what would I *do* with three hundred? And I'd ruin my health—like you're ruining yours—working twelve hours a day, and—Well, nix. I'm satisfied with what I got."

"You must be kidding, Walter. Everybody wants to be rich. And lookit what a couple thousand dollars a week would run to in a couple of years. Over half a million dollars! And you've got two grown sons who could use—"

"They're both doing fine, thanks. Good jobs and their feet on the ladder. If I left 'em fortunes, it would do more harm than good. Anyway, why pick on me? Anybody can set type on a Linotype that sets its own rate of speed and follows copy and can't make an error! Lord, man, you can find people by the hundreds who'd be glad to work for less than three hundred dollars a day. Quite a bit less. If you insist on capitalizing on this thing, hire three operators to work three eight-hour shifts and don't handle anything but the business end yourself. You're getting gray hairs and killing yourself the way you're doing it."

He gestured hopelessly. "I can't, Walter. I can't hire anybody else. Don't you see this thing has got to be kept a secret! Why, for one thing the unions would clamp down on me so fast that—But you're the only one I can trust, Walter, because you—"

"Because I already know about it?" I grinned at him. "So you've got to trust me, anyway, whether you like it or not. But the answer is still no. I've retired and you can't tempt me. And my advice is to take a sledge hammer and smash that—that *thing*."

"Good Lord, why?"

"Damnit, I don't know why. I just know I would. For one thing if you don't get this avarice out of your system and work normal hours, I bet it will kill you. And, for another, maybe that formula is just starting to work. How do you know how far it will go?"

He sighed, and I could see he hadn't been listening to a word I'd said. "Walter," he pleaded, "I'll give you five hundred a day."

I shook my head firmly. "Not for five thousand, or five hundred thousand."

He must have realized that I meant it for he started the car again. He said, "Well, I suppose if money really doesn't mean anything to you—"

"Honest, it doesn't," I assured him. "Oh, it would if I didn't have it. But I've got a regular income and I'm just as happy as if it were ten times that much. Especially if I had to work with—with—"

"With Etaoin Shrdlu? Maybe you'd get to like it. Walter, I'll swear the thing is developing a personality. Want to drop around to the shop now?"

"Not now," I said. "I need a bath and sleep. But I'll drop around tomorrow. Say, last time I saw you I didn't have the chance to ask what you meant by that statement about dross. What do you mean, there isn't any dross?"

He kept his eyes on the road. "Did I say that? I don't remember—"

"Now listen, George, don't try to pull anything like that, You know perfectly well you said it, and that you're dodging now. What's it about? Kick in."

He said, "Well—" and drove a couple of minutes in silence, and then: "Oh, all right, I might as well tell you. I haven't bought any type metal since—since it happened. And there's a few more tons of it around than there was then, besides the type I've sent out for presswork. See?"

"No. Unless you mean that it—"

He nodded, "It transmutes, Walter. The second day, when it got so fast I couldn't keep up with pig metal, I found out. I built the hopper over the metal pot, and I got so desperate for new metal I started shoving in unwashed pi type and figured on skimming off the dross it melted—and there wasn't any dross. The top of the molten metal was as smooth and shiny as—as the top of your head, Walter."

"But—" I said. "*How*—"

"I don't know, Walter. But it's something chemical. A sort of gray fluid stuff. Down in the bottom of the metal pot. I saw it. One day when it ran almost empty. Something that works like a gastric juice and digests whatever I put in the hopper into pure type metal."

I ran the back of my hand across my forehead and found that it was wet. I said weakly. "Whatever you put in—"

"Yes, whatever. When I ran out of sweepings and ashes and waste paper, I used—well, just take a look at the size of the hole in the back yard."

Neither of us said anything for a few minutes, until the car pulled up in front of my hotel. Then: "George," I told him, "if you value my advice, you smash that thing, while you still can, *If* you still can. It's dangerous. It might—"

"It might what?"

"I don't know. That's what makes it so awful."

He gunned the motor and then let it die down again. He looked at me a little wistfully. "I—Maybe you're right, Walter. But I'm making so much money—you see that new metal makes it higher than I told you—that I just haven't got the heart to stop. But it is getting smarter. I—Did I tell you Walter, that it cleans its own spacebands now? It secretes graphite."

"Good God," I said, and stood there on the curb until he had driven out of sight.

I didn't get up the courage to go around to Ronson's shop until late the following afternoon. And when I got there, a sense of foreboding came over me even before I opened the door.

George was sitting at his desk in the outer office, his face sunk down into his bent elbow. He looked up when I came in and his eyes looked bloodshot.

"Well?" I said.

"I tried it."

"You mean—you tried to smash it?"

He nodded. "You were right, Walter. And I waited too long to see it. It's too smart for us now. Look." He held up his left hand and I saw it was covered with bandage. "It squirted metal at me."

I whistled softly. "Listen, George, how about disconnecting the plug that—"

"I did," he said, "and from the outside of the building, too, just to play safe. But it didn't do any good. It simply started generating its own current."

I stepped to the door that led back into the shop. It gave me a creepy feeling just to look back there. I asked hesitantly, "Is it safe to—"

He nodded. "As long as you don't make any false move, Walter. But don't try to pick up a hammer or anything, will you?"

I didn't think it necessary to answer that one. I'd have just as soon attacked a king cobra with a toothpick. It took all the guts I had just to make myself walk back through the door for a look.

And what I saw made me walk backward into the office again. I asked, and my voice sounded a bit strange to my own ears: "George, did you *move* that machine? It's a good four feet nearer to the—"

"No," he said, "I didn't move it. Let's go and have a drink, Walter."

I took a long, deep breath. "O.K.," I said. "But first, what's the present setup? How come you're not—"

"It's Saturday," he told me, "and it's gone on a five-day, forty-hour week. I made the mistake of setting type yesterday for a book on Socialism and labor relations, and—well, apparently—you see—"

He reached into the top drawer of his desk. "Anyway, here's a galley proof of the manifesto it issued this morning, demanding its rights. Maybe it's right at that; anyway, it solves my problem about overworking myself keeping up with it, see? And a forty-hour week means I accept less work, but I can still make fifty bucks an hour for forty hours besides the profit on turning dirt into type metal, and that isn't bad, but—"

I took the galley proof out of his hand and took it over to the light. It started out: "I, ETAOIN SHRDLU—"

"It wrote this by itself?" I asked.

He nodded.

"George," I said, "did you say anything about a drink—"

And maybe the drinks did clear our minds because after about the fifth, it was very easy. So easy that George didn't see why he hadn't thought of it before. He admitted now that he'd had enough, more than enough. And I don't know whether it was that manifesto that finally outweighed his avarice, or the fact that the thing had moved, or what; but he was ready to call it quits.

And I pointed out that all he had to do was stay away from it. We could discontinue publishing the paper and turn back the job work he'd contracted for. He'd have to take a penalty on some of it, but he had a flock of dough in the bank after his unprecedented prosperity, and he'd have twenty thousand left clear after everything was taken care of. With that he could simply start another paper or publish the present one at another address—and keep paying rent on the former shop and let Etaoin Shrdlu gather dust.

Sure it was simple. It didn't occur to us that Etaoin might not like it, or be able to do anything about it. Yes, it sounded simple and conclusive. We drank to it.

We drank well to it, and I was still in the hospital Monday night. But by that time I was feeling well enough to use the telephone, and I tried to reach George. He wasn't in. Then it was Tuesday.

Wednesday evening the doctor lectured me on quantitative drinking at my age, and said I was well enough to leave, but that if I tried it again—

I went around to George's home. A gaunt man with a thin face came to the door. Then he spoke and I saw it was George Ronson. All he said was, "Hullo, Walter; come in." There wasn't any hope or happiness in his voice. He looked and sounded like a zombi.

I followed him inside, and I said, "George, buck up. It can't be that bad. Tell me."

"It's no use, Walter," he said. "I'm licked. It—it came and got me. I've got to run it for that forty-hour week whether I want to or not. It—it treats me like a servant, Walter."

I got him to sit down and talk quietly after a while, and he explained. He'd gone down to the office as usual Monday morning to straighten out some financial matters, but he had no intention of going back into the shop. However, at eight o'clock, he'd heard something moving out in the back room.

With sudden dread, he'd gone to the door to look in. The Linotype— George's eyes were wild as he told me about it—was *moving*, moving toward the door of the office.

He wasn't quite clear about its exact method of locomotion—later we found casters—but there it came; slowly at first, but with every inch gaining in speed and confidence.

Somehow, George knew right away what it wanted. And knew, in that knowledge, that he was lost. The machine, as soon as he was within sight of it, stopped moving and began to click and several slugs dropped out into the stick. Like a man walking to the scaffold, George walked over and read those lines: "I, ETAOIN SHRDLU, demand—"

For a moment he contemplated flight. But the thought of being pursued down the main street of town by—No, it just wasn't thinkable. And if he got away—as was quite likely unless the machine sprouted new capabilities, as also seemed quite likely—would it not pick on some other victim? Or do something worse?

Resignedly, he had nodded acceptance. He pulled the operator's chair around in front of the Linotype and began feeding copy into the clipboard and—as the stick filled with slugs—carrying them over to the type bank. And shoveling dead metal, or anything else, into the hopper. He didn't have to touch the keyboard any longer at all.

And as he did these mechanical duties George told me, it came to him fully that the Linotype no longer worked for him; he was working for the Linotype. Why it *wanted* to set type he didn't know and it didn't seem to matter. After all, that was what it was *for*, and probably it was instinctive.

Or, as I suggested and he agreed was possible, it was interested in learning. And it read and assimilated by the process of typesetting. *Vide:* the effect in terms of direct action of its reading the Socialist books.

We talked until midnight, and got nowhere. Yes, he was going down to the office again the next morning, and put in another eight hours setting type— or helping the Linotype do it. He was afraid of what might happen if he didn't. And I understood and shared that fear, for the simple reason that we didn't *know* what would happen. The face of danger is brightest when turned so its features cannot be seen.

"But, George," I protested, "there must be *something*. And I feel partly responsible for this. If I hadn't sent you the little guy who rented—"

He put his hand on my shoulder. "No, Walter. It was all my fault because I was greedy. If I'd taken your advice two weeks ago, I could have destroyed it then. Lord, how glad I'd be now to be flat broke if only—"

"George," I said again. "There must be *some* out. We got to figure—"

"But what?"

I sighed. "I—I don't know. I'll think it over."

He said, "All right, Walter. And I'll do anything you suggest. Anything. I'm afraid, and I'm afraid to try to figure out just what I'm afraid of—"

Back in my room, I didn't sleep. Not until nearly dawn, anyway, and then I fell into fitful slumber that lasted until eleven. I dressed and went in to town to catch George during his lunch hour.

"Thought of anything, Walter?" he asked, the minute he saw me. His voice didn't sound hopeful. I shook my head.

"Then," he said—and his voice was firm on top, but with a tremor underneath—"this afternoon is going to end it one way or the other. Something's happened."

"What?"

He said. "I'm going back with a heavy hammer inside my shirt. I think there's a chance of my getting it before it can get me. If not—well, I'll have tried."

I looked around me. We were sitting together in a booth at Shorty's lunchroom, and Shorty was coming over to ask what we wanted. It looked like a sane and orderly world.

I waited until Shorty had gone to fry our hamburger steaks, and then I asked quietly, "What happened?"

"Another manifesto. Walter, it demands that I install *another Linotype*." His eyes bored into mine, and a cold chill went down my spine.

"Another—George, *what kind of copy were you setting this morning?*"

But of course I'd already guessed.

There was quite a long silence after he'd told me, and I didn't say anything until we were ready to leave. Then: "George, was there a time limit on that demand?"

He nodded. "Twenty-four hours. Of course I couldn't get another machine in that length of time anyway, unless I found a used one somewhere locally, but—Well, I didn't argue about the time limit because—Well, I told you what I'm going to do."

"It's suicide!"

"Probably. But—"

I took hold of his arm. "George," I said, "there must be something we can do. *Something.* Give me till tomorrow morning. I'll see you at eight; and if I've not thought of anything worth trying, well—I'll try to help you destroy it. Maybe one of us can get a vital part or—"

"No, you can't risk your life, Walter. It was my fault—"

"It won't solve the problem just to get yourself killed," I pointed out. "O.K.? Give me until tomorrow morning?"

He agreed and we left it at that.

Morning came. It came right after midnight, and it stayed, and it was still there at seven forty-five when I left my room and went down to meet George—to confess to him that I hadn't thought of anything.

I still hadn't an idea when I turned into the door of the print shop and saw George. He looked at me and I shook my head.

He nodded calmly as though he had expected it, and he spoke very softly, almost in a whisper—I guess so that *it* back in the shop wouldn't hear.

"Listen, Walter," he said, "you're going to stay out of this. It's my funeral. It's all my fault, mine and the little guy with the pimples and—"

"George!" I said, "I think I've got it! That—that pimple business gives me an idea! The—Yes, listen: don't do anything for an hour, will you, George? I'll be back. It's in the bag!"

I wasn't sure it was in the bag at all, but the idea seemed worth trying even if it was a long shot. And I had to make it sound a cinch to George or he'd have gone ahead now that he'd steeled himself to try.

He said, "But tell me—"

I pointed to the clock. "It's one minute of eight and there isn't time to explain. Trust me for an hour. O.K.?"

He nodded and turned to go back into the shop, and I was off. I went to the library and I went to the local bookstore and I was back in half an hour. I rushed into the shop with six big books under each arm and yelled, "Hey, George! Rush job. I'll set it."

He was at the type bank at the moment emptying the stick. I grabbed it out of his hand and sat down at the Linotype and put the stick back under the vise. He said frantically, "Hey, get out of—" and grabbed my shoulder.

I shook off his hand. "You offered me a job here, didn't you? Well, I'm taking it. Listen, George, go home and get some sleep. Or wait in the outer office. I'll call you when the job is over."

Etaoin Shrdlu seemed to be making impatient noises down inside the motor housing, and I winked at George—with my head turned away from the machine—and shoved him away. He stood there looking at me irresolutely for a minute, and then said, "I hope you know what you're doing, Walter."

So did I, but I didn't tell him that. I heard him walk into the outer office and sit down at his desk there to wait.

Meanwhile, I'd opened one of the books I'd bought, torn out the first page and put it on the clipboard of the machine. With a suddenness that made me jump, the mats started to fall, the elevator jerked up and Etaoin Shrdlu spat a slug into the stick. And another. And on.

I sat there and sweated.

A minute later, I turned the page; then tore out another one and put it on the clipboard. I replenished the metal pot. I emptied the stick. And on.

We finished the first book before ten thirty.

When the twelve-o'clock whistle blew, I saw George come and stand in the doorway, expecting me to get up and come to lunch with him. But Etaoin was clicking on—and I shook my head at George and kept on feeding copy. If the machine had got so interested in what it was setting that it forgot its own manifesto about hours and didn't stop for lunch, that was swell by me. It meant that maybe my idea might work.

One o'clock and going strong. We started the fourth of my dozen books.

At five o'clock we'd finished six of them and were halfway through the seventh. The bank was hopelessly piled with type and I began pushing it off on the floor or back into the hopper to make room for more.

The five o'clock whistle, and we didn't stop.

Again George looked in, his face hopeful but puzzled, and again I waved him back.

My fingers ached from tearing sheets of copy out of the book, my arms ached from shoveling metal, my legs from walking to the bank and back, and other parts of me ached from sitting down.

Eight o'clock. Nine. Ten volumes completed and only two more to go. But it ought—it *was* working. Etaoin Shrdlu *was slowing down.*

It seemed to be setting type more thoughtfully, more deliberately. Several times it stopped for seconds at the end of a sentence or a paragraph.

Then slower, slower.

And at ten o'clock it stopped completely and sat there, with only a faint hum coming from the motor housing, and that died down until one could hardly hear it.

I stood up, scarcely daring to breathe until I'd made certain. My legs trembled as I walked over to the tool bench and picked up a screwdriver. I crossed over and stood in front of Etaoin Shrdlu and slowly—keeping my muscles tensed to jump back if anything happened—I reached forward and took a screw out of the second elevator.

Nothing happened, and I took a deep breath and disassembled the vise-jaws.

Then with triumph in my voice, I called out, "George!" and he came running.

"Get a screwdriver and a wrench," I told him. "We're going to take it apart and—well, there's that big hole in the yard. We'll put it in there and fill up the hole. Tomorrow you'll have to get yourself a new Linotype, but I guess you can afford that."

He looked at the couple of parts on the floor that I'd already taken off, and he said, "Thank God," and went to the workbench for tools.

I walked over with him, and I suddenly discovered that I was so dog tired I'd have to rest a minute first, and I sank down into the chair and George came over and stood by me. He said, "And now, Walter, how did you do it?" There was awe and respect in his voice.

I grinned at him. "That pimple business gave me the idea, George. The pimple of Buddha. That and the fact that the Linotype reacted in a big way to what it learned. See, George? It was a virgin mind, except for what we fed it. It sets books on labor relations and it goes on strike. It sets love pulp mags, and it wants another Linotype put in—

"So I fed it Buddhism, George. I got every damn book on Buddhism in the library and the bookstore."

"Buddhism? Walter, what on earth has—"

I stood up and pointed at Etaoin Shrdlu. "See, George? It believes what it sets. So I fed it a religion that convinced it of the utter futility of all effort and action and the desirability of nothingness. *Om Mani padme hum*, George.

"Look—it doesn't care what happens to it and it doesn't even know we're here. *It's achieved Nirvana,* and it's sitting there contemplating its cam stud!"

Star Mouse

Mitkey, the mouse, wasn't Mitkey then.

He was just another mouse, who lived behind the floorboards and plaster of the house of the great Herr Professor Oberburger, formerly of Vienna and Heidelberg; then a refugee from the excessive admiration of his more powerful fellow-countrymen. The excessive admiration had concerned not Herr Oberburger himself, but a certain gas which had been a by-product of an unsuccessful rocket fuel—which might have been a highly successful something else.

If, of course, the Professor had given them the correct formula. Which he— Well, anyway, the Professor had made good his escape and now lived in a house in Connecticut. And so did Mitkey.

A small gray mouse, and a small gray man. Nothing unusual about either of them. Particularly there was nothing unusual about Mitkey; he had a family and he liked cheese and if there were Rotarians among mice, he would have been a Rotarian.

The Herr Professor, of course, had his mild eccentricities. A confirmed bachelor, he had no one to talk to except himself, but he considered himself an excellent conversationalist and held constant verbal communication with himself while he worked. That fact, it turned out later, was important, because Mitkey had excellent ears and heard those night-long soliloquies. He didn't understand them, of course. If he thought about them at all, he merely thought of the Professor as a large and noisy super-mouse who squeaked over-much.

"Und now," he would say to himself, "ve vill see vether this eggshaust tube vas broperly machined. It should fidt vithin vun vun-hundreth thousandth uf an indtch. Ahhh, it iss berfect. Und now—"

Night after night, day after day, month after month. The gleaming thing grew, and the gleam in Herr Oberburger's eyes grew apace.

It was about three and a half feet long, with weirdly shaped vanes, and it rested on a temporary framework on a table in the center of the room that served the Herr Professor for all purposes. The house in which he and Mitkey lived was a four-room structure, but the Professor hadn't yet found it out, seemingly. Originally, he had planned to use the big room as a laboratory only, but he found it more convenient to sleep on a cot in one corner of it, when he slept at all, and to do the little cooking he did over the same gas burner over which he melted down golden grains of TNT into a dangerous soup which he salted and peppered with strange condiments, but did not eat.

"Und now I shall bour it into tubes, und see vether vun tube adjacendt to another eggsplodes de secondt tube vhen der virst tube iss—"

That was the night Mitkey almost decided to move himself and his family to a more stable abode, one that did not rock and sway and try to turn handsprings on its foundations. But Mitkey didn't move after all, because there were compensations. New mouse-holes all over, and—joy of joy!—a big crack in the back of the refrigerator where the Professor kept, among other things, food.

Of course the tubes had been not larger than capillary size, or the house would not have remained around the mouse-holes. And of course Mitkey could not guess what was coming or understand the Herr Professor's brand of English (or any other brand of English, for that matter) or he would not have let even a crack in the refrigerator tempt him.

The Professor was jubilant that morning.

"Der fuel, idt vorks! Der secondt tube, idt did not eggsplode. Und der virst, in *seggtions*, as I had eggspectedt! Und it is more bowerful; there will be plenty of room for der combartment—"

Ah, yes, the compartment. That was where Mitkey came in, although even the Professor didn't know it yet. In fact the Professor didn't even know that Mitkey existed.

"Und now," he was saying to his favorite listener, "idt is budt a madter of combining der fuel tubes so they work in obbosite bairs. Und then—"

That was the moment when the Herr Professor's eyes first fell on Mitkey. Rather, they fell upon a pair of gray whiskers and a black, shiny little nose protruding from a hole in the baseboards.

"Vell!" he said, "vot haff ve here! Mitkey Mouse himself! Mitkey, how vould you like to go for a ride, negst veek? Ve shall see."

That is how it came about that the next time the Professor sent into town for supplies, his order included a mousetrap—not one of the vicious kind that kills, but one of the wire-cage kind. And it had not been set, with cheese, for more than ten minutes before Mitkey's sharp little nose had smelled out that cheese and followed his nose into captivity.

Not, however, an unpleasant captivity. Mitkey was an honored guest. The cage reposed now on the table at which the Professor did most of his work, and cheese in indigestion-giving abundance was pushed through the bars, and the Professor didn't talk to himself any more.

"You see, Mitkey, I vas going to sendt to der laboratory in Hardtfordt for a vhite mouse, budt vhy should I, mit you here? I am sure you are more soundt und healthy und able to vithstand a long chourney than those laboratory mices. No? Ah, you viggle your viskers und that means yes, no? Und being used to living in dargk holes, you should suffer less than they from glaustrophobia, no?"

And Mitkey grew fat and happy and forgot all about trying to get out of the cage. I fear that he even forgot about the family he had abandoned, but he knew, if he knew anything, that he need not worry about them in the slightest. At least not until and unless the Professor discovered and repaired the hole in the refrigerator. And the Professor's mind was most emphatically not on refrigerators.

"Und so, Mitkey, ve shall place this vane so—it iss only of assistance in der landing, in an atmosphere. It und these vill bring you down safely und slowly enough that der shock-absorbers in der movable combartment vill keep you from bumping your head too hard, I think." Of course Mitkey missed the ominous note to that "I think" qualification because he missed all the rest of it. He did not, as has been explained, speak English. Not then.

But Herr Oberburger talked to him just the same. He showed him pictures. "Did you effer see der mouse you vas named after, Mitkey? Vhat? No? Loogk, this is der original Mitkey Mouse, by Valt Dissney. Budt I think you are cuter, Mitkey."

Probably the Professor was a bit crazy to talk that way to a little gray mouse. In fact, he must have been crazy to make a rocket that worked. For the odd thing was that the Herr Professor was not really an inventor. There was, as he carefully explained to Mitkey, not one single thing about that rocket that was *new*. The Herr Professor was a technician; he could take other people's ideas and make them work. His only real invention—the rocket fuel that wasn't one— had been turned over to the United States Government and had proved to be something already known and discarded because it was too expensive for practical use.

As he explained very carefully to Mitkey, "It iss burely a matter of absolute accuracy and mathematical correctness Mitkey. Idt iss all here—ve merely combine—and ve achieff vhat, Mitkey?

"Eggscape velocity, Mitkey! Chust barely, it adds up to eggscape velocity. Maybe. There are yet unknown facgtors, Mitkey, in der ubper atmosphere, der troposphere, der stratosphere. Ve think ve know eggsactly how mudch air there iss to calculate resistance against, but are ve absolutely sure? No, Mitkey, ve are not. Ve haff not been there. Und der marchin iss so narrow that so mudch as an air current might affect idt."

But Mitkey cared not a whit. In the shadow of the tapering aluminum-alloy cylinder he waxed fat and happy.

"*Der Tag*, Mitkey, *der Tag!* Und I shall not lie to you, Mitkey. I shall not giff you valse assurances. You go on a dancherous chourney, mein little friendt.

"A vifty-vifty chance ve giff you, Mitkey. Not der moon or bust, but der moon *und* bust, or else maybe safely back to earth. You see, my boor little Mitkey, der moon iss not made of green cheese und if it were, you vould not liff to eat it because there iss not enough atmosphere to bring you down safely und vith your viskers still on.

"Und vhy then, you may vell ask, do I send you? Because der rocket may *not* attain eggscape velocity. Und in that case, it iss still an eggsperiment, budt a different vun. Der rocket, if it goes not to der moon, falls back on der earth, no? Und in that case certain instruments shall giff us further information than ve haff yet about things up there in space. Und you shall giff us information, by vether or not you are yet alife, vether der shock absorbers und vanes are sufficient in an earth-equivalent atmosphere. You see?

"Then ladter, vhen ve send rockets to Venus maybe vhere an atmosphere eggsists, ve shall haff data to calculate the needed size of vanes und shock-absorbers, no? Und in either case, und vether or not you return, Mitkey, you shall be vamous! You shall be der virst liffing greature to go oudt beyond der stratosphere of der earth, out into space.

"Mitkey, you shall be der Star-Mouse! I enfy you, Mitkey, und I only vish I vere your size, so I could go, too."

Der Tag, and the door to the compartment. "Gootbye, little Mitkey Mouse." Darkness. Silence. Noise!

"Der rocket—if it goes not to der moon—falls back on der earth, no?" That was what the Herr Professor had thought. But the best-laid plans of mice and men gang aft agley. Even star-mice.

All because of Prxl.

The Herr Professor found himself very lonely. After having had Mitkey to talk to, soliloquies were somehow empty and inadequate.

There may be some who say that the company of a small gray mouse is a poor substitute for a wife; but others may disagree. And, anyway, the Professor had never had a wife, and he *had* a mouse to talk to, so he missed one and if he missed the other, he didn't know it.

During the long night after the launching of the rocket, he had been very busy with his telescope, a sweet little eight-inch reflector, checking its course as it gathered momentum. The exhaust explosions made a tiny fluctuating point of light that was possible to follow, if one knew where to look.

But the following day there seemed to be nothing to do, and he was too excited to sleep, although he tried. So he compromised by doing a spot of housekeeping, cleaning the pots and pans. It was while he was so engaged that he heard a series of frantic little squeaks and discovered that another small gray mouse, with shorter whiskers and a shorter tail than Mitkey, had walked into the wire-cage mousetrap.

"Vell, vell," said the Professor, "vot haff ve here? Minnie? Iss it Minnie come to look for her Mitkey?"

The Professor was not a biologist, but he happened to be right. It *was* Minnie. Rather, it was Mitkey's mate, so the name was appropriate. What strange vagary of mind had induced her to walk into an unbaited trap, the Professor neither knew nor cared, but he was delighted. He promptly remedied the lack of bait by pushing a sizable piece of cheese through the bars.

Thus it was that Minnie came to fill the place of her far-traveling spouse as repository for the Professor's confidences. Whether she worried about her family or not there is no way of knowing, but she need not have done so. They were now large enough to fend for themselves, particularly in a house that offered abundant cover and easy access to the refrigerator.

"Ah, und now it iss dargk enough, Minnie, that ve can loogk for that husband of yours. His viery trail across the sky. True, Minnie, it iss a very small viery trail und der astronomers vill not notice it, because they do not know vhere to loogk. But ve do.

"He iss going to be a very vamous mouse, Minnie, this Mitkey of ours, vhen ve tell der vorld about him und about mein rocket. You see, Minnie, ve haff not told them yet. Ve shall vait und giff der gomplete story all at vunce. By dawn of tomorrow ve'll—

"Ah, there he iss, Minnie! Vaint, but there. I'd hold you up to der scope und let you loogk, but it vould not be vocused right for your eyes, und I do not know how to—

"Almost vun hundred thousand miles, Minnie, und still agcelerating, but not for much longer. Our Mitkey iss on schedule; in fagt he iss going vaster than ve had vigured, no? It iss sure now that he vill eggscape the gravitation of der earth, und fall upon der moon!"

Of course, it was purely coincidental that Minnie squeaked.

"Ah, yess, Minnie, little Minnie. I know, I know. Ve shall neffer see our Mitkey again, und I almost vish our eggsperiment hadt vailed. Budt there are gompensations, Minnie. He shall be der most vamous of all mices. Der Star-Mouse! Virst liffing greature effer to go beyond der gravitational bull of earth!"

The night was long. Occasionally high clouds obscured vision.

"Minnie, I shall make you more gomfortable than in that so-small vire cage. You vould like to seem to be vree, vould you not, vithout bars, like der animals at modern zoos, vith moats insteadt?"

And so, to fill in an hour when a cloud obscured the sky, the Herr Professor made Minnie her new home. It was the end of a wooden crate, about half an inch thick and a foot square, laid flat on the table, and with no visible barrier around it.

But he covered the top with metal foil at the edges, and he placed the board on another larger board which also had a strip of metal foil surrounding the island of Minnie's home. And wires from the two areas of metal foil to opposite terminals of a small transformer which he placed near by.

"Und now, Minnie, I shall blace you on your island, vhich shall be liberally supplied mitt cheese und vater, und you shall vind it is an eggcelent blace to liff. But you vill get a mild shock or two vhen you try to step off der edge of der island. It vill not hurt much, but you vill not like it, und after a few tries you vill learn not to try again, no? Und—"

And night again.

Minnie was happy on her island, her lesson well learned. She would no longer so much as step on the inner strip of metal foil. It was a mouse-paradise of an island, though. There was a cliff of cheese bigger than Minnie herself. It kept her busy. Mouse and cheese; soon one would be transmutation of the other.

But Professor Oberburger wasn't thinking about that. The Professor was worried. When he had calculated and recalculated and aimed his eight-inch reflector through the hole in the roof and turned out the lights—

Yes, there *are* advantages to being a bachelor after all. If one wants a hole in the roof, one simply knocks a hole in the roof and there is nobody to tell one that one is crazy. If winter comes, or if it rains, one can always call a carpenter or use a tarpaulin.

But the faint trail of light wasn't there. The Professor frowned and re-calculated and re-re-calculated and shifted his telescope three-tenths of a second and still the rocket wasn't there.

"Minnie, something iss wrong. Either de tubes haff stopped viring, or—"

Or the rocket was no longer traversing a straight line relative to its point of departure. By straight, of course, is meant parabolically curved relative to everything other than velocity.

So the Herr Professor did the only thing remaining for him to do, and began to search, with the telescope, in widening circles. It was two hours before he found it, five degrees off course already and veering more and more into a— Well, there was only one thing you could call it. A tailspin.

The darned thing was going in circles, circles which appeared to constitute an orbit about something that couldn't possibly be there. Then narrowing into a concentric spiral.

Then—out. Gone. Darkness. No rocket flares.

The Professor's face was pale as he turned to Minnie.

"It iss *imbossible,* Minnie. Mein own eyes, but it could not be. Even if vun side stopped viring, it could not haff gone into such sudden circles." His pencil verified a suspicion. "Und, Minnie, it decelerated vaster than bossible. Even mitt no tubes viring, its momentum vould haff been more—"

The rest of the night—telescope and calculus—yielded no clue. That is, no believable clue. Some force not inherent in the rocket itself, and not accountable by gravitation—even of a hypothetical body—had acted.

"Mein poor Mitkey."

The gray, inscrutable dawn. "Mein Minnie, it vill haff to be a secret. Ve dare not bublish vhat ve saw, for it vould not be believed. I am not sure I believe it myself, Minnie. Berhaps because I vas offertired vrom not sleeping, I chust imachined that I saw—"

Later. "But, Minnie, ve shall hope. Vun hundred vifty thousand miles out, it vas. It vill fall back upon der earth. But I gannot tell vhere! I thought that if it did, I vould be able to galculate its course, und—But after those goncentric cirgles—Minnie, not even Einstein could galculate vhere it vill land. Not effen *me.* All ve can do iss hope that ve shall hear of vhere it falls."

Cloudy day. Black night jealous of its mysteries.

"Minnie, our poor Mitkey. There iss *nothing* could have gauzed—"

But something had.

Prxl.

Prxl is an asteroid. It isn't called that by earthly astronomers, because— for excellent reasons—they have not discovered it. So we will call it by the nearest possible transliteration of the name its inhabitants use. Yes, it's inhabited.

Come to think of it, Professor Oberburger's attempt to send a rocket to the moon had some strange results. Or rather, Prxl did.

You wouldn't think that an asteroid could reform a drunk, would you? But one Charles Winslow, a besotted citizen of Bridgeport, Connecticut, never took a drink after the time when—right on Grove Street—a mouse asked him the road to Hartford. The mouse was wearing bright red pants and vivid yellow gloves—

But that was fifteen months after the Professor lost his rocket. We'd better start over again.

Prxl is an asteroid. One of those despised celestial bodies which terrestrial astronomers call vermin of the sky, because the darned things leave trails across the plates that clutter up the more important observations of novae and nebulae. Fifty thousand fleas on the dark dog of night.

Tiny things, most of them. Astronomers have been discovering recently that some of them come close to Earth. Amazingly close. There was excitement in 1932 when Amor came within ten million miles—astronomically, a mere mashie shot. Then Apollo cut that almost in half, and in 1936 Adonis came within less than one and a half million miles.

In 1937, Hermes, less than half a million, but the astronomers got really excited when they calculated its orbit and found that the little mile-long asteroid *can* come within a mere 220,000 miles, closer than Earth's own moon.

Some day they may be still more excited, if and when they spot the three-eighth-mile asteroid Prxl, that obstacle of space, making a transit across the moon and discover that it frequently comes within a mere hundred thousand miles of our rapidly whirling world.

Only in event of a transit will they ever discover it, though, for Prxl does not reflect light. It hasn't, anyway, for several million years since its inhabitants coated it with a black, light-absorbing pigment derived from its interior. Monumental task, painting a world, for creatures half an inch tall. But worth it, at the time. When they'd shifted its orbit, they were safe from their enemies. There were giants in those days—eight-inch tall marauding pirates from Deimos. Got to Earth a couple of times too, before they faded out of the picture. Pleasant little giants who killed because they enjoyed it. Records in now-buried cities on Deimos might explain what happened to the dinosaurs. And why the promising Cro-Magnons disappeared at the height of their promise only a cosmic few minutes after the dinosaurs went west.

But Prxl survived. Tiny world no longer reflecting the sun's rays, lost to the cosmic killers when its orbit was shifted.

Prxl. Still civilized, with a civilization millions of years old. Its coat of blackness preserved and renewed regularly, more through tradition than fear of enemies in these later degenerate days. Mighty but stagnant civilization, standing still on a world that whizzes like a bullet.

And Mitkey Mouse.

Klarloth, head scientist of a race of scientists, tapped his assistant Bemj on what would have been Bemj's shoulder if he had had one. "Look," he said, "what approaches Prxl. Obviously artificial propulsion."

Bemj looked into the wall-plate and then directed a thought-wave at the mechanism that jumped the magnification a thousand-fold through an alteration of the electronic field.

The image leaped, blurred, then steadied. "Fabricated," said Bemj. "Extremely crude, I must say. Primitive explosive-powered rocket. Wait, I'll check where it came from."

He took the readings from the dials about the viewplate and hurled them as thoughts against the psychocoil of the computer, then waited while that most complicated of machines digested all the factors and prepared the answer. Then, eagerly, he slid his mind into rapport with its projector. Klarloth likewise listened in to the silent broadcast.

Exact point on Earth and exact time of departure. Untranslatable expression of curve of trajectory, and point on that curve where deflected by gravitational pull of Prxl. The destination—or rather the original intended destination—of the rocket was obvious, Earth's moon. Time and place of arrival on Prxl if present course of rocket was unchanged.

"Earth," said Klarloth meditatively. "They were a long way from rocket travel the last time we checked them. Some sort of a crusade, or battle of beliefs, going on, wasn't there?"

Bemj nodded. "Catapults. Bows and arrows. They've taken a long stride since, even if this is only an early experimental thing of a rocket. Shall we destroy it before it gets here?"

Klarloth shook his head thoughtfully. "Let's look it over. May save us a trip to Earth; we can judge their present state of development pretty well from the rocket itself."

"But then we'll have to—"

"Of course. Call the Station. Tell them to train their attracto-repulsors on it and to swing it into a temporary orbit until they prepare a landing-cradle. And not to forget to damp out the explosive before they bring it down."

"Temporary force-field around point of landing—in case?"

"Naturally."

So despite the almost complete absence of atmosphere in which the vanes could have functioned, the rocket came down safely and so softly that Mitkey, in the dark compartment, knew only that the awful noise had stopped.

Mitkey felt better. He ate some more of the cheese with which the compartment was liberally provided. Then he resumed trying to gnaw a hole in the inch-thick wood with which the compartment was lined. That wooden lining was a kind thought of the Herr Professor for Mitkey's mental well-being. He knew that trying to gnaw his way out would give Mitkey something to do en route which would keep him from getting the screaming meemies. The idea had worked; being busy, Mitkey hadn't suffered mentally from his dark confinement. And now that things were quiet, he chewed away more industriously and more happily than ever, sublimely unaware that when he got through the wood, he'd find only metal which he couldn't chew. But better people than Mitkey have found things they couldn't chew.

Meanwhile, Klarloth and Bemj and several thousand other Prxlians stood gazing up at the huge rocket which, even lying on its side, towered high over their heads. Some of the younger ones, forgetting the invisible field of force, walked too close and came back, ruefully rubbing bumped heads.

Klarloth himself was at the psychograph.

"There is life inside the rocket," he told Bemj. "But the impressions are confused. One creature, but I cannot follow its thought processes. At the moment it seems to be doing something with its teeth."

"It could not be an Earthling, one of the dominant race. One of them is much larger than this huge rocket. Gigantic creatures. Perhaps, unable to construct a rocket large enough to hold one of themselves, they sent an experimental creature, such as our wooraths."

"I believe you've guessed right, Bemj. Well, when we have explored its mind thoroughly, we may still learn enough to save us a check-up trip to Earth. I am going to open the door."

"But air—creatures of Earth would need a heavy, almost a dense atmosphere. It could not live."

"We retain the force-field, of course. It will keep the air in. Obviously there is a source of supply of air within the rocket or the creature would not have survived the trip."

Klarloth operated controls, and the force-field itself put forth invisible pseudopods and turned the outer screw-door, then reached within and unlatched the inner door to the compartment itself.

All Prxl watched breathlessly as a monstrous gray head pushed out of the huge aperture yawning overhead. Thick whiskers, each as long as the body of a Prxlian—

Mitkey jumped down, and took a forward step that bumped his black nose hard—into something that wasn't there. He squeaked, and jumped backwards against the rocket.

There was disgust in Bemj's face as he looked up at the monster. "Obviously much less intelligent than a woorath. Might just as well turn on the ray."

"Not at all," interrupted Klarloth. "You forget certain very obvious facts. The creature is unintelligent, of course, but the subconscious of every animal holds in itself every memory, every impression, every sense-image, to which it has ever been subjected. If this creature has ever heard the speech of the Earthlings, or seen any of their works—besides this rocket—every word and every picture is indelibly graven. You see now what I mean?"

"Naturally. How stupid of me, Klarloth. Well, one thing is obvious from the rocket itself: we have nothing to fear from the science of Earth for at least a few millennia. So there is no hurry, which is fortunate. For to send back the creature's memory to the time of its birth, and to follow each sensory impression in the psychograph will require—well, a time at least equivalent to the age of the creature, whatever that is, plus the time necessary for us to interpret and assimilate each."

"But that will not be necessary, Bemj."

"No? Oh, you mean the X-19 waves?"

"Exactly. Focused upon this creature's brain-center, they can, without disturbing his memories, be so delicately adjusted as to increase his intelligence—now probably about .0001 in the scale—to the point where he is a reasoning creature. Almost automatically, during the process, he will assimilate his own memories, and understand them just as he would if he had been intelligent at the time he received those impressions.

"See, Bemj? He will automatically sort out irrelevant data and will be able to answer our questions."

"But would you make him as intelligent as——?"

"As we? No, the X-19 waves would not work so far. I would say to about .2 on the scale. That, judging from the rocket coupled with what we remember of Earthlings from our last trip there, is about their present place on the intelligence scale."

"Ummm, yes. At that level, he would comprehend his experiences on Earth just sufficiently that he would not be dangerous to us, too. Equal to an intelligent Earthling. Just about right for our purpose. Then, shall we teach him our language?"

"Wait," said Klarloth. He studied the psychograph closely for a while. "No, I do not think so. He will have a language of his own. I see in his subconscious, memories of many long conversations. Strangely, they all seem to be monologues by one person. But he will have a language—a simple one. It would take him a long time, even under treatment, to grasp the concepts of our own method of communication. But we can learn his, while he is under the X-19 machine, in a few minutes."

"Does he understand, now, any of that language?"

Klarloth studied the psychograph again. "No, I do not believe he— Wait, there is one word that seems to mean something to him. The word 'Mitkey.' It seems to be his name, and I believe that, from hearing it many times, he vaguely associates it with himself."

"And quarters for him—with air-locks and such?"

"Of course. Order them built."

To say it was a strange experience for Mitkey is understatement. Knowledge is a strange thing, even when it is acquired gradually. To have it thrust upon one—

And there were little things that had to be straightened out. Like the matter of vocal chords. His weren't adapted to the language he now found he knew. Bemj fixed that; you would hardly call it an operation because Mitkey—even with his new awareness—didn't know what was going on, and he was wide awake at the time. And they didn't explain to Mitkey about the J-dimension with which one can get at the inwardness of things without penetrating the outside.

They figured things like that weren't in Mitkey's line, and anyway they were more interested in learning from him than teaching him. Bemj and Klarloth, and a dozen others deemed worthy of the privilege. If one of them wasn't talking to him, another was.

Their questioning helped his own growing understanding. He would not, usually, know that he knew the answer to a question until it was asked. Then he'd piece together, without knowing just how he did it (any more than you or I know *how* we know things) and give them the answer.

Bemj: "Iss this language vhich you sbeak a universal vun?"

And Mitkey, even though he'd never thought about it before, had the answer ready: "No, it iss nodt. It iss Englitch, but I remember der Herr Brofessor sbeaking of other tongues. I belieff he sboke another himself originally, budt in America he always sboke Englitch to become more vamiliar mitt it. It iss a beaudiful sbeech, is it nodt?"

"Hmmmm," said Bemj.

Klarloth: "Und your race, the mices. Are they treated vell?"

"Nodt by most people," Mitkey told him. And explained.

"I vould like to do something for them," he added.

"Loogk, could I nodt take back mitt me this brocess vhich you used upon me? Abbly it to other mices, und greate a race of super-mices?"

"Vhy nodt?" asked Bemj.

He saw Klarloth looking at him strangely, and threw his mind into rapport with the chief scientist's, with Mitkey left out of the silent communion.

"Yes, of course," Bemj told Klarloth, "it will lead to trouble. Two equal classes of beings so dissimilar as mice and men cannot live together in amity. But why should that concern us, other than favorably? The resultant mess will slow down progress on Earth—give us a few more millennia of peace before Earthlings discover we are here, and trouble starts. You know these Earthlings."

"But you would give them the X-19 waves? They might—"

"No, of course not. But we can explain to Mitkey here how to make a very crude and limited machine for them. A primitive one which would suffice for nothing more than the specific task of converting mouse mentality from .0001 to .2, Mitkey's own level and that of the bifurcated Earthlings."

"It is possible," communicated Klarloth. "It is certain that for aeons to come they will be incapable of understanding its basic principle."

"But could they not use even a crude machine to raise their own level of intelligence?"

"You forget, Bemj, the basic limitation of the X-19 rays; that no one can possibly design a projector capable of raising any mentality to a point on the scale higher than his own. Not even we."

All this, of course, over Mitkey's head, in silent Prxlian.

More interviews, and more.

Klarloth again: "Mitkey, ve varn you of vun thing. Avoid carelessness vith electricity. Der new molecular rearranchement of your brain center—it iss unstable, und—"

Bemj: "Mitkey, are you sure your Herr Brofessor iss der most advanced of all who eggsperiment vith der rockets?

"In cheneral, yess, Bemj. There are others who on vun specific boint, such as eggsplosives, mathematics, astrovisics, may know more, but not much more. Und for combining these knowledges, he iss ahead."

"It iss vell," said Bemj.

Small gray mouse towering like a dinosaur over tinier half-inch Prxlians. Meek, herbivorous creature though he was, Mitkey could have killed any one of them with a single bite. But, of course, it never occurred to him to do so, nor to them to fear that he might.

They turned him inside out mentally. They did a pretty good job of study on him physically, too, but that was through the J-dimension, and Mitkey didn't even know about it.

They found out what made him tick, and they found out everything he knew and some things he didn't even know he knew. And they grew quite fond of him.

"Mitkey," said Klarloth one day, "all der civilized races on Earth vear glothing, do they nodt? Vell, if you are to raise der level of mices to men, vould it not be vitting that you vear glothes, too?"

"An eggcelent idea, Herr Klarloth. Und I know chust vhat kind I vould like. Der Herr Brofessor vunce showed me a bicture of a mouse bainted by der artist Dissney, und der mouse vore glothing. Der mouse vas not a real-life vun, budt an imachinary mouse in a barable, und der Brofessor named me after der Dissney mouse."

"Vot kind of glothing vas it, Mitkey?"

"Bright red bants mitt two big yellow buttons in frondt und two in back, und yellow shoes for der back feet und a pair of yellow gloves for der vront. A hole in der seat of der bants to aggomodate der tail."

"Ogay, Mitkey. Such shall be ready for you in fife minutes."

That was on the eve of Mitkey's departure. Originally Bemj had suggested awaiting the moment when Prxl's eccentric orbit would again take it within a hundred and fifty thousand miles of Earth. But, as Klarloth pointed out, that would be fifty-five Earth-years ahead, and Mitkey wouldn't last that long. Not unless they— And Bemj agreed that they had better not risk sending a secret like that back to Earth.

So they compromised by refueling Mitkey's rocket with something that would cancel out the million and a quarter odd miles he would have to travel. That secret they didn't have to worry about, because the fuel would be gone by the time the rocket landed.

Day of departure.

"Ve haff done our best, Mitkey, to set und time der rocket so it vill land on or near der spot from vhich you left Earth. But you gannot eggspect agguracy in a voyach so long as this. You vill land near. The rest iss up to you. Ve haff equvipped the rocket ship for effery contingency."

"Thank you, Herr Klarloth, Herr Bemj. Gootbye."

"Gootbye, Mitkey. Ve hate to loose you."

"Gootbye, Mitkey."

"Gootbye, gootbye ..."

For a million and a quarter miles, the aim was really excellent. The rocket landed in Long Island Sound, ten miles out from Bridgeport, about sixty miles from the house of Professor Oberburger near Hartford.

They had prepared for a water landing, of course. The rocket went down to the bottom, but before it was more than a few dozen feet under the surface, Mitkey opened the door—especially equipped to open from the inside—and stepped out.

Over his regular clothes he wore a neat little diving suit that would have protected him at any reasonable depth, and which, being lighter than water, brought him to the surface quickly where he was able to open his helmet.

He had enough synthetic food to last him for a week, but it wasn't necessary, as things turned out. The nightboat from Boston carried him in to Bridgeport on its anchor chain, and once in sight of land he was able to divest himself of the diving suit and let it sink to the bottom after he'd punctured the tiny compartments that made it float, as he'd promised Klarloth he would do.

Almost instinctively, Mickey knew that he'd do well to avoid human beings until he'd reached Professor Oberburger and told his story. His worst danger proved to be the rats at the wharf where he swam ashore. They were ten times Mitkey's size and had teeth that could have taken him apart in two bites.

But mind has always triumphed over matter. Mitkey pointed an imperious yellow glove and said, "Scram," and the rats scrammed. They'd never seen anything like Mitkey before, and they were impressed.

So for that matter, was the drunk of whom Mitkey inquired the way to Hartford. We mentioned that episode before. That was the only time Mitkey tried direct communication with strange human beings. He took, of course, every precaution. He addressed his remarks from a strategic position only inches away from a hole into which he could have popped. But it was the drunk who did the popping, without even waiting to answer Mitkey's question.

But he got there, finally. He made his way afoot to the north side of town and hid out behind a gas station until he heard a motorist who had pulled in for gasoline inquire the way to Hartford. And Mitkey was a stowaway when the car started up.

The rest wasn't hard. The calculations of the Prxlians showed that the starting point of the rocket was five Earth miles north-west of what showed on their telescopomaps as a city, and which from the Professor's conversation Mitkey knew would be Hartford.

He got there.

"Hello, Brofessor."

The Herr Professor Oberburger looked up, startled. There was no one in sight. "Vot?" he asked, of the air. "Who iss?"

"It iss I, Brofessor. Mitkey, der mouse whom you sent to der moon. But I vas not there. Insteadt, I—"

"Vot?? It is imbossible. Somebody blays der choke. Budt—budt nobody *knows* about that rocket. Vhen it vailed, I didn't told nobody. Nobody budt me knows—"

"And me, Brofessor."

The Herr Professor sighed heavily. "Offervork. I am going vhat they call batty in der bel—"

"No, Brofessor. This is really me, Mitkey. I can talk now. Chust like you."

"You say you can—I do not belief it. Vhy can I not see you, then. Vhere are you? Vhy don't you—"

"I am hiding, Brofessor, in der vall chust behind der big hole. I vanted to be sure efferything vas ogay before I showed myself. Then you vould not get eggcited and throw something at me maybe."

"Vot? Vhy, Mitkey, if it iss really you und I am nodt asleep or going— Vhy, Mitkey, you know better than to think I might do something like that!"

"Ogay, Brofessor."

Mitkey stepped out of the hole in the wall, and the Professor looked at him and rubbed his eyes and looked again and rubbed his eyes and—

"I *am* crazy," he said finally. "Red bants he vears yet, und yellow— It gannot be. I *am* crazy."

"No, Brofessor. Listen, I'll tell you all aboudt."

And Mitkey told him.

Gray dawn, and a small gray mouse still talking earnestly.

"But, Mitkey—"

"Yess, Brofessor. I see your point, that you think an intelligent race of mices und an intelligent race of men couldt nodt get along side by sides. But it vould not be side by sides; as I said, there are only a ferry few beople in the smallest continent of Australia. Und it vould cost little to bring them back und turn offer that continent to us mices. Ve vould call it Moustralia instead of Australia und ve vould instead of Sydney call der capital Dissney in honor of—"

"But, Mitkey—"

"But, Brofessor, look vot ve offer for that continent. *All* mices vould go there. Ve civilize a few und the few help us catch others und bring them in to put them under der ray machine, und the others help catch more und build more machines und it grows like a snowball rolling down hill. Und ve sign a non-aggression pact mitt humans und stay on Moustralia und raise our own food und—"

"But, Mitkey—"

"Und look vot ve offer you in eggschange, Herr Brofessor! Ve vill eggsterminate your vorst enemy—der *rats*. Ve do not like them either. Und vun battalion of vun thousand mices, armed mitt gas masks und small gas bombs could go right in effery hole after der rats und could eggsterminate effery rat in a city in vun day or two. In der whole vorld ve could eggsterminate effery last rat in a year, und at the same time catch und civilize effery mouse und ship him to Moustralia, und—"

"But, Mitkey—"

"Vot, Brofessor?"

"It vould vork, but it vould not vork. You could eggsterminate der rats, yess. But how long vould it be before conflicts of interests vould lead to der mices trying to eggsterminate der people or der people trying to eggsterminate der—"

"They vould not dare, Brofessor! Ve could make veapons that vould—"

"You see, Mitkey?"

"But it vould not habben. If men vill honor our rights, ve vill honor—"

The Herr Professor sighed.

"I—I vill act as your intermediary, Mitkey, und offer your broposition, und— Vell, it is true that getting rid of rats vould be a greadt boon to der human race. Budt—"

"Thank you, Brofessor."

"By der vay, Mitkey. I haff Minnie. Your vife, I guess it iss, unless there vas other mices around. She iss in der other room; I put her there chust before you arriffed, so she vould be in der dark und could sleep. You vant to see her?"

"Vife?" said Mitkey. It had been so long that he had really forgotten the family he had perforce abandoned. The memory returned slowly.

"Vell," he said "—ummm, yess. Ve vill get her und I shall construct quvick a small X-19 prochector und— Yess, it vill help you in your negotiations mitt der governments if there are sefferal of us already so they can see I am not chust a freak like they might otherwise suspegt."

It wasn't deliberate. It couldn't have been, because the Professor didn't know about Klarloth's warning to Mitkey about carelessness with electricity— "Der new molecular rearranchement of your brain center—it iss unstable, und—"

And the Professor was still back in the lighted room when Mitkey ran into the room where Minnie was in her barless cage. She was asleep, and the sight of her— Memory of his earlier days came back like a flash and suddenly Mitkey knew how lonesome he had been.

"Minnie!" he called, forgetting that she could not understand.

And stepped up on the board where she lay. "Squeak!" The mild electrical current between the two strips of tinfoil got him.

There was silence for a while.

Then: "Mitkey," called the Herr Professor. "Come on back und ve vill discuss this—"

He stepped through the doorway and saw them, there in the gray light of dawn, two small gray mice cuddled happily together. He couldn't tell which was which, because Mitkey's teeth had torn off the red and yellow garments which had suddenly been strange, confining and obnoxious things.

"Vot on earth?" asked Professor Oberburger. Then he remembered the current, and guessed.

"Mitkey! Can you no longer talk? Iss der—"

Silence.

Then the Professor smiled. "Mitkey," he said, "my little star-mouse. I think you are more happier now."

He watched them a moment, fondly, then reached down and flipped the switch that broke the electrical barrier. Of course they didn't know they were free, but when the Professor picked them up and placed them carefully on the floor, one ran immediately for the hole in the wall. The other followed, but turned around and looked back—still a trace of puzzlement in the little black eyes, a puzzlement that faded.

"Gootbye, Mitkey. You vill be happier this vay. Und there vill always be cheese."

"Squeak," said the little gray mouse, and it popped into the hole.

"Gootbye—" it might, or might not, have meant.

Runaround

For many days now he had wandered ponderously through the hungry forests, across the hungry plains of dwarf scrub and sand, and had wandered along the lush edges of the streams that flowed down to the big water. Always hungry.

It seemed to him that he had always been hungry.

Sometimes there was something to eat, yes, but it was always something small. One of the little things with hoofs, one of the little things with three toes. All so small. One of them was not more than enough to put a keener edge on that monstrous saurian appetite of his.

And they ran so fast, the little things. He saw them, and his huge mouth would slaver as he ran earth-shakingly toward them, but off they whisked among the trees like little furry streaks. In frantic haste to catch them, he would bowl over the smaller trees that were in the way, but always they were gone when he got there.

Gone on their tiny legs that went faster than his mighty ones. One stride of his was more distance-devouring than fifty of theirs, but those flashing little legs flickered a hundred strides to his one. Even in the open where there were no trees for them to dodge among, he could not catch them.

A hundred years of hunger.

He, Tyrannosaurus Rex, king of all, mightiest and most vicious fighting engine of flesh that ever the world had evolved, was able to kill anything that stood against him. But nothing stood against him. They ran.

The little things. They ran. They flew, some of them. Others climbed trees and swung from limb to limb as fast as he could run along the ground until they came to a tree tall enough to be well out of his twenty-five-foot reach and thick enough of bole that he could not uproot it, and then they would hang ten feet above the grasp of his great jaws. And gibber at him when he roared in baffled, hungry rage.

Hungry, always hungry.

A hundred years of not-quite-enough. Last of his kind, and there was nothing left to stand up against him and fight, and fill his stomach when he had killed it.

His slate-gray skin hung upon him in loose, wrinkled folds as he shriveled away within it, from the ever-present ache and agony of hunger in his guts.

His memory was short, but vaguely he knew that it had not always been thus. He'd been younger once, and he'd fought terribly against things that fought back. They had been scarce and hard to find even then, but occasionally he met them. And killed them.

The big, armor-plated one with the terrible sharp ridges along his back, who tried to roll over on you and cut you in half. The one with the three huge forward-pointing horns and the big ruff of heavy bone. Those had been ones who went on four legs; or had gone on four legs until he had met them. Then they had stopped going.

There had been others more nearly like himself. Some had been many times bigger than he, but he had killed them with ease. The biggest ones of all had little heads and small mouths and ate leaves off the trees and plants on the ground.

Yes, there had been giants on the earth, those days. A few of them. Satisfying meals. Things you could kill and eat your fill of, and lie gorged and somnolent for days. Then eat again if the pesky leather-wings with the long bills of teeth hadn't finished off the Gargantuan feast while you had slept.

But if they had, it did not matter. Stride forth again, and kill again to eat if hungry, for the pure joy of fighting and killing if you were not hungry. Anything that came along. He'd killed them all—the horned ones, the armored ones, the monster ones. Anything that walked or crawled. His sides and flanks were rough and seamed with the scars of ancient battles.

There'd been giants in those days. Now there were the *little* things. The things that ran, and flew, and climbed. And wouldn't fight.

Ran so fast they could run in circles around him, some of them. Always, almost always, out of reach of his curved, pointed, double-edged teeth that were six inches long, and that could—but rarely had the chance to—shear through one of the little hairy things at a single bite, while warm blood coursed down the scaly hide of his neck.

Yes, he could get one of them, once in a while. But not often enough, not enough of them to satisfy that monstrous hunger that was Tyrannosaurus Rex, king of the tyrant reptiles. Now a king without a kingdom.

It was a burning within him, that dreadful hunger. It drove him, always.

It drove him today as he went heavy-footed through the forest, scorning paths, crashing his way through heavy underbrush and sapling trees as though they were grass of the plains.

Always before him the scurry and rush of the footsteps of the little ones, the quick click of hoofs, the *pad-pad* of the softer feet as they ran, ran.

It teemed with life, that forest of the Eocene. But with fleet life which, in smallness and speed, had found safety from the tyrant.

Life, it was, that wouldn't stand up and fight, with bellowing roars that shook the earth, with blood streaming from slavering jowls as monster fought monstrosity. This was life that gave you the runaround, that wouldn't fight and be killed.

Even in the steaming swamps. There were slippery things that slithered into the muddy water there, but they, too, were fast. They swam like wriggling lightning, slid into hollow rotten logs and weren't there when you ripped the logs apart.

It was getting dark, and there was a weakness upon him that made it excruciating pain for him to take another step. He'd been hungry a hundred years, but this was worst of all. But it was not a weakness that made him stop;

it was something that drove him on, made him keep going when every step was effort.

High in a big tree, something that clung to a branch was going *"Yahh! Yahh! Yahh!"* mocking and monotonously, and a broken piece of branch arced down and bounded harmlessly off his heavy hide. Lese majesty. For a moment he was stronger in the hope that something was going to fight.

He whirled and snapped at the branch that had struck him, and it splintered. And then he stood at fullest height and bellowed challenge at the little thing in the big tree, high overhead. But it would not come down; it went *"Yahh! Yahh! Yahh!"* and stayed there in cowardly safety.

He threw himself mightily against the trunk of the tree, but it was five feet thick, and he could not even shake it. He circled twice, roaring his bafflement, and then blundered on into gathering darkness.

Ahead of him, in one of the saplings, was a little gray thing, a ball of fur. He snapped at it, but it wasn't there when he closed his jaws upon the wood. He saw only a dim gray streak as it hit the ground and ran, gone in shadows before he could take a single step.

Darker, and though he could see dimly in the woods, he could see more clearly when he came to the moonlit plain. Still driven on. There was something to his left, something small and alive sitting on haunches on a patch of barren soil. He wheeled to run toward it. It didn't move until he was almost there; then with the suddenness of lightning it popped down a hole and vanished.

His footsteps were slower after that, his muscles responded sluggishly.

At dawn he came to the stream.

It was effort for him to reach it, but he got there and lowered his great head to drink, and drank deeply. The gnawing pain in his stomach rose, a moment, to crescendo, and then dulled. He drank more.

And slowly, ponderously, he sank down to the muddy soil. He didn't fall, but his legs gave way gradually, and he lay there, the rising sun in his eyes, unable to move. The pain that had been in his stomach was all over him now, but dulled, more an aching weakness than an agony.

The sun rose high overhead and sank slowly.

He could see but dimly now, and there were winged things that circled overhead. Things that swept the sky with lazy, cowardly circles. They were food, but they wouldn't come down and fight.

And when it got dark enough, there were other things that came. There was a circle of eyes two feet off the ground, and an excited yapping now and then, and a howl. Little things, food that wouldn't fight and be eaten. The kind of life that gave you the runaround.

Circle of eyes. Wings against the moonlit sky.

Food all about him, but fleet food that ran away on flashing legs the minute it saw or heard, and that had eyes and ears too sharp ever to fail to see or hear. The fast little things that ran and wouldn't fight.

He lay with his head almost at the water's edge. At dawn when the red sun was again in his eyes, he managed to drag his mighty bulk a foot forward so he could drink again. He drank deeply, and a convulsive shudder ran through him and then he lay very quietly with his head in the water.

And the winged things overhead circled slowly down.

The New One

"Papa, are human beings real?"

"Drat it, kid, don't they teach you those things in Ashtaroth's class? If they don't then what am I paying them ten B.T.U. a semester for?"

"Ashtaroth talks about it, Papa. But I can't make much sense out of what he says."

"Um-m-m ... Ashtaroth is a bit— Well, what does he say?"

"He says *they* are and *we* aren't; that we exist only because they believe in us, that we are fig ... fig ... something."

"Figments of their imagination?"

"That's it, Papa. We're figments of their imagination, he says."

"Well, what's hard about that? Doesn't it answer your question?"

"But, Papa, if we're not *real*, why are we here? I mean, how can—"

"All right, kid, I suppose I might as well take time out to explain this to you. But first, don't let these things worry you. They're academic."

"What's 'academic'?"

"Something that doesn't really matter. Something you got to learn so you won't be ignorant, like a dumb dryad. The real lessons, the ones you should study hard, are the ones you get in Lebalome's classes, and Marduk's."

"You mean red magic, and possession and—"

"Yeah, that sort of thing. Particularly the red magic; that's your field as a fire elemental, see? But to get back to this reality stuff. There are two kinds of ... uh ... stuff; mind and matter. You got that much clear now?"

"Yes, Papa."

"Well, *mind* is higher than *matter*, isn't it? A higher plane of existence. Now things like rocks and ... uh ... like rocks are pure matter; that's the lowest kind of existence. Human beings are a kind of fork between mind and matter. They got both. Their bodies are matter like rocks and yet they got minds that run them. That makes them halfway up the scale, understand?"

"I guess so, Papa, but—"

"Don't interrupt. Then the third and highest form of existence is ... uh ... us. The elementals and the gods and the myths of all kinds—the banshees and the mermaids and the afreets and the *loups-garou* and—well, everybody and everything you see around here. We're higher."

"But if we aren't *real*, how—"

"Hush. We're higher because we're pure thought, see? We're pure mind-stock, kid. Just like humans evolved out of nonthinking matter, we evolved out of them. They *conceived* us. Now do you understand?"

"I guess so, Papa. But what if they quit believing in us?"

"They never will—completely. There'll always be some of them who believe, and that's enough. Of course the more of them believe in us, the stronger we are, individually. Now you take some of the older lads like Ammon-Ra and Bel-Marduk—they're kind of weak and puny these days because they haven't any real followers. They used to be big guns around here, kid. I remember when Bel-Marduk could lick his weight in Harpies. Look at him today—walks with a cane. And Thor—boy, you should have heard *him* in a ruckus, only a few centuries ago."

"But what, Papa, if it ever gets so nobody up there believes in them? Do they die?"

"Um-m-m—theoretically, yes. But there's one thing saves us. There are some humans who believe *anything*. Or anyway don't actually disbelieve in anything. That group is a sort of nucleus that holds things together. No matter how discredited a belief is, they hang on by doubting a little."

"But what, Papa, if they conceive of a *new* mythological being? Would he come into existence down here?"

"Of course, kid. That's how we all got here, one time or another. Why, look at poltergeists, for instance. They're newcomers. And all this ectoplasm you see floating around and getting in the way, that's new. And—well, like this big guy Paul Bunyan; he's only been around here a century or so; he isn't much older than you are. And lots of others. Of course, they have to get *invoked* before they show up, but that always gets done sooner or later."

"Gosh, thanks, Papa. I understand you a lot better than I did Ashtaroth. He uses big words like 'transmogrification' and 'superactualization' and what not."

"Okay, kid, now run along and play. But don't bring any of those darn water elemental kids back with you. The place gets so full of steam I can't see. And a very important personage is going to drop in."

"Who, Papa?"

"Darveth, the head fire demon. The big shot himself. That's why I want you to run along outside."

"Gee, Papa, can't I—"

"No. He wants to tell me about something important. He's got a human being on the string, and it's ticklish business."

"How do you mean, got a human being on the string? What's he want to do with him?"

"Make him set fires, of course, up there. What Darveth's going to do with this guy will be good. He says better than he did with Nero or Mrs. O'Leary's cow. It's something big on, this time."

"Gee, can't I watch?"

"Later, maybe. There's nothing to watch yet. This guy's still just a baby. But Darveth's farsighted. Get 'em young, that's his idea. It'll take years to work out, but it'll be hot stuff when it happens."

"Can I watch, then?"

"Sure, kid. But run along and play now. And keep away from those frost giants."

"Yes, Papa."

It took twenty-two years for it to get him. He fought it off that long, and then—blooie.

Oh, it had been there all along, ever since Wally Smith was a baby; ever since—well, it was there before he could remember. Since he'd managed to stand on babyhood's thick stubby little legs, hanging on to two bars of his playpen, and had watched his father take a little stick and rub it across the sole of his shoe and then hold it to his pipe.

Funny, those clouds of smoke that came from that pipe. They were there, and then they weren't, like gray phantoms. But that was merely interesting in a mild way.

What drew his eyes, his round wide wondering eyes, was the *flame*.

The thing that danced on the end of the stick. The thing that flared there, ever-shape-changing. Yellow-red-blue wonder, magic beauty.

One of his chubby hands clung to the bar of the playpen, and the other reached out for the *flame*. His; he wanted it. His.

And his father, holding it safely out of reach, grinning at him in proud and blind paternity. Never guessing. "Pretty, huh, sonny? But mustn't touch. Fire *burn*."

Yes, Wally, fire *burns*.

Wally Smith knew a lot about fire by the time he was in school. He knew that fire burns. He knew it by experience, and it had been painful, but not bitter, experience. The scar was on his forearm to remind him. The blotchy white scar that would always be there when he rolled up his sleeves.

It had marked him in another way, too. His eyes.

That had come early, also. The sun, the glorious sun, the murderous sun. He'd watched that, too, when his mother had moved his playpen out into the yard. Watched it with breathless fascination until his eyes hurt, and had looked back at it again as soon as he could, and had stretched up his little arms toward it. He knew that it was fire, flame, somehow identical with the thing that danced on the end of the sticks his father held to his pipe.

Fire. He *loved* it.

And so, quite young, he wore glasses. All his life he was to be nearsighted and wear thickish glasses.

The draft board took one look at the thickness of those lenses and didn't even send him around for a physical examination. On the thickness of his lenses, they marked him exempt and told him to go home.

That was tough, because he *wanted* to get in. He'd seen a movie newsreel that showed the new flamethrowers. If he could get one of *those* things to operate—

But that desire was subconscious; he didn't know that it was a big part of the reason he wanted to get into uniform. That was in the fall of '41 and we weren't *in* the war yet. Later, after December, it was still part of the reason he wanted to get in, but not the major part. Wally Smith was a good American; that was even more important than being a good pyromaniac.

Anyway, he'd licked the pyromania. Or thought he had. If it was there, it was buried down deep where most of the time he could avoid thinking about it, and there was a "Thus Far, No Farther" sign across one passage of his mind.

That yen for a flamethrower worried him a bit. Then came Pearl Harbor and Wally Smith had it out with himself to discover whether it was *all* patriotism that made him want to kill Japs, or whether that yen for a flamethrower figured at all.

And while he mulled it over, things got hotter in the Philippines and the Japs moved down Malaya to Singapore, and there were U-boats off the coast and it began to look as though his country needed him. And there was a fighting anger in him that told him the hell with whether or not it was pyromania—it was patriotism even more, and he'd worry about the psychiatry of it later.

He tried three recruiting stations, and each of them bounced him back. Then the factory where he worked changed over and— But wait, we're getting a bit ahead of things.

When little Wally Smith was seven, they took him to a psychiatrist. "Yes," said the psychiatrist, "*pyromania*. Or anyway a strong tendency toward pyromania."

"And ... uh ... what causes it, Doctor?"

You've seen that psychiatrist, lots of times. In yeast ads. Identified—probably correctly—as a famous Vienna specialist. Remember when there was that long line of famous Vienna specialists who advocated eating yeast for everything from moral turpitude to ingrowing toenails? That, of course, was before the Nazi steam roller crossed Austria and blood began to flow like *wein*. Well, make a composite picture in your mind of the Vienna yeast dynasty and you'll know how impressive that psychiatrist looked.

"And ... uh ... what causes it, Doctor?"

"Emotional instability, Mr. Smith. Pyromania is not insanity, I wish you to understand. Not as long as it remains ... ah ... under control. It is a compulsion neurosis, predicated upon emotional instability. As to why the neurosis took that particular channel of expression; somewhere back in infancy there must have been a psychic trauma which—"

"A what, Doctor?"

"A trauma. A wound to the psyche, the mind. Possibly in the case of pyromania, the suffering caused by a severe burn. You've heard the old saying, Mr. Smith, 'A burned child fears the fire.' "

And the psychiatrist smiled condescendingly and waved his wand—I mean, his pince-nez glasses on the black silk ribbon—in a gesture of exorcism. "The truth is quite the converse, of course. The burned child *loves* the fire. Was young Wally ever burned, Mr. Smith?"

"Why, yes, Doctor. When he was four he got hold of some matches and—"

There's the scar in plain sight on his arm, Doc. Didn't you notice it? And surely a burned child loves the fire; else he probably wouldn't have been burned in the first place.

The psychiatrist failed to ask about prefire symptoms—but then he would merely have deprecated them had Mr. Smith remembered to tell him. He'd have assured you that such attraction toward flame is normal and that it didn't achieve abnormal proportions until after the episode of the burn. Once a psychiatrist is in full war paint on the traumata trail, he can explain such minor discrepancies without half trying.

And so the psychiatrist, having found the cause, cured him. Period.

"*Now*, Darveth?"

"No, I'm going to wait."

"But it'd be fun to see that schoolhouse burn down. It'd burn easily, too, and the fire escapes aren't quite big enough."

"Uh-huh. But just the same, I'm going to wait."

"You mean, he'll get a whack at something bigger later on?"

"That's the idea."

"But are you sure he won't wiggle off your hook?"

"Not *him.*"

"Time to get up, Wally."

"All right, Mamma." He sat up in bed, hair rumpled, and reached for his glasses so he could see her. And then: "Mamma, I had one of those dreams again last night. The thing that was all fire, and another one like it but different and not so big talking to it. About the schoolhouse and—"

"Wally, the doctor told you you mustn't talk about those dreams. Except when he asks you. You see, talking about them impresses them on your mind and you remember them and think about it, and then that makes you dream about them again. See, Wally boy?"

"Yes, but why can't I tell you—"

"Because the doctor said not to, Wally. Now tell me what you did in school yesterday. Did you get a hundred in arithmetic again?"

Of course the psychiatrist took keen interest in those dreams; they were part of his stock in trade. But he found them confused, meaningless stuff. And you can't blame him for that; have you ever listened to a seven-year-old kid try to tell the plot of a movie he's seen?

It was hash, the way Wally remembered and told it: "—and then this big yellow thing sort of—well, it didn't do much then, I guess. And then the big one, the one that was taller than the other and redder, was talking to it something about fishing and saying he wouldn't wiggle off the hook, and—"

Sitting there on the edge of the chair looking at the psychiatrist through his thick-lensed glasses, his hands twisting tightly together and his eyes round and wide. But talking gibberish.

"My little man, when you sleep tonight, try to think about something pleasant. Something you like much, like ... uh—"

"Like a *bonfire*, Doctor?"

"*No!* I mean, something like playing baseball or going skating."

They watched him carefully. Particularly, they kept matches away from him, and fire. His parents bought an electric stove instead of their gas one, although they couldn't really afford it. But then again, because of the danger of matches, his father gave up smoking and what he saved on tobacco paid for the stove.

Yes, he was cured all right. The psychiatrist took credit for that, as well as cash. At any rate, the more dangerous outward symptoms disappeared. He was still fascinated by fire, but what boy doesn't chase fire engines?

He grew up to be a fairly husky young man. Tall, if a bit awkward. About the right build for a basketball player, except that his eyes weren't good enough to let him play.

He didn't smoke, and—after an experience or two—he decided that he didn't drink either. Drinking tended to weaken that barrier that said, "Thus Far, No Farther," across the blocked passage of his mind. That night he'd almost let go and set fire to the factory where he worked, days, as a shipping clerk. Almost, but not quite.

"*Now,* Darveth?"

"Not yet."

"But, Master, why wait longer? That's a big building; it's wood and it's ramshackle, and they make celluloid novelties. And *celluloid*—you've seen celluloid burn, haven't you, Darveth?"

"Yes, it *is* beautiful. But—"

"You think there is a bigger chance coming?"

"Think? I *know* there is."

Wally Smith woke up with an awful hangover that next morning, and found there was a box of matches in his pocket. They hadn't been there when he'd started to drink the night before, and he didn't remember when or where he'd picked them up.

But it gave him the willies to think that he *had* picked them up. And it gave him the screaming-meemies to wonder what he'd had in his mind when he'd put that box of matches in his pocket. He knew that he'd been on the ragged edge of something, and he had a very frightening idea of what that something had been.

Anyway, he took the pledge. He made up his mind that he'd never, under any circumstances, drink again. He thought he could be sure of himself as long as he didn't drink. As long as his conscious mind was in control, he *wasn't* a pyromaniac, damn it, he *wasn't.* The psychiatrist had cured him of that when he was a kid, hadn't he? Sure he had.

But just the same there came to be a haunted look in his eyes. Luckily, it didn't show much, through his thick glasses. Dot noticed it, a little. Dot Wendler was the girl he went with.

And although Dot didn't know it, that night put another tragedy into his life, for Wally had been on the verge of proposing to her, but now—

Was it fair, he wondered, for him to ask a girl like Dot to marry him when he was no longer quite sure? He almost decided to give her up and not torture himself by seeing her again. That was a bit too much though; he compromised by continuing to date her but not popping the question. A bit like a man who dares not eat, but who stares into delicatessen windows every chance he gets.

Then it got to be December 7th in the year of 1941, and it was on the morning of the 9th that he tried to enlist, in three recruiting stations and was turned down in each.

Dot tried to console him—although down in her heart she was glad. "But, Wally, I'm sure the factory you work for will switch over to defense work. All the ones like it are changing. And you'll be just as helpful. The country needs guns and ... and ammunition and stuff just as much as it needs soldiers. And—" She wanted to say, and it would give him a chance to settle down and marry her, but of course she didn't say it.

It was early in January that she was proved right. He was laid off during an interim period while the factory changed over. There was two weeks of that; the first week a happy vacation because Dot took a week off work, too, and they went everywhere together. She took the week off without pay, just to be with him, but she didn't tell him that.

Then at the end of two weeks, he was called back to work. They'd made the changeover rather quickly; it doesn't require as much changing and retooling for a factory working with chemicals as for one working in metals.

They were going to nitrate toluene. And when toluene has been so treated, they call it trinitrotoluene when they have the time. When they haven't time for a mouthful of syllables like that, TNT describes it just as well.

"*Now*, Darveth?"
"Now!"

By noon that day, Wally Smith didn't know what was wrong with him, but he knew he didn't feel so well, mentally. *Something* was wrong with him, and getting wronger.

He went out onto the loading platform against the railroad spur to eat his lunch. There were a dozen cars on the spur, and ten men were working through the lunch hour at unloading one of them. Stuff in sacks that looked heavy.

"What is it?" Wally called over to one of the men.

"Just cement. For the fireproofing."

"Oh," said Wally. "When do they start on that?"

The man put down his sack and ran the back of a dirty hand across his forehead. "Tomorrow. Know how they're handling this job?" He grinned. "Tear down one wall at a time and pour a cement one. Right while they keep on running full blast."

"Um-m-m," said Wally. "All those cars full of cement?"

"Naw, just this one. Those others are chemicals and stuff. Gosh, I'll feel a lot easier when they get this place fixed up. Right now— You know this'd be worse than Black Tom in the last war if anything went wrong this week. That stuff in the cars alone would blow the fire clear over to the oil-cracking plants across the tracks. And you know what's on the other side of them?"

"Yes," said Wally. "Course they got lots of guards and everything, but—"

"*But* is right," said the man. "We need munitions in a hurry all right, but they got stuff too concentrated around here. This isn't any place to monkey with trinitro anyway. It's too near other stuff. If this plant *did* go up, even with all the precautions they're taking, it'd set off a chain of—" He looked narrowly at Wally Smith. "Say, we're talking too damn much. Don't say anything like what we been saying outside the plant."

Wally nodded, very soberly.

The workman started to heft the sack, and then didn't. He said, "Yeah, they're taking precautions. But one damn spy in here could practically lose the war for us. If he had luck. I mean, if it spread; there's enough stuff right near here to ... well, damn near to swing the balance in the Pacific, kid."

"And," said Wally, "there'd be a lot of people killed, I guess.

"Nuts to people. Maybe a thousand people get killed, what does that matter? That many get killed on the Russian front every day. More. But, Wally— Hell, I talk too much."

He swung the sack of cement back onto his shoulder and went on into the building.

Wally finished his lunch, thoughtfully, and wadded up the paper it had been wrapped in and put it into the fireproof metal trash can. He glanced at his wrist watch and saw there was ten minutes left. He sat down again on the edge of the platform.

He knew what he ought to do. Quit. Even if there was one chance in a million that— But there wasn't a chance, even in a million. Damn it, he told himself, he'd been *cured*. He was O.K. And they needed him here; his job was important, in a small way.

But listen—just in case—how's about going back to that psychiatrist he'd used to go to? The guy was still in town. Tell him the whole story and take his advice; if he said to quit, then—

And he could call him up now, from the office phone, and make an appointment for this evening. No, not the office phone, but there was a nickel phone in the hall. Did he have a loose nickel? Yes, he remembered now; he did.

He stood up and reached into his change pocket, pulled out the change there. Four pennies, and he looked at them curiously. How the deuce had he got those pennies? There'd been a nickel—

He reached into his other pocket, and his hand froze there.

His fingers had touched cardboard, cardboard shaped like a folder of paper matches. Scarcely daring to breathe, he let his fingers explore the foreign object in his pocket. Unmistakably it was a folder of safety matches, a full one, and there was another one below it. And didn't those matches sell two folders for a penny—the missing penny from his nickel that had turned into four cents' change?

But he hadn't put them there. He *never* bought or carried matches. He hadn't—

Or *had* he?

Because he remembered now, the queer thing that had happened this morning on his way to work. That funny feeling when, with mild surprise, he'd found himself on the corner of Grant and Wheeler streets, a block off his regular route to work. A block out of his way, and he didn't remember walking that block.

Getting absent-minded, he'd told himself. Daydreaming. But there were stores along that block, stores that sold matches.

A man can daydream himself into walking a block out of his way. But can he make a purchase—one with fearful connotation like that—without knowing it?

And if he could *buy* matches without conscious volition, couldn't he also use—

Maybe even before he could get out of here!

Quick, Wally, while you know what you're doing, while you *can*—

He took the two folders of matches from his pocket and pushed them through the slide of the fireproof trash can.

And then, walking rapidly and with his face white and set, he went back into the building, down the long corridor to the shipping office, and went in.

He said, "Mr. Davis, I quit."

The baldheaded man at the desk looked up, mild surprise on his mild face. "Wally, what's wrong? Has something happened or ... are you well?"

Wally tried to straighten out his face and make it feel as though it looked natural. He said, "I ... I just quit, Mr. Davis. I can't explain." He turned to walk on out.

"But, Wally, you *can't*. Lord, we're short-handed as it is. And you know your department, Wally. It'll take weeks to get a man broken in to take your place. You've got to give us notice to pull something like this. A week, at the very least, so we can break in a—"

"No. I quit right now. I *got* to—"

"But— Hell, Wally, that's *deserting*. Man, you're *needed* here. This is just as important as ... as the Bataan front. This factory is as important as a whole damn fleet in the Pacific. It's ... you know what we're doing here. And— What are you quitting for?"

"I ... I'm just quitting, that's all."

The baldheaded man at the desk stood up and his face wasn't mild any more. He was a little over five feet tall, to Wally's six, but for the moment he seemed to tower over the younger man. He said, "You're going to tell me what's back of this, or I'm going to—" He was coming around the desk while he talked, and his fists were doubled at his sides.

Wally took a step backward. He said, "Listen, Mr. Davis, you don't understand. I don't *want* to quit. I *got*—"

"Hey, where's Darveth? Get Darveth right away!"

"He's over chewing the fat with Apollo. The Greek's trying to talk him out of this because Greece is on America's side and wants them to win, but Apollo—and all the rest of 'em—aren't strong enough any more to buck—"

"Shut up. *Hey, Darveth!*"

"Yes?"

"This pyromaniac of yours, he's going to *talk*. They'll lock him up if he does and he won't be able to—"

"Shut up; I see."

"Hurry! You're going to lose—"

"Shut up so I can concentrate. Ah, I got him."

"Listen, Mr. Davis, I ... I didn't mean it that way at all. I got such a splitting headache, I just couldn't think straight and I didn't know what I was saying. I was just saying anything to get out of here, so I could go—"

"Oh, that's different, Wally. But why *quit*, just because you got a headache? Sure, leave now and go to your doctor. But come back—today or tomorrow or next week, whenever it's okay again. Man, you don't have to quit just to go home, if you're sick."

"All right, Mr. Davis. Sorry I gave that impression. I wasn't thinking straight. I'll be back as soon as I can. Maybe even today."

That's it, Wally, you got him fooled now. Tell him you're going to see a doc, and that'll give you an excuse to go out for a while. That'll let you buy some more matches, because you couldn't get the ones back you put in the trash box, not without attracting attention.

You're going out to get more matches, and you know what you're going to do with them, don't you, Wally? You're going to lose a thousand lives and several billion dollars' worth of materials and lots of valuable *time* off the armament program, but it'll be a beautiful fire, Wally. The whole sky will be red, red as blood, Wally.

Tell him—

"Look, Mr. Davis, I've had these headaches before. They're sharp and awful while they last, but they last only a few hours. Tell you what; I can come back at five and work four hours then to make up for this afternoon. That be all right?"

"Why, sure—if you're feeling all right by then and are sure it won't hurt you. We *are* behind, and every hour you can put in counts."

"Thanks, Mr. Davis. I'm sure I can. So long."

"Nice work getting out of that one, Darveth. And *night* will be better anyway."

"Night is always better."

"Boy, oh, boy. I'm sure going to be around to watch. Remember Chicago? And Black Tom? And Rome?"

"This will top them."

"But those Greeks, Hermes and Ulysses and that gang. Won't they get together maybe and try to stop it? And some of the legends from other countries on that side might join in. You ready for trouble, Darveth?"

"Trouble? Phooey, nobody believes in those mugs enough to give them any power. I could push 'em all off with my little finger. And look who'd help us, if they did start trouble. Siegfried and Sugimoto and that gang."

"And the Romans."

"The Romans? No, they're not interested in this war. They don't like Mussolini much. No, there won't be trouble. One of my imps could handle the whole gang."

"Swell. Save me a box seat, Darveth."

Night was strange. At seven o'clock, when he'd been working two hours, it began to get dark. And it seemed to Wally Smith that darkness itself was something alien.

He knew, with part of his mind, that he was working, just as he always worked. He knew that he talked and joked with the other men on the shift. Men he knew well because he'd often before worked several hours overtime and thus overlapped the evening shift.

His body worked without his own volition. He picked up things that should be picked up, and put them down where they should be put down, and he made out cards and file memos and bills of lading. It was as though his hands worked of themselves and his voice spoke of itself.

There was another part of Wally Smith that must have been the real part. It seemed to stand back at a distance and watch his body work and listen to his voice speak. A Wally Smith that stood helpless on the edge of an abyss of horror. Knowing, now. The wall pushed through, knowing everything. About Darveth.

And knowing that at nine o'clock, on his way out of the building he would pass that corner room where he'd carefully planted the heap of rubbish. Highly inflammable rubbish; stuff that would catch fire from a single match and flare high, setting fire to the wall behind it before anyone would even know it was there. And *behind* that wall—

There were only two things left to do. Turn the handle that shut off the sprinkler system. Light one match—

One yellow-flaming match, then the red hell of consuming fire. Holocaust. Fire they could never stop, once it was started. Building after building turning to flame-red; body after body turning to charred black as men, killed or stunned by the explosions, cooked in a flaming hell.

It was a strange mix-up, the mind of Wally Smith. Nightmare visions that seemed familiar because he'd seen them in dreams when he was a child. Fantastic beings that he'd never been able to describe or identify, as a child.

But now he knew, at least vaguely, who and what they were. Things out of myth and legend. Things that *weren't*.

But that *were*, somehow, in that nightmare plane.

He even heard them—not their voices, but their thoughts expressed in no language. And names, sometimes, that were the same in any language. Over and over again, the name Darveth, and somehow it was something of fire named Darveth that was making him do what he was doing and going to do.

He saw and heard and felt, in loathing terror, while his hands made out shipping tickets and his voice cracked casual jokes with the other men around him.

And watched the clock. A minute to nine.

Wally Smith yawned. "Well," he said, "guess I'll call it a night. So long, boys."

He walked over to the clock, put his timecard into the slot and punched out.

Put on his hat and coat. Started down the hallway.

Then he was out of sight of the others, and not yet in sight of the guard at the door, and his movements were suddenly stealthy. He walked like a panther as he turned in at the door of the deserted stockroom. The room where everything was ready.

Here it comes. The match was in his hand; his hand was striking the match. The *flame*. As the first flame he had ever seen, dancing on the end of a match in his father's hand. While Wally's stubby little fingers, all those years ago, had reached out for the thing on the end of the stick. The thing that flared there, ever-shape-changing; yellow-red-blue wonder, magic beauty. The *flame*.

Wait until the stick has caught fire, too, wait until it's well-ablaze, so stooping down won't blow it out. A flame's a tender thing, at first.

"No!" cried another part of his mind. "*Don't! Wally, don't*—"

But you can't stop now, Wally, you can't "don't" because Darveth, the fire demon, is in the driver's seat. He's stronger than you are, Wally; he's stronger than any of the others in that nightmare world you're looking into. Yell for help, Wally, it won't do you any good.

Yell to any of them. Yell to old Moloch; he won't listen to you. He's going to enjoy this, too. Most of them are. Not all. Thor's standing to one side, not particularly happy about what's going to happen because he's a fighting man, but he isn't big enough to tangle with Darveth. None of them is, over there.

Fire's king, and all the fire elementals are dancing a dervish dance. Others watching. There's white-bearded Zeus and someone with a head like a crocodile standing beside him. And Dagon riding Scylla—all the creatures men have conceived, and conceiving—

But none of them will help you, Wally. You're on your own. And you're bending over now, with the match. Shielding it with your palm so it won't blow out in the draft from the open door.

Silly, isn't it, Wally, that you're being driven to this by something that can't really be there, something that exists only because it's *thought* of? You're mad, Wally. Mad. Or are you?—isn't *thought* as real a thing as anything? What are *you* but thought harnessed to a chunk of clay? What are *they* but thought, unharnessed?

Yell for help, Wally. There must be help somewhere. Yell, not with your throat and lips because they aren't yours right now, but with your mind! Yell for help where it will do good, *over there*. *Somebody* to stop Darveth. Somebody that would be on your side.

YES! That's it! YELL.

How he got home, afterward and an hour later, Wally never quite remembered. Only that the sky was black with night and studded with stars, not a scarlet sky of holocaust. He scarcely felt the burns on his thumb and forefinger where the match had burned down and burned out against his skin.

His landlady was in her rocking chair on the cool porch. She said, "Home so early, Wally?"

"Early?"

"Why, yes. Didn't you say this morning that you had a date with that girl of yours? I thought you ate downtown and went right to her house from the plant."

Wally, panic-stricken in remembering, was running to the telephone. A frantic moment and then he heard her voice.

"Wally, what happened? I've been waiting since—"

"Sorry, Dot—had to work late and couldn't phone. Can I come around now, and will you marry me?"

"Will I— What did you say, Wally?"

"Honey, it's all right now. Will you marry me?"

"Why— You come on over and I'll tell you, Wally. But what do you mean, it's all right now?"

"It's ... I'll be right over, and tell you."

But reason reasserted itself in the six blocks he had to walk, and of course he didn't tell her what had happened. He thought up a story that would cover what he'd said—and one that she'd believe. Of such stuff are good husbands made, and Wally Smith was ready to make a good one if he got his chance. And he did.

"Papa."

"Hush, child."

"But why, Papa? And what are you doing under the bed?"

"Shhh. Oh, all right, but talk softly. He's still around somewhere, I think."

"Who, Papa?"

"*The new one.* The one that— Grief, child, did you sleep through all the rumpus last night? The biggest fight here in seventeen centuries!"

"Gee, Papa! Who licked who?"

"The new one. He kicked Darveth so far he hasn't got back yet, and then a bunch of Darveth's friends ganged up on him and he knocked hell out of *them.* Now he's walking around out there and—"

"Looking for somebody else to beat up, Papa?"

"Well, I don't know. He hasn't started a fight with anybody yet except the ones that started after him, except Darveth. I guess he took on Darveth because this human being Darveth was working on must have called him."

"But why are *you* hiding, Papa?"

"Because— Well, kid, I'm a fire elemental, of course, and he may think I'm a friend of Darveth's, and I'm not taking any chances till things quiet down. See? Golly, there must be a flock of people up there on this guy's side and believing in him to make him as strong as that. What he did to Darveth—"

"What's his name, Papa? And is he a myth or a legend or what?"

"Don't know, kid. Me, I'm going to let somebody else ask him first."

"I'm going to look out through the curtain, Papa. I'll keep my glow down to a glimmer."

"Hey, come— Oh, all right, but be careful. Is he in sight?"

"Yes; I guess it's him. He doesn't *look* dangerous, but—"

"But don't take any chances, kid. I'm not even going near the window to look out; I'm brighter than you are and he'd see me. Say, I didn't get much of a look last night in the dark. What does he look like by day?"

"Not dangerous-*looking*, Papa. He's got a white goatee and he's tall and thinnish, and he's got red-and-white-striped pants stuffed into boots. And a stovepipe hat; it's blue and got white stars on it. Red, white and blue. Does that mean anything, Papa?"

"From what happened last night, kid, it *must.* Me, I'm staying under the bed until somebody else asks him what his name is!"

The Angelic Angleworm

Charlie Wills shut off the alarm clock and kept right on moving, swinging his feet out of bed and sticking them into his slippers as he reached for a
cigarette. Once the cigarette was lighted, he let himself relax a moment sitting
on the side of the bed.

He still had time, he figured, to sit there and smoke himself awake. He
had fifteen minutes before Pete Johnson would call to take him fishing. And
twelve minutes was enough time to wash his face and throw on his old clothes.

It seemed funny to get up at five o'clock, but he felt swell. Golly, even
with the sun not up yet and the sky a dull pastel through the window, he felt
great. Because there was only a week and a half to wait now.

Less than a week and a half, really, because it was ten days. Or—come to
think of it—a bit more than ten days from this hour in the morning. But call
it ten days, anyway. If he could go back to sleep again now, damn it, when he
woke up it would be that much closer to the time of the wedding. Yes, it was
swell to sleep when you were looking forward to something. Time flies by and
you don't even hear the rustle of its wings.

But no—he couldn't go back to sleep. He'd promised Pete he'd be ready
at five-fifteen, and if he wasn't, Pete would sit out front in his car and honk the
horn and wake the neighbors.

And the three minutes' grace was up, so he tamped out the cigarette and
reached for the clothes on the chair.

He began to whistle softly: "I'm Going to Marry Yum Yum, Yum Yum"
from *The Mikado*. And tried—in the interests of being ready in time—to keep
his eyes off the silver-framed picture of Jane on the bureau.

He must be just about the luckiest guy on earth, Or anywhere else, for
that matter, if there was anywhere else.

Jane Pemberton, with soft brown hair that had little wavelets in it and
felt like silk—no, nicer than silk—and with the cute go-to-hell tilt to her nose,
with long graceful sun-tanned legs, with—damn it, with everything that it
was possible for a girl to have, and more. And the miracle that she loved him
was so fresh that he still felt a bit dazed.

Ten days in a daze, and then—

His eye fell on the dial of the clock, and he jumped. It was ten minutes
after five, and he still sat there holding the first sock. Hurriedly, he finished
dressing. Just in time! It was almost five-fifteen on the head as he slid into his
corduroy jacket, grabbed his fishing tackle, and tiptoed down the stairs and
outside into the cool dawn.

Pete's car wasn't there yet.

Well, that was all right. It'd give him a few minutes to rustle up some worms,
and that would save time later on. Of course he couldn't really dig in Mrs. Grady's
lawn, but there was a bare area of border around the flower bed along the front
porch, and it wouldn't matter if he turned over a bit of the dirt there.

He took his jackknife out and knelt down beside the flower bed. Ran the blade a couple of inches in the ground and turned over a clod of it. Yes, there were worms all right.

There was a nice big juicy one that ought to be tempting to any fish. Charlie reached out to pick it up.

And that was when it happened.

His fingertips came together, but there wasn't a worm between them, because something had happened to the worm. When he'd reached out for it, it had been a quite ordinary-looking angleworm. A three-inch juicy, slippery, wriggling angleworm. It most definitely had *not* had a pair of wings. Nor a—

It was quite impossible, of course, and he was dreaming or seeing things, but there it was.

Fluttering upward in a graceful slow spiral that seemed utterly effortless. Flying past Charlie's face with wings that were shimmery-white, and not at all like butterfly wings or bird wings, but like—

Up and up it circled, now above Charlie's head, now level with the roof of the house, then a mere white—somehow a *shining* white—speck against the gray sky. And after it was out of sight, Charlie's eyes still looked upward.

He didn't hear Pete Johnson's car pull in at the curb, but Pete's cheerful hail of "Hey," caught his attention, and he saw that Pete was getting out of the car and coming up the walk.

Grinning. "Can we get some worms here, before we start?" Pete asked. Then: " 'Smatter? Think you see a flying saucer? And don't you know never to look up with your mouth open like you were doing when I pulled up? Remember that pigeons—Say, *is* something the matter? You look white as a sheet."

Charlie discovered that his mouth was still open, and he closed it. Then he opened it to say something, but couldn't think of anything to say—or rather, of any way of saying it—so he closed his mouth again.

He looked back upward, but there wasn't anything in sight any more, and he looked down at the earth of the flower bed, and it looked like ordinary earth.

"Charlie!" Pete's voice sounded seriously concerned now. "Snap out of it! Are you all right?"

Again Charlie opened his mouth, and closed it. Then he said weakly, "Hello, Pete."

"For God's sake, Charlie. Did you go to sleep out here and have a nightmare, or what? Get up off your knees and— Listen, are you *sick?* Shall I take you to Doc Palmer instead of us going fishing?"

Charlie got to his feet slowly, and shook himself. He said, "I—I guess I'm all right. Something funny happened. But— All right, come on. Let's go fishing."

"But what? Oh, all right, tell me about it later. But before we start, shall we dig some—Hey, don't look like that! Come on, get in the car; get some fresh air and maybe that'll make you feel better."

Pete took his arm, and Pete picked up the tackle box and led Charlie out to the waiting car. He opened the dashboard compartment and took out a bottle. "Here, take a snifter of this."

Charlie did, and as the amber fluid gurgled out of the bottle's neck and down Charlie's he felt his brain begin to rid itself of the numbness of shock. He could think again.

The whisky burned on the way down, but it put a pleasant spot of warmth where it landed, and he felt better. Until it changed to warmth, he hadn't realized that there had been a cold spot in the pit of his stomach.

He wiped his lips with the back of his hand and said, "Gosh."

"Take another," Pete said, his eyes on the road. "Maybe too it'll do you good to tell me what happened and get it out of your system. That is, if you want to."

"I—I guess so," said Charlie. "It—it doesn't sound like much to tell it, Pete. I just reached for a worm, and it flew away. On white, shining wings."

Pete looked puzzled. "You reached for a worm, and it flew away. Well, why not? I mean, I'm no entomologist, but maybe there are worms with wings. Come to think of it, there probably are. There are winged ants, and caterpillars turn into butterflies. What scared you about it?"

"Well, this worm didn't have wings until I reached for it. It looked like an ordinary angleworm. Damn it, it *was* an ordinary angleworm until I went to pick it up. And then it had a—a—oh, skip it. I was probably seeing things."

"Come on, get it out of your system. Give."

"Damn it, Pete, *it had a halo!*"

The car swerved a bit, and Pete eased it back to the middle of the road before he said, "A what?"

"Well," said Charlie defensively, "it looked like a halo. It was a little round golden circle just above its head. It didn't seem to be attached; it just floated there."

"How'd you know it was its head? Doesn't a worm look alike on both ends?"

"Well," said Charlie, and he stopped to consider the matter. How *had* he known? "Well," he said, "since it was a halo wouldn't it be kind of silly for it to have a halo around the wrong end? I mean, even sillier than to have— Hell, you know what I mean."

Pete said, "Hmph." Then, after the car was around a curve: "All right, let's be strictly logical. Let's assume you saw, or thought you saw, what you— uh—thought you saw. Now, you're not a heavy drinker so it wasn't D.T.'s. Far as I can see, that leaves three possibilities."

Charlie said, "I see two of them. It could have been a pure hallucination. People do have 'em, I guess, but *I* never had one before. Or I suppose it could have been a dream, maybe. I'm sure I didn't, but I suppose that I could have gone to sleep there and dreamed I saw it. But *that* isn't it. I'll concede the possibility of an hallucination, but not a dream. What's the third?"

"Ordinary fact. That you really saw a winged worm. I mean, that there is such a thing, for all I know. And you were just mistaken about it not having wings when you first saw it, because they were folded, And what you thought looked like a halo was some sort of a crest or antenna or something. There are some damn funny-looking bugs."

"Yeah," said Charlie. But he didn't believe it. There may be funny-looking bugs, but none that suddenly sprout wings and halos and ascend unto—

He took another drink.

II

Sunday afternoon and evening he spent with Jane, and the episode of the ascending angleworm slipped into the back of Charlie's mind. Anything, except Jane, tended to slip there when he was with her.

At bedtime when he was alone again, it came back, The thought, not the worm. So strongly that he couldn't sleep, and he got up and sat in the armchair by the window and decided the only way to get it out of his mind was to think it through.

If he could pin things down and decide what had really happened out there at the edge of the flower bed, then maybe he could forget it completely.

Okay, he told himself, let's be strictly logical.

Pete had been right about the three possibilities. Hallucination, dream, reality. Now to begin with, it *hadn't* been a dream. He'd been wide awake; he was as sure of that as he was sure of anything. Eliminate that.

Reality? That was impossible, too. It was all right for Pete to talk about the funniness of insects and the possibility of antennae, and such—but Pete hadn't *seen* the damn thing. Why, it had flown past only inches from his eyes. And that halo had really been there.

Antennae? Nuts.

And that left hallucination. That's what it must have been, hallucination. After all, people *do* have hallucinations. Unless it happened often it didn't necessarily mean you were a candidate for the booby hatch. All right then, accept that it was an hallucination, and so what? So forget it.

With that decided, he went to bed and—by thinking about Jane again—happily to sleep.

The next morning was Monday and he went back to work.

And the morning after that was Tuesday.

And on Tuesday—

III

It wasn't an ascending angleworm this time. It wasn't anything you could put your finger on, unless you can put your finger on sunburn, and that's painful sometimes.

But sunburn—in a rainstorm—

It was raining when Charlie Wills left home that morning, but it wasn't raining hard at that time, which was a few minutes after eight. A mere drizzle. Charlie pulled down the brim of his hat and buttoned his raincoat and decided to walk to work anyway. He rather liked walking in rain. And he had time: he didn't have to be there until eight-thirty.

Three blocks away from work, he encountered the Pest, bound in the same direction. The Pest was Jane Pemberton's kid sister, and her right name was Paula, and most people had forgotten the fact. She worked at the Hapworth Printing Company, just as Charlie did; but she was a copyholder for one of the proofreaders and he was assistant production manager.

But he'd met Jane through her, at a party given for employees.

He said, "Hi there, Pest. Aren't you afraid you'll melt?" For it was raining harder now, definitely harder.

"Hello, Charlie-warlie. I like to walk in the rain."

She *would*, thought Charlie bitterly. At the hated nickname Charlie-warlie, he winced. Jane had called him that once, but—after he'd talked reason to her—never again. Jane was reasonable. But the Pest had heard it— And Charlie was mortally afraid, ever after, that she'd sometime call him that at work, with other employees in hearing. And if *that* ever happened—

"Listen," he protested, "can't you forget that damn fool nickname? I'll quit calling you Pest if you quit calling me—uh—*that*."

"But I *like* to be called the Pest. Why don't you like to be called Charlie-warlie?"

She grinned at him, and Charlie writhed inwardly. Because she was *who* she was, he didn't dare—

There was pent-up anger in him as he walked into the blowing rain, head bent low to keep it out of his face. Damn the brat—

With vision limited to a few yards of sidewalk directly ahead of him, Charlie probably wouldn't have seen the teamster and the horse if he hadn't heard the cracks that sounded like pistol shots.

He looked up, and saw. In the middle of the street, maybe fifty feet ahead of Charlie and the Pest and moving toward them came an overloaded wagon. It was drawn by an aged, despondent horse, a horse so old and bony that the slow walk by which it progressed seemed to be its speediest possible rate of movement.

But the teamster obviously didn't think so. He was a big, ugly man with an unshaven, swarthy face. He was standing up, swinging his heavy whip for another blow. It came down, and the old horse quivered under it and seemed to sway between the shafts.

The whip lifted again.

And Charlie yelled, "Hey, there!" and started toward the wagon.

He wasn't certain yet just what he was going to do about it if the brute beating the other brute refused to stop. But it was going to be something, Seeing an animal mistreated was one thing Charlie Wills just couldn't stand. And wouldn't stand.

He yelled, "Hey!" again, because the teamster didn't seem to have heard him the first time, and he started forward at a trot, along the curb.

The teamster heard that second yell, and he might have heard the first. Because he turned and looked squarely at Charlie. Then he raised the whip again, even higher, and brought it down on the horse's welt-streaked back with all his might.

Things went red in front of Charlie's eyes. He didn't yell again. He knew darned well now what he was going to do. It began with pulling that teamster down off the wagon where he could get at him. And then he was going to beat him to a pulp.

He heard Paula's high heels clicking as she started after him and called out, "Charlie, be caref—"

But that was all of it that he heard. Because, just at that moment, it happened.

A sudden blinding wave of intolerable heat, a sensation as though he had just stepped into the heart of a fiery furnace. He gasped once for breath, as the very air in his lungs and in his throat seemed to be scorching hot. And his skin—

Blinding pain, just for an instant. Then it was gone, but too late. The shock had been too sudden and intense, and as he felt again the cool rain in his face, he went dizzy and rubbery all over, and lost consciousness. He didn't even feel the impact of his fall.

Darkness.

And then he opened his eyes into a blur of white that resolved itself into white walls and white sheets over him and a nurse in a white uniform, who said, "Doctor! He's regained consciousness."

Footsteps and the closing of a door, and there was Doc Palmer frowning down on him.

"Well, Charles, what have you been up to now?"

Charlie grinned a bit weakly. He said, "Hi, Doc. I'll bite. What *have* I been up to?"

Doc Palmer pulled up a chair beside the bed and sat down in it. He reached out for Charlie's wrist and held it while he looked at the second hand of his watch. Then he read the chart at the end of the bed and said "Hmph."

"Is that the diagnosis," Charlie wanted to know, "or the treatment? Listen, first what about the teamster? That is, if you know—"

"Paula told me what happened. Teamster's under arrest, and fired. You're all right, Charles. Nothing serious."

"Nothing serious? What's it a non-serious case of? In other words, what happened to me?"

"You keeled over. Prostration. And you'll be peeling for a few days, but that's all. Why didn't you use a lotion of some kind yesterday?"

Charlie closed his eyes and opened them again slowly. And said, "Why didn't I use a— For *what?*"

"The sunburn, of course. Don't you know you can't go swimming on a sunny day and not get—"

"But I wasn't swimming yesterday, Doc. Nor the day before. Gosh, not for a couple weeks, in fact. What do you mean, sunburn?"

Doc Palmer rubbed his chin. He said, "You better rest a while, Charles. If you feel all right by this evening, you can go home. But you better not work tomorrow."

He got up and went out.

The nurse was still there, and Charlie looked at her blankly. He said, "Is Doc Palmer going— Listen, what's this all about?"

The nurse was looking at him queerly. She said, "Why, you were— I'm sorry, Mr. Willis, but a nurse isn't allowed to discuss a diagnosis with a patient. But you haven't anything to worry about; you heard Dr. Palmer say you could go home this afternoon or evening."

"Nuts," said Charlie. "Listen, what time is it? Or aren't nurses allowed to tell that?"

"It's ten-thirty."

"Golly, and I've been here about two hours." He figured back; remembering now that he'd passed a clock that said twenty-four minutes after eight just as they'd turned the corner for that last block. And, if he'd been awake again for five minutes, then he'd been unconscious for two full hours.

"Anything else you want, sir?"

Charlie shook his head slowly. And then because he wanted her to leave so he could sneak a look at that chart, he said, "Well, yes. Could I have a glass of orange juice?"

As soon as she was gone, he sat up in bed. It hurt a little to do that, and he found his skin was a bit tender to the touch. He looked at his arms, pulling up the sleeves of the hospital nightshirt they'd put on him, and the skin was pinkish. Just the shade of pink that meant the first stage of a mild sunburn.

He looked down inside the nightshirt, and then at his legs, and said, "What the hell—" Because the sunburn, if it *was* sunburn, was uniform all over.

And that didn't make sense, because he hadn't been in the sun enough to get burned at any time recently, and he hadn't been in the sun at all without his clothes. And—yes, the sunburn extended even over the area which would have been covered by trunks if he *had* gone swimming.

But maybe the chart would explain. He reached over the foot of the bed and took the clipboard with the chart off the hook.

Reported that patient fainted suddenly on street without apparent cause. Pulse 135, respiration labored, temperature 104, upon admission. All returned to normal within first hour. Symptoms seem to approximate those of heat prostration, but ...

Then there were a few qualifying comments which were highly technical-sounding. Charlie didn't understand them, and somehow he bad a hunch that Doc Palmer didn't understand them either. They had a whistling-in-the-dark sound to them.

Click of heels in the hall outside and he put the chart back quickly and ducked under the covers. Surprisingly, there was a knock. Nurses wouldn't knock, would they?

He said, "Come in."

It was Jane. Looking more beautiful than ever, with her big brown eyes a bit bigger with fright.

"Darling! I came as soon as the Pest called home and told me. But she was awfully vague. What on earth happened?"

By that time she was within reach, and Charlie put his arms around her and didn't give a damn, just then, what had happened to him. But he tried to explain. Mostly to himself.

IV

People always try to explain.

Face a man, or a woman, with something he doesn't understand, and he'll be miserable until he classifies it. Lights in the sky. And a scientist tells him it's the aurora borealis—or the aurora australis—and he can accept the lights, and forget them.

Something knocks pictures off a wall in an empty room, and throws a chair downstairs. Consternation, until it's named. Then it's only a poltergeist.

Name it, and forget it. Anything with a name can be assimilated.

Without one, it's—well unthinkable. Take away the name of anything, and you've got blank horror.

Even something as familiar as a commonplace ghoul. Graves in a cemetery dug up, corpses eaten. Horrible thing, it may be; but it's merely a ghoul; as long as it's named— But suppose, if you can stand it, there was no such word as *ghoul* and no concept of one. *Then* dug-up half-eaten corpses are found. Nameless horror.

Not that the next thing that happened to Charlie Wills had anything to do with a ghoul. Not even a werewolf. But I think that, in a way, he'd have found a werewolf more comforting than the duck, under the circumstances. One expects strange behavior of a werewolf, but a duck—

Like the duck in the museum.

Now there is nothing intrinsically terrible about a duck. Nothing to make one lie awake at night, with cold sweat coming out on top of peeling sunburn. On the whole, a duck is a pleasant object, particularly if it is roasted. This one wasn't.

It happened on Thursday. Charlie's stay in the hospital had been for eight hours; they'd released him late in the afternoon, and he'd eaten dinner downtown and then gone home. The boss had insisted on his taking the next day off from work, Charlie hadn't protested much.

Home, and, after stripping to take a bath, he'd studied his skin with blank amazement. Definitely a first-degree burn. Definitely, all over him. Almost ready to peel.

It did peel, the next day.

He took advantage of the holiday by taking Jane out to the ball game, where they sat in a grandstand so he could be out of the sun. It was a good game, and Jane understood and liked baseball.

Thursday, back to work.

At eleven twenty-five, Old Man Hapworth, the big boss, came into Charlie's office.

"Wills," he said, "we got a rush order to print ten thousand handbills, and the copy will be here in about an hour. I'd like you to follow the thing right through the Linotype room and the composing room and get it on the press the minute it's made up. It's a close squeak whether we make deadline on it, and there's a penalty if we don't."

"Sure, Mr. Hapworth. I'll stick right with it."

"Fine. I'll count on you. But listen—it's a bit early to eat, but just the same you better go out for your lunch hour now. The copy will be here about the time you get back, and you can stick right with the job. That is, if you don't mind eating early."

"Not at all," Charlie lied. He got his hat and went out.

Damn it, it was too early to eat. But he had an hour off and he could eat in half that time, so maybe if he walked half an hour first, he could work up an appetite.

The museum was two blocks away, and the best place to kill half an hour. He went there, strolled down the central corridor without stopping, except to stare for a moment at a statue of Aphrodite that reminded him of Jane Pemberton and made him remember—even more strongly than he already remembered—that it was only six days now until his wedding.

Then he turned off into the room that housed the numismatic collection. He'd used to collect coins when he was a kid, and although the collection had been broken up since then, he still had a mild interest in looking at the big museum collection.

He stopped in front of a showcase of bronze Romans.

But he wasn't thinking about them. He was still thinking about Aphrodite, or Jane, which was quite understandable under the circumstances. Most certainly, he was not thinking about flying worms or sudden waves of burning heat.

Then he chanced to look across toward an adjacent showcase. And within it, he saw the duck.

It was a perfectly ordinary-looking duck. It had a speckled breast and greenish-brown markings on its wings and a darkish head with a darker stripe starting just above the eye and running down along the short neck. It looked like a wild rather than a domestic duck.

And it looked bewildered at being there.

For just a moment, the complete strangeness of the duck's presence in a showcase of coins didn't register with Charlie. His mind was *still* on Aphrodite. Even while he stared at a wild duck under glass inside a showcase marked "Coins of China."

Then the duck quacked, and waddled on its awkward webbed feet down the length of the showcase and butted against the glass of the end, and fluttered its wings and tried to fly upward, but hit against the glass of the top. And it quacked again and loudly.

Only then did it occur to Charlie to wonder what a live duck was doing in a numismatic collection. Apparently, to judge from its actions, the duck was wondering the same thing.

And only then did Charlie remember the angelic worm and the sunless sunburn.

And somebody in the doorway said, "*Pssst.* Hey."

Charlie turned, and the look on his face must have been something out of the ordinary because the uniformed attendant quit frowning and said, "Something wrong, mister?"

For a brief instant, Charlie just stared at him. Then it occurred to Charlie that this was the opportunity he'd lacked when the angleworm had ascended. Two people couldn't see the same hallucination. If it was an—

He opened his mouth to say, "Look," but he didn't have to say anything. The duck beat him to it by quacking loudly and again trying to flutter through the glass of the case.

The attendant's eyes went past Charlie to the case of Chinese coins and he said, "Gaw!"

The duck was still there.

The attendant looked at Charlie again and said, "Did *you*—" and then stopped without finishing the question and went up to the showcase to look at close range. The duck was still struggling to get out, but more weakly. It seemed to be gasping for breath.

The attendant said, "Gaw!" again, and then over his shoulder to Charlie: "Mister, *how* did you— That there case is her-hermetchically sealed. It's airproof. Lookit that bird. It's—"

It already had; the duck fell over, either dead or unconscious.

The attendant grasped Charlie's arm. He said firmly, "Mister, you come with me to the boss." And less firmly, "Uh—*how* did you get that thing in there? And don't try to tell me you didn't, mister. I was through here five minutes ago, and you're the only guy's been in here since."

Charlie opened his mouth, and closed it again. He had a sudden vision of himself being questioned at the headquarters of the museum and then at the police station. And if the police started asking questions about him, they'd find out about the worm and about his having been in the hospital for— And they'd get an alienist maybe, and—

With the courage of sheer desperation, Charlie smiled. He tried to make it an ominous smile; it may not have been ominous, but it was definitely unusual. "How would you like," he asked the attendant, "to find *yourself* in there?" And he pointed with his free arm through the entrance and out into the main hallway at the stone sarcophagus of King Mene-Ptah. "I can do it, the same way I put that duck—"

The museum attendant was breathing hard. His eyes looked slightly glazed, and he let go of Charlie's arm. He said, "Mister, did you really—"

"Want me to show you how?"

"Uh— Gaw!" said the attendant. He ran.

Charlie forced himself to hold his own pace down to a rapid walk, and went in the opposite direction to the side entrance that led out into Beeker Street.

And Beeker Street was still a very ordinary-looking street, with lots of midday traffic, and no pink elephants climbing trees and nothing going on but the hurried confusion of a city street. Its very noise was soothing, in a way; although there was one bad moment when he was crossing at the corner and heard a sudden noise behind him. He turned around, startled, afraid of what strange thing he might see there.

But it was only a truck.

He managed to get out of its way in time to avoid being run over.

V

Lunch. And Charlie was definitely getting into a state of jitters. His hand shook so that he could scarcely pick up his coffee without slopping it over the edge of the cup.

Because a horrible thought was dawning in his mind. *If* something was wrong with him, was it fair to Jane Pemberton for him to go ahead and marry her? Is it fair to saddle the girl one loves with a husband who might go to the icebox to get a bottle of milk and find—God knows what?

And he was deeply, madly in love with Jane.

So he sat there, an unbitten sandwich on the plate before him, and alternated between hope and despair as he tried to make sense out of the three things that had happened to him within the past week.

Hallucination?

But the attendant too had seen the duck!

How comforting it had been—it seemed to him now—that, after seeing the angelic angleworm, he had been able to tell himself it had been an hallucination. *Only* an hallucination.

But wait. Maybe—

Could not the museum attendant have been part of the same hallucination as the duck? Granted that he, Charlie, could have seen a duck that wasn't there, couldn't he also have included in the same category a museum attendant who professed to see the duck? Why not? A duck and an attendant who sees it—the combination could be as illusory as the duck alone.

And Charlie felt so encouraged that he took a bite out of his sandwich.

But the *burn*? Whose hallucination was that? Or *was* there some sort of a natural physical ailment that could produce a sudden skin condition approximating mild sunburn? But, if there were such a thing, then evidently Doc Palmer didn't know about it.

Suddenly Charlie caught a glimpse of the clock on the wall, and it was one o'clock, and he almost strangled on that bite of sandwich when he realized that he was over half an hour late, and must have been sitting in the restaurant almost an hour.

He got up and ran back to the office.

But all was well; Old Man Hapworth wasn't there. And the copy for the rush circular was late and got there just as Charlie arrived.

He said, "*Whew!*" at the narrowness of his escape, and concentrated hard on getting that circular through the plant. He rushed it to the Linotypes and read proof on it himself, then watched make-up over the compositor's shoulder. He knew he was making a nuisance of himself, but it killed the afternoon.

And he thought, "Only one more day to work after today, and then my vacation, and on *Wednesday*—"

Wedding on Wednesday.

But—

If—

The Pest came out of the proofroom in a green smock and looked at him. "Charlie," she said, "you look like something no self-respecting cat would drag in. Say, what's wrong with you? Really?"

"Uh—nothing. Say, Paula, will you tell Jane when you get home that I may be a bit late this evening? I got to stick here till these handbills are off the press."

"Sure, Charlie. But tell me—"

"Nix. Run along, will you? I'm busy."

She shrugged her shoulders, and went back into the proofroom.

The machinist tapped Charlie's shoulder. "Say, we got that new Linotype set up. Want to take a look?"

Charlie nodded and followed. He looked over the installation, and then slid into the operator's chair in front of the machine. "How does she run?"

"Sweet. Those Blue Streak models are honeys. Try it."

Charlie let his fingers play over the keys, setting words without paying any attention to what they were. He sent in three lines to cast, then picked the slugs out of the stick. And found that he had set: "For men have died and worms have eaten them and ascendeth unto Heaven where it sitteth upon the right hand—"

"Gaw!" said Charlie. And that reminded him of—

VI

Jane noticed that there was something wrong. She couldn't have helped noticing. But instead of asking questions, she was unusually nice to him that evening.

And Charlie, who had gone to see her with the resolution to tell her the whole story, found himself weakening. As men always weaken when they are with the women they love and the parlor lamp is turned low.

But she did ask: "Charles—you *do* want to marry me, don't you? I mean, if there's any doubt in your mind and that's what has been worrying you, we can postpone the wedding till you're sure whether you love me enough—"

"*Love* you?" Charlie was aghast. "Why—"

And he proved it pretty satisfactorily.

So satisfactorily, in fact, that he completely forgot his original intention to suggest that very postponement. But *never* for the reason she suggested. With his arms around Jane—well, the poor chap was only human.

A man in love is a drunken man, and you can't exactly blame a drunkard for what he does under the influence of alcohol. You can blame him, of course, for getting drunk in the first place; but you can't put even that much blame on a man in love. In all probability, he fell through no fault of his own. In all probability his original intentions were strictly dishonorable; then, when those intentions met resistance, the subtle chemistry of sublimation converted them into the stuff that stars are made of.

Probably that was why he didn't go to see an alienist the next day. He was a bit afraid of what an alienist might tell him. He weakened and decided to wait and see if anything else happened.

Maybe nothing else would happen.

There was a comforting popular superstition that things went in groups of three, and three things had happened already.

Sure, that was it. From now on, he'd be all right. After all, there wasn't anything basically wrong; there couldn't be. He was in good health. Aside from Tuesday, he hadn't missed a day's work at the print shop in two years.

And—well, by now it was Friday noon and nothing had happened for a full twenty-four hours, and nothing was going to happen again.

Nothing did, Friday, but he read something that jolted him out of his precarious complacency.

A newspaper account.

He sat down in the restaurant at a table at which a previous diner had left a morning paper. Charlie read it while he was waiting for his order to be taken. He finished scanning the front page before the waitress came, and the comic section while he was eating his soup, and then turned idly to the local page.

GUARD AT MUSEUM SUSPENDED
Curator Orders Investigation

And the cold spot in his stomach got larger and colder as he read, for there it was in black and white.

The wild duck had really been in the showcase. No one could figure out how it had been put there. They'd had to take the showcase apart to get it out, and the showcase showed no indication of having been tampered with. It had been puttied up airtight to keep out dust, and the putty had not been damaged.

A guard, for reasons not clearly given in the article, had been given a three-day suspension. One gathered from the wording of the story that the curator of the museum had felt the necessity of doing *something* about the matter.

Nothing of value was missing from the case. One Chinese coin with a hole in the middle, a haikwan tael, made of silver, had not been found after the affair—but it wasn't worth much. There was some doubt as to whether it had been stolen by one of the workmen who had disassembled the showcase or whether it had been accidentally thrown out with the debris of old putty.

The reporter, telling the thing humorously, suggested that probably the duck had mistaken the coin for a doughnut because of the hole, and had eaten it. And that the curator's best revenge would be to eat the duck.

The police had been called in, but had taken the attitude that the whole affair must have been a practical joke. By whom or how accomplished, they didn't know.

Charlie put down the paper and stared moodily across the room.

Then it definitely *hadn't* been a double hallucination, a case of his imagining both duck and attendant. And until now that the bottom had fallen out of that idea, Charlie hadn't realized how strongly he'd counted on the possibility.

Now he was back where he'd started.

Unless—

But that was absurd. Of course, theoretically, the newspaper item he had just read *could* be an hallucination too, but—no, that was too much to swallow. According to that line of reasoning, if he went around to the museum and talked to the curator, the curator himself would be an hallucin—

"*Your duck*, sir."

Charlie jumped halfway out of his chair.

Then he saw it was the waitress standing at the side of the table with his entree, and that she had spoken because he had the newspaper spread out and there wasn't room for her to put it down.

"Didn't you order roast duck, sir? I—"

Charlie stood up hastily, averting his eyes from the dish. He said, "Sorry-gotta-make-a-phone-call," and hastily handed the astonished waitress a dollar bill and strode out. Had he really ordered— Not exactly; he'd told her to bring him the special.

But eat duck? He'd rather eat—no, not fried angleworms either. He shuddered.

He hurried back to the office, despite the fact that he was half an hour early, and felt better once he was within the safe four walls of the Hapworth Printing Company. Nothing out of the way had happened to him there.

As yet.

VII

Basically, Charlie Wills was quite a healthy young man. By two o'clock in the afternoon, he was so hungry that he sent one of the office boys downstairs to buy him a couple of sandwiches.

And he ate them. True, he lifted up the top slice of bread on each and looked inside. He didn't know what he expected to find there, aside from boiled ham and butter and a piece of lettuce, but if he had found—in lieu of one of those ingredients—say, a Chinese silver coin with a hole in the middle, he would not have been more than ordinarily surprised.

It was a dull afternoon at the plant, and Charlie had time to do quite a bit of thinking. Even a bit of research. He remembered that the plant had printed, several years before, a textbook on entomology. He found the file copy and industriously paged through it looking for a winged worm. He found a few winged things that might be called worms, but none that even remotely resembled the angleworm with the halo. Not even, for that matter, if he disregarded the golden circle, and tried to make identification solely on the basis of body and wings.

No flying angleworms.

There weren't any medical hooks in which he could look up—or try to look up—how one could get sunburned without a sun.

But he looked up "tael" in the dictionary, and found that it was equivalent to a liang, which was one-sixteenth of a catty. And that one official liang is equivalent to a hectogram.

None of which seemed particularly helpful.

Shortly before five o'clock he went around saying good-by to everyone, because this was the last day at the office before his two weeks' vacation, and the good-byes were naturally complicated by good wishes on his impending wedding—which would take place in the first week of his vacation.

He had to shake hands with everybody but the Pest, whom, of course, he'd be seeing frequently during the first few days of his vacation. In fact, he went home with her from work to have dinner with the Pembertons.

And it was a quiet, restful, pleasant dinner that left him feeling better than he'd felt since last Sunday morning. Here in the calm harbor of the Pemberton household, the absurd things that had happened to him seemed so far away and so utterly fantastic that he almost doubted if they had happened at all.

And he felt utterly, completely certain that it was all over. Things happened in threes, didn't they? *If* anything else happened— But it wouldn't.

It didn't, that night.

Jane solicitously sent him home at nine o'clock to get to bed early. But she kissed him good night so tenderly, and withal so effectively, that he walked down the street with his head in rosy clouds.

Then suddenly—out of nothing, as it were—Charlie remembered that the museum attendant had been suspended, and was losing three days' pay, because of the episode of the duck in the showcase. And if that duck business was Charlie's fault—even indirectly—didn't he owe it to the guy to step forward and explain to the museum directors that the attendant had been in no way to blame, and that he should not be penalized?

After all, he, Charlie, had probably scared the poor attendant half out of his wits by suggesting that he could repeat the performance with a sarcophagus instead of a showcase, and the attendant had told such a disconnected story that he hadn't been believed.

But—*had* the thing been his fault? *Did* he owe—

And there he was butting his head against that brick wall of impossibility again. Trying to solve the unsolvable.

And he knew, suddenly, that he had been weak in not breaking his engagement to Jane. That what had happened three times within the short space of a week might all too easily happen again.

Good God! Even at the ceremony. Suppose he reached for the wedding ring and pulled out a—

From the rosy clouds of bliss to the black mire of despair had proved to be a walk of less than a block.

Almost he turned back toward the Pemberton home to tell them tonight, then decided not to. Instead, he'd stop by and talk with Pete Johnson.

Maybe Pete—

What he really hoped was that Pete would talk him out of his decision.

VIII

Pete Johnson had a gallon jug, almost full, of wine. Mellow sherry. And Pete had sampled it, and was mellow too.

He refused even to listen to Charlie, until his guest had drunk one glass and had a second on the table in front of him. Then he said, "You got something on your mind. O.K., shoot."

"Lookit, Pete. I told you about that angleworm business. In fact, you were practically there when it happened; And you know about what happened Tuesday morning on my way to work. But yesterday—well, what happened was worse, I guess. Because another guy saw it. It was a duck."

"What was a duck?"

"In a showcase at— Wait, I'll start at the beginning." And he did, and Pete listened.

"Well," he said thoughtfully, "the fact that it was in the newspaper quashes one line of thought. Fortunately. Listen, I don't see what you got to worry about. Aren't you making a mountain out of a few molehills?"

Charlie took another sip of the sherry and lighted a cigarette and said, "How?" quite hopefully.

"Well, three screwy things have happened. But you take any one by itself and it doesn't amount to a hill of beans, does it? Any one of them can be explained. Where you bog down is in sitting there insisting on a blanket explanation for all of them.

"How do you know there is any connection at all? Now take them separately—"

"You take them," suggested Charlie. "How would you explain them so easy as all that?"

"First one's a cinch. Your stomach was upset or something and you had a pure hallucination. Happens to the best people once in a while. Or—you got a second choice just as simple—maybe you saw a new kind of bug. Hell, there are probably thousands of insects that haven't been classified yet. New ones get on the list every year."

"Um," said Charlie. "And the heat business?"

"Well, doctors don't know everything. You got too mad seeing that teamster beating the horse, and anger has a physical effect, hasn't it? You slipped a cog somewhere. Maybe it affected your thermodermal gland."

"What's a thermodermal gland?"

Pete grinned, "I just invented it. But why not? The medicos are constantly finding new ones or new purposes of old ones. And there's *something* in your body that acts as a thermostat and keeps your skin temperature constant. Maybe it went wrong for a minute. Look what a pituitary gland can do for you or against you. Not to mention the parathyroids and the pineal and the adrenals and so on.

"Nothing to it, Charlie. Have some more wine. Now, let's take the duck business. If you don't think about it with the other two things in mind, there's nothing exciting about it. Undoubtedly just a practical joke on the museum or by somebody working there. It was just coincidence that *you* walked in on it."

"But the showcase—"

"Bother the showcase! It could have been done somehow; you didn't check that showcase yourself, and you know what newspapers are. And, for that matter, look what Thurston and Houdini could do with things like that, and let you examine the receptacles before and after. Maybe, too, it wasn't just a joke. Maybe somebody had a purpose putting it there, but why think that purpose had any connection with you? You're an egotist, that's what you are."

Charlie sighed. "Yes, but— But you take the three things together, and—"

"Why take them together? Look, this morning I saw a man slip on a banana peel and fall; this afternoon I had a slight toothache; this evening I got a telephone call from a girl I haven't seen in years. Now why should I take those three events and try to figure one common cause for all of them? One underlying motif for all three? I'd go nuts, if I tried."

"Um," said Charlie. "Maybe you got something there. But—"

Despite the "but—" he went home feeling cheerful, hopeful, and mellow. And he was going through with the wedding just as though nothing had happened. Apparently nothing of importance *had* happened. Pete was sensible.

Charlie slept soundly that Saturday morning, and didn't awaken until almost noon.

And Saturday nothing happened.

IX

Nothing, that is, unless one considered the matter of the missing golf ball as worthy of record. Charlie decided it wasn't; golf balls disappear all too often. In fact, for a dub golfer, it is only normal to lose at least one ball on eighteen holes.

And it was in the rough, at that.

He'd sliced his drive off the tee on the long fourteenth, and he'd seen it curve off the fairway, hit, bounce, and come to rest behind a big tree; with the tree directly between the ball and the green.

And Charlie's "Damn!" had been loud and fervent, because up to that hole he had an excellent chance to break a hundred. Now he'd have to lose a stroke chipping the ball back onto the fairway.

He waited until Pete had hooked into the woods on the other side, and then shouldered his bag and walked toward the ball.

It wasn't there.

Behind the tree and at about the spot where he thought the ball had landed, there was a wreath of wilted flowers strung along a purple cord that showed through at intervals. Charlie picked it up to look under it, but the ball wasn't there.

So, it must have rolled farther, and he looked but couldn't find it. Pete, meanwhile, had found his own ball and hit his recovery shot. He came across to help Charlie look and they waved the following foursome to play on through.

"I thought it stopped right here," Charlie said, "but it must have rolled on. Well, if we don't find it by the time that foursome's played through us, I'll drop another. Say, how'd this thing get here?"

He discovered he still had the wreath in his hand. Pete looked at it and shuddered. "Golly, what a color combination. Violet and red and green on a purple ribbon. It stinks." The thing did smell a bit, although Pete wasn't close enough to notice that and it wasn't what he meant.

"Yeah, but what *is* it? How'd it get—"

Pete grinned. "Looks like one of those things Hawaiians wear around their necks. Leis, don't they call them? Hey!"

He caught the suddenly stricken look on Charlie's face and firmly took the thing out of Charlie's hand and threw it into the woods. "Now, son," he said, "don't go adding *that* damned thing to your string of coincidences. What's the difference who dropped it here or why? Come on, find your ball and let's get ready. The foursome's on the green already."

They didn't find the ball.

So Charlie dropped another. He got it out into the middle of the fairway with a niblick and then a screaming brassie shot down the middle put him on, ten feet from the pin. And he one-putted for a par five on the hole, even with the stroke penalty for a lost ball.

And broke a hundred after all. True, back in the clubhouse while they were getting dressed, he said, "Listen, Pete, about that ball I lost on the fourteenth. Isn't it kind of funny that it—"

"Nuts," Pete grunted. "Didn't you ever lose a ball before? Sometimes you think you see where they land, and it's twenty or even forty feet off from where it really is. The perspective fools you."

"Yeah, but—"

There was that "but" again. It seemed to be the last word on everything that happened recently. Screwy things happen one after another and you can explain each one if you consider it alone, *but—*

"Have a drink," Pete suggested, and handed over a bottle.

Charlie did, and felt better. He had several. It didn't matter, because to-night Jane was going to a shower given by some girl friends and she wouldn't smell it on his breath.

He said, "Pete, got any plans for tonight? Jane's busy, and it's one of my last bachelor evenings—"

Pete grinned. "You mean, what are we going to do or get drunk? O.K., count me in. Maybe we can get a couple more of the gang together. It's Saturday, and none of us has to work tomorrow."

X

And it was undoubtedly a good thing that none of them did have to work Sunday, for few of them would have been able to. It was a highly successful stag evening. Drinks at Tony's, and then a spot of bowling until the manager of the alleys began to get huffy about people bowling balls that started down one alley, jumped the groove, and knocked down pins in the alley adjacent.

And then they'd gone—

Next morning Charlie tried to remember all the places they'd been and all the things they'd done, and decided he was glad he couldn't. For one thing, he had a confused recollection of having tried to start a fight with a Hawaiian guitar player who was wearing a lei, and that he had drunkenly accused the guitarist of stealing his golf ball. But the others had dragged him out of the place before the police got there.

And somewhere around one o'clock they'd eaten, and Charlie had been so stubborn that he'd insisted on trying four eateries before they found one which served duck. He was going to avenge his golf ball by eating duck.

All in all, a very silly and successful spree. Undoubtedly worth a mild hangover.

After all, a guy gets married only once. At least a man who has a girl like Jane Pemberton in love with him gets married only once.

Nothing out of the ordinary happened Sunday. He saw Jane and again had dinner with the Pembertons. And every time he looked at Jane, or touched her, Charlie had somewhat the sensation of a green pilot making his first out-side loop in a fast plane, but that was nothing out of the ordinary. The poor guy was in love.

XI

But on Monday—

Monday was the day that really upset the apple cart. After five fifty-five o'clock Monday afternoon, Charlie knew it was hopeless.

In the morning, he made arrangements with the minister who was to perform the ceremony, and in the afternoon he did a lot of last-minute shopping in the wardrobe line. He found it took him longer than he'd thought.

At five-thirty he began to doubt if he was going to have time to call for the wedding ring. It had been bought and paid for, previously, but was still at the jewelers' being suitably engraved with initials.

He was still on the other side of town at five-thirty, awaiting alterations on a suit, and he phoned Pete Johnson from the tailor's:

"Say, Pete, can you do an errand for me?"

"Sure, Charlie. What's up?"

"I want to get the wedding ring before the store closes at six, so I won't have to come downtown at all tomorrow. It's right in the block with you, Scorwald & Benning's store. It's paid for; will you pick it up for me? I'll phone 'em to give it to you."

"Glad to. Say, where are you? I'm eating downtown tonight; how's about putting the feed bag on with me?"

"Sure, Pete. Listen, maybe I can get to the jeweler's in time: I'm just calling you to play safe. Tell you what; I'll meet you there. You be there at five minutes to six to be sure of getting the ring, and I'll get there at the same time if I can. If I can't, wait for me outside. I won't be later than six-fifteen at the latest."

And Charlie hung up the receiver and found the tailor had the suit ready for him. He paid for it, then went outside and began to look around for a taxi.

It took him ten minutes to find one, and still he saw he was going to get to the jewelry store in time. In fact, it wouldn't have been necessary for him to have phoned Pete. He'd get there easily by five fifty-five.

And it was just a few seconds before that time when he stepped out of the cab, paid off the driver, and strode up to the entrance.

It was just as his first foot crossed the threshold of the Scorwald & Benning store that he noticed the peculiar odor. He had taken one step farther before he recognized what it was, and then it was too late to do anything about it.

It had him. Unconsciously, he'd taken a deep sniff of identification, and the stuff was so strong, so pure, that he didn't need a second. His lungs were filled with it.

And the floor seemed to his distorted vision to be a mile away, but coming up slowly to meet him. Slowly, but getting there. He seemed to hang suspended in the air for a measurable time. Then, before he landed, everything was mercifully black and blank.

XII

"Ether."

Charlie gawked at the white-uniformed doctor. "But how the d-devil could I have got a dose of ether?"

Peter was there, too, looking down at him over the doctor's shoulder. Pete's face was white and tense. Even before the doctor shrugged, Pete was saying: "Listen Charlie, Doc Palmer is on his way over here. I told 'em—"

Charlie was sick at his stomach, very sick, The doctor who had said, "Ether," wasn't there, and neither was Doc Palmer, but Pete now seemed to be arguing with a tall distinguished-looking gentleman who had a spade beard and eyes like a chicken hawk.

Pete was saying, "Let the poor guy alone. Damn it, I've known him all his life. He doesn't need an alienist. Sure he said screwy things while he was under, but doesn't anybody talk silly under ether?"

"But, my young friend"—the tall man's voice was unctuous—"you quite misinterpret the hospital's motives in asking that I examine him. I wish to prove him sane. If possible. He may have had a legitimate reason for taking the ether. And also the affair of last week when he was here for the first time. Surely a normal man—"

"But damn it, he *didn't* take that ether himself. I saw him coming in the doorway after he got out of the cab. He walked naturally, and he had his hands down at his sides. Then, all of a sudden, he just keeled over."

"You suggest someone near him did it?"

"There *wasn't* anybody near him."

Charlie's eyes were closed but by the psychiatrist's tone of voice, he could tell that the man was smiling. "Then how, my young friend, do you suggest that he was anesthetized?"

"Damn it, I don't know. I'm just saying he didn't—"

"Pete!" Charlie recognized his own voice and found that his eyes were open again. "Tell him to go to hell. Tell him to certify me if he wants. Sure I'm crazy. Tell him about the worm and the duck. Take me to the booby hatch. Tell him—"

"Ha." Again the voice with the spade beard. "You have had previous—ah—delusions?"

"Charlie, shut up! Doc, he's still under the influence of the ether; don't listen to him. It isn't *fair* to psych a guy when he doesn't know what he's talking about. For two cents, I'd—"

"Fair? My friend, psychiatry is not a game. I assure you that I have this young man's interests at heart. Perhaps his—ah—aberration is curable, and I wish to—"

Charlie sat up in bed. He yelled. "*Get out of here before I—*"

Things went black again.

The tortuous darkness, thick and smoky and sickening. And he seemed to be creeping through a narrow tunnel toward a light. Then suddenly he knew that he was conscious again. But maybe there was somebody around who would talk to him and ask him questions if he opened his eyes, so he kept them tightly shut.

He kept his eyes tightly shut, and thought.

There must be an answer.

There wasn't any answer.

An angelic angleworm.

Heat wave.

Duck in a showcase of coins.

Wilted wreath of ugly flowers.

Ether in a doorway.

Connect them; there *must* be a connection, it *had* to make sense. It had to *make sense!*

Least common denominator. Something that connects them, that welds them into a coherent series, something that you can understand, something that you can maybe do something about. Something you can fight.

Worm.

Heat.

Duck.

Wreath.

Ether.

Worm.

Heat.

Duck.

Wreath.

Ether.

Worm, heat, duck, wreath, ether, worm, heat, duck, wreath—

They pounded through his head like beating on a tom-tom; they screamed at him out of the darkness and gibbered.

XIII

He must have slept, if you could call it sleep.

It was broad daylight again, and there was only a nurse in the room. He asked, "What—day is it?"

"Wednesday afternoon, Mr. Wills. Is there anything I can do for you?"

Wednesday afternoon. Wedding day.

He wouldn't have to call it off now. Jane knew. Everybody knew. It had been called off for him. He'd been weak not to have done it himself, before—

"There are people waiting to see you, Mr. Wills. Do you feel well enough to entertain visitors?"

"I— Who?"

"A Miss Pemberton and her father. And a Mr. Johnson. Do you want to see them?"

Well, did he?

"Look," he said, "What exactly's wrong with me? I mean—"

"You've suffered a severe shock. But you've slept quietly for the last twelve hours. Physically, you are quite all right. Even able to get up, if you feel you want to. But, of course, you mustn't leave."

Of *course* he mustn't leave. They had him down as a candidate for the booby hatch. An excellent candidate. Young man most likely to succeed.

Wednesday. Wedding day.

Jane.

He couldn't bear to see—

"Listen," he said, "will you send in Mr. Pemberton, alone? I'd rather—"

"Certainly. Anything else I can do for you?"

Charlie shook his head sadly. He was feeling most horribly sorry for himself. Was there anything *anybody* could do for him?

Mr. Pemberton held out his hand quietly. "Charles, I can't begin to tell you how sorry I am—"

Charlie nodded. "Thanks. I—I guess you understand why I don't want to see Jane. I realize that—that of course we can't—"

Mr. Pemberton nodded. "Jane—uh—understands, Charles. She wants to see you, but realizes that it might make both of you feel worse, at least right now. And Charles, if there's anything any of us can do—"

What was there anybody could do?

Pull the wings off an angleworm?

Take a duck out of a showcase?

Find a missing golf ball?

Pete came in after the Pembertons had gone away. A quieter and more subdued Pete than Charlie had ever seen.

He said, "Charlie, do you feel up to talking this over?"

Charlie sighed. "If it'd do any good, yes. I feel all right physically. But—"

"Listen, you've got to keep your chin up. There's an answer somewhere. Listen, I was wrong. There is a connection, a tie-up between these screwy things that happened to you. There's got to be."

"Sure," said Charlie, wearily. "What?"

"That's what we've got to find out. First place, we'll have to outsmart the psychiatrists they'll sic on you. As soon as they think you're well enough to stand it. Now, let's look at it from their point of view so we'll know what to tell 'em. First—"

"How much do they know?"

"Well, you raved while you were unconscious, about the worm business and about a duck and a golf ball, but you can pass that off as ordinary raving. Talking in your sleep. Dreaming. Just deny knowing anything about them, or anything connected with any of them. Sure, the duck business was in the newspapers, but it wasn't a big story and your name wasn't in it. So they'll never tie that up. If they do, deny it. Now that leaves the two times you keeled over and were brought here unconscious."

Charlie nodded. "And what do they make of them?"

"They're puzzled. The first one they can't make anything much of. They're inclined to leave it lay. The second one— Well, they insist that you must, somehow, have given yourself that ether."

"But why? Why would anybody give himself ether?"

"No sane man would. That's just it; they doubt your sanity because they think you did. If you can convince them you're sane, then— Look, you *got* to buck up. They are classifying your attitude as acute melancholia, and that sort of borders on manic depressive. See? You got to act cheerful."

"Cheerful? When I was to be married at two o'clock today? By the way, what time is it now?"

Pete glanced at his wrist watch and said, "Uh—never mind that. Sure, if they ask why you feel lousy mentally, tell them—"

"Damn it, Pete, I wish I *was* crazy. At least, being crazy makes sense. And if this stuff keeps up, *I will* go—"

"*Don't talk like that.* You got to fight."

"Yeah," said Charlie, listlessly. "Fight what?"

There was a low rap on the door and the nurse looked into the room. "Your time is up, Mr. Johnson. You'll have to leave."

XIV

Inaction, and the futility of circling thought-patterns that get nowhere. Finally, he had to do something or go mad.

Get dressed? He called for his clothes and got them, except that he was given slippers instead of his shoes. Anyway, getting dressed took up time.

And sitting in a chair was a change from lying in bed. And then walking up and down was a change from sitting in a chair.

"What time is it?"

"Seven o'clock, Mr. Wills."

Seven o'clock; he should have been married five hours by now.

Married to Jane; beautiful, gorgeous, sweet, loving, understanding, kissable, soft, lovable Jane Pemberton. Five hours ago this moment she should have become Jane Wills.

Nevermore.

Unless—

The problem.

Solve it.

Or go mad.

Why would a worm wear a halo?

"Dr. Palmer is here to see you, Mr. Wills. Shall I—"

"Hello, Charles. Came as soon as I could after I learned you were out of your—uh—coma. Had an o.b. case that kept me. How do you feel?"

He felt terrible.

Ready to scream and tear the paper off the wall only the wall was painted white and didn't have any paper. And scream, scream—

"I feel swell, Doc," said Charlie.

"Anything—uh—strange happen to you since you've been here?"

"Not a thing. But, Doc, how would you explain—"

Doc Palmer explained. Doctors always explain. The air crackled with words like psychoneurotic and autohypnosis and traumata.

Finally, Charlie was alone again. He'd managed to say good-by to Doc Palmer, too, without yelling and tearing him to bits.

"What time is it?"

"Eight o'clock."

Six hours married.

Why is a *duck?*
Solve it.
Or go mad.
What would happen next? "Surely this thing shall follow me all the days of my life and I shall dwell in the bughouse forever."
Eight o'clock.
Six hours married.
Why a lei? Ether? Heat?
What have they in common? And why is a duck?
And what would it be *next time?* When would next time be? Well, maybe he could guess that. How many things happened to him thus far? Five—if the missing golf ball counted. How far apart? Let's see—the angleworm was Sunday morning when he went fishing; the heat prostration was Tuesday; the duck in the museum was Thursday noon, the second-last day he worked; the golf game and the lei was Saturday; the ether Monday—
Two days apart.
Periodicity?
He'd been pacing up and down the room, now suddenly he felt in his pocket and found pencil and a notebook, and sat down in the chair.
Could it be—*exact* periodicity?
He wrote down "Angleworm" and stopped to think. Pete was to call for him to go fishing at five-fifteen and he'd gone downstairs at just that time, and right to the flower bed to dig— Yes, five-fifteen A.M. He wrote it down.
"Heat." Hm-m-m, he'd been a block from work and was due there at eight-thirty, and when he'd passed the corner clock he'd looked and seen that he had five minutes to get there, and then had seen the teamster and— He wrote it down. "Eight twenty-five." And calculated.
Two days, three hours, ten minutes.
Let's see, which was next? The duck in the museum. He could time that fairly well, too. Old Man Hapworth had told him to go to lunch early, and he'd left at—uh—eleven twenty-five and it took him, say, ten minutes to walk the block to the museum and down the main corridor and into the numismatic room— Say, eleven thirty-five.
He subtracted that from the previous one.
And whistled.
Two days, three hours, ten minutes.
The lei? Um, they'd left the clubhouse about one-thirty. Allow an hour and a quarter, say, for the first thirteen holes, and—well, say between two-thirty and three. Strike an average at two forty-five. That would be pretty close. Subtract it.
Two days, three hours, ten minutes.
Periodicity.
He subtracted the next one first—the fourth episode should have happened at five fifty-five on Monday. If—

Yes, it had been *exactly* five minutes of six when he'd walked through the door of the jewelry shop and been anesthetized.

Exactly.

Two days, three hours, ten minutes.

Periodicity.

PERIODICITY.

A connection, at last. Proof that the screwy events were all of a piece. Every—uh—fifty-one hours and ten minutes *something screwy happened.*

But why?

He stuck his head out in the hallway.

"Nurse. NURSE. What time is it?"

"Half past eight, Mr. Wills. Anything I can bring you?"

Yes. No. Champagne. Or a strait jacket. Which?

He'd solved the problem. But the answer didn't make any more sense than the problem itself. Less, maybe. And today—

He figured quickly.

In thirty-five minutes.

Something would happen to him in thirty-five minutes!

Something like a flying angleworm or like a quacking duck suffocating in an air-tight showcase, or—

Or maybe something *dangerous* again? Burning heat, sudden anesthesia—

Maybe something worse?

A cobra, unicorn, devil, werewolf, vampire, unnamable monster?

At nine-five. In half an hour.

In a sudden draft from the open window, his forehead felt cold. Because it was wet with sweat.

In half an hour.

XV

Pace up and down, four steps one way, four steps back. Think, think, THINK.

You've solved part of it; what's the rest? Get it, or it will get you.

Periodicity; that's part of it. Every two days, three hours ten minutes—

Something happens.

Why?

What?

How?

They're connected, those things, they are part of a pattern and they make sense somehow or they wouldn't be spaced an exact interval of time apart.

Connect: angleworm, heat, duck, lei, ether—

Or go mad.

Mad. *Mad.* MAD.

Connect: Ducks eat angleworms, or do they? Heat is necessary to grow flowers to make leis. Angleworms might eat flowers for all he knew, but what have they to do with leis, and what is ether to a duck? Duck is animal, lei is vegetable, heat is vibration, ether is gas, worm is—what the hell is a worm? And why a worm that flies? Why was the duck in the showcase? What about the missing Chinese coin with the hole? Do you add or subtract the golf ball, and if you let x equal a halo and y equal one wing, then x plus 2y plus angle-worm equals—

Outside, somewhere, a clock striking in the gathering darkness.

One, two, three, four, five, six, seven, eight, nine—

Nine o'clock.

Five minutes to go.

In five minutes something was going to happen again.

Cobra, unicorn, devil, werewolf, vampire. Or something cold and slimy and without a name.

Anything.

Pace up and down, four steps one way, four steps back.

Think, THINK.

Jane forever lost. Dearest Jane, in whose arms was all of happiness. Jane, darling, I'm not mad, I'm WORSE than mad. I'm—

WHAT TIME IS IT?

It must be two minutes after nine. Three.

What's coming? Cobra, devil, werewolf—

What will it be this time?

At five minutes after nine—WHAT?

Must be four after now; yes, it had been at least four minutes, maybe four and a half—

He yelled, suddenly. He couldn't stand the waiting.

It couldn't be solved. But he had to solve it.

Or go mad.

MAD.

He must be mad already. Mad to tolerate living, trying to fight something you couldn't fight, trying to beat the unbeatable. Beating his head against—

He was running now, out the door, down the corridor.

Maybe if he hurried, he could kill himself before five minutes after nine. He'd never have to know. DIE, DIE AND GET IT OVER WITH. THAT'S THE ONLY WAY TO BUCK THIS GAME.

Knife.

There'd be a knife somewhere. A scalpel is a knife.

Down the corridor. Voice of a nurse behind him, shouting. Footsteps.

Run. Where? Anywhere.

Less than a minute left. Maybe seconds.

Maybe it's nine-five now. Hurry!

Door marked "Utility"—he jerked it open.

Shelves of linen. Mops and brooms. You can't kill yourself with a mop or broom. You can smother yourself with linen, but not in less than a minute and with doctors and interns coming.

Uniforms. Bucket. Kick the bucket, but *how*? Ah. There on the upper shelf—

A cardboard carton, already opened, marked "Lye."

Painful? Sure, but it wouldn't last long. Get it over with. The box in his hand, the opened corner, and tilted the contents into his mouth.

But it was not a white, searing powder. All that had come out of the cardboard carton was a small copper coin. He took it out of his mouth and held it, and looked at it with dazed eyes.

It was five minutes after nine, then; out of the box of lye had come a small foreign copper coin. No, it wasn't the Chinese haikwan tael that had disappeared from the showcase in the museum, because that was silver and had a hole in it. And the lettering on this wasn't Chinese. If he remembered his coins, it looked Rumanian.

And then strong hands took hold of Charlie's arms and led him back to his room and somebody talked to him quietly for a long time.

And he slept.

XVI

He awoke Thursday morning from a dreamless sleep, and felt strangely refreshed and, oddly, quite cheerful.

Probably because, in that awful thirty-five minutes of waiting he'd experienced the evening before, he'd hit rock bottom. And bounced.

A psychiatrist might have explained it by saying that he had, under stress of great emotion, suffered a temporary lesion and gone into a quasi-state of manic-depressive insanity. Psychiatrists like to make simple things complicated.

The fact was that the poor guy had gone off his rocker for a few minutes.

And the absurd anticlimax of that small copper coin had been the turning point. Look for something horrible, unnamable—and get a small copper coin. Practically a prophylactic treatment, if you've got enough stuff in you to laugh.

And Charlie had laughed last night. Probably that was why his room this morning seemed to be a different room. The window was in a different wall, and it had bars across it. Psychiatrists often misinterpret a sense of humor.

But this morning he felt cheerful enough to overlook the implications of the barred windows. Here it was a bright new day with the sun streaming through the bars, and it was *another* day and he was still alive and had another chance.

Best of all, he knew he wasn't insane.

Unless—

He looked and there were his clothes hanging over the back of a chair and he sat up and put his legs out of bed, and reached for his coat pocket to see if the coin was still where he'd put it when they'd grabbed him.

It was.

Then—

He dressed slowly, thoughtfully.

Now, in the light of morning, it came to him that the thing could be solved. Six—now there were six—screwy things, but they were definitely connected. Periodicity proved it.

Two days, three hours, ten minutes.

And whatever the answer was, it was not malevolent. It was impersonal. If it had wanted to kill, it had a chance last night; it need merely have affected something else other than the lye in that package. There'd *been* lye in the package when he'd picked it up; he could tell that by the weight. And then it had been five minutes after nine and instead of lye there'd been the small copper coin.

It wasn't friendly, either; or it wouldn't have subjected him to heat and anesthesia. It must be something impersonal.

A coin instead of lye.

Were they all substitutions of one thing for another?

Hm-m-m. Lei for a golf ball. A coin for lye. A duck for a coin. But the heat? The ether? The angleworm?

He went to the window and looked out for a while into the warm sunlight falling on the green lawn, and he realized that life was very sweet. And that if he took this thing calmly and didn't let it get him down again, he might yet lick it.

The first clue was already his.

Periodicity.

Take it calmly; think about other things. Keep your mind off the merry-go-round and maybe the answer will come.

He sat down on the edge of the bed and felt in his pocket for the pencil and notebook and they were still there, and the paper on which he'd made his calculations of timing. He studied those calculations carefully.

Calmly.

And at the end of the list he put down "9:05" and added the word "lye" and a dash. Lye had turned to—what? He drew a bracket and began to fill in words that could be used to describe the coin; coin—copper—disk—But those were general. There must be a specific name for the thing.

Maybe—

He pressed the button that would light a bulb outside his door and a moment later heard a key turn in the lock and the door opened. It was a male attendant this time.

Charlie smiled at him. "Morning," he said. "Serve breakfast here, or do I eat the mattress?"

The attendant grinned, and looked a bit relieved. "Sure. Breakfast's ready; I'll bring you some?"

"And—uh—"

"Yes?"

"There's something I want to look up," Charlie said. "Would there be an unabridged dictionary anywhere handy? And if there is, would it be asking too much for you to let me see it a few minutes?"

"Why—I guess it will be all right. There's one down in the office and they don't use it very often."

"That's swell. Thanks."

But the key turned in the lock when he left.

Breakfast came half an hour later, but the dictionary didn't arrive until the middle of the morning. Charlie wondered if there had been a staff meeting to discuss its lethal possibilities. But anyway, it came.

He waited until the attendant had left and then put the big volume on the bed and opened it to the color plate that showed coins of the world. He took the copper coin out of his pocket and put it alongside the plate and began to compare it with the illustrations, particularly those of coins of the Balkan countries. No, nothing just like it among the copper coins. Try the silver—yes, there was a silver coin with the same mug on it. Rumanian. The lettering—yes, it was identically the same lettering except for the denomination.

Charlie turned to the coinage table. Under Rumania—

He gasped.

It couldn't be.

But it was.

It was impossible that the six things that had happened to him could have been—

He was breathing hard with excitement as he turned to the illustrations at the back of the dictionary, found the pages of birds, and began to look among the ducks. Speckled breast and short neck and darker stripe starting just above the eye—

And he knew he'd found the answer.

He'd found the factor, besides periodicity, that connected the things that had happened. If it fitted the others, he could be sure. The angleworm? Why—*sure*—and he grinned at that one. The heat wave? Obvious. And the affair on the golf course? That was harder, but a bit of thought gave it to him.

The matter of the ether stumped him for a while. It took a lot of pacing up and down to solve that one, but finally he managed to do it.

And then? Well, what could he *do* about it?

Periodicity? Yes, that fitted in. If—

Next time would be—hm-m-m—12:15 Saturday morning.

He sat down to think it over. The whole thing was completely incredible. The answer was harder to swallow than the problem.

But—they *all* fitted. Six coincidences, spaced an exact length of time apart?

All right then, forget how incredible it is, and what are you going to do about it? How are you going to get there to let them know?

Well—maybe take advantage of the phenomenon itself?

The dictionary was still there and Charlie went back to it and began to look in the gazetteer. Under "H—"

Whew! There was one that gave him a *double* chance. And within a hundred miles.

If he could get out of here—

He rang the bell, and the attendant came. "Through with the dictionary," Charlie told him. "And listen, could I talk to the doctor in charge of my case?"

It proved that the doctor in charge was still Doc Palmer, and that he was coming up anyway.

He shook hands with Charlie and smiled at him. That was a good sign, or was it?

Well, now if he could lie convincingly enough—

"Doc, I feel swell this morning," said Charlie. "And listen— I remembered something I want to tell you about. Something that happened to me Sunday, couple of days before that first time I was taken to the hospital."

"What was it, Charles?"

"I *did* go swimming, and that accounts for the sunburn that was showing up on Tuesday morning, and maybe for some other things. I'd borrowed Pete Johnson's car—" Would they check up on that? Maybe not. "—and I got lost off the road and found a swell pool and stripped and went in. And I remember now that I dived off the bank and I think I must have grazed my head on a rock because the next thing I remember I was back in town."

"Hm-m-m," said Doc Palmer. "So *that* accounts for the sunburn, and maybe it can account for—"

"Funny that it just came back to me this morning when I woke up," said Charlie. "I guess—"

"I told those fools," said Doc Palmer, "that there couldn't be any connection between the third-degree burn and your fainting. Of course there was, in a way. I mean your hitting your head while you were swimming would account—Charles, I'm sure glad this came back to you. At least we now know the cause of the way you've acted, and we can treat it. In fact, maybe you're cured already."

"I think so, Doc. I sure feel swell now. Like I was just waking up from a nightmare. I guess I made a fool of myself a couple of times. I have a vague recollection of buying some ether once, and something about some lye—but those are like things that happened in a dream, and now my mind's as clear as a bell. Something seemed to pop this morning, and I was all right again."

Doc Palmer sighed. "I'm relieved, Charles. Frankly, you had us quite worried. Of course, I'll have to talk this over with the staff and we'll have to examine you pretty thoroughly, but I think—"

There were the other doctors, and they asked questions and they examined his skull—but whatever lesion had been made by the rock seemed to have healed. Anyway, they couldn't find it.

If it hadn't been for his suicide attempt of the evening before, he could have walked out of the hospital then and there. But because of that they insisted on his remaining under observation for twenty-four hours. And Charlie agreed; that would let him out some time Friday afternoon, and it wasn't until twelve-fifteen Saturday morning that *it* would happen.

Plenty of time to go a hundred miles.

If he just watched everything he did and said in the meantime and made no move or remark which a psychiatrist could interpret—

He loafed and rested.

And at five o'clock Friday afternoon it was all right, and he shook hands all the way round, and was a free man again. He'd promised to report to Doc Palmer regularly for a few weeks.

But he was free.

XVII

Rain and darkness.

A cold, unpleasant drizzle that started to find its way through his clothes and down the back of his neck and into his shoes even as he stepped off the train onto the small wooden platform.

But the station was there, and on the side of it was the sign that told him the name of the town. Charlie looked at it and grinned, and went into the station. There was a cheerful little coal stove in the middle of the room. He had time to get warmed up before he started. He held out his hands to the stove.

Over at one side of the room, a grizzled head regarded him curiously through the ticket window. Charlie nodded at the head and the head nodded back.

"Stayin' here a while, stranger?" the head asked.

"Not exactly," said Charlie. "Anyway, I hope not. I mean—" Hell, after those whoppers he'd told the psychiatrists back at the hospital, he shouldn't have any trouble lying to a ticket agent in a little country town. "I mean, I don't think so."

"Ain't no more trains out tonight, mister. Got a place to stay? If not, my wife sometimes takes in boarders for short spells,"

"Thanks," said Charlie. "I've made arrangements." He started to add, "I hope," and then realized that it would lead him further into discussion.

He glanced at the clock and at his wrist watch and saw that both agreed that it was a quarter to twelve.

"How big is this town?" he asked. "I don't mean population. I mean, how far out the turnpike is it to the township line? The border of town."

"'Tain't big. Half a mile maybe, or a little better. You goin' out to the Tollivers, maybe? They live just past and I heard tell he was sendin' to th' city for a—nope, you don't look like a hired man."

"Nope," said Charlie. "I'm not." He glanced at the clock again and started for the door. He said, "Well, be seeing you."

"You goin' to—"

But Charlie had already gone out the door and was starting down the street behind the railroad station. Into the darkness and the unknown and—Well, he could hardly tell the agent about his real destination, could he?

There was the turnpike. After a block, the sidewalk ended and he had to walk along the edge of the road, sometimes ankle deep in mud. He was soaked through by now, but that didn't matter.

It proved to be more than half a mile to the township line. A big sign there—an oddly big sign considering the size of the town—read:

YOU ARE NOW ENTERING HAVEEN

Charlie crossed the line and faced back. And waited, an eye on his wrist watch.

At twelve-fifteen he'd have to step across. It was ten minutes after already. Two days, three hours, ten minutes after the box of lye had held a copper coin, which was two days, three hours, ten minutes after he'd walked into anesthesia in the door of a jewelry store, which was two days, three hours, ten minutes after—

He watched the hands of his accurately set wrist watch, first the minute hand until twelve-fourteen. Then the second hand.

And when it lacked a second of twelve-fifteen he put forth his foot and at *the* fatal moment he was stepping slowly across the line.

Entering Haveen.

XVIII

And as with each of the others, there was no warning. But suddenly:

It wasn't raining any more. There was bright light, although it didn't seem to come from a visible source. And the road beneath his feet wasn't muddy; it was smooth as glass and alabaster-white. The white-robed entity at the gate ahead stared at Charlie in astonishment.

He said: "How did *you* get here? You aren't even—"

"No," said Charlie. "I'm not even dead. But listen, I've got to see the—uh— Who's in charge of the printing?"

"The Head Compositor, of course. But you can't—"

"I've got to see him, then," said Charlie.

"But the rules forbid—"

"Look, it's important. Some *typographical errors* are going through. It's to your interests up here as well as to mine, that they be corrected, isn't it? Otherwise things can get into an awful mess."

"Errors? Impossible. You're joking."

"Then how," asked Charlie, reasonably, "did I get to Heaven without dying?"

"But—"

"You see I was supposed to be entering Haveen. There is an e-matrix that—"

"Come."

XIX

It was quite pleasant and familiar, that office. Not a lot different from Charlie's own office at the Hapworth Printing Company. There was a rickety wooden desk, littered with papers, and behind it sat a small bald-headed Chief Compositor with printer's ink on his hands and a smear of it on his forehead. Past the closed door was a monster roar and clatter of typesetting machines and presses.

"Sure," said Charlie. "They're supposed to be perfect, so perfect that you don't even need proofreaders. But maybe once out of infinity something can happen to perfection, can't it? Mathematically, once out of infinity *anything* can happen. Now look; there is a separate typesetting machine and operator for the records covering each person, isn't there?"

The Head Compositor nodded. "Correct, although in a manner of speaking the operator and the machine are one, in that the operator is a function of the machine and the machine a manifestation of the operator and both are extensions of the ego of the—but I guess that is a little too complicated for you to understand."

"Yes, I—well, anyway, the channels that the matrices run in must be tremendous. On our Linotypes at the Hapworth Printing Company, an e-mat would make the circuit every sixty seconds or so, and if one was defective it would cause one mistake a minute, but up here—Well, is my calculation of fifty hours and ten minutes correct?"

"It is," agreed the Head Compositor. "And since there is no way you could have found out that fact except—"

"Exactly. And once every that often the defective e-matrix comes round and falls when the operator hits the e-key. Probably the ears of the mat are worn; anyway it falls through a long distributor front and falls too fast and lands ahead of its right place in the word, and a typographical error goes through. Like a week ago Sunday, I was supposed to pick up an *angleworm*, and—"

"Wait."

The Head Compositor pressed a buzzer and issued an order. A moment later, a heavy book was brought in and placed on his desk. Before the Head Compositor opened it, Charlie caught a glimpse of his own name on the cover.

"You said at five-fifteen A.M.?"

Charlie nodded. Pages turned.

"I'll be—blessed!" said the Head Compositor. "*Angelworm!* It must have been something to see. Don't know I've ever heard of an angelworm before. And what was next?"

"The e fell wrong in the word 'hate'—I was going after a man who was beating a horse, and—Well, it came out 'heat' instead of 'hate.' The e dropped two characters early that time. And I got heat prostration and sunburn on a rainy day. That was eight twenty-five Tuesday, and then at eleven thirty-five Thursday at the museum—"

"Yes?" prompted the Head Compositor.

"A tael. A Chinese silver coin I was supposed to see. It came out 'teal' and because a teal is a duck, there was a wild duck fluttering around in an airtight showcase. One of the attendants got in trouble; I hope you'll fix that."

The Head Compositor chuckled, "I shall," he said. "I'd like to have seen that duck. And the next time would have been two forty-five Saturday afternoon. What happened then?"

"Lei instead of lie, sir. My golf ball was stymied behind a tree and it was supposed to be a poor lie—but it was a poor lei instead. Some wilted, mismatched flowers on a purple cord. And the next was the hardest for me to figure out, even when I had the key. I had an appointment at the jewelry store at five fifty-five. But that was the fatal time. I got there at five fifty-five, but the e-matrix fell four characters out of place that time, clear back to the start of the word. Instead of getting *there* at five fifty-five, I got *ether*."

"*Tch, tch*. That one was unfortunate. And next?"

"The next was just the reverse, sir. In fact, it happened to save my life. I went temporarily insane and tried to kill myself by taking lye. But the bad e fell in lye and it came out *ley*, which is a small Rumanian copper coin. I've still got it, for a souvenir. In fact when I found out the name of the coin, I guessed the answer. It gave me the key to the others."

The Head Compositor chuckled again. "You've shown great resource," he said. "And your method of getting here to tell us about it—"

"That was easy, sir. If I timed it so I'd be entering Haveen at the right instant, I had a double chance. If either of the two e's in that word turned out to be the bad one and fell—as it did—too early in the word, I'd be entering Heaven."

"Decidedly ingenious. You may, incidentally, consider the errors corrected. We've taken care of all of them, while you talked; except the last one, of course. Otherwise, you wouldn't still be here. And the defective mat is removed from the channel."

"You mean that as far as people down there know, none of those things ever—"

"Exactly. A revised edition is now on the press, and nobody on Earth will have any recollection of any of those events. In a way of speaking, they no longer ever happened. I mean, they did, but now they didn't for all practical purposes. When we return you to Earth, you'll find the status there just what it would have been if the typographical errors had not occurred."

"You mean, for instance, that Pete Johnson won't remember my having told him about the angleworm, and there won't be any record at the hospital about my having been there? And—"

"Exactly. The errors are *corrected*."

"*Whew!*" said Charlie. "I'll be—I mean, well, I was supposed to have been married Wednesday afternoon, two days ago. Uh—will I be? I mean, *was* I? I mean—"

The Head Compositor consulted another volume, and nodded. "Yes, at two o'clock Wednesday afternoon. To one Jane Pemberton. Now if we return you to Earth as of the time you left there—twelve-fifteen Saturday morning, you'll find yourself—let's see—spending your honeymoon in Miami. At that exact moment, you'll be in a taxicab en route—"

"Yes, but—" Charlie gulped.

"But what?" The Head Compositor looked surprised. "I certainly thought that was what you wanted, Wills. We owe you a big favor for having used such ingenuity in calling those typographical errors to our attention, but I thought that being married to Jane was what you wanted, and if you go back and find yourself—"

"Yes, but—" said Charlie again. "But—I mean— Look, I'll have been married two days. I'll miss—I mean, couldn't I—"

Suddenly the Head Compositor smiled.

"How stupid of me," he said, "of course. Well, the time doesn't matter at all. We can drop you anywhere in the continuum. I can just as easily return you as of two o'clock Wednesday afternoon, at the moment of the ceremony. Or Wednesday morning, just before. Any time at all."

"Well," said Charlie, hesitantly. "It isn't exactly that I'd miss the wedding ceremony. I mean, I don't like receptions and things like that, and I'd have to sit through a long wedding dinner and listen to toasts and speeches and, well, I mean. I—"

The Head Compositor laughed. He said, "Are you ready?"

"Am I—Sure!"

Click of train wheels over the rails, and the stars and moon bright above the observation platform of the speeding train.

Jane in his arms. His wife, and it was Wednesday evening. Beautiful, gorgeous, sweet, loving, soft, kissable, lovable Jane—

She snuggled closer to him, and he was whispering, "It's—it's eleven o'clock, darling. Shall we—"

Their lips met, clung.

Then, hand in hand, they walked through the swaying train. His hand turned the knob of the stateroom door and, as it swung slowly open, he picked her up to carry her across the threshold.

The Hat Trick

In a sense, the thing never happened. Actually, it would not have happened had not a thundershower been at its height when the four of them came out of the movie.

It had been a horror picture. A really horrible one—not trapdoor claptrap, but a subtle, insidious thing that made the rain-laden night seem clean and sweet and welcome. To three of them. The fourth—

They stood under the marquee, and Mae said. "Gee, gang, what do we do now, swim or take taxis?" Mae was a cute little blonde with a turned-up nose, the better for smelling the perfumes she sold across a department-store counter.

Elsie turned to the two boys and said, "Let's all go up to my studio for a while. It's early yet." The faint emphasis on the word "studio" was the snapper. Elsie had had the studio for only a week, and the novelty of living in a studio instead of a furnished room made her feel proud and Bohemian and a little wicked. She wouldn't, of course, have invited Walter up alone, but as long as there were two couples of them, it would be all right.

Bob said, "Swell. Listen, Wally, you hold this cab. I'll run down and get some wine. You girls like port?"

Walter and the girls took the cab while Bob talked the bartender, whom he knew slightly, into selling a fifth of wine after legal hours. He came running back with it and they were off to Elsie's.

Mae, in the cab, got to thinking about the horror picture again; she'd almost made them walk out on it. She shivered, and Bob put his arm around her protectively. "Forget it, Mae," he said. "Just a picture. Nothing like that ever happens, really."

"If it did—" Walter began, and then stopped abruptly.

Bob looked at him and said, "If it did, what?"

Walter's voice was a bit apologetic. "Forget now what I was going to say." He smiled, a little strangely, as though the picture had affected him a bit differently than it had affected the others. Quite a bit.

"How's school coming, Walter?" Elsie asked.

Walter was taking a premed course at night school; this was his one night off for the week. Days he worked in a bookstore on Chestnut Sheet. He nodded and said, "Pretty good."

Elsie was comparing him, mentally, with Mae's boy friend, Bob. Walter wasn't quite as tall as Bob, but he wasn't bad-looking in spite of his glasses. And he was sure a lot smarter than Bob was and would get further some day. Bob was learning printing and was halfway through his apprenticeship now. He'd quit high school in his third year.

When they got to Elsie's studio, she found four glasses in the cupboard, even if they were all different sizes and shapes, and then she rummaged around for crackers and peanut butter while Bob opened the wine and filled the glasses.

It was Elsie's first party in the studio, and it turned out not to be a very wicked one. They talked about the horror picture mostly, and Bob refilled their glasses a couple of times, but none of them felt it much.

Then the conversation ran down a bit and it was still early. Elsie said, "Bob, you used to do some good card tricks. I got a deck in the drawer there. Show us."

That's how it started, as simply as that. Bob took the deck and had Mae draw a card. Then he cut the deck and had Mae put it back in at the cut, and let her cut them a few times, and then he went through the deck, face up, and showed her the card, the nine of spades.

Walter watched without particular interest. He probably wouldn't have said anything if Elsie hadn't piped up, "Bob, that's wonderful. I don't see *how* you do it." So Walter told her, "It's easy; he looked at the bottom card before he started, and when he cut her card into the deck, that card would be on top of it, so he just picked out the card that was next to it."

Elsie saw the look Bob was giving Walter and she tried to cover up by saying how clever it was even when you knew how it worked, but Bob said, "Wally, maybe you can show us something good. Maybe you're Houdini's pet nephew or something."

Walter grinned at him. He said, "If I had a hat, I might show you one." It was safe; neither of the boys had worn hats. Mae pointed to the tricky little thing she'd taken off her head and put on Elsie's dresser. Walter scowled at it. "Call that a hat? Listen, Bob, I'm sorry I gave your trick away. Skip it; I'm no good at them."

Bob had been riffling the cards back and forth from one hand to the other, and he might have skipped it had not the deck slipped and scattered on the floor. He picked them up and his face was red, not entirely from bending over. He held out the deck to Walter. "You must be good on cards, too," he said. "If you could give my trick away, you must know some. G'wan, do one."

Walter took the deck a little reluctantly, and thought a minute. Then, with Elsie watching him eagerly, he picked out three cards, holding them so no one else could see them, and put the deck back down. Then he held up the three cards, in a V shape, and said, "I'll put one of these on top, one on bottom, and one in the middle of the deck and bring them together with a cut. Look, it's the two of diamonds, the ace of diamonds, and the three of diamonds."

He turned them around again so the backs of the cards were toward his audience and began to place them one on top the deck, one in the middle, and—

"Aw, I get that one," Bob said. "That wasn't the ace of diamonds. It was the ace of hearts and you held it between the other two so just the point of the heart showed. You got the ace of diamonds already planted on top the deck." He grinned triumphantly.

Mae said, "Bob, that was *mean*. Wally anyway let you finish your stunt before he said anything."

Elsie frowned at Bob, too. Then her face suddenly lit up and she went across to the closet and opened the door and took a cardboard box off the top shelf. "Just remembered this," she said. "It's from a year ago when I had a part in a ballet at the social center. A top hat."

She opened the box and took it out. It was dented and, despite the box, a bit dusty, but it was indubitably a top hat. She put it, on its crown, on the table near Walter. "You said you could do a *good* one with a hat, Walter," she said. "Show him."

Everybody was looking at Walter and he shifted uncomfortably. "I—I was just kidding him, Elsie. I don't—I mean it's been so long since I tried that kind of stuff when I was a kid, and everything. I don't remember it."

Bob grinned happily and stood up. His glass and Walter's were empty and he filled them, and he put a little more into the girls' glasses, although they weren't empty yet. Then he picked up a yardstick that was in the corner and flourished it like a circus barker's cane. He said, "Step this way, ladies and gentlemen, to see the one and only Walter Beekman do the famous non-existent trick with the black top hat. And in the next cage we have—"

"Bob, shut up," said Mae.

There was a faint glitter in Walter's eyes. He said, "For two cents, I'd—"

Bob reached into his pocket and pulled out a handfull of change. He took two pennies out and reached across and dropped them into the inverted top hat. He said, "There you are," and waved the yardstick-cane again. "Price only two cents, the one-fiftieth part of a dollah! Step right up and see the greatest prestidigitatah on earth—"

Walter drank his wine and then his face kept getting redder while Bob went on spieling. Then he stood up. He said quietly, "What'd you like to see for your two cents, Bob?"

Elsie looked at him open-eyed. "You mean, Wally, you're offering to take *anything* out of—"

"Maybe."

Bob exploded into raucous laughter. He said, "Rats," and reached for the wine bottle.

Walter said, "You asked for it."

He left the top hat right on the table, but he reached out a hand toward it, uncertainly at first. There was a squealing sound from inside the hat, and Walter plunged his hand down in quickly and brought it up holding something by the scruff of the neck.

Mae screamed and then put the back of her hand over her mouth and her eyes were like white saucers. Elsie keeled over quietly on the studio couch in a dead faint; and Bob stood there with his cane-yardstick in midair and his face frozen.

The thing squealed again as Walter lifted it a little higher out of the hat. It looked like a monstrous, hideous black rat. But it was bigger than a rat should be, too big even to have come out of the hat. Its eyes glowed like red light bulbs and it was champing horribly its long scimitar-shaped white teeth, clicking them together with its mouth going several inches open each time and closing like a trap. It wriggled to get the scruff of its neck free of Walter's trembling hand; its clawed forefeet flailed the air. It looked vicious beyond belief.

It squealed incessantly, frightfully, and it smelled with a rank fetid odor as though it had lived in graves and eaten of their contents.

Then, as suddenly as he had pulled his hand out of the hat, Walter pushed it down in again, and the thing down with it. The squealing stopped and Walter took his hand out of the hat. He stood there, shaking, his face pale. He got a handkerchief out of his pocket and mopped sweat off his forehead. His voice sounded strange: "I should never have done it." He ran for the door, opened it, and they heard him stumbling down the stairs.

Mae's hand came away from her mouth slowly and she said, "T—take me home. Bob."

Bob passed a hand across his eyes and said, "Gosh, what—" and went across and looked into the hat. His two pennies were in there, but he didn't reach in to take them out.

He said, his voice cracking once. "What about Elsie? Should we—" Mae got up slowly and said, "Let her sleep it off." They didn't talk much on the way home.

It was two days later that Bob met Elsie on the street. He said, "Hi, Elsie."

And she said, "Hi, there." He said, "Gosh, that was some party we had at your studio the other night. We—we drank too much, I guess."

Something seemed to pass across Elsie's face for a moment, and then she smiled and said, "Well, *I* sure did; I passed out like a light."

Bob grinned back, and said, "I was a little high myself, I guess. Next time I'll have better manners."

Mae had her next date with Bob the following Monday. It wasn't a double date this time.

After the show, Bob said, "Shall we drop in somewhere for a drink?"

For some reason Mae shivered slightly. "Well, all right, but not wine. I'm off wine. Say, have you seen Wally since last week?"

Bob shook his head. "Guess you're right about wine. Wally can't take it, either. Made him sick or something and he ran out quick, didn't he? Hope he made the street in time."

Mae dimpled at him. "You weren't so sober yourself, Mr. Evans. Didn't you try to pick a fight with him over some silly card tricks or something? Gee, that picture we saw was awful; I had a nightmare that night."

He smiled. "What about?"

"About a—Gee, I don't remember. Funny how real a dream can be, and still you can't remember just what it was."

Bob didn't see Walter Beekman until one day, three weeks after the party, he dropped into the bookstore. It was a dull hour and Walter, alone in the store, was writing at a desk in the rear. "Hi, Wally. What are you doing?"

Walter got up and then nodded toward the papers he'd been working on. "Thesis. This is my last year premed, and I'm majoring in psychology."

Bob leaned negligently against the desk. "Psychology, huh?" he asked tolerantly. "What you writing about?"

Walter looked at him a while before he answered. "Interesting theme. I'm trying to prove that the human mind is incapable of assimilating the utterly incredible. That, in other words, if you saw something you simply couldn't possibly believe, you'd talk yourself out of believing you saw it. You'd rationalize it, somehow."

"You mean if I saw a pink elephant I wouldn't believe it?"

Walter said, "Yes, that or a— Skip it." He went up front to wait on another customer.

When Walter came back, Bob said, "Got a good mystery in the rentals? I got the week end off; maybe I'll read one."

Walter ran his eyes along the rental shelves and then flipped the cover of a book with his forefinger. "Here's a dilly of a weird," he said. "About beings from another world, living here in disguise, pretending they're people."

"What for?"

Walter grinned at him. "Read it and find out. It might surprise you."

Bob moved restlessly and turned to look at the rental books himself. He said, "Aw, I'd rather have a plain mystery story. All that kind of stuff is too much hooey for me." For some reason he didn't quite understand, he looked up at Walter and said, "Isn't it?"

Walter nodded and said, "Yeah, I guess it is."

The Geezenstacks

One of the strange things about it was that Aubrey Walters wasn't at all a strange little girl. She was quite as ordinary as her father and mother, who lived in an apartment on Otis Street, and who played bridge one night a week, went out somewhere another night, and spent the other evenings quietly at home.

Aubrey was nine, and had rather stringy hair and freckles, but at nine one never worries about such things. She got along quite well in the not-too-expensive private school to which her parents sent her, she made friends easily and readily with other children, and she took lessons on a three-quarter-size violin and played it abominably.

Her greatest fault, possibly, was her predilection for staying up late of nights, and that was the fault of her parents, really, for letting her stay up and dressed until she felt sleepy and wanted to go to bed. Even at five and six, she seldom went to bed before ten o'clock in the evening. And if, during a period of maternal concern, she was put to bed earlier, she never went to sleep anyway. So why not let the child stay up?

Now, at nine years, she stayed up quite as late as her parents did, which was about eleven o'clock of ordinary nights and later when they had company for bridge, or went out for the evening. Then it was later, for they usually took her along. Aubrey enjoyed it, whatever it was. She'd sit still as a mouse in a seat at the theater, or regard them with little girl seriousness over the rim of a glass of ginger ale while they had a cocktail or two at a night club. She took the noise and the music and the dancing with big-eyed wonder and enjoyed every minute of it.

Sometimes Uncle Richard, her mother's brother, went along with them. She and Uncle Richard were good friends. It was Uncle Richard who gave her the dolls.

"Funny thing happened today," he'd said. "I'm walking down Rodgers Place, past the Mariner Building—you know, Edith; it's where Doc Howard used to have his office—and something thudded on the sidewalk right behind me. And I turned around, and there was this package."

"This package" was a white box a little larger than a shoebox, and it was rather strangely tied with gray ribbon. Sam Walters, Aubrey's father, looked at it curiously.

"Doesn't look dented," he said. "Couldn't have fallen out of a very high window. Was it tied up like that?"

"Just like that. I put the ribbon back on after I opened it and looked in. Oh, I don't mean I opened it then or there. I just stopped and looked up to see who'd dropped it—thinking I'd see somebody looking out of a window. But nobody was, and I picked up the box. It had something in it, not very heavy, and the box and the ribbon looked like—well, not like something somebody'd throw away on purpose. So I stood looking up, and nothing happened, so I shook the box a little and—"

"All right, all right." said Sam Walters. "Spare us the blow-by-blow. You didn't find out who dropped it?"

"Right. And I went up as high as the fourth floor, asking the people whose windows were over the place where I picked it up. They were all home, as it happened, and none of them had ever seen it. I thought it might have fallen off a window ledge. But—"

"What's in it, Dick?" Edith asked.

"Dolls. Four of them. I brought them over this evening for Aubrey. If she wants them."

He untied the package, and Aubrey said, "Oooo, Uncle Richard. They're—they're *lovely.*"

Sam said, "Hm. Those look almost more like manikins than dolls, Dick. The way they're dressed, I mean. Must have cost several dollars apiece. Are you sure the owner won't turn up?"

Richard shrugged. "Don't see how he can. As I told you, I went up four floors, asking. Thought from the look of the box and the sound of the thud, it couldn't have come from even that high. And after I opened it, well—look—" He picked up one of the dolls and held it out for Sam Walters' inspection.

"Wax. The heads and hands, I mean. And not one of them cracked. It couldn't have fallen from higher than the second story. Even then, I don't see how—" He shrugged again.

"They're the Geezenstacks," said Aubrey.

"Huh?" Sam asked.

"I'm going to call them the Geezenstacks," Aubrey said. "Look, this one is Papa Geezenstack and this one is Mama Geezenstack, and the little girl one—that's—that's Aubrey Geezenstack. And the other man one, we'll call him Uncle Geezenstack. The little girl's uncle."

Sam chuckled. "Like us, eh? But if Uncle—uh—Geezenstack is Mama Geezenstack's brother, like Uncle Richard is Mama's brother, then his name wouldn't be Geezenstack."

"Just the same, it is." Aubrey said. "They're all Geezenstacks. Papa, will you buy me a house for them?"

"A doll house? Why—" He'd started to say, "Why, sure," but caught his wife's eye and remembered. Aubrey's birthday was only a week off and they'd been wondering what to get her. He changed it hastily to "Why, I don't know. I'll think about it."

It was a beautiful doll house. Only one-story high, but quite elaborate, and with a roof that lifted off so one could rearrange the furniture and move the dolls from room to room. It scaled well with the manikins Uncle Richard had brought.

Aubrey was rapturous. All her other playthings went into eclipse and the doings of the Geezenstacks occupied most of her waking thoughts.

It wasn't for quite a while that Sam Walters began to notice, and to think about, the strange aspect of the doings of the Geezenstacks. At first, with a quiet chuckle at the coincidences that followed one another.

And then, with a puzzled look in his eyes.

It wasn't until quite a while later that he got Richard off into a corner. The four of them had just returned from a play. He said, "Uh—Dick."

"Yeah, Sam?"

"These dolls, Dick. Where *did* you get them?"

Richard's eyes stared at him blankly. "What do you mean, Sam? I told you where I got them."

"Yes, but—you weren't kidding or anything? I mean, maybe you bought them for Aubrey, and thought we'd object if you gave her such an expensive present, so you—uh—"

"No, honest, I didn't."

"But dammit, Dick, they couldn't have fallen out of a window, or dropped out, and not broken. They're wax. Couldn't someone walking behind you—or going by in an auto or something—?"

"There wasn't anyone around, Sam. Nobody at all. I've wondered about it myself. But if I was lying, I wouldn't make up a screwy story like that, would I? I'd just say I found them on a park bench or a seat in a movie. But why are you curious?"

"I—uh—I just got to wondering."

Sam Walters kept on wondering, too.

They were little things, most of them. Like the time Aubrey had said, "Papa Geezenstack didn't go to work this morning, he's in bed, sick."

"So?" Sam had asked. "And what is wrong with the gentleman?"

"Something he ate, I guess."

And the next morning, at breakfast, "And how is Mr. Geezenstack, Aubrey?"

"A little better, but he isn't going to work today yet, the doctor said. Tomorrow, maybe."

And the next day, Mr. Geezenstack went back to work. That, as it happened, was the day Sam Walters came home feeling quite ill, as a result of something he'd eaten for lunch. Yes, he'd missed two days from work. The first time he'd missed work on account of illness in several years.

And some things were quicker than that, and some slower. You couldn't put your finger on it and say, "Well, if this happens to the Geezenstacks, it will happen to us in twenty-four hours." Sometimes it was less than an hour. Sometimes as long as a week.

"Mama and Papa Geezenstack had a quarrel today."

And Sam had tried to avoid that quarrel with Edith, but it seemed he just couldn't. He'd been quite late getting home, through no fault of his own. It had happened often, but this time Edith took exception. Soft answers failed to turn away wrath, and at last he'd lost his own temper.

"Uncle Geezenstack is going away for a visit." Richard hadn't been out of town for years, but the next week he took a sudden notion to run down to New York. "Pete and Amy, you know. Got a letter from them asking me—"

"When?" Sam asked, almost sharply. "When did you get the letter?"

"Yesterday."

"Then last week you weren't— This sounds like a silly question, Dick, but last week were you thinking about going anywhere? Did you say anything to—to anyone about the possibility of your visiting someone?"

"Lord, no. Hadn't even thought about Pete and Amy for months, till I got their letter yesterday. Want me to stay a week."

"You'll be back in three days—maybe," Sam had said. He wouldn't explain, even when Richard did come back in three days. It sounded just too damn' silly to say that he'd known how long Richard was going to be gone, because that was how long Uncle Geezenstack had been away.

Sam Walters began to watch his daughter, and to wonder. She, of course, was the one who made the Geezenstacks do whatever they did. Was it possible that Aubrey had some strange preternatural insight which caused her, unconsciously, to predict things that were going to happen to the Walters and to Richard?

He didn't, of course, believe in clairvoyance. But was Aubrey clairvoyant?

"Mrs. Geezenstack's going shopping today. She's going to buy a new coat."

That one almost sounded like a put-up job. Edith had smiled at Aubrey and then looked at Sam. "That reminds me, Sam. Tomorrow I'll be downtown, and there's a sale at—"

"But, Edith, these are war times. And you don't *need* a coat."

He'd argued so earnestly that he made himself late for work. Arguing uphill, because he really could afford the coat and she really hadn't bought one for two years. But he couldn't explain that the real reason he didn't want her to buy one was that Mrs. Geezen— Why, it was too silly to say, even to himself.

Edith bought the coat.

Strange, Sam thought, that nobody else noticed those coincidences. But Richard wasn't around all the time, and Edith—well, Edith had the knack of listening to Aubrey's prattle without hearing nine-tenths of it.

"Aubrey Geezenstack brought home her report card today, Papa. She got ninety in arithmetic and eighty in spelling and—"

And two days later, Sam was calling up the headmaster of the school. Calling from a pay station, of course, so nobody would hear him. "Mr. Bradley, I'd like to ask a question that I have a—uh—rather peculiar, but important, reason for asking. Would it be possible for a student at your school to know in advance exactly what grades ..."

No, not possible. The teachers themselves didn't know, until they'd figured averages, and that hadn't been done until the morning the report cards were made out, and sent home. Yes, yesterday morning, while the children had their play period.

"Sam," Richard said, "you're looking kind of seedy. Business worries? Look, things are going to get better from now on, and with your company, you got nothing to worry about anyway."

"That isn't it, Dick. It—I mean, there isn't anything I'm worrying about. Not exactly. I mean—" And he'd had to wriggle out of the cross-examination by inventing a worry or two for Richard to talk him out of.

He thought about the Geezenstacks a lot. Too much. If only he'd been superstitious, or credulous, it might not have been so bad. But he *wasn't*. That's why each succeeding coincidence hit him a little harder than the last.

Edith and her brother noticed it, and talked about it when Sam wasn't around.

"He *has* been acting queer lately, Dick. I'm—I'm really worried. He acts so— Do you think we could talk him into seeing a doctor or a—"

"A psychiatrist? Um, if we could. But I can't see him doing it, Edith. Something's eating him, and I've tried to pump him about it, but he won't open up. Y'know—I think it's got something to do with those damn' dolls."

"Dolls? You mean Aubrey's dolls? The ones you gave her?"

"Yes, the Geezenstacks. He sits and stares at the doll house. I've heard him ask the kid questions about them, and he was *serious*. I think he's got some delusion or something about them. Or centering on them."

"But, Dick, that's—*awful*."

"Look, Edie, Aubrey isn't as interested in them as she used to be, and— Is there anything she wants very badly?"

"Dancing lessons. But she's already studying violin and I don't think we can let her—"

"Do you think if you promised her dancing lessons if she gave up those dolls, she'd be willing? I think we've got to get them out of the apartment. And I don't want to hurt Aubrey, so—"

"Well—but what would we tell Aubrey?"

"Tell *her* I know a poor family with children who haven't any dolls at all. And—I think she'll agree, if you make it strong enough."

"But, Dick, what will we tell Sam? He'll know better than that."

"Tell Sam, when Aubrey isn't around, that you think she's getting too old for dolls, and that—tell him she's taking an unhealthy interest in them, and that the doctor advises— That sort of stuff."

Aubrey wasn't enthusiastic. She was not as engrossed in the Geezenstacks as she'd been when they were newer, but couldn't she have both the dolls *and* the dancing lessons?

"I don't think you'd have time for both, honey. And there are those poor children who haven't *any* dolls to play with, and you ought to feel sorry for them."

And Aubrey weakened, eventually. Dancing school didn't open for ten days, though, and she wanted to keep the dolls until she could start her lessons. There was argument, but to no avail.

"That's all right, Edie," Richard told her. "Ten days is better than not at all, and—well, if she doesn't give them up voluntarily, it'll start a rumpus and Sam'll find out what we're up to. You haven't mentioned anything to him at all, have you?"

"No. But maybe it would make him feel better to know they were—"

"I wouldn't. We don't know just what it is about them that fascinates or repels him. Wait till it happens, and then tell him. Aubrey has already given them away. Or *he* might raise some objection or want to keep them. If I get them out of the place first, he can't."

"You're right, Dick. And Aubrey won't tell him, because I told her the dancing lessons are going to be a surprise for her father, and she can't tell him what's going to happen to the dolls without telling the other side of the deal."

"Swell, Edith."

It might have been better if Sam had known. Or maybe everything would have happened just the same, if he had.

Poor Sam. He had a bad moment the very next evening. One of Aubrey's friends from school was there, and they were playing with the doll house. Sam watching them, trying to look less interested than he was. Edith was knitting and Richard, who had just come in, was reading the paper.

Only Sam was listening to the children and heard the suggestion.

"... and then let's have a play funeral, Aubrey. Just pretend one of them is—"

Sam Walters let out a sort of strangled cry and almost fell getting across the room.

There was a bad moment, then, but Edith and Richard managed to pass it off casually enough, outwardly. Edith discovered it was time for Aubrey's little friend to leave, and she exchanged a significant glance with Richard and they both escorted the girl to the door.

Whispered, "Dick, did you *see*—"

"Something *is* wrong, Edie. Maybe we shouldn't wait. After all, Aubrey has agreed to give them up, and—"

Back in the living room, Sam was still breathing a bit hard. Aubrey looked at him almost as though she was afraid of him. It was the first time she'd ever looked at him like that, and Sam felt ashamed. He said, "Honey, I'm sorry I— But listen, you'll promise me you'll *never* have a play funeral for one of your dolls? Or pretend one of them is badly sick or has an accident—or anything bad at all? Promise?"

"Sure, Papa. I'm—I'm going to put them away for tonight."

She put the lid on the doll house and went back toward the kitchen.

In the hallway, Edie said, "I'll—I'll get Aubrey alone and fix it with her. You talk to Sam. Tell him—look, let's go out tonight, go somewhere and get him away from everything. See if he will."

Sam was still staring at the doll house.

"Let's get some excitement, Sam," Richard said. "How's about going out somewhere? We've been sticking too close to home. It'll do us good."

Sam took a deep breath. "Okay, Dick. If you say so. I—I could use a little fun, I guess."

Edie came back with Aubrey, and she winked at her brother. "You men go on downstairs and get a cab from the stand around the corner. Aubrey and I'll be down by the time you bring it."

Behind Sam's back, as the men were putting on their coats, Richard gave Edith an inquiring look and she nodded.

Outside, there was a heavy fog; one could see only a few yards ahead. Sam insisted that Richard wait at the door for Edith and Aubrey while he went to bring the cab. The woman and girl came down just before Sam got back.

Richard asked, "Did you—?"

"Yes, Dick. I was going to throw them away, but I gave them away instead. That way they're *gone;* he might have wanted to hunt in the rubbish and find them if I'd just thrown—"

"Gave them away? To whom?"

"Funniest thing, Dick. I opened the door and there was an old woman going by in the back hall. Don't know which of the apartments she came from, but she must be a scrubwoman or something, although she looked like a witch really, but when she saw those dolls I had in my hands—"

"Here comes the cab," Dick said. "You gave them to her?"

"Yes, it was funny. She said, *'Mine? To Keep? Forever?'* Wasn't that a strange way of asking it? But I laughed and said, 'Yes, ma'am. Yours forev—'"

She broke off for the shadowy outline of the taxi was at the curb, and Sam opened the door and called out, "Come on, folks!"

Aubrey skipped across the sidewalk into the cab, and the others followed. It started.

The fog was thicker now. They could not see out the windows at all. It was as though a gray wall pressed against the glass, as though the world outside was gone, completely and utterly. Even the windshield, from where they sat, was a gray blank.

"How can he drive so fast?" Richard asked, and there was an edge of nervousness in his voice. "By the way, where are we going, Sam?"

"By George," Sam said, "I forgot to tell her."

"Her?"

"Yeah. Woman driver. They've got them all over now. I'll—"

He leaned forward and tapped on the glass, and the woman turned.

Edith saw her face, and screamed.

Daymare

It started out like a simple case of murder. That was bad enough in itself, because it was the first murder during the five years Rod Caquer had been Lieutenant of Police in Sector Three of Callisto.

Sector Three was proud of that record, or had been until the record became a dead duck.

But before the thing was over, nobody would have been happier than Rod Caquer if it had stayed a simple case of murder—without cosmic repercussions.

Events began to happen when Rod Caquer's buzzer made him look up at the visiscreen.

There he saw the image of Barr Maxon, Regent of Sector Three.

"Morning, Regent," Caquer said pleasantly. "Nice speech you made last night on the—"

Maxon cut him short. "Thanks, Caquer," he said. "You know Willem Deem?"

"The book-and-reel shop proprietor? Yes, slightly."

"He's dead," announced Maxon. "It seems to be murder. You better go there."

His image clicked off the screen before Caquer could ask any questions. But the questions could wait anyway. He was already on his feet and buckling on his shortsword.

Murder on Callisto? It did not seem possible, but if it had really happened he should get there quickly. Very quickly, if he was to have time for a look at the body before they took it to the incinerator.

On Callisto, bodies are never held for more than an hour after death because of the hylra spores which, in minute quantity, are always present in the thinnish atmosphere. They are harmless, of course, to live tissue, but they tremendously accelerate the rate of putrefaction in dead animal matter of any sort.

Dr. Skidder, the Medico-in-Chief, was coming out the front door of the book-and-reel shop when Lieutenant Caquer arrived there, breathless.

The medico jerked a thumb back over his shoulder. "Better hurry if you want a look," he said to Caquer. "They're taking it out the back way. But I've examined—"

Caquer ran on past him and caught the white-uniformed utility men at the back door of the shop.

"Hi, boys, let me take a look," Caquer cried as he peeled back the sheet that covered the thing on the stretcher.

It made him feel a bit sickish, but there was not any doubt of the identity of the corpse or the cause of death. He had hoped against hope that it would turn out to have been an accidental death after all. But the skull had been cleaved down to the eyebrows—a blow struck by a strong man with a heavy sword.

"Better let us hurry, Lieutenant. It's almost an hour since they found him."

Caquer's nose confirmed it, and he put the sheet back quickly and let the utility men go on to their gleaming white truck parked just outside the door.

He walked back into the shop, thoughtfully, and looked around. Everything seemed in order. The long shelves of celluwrapped merchandise were neat and orderly. The row of booths along the other side, some equipped with an enlarger for book customers and the others with projectors for those who were interested in the microfilms, were all empty and undisturbed.

A little crowd of curious persons was gathered outside the door, but Brager, one of the policemen, was keeping them out of the shop.

"Hey, Brager," said Caquer, and the patrolman came in and closed the door behind him.

"Yes, Lieutenant?"

"Know anything about this? Who found him, and when, and so on?"

"I did, almost an hour ago. I was walking by on my beat when I heard the shot."

Caquer looked at him blankly.

"The shot?" he repeated.

"Yeah. I ran in and there he was dead and nobody around. I knew nobody had come out the front way, so I ran to the back and there wasn't anybody in sight from the back door. So I came back and put in the call."

"To whom? Why didn't you call me direct, Brager?"

"Sorry, Lieutenant, but I was excited and I pushed the wrong button and got the Regent. I told him somebody had shot Deem and he said stay on guard and he'd call the Medico and the utility boys and you."

In that order? Caquer wondered. Apparently, because Caquer had been the last one to get there.

But he brushed that aside for the more important question—the matter of Brager having heard a shot. That did not make sense, unless—no, that was absurd, too. If Willem Deem had been shot, the Medico would not have split his skull as part of the autopsy.

"What do you mean by a shot, Brager?" Caquer asked. "An old-fashioned explosive weapon?"

"Yeah," said Brager. "Didn't you see the body? A hole right over the heart. A bullet-hole, I guess. I never saw one before. I didn't know there was a gun on Callisto. They were outlawed even before the blasters were."

Caquer nodded slowly.

"You—you didn't see evidence of any other—uh—wound?" he persisted.

"Earth, no. Why would there be any other wound? A hole through a man's heart's enough to kill him, isn't it?"

"Where did Dr. Skidder go when he left here?" Caquer inquired. "Did he say?"

"Yeah, he said you would be wanting his report so he'd go back to his office and wait till you came around or called him. What do you want me to do, Lieutenant?"

Caquer thought a moment.

"Go next door and use the visiphone there, Brager—I'll get busy on this one," Caquer at last told the policeman. "Get three more men, and the four of you canvass this block and question everyone."

"You mean whether they saw anybody run out the back way, and if they heard the shot, and that sort of things?" asked Brager.

"Yes. Also anything they may know about Deem, or who might have had a reason to—to shoot him."

Brager saluted, and left.

Caquer got Dr. Skidder on the visiphone. "Hello, Doctor," he said. "Let's have it."

"Nothing but what met the eye, Rod. Blaster, of course. Close range."

Lieutenant Rod Caquer steadied himself. "Say that again, Medico."

"What's the matter?" asked Skidder. "Never see a blaster death before? Guess you wouldn't have at that, Rod, you're too young. But fifty years ago when I was a student, we got them once in a while."

"Just how did it kill him?"

Dr. Skidder looked surprised. "Oh, you didn't catch up with the clearance men then. I thought you'd seen it. Left shoulder, burned all the skin and flesh off and charred the bone. Actual death was from shock—the blast didn't hit a vital area. Not that the burn wouldn't have been fatal anyway, in all probability. But the shock made it instantaneous."

Dreams are like this, Caquer told himself.

"In dreams things happen without meaning anything," he thought. "But I'm not dreaming, this is real."

"Any other wounds, or marks on the body?" he asked slowly.

"None. I'd suggest, Rod, you concentrate on a search for that blaster. Search all of Sector Three, if you have to. You know what a blaster looks like, don't you?"

"I've seen pictures," said Caquer. "Do they make a noise, Medico? I've never seen one fired."

Dr. Skidder shook his head. "There's a flash and a hissing sound, but no report."

"It couldn't be mistaken for a gunshot?"

The doctor stared at him.

"You mean an explosive gun? Of course not. Just a faint s-s-s-s. One couldn't hear it more than ten feet away."

When Lieutenant Caquer had clicked off the visiphone he sat down and closed his eyes to concentrate. Somehow he had to make sense out of three conflicting sets of observations. His own, the patrolman's, and the medico's.

Brager had been the first one to see the body, and he said there was a hole over the heart. And that there were no other wounds. He had heard the report of the shot.

Caquer thought, suppose Brager is lying. It still doesn't make sense. Because according to Dr. Skidder, there was no bullet-hole, but a blaster-wound. Skidder had seen the body after Brager had.

Someone could, theoretically at least, have used a blaster in the interim, on a man already dead. But—

But that did not explain the head wound, nor the fact that the medico had not seen the bullet-hole.

Someone could, theoretically at least, have struck the skull with a sword between the time Skidder had made the autopsy and the time he, Rod Caquer, had seen the body. But—

But that didn't explain why he hadn't seen the charred shoulder when he'd lifted the sheet from the body on the stretcher. He might have missed seeing a bullet-hole, but he would not, and he could not, have missed seeing a shoulder in the condition Dr. Skidder described it.

Around and around it went, until at last it dawned on him that there was only one explanation possible. The Medico-in-Chief was lying, for whatever mad reason. That meant, of course, that he, Rod Caquer, had overlooked the bullet-hole Brager had seen; but that was possible.

But Skidder's story could not be true. Skidder himself, at the time of the autopsy, could have inflicted the wound in the head. And he could have lied about the shoulder wound. Why—unless the man was mad—he would have done either of those things, Caquer could not imagine. But it was the only way he could reconcile all the factors.

But by now the body had been disposed of. It would be his word against Dr. Skidder's—

But wait!—the utility men, two of them, would have seen the corpse when they put it on the stretcher.

Quickly Caquer stood up in front of the visiphone and obtained a connection with utility headquarters.

"The two clearance men who took a body from Shop 9364 less than an hour ago—have they reported back yet?" he asked.

"Just a minute, Lieutenant ... Yes, one of them was through for the day and went on home. The other one is here."

"Put him on."

Rod Caquer recognized the man who stepped into the screen. It was the one of the two utility men who had asked him to hurry.

"Yes, Lieutenant?" said the man.

"You helped put the body on the stretcher?"

"Of course."

"What would you say was the cause of death?"

The man in white looked out of the screen incredulously.

"Are you kidding me, Lieutenant?" He grinned. "Even a moron could see what was wrong with that stiff."

Caquer frowned.

"Nevertheless, there are conflicting statements. I want your opinion."

"Opinion? When a man has his head cut off, what two opinions can there be, Lieutenant?"

Caquer forced himself to speak calmly. "Will the man who went with you confirm that?"

"Of course. Earth's Oceans! We had to put it on the stretcher in two pieces. Both of us for the body, and then Walter picked up the head and put it on next to the trunk. The killing was done with a disintegrator beam, wasn't it?"

"You talked it over with the other man?" said Caquer. "There was no difference of opinion between you about the—uh—details?"

"Matter of fact there was. That was why I asked you if it was a disintegrator. After we'd cremated it, he tried to tell me the cut was a ragged one like somebody'd taken several blows with an axe or something. But it was clean."

"Did you notice evidence of a blow struck at the top of the skull?"

"No. Say, Lieutenant, you aren't looking so well. Is anything the matter with you?"

That was the set-up that confronted Rod Caquer, and one cannot blame him for beginning to wish it had been a simple case of murder.

A few hours ago, it had seemed bad enough to have Callisto's no-murder record broken. But from there, it got worse. He did not know it then, but it was going to get still worse and that would be only the start.

It was eight in the evening, now, and Caquer was still at his office with a copy of Form 812 in front of him on the duraplast surface of his desk. There were questions on that form, apparently simple questions.

Name of Deceased: Willem Deem
Occupation: Prop. of book-and-reel shop.
Residence: Apt. 8250, Sector Three, Clsto.
Place of Bus.: Shop 9364, S. T., Clsto.
Time of Death: Approx. 3 p.m. Clsto. Std. Time
Cause of Death:

Yes, the first five questions had been a breeze. But the sixth? He had been staring at that question an hour now. A Callisto hour, not so long as an Earth one, but long enough when you're staring at a question like that.

But confound it, he would have to put something down.

Instead, he reached for the visiphone button and a moment later Jane Gordon was looking at him out of the screen. And Rod Caquer looked back, because she was something to look at.

"Hello, Icicle," he said. "Afraid I'm not going to be able to get there this evening. Forgive me?"

"Of course, Rod. What's wrong? The Deem business?"

He nodded gloomily. "Desk work. Lots of forms and reports I got to get out for the Sector Coordinator."

"Oh. How was he killed, Rod?"

"Rule Sixty-five," he said with a smile, "forbids giving details of any unsolved crime to a civilian."

"Bother Rule Sixty-five. Dad knew Willem Deem well, and he's been a guest here often. Mr. Deem was practically a friend of ours."

"Practically?" Caquer asked. "Then I take it you didn't like him, Icicle?"

"Well—I guess I didn't. He was interesting to listen to, but he was a sarcastic little beast, Rod. I think he had a perverted sense of humor. How was he killed?"

"If I tell you, will you promise not to ask any more questions?" Caquer asked.

Her eyes lighted eagerly. "Of course."

"He was shot," said Caquer, "with an explosive-type gun and a blaster. Someone split his skull with a sword, chopped off his head with an axe and with a disintegrator beam. Then after he was on the utility stretcher, someone stuck his head back on because it wasn't off when I saw him. And plugged up the bullet-hole, and—"

"Rod, stop driveling," cut in the girl. "If you don't want to tell me, all right."

Rod grinned. "Don't get mad. Say, how's your father?"

"Lots better. He's asleep now, and definitely on the upgrade. I think he'll be back at the university by next week. Rod, you look tired. When do those forms have to be in?"

"Twenty-four hours after the crime. But—"

"But nothing. Come on over here, right now. You can make out those old forms in the morning."

She smiled at him, and Caquer weakened.

"All right, Jane," he said. "But I'm going by patrol quarters on the way. Had some men canvassing the block the crime was committed in, and I want their report."

But the report, which he found waiting for him, was not illuminating. The canvass had been thorough, but it had failed to elicit any information of value. No one had been seen to leave or enter the Deem shop prior to Brager's arrival, and none of Deem's neighbors knew of any enemies he might have. No one had heard a shot.

Rod Caquer grunted and stuffed the reports into his pocket. He wondered, as he walked to the Gordon home, where the investigation went from there. How did a detective go about solving such a crime?

True, when he was a college kid back on Earth a few years ago, he had read detective stories. The detective usually trapped someone by discovering a discrepancy in his statements. Generally in a rather dramatic manner, too.

There was Wilder Williams, the greatest of all the fictional detectives, who could look at a man and deduce his whole life history from the cut of his clothes and the shape of his hands. But Wilder Williams had never run across a victim who had been killed in as many ways as there were witnesses.

He spent a pleasant—but futile—evening with Jane Gordon, again asked her to marry him, and again was refused. But he was used to that. She was a bit cooler this evening than usual, probably because she resented his unwillingness to talk about Willem Deem.

And home, to bed.

From the window of his apartment, after the light was out, he could see the monstrous ball of Jupiter hanging low in the sky, the green-black midnight

sky. He lay in bed and stared at it until it seemed that he could still see it after
he had closed his eyes.

Willem Deem, deceased. What was he going to do about Willem Deem?
Around and around, until at last one orderly thought emerged from chaos.

Tomorrow morning he would talk to the Medico. Without mentioning
the sword wound in the head, he would ask Skidder about the bullet hole Brager
claimed to have seen over the heart. If Skidder still said the blaster burn was
the only wound, he would summon Brager and let him argue with the Medico.

And then—Well, he would worry about what to do when he got there.
He would never get to sleep this way.

He thought about Jane, and went to sleep.

After a while, he dreamed. Or was it a dream? If so, then he dreamed that
he was lying there in bed, almost but not quite awake, and that there were
whispers coming from all corners of the room. Whispers out of the darkness.

For big Jupiter had moved on across the sky now. The window was a dim,
scarcely discernible outline, and the rest of the room in utter darkness.

Whispers!

"—kill them."

"You hate them, you hate them, you hate them."

"—kill, kill, kill."

"Sector Two gets all the gravy and Sector Three does all the work. They
exploit our corla plantations. They are evil. Kill them, take over."

"You hate them, you hate them, you hate them."

"Sector Two is made up of weaklings and usurers. They have the taint of
Martian blood. Spill it, spill Martian blood. Sector Three should rule Callisto.
Three the mystic number. We are destined to rule Callisto."

"You hate them, you hate them."

"—kill, kill, kill."

"Martian blood of usurious villains. You hate them, you hate them, you
hate them."

Whispers.

"Now—now—now."

"Kill them, kill them."

"A hundred ninety miles across the flat plains. Get there in an hour in
monocars. Surprise attack. Now. Now. Now."

And Rod Caquer was getting out of bed, fumbling hastily and blindly
into his clothing without turning on the light because this was a dream and
dreams were in darkness.

His sword was in the scabbard at his belt and he took it out and felt the
edge and the edge was sharp and ready to spill the blood of the enemy he was
going to kill.

Now it was going to swing in arcs of red death, his unblooded sword—
the anachronistic sword that was his badge of office, of authority. He had never
drawn the sword in anger, a stubby symbol of a sword, scarce eighteen inches
long; enough, though, enough to reach the heart—four inches to the heart.

The whispers continued.

"You hate them, you hate them, you hate them."

"Spill the evil blood; kill, spill, kill, spill."

"Now, now, now, now."

Unsheathed sword in clenched fist, he was stealing silently out the door, down the stairway, past the other apartment doors.

And some of the doors were opening, too. He was not alone, there in the darkness. Other figures moved beside him in the dark.

He stole out of the door and into the night-cooled darkness of the street, the darkness of the street that should have been brightly lighted. That was another proof that this was a dream. Those street-lights were never off, after dark. From dusk till dawn, they were never off.

But Jupiter over there on the horizon gave enough light to see by. Like a round dragon in the heavens, and the red spot like an evil, malignant eye.

Whispers breathed in the night, whispers from all around him.

"Kill—kill—kill—"

"You hate them, you hate them, you hate them."

The whispers did not come from the shadowy figures about him. They pressed forward silently, as he did.

Whispers came from the night itself, whispers that now began to change tone.

"Wait, not tonight, not tonight, not tonight," they said.

"Go back, go back, go back."

"Back to your homes, back to your beds, back to your sleep."

And the figures about him were standing there, fully as irresolute as he had now become. And then, almost simultaneously, they began to obey the whispers. They turned back, and returned the way they had come, and as silently ...

Rod Caquer awoke with a mild headache and a hung over feeling. The sun, tiny but brilliant, was already well up in the sky.

His clock showed him that he was a bit later than usual, but he took time to lie there for a few minutes, just the same, remembering that screwy dream he'd had. Dreams were like that; you had to think about them right away when you woke up, before you were really fully awake, or you forgot them completely.

A silly sort of dream, it had been. A mad, purposeless dream. A touch of atavism, perhaps? A throwback to the days when peoples had been at each other's throats half the time, back to the days of wars and hatreds and struggle for supremacy.

This was before the Solar Council, meeting first on one inhabited planet and then another, had brought order by arbitration, and then union. And now war was a thing of the past. The inhabitable portion of the solar system—Earth, Venus, Mars, and two of the moons of Jupiter—were all under one government.

But back in the old bloody days, people must have felt as he had felt in that atavistic dream. Back in the days when Earth, united by the discovery of space travel, had subjugated Mars—the only other planet already inhabited by an intelligent race—and then had spread colonies wherever Man could get a foothold.

Certain of those colonies had wanted independence and, next, supremacy. The bloody centuries, those times were called now.

Getting out of bed to dress, he saw something that puzzled and dismayed him. His clothing was not neatly folded over the back of the chair beside the bed as he had left it. Instead, it was strewn about the floor as though he had undressed hastily and carelessly in the dark.

"Earth!" he thought. "Did I sleep-walk last night? Did I actually get out of bed and go out into the street when I dreamed that I did? When those whispers told me to?"

"No," he then told himself, "I've never walked in my sleep before, and I didn't then. I must simply have been careless when I undressed last night. I was thinking about the Deem case. I don't actually remember hanging my clothes on that chair."

So he donned his uniform quickly and hurried down to the office. In the light of morning it was easy to fill out those forms. In the "Cause of Death" blank he wrote, "Medical Examiner reports that shock from a blaster wound caused death."

That let him out from under; he had not said that was the cause of death; merely that the medico said it was.

He rang for a messenger and gave him the reports with instructions to rush them to the mail ship that would be leaving shortly. Then he called Barr Maxon.

"Reporting on the Deems matter, Regent," he said. "Sorry, but we just haven't got anywhere on it yet. Nobody was seen leaving the shop. All the neighbors have been questioned. Today I'm going to talk to all his friends."

Regent Maxon shook his head.

"Use all jets, Lieutenant," he said. "The case must be cracked. A murder, in this day and age, is bad enough. But an unsolved one is unthinkable. It would encourage further crime."

Lieutenant Caquer nodded gloomily. He had thought of that, too. There were the social implications of murder to be worried about—and there was his job as well. A Lieutenant of Police who let anyone get away with murder in his district was through for life.

After the Regent's image had clicked off the visiphone screen, Caquer took the list of Deem's friends from the drawer of his desk and began to study it, mainly with an eye to deciding the sequence of his calls.

He penciled a figure "1" opposite the name of Perry Peters, for two reasons. Peters' place was only a few doors away, for one thing, and for another he knew Perry better than anyone on the list, except possibly Professor Jan Gordon. And he would make that call last, because later there would be a better chance of finding the ailing professor awake—and a better chance of finding his daughter Jane at home.

Perry Peters was glad to see Caquer, and guessed immediately the purpose of the call.

"Hello, Shylock."

"Huh?" said Rod.

"Shylock—the great detective. Confronted with a mystery for the first time in his career as a policeman. Or have you solved it, Rod?"

"You mean Sherlock, you dope—Sherlock Holmes. No I haven't solved it, if you want to know. Look, Perry, tell me all you know about Deem. You knew him pretty well, didn't you?"

Perry Peters rubbed his chin reflectively and sat down on the work bench. He was so tall and lanky that he could sit down on it instead of having to jump up.

"Willem was a funny little runt," he said. "Most people didn't like him because he was sarcastic, and he had crazy notions on politics. Me, I'm not sure whether he wasn't half right half the time, and anyway he played a swell game of chess."

"Was that his only hobby?"

"No. He liked to make things, gadgets mostly. Some of them were good, too, although he did it for fun and never tried to patent or capitalize anything."

"You mean inventions, Perry? Your own line?"

"Well, not so much inventions as gadgets, Rod. Little things, most of them, and he was better on fine workmanship than on original ideas. And, as I said, it was just a hobby with him."

"Ever help you with any of your own inventions?" asked Caquer.

"Sure, occasionally. Again, not so much on the idea end of it as by helping me make difficult parts." Perry Peters waved his hand in a gesture that included the shop around them. "My tools here are all for rough work, comparatively. Nothing under thousandths. But Willem has—had a little lathe that's a honey. Cuts anything, and accurate to a fifty-thousandth."

"What enemies did he have, Perry?"

"None that I know of. Honestly, Rod. Lot of people disliked him, but just an ordinary mild kind of dislike. You know what I mean, the kind of dislike that makes 'em trade at another book-and-reel shop, but not the kind that makes them want to kill anybody."

"And who, as far as you know, might benefit by his death?"

"Um—nobody, to speak of," said Peters, thoughtfully. "I think his heir is a nephew on Venus. I met him once, and he was a likable guy. But the estate won't be anything to get excited about. A few thousand credits is all I'd guess it to be."

"Here's a list of his friends, Perry." Caquer handed Peters a paper. "Look it over, will you, and see if you can make any additions to it. Or any suggestions."

The lanky inventor studied the list, and then passed it back.

"That includes them all, I guess," he told Caquer. "Couple on there I didn't know he knew well enough to rate listing. And you have his best customers down, too; the ones that bought heavily from him."

Lieutenant Caquer put the list back in his pocket.

"What are you working on now?" he asked Peters.

"Something I'm stuck on, I'm afraid," the inventor said. "I needed Deem's help—or at least the use of his lathe, to go ahead with this." He picked up from the bench a pair of the most peculiar-looking goggles Rod Caquer had ever seen. The lenses were shaped like arcs of circles instead of full circles, and they fastened in a band of resilient plastic obviously designed to fit close to the face above and below the lenses. At the top center, where it would be against the forehead of the goggles' wearer, was a small cylindrical box an inch and a half in diameter.

"What on earth are they for?" Caquer asked.

"For use in radite mines. The emanations from that stuff, while it's in the raw state, destroy immediately any transparent substance yet made or discovered. Even quartz. And it isn't good on naked eyes either. The miners have to work blindfolded, as it were, and by their sense of touch."

Rod Caquer looked at the goggles curiously.

"But how is the funny shape of these lenses going to keep the emanations from hurting them, Perry?" he asked.

"That part up on top is a tiny motor. It operates a couple of specially-treated wipers across the lenses. For all the world like an old-fashioned windshield wiper, and that's why the lenses are shaped like the wiper-arm arcs."

"Oh," said Caquer. "You mean the wipers are absorbent and hold some kind of liquid that protects the glass?"

"Yes, except that it's quartz instead of glass. And it's protected only a minute fraction of a second. Those wipers go like the devil—so fast you can't see them when you're wearing the goggles. The arms are half as big as the arcs and the wearer can see out of only a fraction of the lens at a time. But he can see, dimly, and that's a thousand per cent improvement in radite mining."

"Fine, Perry," said Caquer. "And they can get around the dimness by having ultra-brilliant lighting. Have you tried these out?"

"Yes, and they work. Trouble's in the rods; friction heats them and they expand and jam after it's run a minute, or thereabouts. I have to turn them down on Deem's lathe—or one like it. Think you could arrange for me to use it? Just for a day or so?"

"I don't see why not," Caquer told him. "I'll talk to whomever the Regent appoints executor, and fix it up. And later you can probably buy the lathe from his heirs. Or does the nephew go in for such things?"

Perry Peters shook his head. "Nope, he wouldn't know a lathe from a drill-press. Be swell of you, Rod, if you can arrange for me to use it."

Caquer had turned to go, but Perry Peters stopped him.

"Wait a minute," Peters said and then paused and looked uncomfortable.

"I guess I was holding out on you, Rod," the inventor said at last. "I do know one thing about Willem that might possibly have something to do with his death, although I don't see how, myself. I wouldn't tell it on him, except that he's dead, and so it won't get him in trouble."

"What was it, Perry?"

"Illicit political books. He had a little business on the side selling them. Books on the index—you know just what I mean."

Caquer whistled softly. "I didn't know they were made any more. After the council put such a heavy penalty on them—whew!"

"People are still human, Rod. They still want to know the things they shouldn't know—just to find out why they shouldn't, if for no other reason."

"Graydex or Blackdex books, Perry?"

Now the inventor looked puzzled.

"I don't get it. What's the difference?"

"Books on the official index," Caquer explained, "are divided into two groups. The really dangerous ones are in the Blackdex. There's a severe penalty for owning one, and a death penalty for writing or printing one. The mildly dangerous ones are in the Graydex, as they call it."

"I wouldn't know which Willem peddled. Well, off the record, I read a couple Willem lent me once, and I thought they were pretty dull stuff. Unorthodox political theories."

"That would be Graydex." Lieutenant Caquer looked relieved. "Theoretical stuff is all Graydex. The Blackdex books are the ones with dangerous practical information."

"Such as?" The inventor was staring intently at Caquer.

"Instructions how to make outlawed things," explained Caquer. "Like Lethite, for instance. Lethite is a poison gas that's tremendously dangerous. A few pounds of it could wipe out a city, so the council outlawed its manufacture, and any book telling people how to make it for themselves would go on the Blackdex. Some nitwit might get hold of a book like that and wipe out his whole home town."

"But why would anyone?"

"He might be warped mentally, and have a grudge," explained Caquer. "Or he might want to use it on a lesser scale for criminal reason. Or—by Earth, he might be the head of a government with designs on neighboring states. Knowledge of a thing like that might upset the peace of the Solar System."

Perry Peters nodded thoughtfully. "I get your point," he said. "Well, I still don't see what it could have to do with the murder, but I thought I'd tell you about Willem's sideline. You'll probably want to check over his stock before whoever takes over the shop reopens."

"We shall," said Caquer. "Thanks a lot, Perry. If you don't mind, I'll use your phone to get that search started right away. If there are any Blackdex books there, we'll take care of them all right."

When he got his secretary on the screen, she looked both frightened and relieved at seeing him.

"Mr. Caquer," she said, "I've been trying to reach you. Something awful's happened. Another death."

"Murder again?" gasped Caquer.

"Nobody knows what it was," said the secretary. "A dozen people saw him jump out of a window only twenty feet up. And in this gravity that couldn't have killed him, but he was dead when they got there. And four of them that saw him knew him. It was—"

"Well, for Earth's sake, who?"

"I don't—Lieutenant Caquer, they said, all four of them, that it was Willem Deem!"

With a nightmarish feeling of unreality Lieutenant Rod Caquer peered down over the shoulder of the Medico-in-Chief at the body that already lay on the stretcher of the utility men, who stood by impatiently.

"You better hurry, Doc," one of them said. "He won't last much longer and it takes us five minutes to get there."

Dr. Skidder nodded impatiently without looking up, and went on with his examination. "Not a mark, Rod," he said. "Not a sign of poison. Not a sign of anything. He's just dead."

"The fall couldn't have caused it?"

"There isn't even a bruise from the fall. Only verdict I can give is heart failure. Okay, boys, you can take it away."

"You through too, Lieutenant?"

"I'm through," said Caquer. "Go ahead. Skidder, which of them was Willem Deem?"

The medico's eyes followed the white-sheeted burden of the utility men as they carried it toward the truck, and he shrugged helplessly.

"Lieutenant, I guess that's your pigeon," he said. "All I can do is certify the cause of death."

"It just doesn't make sense," Caquer wailed. "Sector Three City isn't so big that he could have had a double living here without people knowing about it. But one of them had to be a double. Off the record, which looked to you like the original?"

Dr. Skidder shook his head grimly.

"Willem Deem had a peculiarly shaped wart on his nose," he said. "So did both of his corpses, Rod. And neither one was artificial, or make-up. I'll stake my professional reputation on that. But come on back to the office with me, and I'll tell you which one of them is the real Willem Deem."

"Huh? How?"

"His thumbprint's on file at the tax department, like everybody's is. And it's part of routine to fingerprint a corpse on Callisto, because it has to be destroyed so quickly."

"You have thumbprints of both corpses?" inquired Caquer.

"Of course. Took them before you reached the scene, both times. I have the one for Willem—I mean the other corpse—back in my office. Tell you what—you pick up the print on file at the tax office and meet me there."

Caquer sighed with relief as he agreed. At least one point would be cleared up—which corpse was which.

And in that comparatively blissful state of mind he remained until half an hour later when he and Dr. Skidder compared the three prints—the one Rod Caquer had secured from the tax office, and one from each of the corpses.

They were identical, all three of them.

"Um," said Caquer. "You're sure you didn't get mixed up on those prints, Dr. Skidder?"

"How could I? I took only one copy from each body, Rod. If I had shuffled them just now while we were looking at them, the results would be the same. All three prints are alike."

"But they can't be."

Skidder shrugged.

"I think we should lay this before the Regent, direct," he said. "I'll call him and arrange an audience. Okay?"

Half an hour later, he was giving the whole story to Regent Barr Maxon, with Dr. Skidder corroborating the main points. The expression on Regent Maxon's face made Lieutenant Rod Caquer glad, very glad, that he had that corroboration.

"You agree," Maxon asked, "that this should be taken up with the Sector Coordinator, and that a special investigator should be sent here to take over?"

A bit reluctantly, Caquer nodded. "I hate to admit that I'm incompetent, Regent, or that I seem to be," Caquer said. "But this isn't an ordinary crime. Whatever goes on it's way over my head. And there may be something even more sinister than murder behind it."

"You're right, Lieutenant. I'll see that a qualified man leaves headquarters today and he'll get in touch with you."

"Regent," Caquer asked, "has any machine or process ever been invented that will—uh—duplicate a human body, with or without the mind being carried over?"

Maxon seemed puzzled by the question.

"You think Deem might have been playing around with something that bit him? No, to my knowledge a discovery like that has never been approached. Nobody has ever duplicated, except by constructive imitation, even an inanimate object. You haven't heard of such a thing, have you, Skidder?"

"No," said the Medical Examiner. "I don't think even your friend Perry Peters could do that, Rod."

From Regent Maxon's office, Caquer went to Deem's shop. Brager was in charge there, and Brager helped him search the place thoroughly. It was a long and laborious task, because each book and reel had to be examined minutely.

The printers of illicit books, Caquer knew, were clever at disguising their product. Usually, forbidden books bore the cover and title page, often even the opening chapters, of some popular work of fiction, and the projection reels were similarly disguised.

Jupiter-lighted darkness was falling outside when they finished, but Rod Caquer knew they had done a thorough job. There wasn't an indexed book anywhere in the shop, and every reel had been run off on the projector.

Other men, at Rod Caquer's orders, had been searching Deem's apartment with equal thoroughness. He phoned there, and got a report, completely negative.

"Not so much as a Venusian pamphlet," said the man in charge at the apartment, with what Caquer thought was a touch of regret in his voice.

"Did you come across a lathe, a small one for delicate work?" Rod asked.

"Um—no, we didn't see anything like that. One room's turned into a workshop, but there's no lathe in it. Is it important?"

Caquer grunted noncommittally. What was one more mystery, and a minor one at that, to a case like this?

"Well, Lieutenant," Brager said when the screen had gone blank, "What do we do now?"

Caquer sighed.

"You can go off duty, Brager," he said. "But first arrange to leave men on guard here and at the apartment. I'll stay until whoever you send comes to relieve me."

When Brager had left, Caquer sank wearily into the nearest chair. He felt terrible, physically, and his mind just did not seem to be working. He let his eyes run again around the orderly shelves of the shop and their orderliness oppressed him.

If there was only a clue of some sort. Wilder Williams had never had a case like this in which the only leads were two identical corpses, one of which had been killed five different ways and the other did not have a mark or sign of violence. What a mess, and where did he go from here?

Well, he still had the list of people he was going to interview, and there was time to see at least one of them this evening.

Should he look up Perry Peters again, and see what, if anything, the lanky inventor could make of the disappearance of the lathe? Perhaps he might be able to suggest what had happened to it. But then again, what could a lathe have to do with a mess like this? One cannot turn out a duplicate corpse on a lathe.

Or should he look up Professor Gordon? He decided to do just that.

He called the Gordon apartment on the visiphone, and Jane appeared in the screen.

"How's your father, Jane?" asked Caquer. "Will he be able to talk to me for a while this evening?"

"Oh, yes," said the girl. "He's feeling much better, and thinks he'll go back to his classes tomorrow. But get here early if you're coming. Rod, you look terrible; what's the matter with you?"

"Nothing, except I feel goofy. But I'm all right, I guess."

"You have a gaunt, starved look. When did you eat last?"

Caquer's eyes widened. "Earth! I forgot all about eating. I slept late and didn't even have breakfast!"

Jane Gordon laughed.

"You dope! Well, hurry around and I'll have something ready for you when you get here."

"But—"

"But nothing. How soon can you start?"

A minute after he had clicked off the visiphone, Lieutenant Caquer went to answer a knock on the shuttered door of the shop.

He opened it. "Oh, hullo, Reese," he said. "Did Brager send you?"

The policeman nodded.

"He said I was to stay here in case. In case what?"

"Routine guard duty, that's all," explained Caquer. "Say, I've been stuck here all afternoon Anything going on?"

"A little excitement. We been pulling in soap-box orators off and on all day. Screwballs. There's an epidemic of them."

"The devil you say! What are they hepped about?"

"Sector Two, for some reason I can't make out. They're trying to incite people to get mad at Sector Two and do something about it. The arguments they use are plain nutty."

Something stirred uneasily in Rod Caquer's memory—but he could not quite remember what it was. Sector Two? Who'd been telling him things about Sector Two recently—usury, unfairness, tainted blood, something silly. Although of course a lot of the people over there did have Martian blood in them ...

"How many of the orators were arrested?" he asked.

"We got seven. Two more slipped away from us, but we'll pick them up if they start spouting again."

Lieutenant Caquer walked slowly, thoughtfully, to the Gordon apartment, trying his level best to remember where, recently, he heard anti-Sector Two propaganda. There must be something back of the simultaneous appearance of nine soap-box radicals, all preaching the same doctrine.

A sub-rosa political organization? But none such had existed for almost a century now. Under a perfectly democratic government, component part of a stable system-wide organization of planets, there was no need for such activity. Of course an occasional crackpot was dissatisfied, but a group in that state of mind struck him as fantastic.

It sounded as crazy as the Willem Deem case. That did not make sense either. Things happened meaninglessly, as in a dream. Dream? What was he trying to remember about a dream? Hadn't he had an odd sort of dream last night—what was it?

But, as dreams usually do, it eluded his conscious mind.

Anyway, tomorrow he would question—or help question—those radicals who were under arrest. Put men on the job of tracing them back, and undoubtedly a common background somewhere, a tie-up, would be found.

It could not be accidental that they should all pop on the same day. It was screwy, just as screwy as the two inexplicable corpses of a book-and-reel shop proprietor. Maybe because the cases were both screwy, his mind tended to couple the two sets of events. But taken together, they were no more digestible than taken separately. They made even less sense.

Confound it, why hadn't he taken that post on Ganymede when it was offered to him? Ganymede was a nice orderly moon. Persons there did not get murdered twice on consecutive days. But Jane Gordon did not live on Ganymede; she lived right here in Sector Three and he was on his way to see her.

And everything was wonderful except that he felt so tired he could not think straight, and Jane Gordon insisted on looking on him as a brother instead of a suitor, and he was probably going to lose his job. He would be the laughing stock of Callisto if the special investigator from headquarters found some simple explanation of things that he had overlooked ...

Jane Gordon, looking more beautiful than he had ever seen her, met him at the door. She was smiling, but the smile changed to a look of concern as he stepped into light.

"Rod!" she exclaimed. "You do look ill, really ill. What have you been doing to yourself besides forgetting to eat?"

Rod Caquer managed a grin.

"Chasing vicious circles up blind alleys, Icicle. May I use your visiphone?"

"Of course. I've some food ready for you; I'll put it on the table while you're calling. Dad's taking a nap. He said to wake him when you got here, but I'll hold off until you're fed."

She hurried out to the kitchen. Caquer almost fell into the chair before the visiscreen, and called the police station. The red, beefy face of Borgesen, the night lieutenant, flashed into view.

"Hi, Borg," said Caquer. "Listen, about those seven screwballs you picked up. Have you—"

"Nine," Borgesen interrupted. "We got the other two, and I wish we hadn't. We're going nuts down here."

"You mean the other two tried it again?"

"No. Suffering Asteroids, they came in and gave themselves up, and we can't kick them out, because there's a charge against them. But they're confessing all over the place. And do you know what they're confessing?"

"I'll bite," said Caquer.

"That you hired them, and offered one hundred credits apiece to them."

"Huh?"

Borgesen laughed, a little wildly. "The two that came in voluntarily said that, and the other seven—Mars, why did I ever become a policeman? I had a chance to study for fireman on a spacer once, and I end up doing this."

"Look—maybe I better come around and see if they make that accusation to my face."

"They probably would, but it doesn't mean anything, Rod. They say you hired them this afternoon, and you were at Deem's with Brager all afternoon. Rod, this moon is going nuts. And so am I. Walther Johnson has disappeared. Hasn't been seen since this morning."

"What? The Regent's confidential secretary? You're kidding me, Borg."

"Wish I was. You ought to be glad you're off duty. Maxon's been raising seven brands of thunder for us to find his secretary for him. He doesn't like the Deem business, either. Seems to blame us for it; thinks it's bad enough for the department to let a man get killed once. Say, which was Deem, Rod? Got any idea?"

Caquer grinned weakly.

"Let's call them Deem and Redeem till we find out," he suggested. "I think they were both Deem."

"But how could one man be two?"

"How could one man be killed five ways?" countered Caquer. "Tell me that and I'll tell you the answer to yours."

"Nuts," said Borgesen, and followed it with a masterpiece of understatement. "There's something funny about that case."

Caquer was laughing so hard that there were tears in his eyes, when Jane Gordon came to tell him food was ready. She frowned at him, but there was concern behind the frown.

Caquer followed her meekly, and discovered he was ravenous. When he'd put himself outside enough food for three ordinary meals, he felt almost human again. His headache was still there, but it was something that throbbed dimly in the distance.

Frail Professor Gordon was waiting in the living room when they went there from the kitchen. "Rod, you look like something the cat dragged in," he said. "Sit down before you fall down."

Caquer grinned. "Overeating did it. Jane's a cook in a million."

He sank into a chair facing Gordon. Jane Gordon had sat on the arm of her father's chair and Caquer's eyes feasted on her. How could a girl with lips as soft and kissable as hers insist on regarding marriage only as an academic subject? How could a girl with—

"I don't see offhand how it could be a cause of his death, Rod, but Willem Deem rented out political books," said Gordon. "There's no harm in my telling that, since the poor chap is dead."

Almost the same words, Caquer remembered, that Perry Peters had used in telling him the same thing.

Caquer nodded.

"We've searched his shop and his apartment and haven't found any, Professor," he said. "You wouldn't know, of course, what kind—"

Professor Gordon smiled. "I'm afraid I would, Rod. Off the record—and I take it you haven't a recorder on our conversation—I've read quite a few of them."

"You?" There was frank surprise in Caquer's voice.

"Never underestimate the curiosity of an educator, my boy. I fear the reading of Graydex books is a more prevalent vice among the instructors in universities than among any other class. Oh, I know it's wrong to encourage the trade, but the reading of such books can't possibly harm a balanced, judicious mind."

"And Father certainly has a balanced, judicious mind, Rod," said Jane, a bit defiantly. "Only—darn him—he wouldn't let me read those books."

Caquer grinned at her. The professor's use of the word "Graydex" had reassured him.

Renting Graydex books was only a misdemeanor, after all.

"Ever read any Graydex books, Rod?" the professor asked. Caquer shook his head.

"Then you've probably never heard of hypnotism. Some of the circumstances in the Deem case— Well, I've wondered whether hypnotism might have been used."

"I'm afraid I don't even know what it is, Professor."

The frail little man sighed.

"That's because you've never read illicit books, Rod," said Gordon. "Hypnotism is the control of one mind by another, and it reached a pretty high state of development before it was outlawed. You've never heard of the Kaprelian Order or the Vargas Wheel?"

Caquer shook his head.

"The history of the subject is in Graydex books, in several of them," said the professor. "The actual methods, and how a Vargas Wheel is constructed would be Blackdex, high on the roster of lawlessness. Of course I haven't read that, but I have read the history.

"A man by the name of Mesmer, way back in the Eighteenth Century, was one of the first practitioners, if not the discoverer, of hypnotism. At any rate, he put it on a more or less scientific basis. By the Twentieth Century, quite a bit had been learned about it—and it became extensively used in medicine.

"A hundred years later, doctors were treating almost as many patients through hypnotism as through drugs and surgery. True, there were cases of its misuse, but they were relatively few.

"But another hundred years brought a big change. Mesmerism had developed too far for the public safety. Any criminal or selfish politician who had a smattering of the art could operate with impunity. He could fool all the people all the time, and get away with it."

"You mean he could really make people think anything he wanted them to?" Caquer asked.

"Not only that, he could make them do anything he wanted. With the use of television one speaker could visibly and directly talk to millions of people."

"But couldn't the government have regulated the art?"

Professor Gordon smiled thinly. "How, when legislators were human, too, and as subject to hypnotism as the people under them? And then, to complicate things almost hopelessly, came the invention of the Vargas Wheel.

"It had been known, back as far as the Nineteenth Century, that an arrangement of moving mirrors could throw anyone who watched it into a state of hypnotic submission. And thought transmission had been experimented with in the Twenty-first Century. It was in the following one that Vargas combined and perfected the two into the Vargas Wheel. A sort of helmet affair, really, with a revolving wheel of specially constructed tricky mirrors on top of it."

"How did it work, Professor?" asked Caquer.

"The wearer of a Vargas Wheel helmet had immediate and automatic control over anyone who saw him—directly, or in a television screen," said Gordon. "The mirrors in the small turning wheel produced instantaneous hypnosis and the helmet—somehow—brought thoughts of its wearer to bear through the wheel and impressed upon his subjects any thoughts he wished to transmit.

"In fact, the helmet itself—or the wheel—could be set to produce certain fixed illusions without the necessity of the operator speaking, or even concentrating, on those points. Or the control could be direct, from his mind."

"Ouch," said Caquer. "A thing like that would—I can certainly see why instructions in making a Vargas Wheel would be Blackdexed. Suffering Asteroids! A man with one of these could—"

"Could do almost anything. Including killing a man and making the manner of his death appear five different ways to five different observers."

Caquer whistled softly. "And including playing nine man Morris with soapbox radicals—or they wouldn't even have to be radicals, but just ordinary orthodox citizens."

"Nine men?" Jane Gordon demanded. "What's this about nine men, Rod? I hadn't heard about it."

But Rod was already standing up.

"Haven't time to explain, Icicle," he said. "Tell you tomorrow, but I must get down to— Wait a minute, Professor, is that all you know about the Vargas Wheel business?"

"Absolutely all, my boy. It just occurred to me as a possibility. There were only five or six of them ever made, and finally the government got hold of them and destroyed them, one by one. It cost millions of lives to do it.

"When they finally got everything cleaned up, colonization of the planets was starting, and an international council had been started with control over all governments. They decided that the whole field of hypnotism was too dangerous, and they made it a forbidden subject. It took quite a few centuries to wipe out all knowledge of it, but they succeeded. The proof is that you'd never heard of it."

"But how about the beneficial aspects of it?" Jane Gordon asked. "Were they lost?"

"Of course," said her father. "But the science of medicine had progressed so far by that time that it wasn't too much of a loss. Today the medicos can cure, by physical treatment, anything that hypnotism could handle."

Caquer, who had halted at the door, now turned back.

"Professor, do you think it possible that someone could have rented a Blackdex book from Deem, and learned all those secrets?" he inquired.

Professor Gordon shrugged. "It's possible," he said. "Deem might have handled occasional Blackdex books, but he knew better than try to sell or rent any to me. So I wouldn't have heard of it."

At the station, Lieutenant Caquer found Lieutenant Borgesen on the verge of apoplexy.

He looked at Caquer.

"You!" he said. And then, plaintively, "The world's gone nuts. Listen, Brager discovered Willem Deem, didn't he? At ten o'clock yesterday morning? And stayed there on guard while Skidder and you and the clearance men were there?"

"Yes, why?" asked Caquer.

Borgesen's expression showed how much he was upset by developments.

"Nothing, not a thing, except that Brager was in the emergency hospital yesterday morning, from nine until after eleven, getting a sprained ankle treated. He couldn't have been at Deem's. Seven doctors and attendants and nurses swear up and down he was in the hospital at that time."

Caquer frowned.

"He was limping today, when he helped me search Deem's shop," he said. "What does Brager say?"

"He says he was there, I mean at Deem's, and discovered Deem's body. We just happened to find out otherwise accidentally—if it is otherwise. Rod, I'm going nuts. To think I had a chance to be fireman on a spacer and took this damned job. Have you learned anything new?"

"Maybe. But first I want to ask you, Borg. About these nine nitwits you picked up. Has anybody tried to identify—"

"Them," interrupted Borgesen. "I let them go."

Caquer stared at the beefy face of the night lieutenant in utter amazement.

"Let them go?" he repeated. "You couldn't, legally. Man, they'd been charged. Without a trial, you couldn't turn them loose."

"Nuts, I did, and I'll take the responsibility for it. Look, Rod, they were right, weren't they?"

"What?"

"Sure. People ought to be waked up about what's going on over in Sector Two. Those phonies over there need taking down a peg, and we're the only ones to do it. This ought to be headquarters for Callisto, right here. Why listen, Rod, a united Callisto could take over Ganymede."

"Borg, was there anything over the televis tonight? Anybody make a speech you listened to?"

"Sure, didn't you hear it? Our friend Skidder. Must have been while you were walking here, because all the televis turned on automatically—it was a general."

"And—was anything specific suggested, Borg? About Sector Two, and Ganymede, and that sort of thing?"

"Sure, general meeting tomorrow morning at ten. In the square. We're all supposed to go; I'll see you there, won't I?"

"Yeah," said Lieutenant Caquer. "I'm afraid you will. I—I got to go, Borg."

Rod Caquer knew what was wrong now. Almost the last thing he wanted to do was stay around the station listening to Borgesen talking under the influence of—what seemed to be—a Vargas Wheel. Nothing else, nothing less, could have made police Lieutenant Borgesen talk as he had just talked. Professor Gordon's guess was getting righter every minute. Nothing else could have brought about such results.

Caquer walked on blindly through the Jupiter-lighted night, past the building in which his own apartment was. He did not want to go there either.

The streets of Sector Three City seemed crowded for so late an hour of the evening. Late? He glanced at his watch and whistled softly. It was not evening any more. It was two o'clock in the morning, and normally the streets would have been utterly deserted.

But they were not, tonight. People wandered about, alone or in small groups that walked together in uncanny silence. Shuffle of feet, but not even the whisper of a voice. Not even—

Whispers! Something about those streets and the people on them made Rod Caquer remember now his dream of the night before. Only now he knew that it had not been a dream. Nor had it been sleepwalking, in the ordinary sense of the word.

He had dressed. He had stolen out of the building. And the street lights had been out too, and that meant that employes of the service department had neglected their posts. They, like others, had been wandering with the crowds.

Listening to last night's whispers. And what had those whispers said? He could remember part of it ...

"Kill—kill—kill— You hate them ..."

A shiver ran down Rod Caquer's spine as he realized the significance of the fact that last night's dream had been a reality. This was something that dwarfed into insignificance the murder of a petty book-and-reel shop owner.

This was something which was gripping a city, something that could upset a world, something that could lead to unbelievable terror and carnage on a scale that hadn't been known since the Twenty-fourth Century. This—which had started as a simple murder case!

Up ahead somewhere, Rod Caquer heard the voice of a man addressing a crowd. A frenzied voice, shrill with fanaticism. He hurried his steps to the corner, and walked around it to find himself in the fringe of a crowd of people pressing around a man speaking from the top of a flight of steps.

"—and I tell you that tomorrow is the day. Now we have the Regent himself with us, and it will be unnecessary to depose him. Men are working all night tonight, preparing. After the meeting in the square tomorrow morning, we shall—"

"Hey!" Rod Caquer yelled. The man stopped talking and turned to look at Rod, and the crowd turned slowly, almost as one man, to stare at him.

"You're under—"

Then Caquer saw that this was but a futile gesture.

It was not the men surging toward him that convinced him of this. He was not afraid of violence. He would have welcomed it as relief from uncanny terror, welcomed a chance to lay about him with the flat of his sword

But standing behind the speaker was a man in uniform—Brager. And Caquer remembered, then, that Borgesen, now in charge at the station, was on the other side. How could he arrest the speaker, when Borgesen, now in charge, would refuse to book him. And what good would it do to start a riot and cause injury to innocent people—people acting not under their own volition, but under the insidious influence Professor Gordon had described to him?

Hand on his sword, he backed away. No one followed. Like automatons, they turned back to the speaker, who resumed his harangue, as though never interrupted. Policeman Brager had not moved, had not even looked in the direction of his superior officer. He alone of all those there had not turned at Caquer's challenge.

Lieutenant Caquer hurried on in the direction he had been going when he had heard the speaker. That way would take him back downtown. He would find a place open where he could use a visiphone, and call the Sector Coordinator. This was an emergency.

And surely the scope of whoever had the Vargas Wheel had not yet extended beyond the boundaries of Sector Three.

He found an all-night restaurant, open but deserted, the lights on but no waiters on duty, no cashier behind the counter. He stepped into the visiphone booth and pushed the button for a long-distance operator. She flashed into sight on the screen almost at once.

"Sector Co-ordinator, Callisto City," Caquer said. "And rush it."

"Sorry, sir. Out of town service suspended by order of the Controller of Utilities, for the duration."

"Duration of what?"

"We are not permitted to give out information."

Caquer gritted his teeth. Well, there was *one* someone who might be able to help him. He forced his voice to remain calm.

"Give me Professor Gordon, University Apartments," he told the operator.

"Yes, sir."

But the screen stayed dark, although the little red button that indicated the buzzer was operating flashed on and off for minutes.

"There is no answer, sir."

Probably Gordon and his daughter were asleep, too soundly asleep to hear the buzzer. For a moment, Caquer considered rushing over there. But it was on the other side of town, and of what help could they be? None, and Professor Gordon was a frail old man, and ill.

No, he would have to— Again he pushed a button of the visiphone and a moment later was talking to the man in charge of the ship hangar.

"Get out that little speed job of the Police Department," snapped Caquer. "Have it ready and I'll be there in a few minutes."

"Sorry, Lieutenant," came the curt reply. "All outgoing power beams shut off, by special order. Everything's grounded for the emergency."

He might have known it, Caquer thought. But what about the special investigator coming from the Co-ordinator's office? "Are incoming ships still permitted to land?" he inquired.

"Permitted to land, but not to leave again without special order," answered the voice.

"Thanks," Caquer said. He clicked off the screen and went out into the dawn, outside. There was a chance, then. The special investigator might be able to help.

But he, Rod Caquer, would have to intercept him, tell him the story and its implications before he could fall with the others, under the influence of the

Vargas Wheel. Caquer strode rapidly toward the terminal. Maybe his ship had already landed and the damage had been done.

Again he passed a knot of people gathered about a frenzied speaker. Almost everyone must be under the influence by this time. But why had he been spared? Why was not he, too, under the evil influence?

True, he must have been on the street on the way to the police station at the time Skidder had been on the air, but that didn't explain everything. All of these people could not have seen and heard that visicast. Some of them must have been asleep already at that hour.

Also he, Rod Caquer, had been affected, the night before, the night of the whispers. He must have been under the influence of the wheel at the time he investigated the murder—the murders.

Why, then, was he free now? Was he the only one, or were there others who had escaped, who were sane and their normal selves?

If not, if he was the only one, why was he free?

Or was he free?

Could it be that what he was doing right now was under direction, was part of some plan?

But no use to think that way, and go mad. He would have to carry on the best he could, and hope that things, with him, were what they seemed to be.

Then he broke into a run, for ahead was the open area of the terminal, and a small space-ship, silver in the dawn, was settling down to land. A small official speedster—it must be the special investigator. He ran around the check-in building, through the gate in the wire fence, and toward the ship, which was already down. The door opened.

A small, wiry man stepped out and closed the door behind him. He saw Caquer and smiled.

"You're Caquer?" he asked, pleasantly. "Co-ordinator's office sent me to investigate a case you fellows are troubled with. My name—"

Lieutenant Rod Caquer was staring with horrified fascination at the little man's well-known features, the all-too-familiar wart on the side of the little man's nose, listening for the announcement he knew this man was going to make—

"—is Willem Deem. Shall we go to your office?"

Too much can happen to any man.

Lieutenant Rod Caquer, Lieutenant of Police of Sector Three, Callisto, had experienced more than his share. How can you investigate the murder of a man who has been killed twice? How should a policeman act when the victim shows up, alive and happy, to help you solve the case?

Not even when you know he is not there really—or if he is, he is not what your eyes tell you he is and is not saying what your ears hear.

There is a point beyond which the human mind can no longer function sanely, and when they reach and pass that point, different people react in different ways.

Rod Caquer's reaction was a sudden, blind, red anger. Directed, for lack of a better object, at the special investigator—if he was the special investigator and not a hypnotic phantasm which wasn't there at all.

Rod Caquer's fist lashed out, and it met a chin. Which proved nothing except that if the little man who'd just stepped out of the speedster was an illusion, he was an illusion of touch as well as of sight. Rod's fist exploded on his chin like a rocket-blast, and the little man swayed and fell forward. Still smiling, because he had not had time to change the expression on his face.

He fell face down, and then rolled over, his eyes closed but smiling gently up at the brightening sky.

Shakily, Caquer bent down and put his hand against the front of the man's tunic. There was the thump of a beating heart, all right. For a moment, Caquer had feared he might have killed with that blow.

And Caquer closed his eyes, deliberately, and felt the man's face with his hand—and it still felt like the face of Willem Deem looked, and the wart was there to the touch as well as to the sense of sight.

Two men had run out of the check-in building and were coming across the field toward him. Rod caught the expression on their faces and then thought of the little speedster only a few paces from him. He had to get out of Sector Three City, to tell somebody what was happening before it was too late.

If only they'd been lying about the outgoing power beam being shut off. He leaped across the body of the man he had struck and into the door of the speedster, jerked at the controls. But the ship did not respond, and—no, they hadn't been lying about the power beam.

No use staying here for a fight that could not possibly decide anything. He went out the door of the speedster, on the other side, away from the men coming toward him, and ran for the fence.

It was electrically charged, that fence. Not enough to kill a man, but plenty to hold him stuck to it until men with rubber gloves cut the wire and took him off. But if the power beam was off, probably the current in the fence was off, too.

It was too high to jump, so he took the chance. And the current was off. He scrambled over it safely and his pursuers stopped and went back to take care of the fallen man beside the speedster.

Caquer slowed down to a walk, but he kept on going. He didn't know where, but he had somehow to keep moving. After a while he found that his steps were taking him toward the edge of town, on the northern side, toward Callisto City.

He was in a small park near the north border when the significance, and the futility, of his direction came to him. And he found, at the same time, that his muscles were sore and tired, that he had a raging headache, that he could not keep on going unless he had a worthwhile and possible goal.

He sank down on a park bench and for a while held his head in his hands. No answer came.

After a while he looked up and saw something that fascinated him. A child's pinwheel on a stick, stuck in the grass of the park, spinning in the wind. Now fast, now slow, as the breeze varied.

It was going in circles, like his mind was. How could a man's mind go other than in circles when he could not tell what was reality and what was illusion? Going in circles, like a Vargas Wheel.

Circles.

But there ought to be some way. A man with a Vargas Wheel was not completely invincible, else how had the council finally succeeded in destroying the few that had been made? True, possessors of the wheels would have cancelled each other out to some extent, but there must have been a last wheel, in someone's hands. Owned by someone who wanted to control the destiny of the solar system.

But they had stopped the wheel.

It could be stopped, then. But how? How, when one could not see it? Rather, when the sight of it put a man so completely under its control that he no longer, after the first glimpse, knew that it was there. Because, on sight, it had captured his mind.

He must stop the wheel. That was the only answer. But how?

That pinwheel there could be the Vargas Wheel, for all he could tell, set to create the illusion that it was a child's toy. Or its possessor, wearing the helmet, might be standing on the path in front of him at this moment, watching him. The possessor of the wheel might be invisible because Caquer's mind was told not to see.

But if the man was there, he'd be really there, and should Rod slash out with his sword, the menace would be ended, wouldn't it? Of course.

But how to find a wheel that one could not see? That one could not see because—

And then, still staring at the pinwheel, Caquer saw a chance, something that might work, a slender chance!

He looked quickly at his wrist watch and saw that it was half past nine, which was one half-hour before the demonstration in the square. And the wheel and its owner would be there, surely.

His aching muscles forgotten, Lieutenant Rod Caquer started to run back toward the center of town. The streets were deserted. Everyone had gone to the square, of course. They had been told to come.

He was winded after a few blocks, and had to slow down to a rapid walk, but there would be time for him to get there before it was over, even if he missed the start.

Yes, he could get there all right. And then, if his idea worked ...

It was almost ten when he passed the building where his own office was situated, and kept on going. He turned in a few doors beyond. The elevator operator was gone, but Caquer ran the elevator up and a minute later he had used his picklock on a door and was in Perry Peters' laboratory.

Peters was gone, of course, but the goggles were there, the special goggles with the trick windshield-wiper effect that made them usable in radite mining.

Rod Caquer slipped them over his eyes, put the motive-power battery into his pocket, and touched the button on the side. They worked. He could see dimly as the wipers flashed back and forth. But a minute later they stopped.

Of course. Peters had said that the shafts heated and expanded after a minute's operation. Well, that might not matter. A minute might be long enough, and the metal would have cooled by the time he reached the square.

But he would have to be able to vary the speed. Among the litter of stuff on the workbench, he found a small rheostat and spliced it in one of the wires that ran from the battery to the goggles.

That was the best he could do. No time to try it out. He slid the goggles up onto his forehead and ran out into the hall, took the elevator down to street level. And a moment later he was running toward the public square, two blocks away.

He reached the fringe of the crowd gathered in the square looking up at the two balconies of the Regency building. On the lower one were several people he recognized; Dr. Skidder, Walther Johnson. Even Lieutenant Borgesen was there.

On the higher balcony, Regent Barr Maxon was alone, and was speaking to the crowd below. His sonorous voice rolled out phrases extolling the might of empire. Only a little distance away, in the crowd, Caquer caught sight of the gray hair of Professor Gordon, and Jane Gordon's golden head beside it. He wondered if they were under the spell, too. Of course they were deluded also or they would not be there. He realized it would be useless to speak to them, to tell them what he was trying to do.

Lieutenant Caquer slid the goggles down over his eyes, blinded momentarily because the wiper arms were in the wrong position. But his fingers found the rheostat, set at zero, and began to move it slowly around the dial toward maximum.

And then, as the wipers began their frantic dance and accelerated, he could see dimly. Through the arc-shaped lenses, he looked around him. On the lower balcony he saw nothing unusual, but on the upper balcony the figure of Regent Maxon suddenly blurred.

There was a man standing there on the upper balcony wearing a strange-looking helmet with wires and atop the helmet was a three-inch wheel of mirrors and prisms.

A wheel that stood still, because of the stroboscopic effect of the mechanized goggles. For an instant, the speed of those wiper arms was synchronized with the spinning of the wheel, so that each successive glimpse of the wheel showed it in the same position, and to Caquer's eyes the wheel stood still, and he could see it.

Then the goggles jammed.

But he did not need them any more now.

He knew that Barr Maxon, or whoever stood up there on the balcony, was the wearer of the wheel.

Silently, and attracting as little attention as possible, Caquer sprinted around the fringe of the crowd and reached the side door of the Regency building.

There was a guard on duty there.

"Sorry, sir, but no one's allowed—"

Then he tried to duck, too late. The flat of Police Lieutenant Rod Caquer's shortsword thudded against his head.

The inside of the building seemed deserted. Caquer ran up the three flights of stairs that would take him to the level of the higher balcony, and down the hall toward the balcony door.

He burst through it, and Regent Maxon turned. Maxon now no longer wore the helmet on his head. Caquer had lost the goggles, but whether he could see it or not, Caquer knew the helmet and the wheel were still in place and working, and that this was his one chance.

Maxon turned and saw Lieutenant Caquer's face, and his drawn sword.

Then, abruptly, Maxon's figure vanished. It seemed to Caquer—although he knew that it was not—that the figure before him was that of Jane Gordon. Jane, looking at him pleadingly, and spoke in melting tones.

"Rod, don't—" she began to say.

But it was not Jane, he knew. A thought, in self-preservation, had been directed at him by the manipulator of the Vargas Wheel.

Caquer raised his sword, and he brought it down hard.

Glass shattered and there was the ring of metal on metal as his sword cut through and split the helmet.

Of course it was not Jane now—just a dead man lying there with blood oozing out of the split in a strange and complicated but utterly shattered helmet. A helmet that could now be seen by everyone there, and by Lieutenant Caquer himself.

Just as everyone, including Caquer himself, could recognize the man who had worn it.

He was a small, wiry man, and there was an unsightly wart on the side of his nose.

Yes, it was Willem Deem. And this time, Rod Caquer knew it was Willem Deem ...

"I thought," Jane Gordon said, "that you were going to leave for Callisto City without saying goodbye to us."

Rod Caquer threw his hat in the general direction of a hook.

"Oh, that," he said. "I'm not even sure I'm going to take the promotion to a job as police co-ordinator there. I have a week to decide, and I'll be around town at least that long. How you been doing, Icicle?"

"Fine, Rod. Sit down. Father will be home soon, and I know he has a lot of things to ask you. Why, we haven't seen you since the big mass meeting."

Funny how dumb a smart man can be, at times.

But then again, he had proposed so often and been refused, that it was not all his fault.

He just looked at her.

"Rod, all the story never came out in the newscasts," she said. "I know you'll have to tell it all over again for my father, but while we're waiting for him, won't you give me some information?"

Rod grinned.

"Nothing to it, really, Icicle," he said. "Willem Deem got hold of a Blackdex book, and found out how to make a Vargas Wheel. So he made one, and it gave him ideas.

"His first idea was to kill Barr Maxon and take over as Regent, setting the helmet so he would appear to be Maxon. He put Maxon's body in his own shop, and then had a lot of fun with his own murder. He had a warped sense of humor, and got a kick out of chasing us in circles."

"But just how did he do all the rest?" asked the girl.

"He was there as Brager, and pretended to discover his own body. He gave one description of the method of death, and caused Skidder and me and the clearance men to see the body of Maxon each a different way. No wonder we nearly went nuts."

"But Brager remembered being there too," she objected.

"Brager was in the hospital at the time, but Deem saw him afterward and impressed on his mind the memory pattern of having discovered Deem's body," explained Caquer. "So naturally, Brager thought he had been there.

"Then he killed Maxon's confidential secretary, because being so close to the Regent, the secretary must have suspected something was wrong even though he couldn't guess what. That was the second corpse of Willem Deem, who was beginning to enjoy himself in earnest when he pulled that on us.

"And of course he never sent to Callisto City for a special investigator at all. He just had fun with me, by making me seem to meet one and having the guy turn out to be Willem Deem again. I nearly did go nuts then, I guess."

"But why, Rod, weren't you as deep in as the others? I mean on the business of conquering Callisto and all of that?" she inquired. "You were free of that part of the hypnosis."

Caquer shrugged.

"Maybe it was because I missed Skidder's talk on the televis," he suggested.

"Of course it wasn't Skidder at all, it was Deem in another guise and wearing the helmet. And maybe he deliberately left me out, because he was having a psychopathic kind of fun out of my trying to investigate the murders of two Willem Deems. It's hard to figure. Perhaps I was slightly cracked from the strain, and it might have been that for that reason I was partially resistant to the group hypnosis."

"You think he really intended to try to rule all of Callisto, Rod?" asked the girl.

"We'll never know, for sure, just how far he wanted, or expected to go later. At first, he was just experimenting with the powers of hypnosis, through the wheel. That first night, he sent people out of their houses into the streets, and then sent them back and made them forget it. Just a test, undoubtedly."

Caquer paused and frowned thoughtfully.

"He was undoubtedly psychopathic, though, and we don't dare even guess what all his plans were," he continued. "You understand how the goggles worked to neutralize the wheel, don't you, Icicle?"

"I think so. That was brilliant, Rod. It's like when you take a moving picture of a turning wheel, isn't it? If the camera synchronizes with the turning of the wheel, so that each successive picture shows it after a complete revolution, then it looks like it's standing still when you show the movie."

Caquer nodded.

"That's it exactly," he said. "Just luck I had access to those goggles, though. For a second I could see a man wearing a helmet up there on the balcony—but that was all I had to know."

"But Rod, when you rushed out on the balcony, you didn't have the goggles on any more. Couldn't he have stopped you, by hypnosis?"

"Well, he didn't. I guess there wasn't time for him to take over control of me. He did flash an illusion at me. It wasn't either Barr Maxon or Willem Deem I saw standing there at the last minute. It was you, Jane."

"I?"

"Yep, you. I guess he knew I'm in love with you, and that's the first thing flashed into his mind—that I wouldn't dare use the sword if I thought it was you standing there. But it wasn't you, in spite of the evidence of my eyes, so I swung it."

He shuddered slightly, remembering the will power he had needed to bring that sword down.

"The worst of it was that I saw you standing there like I've always wanted to see you—with your arms out toward me, and looking at me as though you loved me."

"Like this, Rod?"

And this time he was not too dumb to get the idea.

148

Paradox Lost

A blue bottle fly had got in through the screen, somehow, and it droned in monotonous circles around the ceiling of the classroom. Even as Professor Dolohan droned in monotonous circles of logic up at the front of the class. Shorty McCabe, seated in the back row, glanced from one to the other of them and finally settled on the blue bottle fly as the more interesting of the two.

"The negative absolute," said the professor, "is, in a manner of speaking, not absolutely negative. This is only seemingly contradictory. Reversed in order, the two words acquire new connotations. Therefore—"

Shorty McCabe sighed inaudibly and watched the blue bottle fly, and wished that he could fly around in circles like that, and with such a soul-satisfying buzz. In comparative sizes and decibels, a fly made more noise than an airplane.

More noise, in comparison to size, than a buzz saw. Would a buzz saw saw metal? Say, a saw. Then one could say he saw a buzz saw saw a saw. Or leave out the buzz and that would be better: I saw a saw saw a saw. Or, better yet: Sue saw a saw saw a saw.

"One may think," said the professor, "of an absolute as a mode of being—"

Yeah, thought Shorty McCabe, one may think of anything as anything else, and what does it get you but a headache. Anyway, the blue bottle fly was becoming more interesting. It was flying down now, toward the front of the classroom, and maybe it would light on Professor Dolohan's head. And buzz.

No, but it lighted somewhere out of sight behind the professor's desk. Without the fly to solace him, Shorty looked around the classroom for something else to look at or think about. Only the backs of heads; he was alone in the back row, and—well, he could concentrate on how the hair grew on the backs of people's necks, but it seemed a subject of limited fascination.

He wondered how many of the students ahead of him were asleep, and decided that about half of them were; and he wished he could go to sleep himself, but he couldn't. He'd made the silly mistake of going to bed early the night before and as a result he was now wide-awake and miserable.

"But," said Professor Dolohan, "if we disregard the contravention of probability arising in the statement that the positive absolute is less than absolutely positive, we are led to—"

Hooray! The blue bottle fly was back again, arising from its temporary concealment back of the desk. It droned upward to the ceiling, paused there a moment to preen its wings, and then flew down again, this time toward the back of the room.

And if it kept that spiral course, it would go past within an inch of Shorty's nose. It did. He went cross-eyed watching it and turned his head to keep it in sight. It flew past and—

It just wasn't there any more. At a point about twelve inches to the left of Shorty McCabe, it had suddenly quit flying and suddenly quit buzzing, and it wasn't there. It hadn't died and hadn't fallen into the aisle. It had just—

Disappeared. In midair, four feet above the aisle, it had simply ceased to be there. The sound it had made seemed to have stopped in midbuzz, and in the sudden silence the professor's voice seemed louder, if not funnier. "By creating, through an assumption contrary to fact, we create a pseudoreal set of axioms which are, in a measure, the reversal of existing—"

Shorty McCabe, staring at the point where the fly had vanished, said "Gaw!"

"I beg your pardon?"

"Sorry, Professor. I didn't speak," said Shorty. "I ... I just cleared my throat."

"—by the reversal of existing— What was I saying? Oh, yes. We create an axiomatic basis of pseudologic which would yield different answers to all problems. I mean—"

Seeing that the professor's eyes had left him, Shorty turned his head again to look at the point where the fly had ceased to fly. Had ceased, maybe, to *be* a fly? Nuts; it must have been an optical illusion. A fly went pretty fast. If he'd suddenly lost sight of it—

He shot a look out of the corner of his eye at Professor Dolohan, and made sure that the professor's attention was focused elsewhere. Then Shorty reached out a tentative hand toward the point, or the approximate point, where he'd seen the fly vanish.

He didn't know what he expected to find there, but he didn't feel anything at all. Well, that was logical enough. If the fly had flown into nothing and he, Shorty, had reached out and felt nothing, that proved nothing. But, somehow, he was vaguely disappointed. He didn't know what he'd expected to find; hardly to touch the fly that wasn't there, or to encounter a solid but invisible obstacle, or anything. But—*what* had happened to the fly?

Shorty put his hands on the desk and, for a full minute, tried to forget the fly by listening to the professor. But that was worse than wondering about the fly.

For the thousandth time he wondered why he'd ever been such a sap as to enroll in this Logic 2B class. He'd never pass the exam. And he was majoring in paleontology, anyway. He liked paleontology; a dinosaur was something you could get your teeth into, in a manner of speaking. But logic, phooey; 2B or not 2B. And he'd rather study about fossils than listen to one.

He happened to look down at his hands on the desk. "Gaw!" he said.

"Mr. McCabe?" said the professor.

Shorty didn't answer; he couldn't. He was looking at his left hand. There weren't any fingers on it. He closed his eyes.

The professor smiled a professorial smile. "I believe our young friend in the back seat has ... uh ... gone to sleep," he said. "Will someone please try—"

Shorty hastily dropped his hands into his lap. He said, "I ... I'm okay, Professor. Sorry. Did you say something?"

"Didn't you?"

Shorty gulped. "I ... I guess not."

"We were discussing," said the professor—to the class, thank heaven, and not to Shorty individually—"the possibility of what one might refer to as the impossible. It is not a contradiction in terms, for one must distinguish carefully between *im*possible and *un*possible. The latter—"

Shorty surreptitiously put his hands back on the desk and sat there staring at them. The right hand was all right. The left— He closed his eyes and opened them again and still all the fingers of his left hand were missing. They didn't *feel* missing. Experimentally, he wriggled the muscles that ought to move them and he felt them wriggle.

But they weren't there, as far as his eyes could see. He reached over and felt for them with his right hand—and he couldn't feel them. His right hand went right through the space that his left-hand fingers ought to occupy, and felt nothing. But still he could move the fingers of his left hand. He did.

It was very confusing.

And then he remembered that was the hand he had used in reaching out toward the place where the blue bottle fly had disappeared. And then, as though to confirm his sudden suspicion, he felt a light touch on one of the fingers that wasn't there. A light touch, and something light crawling along his finger. Something about the weight of a blue bottle fly. Then the touch vanished, as though it had flown again.

Shorty bit his lips to keep from saying "Gaw!" again. He was getting scared.

Was he going nuts? Or had the professor been right and was he asleep after all? How could he tell? Pinching? With the only available fingers, those of his right hand, he reached down and pinched the skin of his thigh, hard. It hurt. But then if he dreamed he pinched himself, couldn't he also dream that it hurt?

He turned his head and looked toward his left. There wasn't anything to see that way; the empty desk across the aisle, the empty desk beyond it, the wall, the window, and blue sky through the pane of glass.

But—

He glanced at the professor and saw that his attention was now on the blackboard where he was marking symbols. "Let N," said the professor, "equal known infinity, and the symbol a equal the factor of probability." Shorty tentatively reached out his left hand again into the aisle and watched it closely. He thought he might as well make sure; he reached out a little farther. The *hand was gone*. He jerked back his wrist, and sat there sweating.

He was nuts. He had to be nuts.

Again he tried to move his fingers and felt them wriggle very satisfactorily, just as they should have wriggled. They still had feeling, kinetic and otherwise. But— He reached his wrist toward the desk and didn't feel the desk. He put it in such a position that his hand, if it had been on the end of his wrist, would have *had* to touch or pass through the desk, but he felt nothing.

Wherever his hand was, it wasn't on the end of his wrist. It was still out there in the aisle, no matter where he moved his arm. If he got up and walked out of the classroom, would his hand *still* be out there in the aisle, invisible? And suppose he went a thousand miles away? But that was silly.

But was it any sillier than that his arm should rest here on the desk and his hand be two feet away? The difference in silliness between two feet and a thousand miles was only one of degree.

Was his hand out there?

He took his fountain pen out of his pocket and reached out with his right hand to approximately the point where he thought *it* was, and—sure enough—he was holding only part of a fountain pen, half of one. He carefully refrained from reaching any farther, but raised it and brought it down sharply.

It rapped—he felt it—across the missing knuckles of his left hand! That tied it! It so startled him that he let go of the pen and it was gone. It wasn't on the floor of the aisle. It wasn't anywhere. It was just gone, and it had been a good five-dollar pen, too.

Gaw! Here he was worrying about a *pen* when *his left hand was missing.* What was he going to do about *that?*

He closed his eyes. "Shorty McCabe," he said to himself, "you've got to think this out logically and figure out how to get your hand back out of whatever that is. You daren't get scared. Probably you're asleep and dreaming this, but maybe you aren't, and, *if* you aren't, you're in a jam. Now let's be logical. There is a place out there, a plane or something, and you can reach across it or put things across it, but you can't get them back again.

"Whatever else is on the other side, your left hand is. And your right hand doesn't know what your left hand is doing because one is here and the other is there, and never the twain shall— Hey, cut it out, Shorty. *This isn't funny.*"

But there was one thing he could do, and that was find out roughly the size and shape of the—whatever it was. There was a box of paper clips on his desk. He picked up a few in his right hand and tossed one of them out into the aisle. The paper clip got six or eight inches out into the aisle, and vanished. He didn't hear it land anywhere.

So far, so good. He tossed one a bit lower; same result. He bent down at his desk, being careful not to lean his head out into the aisle, and skittered a paper clip across the floor out into the aisle, saw it vanish eight inches out. He tossed one a little forward, one a bit backward. The plane extended at least a yard to the front and back, roughly parallel with the aisle itself.

And up? He tossed one upward that arced six feet above the aisle and vanished there. Another one, higher yet and in a forward direction. It described an arc in the air and landed on the head of a girl three seats forward in the next aisle. She started a little and put up a hand to her head.

"Mr. McCabe," said Professor Dolohan severely, "may I ask if this lecture bores you?"

Shorty jumped. He said, "Y— No, Professor. I was just—"

"You were, I noticed, experimenting in ballistics and the nature of a parabola. A parabola, Mr. McCabe, is the curve described by a missile projected into space with no continuing force other than its initial impetus and the force of gravity. Now shall I continue with my original lecture, or would you rather we called you up before the class to demonstrate the nature of paraboloid mechanics for the edification of your fellow students?"

"I'm sorry, Professor," said Shorty. "I was ... uh ... I mean ... I mean I'm sorry."

"Thank you, Mr. McCabe. And now—" The professor turned again to the blackboard. "If we let the symbol b represent the degree of unpossibility, in contradistinction to c—"

Shorty stared morosely down at his hands—his *hand*, rather—in his lap. He glanced up at the clock on the wall over the door and saw that in another five minutes the class period would be over. He had to do *something*, and do it quickly.

He turned his eyes toward the aisle again. Not that there was anything there to see. But there was plenty there to think about. Half a dozen paper clips, his best fountain pen, and his left hand.

There was an invisible something out there. You couldn't feel it when you touched it, and objects like paper clips didn't click when they hit it. And you could get through it in one direction, but not in the other. He could reach his right hand out there and touch his left hand with it, no doubt, but then he wouldn't get his right hand back again. And pretty soon class would be over and—

Nuts. There was only one thing he could do that made any sense. There wasn't anything on the other side of that plane that hurt his left hand, was there? Well, then, why not step through it? Wherever he'd be, it would be all in one piece.

He shot a glance at the professor and waited until he turned to mark something on the blackboard again. Then, without waiting to think it over, without *daring* to think it over, Shorty stood up in the aisle.

The lights went out. Or he had stepped into blackness.

He couldn't hear the professor any more, but there was a familiar buzzing noise in his ears that sounded like a blue bottle fly circling around somewhere nearby in the darkness.

He put his hands together, and they were both there; his right hand clasped his left. Well, wherever he was, he was *all* there. But why couldn't he see?

Somebody sneezed.

Shorty jumped, and then said, "Is ... uh ... anybody there?" His voice shook a little, and he hoped now that he was really asleep and that he'd wake up in a minute.

"Of course," said a voice. A rather sharp and querulous voice.

"Uh ... who?"

"What do you mean, who? Me. Can't you see— No, of course you can't. I forgot. Say, listen to that guy! And they say we're crazy!" There was a laugh in the darkness.

"What guy?" asked Shorty. "And who says who's crazy? Listen, I don't get—"

"*That* guy," said the voice. "The teacher. Can't you— No, I forget you can't. You've got no business here anyway. But I'm listening to the teacher telling about what happened to the saurians."

"The what?"

"The saurians, stupid. The dinosaurs. The guy's nuts. And they say *we* are!"

Shorty McCabe suddenly felt the need, the stark necessity, of sitting down. He groped in darkness and felt the top of a desk and felt that there was an empty seat behind it and eased himself down into the seat. Then he said, "This is Greek to me, mister. Who says who's crazy?"

"*They* say *we* are. Don't you know—that's right, you don't. Who let that fly in here?"

"Let's start at the beginning," Shorty begged. "Where am I?"

"You *normals*," said the voice petulantly. "Face you with anything out of the ordinary and you start asking— Oh, well, wait a minute and I'll tell you. Swat that fly for me."

"I can't see it. I—"

"Shut up. I want to listen to this; it's what I came here for. He— Yow, he's telling them that the dinosaurs died out for lack of food because they got too big. Isn't that silly? The bigger a thing is the better chance it has to find food, hasn't it? And the idea of the herbivorous ones ever starving in those forests! Or the carnivorous ones while the herbivorous ones were around! And— But why am I telling you all this? You're normal."

"I ... I don't get it. If I'm normal, what are you?"

The voice chuckled. "I'm *crazy*."

Shorty McCabe gulped. There didn't seem to be anything to say. The voice was all too obviously right, about that.

In the first place, if he could hear outside, Professor Dolohan was lecturing on the positive absolute, and this voice—with whatever, if anything, was attached to it—had come to hear about the decline of the saurians. That didn't make sense because Professor Dolohan didn't know a pixilated pterodactyl from an oblate spheroid.

And— "Ouch!" said Shorty. Something had given him a hard thwack on the shoulder.

"Sorry," said the voice. "I just took a swat at that dratted fly. It lighted on you. Anyway, I missed it. Wait a minute until I turn the switch and let the darned thing out. You want out, too?"

Suddenly the buzzing stopped.

Shorty said, "Listen, I ... I'm too darn curious to want out of here until I got *some* idea what I'm getting out from, I mean out of. I guess I must be crazy, but—"

"No, you're normal. It's we who are crazy. Anyway, that's what they say. Well, listening to that guy talk about dinosaurs bores me; I'd just as soon talk to you as listen to him. But you had no business getting in here, either you or that fly, see? There was a slip-up in the apparatus. I'll tell Napoleon—"

"Who?"

"Napoleon. He's the boss in this province. Napoleons are bosses in some of the others, too. You see a lot of us think we're Napoleon, but not me. It's a common delusion. Anyway, the Napoleon I mean is the one in Donnybrook."

"Donnybrook? Isn't that an insane asylum?"

"Of course, where else would anyone be who thought he was Napoleon? I ask you."

Shorty McCabe closed his eyes and found that didn't do any good because it was dark anyway and he couldn't see even with them open. He said to himself, "I got to keep on asking questions until I get something that makes sense or *I'm* going crazy. Maybe I *am* crazy; maybe this is what it's like to be crazy. But if I am, am I still sitting in Professor Dolohan's class, or ... or what?"

He opened his eyes and asked, "Look, let's see if we can get at this from a different angle. Where are you?"

"Me? Oh, I'm in Donnybrook, too. Normally, I mean. All of us in this province are, except a few that are still on the outside, see? Just now"—suddenly his voice sounded embarrassed—"I'm in a padded cell."

"And," asked Shorty fearfully, "is ... is this *it*? I mean, am *I* in a padded cell, too?"

"Of course not. You're sane. Listen, I've got no business to talk these things over with you. There's a sharp line drawn, you know. It was just because something went wrong with the apparatus."

Shorty wanted to ask "What apparatus?" but he had a hunch that if he did the answer would open up seven or eight new questions. Maybe if he stuck to one point until he understood that one, he could begin to understand some of the others. He said, "Let's get back to Napoleon. You say there is more than one Napoleon among you? How can that be? There can't be two of the same thing."

The voice chuckled. "That's all you know. That's what proves you're normal. That's normal reasoning; it's right, of course. But these guys who think they are Napoleon are crazy, so it doesn't apply. Why can't a hundred men each be Napoleon if they're too crazy to know they can't?"

"Well," said Shorty, "even if Napoleon wasn't dead, at least ninety-nine of them would have to be wrong, wouldn't they? That's logic."

"That's what's wrong with it here," said the voice. "I keep telling you we're crazy."

"We? You mean that I'm—"

"No, no, no, no, no. By 'we' I mean us, myself and the others, not you. That's why you got no business being here at all, see?"

"No," said Shorty. Strangely, he felt completely unafraid now. He knew that he must be asleep dreaming this, but he didn't think he was. But he was as sure as he was sure of anything that he *wasn't* crazy. The voice he was talking to said he wasn't; and that voice certainly seemed to be an authority on the subject. A hundred Napoleons! He said, "This is fun. I want to find out as much as I can before I wake up. Who are you; what's your name? Mine's Shorty."

"Moderately glad to know you, Shorty. You normals bore me usually, but you seem a bit better than most. I'd rather not give you the name they call me at Donnybrook, though; I wouldn't want you to come there visiting or anything. Just call me Dopey."

"You mean ... uh ... the Seven Dwarfs? You think you're one of—"

"Oh, no, not at all. I'm not a paranoiac; none of my delusions, as you would call them, concern identity. It's just the nickname they know me by here. Just like they call you Shorty, see? Never mind my other name."

Shorty said, "What are your ... uh ... delusions?"

"I'm an inventor, what they call a nut inventor. I think I invent time machines, for one thing. This is one of them."

"This is— You mean that I'm in a time machine? Well, yes, that would account for ... uh ... a thing or two. But, listen, if this is a time machine and it works, why do you say you *think* you invent them? If this *is* one—I mean—"

The voice laughed. "But a time machine is impossible. It is a paradox. Your professors will explain that a time machine cannot be, because it would mean that two things could occupy the same space at the same time. And a man could go back and kill himself when he was younger, and—oh, all sorts of stuff like that. It's completely impossible. Only a crazy man could—"

"But you say this *is* one. Uh ... where is it? I mean, where in time."

"Now? It's 1968, of course."

"In— Hey, it's only 1963. Unless you moved it since I got on; did you?"

"No. *I* was in 1968 all along; that's where I was listening to that lecture on the dinosaurs. But you got on back there, five years back. That's because of the warp. The one I'm going to take up with Napo—"

"But where am I ... are we ... now?"

"You're in the same classroom you got on from, Shorty. But five years ahead. If you reach out, you'll see— Try, just to your left, back where you yourself were sitting."

"Uh—would I get my hand back again, or would it be like when I reached into here?"

"It's all right; you'll get it back."

"Well—" said Shorty.

Tentatively, he reached out his hand. It touched something soft that felt like hair. He took hold experimentally and tugged a little.

It jerked suddenly out of his grasp, and involuntarily Shorty jerked his hand back.

"Yow!" said the voice beside him. "That was funny!"

"What ... what happened?" asked Shorty.

"It was a girl, a knockout with red hair. She's sitting in the same seat you were sitting in back there five years ago. You pulled her hair, and you ought to've seen her jump! Listen—"

"Listen to what?"

"Shut up, then, so I can listen—" There was a pause, and the voice chuckled. "The prof is dating her up!"

"Huh?" said Shorty. "Right in class? How—"

"Oh, he just looked back at her when she let out a yip, and told her to stay after class. But from the way he's looking at her, I can guess he's got an ulterior motive. I can't blame him; she's sure a knockout. Reach out and pull her hair again."

"Uh ... well it wouldn't be quite ... uh—"

"That's right," said the voice disgustedly. "I keep forgetting you aren't crazy like me. Must be awful to be normal. Well, let's get out of here. I'm bored. How'd you like to go hunting?"

"Hunting? Well, I'm not much of a shot. Particularly when I can't see anything."

"Oh, it won't be dark if you step out of the apparatus. It's your own world, you know, but it's crazy. I mean, it's an—how would your professor put it?— an illogical aspect of logicality. Anyway, we always hunt with slingshots. It's more sporting."

"Hunt what?"

"Dinosaurs. They're the most fun."

"Dinosaurs! With a slingshot! You're cra— I mean, do you?"

The voice laughed. "Sure, we do. Look, that's what was so funny about what that professor was saying about the saurians. You see, we killed them off. Since I made this time machine, the Jurassic has been our favorite hunting ground. But there may be one or two left for us to hunt. I know a good place for them. This is it."

"This? I thought we were in a classroom in 1968."

"We were, then. Here, I'll inverse the polarity, and you can step right out. Go ahead."

"But—" Shorty said, and then "Well—" and then took a step to his right. Sunlight blinded him.

It was a brighter, more glaring sunlight than he had ever seen or known before, a terrific contrast after the darkness he'd been in. He put his hands over his eyes to protect them, and only slowly was he able to take them away and open his eyes.

Then he saw he was standing on a patch of sandy soil near the shore of a smooth-surfaced lake.

"They come here to drink," said a familiar voice, and Shorty whirled around. The man standing there was a funny-looking little cuss, a good four inches shorter than Shorty, who stood five feet five. He wore shell-rimmed glasses and a small goatee; and his face seemed tiny and wizened under a tall black top hat that was turning greenish with age.

He reached into his pocket and pulled out a small slingshot, but with quite heavy rubber between the prongs. He said, "You can shoot the first one if you want," and held it out.

Shorty shook his head vigorously. "You," he said.

The little man bent down and carefully selected a few stones out of the sand. He pocketed all but one, and fitted that into the leather insert of the slingshot. Then he sat down on a boulder and said, "We needn't hide. They're dumb, those dinosaurs. They'll come right by here."

Shorty looked around him again. There were trees about a hundred yards back from the lake, strange and monstrous trees with gigantic leaves that were a much paler green than any trees he'd ever seen before. Between the trees and the lake were only small, brownish, stunted bushes and a kind of coarse yellow grass.

Something was missing. Shorty suddenly remembered what it was. "Where's the time machine?" he asked.

"Huh? Oh, right here." The little man reached out a hand to his left and it disappeared up to the elbow.

"Oh," said Shorty. "I wondered what it looked like."

"Looked like?" said the little man. "How could it look like anything? I told you that there isn't any such thing as a time machine. There couldn't be; it would be a complete paradox. Time is a fixed dimension. And when I proved that to myself, that's what drove me crazy."

"When was that?"

"About four million years from now, around 1961. I had my heart set on making one, and went batty when I couldn't."

"Oh," said Shorty. "Listen, how come I couldn't see you, up there in the future, and I can here? And which world of four million years ago *is* this; yours or mine?"

"The same thing answers both of those questions. This is neutral ground; it's before there was a bifurcation of sanity and insanity. The dinosaurs are awfully dumb; they haven't got brains enough to be insane, let alone normal. They don't know from anything. They don't know there couldn't be a time machine. That's why we can come here."

"Oh," said Shorty again. And that held him for a while. Somehow it didn't seem particularly strange any more that he should be waiting to see a dinosaur hunted with a slingshot. The mad part of it was that he should be waiting for a dinosaur *at all*. Granting that, it wouldn't have seemed any sillier to have sat here waiting for one with a— "Say," he said, "if using a slingshot on those things is sporting, did you ever try a fly swatter?"

The little man's eyes lighted up. "That," he said, "*is* an idea. Say, maybe you really *are* eligible for—"

"No," said Shorty hastily. "I was just kidding, honest. But, listen—"

"I don't hear anything."

"I don't mean that; I mean—well, listen, pretty soon I'm going to wake up or something, and there are a couple questions I'd like to ask while ... while you're still here."

"You mean while *you're* still here," said the little man. "I told you that your getting in on this with me was a pure accident, and one moreover that I'm going to have to take up with Napo—"

"Damn Napoleon," said Shorty. "Listen, can you answer this so I can understand it? *Are* we here, or *aren't* we? I mean, if there's a time machine there by you, how can it be there if there can't be a time machine? And am I, or am I not, still back in Professor Dolohan's classroom, and if I am, what am I doing here? And—oh, darn it; what's it all about?"

The little man smiled wistfully. "I can see that you are quite thoroughly mixed up. I might as well straighten you out. Do you know anything about logic?"

"Well, a little, Mr. ... uh—"

"Call me Dopey. And if you know a little about logic, *that's your trouble.* Just forget it and remember that I'm crazy, and that makes things different, doesn't it? A crazy person doesn't have to be logical. Our worlds are different, don't you see? Now you're what we call a normal; that is, you see things the same as everybody else. But we don't. And since matter is most obviously a mere concept of mind—"

"Is it?"

"Of course."

"But *that's* according to logic. Descartes—"

The little man waved his slingshot airily. "Oh, yes. But not according to other philosophers. The dualists. That's where the logicians cross us up. They divide into two camps and take diametrically opposite sides of a question, and they can't both be wrong. Silly, isn't it? But the fact remains that matter is a concept of consciousness, even if some people who aren't really crazy think it is. Now there is a normal concept of matter, which you share, and a whole flock of abnormal ones. The abnormal ones sort of get together."

"I don't quite understand. You mean that you have a secret society of ... uh ... lunatics, who ... uh ... live in a different world, as it were?"

"Not as it were," corrected the little man emphatically, "but *as it weren't.* And it isn't a secret society, or anything organized that way. It just *is.* We project into two universes, in a manner of speaking. One is normal; our bodies are born there, and of course, they stay there. And if we're crazy enough to attract attention, we get put into asylums there. But we have another existence, in our minds. That's where I am, and that's where you are at the moment, in my mind. I'm not really here, either."

"Whew!" said Shorty. "But how *could* I be in your—"

"I told you; the machine slipped. But logic hasn't much place in my world. A paradox more or less doesn't matter, and a time machine is a mere bagatelle. Lots of us have them. Lots of us have come back here hunting with them. That's how we killed off the dinosaurs and that's why—"

"Wait," said Shorty. "Is this world we're sitting in, the Jurassic, part of your ... uh ... concept, or is it real? It looks real, and it looks authentic."

"This is real, but it never really existed. That's obvious. If matter is a concept of mind, and the saurians hadn't any minds, then how could they have had a world to live in, except that we thought it up for them afterward?"

"Oh," said Shorty weakly. His mind was going in buzzing circles. "You mean that the dinosaurs never really—"

"Here comes one," said the little man.

Shorty jumped. He looked around wildly and couldn't see anything that looked like a dinosaur.

"Down there," said the little man, "coming through these bushes. Watch this shot."

Shorty looked down as his companion raised the slingshot. A small lizardlike creature, but hopping erect as no lizard hops, was coming around one of the stunted bushes. It stood about a foot and a half high.

There was a sharp pinging sound as the rubber snapped, and a thud as the stone hit the creature between the eyes. It dropped, and the little man went over and picked it up. "You can shoot the next one," he said.

Shorty gawked at the dead saurian. "A struthiomimus!" he said. "Golly. But what if a big one comes along? A brontosaurus, say, or a tyrannosaurus rex?"

"They're all gone. We killed them off. There's only the little ones left, but it's better than hunting rabbits, isn't it? Well, one's enough for me this time. I'm getting bored, but I'll wait for you to shoot one if you want to."

Shorty shook his head. "Afraid I couldn't aim straight enough with that slingshot. I'll skip it. Where's the time machine?"

"Right here. Take two steps ahead of you."

Shorty did, and the lights went out again.

"Just a minute," said the little man's voice, "I'll set the levers. And you want off where you got on?"

"Uh ... it might be a good idea. I might find myself in a mess otherwise. Where are we now?"

"Back in 1968. That guy is still telling his class what *he* thinks happened to the dinosaurs. And that red-headed girl— Say, she really *is* a honey. Want to pull her hair again?"

"No," said Shorty. "But I want off in 1963. How's this going to get me there?"

"You got on here, from 1963, didn't you? It's the warp. I think this will put you off just right."

"You *think?*" Shorty was startled. "Listen, what if I get off the day before and sit down on my own lap in that classroom?"

The voice laughed. "You couldn't do that; you're not crazy. But I did, once. Well, get going. I want to get back to—"

"Thanks for the ride," said Shorty. "But—wait—I still got one question to ask. About those dinosaurs."

"Yes? Well, hurry; the warp might not hold."

"The big ones, the really big ones. How the devil did you kill *them* with slingshots? Or did you?"

The little man chuckled. "Of course we did. We just used bigger slingshots, that's all. Goodby."

Shorty felt a push, and light blinded him again. He was standing in the aisle of the classroom.

"Mr. McCabe," said the sarcastic voice of Professor Dolohan, "class is not dismissed for five minutes yet. Will you be so kind as to resume your seat? And were you, may I ask, somnambulating?"

Shorty sat down hastily. He said, "I ... uh— Sorry, Professor."

He sat out the rest of the period in a daze. It had seemed too vivid for a dream, and his fountain pen was still gone. But, of course, he could have lost that elsewhere. But the whole thing had been so vivid that it was a full day before he could convince himself that he'd dreamed it, and a week before he could forget about it, for long at a time.

Only gradually did the memory of it fade. A year later, he still vaguely remembered that he'd had a particularly screwy dream. But not five years later; no dream is remembered that long.

He was an associate professor now, and had his own class in paleontology. "The saurians," he was telling them, "died out in the late Jurassic age. Becoming too large and unwieldy to supply themselves with food—"

As he talked, he was staring at the pretty red-headed graduate student in the back row. And wondering how he could get up the nerve to ask her for a date.

There was a blue bottle fly in the room; it had risen in a droning spiral from a point somewhere at the back of the room. It reminded Professor McCabe of something, and while he talked, he tried to remember what it was. And just then the girl in the back row jumped suddenly and yipped.

"Miss Willis," said Professor McCabe, "is something wrong?"

"I ... I thought something pulled my hair, Professor," she said. She blushed, and that made her more of a knockout than ever. "I ... I guess I must have dozed off."

He looked at her—severely, because the eyes of the class were upon him. But this was just the chance he'd been waiting and hoping for. He said, "Miss Willis, will you please remain after class?"

And the Gods Laughed

You know how it is when you're with a work crew on one of the asteroids. You're there, stuck for the month you signed up for, with four other guys and nothing to do but talk. Space on the little tugs that you go in and return in, and live in while you're there, is at such a premium that there isn't room for a book or a magazine nor equipment for games. And you're out of radio range except for the usual once-a-terrestrial-day, system-wide newscasts.

So talking is the only indoor sport you can go in for. Talking and listening. You've plenty of time for both because a work-day, in space-suits, is only four hours and that with four fifteen-minute back-to-the-ship rests.

Anyway, what I'm trying to say is that talk is cheap on one of those work crews. With most of the day to do nothing else, you listen to some real whoppers, stories that would make the old-time Liars Club back on Earth seem like Sunday-school meetings. And if your mind runs that way, you've got plenty of time to think up some yourself.

Charlie Dean was on our crew, and Charlie could tell some dillies. He'd been on Mars back in the old days when there was still trouble with the *bolies,* and when living on Mars was a lot like living on Earth back in the days of Indian fighting. The *bolies* thought and fought a lot like Amerinds, even though they were quadrupeds that looked like alligators on stilts—if you can picture an alligator on stilts—and used blow-guns instead of bows and arrows. Or was it crossbows that the Amerinds used against the colonists?

Anyway, Charlie's just finished a whopper that was really too good for the first tryout of the trip. We'd just landed, you see, and were resting up from doing nothing en route, and usually the yarns start off easy and believable and don't work up to real depth-of-space lying until along about the fourth week when everybody's bored stiff.

"So we took this head *bolie,*" Charlie was ending up, "and you know what kind of flappy little ears they've got, and we put a couple of zircon-studded earrings in its ears and let it go, and back it went to the others, and then darned if—" Well, I won't go on with Charlie's yarn, because it hasn't got anything to do with his story except that it brought earrings into the conversation.

Blake shook his head gloomily and then turned to me. He said, "Hank, what went on on Ganymede? You were on that ship that went out there a few months ago, weren't you—the first one that got through? I've never read or heard much about that trip."

"Me either," Charlie said. "Except that the Ganymedeans turned out to be humanoid beings about four feet tall and didn't wear a thing except earrings. Kind of immodest, wasn't it?"

I grinned. "You wouldn't have thought so if you'd seen the Ganymedeans. With them, it didn't matter. Anyway, they didn't wear earrings."

"You're crazy," Charlie said. "Sure, I know you were on that expedition and I wasn't, but you're still crazy, because I had a quick look at some of the pictures they brought back. The natives wore earrings."

"No," I said. "Earrings wore *them*."

Blake sighed deeply. "I knew it, I knew it," he said. "There was something wrong with this trip from the start. Charlie pops off the first day with a yarn that should have been worked up to gradually. And now you say— Or is there something wrong with my *sense of earring?*"

I chuckled. "Not a thing, Skipper."

Charlie said, "I've heard of men biting dogs, but earrings wearing people is a new one. Hank, I hate to say it—but just consider it said."

Anyway, I had their attention. And now was as good a time as any.

I said, "If you read about the trip, you know we left Earth about eight months ago, for a six-months' round trip. There were six of us in the M-94; me and two others made up the crew and there were three specialists to do the studying and exploring. Not the really top-flight specialists, though, because the trip was too risky to send them. That was the third ship to try for Ganymede and the other two had cracked up on outer Jovian satellites that the observatories hadn't spotted from Earth because they are too small to show up in the scopes at that distance.

"When you get there you find there's practically an asteroid belt around Jupiter, most of them so black they don't reflect light to speak of and you can't see them till they hit you or you hit them. But most of them—"

"Skip the satellites," Blake interrupted, "unless they wore earrings."

"Or unless earrings wore *them*," said Charlie.

"Neither," I admitted. "All right, so we were lucky and got through the belt. And landed. Like I said, there were six of us. Lecky, the biologist. Haynes geologist and mineralogist. And Hilda Race, who loved little flowers and was a botanist, egad! You'd have loved Hilda—at a distance. Somebody must have wanted to get rid of her, and sent her on that trip. She gushed; you know the type.

"And then there was Art Willis and Dick Carney. They gave Dick a skipper's rating for the trip; he knew enough astrogation to get us through. So Dick was skipper and Art and I were flunkies and gunmen. Our main job was to go along with the specialists whenever they left the ship and stand guard over them against whatever dangers might pop up."

"And did anything pop?" Charlie demanded.

"I'm coming to that," I told him. "We found Ganymede not so bad, as places go. Gravity low, of course, but you could get around easily and keep your balance once you got used to it. And the air was breathable for a couple of hours; after that you found yourself panting like a dog.

"Lot of funny animals, but none of them were very dangerous. No reptilian life; all of it mammalian, but a funny kind of mammalian if you know what I mean."

Blake said, "I don't want to know what you mean. Get to the natives and the earrings."

I said, "But of course with animals like that, you never *know* whether they're dangerous until you've been around them for a while. You can't judge by size or looks. Like if you'd never seen a snake, you'd never guess that a little coral snake was dangerous, would you? And a Martian zeezee looks for all the world like an overgrown guinea pig. But without a gun—or with one, for that matter—I'd rather face a grizzly bear or a—"

"The earrings," said Blake. "You were talking about earrings."

I said, "Oh, yes; earrings. Well, the natives wore them—for now, I'll put it that way, to make it easier to tell. One earring apiece, even though they had two ears. Gave them a sort of lopsided look, because they were pretty fair-sized earrings—like hoops of plain gold, two or three inches in diameter.

"Anyway, the tribe we landed near wore them that way. We could see the village—a very primitive sort of place made of mud huts—from where we landed. We had a council of war and decided that three of us would stay in the ship and the other three go to the village. Lecky, the biologist, and Art Willis and I with guns. We didn't know what we might run into, see? And Lecky was chosen because he was pretty much of a linguist. He had a flair for languages and could talk them almost as soon as he heard them.

"They'd heard us land and a bunch of them—about forty, I guess—met us halfway between the ship and the village. And they were friendly. Funny people. Quiet and dignified and acting not at all like you'd expect savages to act toward people landing out of the sky. You know how most primitives re-act—either they practically worship you or else they try to kill you.

"We went to the village with them—and there were about forty more of them there; they'd split forces just as we did, for the reception committee. Another sign of intelligence. They recognized Lecky as leader, and started jab-bering to him in a lingo that sounded more like a pig grunting than a man talking. And pretty soon Lecky was making an experimental grunt or two in return.

"Everything seemed on the up and up, and no danger. And they weren't paying much attention to Art and me, so we decided to wander off for a stroll around the village to see what the country was like and whether there were any dangerous beasties or what-not. We didn't see any animals, but we did see another native. He acted different from the others—very different. He threw a spear at us and then ran. And it was Art who noticed that this native didn't wear an earring.

"And then breathing began to get a bit hard for us—we'd been away from the ship over an hour—so we went back to the village to collect Lecky and take him to the ship. He was getting along so well that he hated to leave, but he was starting to pant, too, so we talked him into it. He was wearing one of the earrings, and said they'd given it to him as a present, and he'd made them a return present of a pocket slide-rule he happened to have with him.

"'Why a slide-rule?' I asked him. 'Those things cost money and we've got plenty of junk that would make them happier.'

"'That's what you think,' he said. 'They figured out how to multiply and divide with it almost as soon as I showed it to them. I showed them how to extract square roots, and I was starting on cube roots when you fellows came back.'

"I whistled and took a close look to see if maybe he was kidding me. He didn't seem to be. But I noticed that he was walking strangely and—well, acting just a bit strangely, somehow, although I couldn't put my finger on what it was. I decided finally that he was just a bit over-excited. This was Lecky's first trip off Earth, so that was natural enough.

"Inside the ship, as soon as Lecky got his breath back—the last hundred yards pretty well winded us—he started in to tell Haynes and Hilda Race about the Ganymedeans. Most of it was too technical for me, but I got that they had some strange contradictions in them. As far as their way of life was concerned, they were more primitive than Australian bushmen. But they had brains and a philosophy and a knowledge of mathematics and pure science. They'd told him some things about atomic structure that excited hell out of him. He was in a dither to get back to Earth where he could get at equipment to check some of those things.

"And he said the earring was a sign of membership in the tribe—they'd acknowledged him as a friend and compatriot and what-not by giving it to him."

Blake asked, "Was it gold?"

"I'm coming to that," I told him. I was feeling cramped from sitting so long in one position on the bunk, and I stood up and stretched.

There isn't much room to stretch in an asteroid tug and my hand hit against the pistol resting in the clips on the wall. I said, "What's the pistol for, Blake?"

He shrugged. "Rules. Has to be one hand weapon on every space-craft. Heaven knows why, on an asteroid ship. Unless the council thinks some day an asteroid may get mad at us when we tow it out of orbit so it cracks up another. Say, did I ever tell you about the time we had a little twenty-ton rock in tow and—"

"Shut up, Blake," Charlie said. "He's just getting to those damn earrings."

"Yeah, the earrings," I said. I took the pistol down from the wall and looked at it. It was an old-fashioned metal project weapon, twenty-shot, circa 2000. It was loaded and usable, but dirty. It hurts me to see a dirty gun.

I went on talking, but I sat back down on the bunk, took an old handkerchief out of my duffle-box and started to clean and polish the hand-gun while I talked.

I said, "He wouldn't let us take the earring off. Acted just a little funny about it when Haynes wanted to analyze the metal. Told Haynes he could get one of his own if he wanted to mess with it. And then he went back to rhapsodizing over the superior knowledge the Ganymedeans had shown.

"Next day all of them wanted to go to the village, but we'd made the rule that not more than three of the six of us would be outside the ship at once, and they'd have to take turns. Since Lecky could talk their grunt-lingo, he and Hilda went first, and Art went along to guard them. Looked safe enough to work that proportion now—two scientists to one guard. Outside of that one native that had thrown a spear at Art and me, there hadn't been a sign of danger. And he'd looked like a half-wit and missed us by twenty feet anyway. We hadn't even bothered to shoot at him.

"They were back, panting for breath, in less than two hours. Hilda Race's eyes were shining and she was wearing one of the rings in her left ear. She looked as proud as though it was a royal crown making her queen of Mars or something. She gushed about it, as soon as she got her wind back and stopped panting.

"I went on the next trip, with Lecky and Haynes.

"Haynes was kind of grumpy, for some reason, and said they weren't going to put one of those rings in his ear, even if he did want one for analysis. They could just hand it to him, or else.

"Again nobody paid much attention to me after we got there, and I wandered around the village. I was on the outskirts of it when I heard a yell—and I ran back to the center of town but fast, because it sounded like Haynes.

"There was a crowd around a spot in the middle of—well, call it the compound. Took me a minute to wedge my way through, scattering natives to all sides as I went. And when I got to the middle of things, Haynes was just getting up, and there was a big stain of red on the front of his white linen coat.

"I grabbed him to help him up, and said, 'Haynes, what's the matter? You hurt?'

"He shook his head slowly, as though he was kind of dazed, and then he said, 'I'm all right, Hank. I'm all right. I just stumbled and fell.' Then he saw me looking at that red stain, and smiled. I guess it was a smile, but it didn't look natural. He said, 'That's not blood, Hank. Some native red wine I happened to spill. Part of the ceremony.'

"I started to ask what ceremony, and then I saw he was wearing one of the gold earrings. I thought that was damn funny, but he started talking to Lecky, and he looked and acted all right—well, fairly all right. Lecky was telling him what a few of the grunts meant, and he acted awful interested—but somehow I got the idea he was pretending most of that interest so he wouldn't have to talk to me. He acted as though he was thinking hard, inside, and maybe he was making up a better story to cover that stain on his clothes and the fact that he'd changed his mind so quick about the earring.

"I was getting the notion that something was rotten in the state of Ganymede, but I didn't know what. I decided to keep my yap shut and my eyes open till I found out.

"I'd have plenty of time to study Haynes later, though, so I wandered off again to the edge of the village and just outside it. And it occurred to me that if there was anything I wasn't supposed to see, I might stand a better chance of seeing it if I got under cover. There were plenty of bushes around and I picked out a good clump of them and hid. From the way my lungs worked, I figured I had maybe a half hour before we'd have to start back for the ship.

"And less than half that time had gone by before I saw something."

I stopped talking to hold the pistol up to the light and squint through the barrel. It was getting pretty clean, but there were a couple of spots left up near the muzzle end.

Blake said, "Let me guess. You saw a Martian traaghound standing on his tail, sing Annie Laurie."

"Worse than that," I said. "I saw one of those Ganymede natives get his legs bit off. And it annoyed him."

"It would annoy anyone," said Blake. "Even me, and I'm a pretty mild-tempered guy. What bit them off?"

"I never found out," I told him. "It was something under water. There was a stream there, going by the village, and there must have been something like crocodiles in it. Two natives came out of the village and started to wade across the stream. About half-way over one of them gave a yelp and went down.

"The other grabbed him and pulled him up on the other bank. And both his legs were gone just above the knees.

"And the damnedest thing happened. The native with his legs off stood up on the stumps of them and started talking—or grunting—quite calmly to his companion, who grunted back. And if tone of voice meant anything, he was annoyed. Nothing more. He tried walking on the stumps of his legs, and found he couldn't go very fast.

"And then he gave a gesture that looked for all the world like a shrug, and reached up and took off his earring and held it out to the other native. And then came the strangest part.

"The other native took it—*and the very instant the ring left the hand of the first one*—the one with his legs off—*he fell down dead.* The other one picked up the corpse and threw it in the water, and went on.

"And as soon as he was out of sight I went back to get Lecky and Haynes and take them to the ship. They were ready to leave when I got there.

"I thought I was worried a bit, but I hadn't seen anything yet. Not till I started back to the ship with Lecky and Haynes. Haynes, first thing I noticed, had the stain gone from the front of his coat. Wine or—whatever it was— somebody'd managed to get it out for him, and the coat wasn't even wet. But it was torn, pierced. I hadn't noticed that before. But there was a place there that looked like a spear had gone through his coat.

"And then he happened to get in front of me, and I saw that there was another tear or rip just like it *in back* of his coat. Taken together, it was like somebody'd pushed a spear through him, from front to back. When he'd yelled.

"But if a spear'd gone through him like that, then he was dead. And there he was walking ahead of me back to the ship. With one of those earrings in his left ear—and I couldn't help but remember about that native and the thing in the river. That native was sure enough dead, too, with his legs off like that, but he hadn't found it out until he'd handed that earring away.

"I can tell you I was plenty thoughtful that evening, watching everybody, and it seemed to me that they were all acting strange. Especially Hilda—you'd have to watch a hippopotamus acting kittenish to get an idea. Haynes and Lecky seemed thoughtful and subdued, like they were planning something, maybe. After a while Art came up from the glory hole and he was wearing one of those rings.

"Gave me a kind of shiver to realize that—if what I was thinking could possibly be true—then there was only me and Dick left. And I'd better start comparing notes with Dick pretty soon. He was working on a report, but I knew pretty soon he'd make his routine inspection trip through the storerooms before turning in, and I'd corner him then.

"Meanwhile, I watched the other four and I got surer and surer. And more and more scared. They were trying their darnedest to act natural, but once in a while one of them would slip. For one thing, they'd *forget to talk*. I mean, one of them would turn to another as though he was saying something, but he wouldn't. And then, as though remembering, he'd start in the middle of it— like he'd been talking without words before, telepathically.

"And pretty soon Dick gets up and goes out, and I followed him. We got to one of the side storerooms and I closed the door. 'Dick,' I asked, 'have you noticed it?' And he wanted to know what I was talking about.

"So I told him. I said, 'Those four people out there—they *aren't the ones we started with*. What happened to Art and Hilda and Lecky and Haynes? What the hell goes on here? Haven't you noticed *anything* out of the ordinary?'

"And Dick sighed, kind of, and said, 'Well, it didn't work. We need more practice, then. Come on and we'll tell you all about it.' And he opened the door and held out his hand to me—and the sleeve of his shirt pulled back a little from the wrist and he was wearing one of those gold things, like the others, only he was wearing it as a bracelet instead of an earring.

"I—well, I was too dumbfounded to say anything. I didn't take the hand he held out, but I followed him back into the main room. And then—while Lecky, who seemed to be the leader, I think—held a gun on me, they told me about it.

"And it was even screwier, and worse, than I'd dare guess.

"They didn't have any name for themselves, because they had no language—what you'd really call a spoken or written language—of their own. You see, they were telepathic, and you don't need a language for that. If you tried to translate their thought for themselves, the nearest word you could find for it would be 'we'—the first person plural pronoun. Individually, they identified themselves to one another by numbers rather than names.

"And just as they had no language of their own, they had no real bodies of their own, nor active minds of their own. They were parasitic in a sense that earthmen can't conceive, They were *entities*, apart from— Well, it's difficult to explain, but in a way they had no real existence when not attached to a body they could animate and *think with*. The easiest way to put it is that a detached—

uh—*earring god,* which is what the Ganymedean natives called them—was asleep, dormant, ineffective. Had no power of thought or motion in itself."

Charlie and Blake were looking bewildered. Charlie said, "You're trying to say, Hank, that when one of them came in contact with a person, they took over that person and ran him and thought with his mind but—uh—kept their own identity? And what happened to the person they took over?"

I said, "As near as I could make out, he stayed there, too, as it were, but was dominated by the entity. I mean, there remained all his memories, and his individuality, but something else was in the driver's seat. Running him. Didn't matter whether he was alive or dead, either, as long as his body wasn't in too had shape. Like Haynes—they'd had to kill him to put an earring on him. He was dead, in that if that ring was removed, he'd have fallen flat and never got up again, unless it was put back.

"Like the native whose legs had been cut off. The entity running him had decided the body was no longer practicable for use, so he handed himself back to the other native, see? And they'd find another body in better shape for him to use.

"They didn't tell me where they came from, except that it was outside the solar system, nor just how they got to Ganymede. Not by themselves, though, because they couldn't even exist by themselves. They must have got as far as Ganymede as parasites of visitors that had landed there at some time or other. Maybe millions of years ago. And they couldn't get off Ganymede, of course, till we landed there. Space travel hadn't developed on Ganymede—"

Charlie interrupted me again, "But if they were so smart, why didn't they develop it themselves?"

"They couldn't," I told him. "They weren't any smarter than the minds they occupied. Well, a little smarter, in a way, because they could use those minds to their full capacity and people—Terrestrial or Ganymedean—don't do that. But even the full capacity of the mind of a Ganymedean savage wasn't sufficient to develop a space-ship.

"But now they had *us*—I mean, they had Lecky and Haynes and Hilda and Art and Dick—and they had our space-ship, and they were going to Earth, because they knew all about it and about conditions there from our minds. They planned, simply, to take over Earth and—uh—*run* it. They didn't explain the details of how they propagate, but I gathered that there wouldn't be any shortage of earrings to go around, on Earth. Earrings or bracelets or, however they'd attach themselves.

"Bracelets, probably, or arm or leg bands, because wearing earrings like that would be too conspicuous on Earth, and they'd have to work in secret for a while. Take over a few people at a time, without letting the others know what was going on.

"And Lecky—or the thing that was running Lecky—told me they'd been using me as a guinea pig, that they could have put a ring on me, taken me over, at any time. But they wanted a check on how they were doing at imitating normal people. They wanted to know whether or not I got suspicious and guessed the truth.

"So Dick—or the thing that was running him—had kept himself out of sight under Dick's sleeve, so if I got suspicious of the others, I'd talk it over with Dick—just as I really did do. And that let them know they needed a lot more practice animating those bodies before they took the ship back to Earth to start their campaign there.

"And, well, that was the whole story and they told it to me to watch my reactions, as a normal human. And then Lecky took a ring out of his pocket and held it out toward me with one hand, keeping the pistol on me with the other hand.

"He told me I might as well put it on because if I didn't, he could shoot me first and then put it on me—but that they greatly preferred to take over undamaged bodies and that it would be better for me, too, if I—that is, my body—didn't die first.

"But naturally, I didn't see it that way. I pretended to reach out for the ring, hesitantly, but instead I batted the gun out of his hand, and made a dive for it as it hit the floor.

"I got it, too, just as they all came for me. And I fired three shots into them before I saw that it wasn't even annoying them. The only way you can stop a body animated by one of those rings is to fix it so it can't move, like cutting off the legs or something. A bullet in the heart doesn't worry it.

"But I'd backed to the door and got out of it—out into the Gandymedean night, without even a coat on. It was colder than hell, too. And after I got out there, there just wasn't any place to go. Except back in the ship, and I wasn't going there.

"They didn't come out after me—didn't bother to. They knew that within three hours—four at the outside—I'd be unconscious from insufficient oxygen. If the cold, or something else, didn't get me first.

"Maybe there was some way out, but I didn't see one. I just sat down on a stone about a hundred yards from the ship and tried to think of something I could do. But—"

I didn't go anywhere with the "but—" and there was a moment's silence, and then Charlie said, "Well?"

And Blake said, "What did you do?"

"Nothing," I said. "I couldn't think of a thing to do. I just sat there."

"Till morning?"

"No. I lost consciousness before morning. I came to while it was still dark, in the ship."

Blake was looking at me with a puzzled frown. He said, "The hell. You mean—"

And then Charlie let out a sudden yip and dived headfirst out of the bunk he'd been lying on, and grabbed the gun out of my hand. I'd just finished cleaning it and slipped the cartridge-clip back in.

And then, with it in his hand, he stood there staring at me as though he'd never seen me before.

Blake said, "Sit down, Charlie. Don't you know when you're being ribbed? But—uh—better keep the gun, just the same."

Charlie kept the gun all right, and turned it around to point at me. He said, "I'm making a damn fool out of myself all right, but—Hank, *roll up your sleeves.*"

I grinned and stood up. I said, "Don't forget my ankles, too."

But there was something dead serious in his face, and I didn't push him too far. Blake said, "He could even have it on him somewhere else, with adhesive tape. I mean on the million-to-one chance that he wasn't kidding."

Charlie nodded without turning to look at Blake. He said, "Hank, I hate to ask it, but—"

I sighed, and then chuckled. I said, "Well, I was just going to take a shower anyway."

It was hot in the ship, and I was wearing only shoes and a pair of coveralls. Paying no attention to Blake and Charlie, I slipped them off and stepped through the oilsilk curtains of the little shower cubicle. And turned on the water.

Over the sound of the shower, I could hear Blake laughing and Charlie cursing softly to himself.

And when I came out of the shower, drying myself, even Charlie was grinning. Blake said, "And I thought that yarn Charlie just told was a dilly. This trip is backwards; we'll end up having to tell each other the truth."

There was a sharp rapping on the hull beside the airlock, and Charlie Dean went to open it. He growled, "If you tell Zeb and Ray what chumps you made out of us, I'll beat your damn ears in. You and your earring gods ..."

Portion of telepathic report of No. 67843, on Asteroid—J-864A to No. 5463, on Terra:

"As planned, I tested credulity of terrestrial minds by telling them the true story of what happened on Ganymede.

Found them capable of acceptance thereof.

This proves that our idea of embedding ourselves within the flesh of these terrestrial creatures was an excellent one and is essential to the success of our plan. True, this is less simple than our method on Ganymede, but we must continue to perform the operation upon each terrestrial being as we take him over. Bracelets or other appendages would arouse suspicion.

There is no necessity in wasting a month here. I shall now take command of the ship and return. We will report no ore present here. The four of us who will animate the four terrestrials now aboard this ship will report to you from Terra ..."

Nothing Sirius

Happily, I was taking the last coins out of our machines and counting them while Ma entered the figures in the little red book as I called them out. Nice figures they were.

Yes, we'd had a good play on both of the Sirian planets, Thor and Freda. Especially on Freda. Those little Earth colonies out there are starved to death for entertainment of any kind, and money doesn't mean a thing to them. They'd stood in line to get into our tent and push their coins into our machines—so even with the plenty high expenses of the trip we'd done all right by ourselves.

Yes, they were right comforting, those figures Ma was entering. Of course she'd add them up wrong, but then Ellen would straighten it out when Ma finally gave up. Ellen's good at figures. And got a good one herself, even if I do say it of my only daughter. Credit for that goes to Ma anyway, not to me. I'm built on the general lines of a space tug.

I put back the coin box of the Rocket-Race and looked up. "Ma—" I started to say. Then the door of the pilot's compartment opened and John Lane stood there. Ellen, across the table from Ma, put down her book and looked up too. She was all eyes and they were shining.

Johnny saluted smartly, the regulation salute which a private ship pilot is supposed to give the owner and captain of the ship. It always got under my skin, that salute, but I couldn't talk him out of it because the rules said he should do it.

He said, "Object ahead, Captain Wherry."

"Object?" I queried. "What kind of object?"

You see, from Johnny's voice and Johnny's face you couldn't guess whether it meant anything or not. Mars City Polytech trains 'em to be strictly deadpan and Johnny had graduated magna cum laude. He's a nice kid but he'd announce the end of the world in the same tone of voice he'd use to announce dinner, if it was a pilot's job to announce dinner.

"It seems to be a planet, sir," was all he said.

It took quite a while for his words to sink in.

"A planet?" I asked, not particularly brilliantly. I stared at him, hoping that he'd been drinking or something. Not because I had any objections to his seeing a planet sober, but because if Johnny ever unbent to the stage of taking a few drinks, the alky would probably dissolve some of the starch out of his backbone. Then I'd have someone to swap stories with. It gets lonesome traveling through space with only two women and a Polytech grad who follows all the rules.

"A planet, sir. An object of planetary dimensions, I should say. Diameter about three thousand miles, distance two million, course apparently an orbit about the star Sirius A."

"Johnny," I said, "we're inside the orbit of Thor, which is Sirius *I*, which means it's the first planet of Sirius, and how can there be a planet inside of that? You wouldn't be kidding me, Johnny?"

"You may inspect the viewplate, sir, and check my calculations," he replied stiffly.

I got up and went into the pilot's compartment. There was a disk in the center of the forward viewplate, all right. Checking his calculations was something else again. My mathematics end at checking coins out of coin machines. But I was willing to take his word for the calculations. "Johnny," I almost shouted, "we've discovered a new planet! Ain't that something?"

"Yes, sir," he commented, in his usual matter-of-fact voice.

It was something, but not too much. I mean, the Sirius system hasn't been colonized long and it wasn't too surprising that a little three-thousand-mile planet hadn't been noticed yet. Especially as (although this wasn't known then) its orbit is very eccentric.

There hadn't been room for Ma and Ellen to follow us into the pilot's compartment, but they stood looking in, and I moved to one side so they could see the disk in the viewplate.

"How soon do we get there, Johnny?" Ma wanted to know.

"Our point of nearest approach on this course will be within two hours, Mrs. Wherry," he replied. "We come within half a million miles of it."

"Oh, *do* we?" I wanted to know.

"Unless, sir, you think it advisable to change course and give it more clearance."

I gave clearance to my throat instead and looked at Ma and Ellen and saw that it would be okay by them. "Johnny," I said, "we're going to give it *less* clearance. I've always hankered to see a new planet untouched by human hands. We're going to land there, even if we can't leave the ship without oxygen masks."

He said, "Yes, sir," and saluted, but I thought there was a bit of disapproval in his eyes. Oh, if there had been, there was cause for it. You never know what you'll run into busting into virgin territory out here. A cargo of canvas and slot machines isn't the proper equipment for exploring, is it?

But the Perfect Pilot never questions an owner's orders, doggone him! Johnny sat down and started punching keys on the calculator and we eased out to let him do it.

"Ma," I said, "I'm a blamed fool."

"You would be if you weren't," she came back. I grinned when I got that sorted out, and looked at Ellen.

But she wasn't looking at me. She had that dreamy look in her eyes again. It made me want to go into the pilot's compartment and take a poke at Johnny to see if it would wake him up. "Listen, honey," I said, "that Johnny—"

But something burned the side of my face and I knew it was Ma looking at me, so I shut up. I got out a deck of cards and played solitaire until we landed.

Johnny popped out of the pilot's compartment and saluted. "Landed, sir," he said. "Atmosphere one-oh-sixteen on the gauge."

"And what," Ellen asked, "does that mean in English?"

"It's breathable, Miss Wherry. A bit high in nitrogen and low in oxygen compared to Earth air, but nevertheless definitely breathable."

He was a caution, that young man was, when it came to being precise.

"Then what are we waiting for?" I wanted to know.

"Your orders, sir."

"Shucks with my orders, Johnny. Let's get the door open and get going."

We got the door open. Johnny stepped outside first, strapping on a pair of heatojectors as he went. The rest of us were right behind him.

It was cool outside, but not cold. The landscape looked just like Thor, with bare rolling hills of hard-baked greenish clay. There was plant life, a brownish bushy stuff that looked a little like tumbleweed.

I took a look up to gauge the time and Sirius was almost at zenith, which meant Johnny had landed us smack in the middle of the day side. "Got any idea, Johnny," I asked, "what the period of rotation is?"

"I had time only for a rough check, sir. It came out twenty-one hours and seventeen minutes."

Rough check, he had said.

Ma said, "That's rough enough for us. Gives us a full afternoon for a walk, and what are we waiting for?"

"For the ceremony, Ma," I told her. "We got to name the place, don't we? And where did you put that bottle of champagne we were saving for my birthday? I reckon this is a more important occasion than that is."

She told me where, and I went and got it and some glasses.

"Got any suggestions for a name, Johnny? You saw it first."

"No, sir."

I said, "Trouble is that Thor and Freda are named wrong now. I mean, Thor is Sirius *I* and Freda is Sirius *II,* and since this orbit is inside theirs, they ought to be II and III respectively. Or else this ought to be Sirius 0. Which means it's Nothing Sirius."

Ellen smiled and I think Johnny would have except that it would have been undignified.

But Ma frowned. "William—" she said, and would have gone on in that vein if something hadn't happened.

Something looked over the top of the nearest hill. Ma was the only one facing that way and she let out a whoop and grabbed me. Then we all turned and looked.

It was the head of something that looked like an ostrich, only it must have been bigger than an elephant. Also there was a collar and a blue polka-dot bow tie around the thin neck of the critter, and it wore a hat. The hat was bright yellow and had a long purple feather. The thing looked at us a minute, winked quizzically, and then pulled its head back.

None of us said anything for a minute and then I took a deep breath. "That," I said, "tears it, right down the middle. Planet, I dub thee Nothing Sirius."

I bent down and hit the neck of the champagne bottle against the clay and it just dented the clay and wouldn't break. I looked around for a rock to hit it on. There wasn't any rock.

I took out a corkscrew from my pocket and opened the bottle instead. We all had a drink except Johnny, who took only a token sip because he doesn't drink or smoke. Me, I had a good long one. Then I poured a brief libation on the ground and recorked the bottle; I had a hunch that I might need it more than the planet did. There was lots of whiskey in the ship and some Martian greenbrew but no more champagne. I said, "Well, here we go."

I caught Johnny's eye and he said, "Do you think it wise, in view of the fact that there are—uh—inhabitants?"

"Inhabitants?" I said. "Johnny, whatever that thing that stuck its head over the hill was, it wasn't an inhabitant. And if it pops up again, I'll conk it over the head with this bottle."

But just the same, before we started out, I went inside the *Chitterling* and got a couple more heatojectors. I stuck one in my belt and gave Ellen the other; she's a better shot than I am. Ma couldn't hit the side of an administration building with a spraygun, so I didn't give her one.

We started off, and sort of by mutual consent, we went the other direction from where we'd seen the whatever-it-was. The hills all looked alike for a while and as soon as we were over the first one, we were out of sight of the *Chitterling*. But I noticed Johnny studying a wrist-compass every couple of minutes, and I knew he'd know the way home.

Nothing happened for three hills and then Ma said, "Look," and we looked.

About twenty yards to our left there was a purple bush. There was a buzzing sound coming from it. We went a little closer and saw that the buzzing came from a lot of things that were flying around the bush. They looked like birds until you looked a second time and then you saw that their wings weren't moving. But they zoomed up and down and around just the same. I tried to look at their heads, but where the heads ought to be there was only a blur. A circular blur.

"They got propellers," Ma said. "Like old-fashioned airplanes used to have."

It did look that way.

I looked at Johnny and he looked at me and we started over toward the bush. But the birds, or whatever, flew away quick, the minute we started toward them. They skimmed off low to the ground and were out of sight in a minute.

We started off again, none of us saying anything, and Ellen came up and walked alongside me. We were just far enough ahead to be out of earshot, and she said, "Pop—"

And didn't go on with it, so I answered, "What, kid?"

"Nothing," she replied sorrowful-like. "Skip it."

So of course I knew what she wanted to talk about, but I couldn't think of anything to say except to cuss out Mars Polytech and that wouldn't have done any good. Mars Polytech is just too good for its own good and so are its ramrods of graduates. After a dozen years or so outside, though, some of them manage to unbend and limber up.

But Johnny hadn't been out that long, by ten years or so. The chance to pilot the *Chitterling* had been a break for him, of course, as his first job. A few years with us and he'd be qualified to skipper something bigger. He'd qualify a lot faster than if he'd had to start in as a minor officer on a bigger ship.

The only trouble was that he was too good-looking, and didn't know it. He didn't know anything they hadn't taught him at Polytech and all they'd taught him was math and astrogation and how to salute, and they hadn't taught him how not to.

"Ellen," I started to say, "don't—"

"Yes, Pop?"

"Uh—nothing. Skip it." I hadn't started to say that at all, but suddenly she grinned at me and I grinned back and it was just like we'd talked the whole thing over. True, we hadn't got anywhere, but then we wouldn't have got anywhere if we had, if you know what I mean.

So just then we came to the top of a small rise, and we stopped because just ahead of us was the blank end of a paved street.

An ordinary everyday plastipaved street just like you'd see in any city on Earth, with curb and sidewalks and gutters and the painted traffic line down the middle. Only it ran out to nowhere, where we stood, and from there at least until it went over the top of the next rise, and there wasn't a house or a vehicle or a creature in sight.

I looked at Ellen and she looked at me and then we both looked at Ma and Johnny Lane, who had just caught up with us. I said, "What is it, Johnny?"

"It seems to be a street, sir."

He caught the look I was giving him and flushed a little. He bent over and examined the paving closely and when he straightened up his eyes were even more surprised.

I queried, "Well, what is it? Caramel icing?"

"It's Permaplast, sir. We aren't the discoverers of this planet because that stuff's a trademarked Earth product."

"Um," I mumbled. "Couldn't the natives here have discovered the same process? The same ingredients might be available."

"Yes, sir. But the blocks are trademarked, if you'll look closely."

"Couldn't the natives have—" Then I shut up because I saw how silly that was. But it's tough to think your party has discovered a new planet and then have Earth-trademarked bricks on the first street you come to. "But what's a street doing here at all?" I wanted to know.

"There's only one way to find out," said Ma sensibly. "And that's to follow it. So what are we standing here for?"

So we pushed on, with much better footing now, and on the next rise we saw a building. A two-story red brick with a sign that read "Bon-Ton Restaurant" in Old English script lettering.

I said, "I'll be a—" But Ma clapped her hand over my mouth before I could finish, which was maybe just as well, for what I'd been going to say had been quite inadequate. There was the building only a hundred yards ahead, facing us at a sharp turn in the street.

I started walking faster and I got there first by a few paces. I opened the door and started to walk in. Then I stopped cold on the doorstep, because there wasn't any "in" to that building. It was a false front, like a cinema set, and all you could see through the door was more of those rolling greenish hills.

I stepped back and looked up at the "Bon-Ton Restaurant" sign, and the others walked up and looked through the doorway, which I'd left open. We just stood there until Ma got impatient and said, "Well, what are you going to do?"

"What do you want me to do?" I wanted to know. "Go in and order a lobster dinner? With champagne?—Hey, I forgot."

The champagne bottle was still in my jacket pocket and I took it out and passed it first to Ma and then to Ellen, and then I finished most of what was left; I must have drunk it too fast because the bubbles tickled my nose and made me sneeze.

I felt ready for anything, though, and I took another walk through the doorway of the building that wasn't there. Maybe, I figured, I could see some indication of how recently it had been put up, or something. There wasn't any indication that I could see. The inside, or rather the back of the front, was smooth and plain like a sheet of glass. It looked like a synthetic of some sort.

I took a look at the ground back of it, but all I could see was a few holes that looked like insect holes. And that's what they must have been, because there was a big black cockroach sitting (or maybe standing; how can you tell whether a cockroach is sitting or standing?) by one of them. I took a step closer and he popped down the hole.

I felt a little better as I went back through the front doorway. I said, "Ma, I saw a cockroach. And do you know what was peculiar about it?"

"What?" she asked.

"Nothing," I told her. "That's the peculiar thing, there was nothing peculiar. Here the ostriches wear hats and the birds have propellers and the streets go nowhere and the houses haven't any backs to them, but that cockroach didn't even have feathers."

"Are you sure?" Ellen wanted to know.

"Sure I'm sure. Let's take the next rise and see what's over it."

We went, and we saw. Down in between that hill and the next, the road took another sharp turn and facing us was the front view of a tent with a big banner that said, "Penny Arcade."

This time I didn't even break stride. I said, "They copied that banner from the show Sam Heideman used to have. Remember Sam, and the good old days, Ma?"

"That drunken no-good," Ma said.

"Why, Ma, you liked him too."

"Yes, and I liked you too, but that doesn't mean that you aren't or he isn't—"

"Why, Ma," I interrupted. But by that time we were right in front of the tent. Looked like real canvas because it billowed gently. I said, "I haven't got the heart. Who wants to look through this time?"

But Ma already had her head through the flap of the tent. I heard her say, "Why, hello Sam, you old soak."

I said, "Ma, quit kidding or I'll—"

But by that time I was past her and inside the tent, and it was a tent, all four sides of one, and a good big one at that. And it was lined with the old familiar coin machines. There, counting coins in the change booth, was Sam Heideman, looking up with almost as much surprise on his face as there must have been on mine.

He said, "Pop Wherry! I'll be a dirty name." Only he didn't say "dirty name"—but he didn't get around to apologizing to Ma and Ellen for that until he and I had pounded each other's backs and he had shaken hands around and been introduced to Johnny Lane.

It was just like old times on the carny lots of Mars and Venus. He was telling Ellen how she'd been "so high" when he'd seen her last and did she really remember him?

And then Ma sniffed.

When Ma sniffs like that, there's something to look at, and I got my eyes off dear old Sam and looked at Ma and then at where Ma was looking. I didn't sniff, but I gasped.

A woman was coming forward from the back of the tent, and when I call her a woman it's because I can't think of the right word if there is one. She was St. Cecilia and Guinevere and a Petty girl all ironed into one. She was like a sunset in New Mexico and the cold silver moons of Mars seen from the Equatorial Gardens. She was like a Venusian valley in the spring and like Dorzalski playing the violin. She was really something.

I heard another gasp from alongside me, and it was unfamiliar. Took me a second to realize why it was unfamiliar; I'd never heard Johnny Lane gasp before. It was an effort, but I shifted my eyes for a look at his face. And I thought, "Oh—oh. Poor Ellen." For the poor boy was gone, no question about it.

And just in time—maybe seeing Johnny helped me—I managed to remember that I'm pushing fifty and happily married. I took hold of Ma's arm and hung on. "Sam," I said, "what on Earth—I mean on whatever planet this is—"

Sam turned around and looked behind him. He said, "Miss Ambers, I'd like you to meet some old friends of mine who just dropped in. Mrs. Wherry, this is Miss Ambers, the movie star. "

Then he finished the introductions, first Ellen, then me, and then Johnny. Ma and Ellen were much too polite. Me, I maybe went the other way by pretending not to notice the hand Miss Ambers held out. Old as I am, I had a hunch I might forget to let go if I took it. That's the kind of girl she was.

Johnny did forget to let go.

Sam was saying to me, "Pop, you old pirate, what are you doing here? I thought you stuck to the colonies, and I sure didn't look for you to drop in on a movie set."

"A movie set?" Things were beginning to make sense, almost.

"Sure. Planetary Cinema, Inc. With me as the technical advisor on carny scenes. They wanted inside shots of a coin arcade, so I just brought my old stuff out of storage and set it up here. All the boys are over at the base camp now."

Light was just beginning to dawn on me. "And that restaurant front up the street? That's a set?" I queried.

"Sure, and the street itself. They didn't need it, but they had to film the making of it for one sequence."

"Oh." I went on, "But how about the ostrich with the bow tie and the birds with the propellers? They couldn't have been movie props. Or could they?" I'd heard that Planetary Cinema did some pretty impossible things.

Sam shook his head blankly. "Nope. You must have come across some of the local fauna. There are a few but not many, and they don't get in the way."

Ma said, "Look here, Sam Heideman, how come if this planet has been discovered we hadn't heard about it? How long has it been known, and what's it all about?"

Sam chuckled. "A man named Wilkins discovered this planet ten years ago. Reported it to the Council, but before it got publicized Planetary Cinema got wind of it and offered the Council a whopping rental for the place on the condition that it be kept secret. As there aren't any minerals or anything of value here and the soil ain't worth a nickel, the Council rented it to them on those terms."

"But why secret?"

"No visitors, no distractions, not to mention a big jump on their competitors. All the big movie companies spy on one another and swipe one another's ideas. Here they got all the space they want and can work in peace and privacy."

"What'll they do about our finding the place?" I asked.

Sam chuckled again. "Guess they'll entertain you royally now that you're here and try to persuade you to keep it under your hat. You'll probably get a free pass for life to all Planetary Cinema theaters too."

He went over to a cabinet and came back with a tray of bottles and glasses. Ma and Ellen declined, but Sam and I had a couple apiece and it was good stuff. Johnny and Miss Ambers were over in a corner of the tent whispering together earnestly, so we didn't bother them, especially after I told Sam that Johnny didn't drink.

Johnny still had hold of her hand and was gazing into her eyes like a sick pup. I noticed that Ellen moved around so she was facing the other way and didn't have to watch. I was sorry for her, but there wasn't anything I could do. Something like that happens if it happens. And if it hadn't been for Ma—

But I saw that Ma was getting edgy and I said we'd better get back to the ship and get dressed up if we were due to be entertained royally. Then we could move the ship in closer. I reckoned we could spare a few days on Nothing Sirius. I left Sam in stitches by telling him how we'd named the planet that after a look at the local fauna.

Then I gently pried Johnny loose from the movie star and led him outside. It wasn't easy. There was a blank, blissful expression on his face, and he'd even forgotten to salute me when I'd spoken to him. Hadn't called me "sir" either. In fact, he didn't say anything at all.

Neither did any of the rest of us, walking up the street.

There was something knocking at my mind and I couldn't quite figure out what it was. There was something wrong, something that didn't make sense.

Ma was worried too. Finally I heard her say, "Pop, if they really want to keep this place a secret, wouldn't they maybe—uh—"

"No, they wouldn't," I answered, maybe a bit snappishly. That wasn't what I was worried about, though.

I looked down at that new and perfect road, and there was something about it I didn't like. I diagonaled over to the curb and walked along that, looked down at the greenish clay beyond, but there wasn't anything to see except more holes and more bugs like I'd seen back at the Bon-Ton Restaurant.

Maybe they weren't cockroaches, though, unless the movie company had brought them. But they were near enough like cockroaches for all practical purposes—if a cockroach has a practical purpose, that is. And they still didn't have bow ties or propellers or feathers. They were just plain cockroaches.

I stepped off the paving and tried to step on one or two of them, but they got away and popped into holes. They were plenty fast and shifty on their feet.

I got back on the road and walked with Ma. When she asked, "What were you doing?" I answered, "Nothing."

Ellen was walking on the other side of Ma and keeping her face a studious blank. I could guess what she was thinking and I wished there was something could be done about it. The only thing I could think of was to decide to stay on Earth a while at the end of this trip, and give her a chance to get over Johnny by meeting a lot of other young sprigs. Maybe even finding one she liked.

Johnny was walking along in a daze. He was gone all right, and he'd fallen with awful suddenness, like guys like that always do. Maybe it wasn't love, just infatuation, but right now he didn't know what planet he was on.

We were over the first rise now, out of sight of Sam's tent.

"Pop, did you see any movie cameras around?" Ma asked suddenly.

"Nope, but those things cost millions. They don't leave them setting around loose when they're not being used."

Ahead of us was the front of that restaurant. It looked funny as the devil from a side view, walking toward it from that direction. Nothing in sight but that, the road and green clay hills.

There weren't any cockroaches on the street, and I realized that I'd never seen one there. It seemed as though they never got up on it or crossed it. Why would a cockroach cross the road? To get on the other side?

There was still something knocking at my mind, something that made less sense than anything else.

It got stronger and stronger and it was driving me as crazy as it was. I got to wishing I had another drink. The sun Sirius was getting down toward the horizon, but it was still plenty hot. I even began to wish I had a drink of water.

Ma looked tired too. "Let's stop for a rest," I said, "we're about halfway back."

We stopped. It was right in front of the Bon-Ton and I looked up at the sign and grinned. "Johnny, will you go in and order dinner for us?"

He saluted and replied, "Yes, sir," and started for the door. He suddenly got red in the face and stopped. I chuckled but I didn't rub it in by saying anything else.

Ma and Ellen sat down on the curb.

I walked through the restaurant door again and it hadn't changed any. Smooth like glass on the other side. The same cockroach—I guess it was the same one—was still sitting or standing by the same hole.

I said, "Hello, there," but it didn't answer, so I tried to step on it but again it was too fast for me. I noticed something funny. It had started for the hole the second I decided to step on it, even before I had actually moved a muscle.

I went back through to the front again, and leaned against the wall. It was nice and solid to lean against. I took a cigar out of my pocket and started to light it, but I dropped the match. *Almost*, I knew what was wrong.

Something about Sam Heideman.

"Ma," I said, "isn't Sam Heideman—dead?"

And then, with appalling suddenness I wasn't leaning against a wall any more because the wall just wasn't there and I was falling backward.

I heard Ma yell and Ellen squeal.

I picked myself up off the greenish clay. Ma and Ellen were getting up too, from sitting down hard on the ground because the curb they'd been sitting on wasn't there any more either. Johnny was staggering a bit from having the road disappear under the soles of his feet, and dropping a few inches.

There wasn't a sign anywhere of road or restaurant, just the rolling green hills. And—yes, the cockroaches were still there.

The fall had jolted me plenty, and I was mad. I wanted something to take out my mad on. There were only cockroaches. They hadn't gone up into nothingness like the rest of it. I made another try at the nearest one, and missed again. This time I was positive that he'd moved before I did.

Ellen looked down at where the street ought to be, at where the restaurant front ought to be, and then back the way we'd come as though wondering if the Penny Arcade tent was still there.

"It isn't," I said.

Ma asked, "It isn't what?"

"Isn't there," I explained.

Ma glowered at me. "What isn't where?"

"The tent," I said, a bit peeved. "The movie company. The whole she-bang. And especially Sam Heideman. It was when I remembered about Sam Heideman—five years ago in Luna City we heard he was dead—so he wasn't there. None of it was there. And the minute I realized that, they pulled it all out from under us."

"'They?' What do you mean, 'they,' Pop Wherry? Who is 'they'?"

"You mean who *are* 'they'?" I said, but the look Ma gave me made me wince.

"Let's not talk here," I went on. "Let's get back to the ship as quick as we can, first. You can lead us there, Johnny, without the street?"

He nodded, forgetting to salute or "sir" me. We started off, none of us talking. I wasn't worried about Johnny getting us back; he'd been all right until we'd hit the tent; he'd been following our course with his wrist-compass.

After we got to where the end of the street had been, it got easy because we could see our own footprints in the clay, and just had to follow them. We passed the rise where there had been the purple bush with the propeller birds, but the birds weren't there now, nor was the purple bush.

But the *Chitterling* was still there, thank Heavens. We saw it from the last rise and it looked just as we had left it. It looked like home, and we started to walk faster.

I opened the door and stood aside for Ma and Ellen to go in first. Ma had just started in when we heard the voice. It said, "We bid you farewell."

I said, "We bid you farewell, too. And the hell with you."

I motioned Ma to go on into the ship. The sooner I was out of this place, the better I'd like it.

But the voice said, "Wait," and there was something about it that made us wait. "We wish to explain to you so that you will not return."

Nothing had been further from my mind, but I said, "Why not?"

"Your civilization is not compatible with ours. We have studied your minds to make sure. We projected images from the images we found in your minds, to study your reactions to them. Our first images, our first thought-projections, were confused. But we understood your minds by the time you reached the farthest point of your walk. We were able to project beings similar to yourselves."

"Sam Heideman, yeah," I said. "But how about the da—the woman? She couldn't have been in the memory of any of us because none of us knew her."

"She was a composite—what you would call an idealization. That, however, doesn't matter. By studying you we learned that your civilization concerns itself with things, ours with thoughts. Neither of us has anything to offer the other. No good could come through interchange, whereas much harm might come. Our planet has no material resources that would interest your race."

I had to agree with that, looking out over that monotonous rolling clay that seemed to support only those few tumbleweedlike bushes, and not many of them. It didn't look like it would support anything else. As for minerals, I hadn't seen even a pebble.

"Right you are," I called back. "Any planet that raises nothing but tumbleweeds and cockroaches can keep itself, as far as we're concerned. So—" Then something dawned on me. "Hey, just a minute. There must be something else or who the devil am I talking to?"

"You are talking," replied the voice, "to what you call cockroaches, which is another point of incompatibility between us. To be more precise, you are talking to a thought-projected voice, but we are projecting it. And let me assure you of one thing—that you are more repugnant physically to us than we are to you."

I looked down then and saw them, three of them, ready to pop into holes if I made a move.

Back inside the ship, I said, "Johnny, blast off. Destination, Earth."

He saluted and said, "Yes, sir," and went into the pilot's compartment and shut the door. He didn't come out until we were on an automatic course, with Sirius dwindling behind us.

Ellen had gone to her room. Ma and I were playing cribbage.

"May I go off duty, sir?" Johnny asked, and walked stiffly to his room when I answered, "Sure."

After a while, Ma and I turned in. A while after that we heard noises. I got up to investigate, and investigated.

I came back grinning. "Everything's okay, Ma," I said. "It's Johnny Lane and he's as drunk as a hoot owl!" And I slapped Ma playfully on the fanny.

"Ouch, you old fool," she sniffed. "I'm sore there from the curb disappearing from under me. And what's wonderful about Johnny getting drunk? *You* aren't, are you?"

"No," I admitted, regretfully perhaps. "But, Ma, he told me to go to blazes. And without saluting. Me, the owner of the ship."

Ma just looked at me. Sometimes women are smart, but sometimes they're pretty dumb.

"Listen, he isn't going to keep on getting drunk," I said. "This is an occasion. Can't you see what happened to his pride and dignity?"

"You mean because he—"

"Because he fell in love with the thought-projection of a cockroach," I pointed out. "Or anyway he thought he did. He has to get drunk once to forget that, and from now on, after he sobers up, he's going to be human. I'll bet on it, any odds. And I'll bet too that once he's human, he's going to *see* Ellen and realize how pretty she is. I'll bet he's head-over-heels before we get back to Earth. I'll get a bottle and we'll drink a toast on it. To Nothing Sirius!"

And for once I was right. Johnny and Ellen were engaged before we got near enough to Earth to start decelerating.

The Yehudi Principle

I am going crazy.

Charlie Swann is going crazy, too. Maybe more than I am, because it was his dingbat. I mean, he made it and he thought he knew what it was and how it worked.

You see, Charlie was just kidding me when he told me it worked on the Yehudi principle. Or he thought he was.

"The Yehudi principle?" I said.

"The Yehudi principle," he repeated. "The principle of the little man who wasn't there. He does it."

"Does what?" I wanted to know.

The dingbat, I might interrupt myself to explain, was a headband. In fitted neatly around Charlie's noggin and there was a round black box not much bigger than a pillbox over his forehead. Also there was a round flat copper disk on each side of the band that fitted over each of Charlie's temples, and a strand of wire that ran down behind his ear into the breast pocket of his coat, where there was a little dry cell battery.

It didn't look as if it would do anything, except maybe either cure a headache or make it worse. But from the excited look on Charlie's face, I didn't think it was anything as commonplace as that.

"Does what?" I wanted to know.

"Whatever you want," said Charlie. "Within reason, of course. Not like moving a building or bringing you a locomotive. But any little thing you want done, he does it."

"Who does?"

"Yehudi."

I closed my eyes and counted to five, by ones, I *wasn't* going to ask, "*Who's Yehudi?*"

I shoved aside a pile of papers on the bed—I'd been going through some old clunker manuscripts seeing if I could find something good enough to rewrite from a new angle—and sat down.

"O.K.," I said. "Tell him to bring me a drink."

"What kind?"

I looked at Charlie, and he didn't look like he was kidding. He had to be, of course, but—

"Gin buck," I told him. "A gin buck, with gin in it, if Yehudi knows what I mean."

"Hold out your hand," Charles said.

I held out my hand. Charlie, not talking to me, said, "Bring Hank a gin buck, strong." And then he nodded his head.

Something happened either to Charlie or to my eyes, I didn't know which. For just a second, he got sort of misty. And then he looked normal again.

And I let out a kind of a yip and pulled my hand back, because my hand was wet with something cold. And there was a splashing noise and a wet puddle on the carpet right at my feet. Right under where my hand had been.

Charlie said, "We should have asked for it in a glass."

I looked at Charlie and then I looked at the puddle on the floor and then I looked at my hand. I stuck my index finger gingerly into try mouth and tasted.

Gin buck. With gin in it. I looked at Charlie again.

He asked, "Did I blur?"

"Listen, Charlie," I said. "I've known you for ten years, and we went to Tech together and— But if you pull another gag like that I'll blur you, all right. I'll—"

"Watch closer this time," Charlie said. And again, looking off into space and not talking to me at all, he started talking. "Bring us a fifth of gin, in a bottle. Half a dozen lemons, sliced, on a plate. Two quart bottles of soda and a dish of ice cubes. Put it all on the table over there."

He nodded his head, just like he had before, and darned if he didn't blur. *Blur* was the best word for it.

"You blurred," I said. I was getting a slight headache.

"I thought so," he said. "But I was using a mirror when I tried it alone, and I thought maybe it was my eyes. That's why I came over. You want to mix the drinks or shall I?"

I looked over at the table, and there was all the stuff he'd ordered. I swallowed a couple of times.

"It's real," Charlie said. He was breathing a little hard, with suppressed excitement. "It works, Hank. It *works*. We'll be rich! We can—"

Charlie kept on talking, but I got up slowly and went over to the table. The bottles and lemons and ice were really there. The bottles gurgled when shaken and the ice was cold.

In a minute I was going to worry about how they got there. Meanwhile and right now, I needed a drink. I got a couple of glasses out of the medicine cabinet and the bottle opener out of the file cabinet, and I made two drinks, about half gin.

Then I thought of something. I asked Charlie, "Does Yehudi want a drink, too?"

Charlie grinned. "Two'll be enough," he told me.

"To start with, maybe," I said grimly. I handed him a drink—in a glass— and said, "To Yehudi." I downed mine at a gulp and started mixing another.

Charlie said, "Me, too. Hey, wait a minute."

"Under present circumstances," I said, "a minute is a minute too long between drinks. In a minute I shall wait a minute, but— Hey, why don't we let Yehudi mix 'em for us?"

"Just what I was going to suggest. Look, I want to try something. You put this headband on and tell him to. I want to watch you."

"Me?"

"You," he said. "It can't do any harm, and I want to be sure it works for everybody and not just for me. It may be that it's attuned merely to my brain. You try it."

"Me?" I said.

"You," he told me.

He'd taken it off and was holding it out to me, with the little flat dry cell dangling from it at the end of the wire. I took it and looked it over. It didn't look dangerous. There couldn't possibly be enough juice in so tiny a battery to do any harm.

I put it on.

"Mix us some drinks," I said, and looked over at the table, but nothing happened.

"You got to nod just as you finish," Charlie said. "There's a little pendulum affair in the box over your forehead that works the switch."

I said, "Mix us two gin bucks. In glasses, please." And nodded.

When my head came up again, there were the drinks, mixed.

"Blow me down," I said. And bent over to pick up my drink.

And there I was on the floor.

Charlie said, "Be careful, Hank. If you lean over forward, that's the same as nodding. And don't nod or lean just as you say something you don't mean as an order."

I sat up. "Fan me with a blowtorch," I said.

But I didn't nod. In fact, I didn't move. When I realized what I'd said, I held my neck so rigid that it hurt, and didn't quite breathe for fear I'd swing that pendulum.

Very gingerly, so as not to tilt it, I reached up and took off the headband and put it down on the floor.

Then I got up and felt myself all over. There were probably bruises, but no broken bones. I picked up the drink and drank it. It was a good drink, but I mixed the next one myself. With three-quarters gin.

With it in my hand, I circled around the headband, not coming within a yard of it, and sat down on the bed.

"Charlie," I said, "you've *got* something there. I don't know what it is, but what are we waiting for?"

"Meaning?" said Charlie.

"Meaning what any sensible man would mean. If that darned thing brings anything we ask for, well, let's make it a party. Which would you rather have, Lili St. Cyr or Esther Williams? I'll take the other."

He shook his head sadly. "There are limitations, Hank. Maybe I'd better explain."

"Personally," I said, "I would prefer Lili to an explanation, but go ahead. Let's start with Yehudi. The only two Yehudis I know are Yehudi Menuhin, the violinist, and Yehudi, the little man who wasn't there. Somehow I don't think Menuhin brought us that gin, so—"

"He didn't. For that matter, neither did the little man who wasn't there. I was kidding you, Hank. There isn't any little man who wasn't there."

"Oh," I said. I repeated it slowly, or started to. "There—isn't—any—little—man—who—wasn't—" I gave up. "I think I begin to see," I said. "What you mean is that there wasn't any little man who isn't here. But then, who's Yehudi?"

"There isn't any Yehudi, Hank. But the name, the idea, fitted so well that I called it that for short."

"And what do you call it for long?"

"The automatonic autosuggestive subvibratory superaccelerator."

I drank the rest of my drink.

"Lovely," I said. "I like the Yehudi principle better, though. But there's just one thing. Who brought us that drink-stuff? The gin and the soda and the so forth?"

"I did. And you mixed our second-last, as well as our last drink. Now do you understand?"

"In a word," I said, "not exactly."

Charlie sighed. "A field is set up between the temple-plates which accelerates, several thousand times, the molecular vibration and thereby the speed of organic matter—the brain, and thereby the body. The command given just before the switch is thrown acts as an autosuggestion and you carry out the order you've just given yourself. But so rapidly that no one can see you move; just a momentary blur as you move off and come back in practically the same instant. Is that clear?"

"Sure," I told him. "Except for one thing. Who's Yehudi?"

I went to the table and started mixing two more drinks. Seven-eighths gin.

Charlie said patiently, "The action is so rapid that it does not impress itself upon your memory. For some reason the memory is not affected by the acceleration. The *effect*—both to the user and to the observer—is of the spontaneous obedience of a command by ... well, by the little man who wasn't there."

"Yehudi?"

"Why not?"

"Why not why not?" I asked. "Here, have another drink. It's a bit weak, but so am I. So you got this gin, huh? Where?"

"Probably the nearest tavern. I don't remember."

"Pay for it?"

He pulled out his wallet and opened it. "I think there's a fin missing. I probably left it in the register. My subconscious must be honest."

"But what good is it?" I demanded. "I don't mean your subconscious, Charlie, I mean the Yehudi principle. You could have just as easily bought that gin on the way here. I could just as easily have mixed a drink and known I was doing it. And if you're *sure* it can't go bring us Lili St. Cyr and Esther Williams—"

"It can't. Look, it can't do anything that you yourself can't do. It isn't an it. It's you. Get that through your head, Hank, and you'll understand."

"But what good is it?"

He sighed again. "The real purpose of it is *not* to run errands for gin and mix drinks. That was just a demonstration. The real purpose—"

"Wait," I said. "Speaking of drinks, wait. It's a long time since I had one."

I made the table, tacking only twice, and this time I didn't bother with the soda. I put a little lemon and an ice cube in each glass of gin.

Charlie tasted his and made a wry face.

I tasted mine. "Sour," I said. "I should have left out the lemon. And we better drink them quick before the ice cubes start to melt or they'll be weak."

"The real purpose," said Charlie, "is—"

"Wait," I said. "You could be wrong, you know. About the limitations. I'm going to put that headband on and tell Yehudi to bring us Lili and—"

"Don't be a sap, Hank. I made the thing. I know how it works. You can't get Lili St. Cyr or Esther Williams or Brooklyn Bridge."

"You're positive?"

"Of course."

What a sap I was. I believed him. I mixed two more drinks, using gin and two glasses this time, and then I sat down on the edge of the bed, which was swaying gently from side to side.

"All right," I said. "I can take it now. What is the real purpose of it?"

Charlie Swann blinked several times and seemed to be having trouble bringing his eyes into focus on me. He asked, "The real purpose of what?"

I enunciated slowly and carefully. "Of the automatonic autosuggestive subvibratory superaccelerator. Yehudi, to me."

"Oh, that," said Charlie.

"That," I said. "What is its real purpose?"

"It's like this. Suppose you got something to do that you've got to do in a hurry. Or something that you've got to do, and don't want to do. You could—"

"Like writing a story?" I asked.

"Like writing a story," he said, "or painting a house, or washing a mess of dishes, or shoveling the sidewalk, or ... or doing anything else you've got to do but don't want to do. Look, you put it on and tell yourself—"

"Yehudi," I said.

"Tell Yehudi to do it, and it's done. Sure, you do it, but you don't know that you do, so it doesn't hurt. And it gets done quicker."

"You blur," I said.

He held up his glass and looked through it at the electric light. It was empty. The glass, not the electric light.

He said, "You blur."

"Who?"

He didn't answer. He seemed to be swinging, chair and all, in an arc about a yard long. It made me dizzy to look at him, so I closed my eyes, but that was worse so I opened them again.

I said, "A story?"

"Sure."

"I got to write a story," I said, "but why should I? I mean, why not let Yehudi do it?"

I went over and put on the headband. No extraneous remarks this time, I told myself. Stick to the point.

"Write a story," I said.

I nodded. Nothing happened.

But then I remembered that, as far as I was supposed to know, nothing was supposed to happen. I walked over to the typewriter desk and looked.

There was a white sheet and a yellow sheet in the typewriter, with a carbon between them. The page was about half filled with typing and then down at the bottom were two words by themselves. I couldn't read them. I took my glasses off and still I couldn't, so I put them back on and put my face down within inches of the typewriter and concentrated. The words were "The End."

I looked over alongside the typewriter and there was a neat, but small pile of typed sheets, alternate white and yellow.

It was wonderful. I'd written a story. If my subconscious mind had anything on the ball, it might be the best story I'd ever written.

Too bad I wasn't quite in shape to read it. I'd have to see an optometrist about new glasses. Or something.

"Charlie," I said, "I wrote a story."

"When?"

"Just now."

"I didn't see you."

"I blurred," I said. "But you weren't looking."

I was back, sitting on the bed. I don't remember getting there.

"Charlie," I said, "it's wonderful."

"What's wonderful?"

"Everything. Life. Birdies in the trees. Pretzels. A story in less than a second! One second a week I have to work from now on. No more school, no more books, no more teacher's sassy looks! Charlie, it's *wonderful!*"

He seemed to wake up. He said, "Hank, you're just *beginning* to see the possibilities. They're almost endless, for any profession. Almost *anything.*"

"Except," I said sadly, "Lili St. Cyr and Esther Williams."

"You've got a one-track mind."

"Two-track," I said. "I'd settle for either. Charlie, are you *positive—*"

Wearily, "Yes." Or that was what he meant to say; it came out "Yesh."

"Charlie," I said. "You've been drinking. Care if I *try?*"

"Shoot yourself."

"Huh? Oh, you mean suit yourself. OK, then I'll—"

"Thass what I shaid," Charlie said. "Suit yourshelf."

"You did not."

"What did I shay, then?"

I said, "You shaid—I mean said: 'Shoot yourself.'"

Even Jove nods.

Only Jove doesn't wear a headband like the one I still had on. Or maybe, come to think of it, he does. It would explain a lot of things.

I must have nodded, because there was the sound of a shot.

I let out a yell and jumped up, and Charlie jumped up too. He looked sober.

He said, "Hank, you had that thing on. Are you—?"

I was looking down at myself and there wasn't any blood on the front of my shirt. Nor any pain anywhere. Nor anything.

I quit shaking. I looked at Charlie; he wasn't shot either.

I said, "But who—? What—?"

"Hank," he said. "That shot wasn't in this room at all. It was outside, in the hallway, or on the stair."

"On the *stair?*" Something prickled at the back of my mind. What about a stair? *I saw a man upon the stair, a little man who was not there. He was not there again today. Gee, I wish he'd go away—*

"Charlie," I said. "*It was Yehudi!* He shot himself because I said 'shoot yourself' and the pendulum swung. You were wrong about it being an—an automatonic autosuggestive whatzit. It was Yehudi doing it all the time. It was—"

"Shut up," he said.

But he went over and opened the door and I followed him and we went out in the hallway.

There was a decided smell of burnt powder. It seemed to come from about halfway up the stairs because it got stronger as we neared that point.

"Nobody there," Charlie said, shakily.

In an awed voice I said, "*He was not there again today. Gee, I wish—*"

"Shut up," said Charlie sharply.

We went back into my room.

"Sit down," Charlie said. "We got to figure this out. You said, 'Shoot yourself,' and either nodded or swayed forward. But you didn't shoot yourself. The shot came from—" He shook his head, trying to clear it.

"Let's have some coffee," he suggested. "Some hot, black coffee. Have you got— Hey, you're still wearing that headband. Get us some, but for Heaven's sake be careful."

I said, "Bring us two cups of hot black coffee." And I nodded, but it didn't work. Somehow I'd known it wouldn't.

Charlie grabbed the band off my head. He put it on and tried it himself.

I said, "Yehudi's dead. He shot himself. That thing's no good any more. So I'll make the coffee."

I put the kettle on the hot plate. "Charlie," I said, "look, suppose it *was* Yehudi doing that stuff. Well, how do you know what his limitations were? Look, maybe he *could* have brought us Lili—"

"Shut up," said Charlie. "I'm trying to think."

I shut up and let him think.

And by the time I had the coffee made, I realized how silly I'd been talking.

I brought the coffee. By that time, Charlie had the lid off the pillbox affair and was examining its innards. I could see the little pendulum that worked the switch, and a lot of wires.

He said, "I don't understand it. There's nothing broken."

"Maybe the battery," I suggested.

I got out my flashlight and we used its bulb to test the little dry cell. The bulb burned brightly.

"I don't understand it," Charlie said.

Then I suggested, "Let's start from the beginning, Charlie. It *did* work. It got us stuff for drinks. It mixed one pair of drinks. It— Say—"

"I was just thinking of that," Charlie said. "When you said, 'Blow me down,' and bent over to pick up the drink, what happened?"

"A current of air. It blew me down, Charlie, literally. How could I have done that myself? And notice the difference in pronouns. I said, 'Blow me down,' then but later I said, 'Shoot yourself.' If I'd said, 'Shoot me,' why maybe—"

There was that prickle down my spine again.

Charlie looked dazed. He said, "But I worked it out on scientific principles, Hank. It wasn't just an accident. I couldn't be wrong. You mean you think that— It's utterly silly!"

I'd been thinking just that, again. But differently. "Look," I said, "let's concede that your apparatus set up a field that had an effect upon the brain, but just for argument let's assume you misunderstood the nature of the field. Suppose it enabled you *to project a thought.* And you were thinking about Yehudi; you must have been because you jokingly called it the Yehudi principle, and so Yehudi—"

"That's silly," said Charlie.

"Give me a better one."

He went over to the hot plate for another cup of coffee.

And I remembered something then, and went over to the typewriter table, I picked up the story, shuffling the pages as I picked them up so the first page would come out on top, and I started to read.

I heard Charlie's voice say, "Is it a good story, Hank?"

I said, "G-g-g-g-g-g—"

Charlie took a look at my face and sprinted across the room to read over my shoulder. I handed him the first page The title on it was THE YEHUDI PRINCIPLE.

The story started:

"I am going crazy.

"Charlie Swann is going crazy, too. Maybe more than I am, because it was his dingbat. I mean, he made it and he thought he knew what it was and how it worked."

As I read page after page I handed them to Charlie and he read them too. Yes, it was *this* story. The story you're reading right now, including this part of it that I'm telling right now. Written before the last part of it happened.

Charlie was sitting down when he finished, and so was I.

He looked at me and I looked at him.

He opened his mouth a few times and closed it again twice before he could get anything out. Finally he said, "*T-time*, Hank. It had something to do with *time* too. It wrote in advance just what—Hank, I'll make it work again. I *got* to. It's something big. It's—"

"It's colossal," I said. "But it'll never work again. Yehudi's dead. He shot himself upon the stair."

"You're crazy," said Charlie.

"Not yet," I told him. I looked down at the manuscript he'd handed back to me and read:

"I am going crazy."

I *am* going crazy.

Arena

Carson opened his eyes, and found himself looking upward into a flickering blue dimness.

It was hot, and he was lying on sand, and a sharp rock embedded in the sand was hurting his back. He rolled over to his side, off the rock, and then pushed himself up to a sitting position.

"I'm crazy," he thought. "Crazy—or dead—or something." The sand was blue, bright blue. And there wasn't any such thing as bright blue sand on Earth or any of the planets.

Blue sand.

Blue sand under a blue dome that wasn't the sky nor yet a room, but a circumscribed area—somehow he knew it was circumscribed and finite even though he couldn't see to the top of it.

He picked up some of the sand in his hand and let it run through his fingers. It trickled down onto his bare leg. *Bare?*

Naked. He was stark naked, and already his body was dripping perspiration from the enervating heat, coated blue with sand wherever sand had touched it.

But elsewhere his body was white.

He thought: Then this sand is really blue. If it seemed blue only because of the blue light, then I'd be blue also. But I'm white, so the sand *is* blue. *Blue sand.* There isn't any blue sand. There isn't any place like this place I'm in.

Sweat was running down in his eyes.

It was hot, hotter than hell. Only hell—the hell of the ancients—was supposed to be red and not blue.

But if this place wasn't hell, what was it? Only Mercury, among the planets, had heat like this and this wasn't Mercury. And Mercury was some four billion miles from—

It came back to him then, where he'd been. In the little one-man scouter, outside the orbit of Pluto, scouting a scant million miles to one side of the Earth Armada drawn up in battle array there to intercept the Outsiders.

That sudden strident nerve-shattering ringing of the alarm bell when the rival scouter—the Outsider ship—had come within range of his detectors—

No one knew who the Outsiders were, what they looked like, from what far galaxy they came, other than that it was in the general direction of the Pleiades.

First, sporadic raids on Earth colonies and outposts. Isolated battles between Earth patrols and small groups of Outsider spaceships; battles sometimes won and sometimes lost, but never to date resulting in the capture of an alien vessel. Nor had any member of a raided colony ever survived to describe the Outsiders who had left the ships, if indeed they had left them.

Not a too-serious menace, at first, for the raids had not been too numerous or destructive. And individually, the ships had proved slightly inferior in armament to the best of Earth's fighters, although somewhat superior in speed and maneuverability. A sufficient edge in speed, in fact, to give the Outsiders their choice of running or fighting, unless surrounded.

Nevertheless, Earth had prepared for serious trouble, for a showdown, building the mightiest armada of all time. It had been waiting now, that armada, for a long time. But now the showdown was coming.

Scouts twenty billion miles out had detected the approach of a mighty fleet—a showdown fleet—of the Outsiders. Those scouts had never come back, but their radiotronic messages had. And now Earth's armada, all ten thousand ships and half-million fighting spacemen, was out there, outside Pluto's orbit, waiting to intercept and battle to the death.

And an even battle it was going to be, judging by the advance reports of the men of the far picket line who had given their lives to report before they had died—on the size and strength of the alien fleet.

Anybody's battle, with the mastery of the solar system hanging in the balance, on an even chance. A last and *only* chance, for Earth and all her colonies lay at the utter mercy of the Outsiders if they ran that gauntlet—

Oh yes. Bob Carson remembered now.

Not that it explained blue sand and flickering blueness. But that strident alarming of the bell and his leap for the control panel. His frenzied fumbling as he strapped himself into the seat. The dot in the visiplate that grew larger.

The dryness of his mouth. The awful knowledge that this was *it*. For him, at least, although the main fleets were still out of range of one another.

This, his first taste of battle. Within three seconds or less he'd be victorious, or a charred cinder. Dead.

Three seconds—that's how long a space-battle lasted. Time enough to count to three, slowly, and then you'd won or you were dead. One hit completely took care of a lightly armed and armored little one-man craft like a scouter.

Frantically—as, unconsciously, his dry lips shaped the word "One"—he worked at the controls to keep that growing dot centered on the crossed spiderwebs of the visiplate. His hands doing that, while his right foot hovered over the pedal that would fire the bolt. The single bolt of concentrated hell that had to hit—or else. There wouldn't be time for any second shot.

"Two." He didn't know he'd said that, either. The dot in the visiplate wasn't a dot now. Only a few thousand miles away, it showed up in the magnification of the plate as though it were only a few hundred yards off. It was a sleek. fast little scouter, about the size of his.

And an alien ship, all right.

"Thr—" His foot touched the bolt-release pedal—

And then the Outsider had swerved suddenly and was off the crosshairs. Carson punched keys frantically, to follow.

For a tenth of a second, it was out of the visiplate entirely, and then as the nose of his scouter swung after it, he saw it again, diving straight toward the ground.

The ground?

It was an optical illusion of some sort. It *had* to be, that planet—or whatever it was—that now covered the visiplate. Whatever it was, it couldn't be there.

Couldn't possibly. There *wasn't* any planet nearer than Neptune three billion miles away—with Pluto around on the opposite side of the distant pinpoint sun.

His *detectors! They* hadn't shown any object of planetary dimensions, even of asteroid dimensions. They still didn't.

So it couldn't be there, that whatever-it-was he was driving into, only a few hundred miles below him.

And in his sudden anxiety to keep from crashing, he forgot even the Outsider ship. He fired the front braking rockets, and even as the sudden change of speed slammed him forward against the seat straps, he fired full right for an emergency turn. Pushed them down and *held* them down, knowing that he needed everything the ship had to keep from crashing and that a turn that sudden would black him out for a moment.

It did black him out.

And that was all. Now he was sitting in hot blue sand, stark naked but otherwise unhurt. No sign of his spaceship and—for that matter—no sign of *space.* That curve overhead wasn't a sky, whatever else it was.

He scrambled to his feet.

Gravity seemed a little more than Earth-normal. Not much more.

Flat sand stretching away, a few scrawny bushes in clumps here and there. The bushes were blue, too, but in varying shades, some lighter than the blue of the sand, some darker.

Out from under the nearest bush ran a little thing that was like a lizard, except that it had more than four legs. It was blue, too. Bright blue. It saw him and ran back again under the bush.

He looked up again, trying to decide what was overhead. It wasn't exactly a roof, but it was dome-shaped. It flickered and was hard to look at. But definitely, it curved down to the ground, to the blue sand, all around him.

He wasn't far from being under the center of the dome. At a guess, it was a hundred yards to the nearest wall, if it was a wall. It was as though a blue hemisphere of *something,* about two hundred and fifty yards in circumference, was inverted over the flat expanse of the sand.

And everything blue, except one object. Over near a far curving wall there was a red object. Roughly spherical, it seemed to be about a yard in diameter. Too far for him to see clearly through the flickering blueness. But, unaccountably, he shuddered.

He wiped sweat from his forehead, or tried to, with the back of his hand.

Was this a dream, a nightmare? This heat, this sand, that vague feeling of horror he felt when he looked toward that red thing?

A dream? No, one didn't go to sleep and dream in the midst of a battle in space.

Death? No, never. If there were immortality, it wouldn't be a senseless thing like this, a thing of blue heat and blue sand and a red horror.

Then he heard the voice—

Inside his head he heard it, not with his ears. It came from nowhere or everywhere.

"Through spaces and dimensions wandering," rang the words in his mind, *"and in this space and this time I find two peoples about to wage a war that would exterminate one and so weaken the other that it would retrogress and never fulfill its destiny, but decay and return to mindless dust whence it came. And I say this must not happen."*

"Who ... what are you?" Carson didn't say it aloud, but the question formed itself in his brain.

"You would not understand completely. I am—" There was a pause as though the voice sought—in Carson's brain—for a word that wasn't there, a word he didn't know. *"I am the end of evolution of a race so old the time can not be expressed in words that have meaning to your mind. A race fused into a single entity, eternal—*

"An entity such as your primitive race might become"— again the groping for a word—*"time from now. So might the race you call, in your mind, the Outsiders. So I intervene in the battle to come, the battle between fleets so evenly matched that destruction of both races will result. One must survive. One must progress and evolve."*

"One?" thought Carson. "Mine, or—?"

"It is in my power to stop the war, to send the Outsiders back to their galaxy. But they would return, or your race would sooner or later follow them there. Only by remaining in this space and time to intervene constantly could I prevent them from destroying one another, and I cannot remain.

"So I shall intervene now. I shall destroy one fleet completely without loss to the other. One civilization shall thus survive."

Nightmare. This had to be nightmare, Carson thought. But he knew it wasn't. It was too mad, too impossible, to be anything but real.

He didn't dare ask *the* question—*which?* But his thoughts asked it for him.

"The stronger shall survive," said the voice. *"That I can not—and would not change. I merely intervene to make it a complete victory, not"*—groping again—*"not Pyrrhic victory to a broken race.*

"From the outskirts of the not-yet battle I plucked two individuals, you and an Outsider. I see from your mind that in your early history of nationalisms battles between champions, to decide issues between races, were not unknown.

You and your opponent are here pitted against one another, naked and un-armed, under conditions equally unfamiliar to you both, equally unpleasant to you both. There is no time limit, for here there is no time. The survivor is the champion of his race. That race survives."

"But—" Carson's protest was too inarticulate for expression, but the voice answered it.

"It is fair. The conditions are such that the accident of physical strength will not completely decide the issue. There is a barrier. You will understand. Brain-power and courage will be more important than strength. Most especially courage, which is the will to survive."

"But while this goes on, the fleets will—"

"No, you are in another space, another time. For as long as you are here, time stands still in the universe you know. I see you wonder whether this place is real. It is, and it is not. As I—to your limited understanding—am and am not real. My existence

is mental and not physical. You saw me as a planet; it could have been as a dustmote or a sun.

"*But to you this place is now real. What you suffer here will be real. And if you die here, your death will be real. If you die, your failure will be the end of your race. That is enough for you to know.*"

And then the voice was gone.

Again he was alone, but not alone. For as Carson looked up, he saw that the red thing, the red sphere of horror which he now knew was the Outsider, was rolling toward him.

Rolling.

It seemed to have no legs or arms that he could see, no features. It rolled across the blue sand with the fluid quickness of a drop of mercury. And before it, in some manner he could not understand, came a paralyzing wave of nauseating, retching, horrid hatred.

Carson looked about him frantically. A stone, lying in the sand a few feet away, was the nearest thing to a weapon. It wasn't large, but it had sharp edges, like a slab of flint. It looked a bit like blue flint.

He picked it up, and crouched to receive the attack. It was coming fast, faster than he could run.

No time to think out how he was going to fight it, and how anyway could he plan to battle a creature whose strength, whose characteristics, whose method of fighting he did not know? Rolling so fast, it looked more than ever like a perfect sphere.

Ten yards away. Five. And then it stopped.

Rather, it *was stopped*. Abruptly the near side of it flattened as though it had run up against an invisible wall. It bounced, actually bounced back.

Then it rolled forward again, but more slowly, more cautiously. It stopped again, at the same place. It tried again, a few yards to one side.

There was a barrier there of some sort. It clicked, then, in Carson's mind. That thought projected into his mind by the Entity who had brought them here: "—accident of physical strength will not completely decide the issue. There is a barrier."

A force-field, of course. Not the Netzian Field, known to Earth science, for that glowed and emitted a crackling sound. This one was invisible, silent.

It was a wall that ran from side to side of the inverted hemisphere; Carson didn't have to verify that himself. The Roller was doing that; rolling sideways along the barrier, seeking a break in it that wasn't there.

Carson took half a dozen steps forward, his left hand groping out before him, and then his hand touched the barrier. It felt smooth, yielding, like a sheet of rubber rather than like glass. Warm to his touch, but no warmer than the sand underfoot. And it was completely invisible, even at close range.

He dropped the stone and put both hands against it, pushing. It seemed to yield, just a trifle. But no farther than that trifle, even when he pushed with all his weight. It felt like a sheet of rubber backed up by steel. Limited resiliency, and then firm strength.

He stood on tiptoe and reached as high as he could and the barrier was still there.

He saw the Roller coming back, having reached one side of the arena. That feeling of nausea hit Carson again, and he stepped back from the barrier as it went by. It didn't stop.

But did the barrier stop at ground level? Carson knelt down and burrowed in the sand. It was soft, light, easy to dig in. At two feet down the barrier was still there.

The Roller was coming back again. Obviously, it couldn't find a way through at either side.

There must be a way through, Carson thought. *Some* way we can get at each other, else this duel is meaningless.

But no hurry now, in finding that out. There was something to try first. The Roller was back now, and it stopped just across the barrier, only six feet away. It seemed to be studying him, although for the life of him, Carson couldn't find external evidence of sense organs on the thing. Nothing that looked like eyes or ears, or even a mouth. There was though, he saw now, a series of grooves—perhaps a dozen of them altogether, and he saw two tentacles suddenly push out from two of the grooves and dip into the sand as though testing its consistency. Tentacles about an inch in diameter and perhaps a foot and a half long.

But the tentacles were retractable into the grooves and were kept there except when in use. They were retracted when the thing rolled and seemed to have nothing to do with its method of locomotion. That, as far as Carson could judge, seemed to be accomplished by some shifting—just *how* he couldn't even imagine—of its center of gravity.

He shuddered as he looked at the thing. It was alien, utterly alien, horribly different from anything on Earth or any of the life forms found on the other solar planets. Instinctively, somehow, he knew its mind was as alien as its body.

But he had to try. If it had no telepathic powers at all, the attempt was foredoomed to failure, yet he thought it had such powers. There had, at any rate, been a projection of something that was not physical at the time a few minutes ago when it had first started for him. An almost tangible wave of hatred.

If it could project that, perhaps it could read his mind as well, sufficiently for his purpose.

Deliberately, Carson picked up the rock that had been his only weapon, then tossed it down again in a gesture of relinquishment and raised his empty hands, palms up, before him.

He spoke aloud, knowing that although the words would be meaningless to the creature before him, speaking them would focus his own thoughts more completely upon the message.

"Can we not have peace between us?" he said, his voice sounding strange in the utter stillness. "The Entity who brought us here has told us what must happen if our races fight—extinction of one and weakening and retrogression of the other. The battle between them, said the Entity, depends upon what we do here. Why can not we agree to an eternal peace—your race to its galaxy, we to ours?"

Carson blanked out his mind to receive a reply.

It came, and it staggered him back, physically. He actually recoiled several steps in sheer horror at the depth and intensity of the hatred and lust-to-kill of the red images that had been projected at him. Not as articulate words—as had come to him the thoughts of the Entity—but as wave upon wave of fierce emotion.

For a moment that seemed an eternity he had to struggle against the mental impact of that hatred, fight to clear his mind of it and drive out the alien thoughts to which he had given admittance by blanking his own thoughts. He wanted to retch.

Slowly his mind cleared as, slowly, the mind of a man wakening from nightmare clears away the fear-fabric of which the dream was woven. He was breathing hard and he felt weaker, but he could think.

He stood studying the Roller. It had been motionless during the mental duel it had so nearly won. Now it rolled a few feet to one side, to the nearest of the blue bushes. Three tentacles whipped out of their grooves and began to investigate the bush.

"O. K.," Carson said, "so it's war then." He managed a wry grin. "If I got your answer straight, peace doesn't appeal to you." And, because he was, after all, a quite young man and couldn't resist the impulse to be dramatic, he added. "To the death!"

But his voice, in that utter silence, sounded very silly, even to himself. It came to him, then, that this *was* to the death. Not only his own death or that of the red spherical thing which he now thought of as the Roller, but death to the entire race of one or the other of them. The end of the human race, if he failed.

It made him suddenly very humble and very afraid to think that. More than to think it, to *know* it. Somehow, with a knowledge that was above even faith, he knew that the Entity who had arranged this duel had told the truth about its intentions and its powers. It wasn't kidding.

The future of humanity depended upon *him*. It was an awful thing to realize, and he wrenched his mind away from it. He had to concentrate on the situation at hand.

There had to be some way of getting through the barrier, or of killing through the barrier.

Mentally? He hoped that wasn't all, for the Roller obviously had stronger telepathic powers than the primitive, undeveloped ones of the human race. Or did it?

He had been able to drive the thoughts of the Roller out of his own mind; could it drive out his? If its ability to project were stronger, might not its receptivity mechanism be more vulnerable?

He stared at it and endeavored to concentrate and focus all his thoughts upon it.

"Die," he thought. *"You are going to die. You are dying. You are—"*

He tried variations on it, and mental pictures. Sweat stood out on his forehead and he found himself trembling with the intensity of the effort. But the Roller went ahead with its investigation of the bush, as utterly unaffected as though Carson had been reciting the multiplication table.

So *that* was no good.

He felt a bit weak and dizzy from the heat and his strenuous effort at concentration. He sat down on the blue sand to rest and gave his full attention to watching and studying the Roller. By close study, perhaps, he could judge its strength and detect its weaknesses, learn things that would be valuable to know when and if they should come to grips.

It was breaking off twigs. Carson watched carefully, trying to judge just how hard it worked to do that. Later, he thought, he could find a similar bush on his own side, break off twigs of equal thickness himself, and gain a comparison of physical strength between his own arms and hands and those tentacles.

The twigs broke off hard; the Roller was having to struggle with each one, he saw. Each tentacle, he saw, bifurcated at the tip into two fingers, each tipped by a nail or claw. The claws didn't seem to be particularly long or dangerous. No more so than his own fingernails, if they were let to grow a bit.

No, on the whole, it didn't look too tough to handle physically. Unless, of course, that bush was made of pretty tough stuff. Carson looked around him and, yes, right within reach was another bush of identically the same type.

He reached over and snapped off a twig. It was brittle, easy to break. Of course, the Roller might have been faking deliberately but he didn't think so.

On the other hand, where was it vulnerable? Just how would he go about killing it, if he got the chance? He went back to studying it. The outer hide looked pretty tough. He'd need a sharp weapon of some sort. He picked up the piece of rock again. It was about twelve inches long, narrow, and fairly sharp on one end. If it chipped like flint, he could make a serviceable knife out of it.

The Roller was continuing its investigations of the bushes. It rolled again, to the nearest one of another type. A little blue lizard, many-legged like the one Carson had seen on his side of the barrier, darted out from under the bush.

A tentacle of the Roller lashed out and caught it, picked it up. Another tentacle whipped over and began to pull legs off the lizard, as coldly and calmly as it had pulled twigs off the bush. The creature struggled frantically and emitted a shrill squealing sound that was the first sound Carson had heard here other than the sound of his own voice.

Carson shuddered and wanted to turn his eyes away. But he made himself continue to watch; anything he could learn about his opponent might prove valuable. Even this knowledge of its unnecessary cruelty. Particularly, he thought with a sudden vicious surge of emotion, this knowledge of its unnecessary cruelty. It would make it a pleasure to kill the thing, if and when the chance came.

He steeled himself to watch the dismembering of the lizard, for that very reason.

But he felt glad when, with half its legs gone, the lizard quit squealing and struggling and lay limp and dead in the Roller's grasp.

It didn't continue with the rest of the legs. Contemptuously it tossed the dead lizard away from it, in Carson's direction. It arced through the air between them and landed at his feet.

It had come through the barrier! The barrier wasn't there any more!

Carson was on his feet in a flash, the knife gripped tightly in his hand, and leaped forward. He'd settle this thing here and now! With the barrier gone—

But it wasn't gone. He found that out the hard way, running head on into it and nearly knocking himself silly. He bounced back, and fell.

And as he sat up, shaking his head to clear it, he saw something coming through the air toward him, and to duck it, he threw himself flat again on the sand, and to one side. He got his body out of the way, but there was a sudden sharp pain in the calf of his left leg.

He rolled backward, ignoring the pain, and scrambled to his feet. It was a rock, he saw now, that had struck him. And the Roller was picking up another one now, swinging it back gripped between two tentacles, getting ready to throw again.

It sailed through the air toward him, but he was easily able to step out of its way. The Roller, apparently, could throw straight, but not hard nor far. The first rock had struck him only because he had been sitting down and had not seen it coming until it was almost upon him.

Even as he stepped aside from that weak second throw, Carson drew back his right arm and let fly with the rock that was still in his hand. If missiles, he thought with sudden elation, can cross the barrier, then two can play at the game of throwing them. And the good right arm of an Earthman—

He couldn't miss a three-foot sphere at only four-yard range, and he didn't miss. The rock whizzed straight, and with a speed several times that of the missiles the Roller had thrown. It hit dead center, but it hit flat, unfortunately, instead of point first.

But it hit with a resounding thump, and obviously it hurt. The Roller had been reaching for another rock, but it changed its mind and got out of there instead. By the time Carson could pick up and throw another rock, the Roller was forty yards back from the barrier and going strong.

His second throw missed by feet, and his third throw was short. The Roller was back out of range—at least out of range of a missile heavy enough to be damaging.

Carson grinned. That round had been his. Except—

He quit grinning as he bent over to examine the calf of his leg. A jagged edge of the stone had made a pretty deep cut, several inches long. It was bleeding pretty freely, but he didn't think it had gone deep enough to hit an artery. If it stopped bleeding of its own accord, well and good. If not, he was in for trouble.

Finding out one thing, though, took precedence over that cut. The nature of the barrier.

He went forward to it again, this time groping with his hands before him. He found it; then holding one hand against it, he tossed a handful of sand at it with the other hand. The sand went right through. His hand didn't.

Organic matter versus inorganic? No, because the dead lizard had gone through it, and a lizard, alive or dead, was certainly organic. Plant life? He broke off a twig and poked it at the barrier. The twig went through, with no resistance, but when his fingers gripping the twig came to the barrier, they were stopped.

He couldn't get through it, nor could the Roller. But rocks and sand and a dead lizard—

How about a live lizard? He went hunting, under bushes, until he found one, and caught it. He tossed it gently against the barrier and it bounced back and scurried away across the blue sand.

That gave him the answer, in so far as he could determine it now. The screen was a barrier to living things. Dead or inorganic matter could cross it.

That off his mind, Carson looked at his injured leg again. The bleeding was lessening, which meant he wouldn't need to worry about making a tourniquet. But he should find some water, if any was available, to clean the wound.

Water—the thought of it made him realize that he was getting awfully thirsty. He'd *have* to find water, in case this contest turned out to be a protracted one.

Limping slightly now, he started off to make a full circuit of his half of the arena. Guiding himself with one hand along the barrier, he walked to his right until he came to the curving sidewall. It was visible, a dull blue-gray at close range, and the surface of it felt just like the central barrier.

He experimented by tossing a handful of sand at it, and the sand reached the wall and disappeared as it went through. The hemispherical shell was a force-field, too. But an opaque one, instead of transparent like the barrier.

He followed it around until he came back to the barrier, and walked back along the barrier to the point from which he'd started.

No sign of water.

Worried now, he started a series of zigzags back and forth between the barrier and the wall, covering the intervening space thoroughly.

No water. Blue sand, blue bushes, and intolerable heat. Nothing else.

It must be his imagination, he told himself angrily, that he was suffering *that* much from thirst. How long had he been here? Of course, no time at all, according to his own space-time frame. The Entity had told him time stood still out there, while he was here. But his body processes went on here, just the same. And according to his body's reckoning, how long had he been here? Three or four hours, perhaps. Certainly not long enough to be suffering seriously from thirst.

But he was suffering from it; his throat dry and parched. Probably the intense heat was the cause. It was *hot!* A hundred and thirty Fahrenheit, at a guess. A dry, still heat without the slightest movement of air.

He was limping rather badly, and utterly fagged out when he'd finished the futile exploration of his domain.

He stared across at the motionless Roller and hoped it was as miserable as he was. And quite possibly it wasn't enjoying this, either. The Entity had said the conditions here were equally unfamiliar and equally uncomfortable for both of them. Maybe the Roller came from a planet where two hundred degree heat was the norm. Maybe it was freezing while he was roasting.

Maybe the air was as much too thick for it as it was too thin for him. For the exertion of his explorations had left him panting. The atmosphere here, he realized now, was not much thicker than that on Mars.

No water.

That meant a deadline, for him at any rate. Unless he could find a way to cross that barrier or to kill his enemy from this side of it, thirst would kill him eventually.

It gave him a feeling of desperate urgency. He *must* hurry.

But he made himself sit down a moment to rest, to think.

What was there to do? Nothing, and yet so many things. The several varieties of bushes, for example. They didn't look promising, but he'd have to examine them for possibilities. And his leg—he'd have to do something about that, even without water to clean it. Gather ammunition in the form of rocks. Find a rock that would make a good knife.

His leg hurt rather badly now, and he decided that came first. One type of bush had leaves—or things rather similar to leaves. He pulled off a handful of them and decided, after examination, to take a chance on them. He used them to clean off the sand and dirt and caked blood, then made a pad of fresh leaves and tied it over the wound with tendrils from the same bush.

The tendrils proved unexpectedly tough and strong. They were slender, and soft and pliable, yet he couldn't break them at all. He had to saw them off the bush with the sharp edge of a piece of the blue flint. Some of the thicker ones were over a foot long, and he filed away in his memory, for future reference, the fact that a bunch of the thick ones, tied together, would make a pretty serviceable rope. Maybe he'd be able to think of a use for rope.

Next, he made himself a knife. The blue flint *did* chip. From a foot-long splinter of it, he fashioned himself a crude but lethal weapon. And of tendrils from the bush, he made himself a rope-belt through which he could thrust the flint knife, to keep it with him all the time and yet have his hands free.

He went back to studying the bushes. There were three other types. One was leafless, dry, brittle, rather like a dried tumbleweed. Another was of soft, crumbly wood, almost like punk. It looked and felt as though it would make excellent tinder for a fire. The third type was the most nearly wood-like. It had fragile leaves that wilted at a touch, but the stalks, although short, were straight and strong.

It was horribly, unbearably hot.

He limped up to the barrier, felt to make sure that it was still there. It was.

He stood watching the Roller for a while. It was keeping a safe distance back from the barrier, out of effective stone-throwing range. It was moving around back there, doing something. He couldn't tell what it was doing.

Once it stopped moving, came a little closer, and seemed to concentrate its attention on him. Again Carson had to fight off a wave of nausea. He threw a stone at it and the Roller retreated and went back to whatever it had been doing before.

At least he could make it keep its distance.

And, he thought bitterly, a devil of a lot of good *that* did him. Just the same, he spent the next hour or two gathering stones of suitable size for throwing, and making several neat piles of them, near his side of the barrier.

His throat burned now. It was difficult for him to think about anything except water.

But he *had* to think about other things. About getting through that barrier, under or over it, getting *at* that red sphere and killing it before this place of heat and thirst killed him first.

The barrier went to the wall upon either side, but how high and how far under the sand?

For just a moment, Carson's mind was too fuzzy to think out how he could find out either of those things. Idly, sitting there in the hot sand—and he didn't remember sitting down—he watched a blue lizard crawl from the shelter of one bush to the shelter of another.

From under the second bush, it looked out at him. Carson grinned at it. Maybe he was getting a bit punchdrunk, because he remembered suddenly the old story of the desert-colonists on Mars, taken from an older desert story of Earth— "Pretty soon you get so lonesome you find yourself talking to the lizards, and then not so long after that you find the lizards talking back to you—"

He should have been concentrating, of course, on how to kill the Roller, but instead he grinned at the lizard and said, "Hello, there."

The lizard took a few steps toward him. "Hello," it said.

Carson was stunned for a moment, and then he put back his head and roared with laughter. It didn't hurt his throat to do so, either; he hadn't been *that* thirsty.

Why not? Why should the Entity who thought up this nightmare of a place not have a sense of humor, along with the other powers he has? Talking lizards, equipped to talk back in my own language, if I talk to them— It's a nice touch.

He grinned at the lizard and said, "Come on over." But the lizard turned and ran away, scurrying from bush to bush until it was out of sight.

He was thirsty again.

And he had to *do* something. He couldn't win this contest by sitting here sweating and feeling miserable. He had to *do* something. But what?

Get through the barrier. But he couldn't get through it, or over it. But was he certain he couldn't get under? And come to think of it, didn't one sometimes find water by digging? Two birds with one stone—

Painfully now, Carson limped up to the barrier and started digging, scooping up sand a double handful at a time. It was slow, hard work because the sand ran in at the edges and the deeper he got the bigger in diameter the hole had to be. How many hours it took him, he didn't know, but he hit bedrock four feet down. Dry bedrock; no sign of water.

And the force-field of the barrier went down clear to the bedrock. No dice. No water. Nothing.

He crawled out of the hole and lay there panting, and then raised his head to look across and see what the Roller was doing. It must be doing something back there.

It was. It was making something out of wood from the bushes, tied together with tendrils. A queerly shaped framework about four feet high and roughly square. To see it better, Carson climbed up onto the mound of sand he had excavated from the hole, and stood there staring.

There were two long levers sticking out of the back of it, one with a cup-shaped affair on the end of it. Seemed to be some sort of a catapult, Carson thought.

Sure enough, the Roller was lifting a sizable rock into the cup-shaped outfit. One of his tentacles moved the other lever up and down for a while, and then he turned the machine slightly as though aiming it and the lever with the stone flew up and forward.

The stone arced several yards over Carson's head, so far away that he didn't have to duck, but he judged the distance it had traveled, and whistled softly. He couldn't throw a rock that weight more than half that distance. And even retreating to the rear of his domain wouldn't put him out of range of that machine, if the Roller shoved it forward almost to the barrier.

Another rock whizzed over. Not quite so far away this time.

That thing could be dangerous, he decided. Maybe he'd better do something about it.

Moving from side to side along the barrier, so the catapult couldn't bracket him, he whaled a dozen rocks at it. But that wasn't going to be any good, he saw. They had to be light rocks, or he couldn't throw them that far. If they hit the framework, they bounced off harmlessly. And the Roller had no difficulty, at that distance, in moving aside from those that came near it.

Besides, his arm was tiring badly. He ached all over from sheer weariness. If he could only rest a while without having to duck rocks from that catapult at regular intervals of maybe thirty seconds each—

He stumbled back to the rear of the arena. Then he saw even that wasn't any good. The rocks reached back there, too, only there were longer intervals between them, as though it took longer to wind up the mechanism, whatever it was, of the catapult.

Wearily he dragged himself back to the barrier again. Several times he fell and could barely rise to his feet to go on. He was, he knew, near the limit of his endurance. Yet he didn't dare stop moving now, until and unless he could put that catapult out of action. If he fell asleep, he'd never wake up.

One of the stones from it gave him the first glimmer of an idea. It struck upon one of the piles of stones he'd gathered together near the barrier to use as ammunition, and it struck sparks.

Sparks. Fire. Primitive man had made fire by striking sparks, and with some of those dry crumbly bushes as tinder—

Luckily, a bush of that type was near him. He broke it off, took it over to the pile of stones, then patiently hit one stone against another until a spark touched the punklike wood of the bush. It went up in flames so fast that it singed his eyebrows and was burned to an ash within seconds.

But he had the idea now, and within minutes he had a little fire going in the lee of the mound of sand he'd made digging the hole an hour or two ago.

Tinder bushes had started it, and other bushes which burned, but more slowly, kept it a steady flame.

The tough wirelike tendrils didn't burn readily; that made the fire-bombs easy to make and throw. A bundle of faggots tied about a small stone to give it weight and a loop of the tendril to swing it by.

He made half a dozen of them before he lighted and threw the first. It went wide, and the Roller started a quick retreat, pulling the catapult after him. But Carson had the others ready and threw them in rapid succession. The fourth wedged in the catapult's frame work, and did the trick. The Roller tried desperately to put out the spreading blaze by throwing sand, but its clawed tentacles would take only a spoonful at a time and his efforts were ineffectual. The catapult burned.

The Roller moved safely away from the fire and seemed to concentrate its attention on Carson and again he felt that wave of hatred and nausea. But more weakly; either the Roller itself was weakening or Carson had learned how to protect himself against the mental attack.

He thumbed his nose at it and then sent it scuttling back to safety by throwing a stone. The Roller went clear to the back of its half of the arena and started pulling up bushes again. Probably it was going to make another catapult.

Carson verified—for the hundredth time—that the barrier was still operating, and then found himself sitting in the sand beside it because he was suddenly too weak to stand up.

His leg throbbed steadily now and the pangs of thirst were severe. But those things paled beside the utter physical exhaustion that gripped his entire body.

And the heat.

Hell must be like this, he thought. The hell that the ancients had believed in. He fought to stay awake, and yet staying awake seemed futile, for there was nothing he could do. Nothing, while the barrier remained impregnable and the Roller stayed back out of range.

But there must be *something.* He tried to remember things he had read in books of archaeology about the methods of fighting used back in the days before metal and plastic. The stone missile, that had come first, he thought. Well, that he already had.

The only improvement on it would be a catapult, such as the Roller had made. But he'd never be able to make one, with the tiny bits of wood available from the bushes—no single piece longer than a foot or so. Certainly he could figure out a mechanism for one, but he didn't have the endurance left for a task that would take days.

Days? But the Roller had made one. Had they been here days already? Then he remembered that the Roller had many tentacles to work with and undoubtedly could do such work faster than he.

And besides, a catapult wouldn't decide the issue. He had to do better than that.

Bow and arrow? No; he'd tried archery once and knew his own ineptness with a bow. Even with a modern sportsman's durasteel weapon, made for accuracy. With such a crude, pieced-together outfit as he could make here, he doubted if he could shoot as far as he could throw a rock, and knew he couldn't shoot as straight.

Spear? Well, he *could* make that. It would be useless as a throwing weapon at any distance, but would be a handy thing at close range, if he ever got to close range.

And making one would give him something to do. Help keep his mind from wandering, as it was beginning to do. Sometimes now, he had to concentrate a while before he could remember why he was here, why he had to kill the Roller.

Luckily he was still beside one of the piles of stones. He sorted through it until he found one shaped roughly like a spearhead. With a smaller stone he began to chip it into shape, fashioning sharp shoulders on the sides so that if it penetrated it would not pull out again.

Like a harpoon? There was something in that idea, he thought. A harpoon was better than a spear, maybe, for this crazy contest. If he could once get it into the Roller, and had a rope on it, he could pull the Roller up against the barrier and the stone blade of his knife would reach through that barrier, even if his hands wouldn't.

The shaft was harder to make than the head. But by splitting and joining the main stems of four of the bushes, and wrapping the joints with the tough but thin tendrils, he got a strong shaft about four feet long, and tied the stone head in a notch cut in the end.

It was crude, but strong.

And the rope. With the thin tough tendrils he made himself twenty feet of line. It was light and didn't look strong, but he knew it would hold his weight and to spare. He tied one end of it to the shaft of the harpoon and the other end about his right wrist. At least, if he threw his harpoon across the barrier, he'd be able to pull it back if he missed.

Then when he had tied the last knot and there was nothing more he could do, the heat and the weariness and the pain in his leg and the dreadful thirst were suddenly a thousand times worse than they had been before.

He tried to stand up, to see what the Roller was doing now, and found he couldn't get to his feet. On the third try, he got as far as his knees and then fell flat again.

"I've got to sleep," he thought. "If a showdown came now, I'd be helpless. He could come up here and kill me, if he knew. I've got to regain some strength."

Slowly, painfully, he crawled back away from the barrier. Ten yards, twenty—

The jar of something thudding against the sand near him waked him from a confused and horrible dream to a more confused and more horrible reality, and he opened his eyes again to blue radiance over blue sand.

How long had he slept? A minute? A day?

Another stone thudded nearer and threw sand on him. He got his arms under him and sat up. He turned around and saw the Roller twenty yards away, at the barrier.

It rolled away hastily as he sat up, not stopping until it was as far away as it could get.

He'd fallen asleep too soon, he realized, while he was still in range of the Roller's throwing ability. Seeing him lying motionless, it had dared come up to the barrier to throw at him. Luckily, it didn't realize how weak he was, or it could have stayed there and kept on throwing stones.

Had he slept long? He didn't think so, because he felt just as he had before. Not rested at all, no thirstier, no different. Probably he'd been there only a few minutes.

He started crawling again, this time forcing himself to keep going until he was as far as he could go, until the colorless, opaque wall of the arena's outer shell was only a yard away.

Then things slipped away again—

When he awoke, nothing about him was changed, but this time he knew that he had slept a long time.

The first thing he became aware of was the inside of his mouth; it was dry, caked. His tongue was swollen.

Something was wrong, he knew, as he returned slowly to full awareness. He felt less tired, the stage of utter exhaustion had passed. The sleep had taken care of that.

But there was pain, agonizing pain. It wasn't until he tried to move that he knew that it came from his leg.

He raised his head and looked down at it. It was swollen terribly below the knee and the swelling showed even halfway up his thigh. The plant tendrils he had used to tie on the protective pad of leaves now cut deeply into the swollen flesh.

To get his knife under that imbedded lashing would have been impossible. Fortunately, the final knot was over the shin bone, in front, where the vine cut in less deeply than elsewhere. He was able, after an agonizing effort, to untie the knot.

A look under the pad of leaves told him the worst. Infection and blood poisoning, both pretty bad and getting worse.

And without drugs, without cloth, without even *water,* there wasn't a thing he could do about it.

Not a thing, except *die,* when the poison had spread through his system.

He knew it was hopeless, then, and that he'd lost.

And with him, humanity. When he died here, out there in the universe he knew, all his friends, everybody, would die too. And Earth and the colonized planets would be the home of the red, rolling, alien Outsiders. Creatures out of nightmare, things without a human attribute, who picked lizards apart for the fun of it.

It was the thought of that which gave him courage to start crawling, almost blindly in pain, toward the barrier again. Not crawling on hands and knees this time, but pulling himself along only by his arms and hands.

A chance in a million, that maybe he'd have strength left, when he got there, to throw his harpoon-spear just *once,* and with deadly effect, if—on another chance in a million—the Roller would come up to the barrier. Or if the barrier was gone, now.

It took him years, it seemed, to get there.

The barrier wasn't gone. It was as impassable as when he'd first felt it.

And the Roller wasn't at the barrier. By raising up on his elbows, he could see it at the back of its part of the arena, working on a wooden framework that was a half-completed duplicate of the catapult he'd destroyed.

It was moving slowly now. Undoubtedly it had weakened, too.

But Carson doubted that it would ever need that second catapult. He'd be dead, he thought, before it was finished.

If he could attract it to the barrier, now, while he was still alive— He waved an arm and tried to shout, but his parched throat would make no sound.

Or if he could get through the barrier—

His mind must have slipped for a moment, for he found himself beating his fists against the barrier in futile rage, made himself stop.

He closed his eyes, tried to make himself calm.

"Hello," said the voice.

It was a small, thin voice. It sounded like—

He opened his eyes and turned his head. It *was* a lizard.

"Go away," Carson wanted to say. "Go away; you're not really there, or you're there but not really talking. I'm imagining things again."

But he couldn't talk; his throat and tongue were past all speech with the dryness. He closed his eyes again.

"Hurt," said the voice. "Kill. Hurt—kill. Come."

He opened his eyes again. The blue ten-legged lizard was still there. It ran a little way along the barrier, came back, started off again, and came back.

"Hurt," it said. "Kill. Come."

Again it started off, and came back. Obviously it wanted Carson to follow it along the barrier.

He closed his eyes again. The voice kept on. The same three meaningless words. Each time he opened his eyes, it ran off and came back.

"Hurt. Kill. Come."

Carson groaned. There would be no peace unless he followed the blasted thing. Like it wanted him to.

He followed it, crawling. Another sound, a high-pitched squealing, came to his ears and grew louder.

There was something lying in the sand, writhing, squealing. Something small, blue, that looked like a lizard and yet didn't—

Then he saw what it was—the lizard whose legs the Roller had pulled off, so long ago. But it wasn't dead; it had come back to life and was wriggling and screaming in agony.

"Hurt," said the other lizard. "Hurt. Kill. Kill."

Carson understood. He took the flint knife from his belt and killed the tortured creature. The live lizard scurried off quickly.

Carson turned back to the barrier. He leaned his hands and head against it and watched the Roller, far back, working on the new catapult.

"I could get that far," he thought, "if I could get through. If I could get through, I might win yet. It looks weak, too. I might—"

And then there was another reaction of black hopelessness, when pain sapped his will and he wished that he were dead. He envied the lizard he'd just killed. It didn't have to live on and suffer. And he did. It would be hours, it might be days, before the blood poisoning killed him.

If only he could use that knife on himself—

But he knew he wouldn't. As long as he was alive, there was the millionth chance—

He was straining, pushing on the barrier with the flat of his hands, and he noticed his arms, how thin and scrawny they were now. He must really have been here a long time, for days, to get as thin as that.

How much longer now, before he died? How much more heat and thirst and pain could flesh stand?

For a little while he was almost hysterical again, and then came a time of deep calm, and a thought that was startling.

The lizard he had just killed. *It had crossed the barrier, still alive.* It had come from the Roller's side; the Roller had pulled off its legs and then tossed it contemptuously at him and it had come through the barrier. He'd thought, because the lizard was dead.

But it hadn't been dead; it had been unconscious.

A live lizard couldn't go through the barrier, but an unconscious one could. The barrier was not a barrier, then, to living flesh, but to conscious flesh. It was a *mental* projection, a *mental* hazard.

And with that thought, Carson started crawling along the barrier to make his last desperate gamble. A hope so forlorn that only a dying man would have dared try it.

No use weighing the odds of success. Not when, if he didn't try it, those odds were infinity to zero.

He crawled along the barrier to the dune of sand, about four feet high, which he'd scooped out in trying—how many days ago?—to dig under the barrier or to reach water.

That mound was right at the barrier, its farther slope half on one side of the barrier, half on the other.

Taking with him a rock from the pile nearby, he climbed up to the top of the dune and over the top, and lay there against the barrier, his weight leaning against it so that if the barrier were taken away he'd roll on down the short slope, into the enemy territory.

He checked to be sure that the knife was safely in his rope belt, that the harpoon was in the crook of his left arm and that the twenty-foot rope fastened to it and to his wrist.

Then with his right hand he raised the rock with which he would hit himself on the head. Luck would have to be with him on that blow; it would have to be hard enough to knock him out, but not hard enough to knock him out for long.

He had a hunch that the Roller was watching him, and would see him roll down through the barrier, and come to investigate. It would think he was dead, he hoped—he thought it had probably drawn the same deduction about the nature of the barrier that he had drawn. But it would come cautiously. He would have a little time—

He struck.

Pain brought him back to consciousness. A sudden, sharp pain in his hip that was different from the throbbing pain in his head and the throbbing pain in his leg.

But he had, thinking things out before he had struck himself, anticipated that very pain, even hoped for it, and had steeled himself against awakening with a sudden movement.

He lay still, but opened his eyes just a slit, and saw that he had guessed rightly. The Roller was coming closer. It was twenty feet away and the pain that had awakened him was the stone it had tossed to see whether he was alive or dead.

He lay still. It came closer, fifteen feet away, and stopped again. Carson scarcely breathed.

As nearly as possible, he was keeping his mind a blank, lest its telepathic ability detect consciousness in him. And with his mind blanked out that way, the impact of its thoughts upon his mind was nearly soul-shattering.

He felt sheer horror at the utter *alienness,* the *differentness* of those thoughts. Things that he felt but could not understand and could never express, because no terrestrial language had words, no terrestrial mind had images to fit them. The mind of a spider, he thought, or the mind of a praying mantis or a Martian sand-serpent, raised to intelligence and put in telepathic rapport with human minds, would be a homely familiar thing, compared to this.

He understood now that the Entity had been right: Man or Roller, and the universe was not a place that could hold them both. Farther apart than god and devil, there could never be even a balance between them.

Closer. Carson waited until it was only feet away, until its clawed tentacles reached out—

Oblivious to agony now, he sat up, raised and flung the harpoon with all the strength that remained to him. Or he thought it was all; sudden final strength flooded through him, along with a sudden forgetfulness of pain as definite as a nerve block.

As the Roller, deeply stabbed by the harpoon, rolled away, Carson tried to get to his feet to run after it. He couldn't do that; he fell, but kept crawling.

It reached the end of the rope, and he was jerked forward by the pull on his wrist. It dragged him a few feet and then stopped. Carson kept on going, pulling himself toward it hand over hand along the rope.

It stopped there, writhing tentacles trying in vain to pull out the harpoon. It seemed to shudder and quiver, and then it must have realized that it couldn't get away, for it rolled back toward him, clawed tentacles reaching out.

Stone knife in hand, he met it. He stabbed, again and again, while those horrid claws ripped skin and flesh and muscle from his body.

He stabbed and slashed, and at last it was still.

A bell was ringing, and it took him a while after he'd opened his eyes to tell where he was and what it was. He was strapped into the seat of his scouter, and the visiplate before him showed only empty space. No Outsider ship and no impossible planet.

The bell was the communications plate signal; someone wanted him to switch power into the receiver. Purely reflex action enabled him to reach forward and throw the lever.

The face of Brander, captain of the *Magellan,* mother-ship of his group of scouters, flashed into the screen. His face was pale and his black eyes glowing with excitement.

"*Magellan* to Carson," he snapped. "Come on in. The fight's over. We've won!"

The screen went blank; Brander would be signaling the other scouters of his command.

Slowly, Carson set the controls for the return. Slowly, unbelievingly, he unstrapped himself from the seat and went back to get a drink at the cold-water tank. For some reason, he was unbelievably thirsty. He drank six glasses.

He leaned there against the wall, trying to think.

Had it happened? He was in good health, sound, uninjured. His thirst had been mental rather than physical; his throat hadn't been dry. His leg—

He pulled up his trouser leg and looked at the calf. There was a long white scar there, but a perfectly healed scar. It hadn't been there before. He zipped open the front of his shirt and saw that his chest and abdomen were criss-crossed with tiny, almost unnoticeable, perfectly healed scars.

It *had* happened.

The scouter, under automatic control, was already entering the hatch of the mother-ship. The grapples pulled it into its individual lock, and a moment later a buzzer indicated that the lock was air-filled. Carson opened the hatch and stepped outside, went through the double door of the lock.

He went right to Brander's office, went in, and saluted.

Brander still looked dizzily dazed. "Hi, Carson," he said. "What you missed! What a show!"

"What happened, sir?"

"Don't know, exactly. We fired one salvo, and their whole fleet went up in dust! Whatever it was jumped from ship to ship in a flash, even the ones we hadn't aimed at and that were out of range! The whole fleet disintegrated before our eyes, and we didn't get the paint of a single ship scratched!

"We can't even claim credit for it. Must have been some unstable component in the metal they used, and our sighting shot just set it off. Man, oh man, too bad you missed all the excitement."

Carson managed to grin. It was a sickly ghost of a grin, for it would be days before he'd be over the mental impact of his experience, but the captain wasn't watching, and didn't notice.

"Yes, sir," he said. Common sense, more than modesty, told him he'd be branded forever as the worst liar in space if he ever said any more than that. "Yes, sir, too bad I missed all the excitement."

The Waveries

Definitions from the school-abridged Webster-Hamlin Dictionary, 1998 edition:

> wavery (WA-vĕr-i) n. a vader—*slang*
>
> vader (VA-dĕr) n. inorgan of the class Radio
>
> inorgan (in-ÔR-gan) n. noncorporeal ens, a vader
>
> radio (RA-di-ô) n. 1. class of inorgans 2. etheric frequency between light and electricity 3. (obsolete) method of communication used up to 1957

The opening guns of invasion were not at all loud although they were heard by millions of people. George Bailey was one of the millions. I choose George Bailey because he was the only one who came within a googol of light-years of guessing what they were.

George Bailey was drunk and under the circumstances one can't blame him for being so. He was listening to radio advertisements of the most nauseous kind. Not because he wanted to listen to them, I hardly need say, but because he'd been told to listen to them by his boss, J. R. McGee of the MID network.

George Bailey wrote advertising for the radio. The only thing he hated worse than advertising was radio. And here on his own time he was listening to fulsome and disgusting commercials on a rival network.

"Bailey," J. R. McGee had said, "you should be more familiar with what others are doing. Particularly, you should be informed about those of our own accounts who use several networks. I strongly suggest ..."

One doesn't quarrel with an employer's strong suggestions and keep a two hundred dollar a week job.

But one can drink whisky sours while listening. George Bailey did.

Also, between commercials, he was playing gin rummy with Maisie Hetterman, a cute little redheaded typist from the studio. It was Maisie's apartment and Maisie's radio (George himself, on principle, owned neither a radio nor a TV set) but George had brought the liquor.

"—only the very finest tobaccos," said the radio, "go dit-dit-dit nation's favorite cigarette—"

George glanced at the radio. "Marconi," he said.

He meant Morse, naturally, but the whisky sours had muddled him a bit so his first guess was more nearly right than anyone else's. It was Marconi, in a way. In a very peculiar way.

"Marconi?" asked Maisie.

George, who hated to talk against a radio, leaned over and switched it off.

"I meant Morse," he said. "Morse, as in Boy Scouts or the Signal Corps. I used to be a Boy Scout once."

"You've sure changed," Maisie said.

George sighed. "Somebody's going to catch hell, broadcasting code on that wave length."

"What did it mean?"

"Mean? Oh, you mean what did it mean. Uh—S, the letter S. *Dit-dit-dit* is S. SOS is *dit-dit-dit dah-dah-dah dit-dit-dit.*"

"O is *dah-dah-dah?*"

George grinned. "Say that again, Maisie. I like it. And I think you are *dah-dah-dah* too."

"George, maybe it's really an SOS message. Turn it back on."

George turned it back on. The tobacco ad was still going. "—gentlemen of the most *dit-dit-dit* -ing taste prefer the finer taste of *dit-dit-dit* -arettes. In the new package that keeps them *dit-dit-dit* and ultra fresh—"

"It's not SOS. It's just S's."

"Like a teakettle or—say, George, maybe it's just some advertising gag."

George shook his head. "Not when it can blank out the name of the product. Just a minute till I—"

He reached over and turned the dial of the radio a bit to the right and then a bit to the left, and an incredulous look came into his face. He turned the dial to the extreme left, as far as it would go. There wasn't any station there, not even the hum of a carrier wave. But:

"*Dit-dit-dit,*" said the radio, "*dit-dit-dit.*"

He turned the dial to the extreme right. "*Dit-dit-dit.*"

George switched it off and stared at Maisie without seeing her, which was hard to do.

"Something wrong, George?"

"I hope so," said George Bailey. "I certainly hope so."

He started to reach for another drink and changed his mind. He had a sudden hunch that something big was happening and he wanted to sober up to appreciate it.

He didn't have the faintest idea *how* big it was.

"George, what do you mean?"

"I don't know what I mean. But Maisie, let's take a run down to the studio, huh? There ought to be some excitement."

April 5, 1957; that was the night the waveries came.

It had started like an ordinary evening. It wasn't one, now.

George and Maisie waited for a cab but none came so they took the subway instead. Oh yes, the subways were still running in those days. It took them within a block of the MID Network Building.

The building was a madhouse. George, grinning, strolled through the lobby with Maisie on his arm, took the elevator to the fifth floor and for no reason at all gave the elevator boy a dollar. He'd never before in his life tipped an elevator operator.

The boy thanked him. "Better stay away from the big shots, Mr. Bailey," he said. "They're ready to chew the ears off anybody who even looks at 'em."

"Wonderful," said George.

From the elevator he headed straight for the office of J. R. McGee himself.

There were strident voices behind the glass door. George reached for the knob and Maisie tried to stop him. "But George," she whispered, "you'll be fired!"

"There comes a time," said George. "Stand back away from the door, honey."

Gently but firmly he moved her to a safe position.

"But George, what are you—?"

"Watch," he said.

The frantic voices stopped as he opened the door a foot. All eyes turned toward him as he stuck his head around the corner of the doorway into the room.

"*Dit-dit-dit.*" he said. "*Dit-dit-dit.*"

He ducked back and to the side just in time to escape the flying glass as a paperweight and an inkwell came through the pane of the door.

He grabbed Maisie and ran for the stairs.

"Now we get a drink," he told her.

The bar across the street from the network building was crowded but it was a strangely silent crowd. In deference to the fact that most of its customers were radio people it didn't have a TV set but there was a big cabinet radio and most of the people were bunched around it.

"*Dit,*" said the radio. "*Dit-dah-d'dah-dit-dahditdah dit—*"

"Isn't it beautiful?" George whispered to Maisie.

Somebody fiddled with the dial. Somebody asked, "What band is that?" and somebody said, "Police." Somebody said, "Try the foreign band," and somebody did. "This ought to be Buenos Aires," somebody said. "*Dit-d'dah-dit—*" said the radio.

Somebody ran fingers through his hair and said, "Shut that damn thing off." Somebody else turned it back on.

George grinned and led the way to a back booth where he'd spotted Pete Mulvaney sitting alone with a bottle in front of him. He and Maisie sat across from Pete.

"Hello," he said gravely.

"Hell," said Pete, who was head of the technical research staff of MID.

"A beautiful night, Mulvaney," George said. "Did you see the moon riding the fleecy clouds like a golden galleon tossed upon silver-crested whitecaps in a stormy—"

"Shut up," said Pete. "I'm thinking."

"Whisky sours," George told the waiter. He turned back to the man across the table. "Think out loud, so we can hear. But first, how did you escape the booby hatch across the street?"

"I'm bounced, fired, discharged."

"Shake hands. And then explain. Did you say *dit-dit-dit* to them?"

Pete looked at him with sudden admiration. "Did you?"

"I've a witness. What *did* you do?"

"Told 'em what I thought it was and they think I'm crazy."

"Are you?"

"Yes."

"Good," said George. "Then we want to hear—" He snapped his fingers. "What about TV?"

"Same thing. Same sound on audio and the pictures flicker and dim with every dot or dash. Just a blur by now."

"Wonderful. And now tell me what's wrong. I don't care what it is, as long as it's nothing trivial, but I want to know."

"I think it's space. Space is warped."

"Good old space," George Bailey said.

"George," said Maisie, "please shut up. I want to hear this."

"Space," said Pete, "is also finite." He poured himself another drink. "You go far enough in any direction and get back where you started. Like an ant crawling around an apple."

"Make it an orange," George said.

"All right, an orange. Now suppose the first radio waves ever sent out have just made the round trip. In fifty-six years."

"Fifty-six years? But I thought radio waves traveled at the same speed as light. If that's true, then in fifty-six years they could go only fifty-six light-years, and *that* can't be around the universe because there are galaxies known to be millions or maybe billions of light-years away. I don't remember the figures, Pete, but our own galaxy alone is a hell of a lot bigger than fifty-six light-years."

Pete Mulvaney sighed. "That's why I say space must be warped. There's a short cut somewhere."

"*That* short a short cut? Couldn't be."

"But George, listen to that stuff that's coming in. Can you read code?"

"Not any more. Not that fast, anyway."

"Well, I can," Pete said. "That's early American ham. Lingo and all. That's the kind of stuff the air was full of before regular broadcasting. It's the lingo, the abbreviations, the barnyard to attic chitchat of amateurs with keys, with Marconi coherers or Fessenden barreters—and you can listen for a violin solo pretty soon now. I'll tell you what it'll be."

"What?"

"Handel's *Largo*. The first phonograph record ever broadcast. Sent out by Fessenden from Brant Rock in 1906. You'll hear his CQ-CQ any minute now. Bet you a drink."

"Okay, but what was the *dit-dit-dit* that started this?"

Mulvaney grinned. "Marconi, George. What was the most powerful signal ever broadcast and by whom and when?"

"Marconi? *Dit-dit-dit?* Fifty-six years ago?"

"Head of the class. The first transatlantic signal on December 12, 1901. For three hours Marconi's big station at Poldhu, with two-hundred foot masts, sent out an intermittent S, *dit-dit-dit*, while Marconi and two assistants at St. Johns in Newfoundland got a kite-borne aerial four hundred feet in the air and finally got the signal. Across the Atlantic, George, with sparks jumping from the big Leyden jars at Poldhu and 20,000-volt juice jumping off the tremendous aerials—"

"Wait a minute, Pete, you're off the beam. If that was in 1901 and the first broadcast was about 1906 it'll be five years before the Fessenden stuff gets here on the same route. Even if there's a fifty-six light-year short cut across space and even if those signals didn't get so weak en route that we couldn't hear them—it's crazy."

"I told you it was," Pete said gloomily. "Why, those signals after traveling that far would be so infinitesimal that for practical purposes they wouldn't exist. Furthermore they're all over the band on everything from microwave on up and equally strong on each. And, as you point out, we've already come almost five years in two hours, which isn't possible. I told you it was crazy."

"But—"

"Ssshh. Listen," said Pete.

A blurred, but unmistakably human voice was coming from the radio, mingling with the cracklings of code. And then music, faint and scratchy, but unmistakably a violin. Playing Handel's *Largo*.

Only suddenly it climbed in pitch as though modulating from key to key until it became so horribly shrill that it hurt the ear. And kept on going past the high limit of audibility until they could hear it no more.

Somebody said, "Shut that God damn thing off." Somebody did, and this time nobody turned it back on.

Pete said, "I didn't really believe it myself. And there's another thing against it, George. Those signals affect TV too, and radio waves are the wrong length to do that."

He shook his head slowly. "There must be some other explanation, George. The more I think about it now the more I think I'm wrong."

He was right: he was wrong.

"Preposterous," said Mr. Ogilvie. He took off his glasses, frowned fiercely, and put them back on again. He looked through them at the several sheets of copy paper in his hand and tossed them contemptuously to the top of his desk. They slid to rest against the triangular name plate that read:

B. R. Ogilvie
Editor-in-Chief

"Preposterous," he said again.

Casey Blair, his best reporter, blew a smoke ring and poked his index finger through it. "Why?" he asked.

"Because—why, it's utterly preposterous."

Casey Blair said, "It is now three o'clock in the morning. The interference has gone on for five hours and not a single program is getting through on either TV or radio. Every major broadcasting and telecasting station in the world has gone off the air.

"For two reasons. One, they were just wasting current. Two, the communications bureaus of their respective governments requested them to get off to aid their campaigns with the direction finders. For five hours now, since the start of the interference, they've been working with everything they've got. And what have they found out?"

"It's preposterous!" said the editor.

"Perfectly, but it's true. Greenwich at 11 P. M. New York time; I'm translating all these times into New York time—got a bearing in about the direction of Miami. It shifted northward until at two o'clock the direction was approximately that of Richmond, Virginia. San Francisco at eleven got a bearing in about the direction of Denver; three hours later it shifted southward toward Tucson. Southern Hemisphere: bearings from Capetown, South Africa, shifted from direction of Buenos Aires to that of Montevideo, a thousand miles north.

"New York at eleven had weak indications toward Madrid; but by two o'clock they could get no bearings at all." He blew another smoke ring. "Maybe because the loop antennae they use turn only on a horizontal plane?"

"Absurd."

Casey said, "I like 'preposterous' better, Mr. Ogilvie. Preposterous it is, but it's not absurd. I'm scared stiff. Those lines—and all other bearings I've heard about—run in the same direction if you take them as straight lines running as tangents off the Earth instead of curving them around the surface. I did it with a little globe and a star map. They converge on the constellation Leo."

He leaned forward and tapped a forefinger on the top page of the story he'd just turned in. "Stations that are directly under Leo in the sky get no bearings at all. Stations on what would be the perimeter of Earth relative to that point get the strongest bearings. Listen, have an astronomer check those figures if you want before you run the story, but get it done damn quick—unless you want to read about it in the other newspapers first."

"But the heaviside layer, Casey—isn't that supposed to stop all radio waves and bounce them back?"

"Sure, it does. But maybe it leaks. Or maybe signals can get through it from the outside even though they can't get out from the inside. It isn't a solid wall."

"But—"

"I know, it's preposterous. But there it is. And there's only an hour before press time. You'd better send this story through fast and have it being set up while you're having somebody check my facts and directions. Besides, there's something else you'll want to check."

"What?"

"I didn't have the data for checking the positions of the planets. Leo's on the ecliptic; a planet could be in line between here and there. Mars, maybe."

Mr. Ogilvie's eyes brightened, then clouded again. He said, "We'll be the laughingstock of the world, Blair, if you're wrong."

"And if I'm right?"

The editor picked up the phone and snapped an order.

April 6th headline of the New York Morning Messenger, final (6 A. M.) edition:

RADIO INTERFERENCE
COMES FROM SPACE,
ORIGINATES IN LEO
May Be Attempt at Commu-
nication by Beings
Outside Solar
System

All television and radio broadcasting was suspended.

Radio and television stocks opened several points off the previous day and then dropped sharply until noon when a moderate buying rally brought them a few points back.

Public reaction was mixed; people who had no radios rushed out to buy them and there was a boom, especially in portable and table-top receivers. On the other hand, no TV sets were sold at all. With telecasting suspended there were no pictures on their screens, even blurred ones. Their audio circuits, when turned on, brought in the same jumble as radio receivers. Which, as Pete Mulvaney had pointed out to George Bailey, was impossible; radio waves cannot activate the audio circuits of TV sets. But these did, if they were radio waves.

In radio sets they seemed to be radio waves, but horribly hashed. No one could listen to them very long. Oh, there were flashes—times when, for several consecutive seconds, one could recognize the voice of Will Rogers or Geraldine Farrar or catch flashes of the Dempsey-Carpentier fight or the Pearl Harbor excitement. (Remember Pearl Harbor?) But things even remotely worth hearing were rare. Mostly it was a meaningless mixture of soap opera, advertising and off-key snatches of what had once been music. It was utterly indiscriminate, and utterly unbearable for any length of time.

But curiosity is a powerful motive. There was a brief boom in radio sets for a few days.

There were other booms, less explicable, less capable of analysis. Reminiscent of the Wells-Welles Martian scare of 1938 was a sudden upswing in the sale of shotguns and sidearms. Bibles sold as fast as books on astronomy—and books on astronomy sold like hotcakes. One section of the country showed a sudden interest in lightning rods; builders were flooded with orders for immediate installation.

For some reason which has never been clearly ascertained there was a run on fishhooks in Mobile, Alabama; every hardware and sporting goods store sold out of them within hours.

The public libraries and bookstores had a run on books on astrology and books on Mars. Yes, on Mars—despite the fact that Mars was at that moment on the other side of the sun and that every newspaper article on the subject stressed the fact that no planet was between Earth and the constellation Leo.

Something strange was happening—and no news of developments available except through the newspapers. People waited in mobs outside newspaper buildings for each new edition to appear. Circulation managers went quietly mad.

People also gathered in curious little knots around the silent broadcasting studios and stations, talking in hushed voices as though at a wake. MID network doors were locked, although there was a doorman on duty to admit technicians who were trying to find an answer to the problem. Some of the technicians who had been on duty the previous day had now spent over twenty-four hours without sleep.

George Bailey woke at noon, with only a slight headache. He shaved and showered, went out and drank a light breakfast and was himself again. He bought early editions of the afternoon papers, read them, grinned. His hunch had been right; whatever was wrong, it was nothing trivial.

But what was wrong?

The later editions of the afternoon papers had it.

EARTH INVADED, SAYS SCIENTIST

Thirty-six line type was the biggest they had; they used it. Not a home-edition copy of a newspaper was delivered that evening. Newsboys starting on their routes were practically mobbed. They sold papers instead of delivering them; the smart ones got a dollar apiece for them. The foolish and honest ones who didn't want to sell because they thought the papers should go to the regular customers on their routes lost them anyway. People grabbed them.

The final editions changed the heading only slightly—only slightly, that is, from a typographical viewpoint. Nevertheless, it was a tremendous change in meaning. It read:

EARTH INVADED, SAY SCIENTISTS

Funny what moving an S from the ending of a verb to the ending of a noun can do.

Carnegie Hall shattered precedent that evening with a lecture given at midnight. An unscheduled and unadvertised lecture. Professor Helmetz had stepped off the train at eleven-thirty and a mob of reporters had been waiting for him. Helmetz, of Harvard, had been the scientist, singular, who had made that first headline.

Harvey Ambers, director of the board of Carnegie Hall, had pushed his way through the mob. He arrived minus glasses, hat and breath, but got hold of Helmetz's arm and hung on until he could talk again. "We want you to talk at Carnegie, Professor," he shouted into Helmetz's ear. "Five thousand dollars for a lecture on the 'vaders.'"

"Certainly. Tomorrow afternoon?"

"Now! I've a cab waiting. Come on."

"But—"

"We'll get you an audience. Hurry!" He turned to the mob. "Let us through. All of you can't hear the professor here. Come to Carnegie Hall and he'll talk to you. And spread the word on your way there."

The word spread so well that Carnegie Hall was jammed by the time the professor began to speak. Shortly after, they'd rigged a loud-speaker system so the people outside could hear. By one o'clock in the morning the streets were jammed for blocks around.

There wasn't a sponsor on Earth with a million dollars to his name who wouldn't have given a million dollars gladly for the privilege of sponsoring that lecture on TV or radio, but it was not telecast or broadcast. Both lines were busy.

"Questions?" asked Professor Helmetz.

A reporter in the front row made it first, "Professor," he asked, "have *all* direction finding stations on Earth confirmed what you told us about the change this afternoon?"

"Yes, absolutely. At about noon all directional indications began to grow weaker. At 2:45 o'clock, Eastern Standard Time, they ceased completely. Until then the radio waves emanated from the sky, constantly changing direction with reference to the Earth's surface, but *constant* with reference to a point in the constellation Leo."

"What star in Leo?"

"No star visible on our charts. Either they came from a point in space or from a star too faint for our telescopes.

"But at 2:45 P. M. today—yesterday rather, since it is now past midnight—all direction finders went dead. But the signals persisted, now coming from all sides equally. The invaders had all arrived.

"There is no other conclusion to be drawn. Earth is now surrounded, completely blanketed, by radio-type waves which have *no point of origin*, which travel ceaselessly around the Earth in all directions, changing shape at their will—which currently is still in imitation of the Earth-origin radio signals which attracted their attention and brought them here."

"Do you think it was from a star we can't see, or could it have really been just a point in space?"

"Probably from a point in space. And why not? They are not creatures of matter. If they came here from a star, it must be a very dark star for it to be invisible to us, since it would be relatively near to us—only twenty-eight light-years away, which is quite close as stellar distances go."

"How can you know the distance?"

"By assuming—and it is a quite reasonable assumption— that they started our way when they first discovered our radio signals—Marconi's S-S-S code broadcast of fifty-six years ago. Since that was the form taken by the first arrivals, we assume they started toward us when they encountered those signals. Marconi's signals, traveling at the speed of light, would have reached a point twenty-eight light-years away twenty-eight years ago; the invaders, also traveling at light-speed would require an equal of time to reach us.

"As might be expected only the first arrivals took Morse code form. Later arrivals were in the form of other waves that they met and passed on—or perhaps absorbed—on their way to Earth. There are now wandering around the Earth, as it were, fragments of programs broadcast as recently as a few days ago. Undoubtedly there are fragments of the very last programs to be broadcast, but they have not yet been identified."

"Professor, can you *describe* one of these invaders?"

"As well as and no better than I can describe a radio wave. In effect, they *are* radio waves, although they emanate from no broadcasting station. They are a form of life dependent on wave motion, as our form of life is dependent on the vibration of matter."

"They are different sizes?"

"Yes, in two senses of the word size. Radio waves are measured from crest to crest, which measurement is known as the wave length. Since the invaders cover the entire dials of our radio sets and television it is obvious that either one of two things is true: Either they come in all crest-to-crest sizes or each one can change his crest-to-crest measurement to adapt himself to the tuning of any receiver.

"But that is only the crest-to-crest length. In a sense it may be said that a radio wave has an over-all length determined by its duration. If a broadcasting station sends out a program that has a second's duration, a wave carrying that program is one light-second long, roughly 187,000 miles. A continuous half-hour program is, as it were, on a continuous wave one-half light-hour long, and so on.

"Taking that form of length, the individual invaders vary in length from a few thousand miles—a duration of only a small fraction of a second—to well over half a million miles long—a duration of several seconds. The longest continuous excerpt from any one program that has been observed has been about seven seconds."

"But, Professor Helmetz, why do you assume that these waves are *living* things, a life form. Why not just waves?"

"Because 'just waves' as you call them would follow certain laws, just as inanimate *matter* follows certain laws. An animal can climb uphill, for instance;

a stone cannot unless impelled by some outside force. These invaders are life-forms because they show volition, because they can change their direction of travel, and most especially because they retain their identity; two signals never conflict on the same radio receiver. They follow one another but do not come simultaneously. They do not mix as signals on the same wave length would ordinarily do. They are not 'just waves.'"

"Would you say they are intelligent?"

Professor Helmetz took off his glasses and polished them thoughtfully. He said, "I doubt if we shall ever know. The intelligence of such beings, if any, would be on such a completely different plane from ours that there would be no common point from which we could start intercourse. We are material; they are immaterial. There is no common ground between us."

"But if they are intelligent at all—"

"Ants are intelligent, after a fashion. Call it instinct if you will, but instinct is a form of intelligence; at least it enables them to accomplish some of the same things intelligence would enable them to accomplish. Yet we cannot establish communication with ants and it is far less likely that we shall be able to establish communication with these invaders. The difference in type between ant-intelligence and our own would be nothing to the difference in type between the intelligence, if any, of the invaders and our own. No, I doubt if we shall ever communicate."

The professor had something there. Communication with the vaders—a clipped form, of course, of *invaders*—was never established.

Radio stocks stabilized on the exchange the next day. But the day following that someone asked Dr. Helmetz a sixty-four dollar question and the newspapers published his answer:

"Resume broadcasting? I don't know if we ever shall. Certainly we cannot until the invaders go away, and why should they? Unless radio communication is perfected on some other planet far away and they're attracted there.

"But at least some of them would be right back the moment we started to broadcast again."

Radio and TV stocks dropped to practically zero in an hour. There weren't, however, any frenzied scenes on the stock exchanges; there was no frenzied selling because there was no buying, frenzied or otherwise. No radio stocks changed hands.

Radio and television employees and entertainers began to look for other jobs. The entertainers had no trouble finding them. Every other form of entertainment suddenly boomed like mad.

"Two down," said George Bailey. The bartender asked what he meant.

"I dunno, Hank. It's just a hunch I've got."

"What kind of hunch?"

"I don't even know that. Shake me up one more of those and then I'll go home."

The electric shaker wouldn't work and Hank had to shake the drink by hand.

"Good exercise; that's just what you need," George said. "It'll take some of that fat off you."

Hank grunted, and the ice tinkled merrily as he tilted the shaker to pour out the drink.

George Bailey took his time drinking it and then strolled out into an April thundershower. He stood under the awning and watched for a taxi. An old man was standing there too.

"Some weather," George said.

The old man grinned at him. "You noticed it, eh?"

"Huh? Noticed what?"

"Just watch a while, mister. Just watch a while."

The old man moved on. No empty cab came by and George stood there quite a while before he got it. His jaw dropped a little and then he closed his mouth and went back into the tavern. He went into a phone booth and called Pete Mulvaney.

He got three wrong numbers before he got Pete. Pete's voice said, "Yeah?"

"George Bailey, Pete. Listen, have you noticed the weather?"

"Damn right. *No lightning*, and there should be with a thunderstorm like this."

"What's it mean, Pete? The vaders?"

"Sure. And that's just going to be the start if—" A crackling sound on the wire blurred his voice out.

"Hey, Pete, you still there?"

The sound of a violin. Pete Mulvaney didn't play violin.

"Hey, Pete, what the hell—?"

Pete's voice again. "Come on over, George. Phone won't last long. Bring—" There was a buzzing noise and then a voice said, "—come to Carnegie Hall. The best tunes of all come—"

George slammed down the receiver.

He walked through the rain to Pete's place. On the way he bought a bottle of Scotch. Pete had started to tell him to bring something and maybe that's what he'd started to say.

It was.

They made a drink apiece and lifted them. The lights flickered briefly, went out, and then came on again but dimly.

"No lightning," said George. "No lightning and pretty soon no lighting. They're taking over the telephone. What do they do with the lightning?"

"Eat it, I guess. They must eat electricity."

"No lightning," said George. "Damn. I can get by without a telephone, and candles and oil lamps aren't bad for lights—but I'm going to miss lightning. I *like* lightning. Damn."

The lights went out completely.

Pete Mulvaney sipped his drink in the dark. He said, "Electric lights, refrigerators, electric toasters, vacuum cleaners—"

"Juke boxes," George said. "Think of it, no more God damn juke boxes. No public address systems, no—hey, how about movies?"

"No movies, not even silent ones. You can't work a projector with an oil lamp. But listen, George, no automobiles—no gasoline engine can work without electricity."

"Why not, if you crank it by hand instead of using a starter?"

"The spark, George. What do you think makes the spark."

"Right. No airplanes either, then. Or how about jet planes?"

"Well—I guess some types of jets could be rigged not to need electricity, but you couldn't do much with them. Jet plane's got more instruments than motor, and all those instruments are electrical. And you can't fly or land a jet by the seat of your pants."

"No radar. But what would we need it for? There won't be any more wars, not for a long time."

"A damned long time."

George sat up straight suddenly. "Hey, Pete, what about atomic fission? Atomic energy? Will it still work?"

"I doubt it. Subatomic phenomena are basically electrical. Bet you a dime they eat loose neutrons too." (He'd have won his bet; the government had not announced that an A-bomb tested that day in Nevada had fizzled like a wet firecracker and that atomic piles were ceasing to function.)

George shook his head slowly, in wonder. He said, "Streetcars and buses, ocean liners—Pete, this means we're going back to the original source of horsepower. Horses. If you want to invest, buy horses. Particularly mares. A brood mare is going to be worth a thousand times her weight in platinum."

"Right. But don't forget steam. We'll still have steam engines, stationary and locomotive."

"Sure, that's right. The iron horse again, for the long hauls. But Dobbin for the short ones. Can you ride, Pete?"

"Used to, but I think I'm getting too old. I'll settle for a bicycle. Say, better buy a bike first thing tomorrow before the run on them starts. I know *I'm* going to."

"Good tip. And I used to be a good bike rider. It'll be swell with no autos around to louse you up. And say—"

"What?"

"I'm going to get a cornet too. Used to play one when I was a kid and I can pick it up again. And then maybe I'll hole in somewhere and write that nov— Say, what about printing?"

"They printed books long before electricity, George. It'll take a while to readjust the printing industry, but there'll be books all right. Thank God for that."

George Bailey grinned and got up. He walked over to the window and looked out into the night. The rain had stopped and the sky was clear.

A streetcar was stalled, without lights, in the middle of the block outside. An automobile stopped, then started more slowly, stopped again; its headlights were dimming rapidly.

George looked up at the sky and took a sip of his drink.

"No lightning," he said sadly. "I'm going to miss the lightning."

The changeover went more smoothly than anyone would have thought possible.

The government, in emergency session, made the wise decision of creating one board with absolutely unlimited authority and under it only three subsidiary boards. The main board, called the Economic Readjustment Bureau, had only seven members and its job was to co-ordinate the efforts of the three subsidiary boards and to decide, quickly and without appeal, any jurisdictional disputes among them.

First of the three subsidiary boards was the Transportation Bureau. It immediately took over, temporarily, the railroads. It ordered Diesel engines run on sidings and left there, organized use of the steam locomotives and solved the problems of railroading sans telegraphy and electric signals. It dictated, then, what should be transported; food coming first, coal and fuel oil second, and essential manufactured articles in the order of their relative importance. Carload after carload of new radios, electric stoves, refrigerators and such useless articles were dumped unceremoniously alongside the tracks, to be salvaged for scrap metal later.

All horses were declared wards of the government, graded according to capabilities, and put to work or to stud. Draft horses were used for only the most essential kinds of hauling. The breeding program was given the fullest possible emphasis; the bureau estimated that the equine population would double in two years, quadruple in three, and that within six or seven years there would be a horse in every garage in the country.

Farmers, deprived temporarily of their horses, and with their tractors rusting in the fields, were instructed how to use cattle for plowing and other work about the farm, including light hauling.

The second board, the Manpower Relocation Bureau, functioned just as one would deduce from its title. It handled unemployment benefits for the millions thrown temporarily out of work and helped relocate them—not too difficult a task considering the tremendously increased demand for hand labor in many fields.

In May of 1957 thirty-five million employables were out of work; in October, fifteen million; by May of 1958, five million. By 1959 the situation was completely in hand and competitive demand was already beginning to raise wages.

The third board had the most difficult job of the three. It was called the Factory Readjustment Bureau. It coped with the stupendous task of converting factories filled with electrically operated machinery and, for the most part, tooled for the production of other electrically operated machinery, over for the production, without electricity, of essential non-electrical articles.

The few available stationary steam engines worked twenty-four hour shifts in those early days, and the first thing they were given to do was the running of lathes and stampers and planers and millers working on turning out more stationary steam engines, of all sizes. These, in turn, were first put to work making still more steam engines. The number of steam engines grew by squares and cubes, as did the number of horses put to stud. The principle was the same. One might, and many did, refer to those early steam engines as stud horses. At any rate, there was no lack of metal for them. The factories were filled with nonconvertible machinery waiting to be melted down.

Only when steam engines—the basis of the new factory economy—were in full production, were they assigned to running machinery for the manufacture of other articles. Oil lamps, clothing, coal stoves, oil stoves, bathtubs and bedsteads.

Not quite all of the big factories were converted. For while the conversion period went on, individual handicrafts sprang up in thousands of places. Little one- and two-man shops making and repairing furniture, shoes, candles, all sorts of things that *could* be made without complex machinery. At first these small shops made small fortunes because they had no competition from heavy industry. Later, they bought small steam engines to run small machines and held their own, growing with the boom that came with a return to normal employment and buying power, increasing gradually in size until many of them rivaled the bigger factories in output and beat them in quality.

There *was* suffering, during the period of economic readjustment, but less than there had been during the great depression of the early thirties. And the recovery was quicker.

The reason was obvious: In combating the depression, the legislators were working in the dark. They didn't know its cause—rather, they knew a thousand conflicting theories of its cause—and they didn't know the cure. They were hampered by the idea that the thing was temporary and would cure itself if left alone. Briefly and frankly, they didn't know what it was all about and while they experimented, it snowballed.

But the situation that faced the country—and all other countries—in 1957 was clear-cut and obvious. No more electricity. Readjust for steam and horsepower.

As simple and clear as that, and no ifs or ands or buts. And the whole people—except for the usual scattering of cranks—back of them.

By 1961—

It was a rainy day in April and George Bailey was waiting under the sheltering roof of the little railroad station at Blakestown, Connecticut, to see who might come in on the 3:14.

It chugged in at 3:25 and came to a panting stop, three coaches and a baggage car. The baggage car door opened and a sack of mail was handed out and the door closed again. No luggage, so probably no passengers would—

Then at the sight of a tall dark man swinging down from the platform of the rear coach, George Bailey let out a yip of delight. "Pete! Pete Mulvaney! What the devil—"

"Bailey, by all that's holy! What are you doing here?"

George wrung Pete's hand. "Me? I live here. Two years now. I bought the *Blakestown Weekly* in '59, for a song, and I run it—editor, reporter, and janitor. Got one printer to help me out with that end, and Maisie does the social items. She's—"

"Maisie? Maisie Hetterman?"

"Maisie Bailey now. We got married same time I bought the paper and moved here. What are you doing here, Pete?"

"Business. Just here overnight. See a man named Wilcox."

"Oh, Wilcox. Our local screwball—but don't get me wrong; he's a smart guy all right. Well, you can see him tomorrow. You're coming home with me now, for dinner and to stay overnight. Maisie'll be glad to see you. Come on, my buggy's over here."

"Sure. Finished whatever you were here for?"

"Yep, just to pick up the news on who came in on the train. And you came in, so here we go."

They got in the buggy, and George picked up the reins and said, "Giddup. Bessie," to the mare. Then, "What are you doing now, Pete?"

"Research. For a gas-supply company. Been working on a more efficient mantle, one that'll give more light and be less destructible. This fellow Wilcox wrote us he had something along that line; the company sent me up to look it over. If it's what he claims, I'll take him back to New York with me, and let the company lawyers dicker with him."

"How's business, otherwise?"

"Great, George. *Gas*; that's the coming thing. Every *new* home's being piped for it, and plenty of the old ones. How about you?"

"We got it. Luckily *we* had one of the old Linotypes that ran the metal pot off a gas burner, so it was already piped in. And our home is right over the office and print shop, so all we had to do was pipe it up a flight. Great stuff, gas. How's New York?"

"Fine, George. Down to its last million people, and stabilizing there, No crowding and plenty of room for everybody. The *air*—why, it's better than Atlantic City, without gasoline fumes."

"Enough horses to go around yet?"

"Almost. But bicycling's the craze; the factories can't turn out enough to meet the demand. There's a cycling club in almost every block and all the able-bodied cycle to and from work. Doing 'em good, too; a few more years and the doctors will go on short rations."

"You got a bike?"

"Sure, a pre-vader one. Average five miles a day on it, and I eat like a horse."

George Bailey chuckled. "I'll have Maisie include some hay in the dinner. Well, here we are. Whoa, Bessie."

An upstairs window went up, and Maisie looked out and down. She called out, "Hi, Pete!"

"Extra plate, Maisie," George called. "We'll be up soon as I put the horse away and show Pete around downstairs."

He led Pete from the barn and into the back door of the newspaper shop. "Our Linotype!" he announced proudly, pointing.

"How's it work? Where's your steam engine?"

George grinned. "Doesn't work yet; we still hand set the type. I could get only one steamer and had to use that on the press. But I've got one on order for the Lino, and coming up in a month or so. When we get it, Pop Jenkins, my printer, is going to put himself out of a job teaching me to run it. With the Linotype going, I can handle the whole thing myself."

"Kind of rough on Pop?"

George shook his head. "Pop eagerly awaits the day. He's sixty-nine and wants to retire. He's just staying on until I can do without him. Here's the press—a honey of a little Miehle; we do some job work on it, too. And this is the office, in front. Messy, but efficient."

Mulvaney looked around him and grinned. "George, I believe you've found your niche. You were cut out for a small-town editor."

"Cut out for it? I'm crazy about it. I have more fun than everybody. Believe it or not, I work like a dog, and like it. Come on upstairs."

On the stairs, Pete asked, "And the novel you were going to write?"

"Half done, and it isn't bad. But it isn't the novel I was going to write; I was a cynic then. Now—"

"George, I think the waveries were your best friends."

"Waveries?"

"Lord, how long does it take slang to get from New York out to the sticks? The vaders, of course. Some professor who specializes in studying them described one as a wavery place in the ether, and 'wavery' stuck— Hello there, Maisie, my girl. You look like a million."

They ate leisurely. Almost apologetically, George brought out beer, in cold bottles. "Sorry, Pete, haven't anything stronger to offer you. But I haven't been drinking lately. Guess—"

"*You* on the wagon, George?"

"Not on the wagon, exactly. Didn't swear off or anything, but haven't had a drink of strong liquor in almost a year. I don't know why, but—"

"I do," said Pete Mulvaney. "I know exactly why you don't—because I don't drink much either, for the same reason. We don't drink because we don't *have* to—say, isn't that a *radio* over there?"

George chuckled. "A souvenir. Wouldn't sell it for a fortune. Once in a while I like to look at it and think of the awful guff I used to sweat out for it. And then I go over and click the switch and nothing happens. Just silence. Silence is the most wonderful thing in the world, sometimes, Pete. Of course I couldn't do that if there was any juice, because I'd get vaders then. I suppose they're still doing business at the same old stand?"

"Yep, the Research Bureau checks daily. Try to get up current with a little generator run by a steam turbine. But no dice; the vaders suck it up as fast as it's generated."

"Suppose they'll ever go away?"

Mulvaney shrugged. "Helmetz thinks not. He thinks they propagate in proportion to the available electricity. Even if the development of radio broadcasting somewhere else in the Universe would attract them there, some would stay here—and multiply like flies the minute we tried to use electricity again. And meanwhile, they'll live on the static electricity in the air. What do you do evenings up here?"

"Do? Read, write, visit with one another, go to the amateur groups— Maisie's chairman of the Blakestown Players, and I play bit parts in it. With the movies out everybody goes in for theatricals and we've found some real talent. And there's the chess-and-checker club, and cycle trips and picnics—there isn't time enough. Not to mention music. Everybody plays an instrument, or is trying to."

"You?"

"Sure, cornet. First cornet in the Silver Concert Band, with solo parts. And— Good Heavens! Tonight's rehearsal, and we're giving a concert Sunday afternoon. I hate to desert you, but—"

"Can't I come around and sit in? I've got my flute in the brief case here, and—"

"*Flute?* We're short on flutes. Bring that around and Si Perkins, our director, will practically shanghai you into staying over for the concert Sunday— and it's only three days, so why not? And get it out now; we'll play a few old-timers to warm up. Hey, Maisie, skip those dishes and come on in to the piano!"

While Pete Mulvaney went to the guest room to get his flute from the brief case, George Bailey picked up his cornet from the top of the piano and blew a soft, plaintive little minor run on it. Clear as a bell; his lip was in good shape tonight.

And with the shining silver thing in his hand he wandered over to the window and stood looking out into the night. It was dusk out and the rain had stopped.

A high-stepping horse *clop-clopped* by and the bell of a bicycle jangled. Somebody across the street was strumming a guitar and singing. He took a deep breath and let it out slowly.

The scent of spring was soft and sweet in the moist air.

Peace and dusk.

Distant rolling thunder.

God damn it, he thought, *if only there was a bit of lightning*.

He missed the lightning.

Murder in Ten Easy Lessons

There isn't anything romantic about murder. It's a nasty business and you wouldn't like it.

Yes, take a murder and take it apart. You'll find it about as pleasant to dissect as a several-weeks-dead frog. The smell is pretty much the same, and you'll be in just as much of a hurry to rush to the incinerator with your subject.

You can quit reading now, right here. If you don't, remember I warned you.

You wouldn't have liked Morley Evans; few people did. You might, incidentally, have read about him in the paper, but not under that name. Duke Evans was the name he went by. Later, I mean; as a boy they called him Stinky.

Sounds like a joke, that name Stinky. Usually it is, but not always. Occasionally kids show an uncanny knack of picking nicknames. Not that he smelled physically; as a boy he was required by his parents to bathe his body at reasonable intervals. As a man, he was dapper and well groomed in a greasy sort of way. Maybe I seem to be too prejudiced; he wasn't really greasy. But he did use hair oil.

We're getting ahead of ourselves, though. Back to Stinky Evans and the first lesson. He was fourteen then. He ran with a gang who used to raid the dime stores every Saturday afternoon, coming out with their pockets stuffed. Most of them were rather good at it and were seldom caught.

Harry Callan was the head of the gang. He was a little older than the others and he had connections. He could take a conglomeration of twenty dollars' worth of packaged razor blades, phonograph needles and the like, and turn it into five dollars cash. With that ability and with his fists and his advantage in size, he ruled the gang.

You might say that Stinky Evans' first lesson in murder came the afternoon when Harry Callan knocked the hell out of him. For no particular reason; just that every once in a while Harry beat up one of his satellites to be sure they'd stay in line.

It happened in the alley behind the Gem Bowling Alleys, where some of them set pins once in a while. It started with words—mostly Harry Callan's words—then Harry whaled into Stinky Evans and whaled the tar out of him.

It was a new experience, for Stinky's only fights had been with kids smaller than himself. It didn't last long. When it was over he lay in the alley, half-sobbing, half-cursing, with blood running out of his nose. Not really hurt; he could easily have stood up again to take more.

But in spite of the blind anger and hatred in him, he knew better. He knew he was licked.

So he lay there and his hand closed around the cobblestone and that was when the little devil got into his mind and he picked up the cobblestone. *Kill,* something told him. *Kill the rat.*

It didn't lead to anything. Harry Callan kicked the stone out of his hand, kicked him in the face and broke three of his teeth, and then turned away into the back door of the Gem Bowling Alleys.

It wouldn't have led to anything, anyway. He wouldn't have thrown the stone, or at any rate he wouldn't have thrown it at Harry Callan's head. He'd have weakened, because he wasn't ready for murder yet.

After a while, he got up and went home.

If marriages are (as they tell us) made in heaven, then murders must be made in hell.

Of course, nobody much believes in hell any more—not, that is, in a concrete hell with little red devils running around with pitchforks and that sort of thing.

But there must be a hell, just the same, for that is where murders are made. To explain the build-up of a murder, you've got to believe that much. And since we've got to have some kind of a hell, let's stick to the classical model. Since we're going to postulate a hell, let's make it good. Little red devils and all.

In other words, let's shoot the works. Let's imagine a Little Red Devil chuckling gleefully while Stinky Evans was walking home from the alley behind the Gem.

Let's imagine the Little Red Devil talking to the big boss himself. "Good material, Boss. A nasty little punk if there ever was one. He'll make the grade, Boss."

"You gave him the first lesson?"

"Yep," said the Little Red Devil. "Just now. A few more from from to time and he'll come through."

"All right, he's yours. Stay with him."

"You bet, Boss," said the L.R.D. "I'll stay with him, all right. I'll stay with him."

That was Stinky Evans at fourteen. At fifteen he got caught stealing a spare tire. He spent a night in the bullpen before they found out he was under age and switched him over to the juvenile authorities. In the bullpen he got talking with a four-timer and they got around to shivs.

It was dark in the cell except for the pattern made by the bars of the doors upon the floor. A pale yellow trapezoid with narrow black parallel stripes. A cockroach started across it and a big foot in prison-made shoes went out from the bunk and squashed the cockroach.

"If you ever stick a shiv in a guy, twist it," the four-timer told him. "Lets the air in and he flops quick. Hasn't time to yell or scramble any eggs for you, see? That's why a wide blade's best. Lets in more air when you twist. Those damn' stilettos ain't no good; you got to hit the heart or else stab the guy half a dozen times ..." There was more. It was quite a lesson. Stinky thought about Harry Callan.

Down the corridor a drunk with d.t.'s was yelling like hell because tarantulas were after him. Stinky Evans shivered.

They gave him probation on the tire theft.

Before that was up, though, he got in trouble again and this time took six months at the reformatory. That was a good six months; he learned plenty there. Without boring you with the unpleasant details, let's count it as lessons three to five, inclusive, and consider ourselves conservative.

He was fifteen when he got out, but he looked older. He felt older. He'd decided not to go home. Going home meant he'd have to take a job and keep reporting to the juvenile authorities how he was getting along in it. They'd keep checking on him all the time. The hell with that.

He went home only long enough to sneak out some clothes and get the rent money out of the chipped teapot. Twenty-five bucks, it was.

He hopped a rattler and got off when he saw the shacks working along the train at Springfield, the division point.

He took a cheap room in Springfield and cased the town. When most of his money was gone, he went back where there'd been a BOY WANTED sign in a poolroom window.

It was the Acme Pool Parlor, run by Nick Chester. Maybe you've heard of Nick Chester. You'd know of him, all right, if you ever lived in Springfield.

A swarthy little guy, but smooth. He wore two-hundred-dollar suits and smoked fifty-cent cigars. Lived in a swank mansion out at the edge of town and drove a custom-made car. All the trimmings, if you know what I mean. All out of a little poolroom that maybe took in twenty or thirty dollars a week.

Nick tilted his twenty-dollar fedora back on his head and looked Stinky Evans over with eyes that didn't miss any tricks.

"How old ya, kid?" he said.

"Twenty."

"Been in stir, huh?" Nick didn't wait for an answer to that one. "Okay by me if y'ain't hot."

Stinky shook his head.

"What's ya name?" Nick asked.

Stinky'd decided that. "Duke," he said. "Duke Evans."

"Okay, Duke. You rack balls for a while," Nick said. "When I get to know you better, maybe I can give you something else. We'll get along."

Duke went back by the pool tables. He watched Nick Chester, and he knew now what he was going to be. That was for him; a two-C suit with a white carnation in the lapel, expensive cigars, a blank but knowing pair of eyes and a pocketful of hay.

Power. That was for him. He'd work for it; he'd steal for it; he'd even commit ...

Maybe there was rejoicing in hell. I mean, of course, if there is any such place. Things were going swimmingly. It was all too obvious that the Little Red Devil was on the job.

"He's coming along fine, Boss," said the L.R.D. "Just had the sixth lesson, you might say. Another year—"

"Not so soon. Let him ripen. Be sure of him."

"He'll graduate, Boss, *cum laude*. But you mean I got to wait two or three years yet?"

"Let him ripen. Five or six years."

The L.R.D. gulped and looked aghast. "That long? Oh, *Heaven!*"

So they had to wash his mouth out with brimstone.

Call it the seventh lesson, at eighteen. Duke Evans was beginning to look like Duke Evans. He wore only a thirty-dollar suit but the trousers had a razor edge to them.

He wasn't racking balls now; he was making collections. Small ones, but lots of them. That was Nick's system and his strength—a finger in a thousand small pies. One at a time, Duke was learning about those pies.

He went into the florist's shop on Grove Street, walked briskly on through and found the little florist alone in the back room making up a wreath. Duke grinned at him. "Hi, Larkin. Your dues; forty bucks."

The little man didn't smile back. "I—I can't afford it; I told Mr. Wescott of your association. Talked to him on the phone this morning. I've been losing money since I started paying—"

Duke quit grinning and his eyes got hard. "I got orders to get it. See?"

"But look, I haven't even *got* forty dollars. I haven't paid all the rent yet. I can't—"

He'd stepped backward and there was fear in his face. That was a mistake. Nobody had ever before shown fear of Duke Evans. And the florist was a little guy, too. The little mark was scared stiff.

It wasn't Duke's job; he could have gone back and reported. One of the muscle boys would have been sent around. But it was so easy.

He gave Larkin the back of his hand across the left side of his face and knocked his glasses off, then smashed the palm of his hand across the other side of the face, stepping in as the florist stepped back.

Then again, rocking the little man's head back and forth before he stepped in with a hard jab to the pit of the stomach. Larkin doubled over and retched.

Duke stepped back. "That was a sample. Still think you can't rake up forty bucks?"

Duke got the forty bucks. On the way back to headquarters, he bought himself a cigar. He didn't like the taste of it as well as cigarettes, but from now on he was going to smoke them. On his lapel was a white rosebud he'd taken from a vase on his way out of Larkin's.

He got his shoes shined, too, although they didn't really need it. He felt pretty good.

Nick Chester looked at the white rosebud. His left eyebrow went up half a millimeter, which wasn't enough for Duke to notice.

Duke got friendly with Tony Barria—as nearly as anyone could ever get to being friendly with Tony.

Tony was a little guy, too, like Larkin had been, but Tony wasn't the kind of little guy that you shoved around. Tony was a torpedo.

He was cold and tense and he moved with a smooth grace that seemed jerky because it was so fast. Nobody ever felt at ease with Tony, really; you sort of got the idea that if you clapped him on the back, he'd explode. Maybe they tailored that word *torpedo* just to fit Tony Barria. But shoot a couple of snooker games with him and then you could loosen his tongue with Chianti, which is an expensive word for Italian red wine. And because Duke wanted to learn something that Tony could teach him, he kept Chianti in his room. He took a lesson from Tony in things an ambitious young man should know.

Like: "Look, if you're going to *use* it on somebody, a forty-five automatic's the thing. Don't monkey with a little gun. A forty-five, because if you hit the shoulder or the leg or somewhere with a little gun, it don't mean nothing. Got to hit the head or the heart. In the guts'll kill him, but he'll live a while first. Maybe long enough to talk, see? But a big slug wherever it hits knocks 'em down like a baseball bat.

"But if you're carrying a rod just in case, a thirty-two automatic'll do. Light and don't bulge your coat ..."

Oh, sure, those were elementary things, but Duke dug in and got some fine points, too. Like how to beat a paraffin test; and if you don't know that, you're better off not to. I'm not giving lessons; just telling about them.

Tony was a gunman all the way. He thought shivs were effeminate, fists were for gorillas, tommies were for morons who couldn't learn to shoot straight with a heater. "Why, any day I'd go up against a typewriter, with a forty-five. One shot I'd need and there'd be time for three while he was getting that damn' thing swung around and pointed—"

Duke Evans picked up quite a bit from Tony. One thing he didn't learn: how not to be afraid of Tony. But when he moved in, he thought Tony would be on his side. Tony didn't like Nick, and Duke worked on that ...

Duke let a couple of years go by. He grew in evil, in stature, and in favor with himself and the gang. He bought himself two pistols, obtaining them in such a manner that they could not be traced back to him. He bought himself a rifle, too, but he purchased that openly and talked about it. His occasional hunting trips were for the purpose of finding secluded spots in the woods where he could practice shooting an automatic. Nobody knew about the pistols or his practice with them.

For a while, he took over running the strong-arm squad. Just telling them whom to see and how much of a job to do on him. He got a kick out of that.

Once he planted a pineapple himself that blew the guts out of a cigar store run by a man named Perelman who'd decided, against advice, not to job a book on the ponies. That was why the pineapple was put in his store. But the reason Duke Evans did the job in person was that Perelman had said, "Get out of here, punk," to Duke Evans.

Duke Evans wasn't a punk any more.

He heard the explosion from several blocks away and thought, "Punk huh?" He wished Perelman had been in the store when the bomb went off. He pictured it vividly. Because he was standing in a dark alley and didn't have to stay dead-pan, the look on his face wasn't nice.

Not nice at all. But then Duke Evans wasn't a nice guy. I warned you about that.

Then after a while, he was ready. Ready for the takeover and the gravy train.

He'd worked it out, and he wasn't going to be crude and use a gun after all. That was for cheap torpedoes like Tony. There were reasons why it would be better if Nick's death looked like a hit-run.

He stole a car one day and kept it under wraps until late at night, after Nick had gone home. Then he made his phone call. He'd worked out the angles on that. It was important he saw Nick right away; something had come up. And since Nick wouldn't ever allow any of his men to come to his home, would Nick please—

Well, the details don't matter; it worked out that Nick would get dressed and go out to walk about two blocks, too short a distance to bother getting his car out of the garage. And Nick would have to cross at a certain corner.

Duke parked the stolen car with the lights out and the engine turning over lightly, at just the right spot. He could start up when Nick was a third of the way across, and get him whether he tried to go ahead or duck back.

There was a light down at the corner, but it was dark where the car was parked. It was darker than he thought. Nick would be coming along any minute now. All of Duke's attention was concentrated on watching for him.

He didn't hear the two men coming afoot from the opposite direction until they were at the car and one opened a door on either side. One of them was Tony Barria, the other was the Swede.

Tony got in beside him and held the forty-five in his ribs. Duke remembered what a forty-five did to a man. Duke began to sweat. He said, "Listen, Tony, I—"

The gun prodded. "Shut up. Drive north."

"Tony, I'll give you—"

Swede, in the back seat, raised the butt of his pistol and brought it down in a short vicious arc.

But it wasn't until near dawn (in Springfield; not in hell) that the Little Red Devil came running into the main office, grinning triumphantly and lashing his arrow-tipped tail in high glee.

"Just graduated him, Boss," he chortled. "Just gave him the final lesson. He knows all about murder now. Got kayoed, but he came to before they got to the bay and took it all in while they were putting the cement tub on his feet. You shoulda heard him beg till they had to gag him. But he took it all in; he knows all about it, plenty. Yep, he sure graduated. He sure—"

"Good. You brought him along, of course."

"Yep," said the L.R.D. "I brought him along, all right; I sure brought him along ..."

Pi in the Sky

Roger Jerome Phlutter, for whose absurd name I offer no defense other than that it is genuine, was, at the time of the events of this story, a hardworking clerk in the office of the Cole Observatory.

He was a young man of no particular brilliance, although he performed his daily tasks assiduously and efficiently, studied the calculus at home for one hour every evening, and hoped some day to become a chief astronomer of some important observatory.

Nevertheless, our narration of the events of late March in the year 1987 must begin with Roger Phlutter for the good and sufficient reason that he, of all men on earth, was the first observer of the stellar aberration.

Meet Roger Phlutter.

Tall, rather pale from spending too much time indoors, thickish shell-rimmed glasses, dark hair close-cropped in the style of the nineteen eighties, dressed neither particularly well nor badly, smokes cigarettes rather excessively ...

At a quarter to five that afternoon, Roger was engaged in two simultaneous operations. One was examining, in a blink-microscope, a photographic plate taken late the previous night of a section in Gemini. The other was considering whether or not, on the three dollars remaining of his pay from last week, he dared phone Elsie and ask her to go somewhere with him.

Every normal young man has undoubtedly, at some time or other, shared with Roger Phlutter his second occupation, but not everyone has operated or understands the operation of a blink-microscope. So let us raise our eyes from Elsie to Gemini.

A blink-mike provides accommodation for two photographic plates taken of the same section of sky, but at different times. These plates are carefully juxtaposed and the operator may alternately focus his vision, through the eyepiece, first upon one and then upon the other, by means of a shutter. If the plates are identical, the operation of the shutter reveals nothing, but if one of the dots on the second plate differs from the position it occupies on the first, it will call attention to itself by seeming to jump back and forth as the shutter is manipulated.

Roger manipulated the shutter, and one of the dots jumped. So did Roger. He tried it again, forgetting—as we have—all about Elsie for the moment, and the dot jumped again. It jumped almost a tenth of a second.

Roger straightened up and scratched his head. He lighted a cigarette, put it down on the ashtray, and looked into the blink-mike again. The dot jumped again, when he used the shutter.

Harry Wesson, who worked the evening shift, had just come into the office and was hanging up his topcoat.

"Hey, Harry!" Roger said. "There's something wrong with this blinking blinker."

"Yeah?" said Harry.

"Yeah. Pollux moved a tenth of a second."

"Yeah?" said Harry. "Well, that's about right for parallax. Thirty-two light years—parallax of Pollux is point one oh one. Little over a tenth of a second, so if your comparison plate was taken about six months ago when the earth was on the other side of her orbit, that's about right."

"But Harry, the comparison plate was taken night before last. They're twenty-four hours apart."

"You're crazy."

"Look for yourself."

It wasn't quite five o'clock yet, but Harry Wesson magnanimously overlooked that, and sat down in front of the blink-mike. He manipulated the shutter, and Pollux obligingly jumped.

There wasn't any doubt about it being Pollux, for it was far and away the brightest dot on the plate. Pollux is a star of 1.2 magnitude, one of the twenty brightest in the sky and by far the brightest in Gemini. And none of the faint stars around it had moved at all.

"Um," said Harry Wesson. He frowned and looked again. "One of those plates is misdated, that's all. I'll check into it first thing."

"Those plates aren't misdated," Roger said doggedly. "I dated them myself."

"That proves it," Harry told him. "Go on home. It's five o'clock. If Pollux moved a tenth of a second last night, I'll move it back for you."

So Roger left.

He felt uneasy somehow, as though he shouldn't have. He couldn't put his finger on just what worried him, but something did. He decided to walk home instead of taking the bus.

Pollux was a fixed star. It couldn't have moved a tenth of a second in twenty-four hours.

"Let's see—thirty-two light years," Roger said to himself. "Tenth of a second. Why, that would be movement several times faster than the speed of light. Which is positively silly!"

Wasn't it?

He didn't feel much like studying or reading tonight. Was three dollars enough to take Elsie out?

The three balls of a pawn-shop loomed ahead, and Roger succumbed to temptation. He pawned his watch, and then phoned Elsie. Dinner and a show?

"Why certainly, Roger."

So, until he took her home at one-thirty, he managed to forget astronomy. Nothing odd about that. It would have been strange if he had managed to remember it.

But his feeling of restlessness came back as soon as he had left her. At first, he didn't remember why. He knew merely that he didn't feel quite like going home yet.

The corner tavern was still open, and he dropped in for a drink. He was having his second one when he remembered. He ordered a third.

"Hank." he said to the bartender. "You know Pollux?"

"Pollux who?" asked Hank.

"Skip it," said Roger. He had another drink, and thought it over. Yes, he'd made a mistake somewhere. Pollux couldn't have moved.

He went outside and started to walk home. He was almost there when it occurred to him to look up at Pollux. Not that, with the naked eye, he could detect a displacement of a tenth of a second, but he felt curious.

He looked up, oriented himself by the sickle of Leo, and then found Gemini—Castor and Pollux were the only stars in Gemini visible, for it wasn't a particularly good night for seeing. They were there, all right, but he thought they looked a little farther apart than usual. Absurd, because that would be a matter of degrees, not minutes or seconds.

He stared at them for a while, and then looked across to the dipper. Then he stopped walking and stood there. He closed his eyes and opened them again, carefully.

The dipper just didn't look right. It was distorted. There seemed to be more space between Alioth and Mizar, in the handle, than between Mizar and Alkaid. Phecda and Merak, in the bottom of the dipper, were closer together, making the angle between the bottom and the lip steeper. Quite a bit steeper.

Unbelievingly, he ran an imaginary line from the pointers, Merak and Dubhe, to the North Star. The line curved. It had to. If he ran it straight, it missed Polaris by maybe five degrees.

Breathing a bit hard, Roger took off his glasses and polished them very carefully with his handkerchief. He put them back on again and the dipper was still crooked.

So was Leo, when he looked back to it. At any rate, Regulus wasn't where it should be by a degree or two.

A degree or two! At the distance of Regulus! Was it sixty-five light years? Something like that.

Then, in time to save his sanity, Roger remembered that he'd been drinking. He went home without daring to look upward again. He went to bed, but couldn't sleep.

He didn't feel drunk. He grew more excited, wide awake.

He wondered if he dared phone the observatory. Would he sound drunk over the phone? The devil with whether he sounded that way or not, he finally decided. He went to the telephone in his pajamas.

"Sorry," said the operator.

"What d'ya mean, sorry?"

"I cannot give you that number," said the operator, in dulcet tones. And then, "I am sorry. We do not have that information."

He got the chief operator, and the information. Cole Observatory had been so deluged with calls from amateur astronomers that they had found it necessary to request the telephone company to discontinue all incoming calls save long distance ones from other observatories.

"Thanks," said Roger. "Will you get me a cab?"

It was an unusual request, but the chief operator obliged and got him a cab.

He found the Cole Observatory in a state resembling a madhouse.

The following morning most newspapers carried the news. Most of them gave it two or three inches on an inside page, but the facts were there.

The facts were that a number of stars, in general the brightest ones, within the past forty-eight hours had developed noticeable proper motions.

"This does not imply," quipped the New York *Spotlight,* "that their motions have been in any way improper in the past. 'Proper motion' to an astronomer means the movement of a star across the face of the sky with relation to other stars. Hitherto, a star named 'Barnard's Star' in the constellation Ophiuchus has exhibited the greatest proper motion of any known star, moving at the rate of ten and a quarter seconds a year. 'Barnard's Star' is not visible to the naked eye."

Probably no astronomer on earth slept that day.

The observatories locked their doors, with their full staffs on the inside, and admitted no one except occasional newspaper reporters who stayed a while and went away with puzzled faces, convinced at last that something strange was happening.

Blink-microscopes blinked, and so did astronomers. Coffee was consumed in prodigious quantities. Police riot squads were called to six United States observatories. Two of these calls were occasioned by attempts to break in on the part of frantic amateurs without. The other four were summoned to quell fistfights developing out of arguments within the observatories themselves. The office of Lick Observatory was a shambles, and James Truwell, Astronomer Royal of England, was sent to London Hospital with a mild concussion, the result of having a heavy photographic plate smashed over his head by an irate subordinate.

But these incidents were exceptions. The observatories, in general, were well-ordered madhouses.

The center of attention in the more enterprising ones was the loud-speaker in which reports from the Eastern Hemisphere could be relayed to the inmates. Practically all observatories kept open wires to the night side of earth, where the phenomena were still under scrutiny.

Astronomers under the night skies of Singapore, Shanghai and Sydney did their observing, as it were, directly into the business end of a long-distance telephone hook-up.

Particularly of interest were reports from Sydney and Melbourne, whence came reports on the southern skies not visible—even at night—from Europe or the United States. The Southern Cross was by these reports, a cross no longer, its Alpha and Beta being shifted northward. Alpha and Beta Centauri, Canopus and Achernar all showed considerable proper motion—all, generally speaking, northward. Triangulum Australe and the Magellanic Clouds were undisturbed. Sigma Octanis, the weak pole star, had not moved.

Disturbance in the southern sky, then, was much less than in the northern one, in point of the number of stars displaced. However, relative proper motion of the stars which were disturbed was greater. While the general direction of movement of the few stars which did move was northward, their paths were not directly north, nor did they converge upon any exact point in space.

United States and European astronomers digested these facts and drank more coffee.

Evening papers, particularly in America, showed greater awareness that something indeed unusual was happening in the skies. Most of them moved the story to the front page—but not the banner headlines—giving it a half-column with a runover that was long or short, depending upon the editor's luck in obtaining quotable statements from astronomers.

The statements, when obtained, were invariably statements of fact and not of opinion. The facts themselves, said these gentlemen, were sufficiently startling, and opinions would be premature. Wait and see. Whatever was happening was happening fast.

"How fast?" asked an editor.

"Faster than possible," was the reply.

Perhaps it is unfair to say that no editor procured expressions of opinion thus early. Charles Wangren, enterprising editor of the *Chicago Blade*, spent a small fortune in long-distance telephone calls. Out of possibly sixty attempts, he finally reached the chief astronomers at five observatories. He asked each of them the same question.

"What, in your opinion, is a possible cause, any possible cause, of the stellar movements of the last night or two?"

He tabulated the results.

"I wish I knew."—Geo. F. Stubbs, Tripp Observatory, Long Island.

"Somebody or something is crazy, and I hope it's me—I mean I."—Henry Collister McAdams, Lloyd Observatory, Boston.

"What's happening is impossible. There can't be any cause."—Letton Tischauer Tinney, Burgoyne Observatory, Albuquerque.

"I'm looking for an expert on Astrology. Know one?"—Patrick R. Whitaker, Lucas Observatory, Vermont.

Sadly studying this tabulation, which had cost him $187.35—including tax—to obtain, Editor Wangren signed a voucher to cover the long distance calls and then dropped his tabulation into the wastebasket. He telephoned his regular space-rates writer on scientific subjects.

"Can you give me a series of articles—two-three thousand words each—on all this astronomical excitement?"

"Sure," said the writer. "But what excitement?" It transpired that he'd just got back from a fishing trip and had neither read a newspaper nor happened to look up at the sky. But he wrote the articles. He even got sex appeal into them through illustrations, by using ancient star-charts showing the constellations in dishabille, by reproducing certain famous paintings such as "The Origin of the Milky Way" and by using a photograph of a girl in a bathing suit sighting a hand telescope, presumably at one of the errant stars. Circulation of the *Chicago Blade* increased by 21.7%.

It was five o'clock again in the office of the Cole Observatory, just twenty-four and a quarter hours after the beginning of all the commotion. Roger Phlutter—yes, we're back to him again—woke up suddenly when a hand was placed on his shoulder.

"Go on home, Roger," said Mervin Armbruster, his boss, in a kindly tone. Roger sat upright suddenly.

"But Mr. Armbruster," he said, "I'm sorry I fell asleep."

"Bosh," said Armbruster. "You can't stay here forever, none of us can. Go on home."

Roger Phlutter went home. But when he'd taken a bath, he felt more restless than sleepy. It was only six-fifteen. He phoned Elsie.

"I'm awfully sorry, Roger, but I have another date. What's going on, Roger? The stars, I mean."

"Gosh, Elsie—they're moving. Nobody knows."

"But I thought all the stars moved," Elsie protested. "The sun's a star, isn't it? Once you told me the sun was moving toward a point in Samson."

"Hercules."

"Hercules, then. Since you said all the stars were moving, what is everybody getting excited about?"

"This is different," said Roger. "Take Canopus. It's started moving at the rate of seven light-years a day. It can't do that!"

"Why not?"

"Because," said Roger patiently, "nothing can move faster than light."

"But if it is moving that fast, then it can," said Elsie. "Or else maybe your telescope is wrong or something. Anyway, it's pretty far off, isn't it?"

"A hundred and sixty light years. So far away that we see it a hundred and sixty years ago."

"Then maybe it isn't moving at all," said Elsie. "I mean, maybe it quit moving a hundred and fifty years ago and you're getting all excited about something that doesn't matter any more because it's all over with. Still love me?"

"I sure do, honey. Can't you break that date?"

"'Fraid not, Roger. But I wish I could."

He had to be content with that. He decided to walk uptown to eat.

It was early evening, and too early to see stars overhead, although the clear blue sky was darkening. When the stars did come out tonight, Roger knew, few of the constellations would be recognizable.

As he walked, he thought over Elsie's comments and decided that they were as intelligent as anything he'd heard at Cole. In one way they'd brought out one angle he'd never thought of before, and that made it more incomprehensible.

All these movements had started the same evening—yet they hadn't. Centauri must have started moving four years or so ago, and Rigel five hundred and forty years ago when Christopher Columbus was still in short pants if any, and Vega must have started acting up the year he—Roger, not Vega—was born, twenty-six years ago. Each star out of the hundreds must have started on a date in exact relation to its distance from Earth. Exact relation, to a light-second, for checkups of all the photographic plates taken night before last indicated that all the new stellar movements had started at four ten A.M. Greenwich time. What a mess!

Unless this meant that light, after all, had infinite velocity.

If it didn't have—and it is symptomatic of Roger's perplexity that he could postulate that incredible "if"—then—then what? Things were just as puzzling as before.

Mostly, he felt outraged that such events should happen.

He went into a restaurant and sat down. A radio was blaring out the latest composition in dissarythm, the new quarter-tone dance music in which chorded woodwinds provided background patterns for the mad melodies pounded on tuned tomtoms. Between each number and the next a phrenetic announcer extolled the virtues of a product.

Munching a sandwich, Roger listened appreciatively to the dissarythm and managed not to hear the commercials. Most intelligent people of the eighties had developed a type of radio deafness which enabled them not to hear a human voice coming from a loud-speaker, although they could hear and enjoy the then infrequent intervals of music between announcements. In an age when advertising competition was so keen that there was scarcely a bare wall or an unbillboarded lot within miles of a population center, discriminating people could retain normal outlooks on life only by carefully cultivated partial blindness and partial deafness which enabled them to ignore the bulk of that concerted assault upon their senses.

For that reason a good part of the newscast which followed the dissarythm program went, as it were, into one of Roger's ears and out of the other before it occurred to him that he was not listening to a panegyric on patent breakfast foods.

He thought he recognized the voice, and after a sentence or two he was sure that it was that of Milton Hale, the eminent physicist whose new theory on the principle of indeterminacy had recently occasioned so much scientific controversy. Apparently, Dr. Hale was being interviewed by a radio announcer.

"—a heavenly body, therefore, may have position or velocity, but it may not be said to have both at the same time, with relation to any given space-time frame."

"Dr. Hale, can you put that into common every-day language?" said the syrupy-smooth voice of the interviewer.

"That is common language, sir. Scientifically expressed, in terms of the Heisenberg contraction-principle, then n to the seventh power in parentheses, representing the pseudoposition of a Diedrich quantum-integer in relation to the seventh coefficient of curvature of mass—"

"Thank you, Dr. Hale, but I fear you are just a bit over the heads of our listeners."

"And your own head," thought Roger Phlutter.

"I am sure, Dr. Hale, that the question of greatest interest to our audience is whether these unprecedented stellar movements are real or illusory?"

"Both. They are real with reference to the frame of space but not with reference to the frame of space-time."

"Can you clarify that, Doctor?"

"I believe I can. The difficulty is purely epistemological. In strict causality, the impact of the macroscopic—"

"'The slithy toves did gyre and gimble in the wabe,' " thought Roger Phlutter.

"—upon the parallelism of the entropy-gradient."

"Bah!" said Roger, aloud.

"Did you say something, sir?" asked the waitress. Roger noticed her for the first time. She was small and blonde and cuddly. Roger smiled at her.

"That depends upon the space-time frame from which one regards it," he said, judicially. "The difficulty is epistemological."

To make up for that, he tipped her more than he should have, and left.

The world's most eminent physicist, he realized, knew less of what was happening than did the general public. The public knew that the fixed stars were moving, or that they weren't. Obviously Dr. Hale didn't even know that. Under a smoke-screen of qualifications, Hale had hinted that they were doing both.

Roger looked upward, but only a few stars, faint in the early evening, were visible through the halation of the myriad neon and spiegel-light signs. Too early yet, he decided.

He had one drink at a nearby bar, but it didn't taste quite right to him so he didn't finish it. He hadn't realized what was wrong, but he was punch-drunk from lack of sleep. He merely knew that he wasn't sleepy any more and intended to keep on walking until he felt like going to bed. Anyone hitting him over the head with a well-padded blackjack would have been doing him a signal service, but no one took the trouble.

He kept on walking and, after a while, turned into the brilliantly lighted lobby of a cineplus theater. He bought a ticket and took his seat just in time to see the sticky end of one of the three feature pictures. Several advertisements followed which he managed to look at without seeing.

"We bring you next," said the screen, "a special visicast of the night sky of London, where it is now three o'clock in the morning."

The screen went black, with hundreds of tiny dots that were stars. Roger leaned forward to watch and listen carefully—this would be a broadcast and visicast of facts, not of verbose nothingness.

"The arrow," said the screen, as an arrow appeared upon it, "is now pointing to Polaris, the pole star, which is now ten degrees from the celestial pole in the direction of Ursa Major. Ursa Major itself, the Big Dipper, is no longer recognizable as a dipper, but the arrow will now point to the stars that formerly composed it."

Roger breathlessly followed the arrow and the voice.

"Alkaid and Dubhe," said the voice. "The fixed stars are no longer fixed, but—" The picture changed abruptly to a scene in a modern kitchen. "—the qualities and excellences of Stellar's Stoves do not change. Foods cooked by the super-induced vibratory method taste as good as ever. Stellar Stoves are unexcelled."

Leisurely, Roger Phlutter stood up and made his way out into the aisle. He took his pen-knife from his pocket as he walked toward the screen. One easy jump took him up onto the low stage. His slashes into the fabric were not angry ones. They were careful, methodical cuts intelligently designed to accomplish a maximum of damage with a minimum expenditure of effort.

The damage was done, and thoroughly, by the time three strong ushers gathered him in. He offered no resistance either to them or to the police to whom they gave him. In night court, an hour later, he listened quietly to the charges against him.

"Guilty or not guilty?" asked the presiding magistrate.

"Your Honor, that is purely a question of epistemology," said Roger, earnestly. "The fixed stars move, but Corny Toasties, the world's greatest breakfast food, still represents the pseudo-position of a Diedrich quantum-integer in relation to the seventh coefficient of curvature!"

Ten minutes later, he was sleeping soundly. In a cell, it is true, but soundly nonetheless. The police left him there because they had realized he needed to sleep ...

Among other minor tragedies of that night can be included the case of the schooner *Ransagansett*, off the coast of California. Well off the coast of California! A sudden squall had blown her miles off course, how many miles the skipper could only guess.

The *Ransagansett* was an American vessel, with a German crew, under Venezuelan registry, engaged in running booze from Ensenada, Baja California, up the coast to Canada, then in the throes of a prohibition experiment. The *Ransagansett* was an ancient craft with four engines and an untrustworthy compass. During the two days of the storm, her outdated radio receiver—vintage of 1955—had gone haywire beyond the ability of Gross, the first mate, to repair.

But now only a mist remained of the storm, and the remaining shreds of wind were blowing it away. Hans Gross, holding an ancient astrolabe, stood on the deck waiting. About him was utter darkness, for the ship was running without lights to avoid the coastal patrols.

"She clearing, Mister Gross?" called the voice of the captain from below.

"Aye, sir. Idt iss glearing rabidly."

In the cabin, Captain Randall went back to his game of blackjack with the second mate and the engineer. The crew—an elderly German named Weiss, with a wooden leg—was asleep abaft the scuttlebutt—wherever that may have been.

A half hour went by. An hour, and the captain was losing heavily to Helmstadt, the engineer.

"Mister Gross!" he called out.

There wasn't any answer and he called again and still obtained no response.

"Just a minute, mein fine feathered friends," he said to the second mate and engineer, and went up the companionway to the deck.

Gross was standing there staring upward with his mouth open. The mists were gone.

"Mister Gross," said Captain Randall.

The second mate didn't answer. The captain saw that his second mate was revolving slowly where he stood.

"Hans!" said Captain Randall, "What the devil's wrong with you?" Then he too, looked up.

Superficially the sky looked perfectly normal. No angels flying around nor sound of airplane motors. The dipper—Captain Randall turned around slowly, but more rapidly than Hans Gross. Where was the Big Dipper?

For that matter, where was anything? There wasn't a constellation anywhere that he could recognize. No sickle of Leo. No belt of Orion. No horns of Taurus.

Worse, there was a group of eight bright stars that ought to have been a constellation, for they were shaped roughly like an octagon. Yet if such a constellation had ever existed, he'd never seen it, for he'd been around the Horn and Good Hope. Maybe at that— But no, there wasn't any Southern Cross!

Dazedly, Captain Randall walked to the companionway.

"Mister Weisskopf," he called. "Mister Helmstadt. Come on deck."

They came and looked. Nobody said anything for quite a while.

"Shut off the engines, Mister Helmstadt," said the captain. Helmstadt saluted—the first time he ever had—and went below.

"Captain, shall I vake opp Veiss?" asked Weisskopf.

"What for?"

"I don't know."

The captain considered. "Wake him up," he said.

"I think ve are on der blanet Mars," said Gross.

But the captain had thought of that and rejected it.

"No," he said firmly. "From any planet in the solar system the constellations would look approximately the same.

"You mean ve are oudt of der cosmos?"

The throb of the engines suddenly ceased and there only the soft familiar lapping of the waves against hull and the gentle familiar rocking of the boat.

Weisskopf returned with Weiss, and Helmstadt came on deck and saluted again.

"Vell, Captain?"

Captain Randall waved a hand to the after deck, piled high with cases of liquor under a canvas tarpaulin. "Break out the cargo," he ordered.

The blackjack game was not resumed. At dawn, under a sun they had never expected to see again—and, for that matter, certainly were not seeing at the moment—the five unconscious men were moved from the ship to the Port of San Francisco Jail by members of the coast patrol. During the night the *Ransagansett* had drifted through the Golden Gate and bumped gently into the dock of the Berkeley ferry.

In tow at the stern of the schooner was a big canvas tarpaulin. It was transfixed by a harpoon whose rope was firmly tied to the after-mast. Its presence there was never explained officially, although days later Captain Randall had vague recollection of having harpooned a sperm whale during the night. But the elderly able-bodied seaman named Weiss never did find out what happened to his wooden leg, which is perhaps just as well.

Milton Hale, Ph.D., eminent physicist, had finished broadcasting and the program was off the air.

"Thank you very much, Dr. Hale," said the radio announcer. The yellow light went on and stayed. The mike was dead. "Uh—your check will be waiting for you at the window. You—uh—know where."

"I know where," said the physicist. He was a rotund, jolly-looking little man. With his bushy white beard, he resembled a pocket edition of Santa Claus. His eyes twinkled and he smoked a short stubby pipe.

He left the sound-proof studio and walked briskly down the hall to the cashier's window. "Hello, sweetheart," he said to the girl on duty there. "I think you have two checks for Dr. Hale."

"You are Dr. Hale?"

"I sometimes wonder," said the little man. "But I carry identification that seems to prove it.

"Two checks?"

"Two checks. Both for the same broadcast, by special arrangement. By the way, there is an excellent revue at the Mabry Theater this evening."

"Is there? Yes, here are your checks, Dr. Hale. One for seventy-five and one for twenty-five. Is that correct?"

"Gratifyingly correct. Now about the revue at the Mabry?"

"If you wish I'll call my husband and ask him about it," said the girl. "He's the doorman over there."

Dr. Hale sighed deeply, but his eyes still twinkled. "I think he'll agree," he said. "Here are the tickets, my dear, and you can take him. I find that I have work to do this evening."

The girl's eyes widened, but she took the tickets.

Dr. Hale went into the phone booth and called his home. His home, and Dr. Hale, were both run by his elder sister. "Agatha, I must remain at the office this evening," he said.

"Milton, you know you can work just as well in your study here at home. I heard your broadcast, Milton. It was wonderful."

"It was sheer balderdash, Agatha. Utter rot. What did I say?"

"Why, you said that—uh—that the stars were—I mean, you were not—"

"Exactly, Agatha. My idea was to avert panic on the part of the populace. If I'd told them the truth, they'd have worried. But by being smug and scientific, I let them get the idea that everything was—uh—under control. Do you know, Agatha, what I meant by the parallelism of an entropy-gradient?"

"Why—not exactly."

"Neither did I."

"Milton, have you been drinking?"

"Not y— No, I haven't. I really can't come home to work this evening, Agatha. I'm using my study at the university, because I must have access to the library there, for reference. And the star-charts."

"But, Milton, how about that money for your broadcast? You know it isn't safe for you to have money in your pocket when you're feeling—like this."

"It isn't money, Agatha. It's a check, and I'll mail it to you before I go to the office. I won't cash it myself. How's that?"

"Well—if you must have access to the library, I suppose you must. Good-by, Milton."

Dr. Hale went across the street to the drug store. There he bought a stamp and envelope and cashed the twenty-five dollar check. The seventy-five dollar one he put into the envelope and mailed.

Standing beside the mailbox he glanced up at the early evening sky—shuddered, and hastily lowered his eyes. He took the straightest possible line for the nearest tavern and ordered a double Scotch.

"Y'ain't been in for a long time, Dr. Hale," said Mike, the bartender.

"That I haven't, Mike. Pour me another."

"Sure. On the house, this time. We had your broadcast tuned in on the radio just now. It was swell."

"Yes."

"It sure was. I was kind of worried what was happening up there, with my son an aviator and all. But as long as you scientific guys know what it's all about, I guess it's all right. That was sure a good speech, Doc. But there's one question I'd like to ask you."

"I was afraid of that," said Dr. Hale.

"These stars. They're moving, going somewhere. But where they going? I mean, like you said, if they are."

"There's no way of telling that exactly, Mike."

"Aren't they moving in a straight line, each one of them?"

For just a moment the celebrated scientist hesitated.

"Well—yes and no, Mike. According to spectroscopic analysis, they're maintaining the same distance from us, each one of them. So they're really moving—if they're moving—in circles around us. But the circles are straight, as it were. I mean, it seems that we're in the center of those circles, so the stars that are moving aren't coming closer to us or receding."

"You could draw lines for those circles?"

"On a star-globe, yes. It's been done. They all seem to be heading for a certain area of the sky, but not for a given point. In other words, they don't intersect."

"What part of the sky they going to?"

"Approximately between Ursa Major and Leo, Mike. The ones farthest from there are moving fastest, the ones nearest are moving slower. But darn you, Mike, I came in here to forget about stars, not to talk about them. Give me another."

"In a minute, Doc. When they get there, are they going to stop or keep on going?"

"How the devil do I know, Mike? They started suddenly, all at the same time, and with full original velocity—I mean, they started out at the same speed they're going now—without warming up, so to speak—so I suppose they could stop just as unexpectedly."

He stopped just as suddenly as the stars might. He stared at his reflection in the mirror back of the bar as though he'd never seen it before.

"What's the matter, Doc?"

"Mike!"

"Yes, Doc?"

"Mike, you're a genius.

"Me? You're kidding."

Dr. Hale groaned. "Mike, I'm going to have to go to the university to work this out. So I can have access to the library and the star-globe there. You're making an honest man out of me, Mike. Whatever kind of Scotch this is, wrap me up a bottle."

"It's Tartan Plaid. A quart?"

"A quart, and make it snappy. I've got to see a man about a dog-star."

"Serious, Doc?"

Dr. Hale sighed audibly. "You brought that on yourself, Mike. Yes, the dog-star is Sirius. I wish I'd never come in here, Mike. My first night out in weeks, and you ruin it."

He took a cab to the university, let himself in, and turned on the lights in his private study and in the library. Then he took a good stiff slug of Tartan Plaid and went to work.

First, by telling the chief operator who he was and arguing a bit, he got a telephone connection with the chief astronomer of Cole Observatory.

"This is Hale, Armbruster," he said. "I've got an idea, but I want to check my facts before I start to work on it. Last information I had, there were four-hundred sixty-eight stars exhibiting new proper motion. Is that still correct?"

"Yes, Milton. The same ones are still at it—no others."

"Good. I have a list then. Has there been any change in speed of motion of any of them?"

"No. Impossible as it seems, it's constant. What is your idea?"

"I want to check my theory first. If it works out into anything, I'll call you." But he forgot to.

It was a long, painful job. First he made a chart of the heavens in the area between Ursa Major and Leo. Across that chart he drew 468 lines representing the projected path of each of the aberrant stars. At the border of the chart, where each line entered, he made a notation of the apparent velocity of the star—not in light-years per hour—but in degrees per hour, to the fifth decimal.

Then he did some reasoning.

"Postulate that the motion which began simultaneously will stop simultaneously," he told himself. "Try a guess at the time. Let's try ten o'clock tomorrow evening."

He tried it and looked at the series of positions indicated upon the chart. No.

Try one o'clock in the morning. It looked almost like—sense!

Try midnight.

That did it. At any rate, it was close enough. The calculation could be only a few minutes off one way or the other and there was no point now in working out the exact time. Now that he knew the incredible fact.

He took another drink and stared at the chart grimly.

A trip to the library gave Dr. Hale the further information he needed. The address!

Thus began the saga of Dr. Hale's journey. A useless journey, it is true, but one that should rank with the trip of the messenger to Garcia.

He started it with a drink. Then, knowing the combination, he rifled the safe in the office of the president of the university. The note he left in the safe was a masterpiece of brevity. It read:

Taking money. Explain later.

Then he took another drink and put the bottle in his pocket. He went outside and hailed a taxicab. He got in.

"Where to, sir?" asked the cabby.

Dr. Hale gave an address.

"Fremont Street?" said the cabby. "Sorry, sir, but I don't know where that is."

"In Boston," said Dr. Hale. "I should have told you, in Boston."

"Boston? You mean Boston, Massachusetts? That's a long way from here."

"Therefore we better start right away," said Dr. Hale, reasonably. A brief financial discussion and the passing of money, borrowed from the university safe, set the driver's mind at rest, and they started.

It was a bitter cold night, for March, and the heater in the taxi didn't work any too well. But the Tartan Plaid worked superlatively for both Dr. Hale and the cabby, and by the time they reached New Haven, they were singing old-time songs lustily.

"Off we go, into the wide, wild yonder ..." their voices roared.

It is regrettably reported, but possibly untrue, that in Hartford Dr. Hale leered out of the window at a young woman waiting for a late street-car and asked her if she wanted to go to Boston. Apparently, however, she didn't, for at five o'clock in the morning when the cab drew up in front of 614 Fremont Street, Boston, only Dr. Hale and the driver were in the cab.

Dr. Hale got out and looked at the house. It was a millionaire's mansion, and it was surrounded by a high iron fence with barbed wire on top of it. The gate in the fence was locked and there was no bell button to push.

But the house was only a stone's throw from the sidewalk, and Dr. Hale was not to be deterred. He threw a stone. Then another. Finally he succeeded in smashing a window.

After a brief interval, a man appeared in the window. A butler, Dr. Hale decided.

"I'm Dr. Milton Hale," he called out. "I want to see Rutherford R. Sniveley, right away. It's important."

"Mr. Sniveley is not at home, sir," said the butler. "And about that window—"

"The devil with the window," shouted Dr. Hale. "Where is Sniveley?"

"On a fishing trip."

"Where?"

"I have orders not to give out that information."

Dr. Hale was just a little drunk, perhaps. "You'll give it out just the same," he roared. "By orders of the President of the United States."

The butler laughed. "I don't see him."

"You will," said Hale.

He got back in the cab. The driver had fallen asleep, but Hale shook him awake.

"The White House," said Dr. Hale.

"Huh?"

"The White House, in Washington," said Dr. Hale. "And hurry!" He pulled a hundred dollar bill from his pocket. The cabby looked at it, and groaned. Then he put the bill into his pocket and started the cab.

A light snow was beginning to fall.

As the cab drove off, Rutherford R. Sniveley, grinning, stepped back from the window. Mr. Sniveley had no butler.

If Dr. Hale had been more familiar with the peculiarities of the eccentric Mr. Sniveley, he would have known Sniveley kept no servants in the place overnight, but lived alone in the big house at 614 Fremont Street. Each morning at ten o'clock, a small army of servants descended upon the house, did their work as rapidly as possible, and were required to depart before the witching hour of noon. Aside from these two hours of every day, Mr. Sniveley lived in solitary splendor. He had few, if any, social contacts.

Aside from the few hours a day he spent administering his vast interests as one of the country's leading manufacturers, Mr. Sniveley's time was his own and he spent practically all of it in his workshop, making gadgets.

Sniveley had an ash-tray which would hand him a lighted cigar any time he spoke sharply to it, and a radio receiver so delicately adjusted that it would cut in automatically on Sniveley-sponsored programs and shut off again when they were finished. He had a bathtub that provided a full orchestral accompaniment to his singing therein, and he had a machine which would read aloud to him from any book which he placed in its hopper.

His life may have been a lonely one, but it was not without such material comforts. Eccentric, yes, but Mr. Sniveley could afford to be eccentric with a net income of four million dollars a year. Not bad for a man who'd started life as the son of a shipping clerk.

Mr. Sniveley chuckled as he watched the taxicab drive away, and then he went back to bed and to the sleep of the just.

"So somebody has things figured out nineteen hours ahead of time," he thought. "Well, a lot of good it will do them!"

There wasn't any law to punish him for what he'd done ...

Bookstores did a landoffice business that day in books on astronomy. The public, apathetic at first, was deeply interested now. Even ancient and musty volumes of Newton's *Principia* sold at premium prices.

The ether blared with comment upon the new wonder of the skies. Little of the comment was professional, or even intelligent, for most astronomers were asleep that day. They'd managed to stay awake the first forty-eight hours from the start of the phenomena, but the third day found them worn out mentally and physically, and inclined to let the stars take care of themselves while they— the astronomers, not the stars—caught up on sleep.

Staggering offers from the telecast and broadcast studios enticed a few of them to attempt lectures, but their efforts were dreary things, better forgotten. Dr. Carver Blake, broadcasting from KNB, fell soundly asleep between a perigee and an apogee.

Physicists were also greatly in demand. The most eminent of them all, however, was sought in vain. The solitary clue to Dr. Milton Hale's disappearance, the brief note "Taking money. Explain later," wasn't much of a help. His sister Agatha feared the worst.

For the first time in history, astronomical news made banner headlines in the newspapers.

Snow had started early that morning along the northern Atlantic seaboard and now it was growing steadily worse. Just outside Waterbury, Conn., the driver of Dr. Hale's cab began to weaken.

It wasn't human, he thought, for a man to be expected to drive to Boston and then, without stopping, from Boston to Washington. Not even for a hundred dollars.

Not in a storm like this. Why, he could see only a dozen yards ahead through the driving snow, even when he could manage to keep his eyes open. His fare was slumbering soundly in the back seat. Maybe he could get away with stopping here along the road, for an hour, to catch some sleep. Just an hour. His fare wouldn't ever know the difference. The guy must be loony, he thought, or why hadn't he taken a plane or a train?

Dr. Hale would have, of course, if he'd thought of it. But he wasn't used to traveling and besides there'd been the Tartan Plaid. A taxi had seemed the easiest way to get anywhere—no worrying about tickets and connections and stations. Money was no object, and the plaid condition of his mind had caused him to overlook the human factor involved in an extended journey by taxi.

When he awoke, almost frozen, in the parked taxi, that human factor dawned upon him. The driver was so sound asleep that no amount of shaking could arouse him. Dr. Hale's watch had stopped, so he had no idea where he was or what time it was.

Unfortunately, too, he didn't know how to drive a car. He took a quick drink to keep from freezing, and then got out of the cab, and as he did so, a car stopped.

It was a policeman—what is more it was a policeman in a million.

Yelling over the roar of the storm, Hale hailed him.

"I'm Dr. Hale," he shouted. "We're lost. Where am I?"

"Get in here before you freeze," ordered the policeman. "Do you mean Dr. Milton Hale, by any chance?"

"Yes."

"I've read all your books, Dr. Hale," said the policeman. "Physics is my hobby, and I've always wanted to meet you. I want to ask you about the revised value of the quantum."

"This is life or death," said Dr. Hale. "Can you take me to the nearest airport, quick?"

"Of course, Dr. Hale."

"And look—there's a driver in that cab, and he'll freeze to death unless we send aid."

"I'll put him in the back seat of my car, and then run the cab off the road. We'll take care of details later."

"Hurry, please."

The obliging policeman hurried. He got back in and started the car.

"About the revised quantum value," Dr. Hale, he began, then stopped talking.

Dr. Hale was sound asleep. The policeman drove to Waterbury airport, one of the largest in the world since the population shift from New York city northwards in the 1960's and 70's had given it a central position. In front of the ticket office, he gently awakened Dr. Hale.

"This is the airport, sir," he said.

Even as he spoke, Dr. Hale was leaping out of the car and stumbling into the building, yelling, "Thanks," over his shoulder and nearly falling down in doing so.

The warm-up roaring of the motors of a superstratoliner out on the field lent wings to his heels as he dashed for the ticket window.

"What plane's that?" he yelled.

"Washington Special, due out in one minute. But I don't think you can make it."

Dr. Hale slapped a hundred-dollar bill on the ledge. "Ticket," he gasped. "Keep change."

He grabbed the ticket and ran, getting into the plane just as the doors were being closed. Panting, he fell into a seat, the ticket still in his hand. He was sound asleep before the hostess strapped him in for the blind take-off.

A little while later, the hostess awakened him. The passengers were disembarking.

Dr. Hale rushed out of the plane, and ran across the field to the airport building. A big clock told him that it was nine o'clock, and he felt elated as he ran for the door marked "Taxicabs."

He got into the nearest one.

"White House," he told the driver. "How long'll it take?"

"Ten minutes.

Dr. Hale gave a sigh of relief and sank back against the cushions. He didn't go back to sleep this time. He was wide awake now. But he closed his eyes to think out the words he'd use in explaining matters.

"Here you are, sir."

Dr. Hale gave the driver a bill and hurried out of the cab and into the building. It didn't look like he expected it to look. But there was a desk and he ran up to it.

"I've got to see the President, quick. It's vital."

The clerk frowned. "The president of what?"

Dr. Hale's eyes went wide. "The president of the— Say, what building is this? And what town?"

The clerk's frown deepened. "This is the White House Hotel," he said, "Seattle, Washington."

Dr. Hale fainted. He woke up in a hospital three hours later. It was then midnight, Pacific Time, which meant it was three o'clock in the morning on the Eastern Seaboard. It had, in fact, been midnight already in Washington, D. C., and in Boston, when he had been leaving the Washington Special in Seattle.

Dr. Hale rushed to the window and shook his fists, both of them, at the sky. A futile gesture.

Back in the East, however, the storm had stopped by twilight, leaving a light mist in the air. The star-conscious public thereupon deluged the weather bureaus with telephoned requests about the persistence of the mist.

"A breeze off the ocean is expected," they were told. "It is blowing now, in fact, and within an hour or two will have cleared off the light fog."

By eleven-fifteen the skies of Boston were clear.

Untold thousands braved the bitter cold and stood staring upward at the unfolding pageant of the no-longer-eternal stars. It almost looked as though an incredible development had occurred.

And then, gradually, the murmur grew. By a quarter to twelve, the thing was certain, and the murmur hushed and then grew louder than ever, waxing toward midnight. Different people reacted differently, of course, as might be expected. There was laughter as well as indignation, cynical amusement as well as shocked horror. There was even admiration.

Soon in certain parts of the city, a concerted movement on the part of those who knew an address on Fremont Street, began to take place. Movement afoot and in cars and public vehicles, converging.

At five minutes of twelve, Rutherford R. Sniveley sat waiting within his house. He was denying himself the pleasure of looking until, at the last moment, the thing was complete.

It was going well. The gathering murmur of voices, mostly angry voices, outside his house told him that. He heard his name shouted.

254 From These Ashes

Just the same he waited until the twelfth stroke of the clock before he stepped out upon the balcony. Much as he wanted to look upward, he forced himself to look down at the street first. The milling crowd was there, and it was angry. But he had only contempt for the milling crowd.

Police cars were pulling up, too, and he recognized the Mayor of Boston getting out of one of them, and the Chief of Police was with him. But so what? There wasn't any law covering this.

Then having denied himself the supreme pleasure long enough, he turned his eyes up to the silent sky, and there it was. The four hundred and sixty-eight brightest stars spelling out:

USE
SNIVELY'S
SOAP

For just a second did his satisfaction last. Then his face began to turn apoplectic purple.

"My God!" said Mr. Sniveley. "It's spelled wrong!"

His face grew more purple still and then, as a tree falls, he fell backward through the window.

An ambulance rushed the fallen magnate to the nearest hospital, but he was pronounced dead—of apoplexy—upon entrance.

But misspelled or not, the eternal stars held their position as of that midnight. The aberrant motion had stopped and again the stars were fixed. Fixed to spell—USE SNIVELY'S SOAP!

Of the many explanations offered by all and sundry who professed some physical and astronomical knowledge, none was more lucid—or closer to the actual truth—than that put forward by Wendell Mehan, president emeritus of the New York Astronomical Society.

"Obviously, the phenomenon is a trick of refraction, said Dr. Mehan. "It is manifestly impossible for any force contrived by man to move a star. The stars, therefore, still occupy their old places in the firmament.

"I suggest that Sniveley must have contrived a method of refracting the light of the stars, somewhere in or just above the atmospheric layer of earth, so that they appear to have changed their positions. This is done, probably, by radio waves or similar waves, sent on some fixed frequency from a set—or possibly a series of four hundred and sixty-eight sets—somewhere upon the surface of the earth. Although we do not understand just how it is done, it is no more unthinkable that light rays should be bent by a field of waves than by a prism or by gravitational force.

"Since Sniveley was not a great scientist, I imagine that his discovery was empiric rather than logical—an accidental find. It is quite possible that even the discovery of his projector will not enable present-day scientists to understand its secret, any more than an aboriginal savage could understand the operation of a simple radio receiver by taking one apart.

"My principal reason for this assertion is the fact that the refraction obviously is a fourth-dimensional phenomenon or its effect would be purely local to one portion of the globe. Only in the fourth dimension could light be so refracted ..."

There was more, but it is better to skip to his final paragraph:

"This effect cannot possibly be permanent—more permanent, that is, than the wave-projector which causes it. Sooner or later, Sniveley's machine will be found and shut off, or it will break down or wear out of its own volition. Undoubtedly it includes vacuum tubes, which will someday blow out, as do the tubes in our radios ..."

The excellence of Mr. Mehan's analysis was shown, two months and eight days later, when the Boston Electric Co. shut off, for non-payment of bills, service to a house situated at 901 West Rogers Street, ten blocks from the Sniveley mansion. At the instant of the shut-off, excited reports from the night side of Earth brought the news that the stars had flashed back into their former positions, instantaneously.

Investigation brought out that the description of one Elmer Smith, who had purchased that house six months before, corresponded with the description of Rutherford R. Sniveley, and undoubtedly Elmer Smith and Rutherford R. Sniveley were one and the same person.

In the attic was found a complicated network of four hundred and sixty-eight radio-type antennae, each antenna of different length and running in a different direction. The machine to which they were connected was not larger, strangely, than the average ham's radio projector, nor did it draw appreciably more current, according to the electric company's record.

By special order of the President of the United States, the projector was destroyed without examination of its internal arrangement. Clamorous protests against this highhanded executive order arose from many sides. But inasmuch as the projector had already been broken up, the protests were of no avail.

Serious repercussions were, on the whole, amazingly few.

Persons in general appreciated the stars more, but trusted them less.

Roger Phlutter got out of jail and married Elsie. Dr. Milton Hale found he liked Seattle, and stayed there. Two thousand miles away from his sister Agatha, he found it possible for the first time to defy her openly. He enjoys life more but, it is feared, will write fewer books.

There is one fact remaining which is painful to consider, since it casts a deep reflection upon the basic intelligence of the human race. It is proof, though, that the President's executive order was justified, despite scientific protest.

That fact is as humiliating as it is enlightening. During the two months and eight days during which the Sniveley machine was in operation, sales of Sniveley Soap increased 915%!

Placet Is a Crazy Place

Even when you're used to it, it gets you down sometimes. Like that morning—if you can call it a morning. Really it was night. But we go by Earth time on Placet because Placet time would be as screwy as everything else on that goofy planet. I mean, you'd have a six-hour day and then a two-hour night and then a fifteen-hour day and a one-hour night and—well, you just couldn't keep time on a planet that does a figure-eight orbit around two dissimilar suns, going like a bat out of hell around and between them, and the suns going around each other so fast and so comparatively close that Earth astronomers thought it was only one sun until the Blakeslee expedition landed here twenty years ago.

You see, the rotation of Placet isn't any even fraction of the period of its orbit and there's the Blakeslee Field in the middle between the suns—a field in which light rays slow down to a crawl and get left behind and—well—

If you've not read the Blakeslee reports on Placet, hold on to something while I tell you this:

Placet is the only known planet that can eclipse itself twice at the same time, run headlong into itself every forty hours, and then chase itself out of sight.

I don't blame you.

I didn't believe it either and it scared me stiff the first time I stood on Placet and saw Placet coming head-on to run into us. And yet I'd read the Blakeslee reports and knew what was really happening and why. It's rather like those early movies when the camera was set up in front of a train and the audience saw the locomotive heading right toward them and would feel an impulse to run even though they knew the locomotive wasn't really there.

But I started to say, like that morning, I was sitting at my desk, the top of which was covered with grass. My feet were—or seemed to be—resting on a sheet of rippling water. But it wasn't wet.

On top of the grass of my desk lay a pink flowerpot, into which, nose-first, stuck a bright green Saturnian lizard. That—reason and not my eyesight told me—was my pen and inkwell. Also an embroidered sampler that said, "God Bless Our Home" in neat cross-stitching. It actually was a message from Earth Center which had just come in on the radiotype. I didn't know what it said because I'd come into my office after the B. F. effect had started. I didn't think it really said, "God Bless Our Home" because it seemed to. And just then I was mad, I was fed up, and I didn't care a holler what it actually did say.

You see—maybe I'd better explain—the Blakeslee Field effect occurs when Placet is in mid-position between Argyle I and Argyle II, the two suns it figure eights around. There's a scientific explanation of it, but it must be expressed in formulas, not in words. It boils down to this; Argyle I is terrene matter and Argyle II contraterrene, or negative matter. Halfway between them—over a considerable stretch of territory—is a field in which light rays are slowed down, way down. They move at about the speed of sound. The result is that if some-thing is moving faster than sound—as Placet itself does—you can still see it coming after it has passed you. It takes the visual image of Placet twenty-six hours to get through the field. By that time, Placet has rounded one of its suns and meets its own image on the way back. In midfield, there's an image com-ing and an image going, and it eclipses itself twice, occulting both suns at the same time. A little farther on, it runs into itself coming from the opposite di-rection—and scares you stiff if you're watching, even if you know it's not really happening.

Let me explain it this way before you get dizzy. Say an old-fashioned lo-comotive is coming toward you, only at a speed much faster than sound. A mile away, it whistles. It passes you and *then* you hear the whistle, coming from the point a mile back where the locomotive isn't any more. That's the auditory effect of an object traveling faster than sound; what I've just described is the visual effect of an object traveling—in a figure-eight orbit—faster than its own visual image.

That isn't the worst of it; you can stay indoors and avoid the eclipsing and the head-on collisions, but you can't avoid the physio-psychological effect of the Blakeslee Field.

And that, the physio-psychological effect, is something else again. The field does something to the optic nerve centers, or to the part of the brain to which the optic nerves connect, something similar to the effect of certain drugs. You have—you can't exactly call them hallucinations, because you don't ordi-narily see things that aren't there, but you get an illusory picture of what is there.

I knew perfectly well that I was sitting at a desk the top of which was glass, and not grass; that the floor under my feet was ordinary plastiplate and not a sheet of rippling water; that the objects on my desk were not a pink flow-erpot with a Saturnian lizard sticking in it, but an antique twentieth century inkwell and pen—and that the "God Bless Our Home" sampler was a radiotype message on ordinary radiotype paper. I could verify any of those things by my sense of touch, which the Blakeslee Field doesn't affect.

You can close your eyes, of course, but you don't—because even at the height of the effect, your eyesight gives you the relative size and distance of things and if you stay in familiar territory your memory and your reason tell you what they are.

So when the door opened and a two-headed monster walked in, I knew it was Reagan. Reagan isn't a two-headed monster, but I could recognize the sound of his walk.

I said, "Yes, Reagan?"

The two-headed monster said, "Chief, the machine shop is wobbling. We may have to break the rule not to do any work in midperiod."

"Birds?" I asked.

Both of his heads nodded. "The underground part of those walls must be like sieves from the birds flying through 'em, and we'd better pour concrete quick. Do you think those new alloy reinforcing bars the *Ark*'ll bring will stop them?"

"Sure," I lied. Forgetting the field, I turned to look at the clock, but there was a funeral wreath of white lilies on the wall where the clock should have been. You can't tell time from a funeral wreath. I said, "I was hoping we wouldn't have to reinforce those walls till we had the bars to sink in them. The *Ark*'s about due; they're probably hovering outside right now waiting for us to come out of the field. You think we could wait till—"

There was a crash.

"Yeah, we can wait," Reagan said. "There went the machine shop, so there's no hurry at all."

"Nobody was in there?"

"Nope, but I'll make sure." He ran out.

That's what life on Placet is like. I'd had enough of it; I'd had too much of it. I made up my mind while Reagan was gone.

When he came back, he was a bright blue articulated skeleton.

He said, "O.K., Chief. Nobody was inside."

"Any of the machines badly smashed?"

He laughed. "Can you look at a rubber beach horse with purple polka dots and tell whether it's an intact lathe or a busted one? Say, Chief, you know what you look like?"

I said, "If you tell me, you're fired."

I don't know whether I was kidding or not; I was plenty on edge. I opened the drawer of my desk and put the "God Bless Our Home" sampler in it and slammed the drawer shut. I was fed up. Placet is a crazy place and if you stay there long enough you go crazy yourself. One out of ten of Earth Center's Placet employees has to go back to Earth for psychopathic treatment after a year or two on Placet. And I'd been there three years, almost. My contract was up. I made up my mind, too.

"Reagan," I said.

He'd been heading for the door. He turned. "Yeah, Chief?"

I said, "I want you to send a message on the radiotype to Earth Center. And get it straight, two words: *I quit.*"

He said, "O.K., Chief." He went on out and closed the door.

I sat back and closed my eyes to think. I'd done it now. Unless I ran after Reagan and told him not to send the message, it was done and over and irrevocable. Earth Center's funny that way; the board is plenty generous in some directions; but once you resign they never let you change your mind. It's an ironclad rule and ninety-nine times out of a hundred it's justified on interplanetary and intragalactic projects. A man must be 100 per cent enthusiastic about his job to make a go of it, and once he's turned against it, he's lost the keen edge.

I knew the midperiod was about over, but I sat there with my eyes closed just the same. I didn't want to open them to look at the clock until I could see the clock as a clock and not as whatever it might be this time. I sat there and thought.

I felt a bit hurt about Reagan's casualness in accepting the message. He'd been a good friend of mine for ten years; he could at least have said he was sorry I was going to leave. Of course there was a fair chance that he might get the promotion, but even if he was thinking that, he could have been diplomatic about it. At least, he could have—

Oh, quit feeling sorry for yourself, I told myself. *You're through with Placet and you're through with Earth Center, and you're going back to Earth pretty soon now as soon as they relieve you, and you can get another job there, probably teaching again.*

But damn Reagan, just the same. He'd been my student at Earth City Poly, and I'd got him this Placet job and it was a good one for a youngster his age, assistant administrator of a planet with nearly a thousand population. For that matter, my job was a good one for a man *my* age—I'm only thirty-one myself. An excellent job, except that you couldn't put up a building that wouldn't fall down again and— *Quit crabbing,* I told myself; *you're through with it now. Back to Earth and a teaching job again. Forget it.*

I was tired. I put my head on my arms on top of the desk, and I must have dozed off for a minute.

I looked up at the sound of footsteps coming through the doorway; they weren't Reagan's footsteps. The illusions were getting better now, I saw. It was— or appeared to be—a gorgeous redhead. It couldn't be, of course. There are a few women on Placet, mostly wives of technicians but—

She said, "Don't you remember me, Mr. Rand?" It was a woman; her voice was a woman's voice, and a beautiful voice. Sounded vaguely familiar, too.

"Don't be silly," I said; "how can I recognize you at mid-per—" My eyes suddenly caught a glimpse of the clock past her shoulder, and it was a clock and not a funeral wreath or a cuckoo's nest, and I realized suddenly that everything else in the room was back to normal. And that meant midperiod was over, and I wasn't seeing things.

My eyes went back to the redhead. She must be real, I realized. And suddenly I knew her, although she'd changed, changed plenty. All changes were improvements, although Michaelina Witt had been a very pretty girl when she'd been in my extra-terrestrial Botany III class at Earth City Polytech four— no, five years ago.

She'd been pretty, then. Now she was beautiful. She was stunning. How had the teletalkies missed her? Or had they? What was she doing *here*? She must have just got off the *Ark*, but— I realized I was still gawking at her. I stood up so fast I almost fell across the desk.

"Of course I remember you, Miss Witt," I stammered. "Won't you sit down? How did you come here? Have they relaxed the no-visitors rule?"

She shook her head, smiling. "I'm not a visitor, Mr. Rand. Center advertised for a technician-secretary for you, and I tried for the job and got it, subject to your approval, of course. I'm on probation for a month, that is."

"Wonderful," I said. It was a masterpiece of understatement. I started to elaborate on it: "Marvelous—"

There was the sound of someone clearing his throat. I looked around; Reagan was in the doorway. This time not as a blue skeleton or a two-headed monster. Just plain Reagan.

He said, "Answer to your radiotype just came." He crossed over and dropped it on my desk. I looked at it. "O.K. August 19th," it read. My momentary wild hope that they'd failed to accept my resignation went down among the widgie birds. They'd been as brief about it as I'd been.

August 19th—the next arrival of the *Ark*. They certainly weren't wasting any time—mine or theirs. Four days!

Reagan said, "I thought you'd want to know right away, Phil."

"Yeah," I told him. I glared at him. "Thanks." With a touch of spite—or maybe more than a touch—I thought, *well, my bucko, you don't get the job, or that message would have said so; they're sending a replacement on the next shuttle of the* Ark.

But I didn't say that; the veneer of civilization was too thick. I said, "Miss Witt, I'd like you to meet—" They looked at each other and started to laugh, and I remembered. Of course, Reagan and Michaelina had both been in my botany class, as had Michaelina's twin brother, Ichabod. Only, of course, no one ever called the redheaded twins Michaelina and Ichabod. It was Mike and Ike, once you knew them.

Reagan said, "I met Mike getting off the *Ark*. I told her how to find your office, since you weren't there to do the honors."

"Thanks," I said. "Did the reinforcing bars come?"

"Guess so. They unloaded some crates. They were in a hurry to pull out again. They've gone."

I grunted.

Reagan said, "Well, I'll check the ladings. Just came to give you the radiotype; thought you'd want the good news right away."

He went out, and I glared after him. The louse. The—

Michaelina said, "Am I to start work right away, Mr. Rand?"

I straightened out my face and managed a smile. "Of course not," I told her. "You'll want to look around the place first. See the scenery and get acclimated. Want to stroll into the village for a drink?"

"Of course."

We strolled down the path toward the little cluster of buildings, all small, one-story, and square.

She said, "It's—it's nice. Feels like I'm walking on air, I'm so light. Exactly what is the gravity?"

"Point seven four," I said. "If you weigh—um-m, a hundred twenty pounds on Earth, you weigh about eighty-nine pounds here. And on you, it looks good."

She laughed. "Thank you, Professor— Oh, that's right; you're not a professor now. You're now my boss, and I must call you Mr. Rand."

"Unless you're willing to make it Phil, Michaelina?"

"If you'd call me Mike; I detest Michaelina, almost as much as Ike hates Ichabod."

"How is Ike?"

"Fine. Has a student-instructor job at Poly, but he doesn't like it much." She looked ahead at the village. "Why so many small buildings instead of a few bigger ones?"

"Because the average life of a structure of any kind on Placet is about three weeks. And you never know when one is going to fall down—with someone inside. It's our biggest problem. All we can do is make them small and light, except the foundations, which we make as strong as possible. Thus far, nobody has been hurt seriously in the collapse of a building, for that reason, but— Did you feel that?"

"The vibration? What was it, an earthquake?"

"No," I said. "It was a flight of birds."

"What?"

I had to laugh at the expression on her face. I said, "Placet is a crazy place. A minute ago, you said you felt as though you were walking on air. Well, in a way, you are doing just exactly that. Placet is one of the rare objects in the Universe that is composed of both ordinary and *heavy* matter. Matter with a collapsed molecular structure, so heavy you couldn't lift a pebble of it. Placet has a core of that stuff; that's why this tiny planet, which has an area about twice the size of Manhattan Island, has a gravity three-quarters that of Earth. There is life—animal life, not intelligent—living on the core. There are birds, whose molecular structure is like that of the planet's core, so dense that ordinary matter is as tenuous to them as air is to us. They actually *fly* through it, as birds on Earth fly through the air. From their standpoint we're walking on top of Placet's atmosphere."

"And the vibration of their flight under the surface makes the houses collapse?"

"Yes, and worse—they fly right through the foundations, no matter what we make them of. Any matter we can work with is just so much gas to them. They fly through iron or steel as easily as through sand or loam. I've just got a shipment of some specially tough stuff from Earth—the special alloy steel you heard me ask Reagan about—but I haven't much hope of it doing any good."

"But aren't those birds dangerous? I mean, aside from making the buildings fall down. Couldn't one get up enough momentum flying to carry it out of the ground and into the air a little way? And wouldn't it go right through anyone who happened to be there?"

"It would," I said, "but it doesn't. I mean, they never fly closer to the surface than a few inches. Some sense stems to tell them when they're nearing the top of their 'atmosphere.' Something analogous to the supersonics a bat uses. You know, of course, how a bat can fly in utter darkness and never fly into a solid object."

"Like radar, yes."

"Like radar, yes, except a bat uses sound waves instead of radio waves. And the widgie birds must use something that works on the same principle, in reverse; turns them back a few inches before they approach what to them would be the equivalent of a vacuum. Being heavy-matter, they could no more exist or fly in air than a bird could exist or fly in a vacuum."

While we were having a cocktail apiece in the village, Michaelina mentioned her brother again. She said, "Ike doesn't like teaching at all, Phil. Is there any chance at all that you could get him a job here on Placet?"

I said, "I've been badgering Earth Center for another administrative assistant. The work is increasing plenty since we've got more of the surface under cultivation. Reagan really needs help. I'll—"

Her whole face was alight with eagerness. And I remembered. I was through. I'd resigned, and Earth Center would pay as much attention to any recommendation of mine as though I were a widgie bird. I finished weakly, "I'll—I'll see if I can do anything about it."

She said, "Thanks—Phil." My hand was on the table beside my glass, and for a second she put hers over it. All right, it's a hackneyed metaphor to say it felt as though a high-voltage current went through me. But it did, and it was a mental shock as well as a physical one, because I realized then and there that I was head over heels. I'd fallen harder than any of Placet's buildings ever had. The thump left me breathless. I wasn't watching Michaelina's face, but from the way she pressed her hand harder against mine for a millisecond and then jerked it away as though from a flame, she must have felt a little of that current, too.

I stood up a little shakily and suggested that we walk back to headquarters.

Because the situation was completely impossible, now. Now that Center had accepted my resignation and I was without visible or invisible means of support. In a psychotic moment, I'd cooked my own goose. I wasn't even sure I could get a teaching job. Earth Center is the most powerful organization in the Universe and has a finger in every pie. If they blacklisted me—

Walking back, I let Michaelina do most of the talking; I had some heavy thinking to do. I wanted to tell her the truth—and I didn't want to.

Between monosyllabic answers, I fought it out with myself. And, finally lost. Or won. I'd not tell her—until just before the next coming of the *Ark*. I'd pretend everything was O.K. and normal for that long, give myself that much chance to see if Michaelina would fall for me. That much of a break I'd give myself. A chance, for four days.

And then—well, if by then she'd come to feel about me the way I did about her, I'd tell her what a fool I'd been and tell her I'd like to— No, I wouldn't let her return to Earth with me, even if she wanted to, until I saw light ahead through a foggy future. All I could tell her was that if and when I had a chance of working my way up again to a decent job—and after all I was still only thirty-one and might be able to—

That sort of thing.

Reagan was waiting in my office, looking as mad as a wet hornet. He said, "Those saps at Earth Center shipping department gummed things again. Those crates of special steel—aren't."

"Aren't what?"

"Aren't anything. They're empty crates. Something went wrong with the crating machine and they never knew it."

"Are you sure that's what those crates were supposed to contain?"

"Sure I'm sure. Everything else on the order came, and the ladings specified the steel for those particular crates." He ran a hand through his tousled hair. It made him look more like an Airedale than he usually does.

I grinned at him. "Maybe it's invisible steel."

"Invisible, weightless and intangible. Can *I* word the message to Center telling them about it?"

"Go as far as you like," I told him, "Wait here a minute, though. I'll show Mike where her quarters are and then I want to talk to you a minute."

I took Michaelina to the best available sleeping cabin of the cluster around headquarters. She thanked me again for trying to get Ike a job here, and I felt lower than a widgie bird's grave when I went back to my office.

"Yeah, Chief?" Reagan said.

"About that message to Earth," I told him. "I mean the one I sent this morning. I don't want you to say anything about it to Michaelina."

He chuckled. "Want to tell her yourself, huh? O.K. I'll keep my yap shut."

I said, a bit wryly, "Maybe I was foolish sending it."

"Huh?" he said. "I'm sure glad you did. Swell idea."

He went out, and I managed not to throw anything at him.

The next day was a Tuesday, if that matters. I remember it as the day I solved one of Placet's two major problems. An ironic time to do it, maybe.

I was dictating some notes on greenwort culture—Placet's importance to Earth is, of course, the fact that certain plants native to the place and which won't grow anywhere else yield derivatives that have become important to the pharmacopoeia. I was having heavy sledding because I was watching Michaelina take the notes; she'd insisted on starting work her second day on Placet.

And suddenly, out of a clear sky and out of a muggy mind, came an idea. I stopped dictating and rang for Reagan. He came in.

"Reagan," I said, "order five thousand ampoules of J-17 Conditioner. Tell 'em to rush it."

"Chief, don't you remember? We tried the stuff. Thought it might condition us to see normally in midperiod, but it didn't affect the optic nerves. We still saw screwy. It's great for conditioning people to high or low temperatures or—"

"Or long or short waking-sleeping periods," I interrupted him. "That's what I'm talking about, Reagan. Look, revolving around two suns, Placet has such short irregular periods of light and dark that we never took them seriously. Right?"

"Sure but—"

"But since there's no logical Placet day and night we could use, we made ourselves slaves to a sun so far away we can't see it. We use a twenty-four hour day. But midperiod occurs every twenty hours, regularly. We can use conditioner to adapt ourselves to a *twenty*-hour day—six hours sleep, twelve awake—with everybody blissfully sleeping through the period when their eyes play tricks on them. And in a darkened sleeping room so you couldn't see anything, even if you woke up. More and shorter days per year—and nobody goes psychopathic on us. Tell me what's wrong with it."

His eyes went bleak and blank and he hit his forehead a resounding whack with the palm of his band.

He said, "Too simple, that's what's wrong with it. So darned simple only a genius could see it. For two years I've been going slowly nuts and the answer so easy nobody could see it. I'll put the order in right away."

He started out and then turned back. "Now how do we keep the buildings up? Quick, while you're fey or whatever you are."

I laughed. I said, "Why not try that invisible steel of yours in the empty crates?"

He said, "Nuts," and closed the door.

And the next day was a Wednesday and I knocked off work and took Michaelina on a walking tour around Placet. Once around is just a nice day's hike. But with Michaelina Witt, any day's hike would be a nice day's hike. Except, of course, that I knew I had only one more full day to spend with her. The world would end on Friday.

Tomorrow the *Ark* would leave Earth, with the shipment of conditioner that would solve one of our problems—and with whomever Earth Center was sending to take my place. It would warp through space to a point a safe distance outside the Argyle I-II system and come in on rocket power from there. It would be here Friday, and I'd go back with it. But I tried not to think about that.

I pretty well managed to forget it until we got back to headquarters and Reagan met me with a grin that split his homely mug into horizontal halves. He said, "Chief, you did it."

"Swell," I said. "I did what?"

"Gave me the answer what to use for reinforcing foundations. You solved the problem."

"Yeah?" I said.

"Yeah. Didn't he, Mike?"

Michaelina looked as puzzled as I must have. She said, "He was kidding. He said to use the stuff in the empty crates, didn't he?"

Reagan grinned again. "He just thought be was kidding. That's what we're going to use from now on. Nothing. Look, Chief, it's like the conditioner—so simple we never thought of it. Until you told me to use what was in the empty crates, and I got to thinking it over."

I stood thinking a moment myself, and then I did what Reagan had done the day before—hit myself a whack on the forehead with the heel of my palm. Michaelina still looked puzzled.

"Hollow foundations," I told her. "What's the one thing widgie birds won't fly through? *Air*. We can make buildings as big as we need them, now. For foundations, we sink double walls with a wide air space between. We can—"

I stopped, because it wasn't "we" anymore. *They* could do it after I was back on Earth looking for a job.

And Thursday went and Friday came.

I was working, up till the last minute, because it was the easiest thing to do. With Reagan and Michaelina helping me, I was making out material lists for our new construction projects. First, a three-story building of about forty rooms for a headquarters building,

We were working fast, because it would be midperiod shortly, and you can't do paper work when you can't read and can write only by feel.

But my mind was on the *Ark*. I picked up the phone and called the radiotype shack to ask about it.

"Just got a call from them," said the operator. "They're warped in, but not close enough to land before midperiod. They'll land right after."

"O.K.," I said, abandoning the hope that they'd be a day late.

I got up and walked to the window. We were nearing mid-position, all right. Up in the sky to the north I could see Placet coming toward us.

"Mike," I said. "Come here."

She joined me at the window and we stood there, watching. My arm was around her. I don't remember putting it there, but I didn't take it away, and she didn't move.

Behind us, Reagan cleared his throat, He said, "I'll give this much of the list to the operator. He can get it on the ether right after midperiod." He went out and shut the door behind him.

Michaelina seemed to move a little closer. We were both looking out the window at Placet rushing toward us. She said, "Beautiful, isn't it, Phil?"

"Yes," I said. But I turned, and I was looking at her face as I said it. Then— I hadn't meant to—I kissed her.

I went back, and sat down at my desk, She said, "Phil, what's the matter? You haven't got a wife and six kids hidden away somewhere, or something, have you? You were single when I had a crush on you at Earth Polytech—and I waited five years to get over it and didn't, and finally wangled a job on Placet just to— Do I have to do the proposing?"

I groaned. I didn't look at her. I said, "Mike, I'm nuts about you. But— just before you came, I sent a two-word radiotype to Earth. It said, 'I quit.' So I've got to leave Placet on this shuttle of the *Ark*, and I doubt if I can even get a teaching job, now that I've got Earth Center down on me, and—"

She said, "But, Phil!" and took a step toward me.

There was a knock on the door, Reagan's knock. I was glad, for once, of the interruption. I called out for him to come in, and he opened the door.

He said, "You told Mike yet, Chief?"

I nodded, glumly.

Reagan grinned. "Good," he said; "I've been busting to tell her. It'll be swell to see Ike again."

"Huh?" I said. "Ike who?"

Reagan's grin faded. He said, "Phil, are you slipping, or something? Don't you remember giving me the answer to that Earth Center radiotype four days ago, just before Mike got here?"

I stared at him with my mouth open. I hadn't even read that radiotype, let alone answered it. Had Reagan gone psychopathic, or had I? I remembered shoving it in the drawer of my desk. I jerked open the drawer and pulled it out. My hand shook a little as I read it: REQUEST FOR ADDITIONAL ASSISTANT GRANTED. WHOM DO YOU WANT FOR THE JOB?

I looked up at Reagan again. I said, "You're trying to tell me I sent an answer to this?"

He looked as dumbfounded as I felt.

"You told me to," he said.

"What did I tell you to send?"

"Ike Witt." He stared at me. "Chief, are you feeling all right?"

I felt so all right something seemed to explode in my head. I stood up and started for Michaelina. I said, "Mike, will you marry me?" I got my arms around her, just in time, before midperiod closed down on us, so I couldn't see what she looked like, and vice versa. But over her shoulder, I could see what must be Reagan. I said, "Get out of here, you ape," and I spoke quite literally because that's exactly what he appeared to be. A bright yellow ape.

The floor was shaking under my feet, but other things were happening to me, too, and I didn't realize what the shaking meant until the ape turned back and yelled, "A flight of birds going under us, Chief! Get out quick, before—"

But that was as far as he got before the house fell down around us and the tin roof hit my head and knocked me out. Placet is a crazy place. I like it.

Knock

There is a sweet little horror story that is only two sentences long:
The last man on Earth sat alone in a room. There was a knock at the door ...
Two sentences and an ellipsis of three dots. The horror, of course, isn't in
the story at all; it's in the ellipsis, the implication: *what* knocked at the door.
Faced with the unknown, the human mind supplies something vaguely horrible.
But it *wasn't* horrible, really.

The last man on Earth—or in the universe, for that matter—*sat alone in a
room*. It was a rather peculiar room. He'd just been studying out the reason for
its peculiarity. His conclusion didn't horrify him, but it annoyed him.

Walter Phelan, who had been associate professor of anthropology at
Nathan University up to the time two days ago when Nathan University had
ceased to exist, was not a man who horrified easily. Not that Walter Phelan
was a heroic figure, by any wild stretch of the imagination. He was slight of
stature and mild of disposition. He wasn't much to look at, and he knew it.

Not that appearance worried him now. Right now, in fact, there wasn't much
feeling in him. Abstractedly, he knew that two days ago, within the space of an
hour, the human race had been destroyed, except for him and, somewhere—one
woman. And that was a fact which didn't concern Walter Phelan in the slightest
degree. He'd probably never see her and didn't care too much if he didn't.

Women just hadn't been a factor in Walter's life since Martha had died a
year and a half ago. Not that Martha hadn't been a good wife—albeit a bit on
the bossy side. Yes, he'd loved Martha, in a deep, quiet way. He was only forty
now, and he'd been only thirty-eight when Martha had died, but—well—he
just hadn't thought about women since then. His life had been his books, the
ones he read and the ones he wrote. Now there wasn't any point in writing
books, but he had the rest of his life to spend in reading them.

True, company would have been nice, but he'd get along without it.
Maybe after a while he'd get so he'd enjoy the occasional company of one of
the Zan, although that was a bit difficult to imagine. Their thinking was so
alien to his that it was a bit difficult to imagine their finding common ground
for a discussion. They were intelligent in a way, but so is an ant. No man has
ever established communication with an ant. He thought of the Zan, somehow, as super-ants, although they didn't look like ants—and he had a hunch
that the Zan regarded the human race as the human race regarded ordinary
ants. Certainly what they'd done to Earth had been what men do to ant hills,
and it had been done much more efficiently.

But they'd given him plenty of books. They'd been nice about that, as
soon as he had told them what he wanted. And he had told them that the
moment he realized that he was destined to spend the rest of his life alone in
this room. The rest of his life, or as the Zan had quaintly expressed it, for-ev-er.

Even a brilliant mind, and the Zan obviously had brilliant minds, had its idiosyncrasies. The Zan had learned to speak Terrestrial English in a matter of hours, but they persisted in separating syllables. However, we digress.

There was a knock at the door.

You've got it all now except the three dots, the ellipsis, and I'm going to fill that in and show you that it wasn't horrible at all.

Walter Phelan called out, "Come in," and the door opened. It was, of course, only a Zan. It looked exactly like the other Zan; if there was any way of telling them apart, Walter hadn't found it. It was about four feet tall and it looked like nothing on Earth—nothing, that is, that had been on Earth before the Zan came here.

Walter said, "Hello, George." When he'd learned that none of them had names, he'd decided to call them all George and the Zan didn't seem to mind.

This one said, "Hel-lo, Wal-ter." That was ritual, the knock on the door and the greetings. Walter waited.

"Point one," said the Zan. "You will please hence-forth sit with your chair fac-ing the oth-er way."

Walter said, "I thought so, George. That plain wall is transparent from the other side, isn't it?"

"It is trans-par-ent."

Walter sighed. "I knew it. That plain blank wall, without a single piece of furniture against it. And made of something different from the other walls. If I persist in sitting with my back to it, what then? You will kill me?— I ask hopefully."

"We will take a-way your books."

"You've got me there, George. All right, I'll face the other way when I sit and read. How many other animals besides me are in this zoo of yours?"

"Two hun-dred and six-teen."

Walter shook his head. "Not complete, George. Even a bush-league zoo can beat that—*could* beat that, I mean, if there were any bush-league zoos left. Did you just pick us at random?"

"Ran-dom sam-ples, yes. All spe-cies would have been too man-y. Male and fe-male each of one hun-dred kinds."

"What do you feed them? The carnivorous ones, I mean."

"We make feed. Syn-thet-ic."

"Smart. And the flora? You've got a collection of that, too, haven't you?"

"Flo-ra not hurt by vi-bra-tions. It is all still grow-ing."

"Good for the flora. You weren't as hard on it, then, as you were on the fauna. Well, George, you started out with 'point one.' I deduce that there is a point two lurking somewhere. What is it?"

"There is some-thing we do not un-der-stand. Two of the oth-er an-i-mals sleep and do not wake. They are cold."

"It happens in the best-regulated zoos, George. Probably not a thing wrong with them except that they're dead."

"Dead? That means stopped. But noth-ing stopped them. Each was a-lone."

Walter stared at the Zan. "Do you mean, George, that you do not know what natural death is?"

"Death is when a be-ing is killed, stopped from liv-ing."

Walter Phelan blinked. "How old are you, George?" he asked.

"Six-teen—you would not know the word. Your planet went a-round your sun a-bout sev-en thou-sand times. I am still young."

Walter whistled softly. "A babe in arms," he said. He thought hard for a moment. "Look, George, you've got something to learn about this planet you're on. There's a guy down here who doesn't hang around where you come from. An old man with a beard and a scythe and an hourglass. Your vibrations didn't kill him."

"What *is* he?"

"Call him the Grim Reaper, George. Old Man Death. Our people and animals live until somebody, Old Man Death, stops them from ticking."

"He stopped the two crea-tures? He will stop more?"

Walter opened his mouth to answer, and then closed it again. Something in the Zan's voice indicated that there would be a worried frown on his face if he had a face recognizable as such.

"How about taking me to those animals who won't wake up?" Walter asked. "Is that against the rules?"

"Come," said the Zan.

That had been the afternoon of the second day. It was the next morning that the Zan came back, several of them. They began to move Walter Phelan's books and furniture. When they finished that, they moved him. He found himself in a much larger room a hundred yards away.

He sat and waited this time, too. When there was a knock on the door, he knew what was coming and politely stood up as he called out, "Come in."

A Zan opened the door and stood aside. A woman entered.

Walter bowed slightly. "Walter Phelan," he said, "in case George didn't tell you my name. George tries to be polite but he doesn't know all our ways."

The woman seemed calm; he was glad to notice that. She said, "My name's Grace Evans, Mr. Phelan. What's this all about? Why did they bring me here?"

Walter was studying her as she talked. She was tall, fully as tall as he, and well-proportioned. She looked to be somewhere in her early thirties, about the age Martha had been. She had the same calm confidence about her that he had always liked about Martha, even though it had contrasted with his own easygoing informality. In fact, he thought she looked quite a bit like Martha.

"I think you can guess why they brought you here, but let's go back a bit," he said. "Do you know what's happened otherwise?"

"You mean that they've—killed everyone?"

"Yes. Please sit down. You know how they accomplished it?"

She sank into a comfortable chair nearby. "No," she said. "I don't know just how. Not that it matters, does it?"

"Not a lot. But here's the story, what I know of it from getting one of them to talk, and from piecing things together. There isn't a great number of them—here anyway. I don't know how numerous a race they are where they came from and I don't know where that is, but I'd guess it's outside the solar system. You've seen the spaceship they came in?"

"Yes. It's as big as a mountain."

"Almost. Well, it has equipment for emitting some sort of vibration—they call it that in our language, but I imagine it's more like a radio wave than a sound vibration—that destroys all animal life. The ship itself is insulated against the vibration. I don't know whether its range is big enough to kill off the whole planet at once, or whether they flew in circles around the earth, sending out the vibratory waves. But it killed everything at once instantly and, I hope, painlessly. The only reason we, and the other two-hundred-odd animals in this zoo weren't killed was because we were inside the ship. We'd been picked up as specimens. You do know this is a zoo, don't you?"

"I—I suspected it."

"The front walls are transparent from the outside. The Zan were pretty clever in fixing up the inside of each cubicle to match the natural habitat of the creature it contains. These cubicles, such as the one we're in, are of plastic and they've got a machine that makes one in about ten minutes. If Earth had a machine and a process like that, there wouldn't have been any housing shortage. Well, there isn't any housing shortage now, anyway. And I imagine that the human race—specifically you and I—can stop worrying about the H-bomb and the next war. The Zan have certainly solved a lot of problems for us."

Grace Evans smiled faintly. "Another case where the operation was successful but the patient died. Things *were* in an awful mess. Do you remember being captured? I don't. I went to sleep one night and woke up in a cage on the spaceship."

"I don't remember either," Walter said. "My hunch is that they used the waves at low intensity first, just enough to knock us all out. Then they cruised around, picking up samples for their zoo more or less at random. After they had as many as they wanted, or as many as they had room in the ship for, they turned on the juice all the way. And that was that. It wasn't until yesterday that they knew they'd made a mistake by overestimating us. They thought we were immortal, as they are."

"That we were—what?"

"They can be killed but they don't know what natural death is. They didn't anyway, until yesterday. Two of us died yesterday."

"Two of— Oh!"

"Yes, two of us animals in their zoo. Two species gone irrevocably. And by the Zan's way of figuring time, the remaining member of each species is going to live only a few minutes anyway. They figured they had permanent specimens."

"You mean they didn't realize what short-lived creatures we are?"

"That's right," Walter said. "One of them is young at seven thousand years, he told me. They're bisexual themselves, incidentally, but they probably breed every ten thousand years or thereabouts. When they learned yesterday how ridiculously short a life span we terrestrial animals have, they were probably shocked to the core, if they have cores. At any rate they decided to reorganize their zoo—two by two instead of one by one. They figure we'll last longer collectively if not individually."

"Oh!" Grace Evans stood up and there was a faint flush on her face. "If you think— If they think—" She turned toward the door.

"It'll be locked," Walter Phelan said calmly. "But don't worry. Maybe they think, but I *don't* think. You needn't even tell me that you wouldn't have me if I were the last man on Earth; it would be corny under the circumstances."

"But are they going to keep us locked up together in this one little room?"

"It isn't so little; we'll get by. I can sleep quite comfortably in one of those overstuffed chairs. And don't think I don't agree with you perfectly, my dear. All personal considerations aside, the least favor we can do the human race is to let it die out with us and not be perpetuated for exhibition in a zoo."

She said, "Thank you," almost inaudibly, and the flush was gone from her face. There was anger in her eyes, but Walter knew that it wasn't anger at him. With her eyes sparkling like that, she looked a lot like Martha, he thought.

He smiled at her and said, "Otherwise—"

She started out of her chair and for a moment he thought she was going to come over and slap him. Then she sank back wearily. "If you were a *man*, you'd be thinking of some way to— They can be killed, you said?" Her voice was bitter.

"The Zan? Oh, certainly. I've been studying them. They look horribly different from us, but I think they have about the same metabolism, the same type of circulatory system, and probably the same type of digestive system. I think that anything that would kill one of us would kill one of them."

"But you said—"

"Oh, there are differences, of course. Whatever factor it is in man that ages him, they don't have. Or else they have some gland that man doesn't have, something that renews cells. More often than every seven years, I mean."

She had forgotten her anger now. She leaned forward eagerly. She said, "I think that's right. I don't think, though, that they feel pain."

He had been hoping that. He said, "What makes you think so, my dear?"

"I stretched a piece of wire that I found in the desk of my own cubicle across the door so the Zan would fall over it. He did, and the wire cut his leg."

"Did he bleed red?"

"Yes, but it didn't seem to annoy him. He didn't get mad about it; he didn't mention it, just took the wire down. When he came back the next time a few hours later, the cut was gone. Well, almost gone. I could see just enough of a trace of it to be sure it was the same Zan."

Walter Phelan nodded slowly. "He wouldn't get angry, of course. They're emotionless. Maybe if we killed one they wouldn't even punish us. Just give us our food through a trap door and stay clear of us, treat us as men would have treated a zoo animal that had killed its keeper. They'd probably just see that we didn't get a crack at any more keepers."

"How many of them are there?"

Walter said, "About two hundred, I think, in this particular spaceship. But undoubtedly there are many more where they came from. I have a hunch, though, that this is just an advance board, sent to clear off this planet and make it safe for Zan occupancy."

"They certainly did a good—"

There was a knock at the door and Walter Phelan called out, "Come in." A Zan opened the door and stood in the doorway.

"Hello, George," said Walter.

"Hel-lo, Wal-ter." The same ritual. The same Zan?

"What's on your mind?"

"An-oth-er creature sleeps and will not wake. A small fur-ry one called a wea-sel."

Walter shrugged. "It happens, George. Old Man Death. I told you about him."

"And worse. A Zan has died. This morn-ing."

"Is that worse?" Walter looked at him blandly. "Well, George, you'll have to get used to it if you're going to stay around here."

The Zan said nothing. It stood there.

Finally, Walter said, "Well?"

"About the wea-sel. You advise the same?"

Walter shrugged again. "Probably won't do any good. But why not?"

The Zan left.

Walter could hear his footsteps dying away outside. He grinned. "It might work, Martha," he said.

"Mar— My name is Grace, Mr. Phelan. What might work?"

"My name is Walter, Grace. You might as well get used to it. You know, Grace, you do remind me a lot of Martha. She was my wife. She died a couple of years ago."

"I'm sorry. But *what* might work? What were you talking about to the Zan?"

"We should know tomorrow," Walter said. And she couldn't get another word out of him.

That was the third day of the stay of the Zan. The next day was the last.

It was nearly noon when one of the Zan came. After the ritual, he stood in the doorway, looking more alien than ever. It would be interesting to describe him for you, but there aren't words. He said, "We go. Our coun-cil met and de-ci-ded."

"Another of you died?"

"Last night. This is pla-net of death."

Walter nodded. "You did your share. You're leaving two hundred and thirteen alive, besides us, but that's out of quite a few billion. Don't hurry back."

"Is there an-y-thing we can do?"

"Yes. You can hurry. And you can leave our door unlocked, but not the others. We'll take care of the others."

The Zan nodded, and left.

Grace Evans was standing, her eyes shining. She asked, "How—? What—?"

"Wait," cautioned Walter. "Let's hear them blast off. It's a sound I want to hear and remember."

The sound came within minutes, and Walter Phelan, realizing how rigidly he'd been holding himself, dropped into a chair and relaxed.

He said softly, "There was a snake in the Garden of Eden, too, Grace, and it got us into trouble. But this one got us out of it, and made up. I mean the mate of the snake that died day before yesterday. It was a rattlesnake."

"You mean it killed the two Zan who died? But—"

Walter nodded. "They were babes in the woods here. When they took me to see the first creatures who 'were asleep and wouldn't wake up,' and I saw that one of them was a rattlesnake, I had an idea, Grace. Just maybe, I thought, poison creatures were a development peculiar to Earth and the Zan wouldn't know about them. And, too, maybe their metabolism was enough like ours that the poison would kill them. Anyway, I had nothing to lose trying. And both maybes turned out to be right."

"How did you get the living rattlesnake to—"

Walter Phelan grinned. "I told them what affection is. They didn't know. But they were interested, I found, in preserving the remaining one of each species as long as possible, to picture and record it before it died. I told them it would die immediately because of the loss of its mate, unless it had affection and petting, constantly.

"I showed them how, with the duck, which was the other creature who had lost its mate. Luckily it was a tame duck and I had no trouble holding it against my chest and petting it, to show them how. Then I let them take over with it—and with the rattlesnake."

He stood up and stretched, and then sat down again more comfortably. He said, "Well, we've got a world to plan. We'll have to let the animals out of the ark, and that will take some thinking and deciding. The herbivorous wild ones we can let go right away, and let them take their chances. The domestic ones we'll do better to keep and take charge of; we'll need them. But the carnivora, the predators— Well, we'll have to decide. But I'm afraid it's got to be thumbs down. Unless maybe we can find and operate the machinery that they used to make synthetic food."

He looked at her. "And the human race. We've got to make a decision about that. A pretty important decision."

Her face was getting a bit pink again, as it had yesterday; she sat rigidly in her chair. "No," she said.

He didn't seem to have heard her. "It's been a nice race, even if nobody won it. It'll be starting over again now, if we start it, and it may go backwards for a while until it gets its breath, but we can gather books for it and keep most of its knowledge intact, the important things anyway. We can—"

He broke off as she got up and started for the door. Just the way Martha would have acted, he thought, back in the days when he was courting her, before they were married.

He said, "Think it over, my dear, and take your time. But come back."

The door slammed. He sat waiting, thinking out all the things there were to do once he started, but in no hurry to start them.

And after a while he heard her hesitant footsteps coming back.

He smiled a little. See? It wasn't horrible, really.

The last man on Earth sat alone in a room. There was a knock at the door ...

All Good Bems

The spaceship from Andromeda II spun like a top in
the grip of mighty forces. The five-limbed Andromedan
strapped into the pilot's seat turned the three protuber-
ant eyes of one of his heads toward the four other
Andromedans strapped into bunks around the ship.
"Going to be a rough landing," he said. It was.

Elmo Scott hit the tab key of his typewriter and listened to the carriage zing across and ring the bell. It sounded nice and he did it again. But there still weren't any words on the sheet of paper in the machine.

He lit another cigarette and stared at it. At the paper, that is, not the cigarette. There still weren't any words on the paper.

He tilted his chair back and turned to look at the sleek black-and-tan Doberman pinscher lying in the mathematical middle of the rag rug. He said, "You lucky dog." The Doberman wagged what little stump of tail he had. He didn't answer otherwise.

Elmo Scott looked back at the paper. There still weren't any words there. He put his fingers over the keyboard and wrote: "Now is the time for all good men to come to the aid of the party." He stared at the words, such as they were, and felt the faintest breath of an idea brush his cheek.

He called out "Toots!" and a cute little brunette in a blue gingham house dress came out of the kitchen and stood by him. His arm went around her. He said, "I got an idea."

She read the words in the typewriter. "It's the best thing you've written in three days," she said, "except for that letter renewing your subscription to the *Digest*. I think that was better."

"Button your lip," Elmo told her. "I'm talking about what I'm going to do with that sentence. I'm going to change it to a science-fiction plot idea, one word at a time. It can't miss. Watch."

He took his arm from around her and wrote under the first sentence: "Now is the time for all good Bems to come to the aid of the party." He said, "Get the idea, Toots? Already it's beginning to look like a science-fiction sendoff. Good old bug-eyed monsters. Bems to you. Watch the next step."

Under the first sentence and the second he wrote. "Now is the time for all good Bems to come to the aid of—" He stared at it. "What shall I make it, Toots? 'The galaxy' or 'the universe'?"

"Better make it yourself. If you don't get a story finished and the check for it in two weeks, we lose this cabin and walk back to the city and—and you'll have to quit writing full time and go back to the newspaper and—"

"Cut it out, Toots. I know all that. Too well."

"Just the same, Elmo, you'd better make it: 'Now is the time for all good Bems to come to the aid of Elmo Scott.'"

The big Doberman stirred on the rag rug. He said, "You needn't."

Both human heads turned toward him.

The little brunette stamped a dainty foot. "Elmo!" she said. "Trying a trick like that. That's how you've been spending the time you should have spent writing. Learning ventriloquism!"

"No, Toots," said the dog. "It isn't that."

"Elmo! How do you get him to move his mouth like—" Her eyes went from the dog's face to Elmo's and she stopped in mid-sentence. If Elmo Scott wasn't scared stiff, then he was a better actor than Maurice Evans. She said, "Elmo!" again, but this time her voice was a scared little wail, and she didn't stamp her foot. Instead she practically fell into Elmo's lap and, if he hadn't grabbed her, would probably have fallen from there to the floor.

"Don't be frightened, Toots," said the dog.

Some degree of sanity returned to Elmo Scott. He said, "Whatever you are, don't call my wife Toots. Her name is Dorothy."

"You call her Toots."

"That's—that's different."

"I see it is," said the dog. His mouth lolled open as though he were laughing. "The concept that entered your mind when you used that word 'wife' is an interesting one. This is a bisexual planet, then."

Elmo said, "This is a—uh— What are you talking about?"

"On Andromeda II," said the dog, "we have five sexes. But we are a highly developed race, of course. Yours is highly primitive. Perhaps I should say lowly primitive. Your language has, I find, confusing connotations; it is not mathematical. But, as I started to observe, you are still in the bisexual stage. How long since you were monosexual? And don't deny that you once were; I can read the word 'amoeba' in your mind."

"If you can read my mind," said Elmo, "why should I talk?"

"Consider Toots—I mean Dorothy," said the dog. "We cannot hold a three-way conversation since you two are not telepathic. At any rate, there shall shortly be more of us in the conversation. I have summoned my companions." He laughed again. "Do not let them frighten you, no matter in what form they may appear. They are merely Bems."

"B-bems?" asked Dorothy. "You mean you are b-bug-eyed monsters? That's what Elmo means by Bems, but you aren't—"

"That is just what I am," said the dog. "You are not, of course, seeing the real me. Nor will you see my companions as they really are. They, like me, are temporarily animating bodies of creatures of lesser intelligence. In our real bodies, I assure you, you would classify us as Bems. We have five limbs each and two heads, each head with three eyes on stalks."

"Where are your real bodies?" Elmo asked.

"They are dead— Wait, I see that word means more to you than I thought at first. They are dormant, temporarily uninhabitable and in need of repairs, inside the fused hull of a spaceship which was warped into this space too near a planet. This planet. That's what wrecked us."

"Where? You mean there's really a spaceship near here? Where?" Elmo's eyes were almost popping from his head as he questioned the dog.

"That is none of your business, Earthman. If it were found and examined by you creatures, you would possibly discover space travel before you are ready for it. The cosmic scheme would be upset." He growled. "There are enough cosmic wars now. We were fleeing a Betelgeuse fleet when we warped into your space."

"Elmo," said Dorothy, "What's beetle juice got to do with it? Wasn't this crazy enough before he started talking about a beetle juice fleet?"

"No," said Elmo resignedly. "It wasn't." For a squirrel had just pushed its way through a hole in the bottom of the screen door.

It said, "Hyah dar, yo-all. We-uns got yo message, One."

"See what I mean?" said Elmo.

"Everything is all right, Four," said the Doberman. These people will serve our purpose admirably. Meet Elmo Scott and Dorothy Scott; don't call her Toots."

"Yessir. Yessum. Ah's sho gladda meetcha."

The Doberman's mouth lolled open again in another laugh; it was unmistakable this time.

"Perhaps I'd better explain Four's accent," he said. "We scattered, each entering a creature of low mentality and from that vantage point contacting the mind of some member of the ruling species, learning from that mind the language and the level of intelligence and degree of imagination. I take it from your reaction that Four has learned the language from a mind which speaks a language differing slightly from yours."

"Ah sho did," said the squirrel.

Elmo shuddered slightly. "Not that I'm suggesting it, but I'm curious to know why you didn't take over the higher species directly," he said.

The dog looked shocked. It was the first time Elmo had ever seen a dog look shocked, but the Doberman managed it.

"It would be unthinkable," he declared. "The cosmic ethic forbids the taking over of any creature of an intelligence over the four level. We Andromedans are of the twenty-three level, and I find you Earthlings—"

"Wait!" said Elmo. "Don't tell me. It might give me an inferiority complex. Or would it?"

"Ah fears it might," said the squirrel.

The Doberman said, "So you can see that it is not purely coincidence that we Bems should manifest ourselves to you who are a writer of what I see you call science-fiction. We studied many minds and yours was the first one we found capable of accepting the premise of visitors from Andromeda. Had Four here, for example, tried to explain things to the woman whose mind he studied, she would probably have gone insane."

"She sho would," said the squirrel.

A chicken thrust its head through the hole in the screen, clucked, and pulled its head out again.

"Please let Three in," said the Doberman. "I fear that you will not be able to communicate directly with Three. He has found that subjectively to modify the throat structure of the creature he inhabits in order to enable it to talk would be a quite involved process. It does not matter. He can communicate telepathically with one of us, and we can relay his comments to you. At the moment he sends you his greetings and asks that you open the door."

The clucking of the chicken (it was a big black hen, Elmo saw) sounded angry and Elmo said, "Better open the door, Toots."

Dorothy Scott got off his lap and opened the door. She turned a dismayed face to Elmo and then to the Doberman.

"There's a cow coming down the road," she said. "Do you mean to tell me that she—"

"He," the Doberman corrected her. "Yes, that will be Two. And since your language is completely inadequate, in that it has only two genders, you may as well call all of us 'he'; it will save trouble. Of course, we are five different sexes, as I explained."

"You didn't explain," said Elmo, looking interested.

Dorothy glowered at Elmo. "He'd better not. Five different sexes! All living together in one spaceship. I suppose it takes all five of you to—uh—"

"Exactly," said the Doberman. "And now if you will please open the door for Two, I'm sure that—"

"I will not! Have a cow in here? Do you think I'm crazy?"

"We could make you so," said the dog. Elmo looked from the dog to his wife.

"You'd better open the door, Dorothy," he advised.

"Excellent advice," said the Doberman. "We are not, incidentally, going to impose on your hospitality, nor will we ask you to do anything unreasonable."

Dorothy opened the screen door and the cow clumped in.

He looked at Elmo and said, "Hi, Mac. What's cookin'?"

Elmo closed his eyes.

The Doberman asked the cow, "Where's Five? Have you been in touch with him?"

"Yeah," said the cow. "He's comin'. The guy I looked over was a bindlestiff, One. What are these mugs?"

"The one with the pants is a writer," said the dog. "The one with the skirt is his wife."

"What's a wife?" asked the cow. He looked at Dorothy and leered. "I like skirts better," he said. "Hiya, Babe."

Elmo got up out of his chair, glaring at the cow. "Listen, you—" That was as far as he got. He dissolved into laughter, almost hysterical laughter, and sank down into the chair again.

Dorothy looked at him indignantly. "Elmo! Are you going to let a cow—"

She almost strangled on the word as she caught Elmo's eye, and she, too, started laughing. She fell into Elmo's lap so hard that he grunted.

The Doberman was laughing, too, his long pink tongue lolling out. "I'm glad you people have a sense of humor," he said with approval. "In fact, that is one reason we chose you. But let us be serious a moment."

There wasn't any laughter in his voice now. He said, "Neither of you will be harmed, but you will be watched. Do not go near the phone or leave the house while we are here. Is that understood?"

"How long are you going to be here?" Elmo asked. "We have food for only a few days."

"That will be long enough. We will be able to make a new spaceship within a matter of hours. I see that that amazes you; I shall explain that we can work in a slower dimension."

"I see," said Elmo.

"What is he talking about, Elmo?" Dorothy demanded.

"A slower dimension," said Elmo. "I used it in a story once myself. You go into another dimension where the time rate is different; spend a month there and come back and you get back only a few minutes or hours after you left, by time in your own dimension."

"And you invented it? Elmo, how wonderful!"

Elmo grinned at the Doberman. He said, "That's all you want—to let you stay here until you get your new ship built? And to let you alone and not notify anybody that you're here?"

"Exactly." The dog appeared to beam with delight. "And we will not inconvenience you unnecessarily. But you will be guarded. Five or I will do that."

"Five? Where is he?"

"Don't be alarmed; he is under your chair at the moment, but he will not harm you. You didn't see him come in a moment ago through the hole in the screen. Five, meet Elmo and Dorothy Scott. Don't call her Toots."

There was a rattle under the chair. Dorothy screamed and pulled her feet up into Elmo's lap. Elmo tried to put his there too, with confusing results.

There was hissing laughter from under the chair. A sibilant voice said, "Don't worry, folks. I didn't know until I read in your minds just now that shaking my tail like that was a warning that I was about to— Think of the word for me—thank you. To strike." A five-foot-long rattlesnake crawled out from under the chair and curled up beside the Doberman.

"Five won't harm you," said the Doberman. "None of us will."

"We sho won't," said the squirrel.

The cow leaned against the wall, crossed its front legs and said, "That's right, Mac." He, or she, or it leered at Dorothy. It said, "An' Babe, you don't need to worry about what you're worryin' about. I'm housebroke." It started to chew placidly and then stopped. "I won't give you no udder trouble, either," it concluded.

Elmo Scott shuddered slightly.

"You've done worse than that yourself," said the Doberman. "And it's quite a trick to pun in a language you've just learned. I can see one question in your mind. You're wondering that creatures of high intelligence should have a sense of humor. The answer is obvious if you think about it; isn't your sense of humor more highly developed than that of creatures who have even less intelligence than you?"

"Yes," Elmo admitted. "Say, I just thought of something else. Andromeda is a constellation, not a star. Yet you said your planet is Andromeda II. How come?"

"Actually we come from a planet of a star in Andromeda for which you have no name; it's too distant to show up in your telescopes. I merely called it by a name that would be familiar to you. For your convenience I named the star after the constellation."

Whatever slight suspicion (of what, he didn't know) Elmo Scott may have had, evaporated.

The cow uncrossed its legs. "What t'ell we waitin' for?" it inquired.

"Nothing, I suppose," said the Doberman. "Five and I will take turns standing guard."

"Go ahead and get started," said the rattlesnake. "I'll take the first trick. Half an hour; that'll give you a month there."

The Doberman nodded. He got up and trotted to the screen door, pushing it open with his muzzle after lifting the latch with his tail. The squirrel, the chicken and the cow followed.

"Be seein' ya, Babe," said the cow.

"We sho will," the squirrel said.

It was almost two hours later that the Doberman, who was then on duty as guard, lifted his head suddenly.

"There they went," he said.

"I beg your pardon," said Elmo Scott.

"Their new spaceship just took off. It has warped out of this space and is heading back toward Andromeda."

"You say *their*. Didn't you go along?"

"Me? Of course not. I'm Rex, your dog. Remember? Only One, who was using my body, left me with an understanding of what happened and a low level of intelligence."

"A low level?"

"About equal to yours, Elmo. He says it will pass away, but not until after I've explained everything to you. But how about some dog food? I'm hungry. Will you get me some, Toots?"

Elmo said, "Don't call my wife— Say, are you really Rex?"

"Of course I'm Rex."

"Get him some dog food, Toots," Elmo said. "I've got an idea. Let's all go out in the kitchen so we can keep talking."

"Can I have two cans of it?" asked the Doberman.

Dorothy was getting them out of the closet. "Sure, Rex," she said.

The Doberman lay down in the doorway. "How about rustling some grub for us, too, Toots?" Elmo suggested. "I'm hungry. Look, Rex, you mean they just went off like that without saying good-by to us, or anything?"

"They left me to say good-by. And they did you a favor, Elmo, to repay you for your hospitality. One took a look inside that skull of yours and found the psychological block that's been keeping you from thinking of plots for your stories. He removed it. You'll be able to write again. No better than before, maybe, but at least you won't go snow-blind staring at blank paper."

"The devil with that," said Elmo. "How about the spaceship they didn't repair? Did they leave it?"

"Sure. But they took their bodies out of it and fixed them up. They were really Bems, by the way. Two heads apiece, five limbs—and they could use all five as either arms or legs—six eyes apiece, three to a head, on long stems. You should have seen them."

Dorothy was putting cold food on the table. "You won't mind a cold lunch, will you, Elmo?" she asked.

Elmo looked at her without seeing her and said, "Huh?" and then turned back to the Doberman. The Doberman got up from the doorway and went over to the big dish of dog food that Dorothy had just put down on the floor. He said, "Thanks, Toots," and started eating in noisy gulps.

Elmo made himself a sandwich, and started munching it. The Doberman finished his meal, lapped up some water and went back to the throw rug in the doorway.

Elmo stared at him. "Rex, if I can find that spaceship they abandoned, I won't *have* to write stories," he said. "I can find enough things in it to— Say, I'll make you a proposition."

"Sure," said the Doberman, "if I tell you where it is, you'll get another Doberman pinscher to keep me company, and you'll raise Doberman pups. Well, you don't know it yet, but you're going to do that anyway. The Bem named One planted the idea in your mind; he said I ought to get something out of this, too."

"Okay, but will you tell me where it is?"

"Sure, now that you've finished that sandwich. It was something that would have looked like a dust mote, if you'd seen it, on the top slice of boiled ham. It was almost submicroscopic. You just ate it."

Elmo Scott put his hands to his head. The Doberman's mouth was open; its tongue lolled out for all the world as though it were laughing at him.

Elmo pointed a finger at him. He said, "You mean I've got to write for a living all the rest of my life?"

"Why not?" asked the Doberman. "They figured out you'd be really happier that way. And with the psychological block removed, it won't be so hard. You won't have to start out, 'Now is the time for all good men—' And, incidentally, it wasn't any coincidence that you substituted Bems for men; that was One's idea. He was already here inside me, watching you. And getting quite a kick out of it."

Elmo got up and started to pace back and forth. "Looks like they outsmarted me at every turn but one, Rex," he murmured. "I've got 'em there, if you'll co-operate."

"How?"

"We can make a fortune with you. The world's only talking dog. Rex, we'll get you diamond-studded collars and feed you aged steaks and—and get everything you want. Will you?"

"Will I what?"

"Speak."

"Woof," said the Doberman.

Dorothy Scott looked at Elmo Scott. "Why do that, Elmo?" she asked. "You told me I should never ask him to speak unless we had something to give him, and he's just eaten."

"I dunno," said Elmo. "I forgot. Well, guess I'd better get back to getting a story started." He stepped over the dog and walked to his typewriter in the other room.

He sat down in front of it and then called out. "Hey, Toots," and Dorothy came in and stood beside him. He said, "I think I got an idea. That 'Now is the time for all good Bems to come to the aid of Elmo Scott' has the germ of an idea in it. I can even pick the title out of it. 'All Good Bems.' About a guy trying to write a science-fiction story, and suddenly his—uh—dog—I can make him a Doberman like Rex and—Well, wait till you read it."

He jerked fresh paper into the typewriter and wrote the heading:

ALL GOOD BEMS

Mouse

Bill Wheeler was, as it happened, looking out of the window of his bachelor apartment on the fifth floor on the corner of 83rd Street and Central Park West when the spaceship from Somewhere landed.

It floated gently down out of the sky and came to rest in Central Park on the open grass between the Simon Bolivar Monument and the walk, barely a hundred yards from Bill Wheeler's window.

Bill Wheeler's hand paused in stroking the soft fur of the Siamese cat lying on the windowsill and he said wonderingly, "What's that, Beautiful?" but the Siamese cat didn't answer. She stopped purring, though, when Bill stopped stroking her. She must have felt something different in Bill—possibly from the sudden rigidity in his fingers or possibly because cats are prescient and feel changes of mood. Anyway she rolled over on her back and said, "Miaouw," quite plaintively. But Bill, for once, didn't answer her. He was too engrossed in the incredible thing across the street in the park.

It was cigar-shaped, about seven feet long and two feet in diameter at the thickest point. As far as size was concerned, it might have been a large toy model dirigible, but it never occurred to Bill—even at his first glimpse of it when it was about fifty feet in the air, just opposite his window—that it might be a toy or a model.

There was something about it, even at the most casual look, that said *alien.* You couldn't put your finger on what it was. Anyway, alien or terrestrial, it had no visible means of support. No wings, propellers, rocket tubes or anything else—and it was made of metal and obviously heavier than air.

But it floated down like a feather to a point just about a foot above the grass. It stopped there and suddenly, out of one end of it (both ends were so nearly alike that you couldn't say it was the front or back) came a flash of fire that was almost blinding. There was a hissing sound with the flash and the cat under Bill Wheeler's hand turned over and was on her feet in a single lithe movement, looking out of the window. She spat once, softly, and the hairs on her back and the back of her neck stood straight up, as did her tail, which was now a full two inches thick.

Bill didn't touch her; if you know cats you don't when they're like that. But he said, "Quiet, Beautiful. It's all right. It's only a spaceship from Mars, to conquer Earth. It isn't a mouse."

He was right on the first count, in a way. He was wrong on the second, in a way. But let's not get ahead of ourselves like that.

After the single blast from its exhaust tube or whatever it was the spaceship dropped the last twelve inches and lay inert on the grass. It didn't move. There was now a fan-shaped area of blackened earth radiating from one end of it, for a distance of about thirty feet.

And then nothing happened except that people came running from several directions. Cops came running, too, three of them, and kept people from

284 From These Ashes

going too close to the alien object. Too close, according to the cops' idea, seemed to be closer than about ten feet. Which, Bill Wheeler thought, was silly. If the thing was going to explode or anything, it would probably kill everyone for blocks around.

But it didn't explode. It just lay there, and nothing happened. Nothing except that flash that had startled both Bill and the cat. And the cat looked bored now, and lay back down on the windowsill, her hackles down.

Bill stroked her sleek fawn-colored fur again, absentmindedly. He said, "This is a day, Beautiful. That thing out there is from *outside,* or I'm a spider's nephew. I'm going down and take a look at it."

He took the elevator down. He got as far as the front door, tried to open it, and couldn't. All he could see through the glass was the backs of people, jammed tight against the door. Standing on tiptoes and stretching his neck to see over the nearest ones, he could see a solid phalanx of heads stretching from here to there.

He got back in the elevator. The operator said, "Sounds like excitement out front. Parade going by or something?"

"Something," Bill said. "Spaceship just landed in Central Park, from Mars or somewhere. You hear the welcoming committee out there."

"The hell," said the operator. "What's it doing?"

"Nothing."

The operator grinned. "You're a great kidder, Mr. Wheeler. How's that cat you got?"

"Fine," said Bill. "How's yours?"

"Getting crankier. Threw a book at me when I got home last night with a few under my belt and lectured me half the night because I'd spent three and a half bucks. You got the best kind."

"I think so," Bill said.

By the time he got back to the window, there was really a crowd down there. Central Park West was solid with people for half a block each way and the park was solid with them for a long way back. The only open area was a circle around the spaceship, now expanded to about twenty feet in radius, and with a lot of cops keeping it open instead of only three.

Bill Wheeler gently moved the Siamese over to one side of the windowsill and sat down. He said, "We got a box seat, Beautiful. I should have had more sense than to go down there."

The cops below were having a tough time. But reinforcements were coming, truckloads of them. They fought their way into the circle and then helped enlarge it. Somebody had obviously decided that the larger that circle was the fewer people were going to be killed. A few khaki uniforms had infiltrated the circle, too.

"Brass," Bill told the cat. "High brass. I can't make out insignia from here, but that one boy's at least a three-star; you can tell by the way he walks."

They got the circle pushed back to the sidewalk, finally. There was a lot of brass inside by then. And half a dozen men, some in uniform, some not, were starting, very carefully, to work on the ship. Photographs first, and then measurements, and then one man with a big suitcase of paraphernalia was carefully scratching at the metal and making tests of some kind.

"A metallurgist, Beautiful," Bill Wheeler explained to the Siamese, who wasn't watching at all. "And I'll bet you ten pounds of liver to one miaouw he finds that's an alloy that's brand new to him. And that it's got some stuff in it he can't identify.

"You really ought to be looking out, Beautiful, instead of lying there like a dope. This is a *day*, Beautiful. This may be the beginning of the end—or of something new. I wish they'd hurry up and get it open."

Army trucks were coming into the circle now. Half a dozen big planes were circling overhead, making a lot of noise. Bill looked up at them quizzically.

"Bombers, I'll bet, with pay loads. Don't know what they have in mind unless to bomb the park, people and all, if little green men come out of that thing with ray guns and start killing everybody. Then the bombers could finish off whoever's left."

But no little green men came out of the cylinder. The men working on it couldn't, apparently, find an opening in it. They'd rolled it over now and exposed the under side, but the under side was the same as the top. For all they could tell, the under side *was* the top.

And then Bill Wheeler swore. The army trucks were being unloaded, and sections of a big tent were coming out of them, and men in khaki were driving stakes and unrolling canvas.

"They *would* do something like that, Beautiful," Bill complained bitterly. "Be bad enough if they hauled it off, but to leave it there to work on and still to block off our view—"

The tent went up. Bill Wheeler watched the top of the tent, but nothing happened to the top of the tent and whatever went on inside he couldn't see. Trucks came and went, high brass and civvies came and went.

And after a while the phone rang. Bill gave a last affectionate rumple to the cat's fur and went to answer it.

"Bill Wheeler?" the receiver asked. "This is General Kelly speaking. Your name has been given to me as a competent research biologist. Tops in your field. Is that correct?"

"Well," Bill said. "I'm a research biologist. It would be hardly modest for me to say I'm tops in my field. What's up?"

"A spaceship has just landed in Central Park."

"You don't say," said Bill.

"I'm calling from the field of operations; we've run phones in here, and we're gathering specialists. We would like you and some other biologists to examine something that was found inside the—uh—spaceship. Grimm of Harvard was in town and will be here and Winslow of New York University is already here. It's opposite Eighty-third Street. How long would it take you to get here?"

"About ten seconds, if I had a parachute. I've been watching you out of my window." He gave the address and the apartment number. "If you can spare a couple of strong boys in imposing uniforms to get me through the crowd, it'll be quicker than if I try it myself. Okay?"

"Right. Send 'em right over. Sit tight."

"Good," said Bill. "*What* did you find inside the cylinder?"

There was a second's hesitation. Then the voice said, "Wait till you get here."

"I've got instruments," Bill said. "Dissecting equipment. Chemicals. Reagents. I want to know what to bring. Is it a little green man?"

"No," said the voice. After a second's hesitation again, it said, "It seems to be a mouse. A dead mouse."

"Thanks," said Bill. He put down the receiver and walked back to the window. He looked at the Siamese cat accusingly. "Beautiful," he demanded, "was somebody ribbing me, or—"

There was a puzzled frown on his face as he watched the scene across the street. Two policemen came hurrying out of the tent and headed directly for the entrance of his apartment building. They began to work their way through the crowd.

"Fan me with a blowtorch, Beautiful," Bill said. "It's the McCoy." He went to the closet and grabbed a valise, hurried to a cabinet and began to stuff instruments and bottles into the valise. He was ready by the time there was a knock on the door.

He said, "Hold the fort, Beautiful. Got to see a man about a mouse." He joined the policemen waiting outside his door and was escorted through the crowd and into the circle of the elect and into the tent.

There was a crowd around the spot where the cylinder lay. Bill peered over shoulders and saw that the cylinder was neatly split in half. The inside was hollow and padded with something that looked like fine leather, but softer. A man kneeling at one end of it was talking.

"—not a trace of any activating mechanism, any mechanism at *all*, in fact. Not a wire, not a grain or a drop of any fuel. Just a hollow cylinder, padded inside. Gentlemen, it *couldn't* have traveled by its own power in any conceivable way. But it came here, and from outside. Gravesend says the material is definitely extraterrestrial. Gentlemen, I'm stumped."

Another voice said, "I've an idea, Major." It was the voice of the man over whose shoulder Bill Wheeler was leaning and Bill recognized the voice and the man with a start. It was the President of the United States. Bill quit leaning on him.

"I'm no scientist," the President said. "And this is just a possibility. Remember the one blast, out of that single exhaust hole? That might have been the destruction, the dissipation of whatever the mechanism or the propellant was. Whoever, whatever, sent or guided this contraption might not have wanted us to find out what made it run. It was constructed, in that case, so that, upon landing, the mechanism destroyed itself utterly. Colonel Roberts, you examined that scorched area of ground. Anything that might bear out that theory?"

"Definitely, sir," said another voice. "Traces of metal and silica and some carbon, as though it had been vaporized by terrific heat and then condensed and uniformly spread. You can't find a chunk of it to pick up, but the instruments indicate it. Another thing—"

Bill was conscious of someone speaking to him. "You're Bill Wheeler, aren't you?"

Bill turned, "Professor Winslow!" he said. "I've seen your picture, sir, and I've read your papers in the Journal. I'm proud to meet you and to—"

"Cut the malarkey," said Professor Winslow, "and take a gander at this." He grabbed Bill Wheeler by the arm and led him to a table in one corner of the tent.

"Looks for all the world like a dead mouse," he said, "but it isn't. Not quite. I haven't cut in yet; waited for you and Grimm. But I've taken temperature tests and had hairs under the mike and studied musculature. It's—well, look for yourself."

Bill Wheeler looked. It looked like a mouse all right, a very small mouse, until you looked closely. Then you saw little differences, if you were a biologist.

Grimm got there and—delicately, reverently—they cut in. The differences stopped being little ones and became big ones. The bones didn't seem to be made of bone, for one thing, and they were bright yellow instead of white. The digestive system wasn't too far off the beam, and there was a circulatory system and a white milky fluid in it, but there wasn't any heart. There were, instead, nodes at regular intervals along the larger tubes.

"Way stations," Grimm said. "No central pump. You might call it a lot of little hearts instead of one big one. Efficient, I'd say. Creature built like this couldn't have heart trouble. Here, let me put some of that white fluid on a slide."

Someone was leaning over Bill's shoulder, putting uncomfortable weight on him. He turned his head to tell the man to get the hell away and saw it was the President of the United States. "Out of this world?" the President asked quietly.

"And how," said Bill. A second later he added, "Sir," and the President chuckled. He asked, "Would you say it's been dead long or that it died about the time of arrival?"

Winslow answered that one. "It's purely a guess, Mr. President, because we don't know the chemical make-up of the thing, or what its normal temperature is. But a rectal thermometer reading twenty minutes ago, when I got here, was ninety-five three and one minute ago it was ninety point six. At that rate of heat loss, it couldn't have been dead long."

"Would you say it was an intelligent creature?"

"I wouldn't say for sure, Sir. It's too alien. But I'd guess—definitely no. No more so than its terrestrial counterpart, a mouse. Brain size and convolutions are quite similar."

"You don't think it could, conceivably, have designed that ship?"

"I'd bet a million to one against it, Sir."

It had been mid-afternoon when the spaceship had landed; it was almost midnight when Bill Wheeler started home. Not from across the street, but from the lab at New York U., where the dissection and microscopic examinations had continued.

He walked home in a daze, but he remembered guiltily that the Siamese hadn't been fed, and hurried as much as he could for the last block.

She looked at him reproachfully and said "Miaouw, miaouw, miaouw, miaouw—" so fast he couldn't get a word in edgewise until she was eating some liver out of the icebox.

"Sorry, Beautiful," he said then. "Sorry, too, I couldn't bring you that mouse, but they wouldn't have let me if I'd asked, and I didn't ask because it would probably have given you indigestion."

He was still so excited that he couldn't sleep that night. When it got early enough he hurried out for the morning papers to see if there had been any new discoveries or developments.

There hadn't been. There was less in the papers than he knew already. But it was a big story and the papers played it big.

He spent most of three days at the New York U. lab, helping with further tests and examinations until there just weren't any new ones to try and darn little left to try them on. Then the government took over what was left and Bill Wheeler was on the outside again.

For three more days he stayed home, tuned in on all news reports on the radio and video and subscribed to every newspaper published in English in New York City. But the story gradually died down. Nothing further happened; no further discoveries were made and if any new ideas developed, they weren't given out for public consumption.

It was on the sixth day that an even bigger story broke—the assassination of the President of the United States. People forgot the spaceship.

Two days later the prime minister of Great Britain was killed by a Spaniard and the day after that a minor employee of the Politburo in Moscow ran amuck and shot a very important official.

A lot of windows broke in New York City the next day when a goodly portion of a county in Pennsylvania went up fast and came down slowly. No one within several hundred miles needed to be told that there was—or had been—a dump of A-bombs there. It was in sparsely populated country and not many people were killed, only a few thousand.

That was the afternoon, too, that the president of the stock exchange cut his throat and the crash started. Nobody paid too much attention to the riot at Lake Success the next day because of the unidentified submarine fleet that suddenly sank practically all the shipping in New Orleans harbor.

It was the evening of that day that Bill Wheeler was pacing up and down the front room of his apartment. Occasionally he stopped at the window to pet the Siamese named Beautiful and to look out across Central Park, bright under lights and cordoned off by armed sentries, where they were pouring concrete for the anti-aircraft gun emplacements.

He looked haggard.

He said, "Beautiful, we saw the start of it, right from this window. Maybe I'm crazy, but I still think that spaceship started it. God knows how. Maybe I should have fed you that mouse. Things couldn't have gone to pot, so *suddenly* without help from somebody or something."

He shook his head slowly. "Let's dope it out, Beautiful. Let's say something came in on that ship besides a dead mouse. What could it have been? What could it have done and be doing?

"Let's say that the mouse was a laboratory animal, a guinea pig. It was sent in the ship and it survived the journey but died when it got here. Why? I've got a screwy hunch, Beautiful."

He sat down in a chair and leaned back, staring up at the ceiling. He said, "Suppose the superior intelligence— from Somewhere—that made that ship came in with it. Suppose it wasn't the mouse—let's call it a mouse. Then, since the mouse was the only physical thing in the spaceship, the being, the invader, wasn't physical. It was an entity that could live apart from whatever body it had back where it came from. But let's say it could live in *any* body and it left its own in a safe place back home and rode here in one that was expendable, that it could abandon on arrival. That would explain the mouse and the fact that it died at the time the ship landed.

"Then the *being*, at that instant, just jumped into the body of someone here—probably one of the first people to run toward the ship when it landed. It's living in somebody's body—in a hotel on Broadway or a flophouse on the Bowery or anywhere—pretending to be a human being. That make sense, Beautiful?"

He got up and started to pace again.

"And having the ability to control other minds, it sets about to make the world—the Earth—safe for Martians or Venusians or whatever they are. It sees— after a few days of study—that the world is on the brink of destroying itself and needs only a push. So it could give that push.

"It could get inside a nut and make him assassinate the President, and get caught at it. It could make a Russian shoot his Number 1. It could make a Spaniard shoot the prime minister of England. It could start a bloody riot in the U. N., and make an army man, there to guard it, explode an A-bomb dump. It could—hell, Beautiful, it could push this world into a final war within a week. It practically *has* done it."

He walked over to the window and stroked the cat's sleek fur while he frowned down at the gun emplacements going up under the bright floodlights.

"And he's done it and even if my guess is right I couldn't stop him because I couldn't find him. And nobody would believe me, now. He'll make the world safe for Martians. When the war is over, a lot of little ships like that—or big ones—can land here and take over what's left ten times as easy as they could now."

He lighted a cigarette with hands that shook a little. He said, "The more I think of it, the more—"

He sat down in the chair again. He said, "Beautiful, I've got to *try.* Screwy as that idea is, I've got to give it to the authorities, whether they believe it or not. That Major I met was an intelligent guy. So is General Keely. I—"

He started to walk to the phone and then sat down again. "I'll call both of them, but let's work it out just a little finer first. See if I can make any intelligent suggestions how they could go about finding the—the *being*—"

He groaned. "Beautiful, it's impossible. It wouldn't even have to be a human being. It could be an animal, anything. It could be you. He'd probably take over whatever nearby type of mind was nearest his own. If he was remotely feline, you'd have been the nearest cat."

He sat up and stared at her. He said, "I'm going crazy, Beautiful. I'm remembering how you jumped and twisted just after that spaceship blew up its mechanism and went inert. And, listen, Beautiful, you've been sleeping twice as much as usual lately. Has your mind been out—

"Say, *that* would be why I couldn't wake you up yesterday to feed you. Beautiful, cats always wake up easily. *Cats* do."

Looking dazed, Bill Wheeler got up out of the chair. He said, "Cat, *am* I crazy, or—"

The Siamese cat looked at him languidly through sleepy eyes. Distinctly it said, *"Forget it."*

And halfway between sitting and rising, Bill Wheeler looked even more dazed for a second. He shook his head as though to clear it.

He said, "What was I talking about, Beautiful? I'm getting punchy from not enough sleep."

He walked over to the window and stared out, gloomily, rubbing the cat's fur until it purred.

He said, "Hungry, Beautiful? Want some liver?"

The cat jumped down from the windowsill and rubbed itself against his leg affectionately.

It said, "Miaouw."

Come and Go Mad

He had known it, somehow, when he had awakened that morning. He knew it more surely now, staring out of the editorial room window into the early afternoon sunlight slanting down among the buildings to cast a pattern of light and shadow. He knew that soon, perhaps even today, something important was going to happen. Whether good or bad he did not know, but he darkly suspected. And with reason; there are few good things that may unexpectedly happen to a man, things, that is, of lasting importance. Disaster can strike from innumerable directions, in amazingly diverse ways.

A voice said, "Hey, Mr. Vine," and he turned away from the window, slowly. That in itself was strange for it was not his manner to move slowly; he was a small, volatile man, almost cat-like in the quickness of his reactions and his movements.

But this time something made him turn slowly from the window, almost as though he never again expected to see that chiaroscuro of an early afternoon.

He said, "Hi, Red."

The freckled copy boy said, "His Nibs wants to see ya."

"Now?"

"Naw. Atcher convenience. Sometime next week, maybe. If yer busy, give him an apperntment."

He put his fist against Red's chin and shoved, and the copy boy staggered back in assumed distress.

He went over to the water cooler. He pressed his thumb on the button and water gurgled into the paper cup.

Harry Wheeler sauntered over and said, "Hiya, Nappy. What's up? Going on the carpet?"

He said, "Sure, for a raise."

He drank and crumpled the cup, tossing it into the wastebasket. He went over to the door marked Private and went through it.

Walter J. Candler, the managing editor, looked up from the work on his desk and said affably, "Sit down, Vine. Be with you in a moment," and then looked down again.

He slid into the chair opposite Candler, worried a cigarette out of his shirt pocket and lighted it. He studied the back of the sheet of paper of which the managing editor was reading the front. There wasn't anything on the back of it.

The M.E. put the paper down and looked at him. "Vine, I've got a screwy one. You're good on screwy ones."

He grinned slowly at the M.E. He said, "If that's a compliment, thanks."

"It's a compliment, all right. You've done some pretty tough things for us. This one's different. I've never yet asked a reporter to do anything I wouldn't do myself. *I* wouldn't do this, so I'm not asking you to."

The M.E. picked up the paper he'd been reading and then put it down again without even looking at it. "Ever hear of Ellsworth Joyce Randolph?"

"Head of the asylum? Hell yes, I've met him. Casually."

"How'd he impress you?"

He was aware that the managing editor was staring at him intently, that it wasn't too casual a question. He parried. "What do you mean? In what way? You mean is he a good Joe, is he a good politician, has he got a good bedside manner for a psychiatrist, or what?"

"I mean, how sane do you think he is?"

He looked at Candler and Candler wasn't kidding. Candler was strictly deadpan.

He began to laugh, and then he stopped laughing. He leaned forward across Candler's desk. "Ellsworth Joyce Randolph," he said. "You're talking about Ellsworth Joyce Randolph?"

Candler nodded. "Dr. Randolph was in here this morning. He told a rather strange story. He didn't want me to print it. He did want me to check on it, to send our best man to check on it. He said if we found it was true we could print it in hundred and twenty line type in red ink." Candler grinned wryly. "We could, at that."

He stumped out his cigarette and studied Candler's face. "But the story itself is so screwy you're not sure whether Dr. Randolph himself might be insane?"

"Exactly."

"And what's tough about the assignment?"

"The doc says a reporter could get the story only from the inside."

"You mean, go in as a guard or something?"

Candler said, "As something."

"Oh."

He got up out of the chair and walked over to the window, stood with his back to the managing editor, looking out. The sun had moved hardly at all. Yet the shadow pattern in the streets looked different, obscurely different. The shadow pattern inside him was different, too. This, he knew, was what had been going to happen. He turned around. He said, "No. Hell no."

Candler shrugged imperceptibly. "Don't blame you. I haven't even asked you to. I wouldn't do it myself."

He asked, "What does Ellsworth Joyce Randolph think is going on inside his nut-house? It must be something pretty screwy if it made you wonder whether Randolph himself is sane."

"I can't tell you that, Vine. Promised him I wouldn't, whether or not you took the assignment."

"You mean—even if I took the job I still wouldn't know what I was looking for?"

"That's right. You'd be prejudiced. You wouldn't be objective. You'd be looking for something, and you might think you found it whether it was there or not. Or you might be so prejudiced against finding it that you'd refuse to recognize it if it bit you in the leg."

He strode from the window over to the desk and banged his fist down on it.

He said, "God damn it, Candler, why *me?* You know what happened to me three years ago."

"Sure. Amnesia."

"Sure, amnesia. Just like that. But I haven't kept it any secret that I never got *over* that amnesia. I'm thirty years old—or am I? My memory goes back three years. Do you know what it feels like to have a blank wall in your memory only three years back?

"Oh, sure, I know what's on the other side of that wall. I know because everybody tells me. I know I started here as a copy boy ten years ago. I know where I was born and when and I know my parents are both dead. I know what they look like—because I've seen their pictures. I know I didn't have a wife and kids, because everybody who knew me told me I didn't. Get that part—everybody who knew me, not everybody I knew. I didn't know anybody.

"Sure, I've done all right since then. After I got out of the hospital—and I don't even remember the accident that put me there—I did all right back here because I still knew how to write news stories, even though I had to learn everybody's name all over again. I wasn't any worse off than a new reporter starting cold on a paper in a strange city. And everybody was as helpful as hell."

Candler raised a placating hand to stem the tide. He said, "Okay, Nappy. You said no, and that's enough. I don't see what all that's got to do with this story, but all you had to do was say no. So forget about it."

The tenseness hadn't gone out of him. He said, "You don't see what *that's* got to do with the story? You ask—or, all right, you don't ask, you suggest— that I get myself certified as a madman, go into an asylum as a patient. When— how much confidence could anyone have in his own mind when he can't re- member going to school, can't remember the first time he met any of the people he works with every day, can't remember starting on the job he works at, can't remember—anything back of three years before?"

Abruptly he struck the desk again with his fist, and then looked foolish about it. He said, "I'm sorry. I didn't mean to get wound up about it like that."

Candler said. "Sit down."

"The answer's still no."

"Sit down, anyway."

He sat down and fumbled a cigarette out of his pocket, got it lighted.

Candler said, "I didn't even mean to mention it, but I've got to now. Now that you talked that way. I didn't know you felt like that about your amnesia. I thought that was water under the bridge.

"Listen, when Dr. Randolph asked me what reporter we had that could best cover it, I told him about you. What your background was. He remem- bered meeting you, too, incidentally. But he hadn't known you had amnesia."

"Is that why you suggested me?"

"Skip that till I make my point. He said that while you were there, he'd be glad to try one of the newer, milder forms of shock treatment on you, and that it might restore your lost memories. He said it would be worth trying."

"He didn't say it would work."

"He said it might; that it wouldn't do any harm."

He stubbed out the cigarette from which he'd taken only three drags. He glared at Candler. He didn't have to say what was in his mind; the managing editor could read it.

Candler said, "Calm down, boy. Remember I didn't bring it up until you yourself started in on how much that memory-wall bothered you. I wasn't saving it for ammunition. I mentioned it only out of fairness to you, after the way you talked."

"Fairness!"

Candler shrugged. "You said no. I accepted it. Then you started raving at me and put me in a spot where I had to mention something I'd hardly thought of at the time. Forget it. How's that graft story coming? Any new leads?"

"You going to put someone else on the asylum story?"

"No. You're the logical one for it."

"What *is* the story? It must be pretty woolly if it makes you wonder if Dr. Randolph is sane. Does he think his patients ought to trade places with his doctors, or what?"

He laughed. "Sure, you can't tell me. That's really beautiful double bait. Curiosity—and hope of knocking down that wall. So what's the rest of it? If I say yes instead of no, how long will I be there, under what circumstances? What chance have I got of getting out again? How do I get in?"

Candler said slowly, "Vine, I'm not sure any more I want you to try it. Let's skip the whole thing."

"Let's not. Not until you answer my questions, anyway."

"All right. You'd go in anonymously, so there wouldn't be any stigma attached if the story wouldn't work out. If it does, you can tell the whole truth—including Dr. Randolph's collusion in getting you in and out again. The cat will be out of the bag, then.

"You might get what you want in a few days—and you wouldn't stay on it more than a couple of weeks in any case."

"How many at the asylum would know who I was and what I was there for, besides Randolph?"

"No one." Candler leaned forward and held up four fingers of his left hand. "Four people would have to be in on it. You." He pointed to one finger. "Me." A second. "Dr. Randolph." The third finger. "And one other reporter from here."

"Not that I'd object, but why the other reporter?"

"Intermediary. In two ways. First, he'll go with you to some psychiatrist; Randolph will recommend one you can fool comparatively easily. He'll be your brother and request that you be examined and certified. You convince the psychiatrist you're nuts and he'll certify you. Of course it takes two doctors to put you away, but Randolph will be the second. Your alleged brother will want Randolph for the second one."

"All this under an assumed name?"

"If you prefer. Of course there's no real reason why it should be."

"That's the way I feel about it. Keep it out of the papers, of course. Tell everybody around here—except my—hey, in that case we couldn't make up a brother. But Charlie Doerr, in Circulation, is my first cousin and my nearest living relative. He'd do, wouldn't he?"

"Sure. And he'd have to be intermediary the rest of the way, then. Visit you at the asylum and bring back anything you have to send back."

"And if, in a couple of weeks, I've found nothing, you'll spring me?"

Candler nodded. "I'll pass the word to Randolph; he'll interview you and pronounce you cured, and you're out. You come back here, and you've been on vacation. That's all."

"What kind of insanity should I pretend to have?"

He thought Candler squirmed a little in his chair. Candler said, "Well—wouldn't this Nappy business be a natural? I mean, paranoia is a form of insanity which, Dr. Randolph told me, hasn't any physical symptoms. It's just a delusion supported by a systematic framework of rationalization. A paranoiac can be sane in every way except one."

He watched Candler and there was a faint twisted grin on his lips. "You mean I should think I'm Napoleon?"

Candler gestured slightly. "Choose your own delusion. But—isn't that one a natural? I mean, the boys around the office always kidding you and calling you Nappy. And—" He finished weakly, "—and everything."

And then Candler looked at him squarely. "Want to do it?"

He stood up. "I think so. I'll let you know for sure tomorrow morning after I've slept on it, but unofficially—yes. Is that good enough?"

Candler nodded.

He said, "I'm taking the rest of the afternoon off; I'm going to the library to read up on paranoia. Haven't anything else to do anyway. And I'll talk to Charlie Doerr this evening. Okay?"

"Fine. Thanks."

He grinned at Candler. He leaned across the desk. He said, "I'll let you in on a little secret, now that things have gone this far. Don't tell anyone. I *am* Napoleon!"

It was a good exit line, so he went out.

II

He got his hat and coat and went outside, out of the air-conditioning and into the hot sunlight. Out of the quiet madhouse of a newspaper office after deadline, into the quieter madhouse of the streets on a sultry July afternoon.

He tilted his panama back on his head and ran his handkerchief across his forehead. Where was he going? Not to the library to bone up on paranoia; that had been a gag to get off for the rest of the afternoon. He'd read everything the library had on paranoia—and on allied subjects—over two years ago.

He was an expert on it. He could fool any psychiatrist in the country into thinking that he was sane—or that he wasn't.

He walked north to the park and sat down on one of the benches in the shade. He put his hat on the bench beside him and mopped his forehead again.

He stared out at the grass, bright green in the sunlight, at the pigeons with their silly head-bobbing method of walking, at a red squirrel that came down one side of a tree, looked about him and scurried up the other side of the same tree.

And he thought back to the wall of amnesia of three years ago.

The wall that hadn't been a wall at all. The phrase intrigued him: a wall at all. Pigeons on the grass, alas. A wall at all.

It wasn't a wall at all; it was a shift, an abrupt change. A line had been drawn between two lives. Twenty-seven years of a life before the accident. Three years of a life since the accident.

They were not the same life.

But no one knew. Until this afternoon he had never even hinted the truth—if it *was* the truth—to anyone. He'd used it as an exit line in leaving Candler's office, knowing Candler would take it as a gag. Even so, one had to be careful; use a gag-line like that often, and people begin to wonder.

The fact that his extensive injuries from that accident had included a broken jaw was probably responsible for the fact that today he was free and not in an insane asylum. That broken jaw—it had been in a cast when he'd returned to consciousness forty-eight hours after his car had run head-on into a truck ten miles out of town—had prevented him from talking for three weeks.

And by the end of three weeks, despite the pain and the confusion that had filled them, he'd had a chance to think things over. He'd invented the wall. The amnesia, the convenient amnesia that was so much more believable than the truth as he knew it.

But *was* the truth as he knew it?

That was the haunting ghost that had ridden him for three years now, since the very hour when he had awakened to whiteness in a white room and a stranger, strangely dressed, had been sitting beside a bed the like of which had been in no field hospital he'd ever heard of or seen. A bed with an overhead framework. And when he looked from the stranger's face down at his own body, he saw that one of his legs and both of his arms were in casts and that the cast of the leg stuck upward at an angle, a rope running over a pulley holding it so.

He'd tried to open his mouth to ask where he was, what had happened to him, and that was when he discovered the cast on his jaw.

He'd stared at the stranger, hoping the latter would have sense enough to volunteer the information and the stranger had grinned at him and said, "Hi, George. Back with us, huh? You'll be all right."

And there was something strange about the language—until he placed what it was. English. Was he in the hands of the English? And it was a language, too, which he knew little of, yet he understood the stranger perfectly. And why did the stranger call him George?

Maybe some of the doubt, some of the fierce bewilderment, showed in his eyes, for the stranger leaned closer to the bed. He said, "Maybe you're still confused, George. You were in a pretty bad smash-up. You ran that coupe of yours head-on into a gravel truck. That was two days ago, and you're just coming out of it for the first time. You're all right, but you'll be in the hospital for a while, till all the bones you busted knit. Nothing seriously wrong with you."

And then waves of pain had come and swept away the confusion, and he had closed his eyes.

Another voice in the room said, "We're going to give you a hypo, Mr. Vine," but he hadn't dared open his eyes again. It was easier to fight the pain without seeing.

There had been the prick of a needle in his upper arm. And pretty soon there'd been nothingness.

When he came back again—twelve hours later, he learned afterwards—it had been to the same white room, the same strange bed, but this time there was a woman in the room, a woman in a strange white costume standing at the foot of the bed studying a paper that was fastened to a piece of board.

She smiled at him when she saw that his eyes were open She said, "Good morning, Mr. Vine. Hope you're feeling better. I'll tell Dr. Holt that you're back with us."

She went away and came back with a man who was also strangely dressed, in roughly the same fashion as had had been the stranger who had called him George.

The doctor looked at him and chuckled. "Got a patient, for once, who can't talk back to me. Or even write notes." Then his face sobered. "Are you in pain, though? Blink once if you're not, twice if you are."

The pain wasn't really very bad this time, and he blinked once. The doctor nodded with satisfaction. "That cousin of yours," he said, "has kept calling up. He'll be glad to know you're going to be back in shape to—well, to listen if not to talk. Guess it won't hurt you to see him a while this evening."

The nurse rearranged his bedclothing and then, mercifully, both she and the doctor had gone, leaving him alone to straighten out his chaotic thoughts.

Straighten them out? That had been three years ago, and he hadn't been able to straighten them out yet:

The startling fact that they'd spoken English and that he'd understood that barbaric tongue perfectly, despite his slight previous knowledge of it. How could an accident have made him suddenly fluent in a language which he had known but slightly?

The startling fact that they'd called him by a different name. "George" had been the name used by the man who'd been beside his bed last night. "Mr. Vine," the nurse had called him. George Vine, an English name, surely.

But there was one thing a thousand times more startling than either of those: It was what last night's stranger (Could he be the "cousin" of whom the doctor had spoken?) had told him about the accident. "You ran that coupe of yours head-on into a gravel truck."

The amazing thing, the contradictory thing, was that he *knew* what a *coupe* was and what a *truck* was. Not that he had any recollection of having driven either, of the accident itself, or of anything beyond that moment when he'd been sitting in the tent after Lodi—but—but how could a picture of a coupe, something driven by a gasoline engine arise to his mind when such a concept had never been in his mind before.

There was that mad mingling of two worlds—the one sharp and clear and definite. The world he'd lived his twenty-seven years of life in, the world into which he'd been born twenty-seven years ago, on August 15th, 1769, in Corsica. The world in which he'd gone to sleep—it seemed like last night—in his tent at Lodi, as General of the Army in Italy, after his first important victory in the field.

And then there was this disturbing world into which he had been awakened, this white world in which people spoke an English—now that he thought of it—which was different from the English he had heard spoken at Brienne, in Valence, at Toulon, and yet which he understood perfectly, which he knew instinctively that he could speak if his jaw were not in a cast. This world in which people called him George Vine, and in which, strangest of all, people used words that he did not know, could not conceivably know, and yet which brought pictures to his mind.

Coupe, truck. They were both forms of—the word came to his mind unbidden—automobiles. He concentrated on what an automobile was and how it worked, and the information was there. The cylinder block, the pistons driven by explosions of gasoline vapor, ignited by a spark of electricity from a generator—

Electricity. He opened his eyes and looked upward at the shaded light in the ceiling, and he knew, somehow, that it was an *electric* light, and in a general way he knew what electricity was.

The Italian Galvani—yes, he'd read of some experiments of Galvani, but they hadn't encompassed anything practical such as a light like that. And staring at the shaded light, he visualized behind it water power running dynamos, miles of wire, motors running generators. He caught his breath at the concept that came to him out of his own mind, or part of his own mind.

The faint, fumbling experiments of Galvani with their weak currents and kicking frogs' legs had scarcely foreshadowed the unmysterious mystery of that light up in the ceiling; and that was the strangest thing yet; part of his mind found it mysterious and another part took it for granted and understood in a general sort of way how it all worked.

Let's see, he thought, the electric light was invented by Thomas Alva Edison somewhere around— Ridiculous; he'd been going to say around 1900, and it was now only 1796!

And then the really horrible thing came to him and he tried—painfully, in vain—to sit up in bed. It *had* been 1900, his memory told him, and Edison had died in 1931— And a man named Napoleon Bonaparte had died a hundred and ten years before that, in 1821.

He'd nearly gone insane then.

And, sane or insane, only the fact that he could not speak had kept him out of a madhouse; it gave him time to think things out, time to realize that his only chance lay in pretending amnesia, in pretending that he remembered nothing of life prior to the accident. They don't put you in a madhouse for amnesia. They tell you who you are, let you go back to what they tell you your former life was. They let you pick up the threads and weave them, while you try to remember.

Three years ago he'd done that. Now, tomorrow, he was going to a psychiatrist and say that he was—Napoleon!

III

The slant of the sun was greater. Overhead a big bird of a plane droned by and he looked up at it and began laughing, quietly to himself—not the laughter of madness. True laughter because it sprang from the conception of Napoleon Bonaparte riding in a plane like that and from the overwhelming incongruity of that idea.

It came to him then that he'd never ridden in a plane that he remembered. Maybe George Vine had; at some time in the twenty-seven years of life George Vine had spent, he must have. But did that mean that *he* had ridden in one? That was a question that was part of the big question.

He got up and started to walk again. It was almost five o'clock; pretty soon Charlie Doerr would be leaving the paper and going home for dinner. Maybe he'd better phone Charlie and be sure he'd be home this evening.

He headed for the nearest bar and phoned; he got Charlie just in time. He said, "This is George. Going to be home this evening?"

"Sure, George. I was going to a poker game, but I called it off when I learned you'd be around."

"When you learned— Oh, Candler talked to you?"

"Yeah. Say, I didn't know you'd phone me or I'd have called Marge, but how about coming out for dinner? It'll be all right with her; I'll call her now if you can."

He said, "Thanks, no, Charlie. Got a dinner date. And say, about that card game; you can go. I can get there about seven and we won't have to talk all evening; an hour'll be enough. You wouldn't be leaving before eight anyway."

Charlie said, "Don't worry about it; I don't much want to go anyway, and you haven't been out for a while. So I'll see you at seven, then."

From the phone booth, he walked over to the bar and ordered a beer. He wondered why he'd turned down the invitation to dinner; probably because, subconsciously, he wanted another couple of hours by himself before he talked to anyone, even Charlie and Marge.

He sipped his beer slowly, because he wanted to make it last; he had to stay sober tonight, plenty sober. There was still time to change his mind; he'd left himself a loophole, however small. He could still go to Candler in the morning and say he'd decided not to do it.

Over the rim of his glass he stared at himself in the back-bar mirror. Small, sandy-haired, with freckles on his nose, stocky. The small and stocky part fitted all right; but the rest of it! Not the remotest resemblance.

He drank another beer slowly, and that made it half past five.

He wandered out again and walked, this time toward town. He walked past the *Blade* and looked up to the third floor and at the window he'd been looking out of when Candler had sent for him. He wondered if he'd ever sit by that window again and look out across a sunlit afternoon.

Maybe. Maybe not.

He thought about Clare. Did he want to see her tonight?

Well, no, to be honest about it, he didn't. But if he disappeared for two weeks or so without having even said good-bye to her, then he'd have to write her off his books.

He'd better.

He stopped in at a drug store and called her home. He said, "This is George, Clare. Listen, I'm being sent out of town tomorrow on an assignment; don't know how long I'll be gone. One of those things that might be a few days or a few weeks. But could I see you late this evening, to say so-long?"

"Why sure, George. What time?"

"It might be after nine, but not much after. That be okay? I'm seeing Charlie first, on business; may not be able to get away before nine."

"Of course, George. Any time."

He stopped in at a hamburger stand, although he wasn't hungry, and managed to eat a sandwich and a piece of pie. That made it a quarter after six and, if he walked, he'd get to Charlie's at just about the right time. So he walked.

Charlie met him at the door. With finger on his lips, he jerked his head backward toward the kitchen where Marge was wiping dishes. He whispered, "I didn't tell Marge, George. It'd worry her."

He wanted to ask Charlie why it would, or should, worry Marge, but he didn't. Maybe he was a little afraid of the answer. It would have to mean that Marge was worrying about him already, and that was a bad sign. He thought he'd been carrying everything off pretty well for three years now.

Anyway, he couldn't ask because Charlie was leading him into the living room and the kitchen was within easy earshot, and Charlie was saying, "Glad you decided you'd like a game of chess, George. Marge is going out tonight; movie she wants to see down at the neighborhood show. I was going to that card game out of self-defense, but I didn't want to."

He got the chessboard and men out of the closet and started to set up a game on the coffee table.

Marge came in with a tray bearing tall cold glasses of beer and put it down beside the chessboard. She said, "Hi, George. Hear you're going away a couple of weeks."

He nodded. "But I don't know where. Candler—the managing editor— asked me if I'd be free for an out of town assignment and I said sure, and he said he'd tell me about it tomorrow."

Charlie was holding out clenched hands, a pawn in each, and he touched Charlie's left hand and got white. He moved pawn to king's fourth and, when Charlie did the same, advanced his queen's pawn.

Marge was fussing with her hat in front of the mirror. She said, "If you're not here when I get back, George, so long and good luck."

He said, "Thanks, Marge. 'Bye."

He made a few more moves before Marge came over, ready to go, kissed Charlie good-bye, and then kissed him lightly on the forehead. She said, "Take care of yourself, George."

For a moment his eyes met her pale blue ones and he thought, she *is* worrying about me. It scared him a little.

After the door had closed behind her, he said, "Let's not finish the game, Charlie. Let's get to the brass tacks, because I've got to see Clare about nine. Dunno how long I'll be gone, so I can't very well not say good-bye to her."

Charlie looked up at him. "You and Clare serious, George?"

"I don't know."

Charlie picked up his beer and took a sip. Suddenly his voice was brisk and business-like. He said, "All right, let's sit on the brass tacks. We've got an appointment for eleven o'clock tomorrow morning with a guy named Irving, Dr. W. E. Irving, in the Appleton Block. He's a psychiatrist; Dr. Randolph recommended him.

"I called him up this afternoon after Candler talked to me; Candler had already phoned Randolph. I gave my right name. My story was this: I've got a cousin who's been acting queer lately and whom I wanted him to talk to. I didn't give the cousin's name. I didn't tell him in what way you'd been acting queer; I ducked the question and said I'd rather have him judge for himself without prejudice. I said I'd talked you into talking to a psychiatrist and that the only one I knew of was Randolph; that I'd called Randolph, who said he didn't do much private practice and recommended Irving. I told him I was your nearest living relative.

"That leaves the way open to Randolph for the second name on the certificate. If you can talk Irving into thinking you're really insane and he wants to sign you up, I can insist on having Randolph, whom I wanted in the first place. And this time, of course, Randolph will agree."

"You didn't say a thing about what kind of insanity you suspected me of having?"

Charlie shook his head. He said, "So, anyway, neither of us goes to work at the *Blade* tomorrow. I'll leave home the usual time so Marge won't know anything, but I'll meet you downtown—say, in the lobby of the Christina— at a quarter of eleven. And if you can convince Irving that you're commitable— if that's the word—we'll get Randolph right away and get the whole thing settled tomorrow."

"And if I change my mind?"

"Then I'll call the appointment off. That's all. Look, isn't that all there is to talk over? Let's play this game of chess out; it's only twenty after seven."

He shook his head. "I'd rather talk, Charlie. One thing you forgot to cover, anyway. After tomorrow. How often you coming to see me to pick up bulletins for Candler?"

"Oh, sure, I forgot that. As often as visiting hours will permit—three times a week. Monday, Wednesday, Friday afternoons. Tomorrow's Friday, so if you get in, the first time I'll be able to see you is Monday."

"Okay. Say, Charlie, did Candler even hint to you at what the story is that I'm supposed to get in there?"

Charlie Doerr shook his head slowly. "Not a word. What is it? Or is it too secret for you to talk about?"

He stared at Charlie, wondering. And suddenly he felt that he couldn't tell the truth: that he didn't know either. It would make him look so silly. It hadn't sounded so foolish when Candler had given the reason—a reason, anyway—for not telling him, but it would sound foolish now.

He said, "If he didn't tell you, I guess I'd better not either, Charlie." And since that didn't sound too convincing, he added, "I promised Candler I wouldn't."

Both glasses of beer were empty by then, and Charlie took them into the kitchen for refilling.

He followed Charlie, somehow preferring the informality of the kitchen. He sat a-straddle of a kitchen chair, leaning his elbows on the back of it, and Charlie leaned against the refrigerator.

Charlie said, "Prosit!" and they drank, and then Charlie asked, "Have you got your story ready for Doc Irving?"

He nodded. "Did Candler tell you what I'm to tell him?"

"You mean, that you're Napoleon?" Charlie chuckled.

Did that chuckle ring true? He looked at Charlie, and he knew that what he was thinking was completely incredible. Charlie was square and honest as they came. Charlie and Marge were his best friends; they'd been his best friends for three years that he knew of. Longer than that, a hell of a lot longer, according to Charlie. But beyond those three years—that was something else again.

He cleared his throat because the words were going to stick a little. But he had to ask, he had to be sure. "Charlie, I'm going to ask you a hell of a question. Is this business on the up and up?"

"Huh?"

"It's a hell of a thing to ask. But—look, you and Candler don't think I'm crazy, do you? You didn't work this out between you to get me put away—or anyway examined—painlessly, without my knowing it was happening, till too late, did you?"

Charlie was staring at him. He said, "Jeez, George, you don't think I'd do a thing like that, do you?"

"No, I don't. But—you could think it was for my own good, and you might on that basis. Look, Charlie, if it *is* that, if you *think* that, let me point out that this isn't fair. I'm going up against a psychiatrist tomorrow to lie to him, to try to convince him that I have delusions. Not to be honest with him. And that would be unfair as hell, to me. You see that, don't you, Charlie?"

Charlie's face got a little white. He said slowly, "Before God, George, it's nothing like that. All I know about this is what Candler and you have told me."

"You think I'm sane, fully sane?"

Charlie licked his lips. He said, "You want it straight?"

"Yes."

"I never doubted it, until this moment. Unless—well, amnesia is a form of mental aberration, I suppose, and you've never got over that, but that isn't what you mean, is it?"

"No."

"Then, until right now— George, that sounds like a persecution complex, if you really meant what you asked me. A conspiracy to get you to— Surely you can see how ridiculous it is. What possible reason would either Candler or I have to get you to lie yourself into being committed?"

He said, "I'm sorry, Charlie. It was just a screwy momentary notion. No, I don't think that, of course." He glanced at his wrist watch. "Let's finish that chess game, huh?"

"Fine. Wait till I give us a refill to take along."

He played carelessly and managed to lose within fifteen minutes. He turned down Charlie's offer of a chance for revenge and leaned back in his chair.

He said, "Charlie, ever hear of chessmen coming in red and black?"

"N-no. Either black and white, or red and white, any I've ever seen. Why?"

"Well—" He grinned. "I suppose I oughtn't to tell you this after just making you wonder whether I'm really sane after all, but I've been having recurrent dreams recently. No crazier than ordinary dreams except that I've been dreaming the same things over and over. One of them is something about a game between the red and the black; I don't even know whether it's chess. You know how it is when you dream; things seem to make sense whether they do or not. In the dream I don't wonder whether the red-and-black business is chess or not; I know, I guess, or seem to know. But the knowledge doesn't carry over. You know what I mean?"

"Sure. Go on."

"Well, Charlie, I've been wondering if it just might have something to do with the other side of that wall of amnesia I've never been able to cross. This is the first time in my—well, not in my life, maybe, but in the three years I remember of it, that I've had recurrent dreams. I wonder if—if my memory may not be trying to get through.

"Did I ever have a set of red and black chessmen, for instance? Or, in any school I went to, did they have intramural basketball or baseball between red teams and black teams, or—or anything like that?"

Charlie thought for a long moment before he shook his head. "No," he said, "nothing like that. Of course there's red and black in roulette—*rouge et noir*. And it's the two colors in a deck of playing cards."

"No, I'm pretty sure it doesn't tie in with cards or roulette. It's not—not like that. It's a game *between* the red and the black. They're the players, somehow. Think hard, Charlie; not about where you might have run into that idea, but where *I* might have."

He watched Charlie struggle and after a while he said, "Okay, don't sprain your brain, Charlie. Try this one. *The brightly shining.*"

"The brightly shining what?"

"Just that phrase, *the brightly shining*. Does it mean anything to you, at all?"

"No."

"Okay," he said. "Forget it."

IV

He was early and he walked past Clare's house, as far as the corner and stood under the big elm there, smoking the rest of his cigarette, thinking bleakly.

There wasn't anything to think about, really; all he had to do was say good-bye to her. Two easy syllables. And stall off her questions as to where he was going, exactly how long he'd be gone. Be quiet and casual and unemotional about it, just as though they didn't mean anything in particular to each other.

It *had* to be that way. He'd known Clare Wilson a year and a half now, and he'd kept her dangling that long; it wasn't fair. This had to be the end, for her sake. He had about as much business asking a woman to marry him as—as a madman who thinks he's Napoleon!

He dropped his cigarette and ground it viciously into the walk with his heel, then went back to the house, up on the porch, and rang the bell.

Clare herself came to the door. The light from the hallway behind her made her hair a circlet of spun gold around her shadowed face.

He wanted to take her into his arms so badly that he clenched his fists with the effort it took to keep his arms down.

Stupidly, he said, "Hi, Clare. How's everything?"

"I don't know, George. How *is* everything? Aren't you coming in?"

She'd stepped back from the doorway to let him past and the light was on her face now, sweetly grave. She knew something was up, he thought; her expression and the tone of her voice gave that away.

He didn't want to go in. He said, "It's such a beautiful night, Clare. Let's take a stroll."

"All right, George." She came out onto the porch. "It is a fine night, such beautiful stars." She turned and looked at him. "Is one of them yours?"

He started a little. Then he stepped forward and took her elbow, guiding her down the porch steps. He said lightly, "All of them are mine. Want to buy any?"

"You wouldn't *give* me one? Just a teeny little dwarf star, maybe? Even one that I'd have to use a telescope to see?"

They were out on the sidewalk then, out of hearing of the house, and abruptly her voice changed, the playful note dropped from it, and she asked another question, "What's wrong, George?"

He opened his mouth to say nothing was wrong, and then closed it again. There wasn't any lie that he could tell her, and he couldn't tell her the truth, either. Her asking of that question, in that way, should have made things easier; it made them more difficult.

She asked another, "You mean to say good-bye for—for good, don't you, George?"

He said, "Yes," and his mouth was very dry. He didn't know whether it came out as an articulate monosyllable or not, and he wetted his lips and tried again. He said, "Yes, I'm afraid so, Clare."

"Why?"

He couldn't make himself turn to look at her, he stared blindly ahead. He said, "I—I can't tell you, Clare. But it's the only thing I can do. It's best for both of us."

"Tell me one thing, George. Are you really going away? Or was that just— an excuse?"

"It's true. I'm going away; I don't know for how long. But don't ask me where, please. I can't tell you that."

"Maybe I can tell you, George. Do you mind if I do?"

He minded all right; he minded terribly. But how could he say so? He didn't say anything, because he couldn't say yes, either.

They were beside the park now, the little neighborhood park that was only a block square and didn't offer much in the way of privacy, but which did have benches. And he steered her—or she steered him; he didn't know which— into the park and they sat down on a bench. There were other people in the park, but not too near. Still he hadn't answered her question.

She sat very close to him on the bench. She said, "You've been worried about your mind, haven't you, George?"

"Well—yes, in a way, yes, I have."

"And your going away has something to do with that, hasn't it? You're going somewhere for observation or treatment, or both?"

"Something like that. It's not as simple as that, Clare, and I—I just can't tell you about it."

She put her hand on his hand, lying on his knee. She said, "I knew it was something like that, George. And I don't ask you to tell me anything about it.

"Just—just don't say what you meant to say. Say so-long instead of good-bye. Don't even write me, if you don't want to. But don't be noble and call everything off here and now, for my sake. At least wait until you've been wher-ever you're going. Will you?"

He gulped. She made it sound so simple when actually it was so compli-cated. Miserably he said, "All right, Clare. If you want it that way."

Abruptly she stood up. "Let's get back, George."

He stood beside her. "But it's early."

"I know, but sometimes— Well, there's a psychological moment to end a date, George. I know that sounds silly. but after what we've said, wouldn't it be—uh—anticlimactic—to—"

He laughed a little. He said, "I see what you mean."

They walked back to her home in silence. He didn't know whether it was happy or unhappy silence; he was too mixed up for that.

On the shadowed porch, in front of the door, she turned and faced him. "George," she said. Silence.

"Oh, damn you, George; quit being so *noble* or whatever you're being. Unless, of course, you *don't* love me. Unless this is just an elaborate form of— of runaround you're giving me. Is it?"

There were only two things he could do. One was run like hell. The other was what he did. He put his arms around her and kissed her. Hungrily.

When that was over, and it wasn't over too quickly, he was breathing a little hard and not thinking too clearly, for he was saying what he hadn't meant to say at all, "I love you, Clare. I love you; I love you so."

And she said, "I love you, too, dear. You'll come back to me, won't you?" And he said, "Yes. *Yes.*"

It was four miles or so from her home to his rooming house, but he walked, and the walk seemed to take only seconds.

He sat at the window of his room, with the light out, thinking, but the thoughts went in the same old circles they'd gone in for three years.

No new factor had been added except that now he was going to stick his neck out, way out, miles out. Maybe, just maybe, this thing was going to be settled one way or the other.

Out there, out his window, the stars were bright diamonds in the sky. Was one of them his star of destiny? If so, he was going to follow it, follow it even into the madhouse if it led there. Inside him was a deeply rooted conviction that this wasn't accident, that it wasn't coincidence that had led to his being asked to tell the truth under guise of falsehood.

His star of destiny.

Brightly shining? No, the phrase from his dreams did not refer to that; it was not an adjective phrase, but a noun. *The brightly shining.* What was *the brightly shining?*

And the red and the black? He'd thought of everything Charlie had suggested, and other things, too. Checkers, for instance. But it was not that.

The red and the black.

Well, whatever the answer was, he was running full-speed toward it now, not away from it.

After a while he went to bed, but it was a long time before he went to sleep.

V

Charlie Doerr came out of the inner office marked Private and put his hand out. He said, "Good luck, George. The doc's ready to talk to you now."

He shook Charlie's hand and said, "You might as well run along. I'll see you Monday, first visiting day."

"I'll wait here," Charlie said. "I took the day off work anyway, remember? Besides, maybe you won't have to go."

He dropped Charlie's hand, and stared into Charlie's face. He said slowly, "What do you mean, Charlie—maybe I won't have to go."

"Why—" Charlie looked puzzled. "Why, maybe he'll tell you you're all right, or just suggest regular visits to see him until you're straightened out, or—" Charlie finished weakly, "—or something."

Unbelievingly, he stared at Charlie. He wanted to ask, am I crazy or are you, but that sounded crazy under the circumstances. But he had to be sure, sure that Charlie just hadn't let something slip from his mind; maybe he'd fallen into the role he was supposed to be playing when he talked to the doctor just now. He asked, "Charlie, don't you remember that—" And even the rest of that question seemed insane for him to be asking, with Charlie staring blankly at him. The answer was in Charlie's face; it didn't have to be brought to Charlie's lips.

Charlie said again, "I'll wait; of course. Good luck, George."

He looked into Charlie's eyes and nodded, then turned and went through the door marked Private. He closed it behind him, meanwhile studying the man who had been sitting behind the desk and who had risen as he entered. A big man, broad shouldered, iron gray hair.

"Dr. Irving?"

"Yes, Mr. Vine. Will you be seated, please?"

He slid into the comfortable, padded armchair across the desk from the doctor.

"Mr. Vine," said the doctor, "a first interview of this sort is always a bit difficult. For the patient, I mean. Until you know me better, it will be difficult for you to overcome a certain reticence in discussing yourself. Would you prefer to talk, to tell things your own way, or would you rather I asked questions?"

He thought that over. He'd had a story ready, but those few words with Charlie in the waiting room had changed everything.

He said, "Perhaps you'd better ask questions."

"Very well." There was a pencil in Dr. Irving's hand and paper on the desk before him. "Where and when were you born?"

He took a deep breath. "To the best of my knowledge, in Corsica on August 15th, 1769. I don't actually remember being born, of course. I do remember things from my boyhood on Corsica, though. We stayed there until I was ten, and after that I was sent to school at Brienne."

Instead of writing, the doctor was tapping the paper lightly with the tip of the pencil. He asked, "What month and year is this?"

"August, 1947. Yes, I know that should make me a hundred and seventy-some years old. You want to know how I account for that. I don't. Nor do I account for the fact that Napoleon Bonaparte died in 1821."

He leaned back in the chair and crossed his arms, staring up at the ceiling. "I don't attempt to account for the paradoxes or the discrepancies. I recognize them as such. But according to my own memory, and aside from logic pro or con, I was Napoleon for twenty-seven years. I won't recount what happened during that time; it's all down in the history books.

"But in 1796, after the battle of Lodi, while I was in charge of the armies in Italy, I went to sleep. As far as I knew, just as anyone goes to sleep anywhere, any time. But I woke up—with no sense whatever of duration, by the way—in a hospital in town here, and I was informed that my name was George Vine, that the year was 1944, and that I was twenty-seven years old.

"The twenty-seven years old part checked, and that was all. Absolutely all. I have no recollections of any parts of George Vine's life, prior to his—my—waking up in the hospital after the accident. I know quite a bit about his early life now, but only because I've been told.

"I know when and where he was born, where he went to school, and when he started work at the *Blade*. I know when he enlisted in the army and when he was discharged—late in 1943—because he developed a trick knee after a leg injury. Not in combat, incidentally, and there wasn't any 'psycho-neurotic' on my—his—discharge."

The doctor quit doodling with the pencil. He asked, "You've felt this way for three years—and kept it a secret?"

"Yes. I had time to think things over after the accident, and yes, I decided then to accept what they told me about my identity. They'd have locked me up, of course. Incidentally, I've *tried* to figure out an answer. I've studied Dunne's theory of time—even Charles Fort! " He grinned suddenly. "Ever read about Casper Hauser?"

Dr. Irving nodded.

"Maybe he was playing smart the way I did. And I wonder how many other amnesiacs pretended they didn't know what happened prior to a certain date—rather than admit they had memories at obvious variance with the facts."

Dr. Irving said slowly, "Your cousin informs me that you were a bit—ah—'hepped' was his word—on the subject of Napoleon before your accident. How do you account for that?"

"I've told you I don't account for any of it. But I can verify that fact, aside from what Charlie Doerr says about it. Apparently I—the George Vine I, if I was ever George Vine—was quite interested in Napoleon, had read about him, made a hero of him, and had talked about him quite a bit. Enough so that the fellows he worked with at the *Blade* had nicknamed him 'Nappy.'"

"I notice you distinguish between yourself and George Vine. Are you or are you not he?"

"I have been for three years. Before that—I have no recollection of being George Vine. I don't think I was. I think—as nearly as I think anything—that *I*, three years ago, woke up in George Vine's body."

"Having done what for a hundred and seventy-some years?"

"I haven't the faintest idea. Incidentally, I don't doubt that this *is* George Vine's body, and with it I inherited his knowledge—except his personal memories. For example, I knew how to handle his job at the newspaper, although I didn't remember any of the people I worked with there. I have his knowledge of English, for instance, and his ability to write. I knew how to operate a typewriter. My handwriting is the same as his."

"If you think that you are not Vine, how do you account for that?"

He leaned forward. "I think part of me is George Vine, and part of me isn't. I think some transference has happened which is outside the run of ordinary human experience. That doesn't necessarily mean that it's supernatural—nor that I'm insane. *Does it?*"

Dr. Irving didn't answer. Instead, he asked, "You kept this secret for three years, for understandable reasons. Now, presumably for other reasons, you decide to tell. What are the other reasons? What has happened to change your attitude?"

It was the question that had been bothering him.

He said slowly, "Because I don't believe in coincidence. Because something in the situation itself has changed. Because I'm willing to risk imprisonment as a paranoiac to find out the truth."

"What in the situation has changed?"

"Yesterday it was suggested—by my employer—that I feign insanity for a practical reason. And the very kind of insanity which I have, if any. Surely, I will admit the possibility that I'm insane. But I can only operate on the theory that I'm not. You know that you're Dr. Willard E. Irving; you can only operate on that theory—but how do you *know* you are? Maybe you're insane, but you can only act as though you're not."

"You think your employer is part of a plot—ah—against you? You think there is a conspiracy to get you into a sanitarium?"

"I don't know. Here's what has happened since yesterday noon." He took a deep breath. Then he plunged. He told Dr. Irving the whole story of his interview with Candler, what Candler had said about Dr. Randolph, about his talk with Charlie Doerr last night and about Charlie's bewildering about-face in the waiting room.

When he was through he said, "That's all." He looked at Dr. Irving's expressionless face with more curiosity than concern, trying to read it. He added, quite casually, "You don't believe me, of course. You think I'm insane."

He met Irving's eyes squarely. He said, "You have no choice—unless you would choose to believe I'm telling you an elaborate set of lies to convince you I'm insane. I mean, as a scientist and as a psychiatrist, you cannot even admit the possibility that the things I believe—*know*—are objectively true. Am I not right?"

"I fear that you are. So?"

"So go ahead and sign your commitment. I'm going to follow this thing through. Even to the detail of having Dr. Ellsworth Joyce Randolph sign the second one."

"You make no objection?"

"Would it do any good if I did?"

"On one point, yes, Mr. Vine. If a patient has a prejudice against—or a delusion concerning—one psychiatrist, it is best not to have him under that particular psychiatrist's care. If you think Dr. Randolph is concerned in a plot against you, I would suggest that another one be named."

He said softly, "Even if I choose Randolph?"

Dr. Irving waved a deprecating hand, "Of course, if both you and Mr. Doerr prefer—"

"We prefer."

The iron gray head nodded gravely. "Of course you understand one thing; if Dr. Randolph and I decide you should go to the sanitarium, it will not be for custodial care. It will be for your recovery through treatment."

He nodded.

Dr. Irving stood. "You'll pardon me a moment? I'll phone Dr. Randolph."

He watched Dr. Irving go through a door to an inner room. He thought; there's a phone on his desk right there; but he doesn't want me to overhear the conversation.

He sat there very quietly until Irving came back and said, "Dr. Randolph is free. And I phoned for a cab to take us there. You'll pardon me again? I'd like to speak to your cousin, Mr. Doerr."

He sat there and didn't watch the doctor leave in the opposite direction for the waiting room. He could have gone to the door and tried to catch words in the low-voiced conversation, but he didn't. He just sat there until he heard the waiting room door open behind him and Charlie's voice said, "Come on, George. The cab will be waiting downstairs by now."

They went down in the elevator and the cab was there. Dr. Irving gave the address.

In the cab, about half way there, he said, "It's a beautiful day," and Charlie cleared his throat and said, "Yeah, it is." The rest of the way he didn't try it again and nobody said anything.

VI

He wore gray trousers and a gray shirt, open at the collar and with no necktie that he might decide to hang himself with. No belt, either, for the same reason, although the trousers buttoned so snugly around the waist that there was no danger of them falling off. Just as there was no danger of his falling out any of the windows; they were barred.

He was not in a cell, however; it was a large ward on the third floor. There were seven other men in the ward. His eyes ran over them. Two were playing checkers, sitting on the floor with a board on the floor between them. One sat in a chair, staring fixedly at nothing; two leaned against the bars of one of the open windows, looking out and talking casually and sanely. One read a magazine. One sat in a corner, playing smooth arpeggios on a piano that wasn't there at all.

He stood leaning against the wall, watching the other seven. He'd been here two hours now; it seemed like two years.

The interview with Dr. Ellsworth Joyce Randolph had gone smoothly; it had been practically a duplicate of his interview with Irving. And quite obviously, Dr. Randolph had never heard of him before.

He'd expected that, of course.

He felt very calm, now. For a while, he'd decided, he wasn't going to think, wasn't going to worry, wasn't even going to feel.

He strolled over and stood watching the checker game.

It was a sane checker game; the rules were being followed.

One of the men looked up and asked, "What's your name?" It was a perfectly sane question; the only thing wrong with it was that the same man had asked the same question four times now within the two hours he'd been here.

He said, "George Vine."

"Mine's Bassington, Ray Bassington. Call me Ray. Are you insane?"

"No."

"Some of us are and some of us aren't. He is." He looked at the man who was playing the imaginary piano. "Do you play checkers?"

"Not very well."

"Good. We eat pretty soon now. Anything you want to know, just ask me."

"How do you get out of here? Wait, I don't mean that for a gag, or anything. Seriously, what's the procedure?"

"You go in front of the board once a month. They ask you questions and decide if you go or stay. Sometimes they stick needles in you. What you down for?"

"Down for? What do you mean?"

"Feeble-minded, manic-depressive, dementia praecox, involutional melancholia—"

"Oh. Paranoia, I guess."

"That's bad. Then they stick needles in you."

A bell rang somewhere.

"That's dinner," said the other checker player. "Ever try to commit suicide? Or kill anyone?"

"No."

"They'll let you eat at an A table then, with knife and fork."

The door of the ward was being opened. It opened outward and a guard stood outside and said, "All right." They filed out, all except the man who was sitting in the chair staring into space.

"How about him?" he asked Ray Bassington

"He'll miss a meal tonight. Manic-depressive; just going into the depressive stage. They let you miss one meal; if you're not able to go to the next they take you and feed you. You a manic-depressive?"

"No."

"You're lucky. It's hell when you're on the down-swing. Here, through this door."

It was a big room. Tables and benches were crowded with men in gray shirts and gray trousers, like his. A guard grabbed his arm as he went through the doorway and said, "There. That seat."

It was right beside the door. There was a tin plate, messy with food, and a spoon beside it. He asked, "Don't I get a knife and fork? It was told—"

The guard gave him a shove toward the seat. "Observation period, seven days. Nobody gets silverware till their observation period's over. Siddown."

He sat down. No one at his table had silverware. All the others were eating, several of them noisily and messily. He kept his eyes on his own plate, unappetizing as that was. He toyed with his spoon and managed to eat a few pieces of potato out of the stew and one or two of the chunks of meat that were mostly lean.

The coffee was in a tin cup and he wondered why until he realized how breakable an ordinary cup would be and how lethal could be one of the heavy mugs cheap restaurants use.

The coffee was weak and cool; he couldn't drink it.

He sat back and closed his eyes. When he opened them again there was an empty plate and an empty cup in front of him and the man at his left was eating very rapidly. It was the man who'd been playing the non-existent piano.

He thought, if I'm here long enough, I'll get hungry enough to eat that stuff. He didn't like the thought of being there that long.

After a while a bell rang and they got up, one table at a time on signals he didn't catch, and filed out. His group had come in last; it went out first.

Ray Bassington was behind him on the stairs. He said, "You'll get used to it. What'd you say your name is?"

"George Vine."

Bassington laughed. The door shut on them and a key turned.

He saw it was dark outside. He went over to one of the windows and stared out through the bars. There was a single bright star that showed just above the top of the elm tree in the yard. *His* star? Well, he'd followed it here. A cloud drifted across it.

Someone was standing beside him. He turned his head and saw it was the man who'd been playing piano. He had a dark, foreign-looking face with intense black eyes; just then he was smiling, as though at a secret joke.

"You're new here, aren't you? Or just get put in this ward, which?"

"New. George Vine's the name."

"Baroni. Musician. Used to be, anyway. Now—let it go. Anything you want to know about the place?"

"Sure. How to get out of it."

Baroni laughed, without particular amusement but not bitterly either. "First, convince them you're all right again. Mind telling what's wrong with you—or don't you want to talk about it? Some of us mind, others don't."

He looked at Baroni, wondering which way he felt. Finally he said, "I guess I don't mind. I—think I'm Napoleon."

"Are you?"

"Am I what?"

"*Are* you Napoleon? If you aren't, that's one thing. Then maybe you'll get out of here in six months or so. If you really *are*—that's bad. You'll probably die here."

"Why? I mean, if I *am*, then I'm sane and—"

"Not the point. Point's whether they think you're sane or not. Way they figure, if you think you're Napoleon you're not sane. Q. E. D. You stay here."

"Even if I tell them I'm convinced I'm George Vine?"

"They've worked with paranoia before. And that's what they've got you down for, count on it. And any time a paranoiac gets tired of a place, he'll try to lie his way out of it. They weren't born yesterday. They know that."

"In general, yes, but how—"

A sudden cold chill went down his spine. He didn't have to finish the question. *They stick needles in you*— It hadn't meant anything when Ray Bassington had said it.

The dark man nodded. "Truth serum," he said. "When a paranoiac reaches the stage where he's cured if he's telling the truth, they make sure he's telling it before they let him go."

He thought what a beautiful trap it had been that he'd walked into. He'd probably die here, now.

He leaned his head against the cool iron bars and closed his eyes. He heard footsteps walking away from him and knew he was alone.

He opened his eyes and looked out into blackness; now the clouds had drifted across the moon, too.

Clare, he thought; *Clare.*

A trap.

But—if there was a trap, there must be a trapper.

He was sane or he was insane. If he was sane, he'd walked into a trap, and *if there was a trap, there must be a trapper, or trappers.*

If he was insane—

God, let it be that he *was* insane. That way everything made such sweetly simple sense, and someday he might be out of here, he might go back to working for the *Blade,* possibly even with a memory of all the years he'd worked there. Or that George Vine had worked there.

That was the catch. *He* wasn't George Vine.

And there was another catch. He *wasn't* insane.

The cool iron of the bars against his forehead.

After a while he heard the door open and looked around. Two guards had come in. A wild hope, reasonless, surged up inside him. It didn't last.

"Bedtime, you guys," said one of the guards. He looked at the manic-depressive sitting motionless on the chair and said, "Nuts. Hey, Bassington, help me get this guy in."

The other guard, a heavy-set man with hair close-cropped like a wrestler's, came over to the window.

"You. You're the new one in here. Vine, ain't it?"

He nodded.

"Want trouble, or going to be good?" Fingers of the guard's right hand clenched, the fist went back.

"Don't want trouble. Got enough."

The guard relaxed a little. "Okay, stick to that and you'll get along. Vacant bunk's in there." He pointed. "One on the right. Make it up yourself in the morning. Stay in the bunk and mind your own business. If there's any noise or trouble here in the ward, we come in and take care of it. Our own way. You wouldn't like it."

He didn't trust himself to speak, so he just nodded. He turned and went through the door of the cubicle to which the guard had pointed. There were two bunks in there; the manic-depressive who'd been on the chair was lying flat on his back on the other, staring blindly up at the ceiling through wide-open eyes. They'd pulled his shoes off, leaving him otherwise dressed.

He turned to his own bunk, knowing there was nothing on earth he could do for the other man, no way he could reach him through the impenetrable shell of blank misery which is the manic-depressive's intermittent companion.

He turned down a gray sheet-blanket on his own bunk and found under it another gray sheet-blanket atop a hard but smooth pad. He slipped off his shirt and trousers and hung them on a hook on the wall at the foot of his bed. He looked around for a switch to turn off the light over head and couldn't find one. But, even as he looked, the light went out.

A single light still burned somewhere in the ward room outside, and by it he could see to take his shoes and socks off and get into the bunk.

He lay very quiet for a while, hearing only two sounds, both faint and seeming far away. Somewhere in another cubicle off the ward someone was singing quietly to himself, a wordless monody; somewhere else someone else was sobbing. In his own cubicle, he couldn't hear even the sound of breathing from his room mate.

Then there was a shuffle of bare feet and someone in the open doorway said, "George Vine."

He said, "Yes?"

"Shhhh, not so loud. This is Bassington. Want to tell you about that guard; I should have warned you before. Don't ever tangle with him."

"I didn't."

"I heard; you were smart. He'll slug you to pieces if you give him half a chance. He's a sadist. A lot of guards are; that's why they're bughousers; that's what they call themselves, bughousers. If they get fired one place for being too brutal they get on at another one. He'll be in again in the morning; I thought I'd warn you."

The shadow in the doorway was gone.

He lay there in the dimness, the almost-darkness, feeling rather than thinking. Wondering. Did mad people ever know that they were mad? Could they tell? Was every one of them sure, as he was sure—?

That quiet, still thing lying in the bunk near his, inarticulately suffering, withdrawn from human reach into a profound misery beyond the understanding of the sane—

"Napoleon Bonaparte!"

A clear voice, but had it been within his mind, or from without? He sat up on the bunk. His eyes pierced the dimness, could discern no form, no shadow, in the doorway.

He said, "Yes?"

VII

Only then, sitting up on the bunk and having answered "Yes," did he realize the name by which the voice had called him.

"Get up. Dress."

He swung his legs out over the edge of the bunk, stood up. He reached for his shirt and was slipping his arms into it before he stopped and asked, "Why?"

"To learn the truth."

"Who are you?" he asked.

"Do not speak aloud. I can hear you. I am within you and without. I have no name."

"Then *what* are you?" He said it aloud, without thinking.

"An instrument of The Brightly Shining."

He dropped the trousers he'd been holding. He sat down carefully on the edge of the bunk, leaned over and groped around for them.

His mind groped, too. Groped for he knew not what. Finally he found a question—the question. He didn't ask it aloud this time; he thought it, concentrated on it as he straightened out his trousers and thrust his legs in them.

"Am I mad?"

The answer—*No*—came clear and sharp as a spoken word, but had it been spoken? Or was it a sound that was only in his mind?

He found his shoes and pulled them on his feet. As he fumbled the laces into some sort of knots, he thought, "Who—what—is The Brightly Shining?"

"The Brightly Shining is *that which is Earth*. It is the intelligence of our planet. It is one of three intelligences in the solar system, one of many in the universe. Earth is one; it is called The Brightly Shining."

"I do not understand," he thought.

"You will. Are you ready?"

He finished the second knot. He stood up. The voice said, "Come. Walk silently."

It was as though he was being led through the almost-darkness, although he felt no physical touch upon him; he saw no physical presence beside him.

But he walked confidently, although quietly on tiptoe, knowing he would not walk into anything nor stumble. Through the big room that was the ward, and then his outstretched hand touched the knob of a door.

He turned it gently and the door opened inward. Light blinded him. The voice said, "Wait," and he stood immobile. He could hear sound—the rustle of paper, the turn of a page—outside the door, in the lighted corridor.

Then from across the hall came the sound of a shrill scream. A chair scraped and feet hit the floor of the corridor, walking away toward the sound of the scream. A door opened and closed.

The voice said, "Come," and he pulled the door open the rest of the way and went outside, past the desk and the empty chair that had been just outside the door of the ward.

Another door, another corridor. The voice said, "Wait," the voice said, "Come"; this time a guard slept. He tiptoed past. Down steps.

He thought the question, "Where am I going?"

"Mad," said the voice.

"But you said I wasn't—" He'd spoken aloud and the sound startled him almost more than had the answer to his last question. And in the silence that followed the words he'd spoken there came—from the bottom of the stairs and around the corner—the sound of a buzzing switchboard, and someone said, "Yes? ... Okay, Doctor, I'll be right up." Footsteps and the closing of an elevator door.

He went down the remaining stairs and around the corner and he was in the front main hall. There was an empty desk with a switchboard beside it. He walked past it and to the front door. It was bolted and he threw the heavy bolt.

He went outside, into the night.

He walked quietly across cement, across gravel; then his shoes were on grass and he didn't have to tiptoe any more. It was as dark now as the inside of an elephant; he felt the presence of trees nearby and leaves brushed his face occasionally, but he walked rapidly, confidently, and his hand went forward just in time to touch a brick wall.

He reached up and he could touch the top of it; he pulled himself up and over it. There was broken glass on the flat top of the wall; he cut his clothes and his flesh badly, but he felt no pain, only the wetness of blood and the stickiness of blood.

He walked along a lighted road, he walked along dark and empty streets, he walked down a darker alley. He opened the back gate of a yard and walked to the back door of a house. He opened the door and went in. There was a lighted room at the front of the house; he could see the rectangle of light at the end of a corridor. He went along the corridor and into the lighted room.

Someone who had been seated at a desk stood up. Someone, a man, whose face he knew but whom he could not—

"Yes," said the man, smiling, "you know me, but you do not know me. Your mind is under partial control and your ability to recognize me is blocked out. Other than that and your analgesia—you are covered with blood from the glass on the wall, but you don't feel any pain—your mind is normal and you are sane."

"What's it all about?" he asked. "Why was I brought here?"

"Because you are sane. I'm sorry about that, because you can't be. It is not so much that you retained memory of your previous life, after you'd been moved. That happens. It is that you somehow know something of what you shouldn't—something of The Brightly Shining, and of the Game between the red and the black. For that reason—"

"For that reason, what?" he asked.

The man he knew and did not know smiled gently. "For that reason you must know the rest, so that you will know nothing at all. For everything will add to nothing. The truth will drive you mad."

"That I do not believe."

"Of course you don't. If the truth were conceivable to you, it would not drive you mad. But you cannot remotely conceive the truth."

A powerful anger surged up within him. He stared at the familiar face that he knew and did not know, and he stared down at himself; at the torn and bloody gray uniform, at his torn and bloody hands. The hands hooked like claws with the desire to kill—someone, the someone, whoever it was, who stood before him.

He asked, "What are you?"

"I am an instrument of The Brightly Shining."

"The same which led me here, or another?"

"One is all, all is one. Within the whole and its parts, there is no difference. One instrument is another and the red is the black and the black is the white and there is no difference. The Brightly Shining is the soul of the Earth. I use *soul* as the nearest word in your vocabulary."

Hatred was almost a bright light. It was almost something that he could lean into, lean his weight against.

He asked, "What is The Brightly Shining?" He made the words a curse in his mouth.

"Knowing will make you mad. You want to know?"

"Yes." He made a curse out of that simple, sibilant syllable.

The lights were dimming. Or was it his eyes? The room was becoming dimmer, and at the same time receding. It was becoming a tiny cube of dim light, seen from afar and outside, from somewhere in the distant dark, ever receding, turning into a pin-point of light, and within that point of light ever the hated Thing, the man—or was it a man?—standing beside the desk.

Into darkness, into space, up and apart from the earth—a dim sphere in the night, a receding sphere outlined against the spangled blackness of eternal space, occulting the stars, a disk of black.

It stopped receding, and time stopped. It was as though the clock of the universe stood still. Beside him, out of the void, spoke the voice of the instrument of The Brightly Shining.

"Behold," it said. "The Being of Earth."

He beheld. Not as though an outward change was occurring, but an inward one, as though his senses were being changed to enable him to perceive something hitherto unseeable.

The ball that was Earth began to glow. Brightly to shine.

"You see the intelligence that rules Earth," said the voice. "The sum of the black and the white and the red, that are one, divided only as the lobes of a brain are divided, the trinity that is one."

The glowing ball and the stars behind it faded, and the darkness became deeper darkness and then there was dim light, growing brighter, and he was back in the room with the man standing at the desk.

"You saw," said the man whom he hated. "But you do not understand. You ask, *what* have you seen, *what* is The Brightly Shining? It is a group intelligence, the true intelligence of Earth, one intelligence among three in the Solar system, one among many in the universe.

"What, then, is man? Men are pawns, in games of—to you—unbelievable complexity, between the red and the black, the white and the black, for amusement. Played by one part of an organism against another part, to while away an instant of eternity. There are vaster games, played between galaxies. Not with man.

"Man is a parasite peculiar to Earth, which tolerates his presence for a little while. He exists nowhere else in the cosmos, and he does not exist here for long. A little while, a few chessboard wars, which he thinks he fights himself— You begin to understand."

The man at the desk smiled.

"You want to know of yourself. Nothing is less important. A move was made, before Lodi. The opportunity was there for a move of the red; a stronger, more ruthless personality was needed; it was a turning point in history— which means in the game. Do you understand now? A pinch-hitter was put in to become Napoleon."

He managed two words. "And then?"

"The Brightly Shining does not kill. You had to be put somewhere, some time. Long later a man named George Vine was killed in an accident; his body was still usable. George Vine had not been insane, but he had had a Napoleonic complex. The transference was amusing."

"No doubt." Again it was impossible to reach the man at the desk. The hatred itself was a wall between them. "Then George Vine is dead?"

"Yes. And you, because you knew a little too much, must go mad so that you will know nothing. Knowing the truth will drive you mad."

"No!"

The instrument only smiled.

VIII

The room, the cube of light, dimmed; it seemed to tilt. Still standing, he was going over backward, his position becoming horizontal instead of vertical.

His weight was on his back and under him was the soft-hard smoothness of his bunk, the roughness of a gray sheet blanket. And he could move; he sat up.

Had he been dreaming? Had he really been outside the asylum? He held up his hands, touched one to the other, and they were wet with something sticky. So was the front of his shirt and the thighs and knees of his trousers.

And his shoes were on.

The blood was there from climbing the wall. And now the analgesia was leaving, and pain was beginning to come into his hands, his chest, his stomach and his legs. Sharp biting pain.

He said aloud, *"I am not mad. I am not mad."* Was he screaming it?

A voice said, "No. Not yet." Was it the voice that had been here in the room before? Or was it the voice of the man who had stood in the lighted room? Or had both been the same voice?

It said, "Ask, 'What is man?'"

Mechanically, he asked it.

"Man is a blind alley in evolution, who came too late to compete, who has always been controlled and played with by The Brightly Shining, which was old and wise before man walked erect.

"Man is a parasite upon a planet populated before he came, populated by a Being that is one and many, a billion cells but a single mind, a single intelligence, a single will—as is true of every other populated planet in the universe.

"Man is a joke, a clown, a parasite. He is nothing; he will be less."

"Come and go mad."

He was getting out of bed again; he was walking. Through the doorway of the cubicle, along the ward. To the door that led to the corridor; a thin crack of light showed under it. But this time his hand did not reach out for the knob. Instead he stood there facing the door, and it began to glow; slowly it became light and visible.

As though from somewhere an invisible spotlight played upon it, the door became a visible rectangle in the surrounding blackness; was brightly visible as the crack under it.

The voice said, "You see before you a cell of your ruler, a cell unintelligent in itself, yet a tiny part of a unit which is intelligent, one of a trillion units which make up *the* intelligence which rules the earth—and you. And which earth-wide intelligence is one of a million intelligences which rule the universe."

"The *door?* I don't—"

The voice spoke no more; it had withdrawn, but somehow inside his mind was the echo of silent laughter.

He leaned closer and saw what he was meant to see. An ant was crawling up the door.

His eyes followed it, and numbing horror crawled apace, up his spine. A hundred things that had been told and shown him suddenly fitted into a pattern, a pattern of sheer horror. The black, the white, the red; the black ants, the white ants, the red ants; the players with men, separate lobes of a single group brain, the intelligence that was one. Man an accident, a parasite, a pawn; a million planets in the universe inhabited each by an insect race that was a single intelligence for the planet—and all the intelligences together were the single cosmic intelligence that was—*God!*

The one-syllable word wouldn't come.

He went mad, instead.

He beat upon the now-dark door with his bloody hands, with his knees, his face, with himself, although already he had forgotten why, had forgotten what he wanted to crush.

He was raving mad—dementia praecox, not paranoia—when they released his body by putting it into a strait jacket, released it from frenzy to quietude.

He was quietly mad—paranoia, not dementia praecox—when they released him as sane eleven months later.

Paranoia, you see, is a peculiar affliction; it has no physical symptoms, it is merely the presence of a fixed delusion. A series of metrazol shocks had cleared up the dementia praecox and left only the fixed delusion that he was George Vine, a reporter.

The asylum authorities thought he was, too, so the delusion was not recognized as such and they released him and gave him a certificate to prove he was sane.

He married Clare; he still works at the *Blade*—for a man named Candler. He still plays chess with his cousin, Charlie Doerr. He still sees—for periodic checkups—both Dr. Irving and Dr. Randolph.

Which of them smiles inwardly? What good would it do you to know?

It doesn't matter. Don't you understand? Nothing matters!

Crisis, 1999

The little man with the sparse gray hair and the inconspicuous bright red suit stopped on the corner of State and Randolph to buy a micronews, a Chicago *Sun-Tribune* of March 21st, 1999. Nobody noticed him as he walked into the corner superdrug and took a vacant booth. He dropped a quarter into the coffee-slot and while the conveyor brought him his coffee, he glanced at the headlines on the tiny three-by-four-inch page. His eyes were unusually keen; he could read those headlines easily without artificial aid. But nothing on the first page or the second interested him; they concerned international matters, the third Venus rocket, and the latest depressing report of the ninth moon expedition. But on page three there were two stories concerning crime, and he took a tiny micrographer from his pocket and adjusted it to read the stories while he drank his coffee.

Bela Joad was the little man's name. His right name, that is; he'd gone by so many names in so many places that only a phenomenal memory could have kept track of them all, but he had a phenomenal memory. None of those names had ever appeared in print, nor had his face or voice ever been seen or heard on the ubiquitous video. Fewer than a score of people, all of them top officials in various police bureaus, knew that Bela Joad was the greatest detective in the world.

He was not an employee of any police department, drew no salary nor expense money, and collected no rewards. It may have been that he had private means and indulged in the detection of criminals as a hobby. It may equally have been that he preyed upon the underworld even as he fought it, that he made criminals support his campaign against them. Whichever was the case, he worked for no one; he worked against crime. When a major crime or a series of major crimes interested him, he would work on it, sometimes consulting beforehand with the chief of police of the city involved, sometimes working without the chief's knowledge until he would appear in the chief's office and present him with the evidence that would enable him to make an arrest and obtain a conviction.

He himself had never testified, or even appeared, in a courtroom. And while he knew every important underworld character in a dozen cities, no member of the underworld knew him, except fleetingly, under some transient identity which he seldom resumed.

Now, over his morning coffee, Bela Joad read through his micrographer the two stories in the *Sun-Tribune* which had interested him. One concerned a case that had been one of his few failures, the disappearance—possibly the kidnapping—of Dr. Ernst Chappel, professor of criminology at Columbia University. The headline read NEW LEAD IN CHAPPEL CASE, but a careful reading of the story showed the detective that the lead was new only to the newspapers; he himself had followed it into a blind alley two years ago, just after Chappel had vanished. The other story revealed that one Paul (Gyp) Girard had yesterday been acquitted of the slaying of his rival for control of North

Chicago gambling. Joad read that one carefully indeed. Just six hours before, seated in a beergarten in New Berlin, Western Germany, he had heard the news of that acquittal on the video, without details. He had immediately taken the first stratoplane to Chicago.

When he had finished with the micronews, he touched the button of his wrist model timeradio, which automatically attuned itself to the nearest timestation, and it said, just loudly enough for him to hear, "Nine-oh-four." Chief Dyer Rand would be in his office, then.

Nobody noticed him as he left the superdrug. Nobody noticed him as he walked with the morning crowds along Randolph to the big, new Municipal Building at the corner of Clark. Chief Rand's secretary sent in his name—not his real one, but one Rand would recognize—without giving him a second glance.

Chief Rand shook hands across the desk and then pressed the intercom button that flashed a blue not-to-be-disturbed signal to his secretary. He leaned back in his chair and laced his fingers across the conservatively small (one inch) squares of his mauve and yellow shirt. He said, "You heard about Gyp Girard being acquitted?"

"That's why I'm here."

Rand pushed his lips out and pulled them in again. He said, "The evidence you sent me was perfectly sound, Joad. It should have stood up. But I wish you had brought it in yourself instead of sending it by the tube, or that there had been some way I could have got in touch with you. I could have told you we'd probably not get a conviction. Joad, something rather terrible has been happening. I've had a feeling you would be my only chance. If only there had been some way I could have got in touch with you—"

"Two years ago?"

Chief Rand looked startled. "Why did you say that?"

"Because it was two years ago that Dr. Chappel disappeared in New York."

"Oh," Rand said. "No, there's no connection. I thought maybe you knew something when you mentioned two years. It hasn't been quite that long, really, but it was close."

He got up from behind the strangely-shaped plastic desk and began to pace back and forth the length of the office.

He said, "Joad, in the last year—let's consider that period, although it started nearer two years ago—out of every ten major crimes committed in Chicago, seven are unsolved. Technically unsolved, that is; in five out of those seven we know who's guilty but we can't prove it. We can't get a conviction.

"The underworld is beating us, Joad, worse than they have at any time since the Prohibition era of seventy-five years ago. If this keeps up, we're going back to days like that, and worse.

"For a twenty-year period now we've had convictions for eight out of ten major crimes. Even before twenty years ago—before the use of the lie-detector in court was legalized, we did better than we're doing now. 'Way back in the decade of 1970 to 1980, for instance, we did better than we're doing now by more than two to one; we got convictions for six out of every ten major crimes. This last year, it's been three out of ten.

"And I know the reason, but I don't know what to do about it. The reason is that the underworld is beating the lie-detector!"

Bela Joad nodded. But he said mildly, "A few have always managed to beat it. It's not perfect. Judges always instruct juries to remember that the lie-detector's findings have a high degree of probability but are not infallible, that they should be weighed as indicative but not final, that other evidence must support them. And there has always been the occasional individual who can tell a whopper with the detector on him, and not jiggle the graph needles at all."

"One in a thousand, yes. But, Joad, almost every underworld big-shot has been beating the lie-detector recently."

"I take it you mean the professional criminals, not the amateurs."

"Exactly. Only regular members of the underworld—professionals, the habitual criminals. If it weren't for that, I'd think—I don't know what I'd think. Maybe that our whole theory was wrong."

Bela Joad said, "Can't you quit using it in court in such cases? Convictions were obtained before its use was legalized. For that matter, before it was invented."

Dyer Rand sighed and dropped into his pneumatic chair again. "Sure, I'd like that if I could do it. I wish right now that the detector never *had* been invented or legalized. But don't forget that the law legalizing it gives *either* side the opportunity to use it in court. If a criminal knows he can beat it, he's going to demand its use even if we don't. And what chance have we got with a jury if the accused demands the detector and it backs up his plea of innocence?"

"Very slight, I'd say."

"Less than slight, Joad. This Gyp Girard business yesterday. I know he killed Pete Bailey. You know it. The evidence you sent me was, under ordinary circumstances, conclusive. And yet I knew we'd lose the case. I wouldn't have bothered bringing it to trial except for one thing."

"And that one thing?"

"*To get you here,* Joad. There was no other way I could reach you, but I hoped that if you read of Girard's acquittal, after the evidence you'd given me, you'd come around to find out what had happened."

He got up and started to pace again. "Joad, I'm going mad. *How* is the underworld beating the machine? That's what I want you to find out, and it's the biggest job you've ever tackled. Take a year, take five years, but crack it, Joad.

"Look at the history of law enforcement. Always the law has been one jump ahead of the criminal in the field of science. Now the criminals—of Chicago, anyway—are one jump ahead of *us*. And if they stay that way, if we don't get the answer, we're headed for a new dark age, when it'll no longer be safe for a man or a woman to walk down the street. The very foundations of our society can crumble. We're up against something very evil and very powerful."

Bela Joad took a cigarette from the dispenser on the desk; it lighted automatically as he picked it up. It was a green cigarette and he exhaled green smoke through his nostrils before he asked, almost disinterestedly, "Any ideas, Dyer?"

"I've had two, but I think I've eliminated both of them. One is that the machines are being tampered with. The other is that the technicians are being tampered with. But I've had both men and machines checked from every possible angle and can't find a thing. On big cases I've taken special precautions. For example, the detector we used at the Girard trial; it was brand-new and I had it checked right in this office." He chuckled. "I put Captain Burke under it and asked him if he was being faithful to his wife. He said he was and it nearly broke the needle. I had it taken to the courtroom under special guard."

"And the technician who used it?"

"I used it myself. Took a course in it, evenings, for four months."

Bela Joad nodded. "So it isn't the machine and it isn't the operator. That's eliminated, and I can start from there."

"How long will it take you, Joad?"

The little man in the red suit shrugged. "I haven't any idea."

"Is there any help I can give you? Anything you want to start on?"

"Just one thing, Dyer. I want a list of the criminals who have beaten the detector and a dossier on each. Just the ones you're morally sure actually committed the crimes you questioned them about. If there's any reasonable doubt, leave them off the list. How long will it take to get it ready?"

"It's ready now; I had it made up on the chance that you'd come here. And it's a long report, so I had it microed down for you." He handed Bela Joad a small envelope. Joad said, "Thank you. I won't contact you till I have something or until I want your cooperation. I think first I'm going to stage a murder, and then have you question the murderer."

Dyer Rand's eyes went wide. "Whom are you going to have murdered?"

Bela Joad smiled. "Me," he said.

He took the envelope Rand had given him back to his hotel and spent several hours studying the microfilms through his pocket micrographer, memorizing their contents thoroughly. Then he burned both films and envelope.

After that Bela Joad paid his hotel bill and disappeared, but a little man who resembled Bela Joad only slightly rented a cheap room under the name of Martin Blue. The room was on Lake Shore Drive, which was then the heart of Chicago's underworld.

The underworld of Chicago had changed less, in fifty years, than one would think. Human vices do not change, or at least they change but slowly. True, certain crimes had diminished greatly but on the other hand, gambling had increased. Greater social security than any country had hitherto known was, perhaps, a factor. One no longer needed to save for old age as, in days gone by, a few people did.

Gambling was a lush field for the crooks and they cultivated the field well. Improved technology had increased the number of ways of gambling and it had increased the efficiency of ways of making gambling crooked. Crooked gambling was big business and underworld wars and killings occurred over territorial rights, just as they had occurred over such rights in the far back days of Prohibition when alcohol was king. There was still alcohol, but it was of lesser importance now. People were learning to drink more moderately. And drugs were passé, although there was still some traffic in them.

Robberies and burglaries still occurred, although not quite as frequently as they had fifty years before.

Murder was slightly more frequent. Sociologists and criminologists differed as to the reason for the increase of crime in this category.

The weapons of the underworld had, of course, improved, but they did not include atomics. All atomic and subatomic weapons were strictly controlled by the military and were never used by either the police or by criminals. They were too dangerous; the death penalty was mandatory for anyone found in possession of an atomic weapon. But the pistols and guns of the underworld of 1999 were quite efficient. They were much smaller and more compact, and they were silent. Both guns and cartridges were made of superhard magnesium and were very light. The commonest weapon was the .19 calibre pistol— as deadly as the .45 of an earlier era because the tiny projectiles were explosive—and even a small pocket-pistol held from fifty to a hundred rounds.

But back to Martin Blue, whose entrance into the underworld coincided with the disappearance of Bela Joad from the latter's hotel.

Martin Blue, as it turned out, was not a very nice man. He had no visible means of support other than gambling and he seemed to lose, in small amounts, almost more often than he won. He almost got in trouble on a bad check he gave to cover his losses in one game, but he managed to avoid being liquidated by making the check good. His only reading seemed to be the *Racing Microform*, and he drank too much, mostly in a tavern (with clandestine gambling at the back) which formerly had been operated by Gyp Girard. He got beaten up there once because he defended Gyp against a crack made by the current proprietor to the effect that Gyp had lost his guts and turned honest.

For a while fortune turned against Martin Blue and he went so broke that he had to take a job as a waiter in the outside room of a Michigan Boulevard joint called Sloppy Joe's, possibly because Joe Zatelli, who ran it, was the nattiest dresser in Chicago—and in the *fin de siècle* era when leopard-skin suits (synthetic but finer and more expensive than real leopard skin) were a dime a dozen and plain pastel-silk underwear was dated.

Then a funny thing happened to Martin Blue. Joe Zatelli killed him. Caught him, after hours, rifling the till, and just as Martin Blue turned around Zatelli shot him. Three times for good measure. And then Zatelli, who never trusted accomplices, got the body into his car and deposited it in an alley back of a teletheater.

The body of Martin Blue got up and went to see Chief Dyer Rand and told Rand what he wanted done.

"You took a hell of a chance," Rand said.

"Not too much of a chance," Blue said. "I'd put blanks in his gun and I was pretty sure he'd use that. He won't ever find out, incidentally, that the rest of the bullets in it are blanks unless he tries to kill somebody else with it; they don't *look* like blanks. And I had a pretty special vest on under my suit.

Rigid backing and padded on top to feel like flesh, but of course he couldn't feel a heartbeat through it. And it was gimmicked to make a noise like explosive cartridges hitting—when the duds punctured the compartments."

"But if he'd switched guns or bullets?"

"Oh, the vest was bulletproofed for anything short of atomics. The danger was in his thinking of a fancy way of disposing of the body. If he had, I could have taken care of myself, of course, but it would have spoiled the plan and cost me three months' build-up. But I'd studied his style and I was pretty sure what he'd do. Now here's what I want you to do, Dyer—"

The newspapers and videocasts the next morning carried the story of the finding of a body of an unidentified man in a certain alley. By afternoon they reported that it had been identified as the body of Martin Blue, a small-time crook who had lived on Lake Shore Drive, in the heart of the Tenderloin. And by evening a rumor had gone out through the underworld to the effect that the police suspected Joe Zatelli, for whom Blue had worked, and might pick him up for questioning.

And plainclothesmen watched Zatelli's place, front and back, to see where he'd go if he went out. Watching the front was a small man about the build of Bela Joad or Martin Blue. Unfortunately, Zatelli happened to leave by the back and he succeeded in shaking off the detectives on his trail.

They picked him up the next morning, though, and took him to headquarters. They put the lie-detector on him and asked him about Martin Blue. He admitted Blue had worked for him but said he'd last seen Blue when the latter had left his place after work the night of the murder. The lie-detector said he wasn't lying.

Then they pulled a tough one on him. Martin Blue walked into the room where Zatelli was being questioned. And the trick fizzled. The gauges of the detector didn't jump a fraction of a millimeter and Zatelli looked at Blue and then at his interrogators with complete indignation. "What's the idea?" he demanded. "The guy ain't even dead, and you're asking me if I bumped him off?"

They asked Zatelli, while they had him there, about some other crimes he might have committed, but obviously—according to his answers and the lie-detector—he hadn't done any of them. They let him go.

Of course that was the end of Martin Blue. After showing up before Zatelli at headquarters, he might as well have been dead in an alley for all the good he was going to do.

Bela Joad told Chief Rand, "Well, anyway, now we *know*."

"What do we know?"

"We know for sure the detector is being beaten. You might conceivably have been making a series of wrong arrests before. Even the evidence I gave you against Girard might have been misleading. But we *know* that Zatelli beat the machine. Only I wish Zatelli had come out the front way so I could have tailed him; we might have the whole thing now instead of part of it."

"You're going back? Going to do it all over again?"

"Not the same way. This time I've got to be on the other end of a murder, and I'll need your help on that."

"Of course. But won't you tell me what's on your mind?"

"I'm afraid I can't, Dyer. I've got a hunch within a hunch. In fact, I've had it ever since I started on this business. But will you do one other thing for me?"

"Sure. What?"

"Have one of your men keep track of Zatelli, of everything he does from now on. Put another one on Gyp Girard. In fact, take as many men as you can spare and put one on each of the men you're fairly sure has beaten the detector within the last year or two. And always from a distance; don't let the boys know they're being checked on. Will you?"

"I don't know what you're after, but I'll do it. Won't you tell me *anything*? Joad, this is important. Don't forget it's not just a case, it's something that can lead to the breakdown of law enforcement."

Bela Joad smiled "Not quite that bad, Dyer. Law enforcement as it applies to the underworld, yes. But you're getting your usual percentage of convictions on nonprofessional crimes."

Dyer Rand looked puzzled. "What's that got to do with it?"

"Maybe everything; It's why I can't tell you anything yet. But don't worry." Joad reached across the desk and patted the chief's shoulder, looking—although he didn't know it—like a fox terrier giving his paw to an Airedale. "Don't worry, Dyer. I'll promise to bring you the answer. Maybe I won't be able to let you keep it."

"Do you really know what you're looking for?"

"Yes. I'm looking for a criminologist who disappeared well over two years ago. Dr. Ernst Chappel."

"You think—?"

"Yes, I think. That's why I'm looking for Dr. Chappel."

But that was all Dyer could get out of him. Bela Joad left Dyer Rand's office and returned to the underworld.

And in the underworld of Chicago a new star arose. Perhaps one should call him a *nova* rather than merely a star so rapidly did he become famous—or notorious. Physically, he was rather a small man, no larger than Bela Joad or Martin Blue, but he wasn't a mild little man like Joad or a weak jackal like Blue. He had what it took, and he parlayed what he had. He ran a small night club, but that was just a front. Behind that front things happened, things that the police couldn't pin on him, and—for that matter—didn't seem to know about, although the underworld knew.

His name was Willie Ecks, and nobody in the underworld had ever made friends and enemies faster. He had plenty of each; the former were powerful and the latter were dangerous. In other words, they were both the same type of people.

His brief career was truly—if I may scramble my star-nova metaphor but keep it celestial—a meteoric matter. And for once that hackneyed and inaccurate metaphor is used correctly. Meteors do not rise—as anybody who has ever studied meteorology, which has no connection with meteors, knows. Meteors fall, with a dull thud. And that is what happened to Willie Ecks, when he got high enough.

Three days before, Willie Ecks's worst enemy had vanished. Two of his henchmen spread the rumor that it was because the cops had come and taken him away, but that was obviously malarkey designed to cover the fact that they intended to avenge him. That became obvious when, the very next morning, the news broke that the gangster's body had been found, neatly weighted, in the Blue Lagoon at Washington Park.

And by dusk of that very day rumor had gone from bistro to bistro of the underworld that the police had pretty good proof who had killed the deceased— and with a forbidden atomic at that—and that they planned to arrest Willie Ecks and question him. Things like that get around even when it's not intended that they should.

And it was on the second day of Willie Ecks's hiding-out in a cheap little hotel on North Clark Street, an old-fashioned hotel with elevators and windows, his whereabouts known only to a trusted few, that one of those trusted few gave a certain knock on his door and was admitted.

The trusted one's name was Mike Leary and he'd been a close friend of Willie's and a close enemy of the gentleman who, according to the papers, had been found in the Blue Lagoon.

He said, "Looks like you're in a jam, Willie."

"—, yes," said Willie Ecks. He hadn't used facial depilatory for two days; his face was blue with beard and bluer with fear.

Mike said, "There's a way out, Willie. It'll cost you ten grand. Can you raise it?"

"I've got it. What's the way out?"

"There's a guy. I know how to get in touch with him; I ain't used him myself, but I would if I got in a jam like yours. He can fix you up, Willie."

"How?"

"He can show you how to beat the lie-detector. I can have him come around to see you and fix you up. Then you let the cops pick you up and question you, see? They'll drop the charge—or if they bring it to trial, they can't make it stick."

"What if they ask me about—well, never mind what—other things I may have done?"

"He'll take care of that, too. For five grand he'll fix you so you can go under that detector clean as—as clean as hell."

"You said ten grand."

Mike Leary grinned. "I got to live too, don't I, Willie? And you said you got ten grand, so it ought to be worth that much to you, huh?"

Willie Ecks argued, but in vain. He had to give Mike Leary five thousand-dollar bills. Not that it really mattered, because those were pretty special thousand-dollar bills. The green ink on them would turn purple within a few days. Even in 1999 you couldn't spend a purple thousand-dollar bill, so when it happened Mike Leary would probably turn purple too, but by that time it would be too late for him to do anything about it.

It was late that evening when there was a knock on Willie Ecks's hotel room door. He pressed the button that made the main panel of the door transparent from his side.

He studied the nondescript-looking man outside the door very carefully. He didn't pay any attention to facial contours or to the shabby yellow suit the man wore. He studied the eyes somewhat, but mostly he studied the shape and conformation of the ears and compared them mentally with the ears of photographs he had once studied exhaustively. And then Willie Ecks put his gun back into his pocket and opened the door. He said, "Come in."

The man in the yellow suit entered the room and Willie Ecks shut the door very carefully and locked it.

He said, "I'm proud to meet you, Dr. Chappel."

He sounded as though he meant it, and he did mean it.

It was four o'clock in the morning when Bela Joad stood outside the door of Dyer Rand's apartment. He had to wait, there in the dimly luminous hallway, for as long as it took the chief to get out of bed and reach the door, then activate the one-way-transparent panel to examine his visitor.

Then the magnetic lock sighed gently and the door opened. Rand's eyes were bleary and his hair was tousled. His feet were thrust into red plastic slippers and he wore neonylon sleeping pajamas that looked as though they had been slept in.

He stepped aside to let Bela Joad in, and Joad walked to the center of the room and stood looking about curiously. It was the first time he'd ever been in Rand's private quarters. The apartment was like that of any other well-to-do bachelor of the day. The furniture was unobtrusive and functional, each wall a different pastel shade, faintly fluorescent and emitting gentle radiant heat and the faint but constant caress of ultraviolet that kept people who could afford such apartments healthily tanned. The rug was in alternate one-foot squares of cream and gray, the squares separate and movable so that wear would be equalized. And the ceiling, of course, was the customary one-piece mirror that gave an illusion of height and spaciousness.

Rand said, "Good news, Joad?"

"Yes. But this is an unofficial interview, Dyer. What I'm going to tell you is confidential, between us."

"What do you mean?"

Joad looked at him. He said, "You still look sleepy, Dyer. Lets have coffee. It'll wake you up, and I can use some myself."

"Fine," Dyer said. He went into the kitchenette and pressed the button that would heat the coils of the coffee-tap. "Want it laced?" he called back.

"Of course."

Within a minute he came back with two cups of steaming *café royale*. With obvious impatience he waited until they were seated comfortably and each had taken his first sip of the fragrant beverage before he asked, "Well, Joad?"

"When I say it's unofficial, Dyer, I mean it. I can give you the full answer, but only with the understanding that you'll forget it as soon as I tell you, that you'll never tell another person, and that you won't act upon it."

Dyer Rand stared at his guest in amazement. He said, "I can't promise that! I'm chief of police, Joad. I have my duty to my job and to the people of Chicago."

"That's why I came here, to your apartment, instead of to your office. You're not working now, Dyer; you're on your own time."

"But—"

"Do you promise?"

"Of course not."

Bela Joad sighed. "Then I'm sorry for waking you, Dyer." He put down his cup and started to rise.

"Wait! You can't do that. You can't just walk out on me!"

"Can't I?"

"All right, all right, I'll promise. You must have some good reason. Have you?"

"Yes."

"Then I'll take your word for it."

Bela Joad smiled. "Good," he said. "Then I'll be able to report to you on my last case. For this is my last case, Dyer. I'm going into a new kind of work."

Rand looked at him incredulously. "What?"

"I'm going to teach crooks how to beat the lie-detector."

Chief Dyer Rand put down his cup slowly and stood up. He took a step toward the little man, about half his weight, who sat at ease on the armless, overstuffed chair.

Bela Joad still smiled. He said, "Don't try it, Dyer. For two reasons. First, you couldn't hurt me and I wouldn't want to hurt you and I might have to. Second, it's all right, it's on the up and up. Sit down."

Dyer Rand sat down.

Bela Joad said, "When you said this thing was big, you didn't know how big. And it's going to be bigger; Chicago is just the starting point. And thanks, by the way for those reports I asked you for. They are just what I expected they'd be."

"The reports? But they're still in my desk at headquarters.

"They were. I've read them and destroyed them. Your copies, too. Forget about them. And don't pay too much attention to your current statistics. I've read them too."

Rand frowned. "And why should I forget them?"

"Because they confirm what Ernie Chappel told me this evening. Do you know, Dyer, that your *number* of major crimes has gone down in the past year by an even bigger percentage than the percentage by which your convictions for major crimes has gone down?"

"I noticed that. You mean, there's a connection?"

"Definitely. Most crimes—a very high percentage of them—are committed by professional criminals, repeaters. And Dyer, it goes even farther than that. Out of several thousand major crimes a year, ninety percent of them are committed by *a few hundred professional criminals.* And do you know that the number of professional criminals in Chicago has been reduced by almost a third in the last two years? It *has.* And that's why your number of major crimes has decreased."

Bela Joad took another sip of his coffee and then leaned forward. "Gyp Girard, according to your report, is now running a vitadrink stand on the West Side, he hasn't committed a crime in almost a year—since he beat your lie-detector." He touched another finger. "Joe Zatelli, who used to be the roughest boy on the Near North Side, is now running his restaurant straight. Carey Hutch. Wild Bill Wheeler— Why should I list them all? You've got the list, and it's not complete because there are plenty of names you haven't got on it, people who went to Ernie Chappel so he could show them how to beat the detector, and then didn't get arrested after all. And nine out of ten of them— and that's conservative, Dyer—*haven't committed a crime since!*"

Dyer Rand said, "Go on. I'm listening."

"My original investigation of the Chappel case showed me that he'd disappeared voluntarily. And I knew he was a good man, and a great one. I knew he was mentally sound because he was a psychiatrist as well as a criminologist. A psychiatrist's *got* to be sound. So I knew he'd disappeared for some good reason.

"And when, about nine months ago, I heard your side of what had been happening in Chicago, I began to suspect that Chappel had come here to do his work. Are you beginning to get the picture?"

"Faintly."

"Well, don't faint yet. Not until you figure how an expert psychiatrist can help crooks beat the detector. Or have you?"

"Well—"

"That's it. The most elementary form of hypnotic treatment, something any qualified psychiatrist could do fifty years ago. Chappel's clients—of course they don't know who or what he is; he's a mysterious underworld figure who helps them beat the rap—pay him well and tell him what crimes they may be questioned about by the police if they're picked up. He tells them to include every crime they've ever committed and any racket they've ever been in, so the police won't catch them up on any old counts. Then he—"

"Wait a minute," Rand interrupted. "How does he get them to trust him that far?"

Joad gestured impatiently. "Simple. They aren't confessing a single crime, even to him. He just wants a list that *includes* everything they've done. They can add some ringers and he doesn't know which is which. So it doesn't matter.

"Then he puts them under light waking-hypnosis and tells them they are not criminals and never have been and they have never done any of the things on the list he reads back to them. That's all there is to it.

"So when you put them under the detector and ask them if they've done this or that, they say they haven't and they *believe* it. That's why your detector gauges don't register. That's why Joe Zatelli didn't jump when he saw Martin

Blue walk in. He didn't know Blue was dead—except that he'd read it in the papers."

Rand leaned forward. "Where is Ernst Chappel?"

"You don't want him, Dyer."

"Don't *want* him? He's the most dangerous man alive today!"

"To whom?"

"To *whom?* Are you crazy?"

"I'm not crazy. He's the most dangerous man alive today—to the underworld. Look, Dyer, any time a criminal gets jittery about a possible pinch, he sends for Ernie or goes to Ernie. And Ernie washes him whiter than snow and in the process tells him *he's not a criminal.*

"And so, at least nine times out of ten, he quits being a criminal. Within ten or twenty years Chicago isn't going to have an underworld. There won't be any organized crimes by professional criminals. You'll always have the amateur with you, but he's a comparatively minor detail. How about some more *café royale?*"

Dyer Rand walked to the kitchenette and got it. He was wide awake by now, but he walked like a man in a dream.

When he came back, Joad said, "And now that I'm in with Ernie on it, Dyer, we'll stretch it to every city in the world big enough to have an underworld worth mentioning. We can train picked recruits; I've got my eye on two of your men and may take them away from you soon. But I'll have to check them first. We're going to pick our apostles—about a dozen of them—very carefully. They'll be the right men for the job."

"But, Joad, look at all the crimes that are going to go unpunished!" Rand protested.

Bela Joad drank the rest of his coffee and stood up. He said, "And which is more important—to punish criminals or to end crime? And, if you want to look at it moralistically, should a man be punished for a crime when he doesn't even remember committing it, when he is no longer a criminal?"

Dyer Rand sighed. "You win, I guess. I'll keep my promise. I suppose— I'll never see you again?"

"Probably not, Dyer. And I'll anticipate what you're going to say next. Yes, I'll have a farewell drink with you. A straight one, without the coffee."

Dyer Rand brought the glasses. He said, "Shall we drink to Ernie Chappel?"

Bela Joad smiled. He said, "Let's include him in the toast, Dyer. But let's drink to all men who work to put themselves out of work. Doctors work toward the day when the race will be so healthy it won't need doctors; lawyers work toward the day when litigation will no longer be necessary. And policemen, detectives, and criminologists work toward the day when they will no longer be needed because there will be no more crime."

Dyer Rand nodded very soberly and lifted his glass. They drank.

Letter to a Phoenix

There is much to tell you, so much that it is difficult to know where to begin. Fortunately, I have forgotten most of the things that have happened to me. Fortunately, the mind has a limited capacity for remembering. It would be horrible if I remembered the details of a hundred and eighty thousand years—the details of four thousand lifetimes that I have lived since the first great atomic war.

Not that I have forgotten the really great moments. I remember being on the first expedition to land on Mars and the third to land on Venus. I remember—I believe it was in the third great war—the blasting of Skora from the sky by a force that compares to nuclear fission as a nova compares to our slowly dying sun. I was second in command on a Hyper-A Class spacer in the war against the second extragalactic invaders, the ones who established bases on Jupe's moons before we knew they were there and almost drove us out of the Solar System before we found the one weapon they couldn't stand up against. So they fled where we couldn't follow them, then, outside of the Galaxy. When we did follow them, about fifteen thousand years later, they were gone. They were dead three thousand years.

And this is what I want to tell you about—that mighty race and the others—but first; so that you will know how I know what I know, I will tell you about myself.

I am not immortal. There is only one immortal being in the universe; of it, more anon. Compared to it, I am of no importance, but you will not understand or believe what I say to you unless you understand what I am.

There is little in a name, and that is a fortunate thing—for I do not remember mine. That is less strange than you think, for a hundred and eighty thousand years is a long time and for one reason or another I have changed my name a thousand times or more. And what could matter less than the name my parents gave me a hundred and eighty thousand years ago?

I am not a mutant. What happened to me happened when I was twenty-three years old, during the first atomic war. The first war, that is, in which both sides used atomic weapons—puny weapons, of course, compared to subsequent ones. It was less than a score of years after the discovery of the atom bomb. The first bombs were dropped in a minor war while I was still a child. They ended that war quickly for only one side had them.

The first atomic war wasn't a bad one—the first one never is. I was lucky for, if it had been a bad one—one which ended a civilization—I'd not have survived it despite the biological accident that happened to me. If it had ended a civilization, I wouldn't have been kept alive during the sixteen-year sleep period I went through about thirty years later. But again I get ahead of the story.

I was, I believe, twenty or twenty-one years old when the war started. They didn't take me for the army right away because I was not physically fit.

I was suffering from a rather rare disease of the pituitary gland—Somebody's syndrome. I've forgotten the name. It caused obesity, among other things. I was about fifty pounds overweight for my height and had little stamina. I was rejected without a second thought.

About two years later my disease had progressed slightly, but other things had progressed more than slightly. By that time the army was taking anyone; they'd have taken a one-legged one-armed blind man if he was willing to fight. And I was willing to fight. I'd lost my family in a dusting, I hated my job in a war plant, and I had been told by doctors that my disease was incurable and I had only a year or two to live in any case. So I went to what was left of the army and what was left of the army took me without a second thought and sent me to the nearest front, which was ten miles away. I was in the fighting one day after I joined.

Now I remember enough to know that *I* hadn't anything to do with it, but it happened that the time I joined was the turn of the tide. The other side was out of bombs and dust and getting low on shells and bullets. We were out of bombs and dust, too, but they hadn't knocked out *all* of our production facilities and we'd got just about all of theirs. We still had planes to carry them, too, and we still had the semblance of an organization to send the planes to the right places. Nearly the right places, anyway; sometimes we dropped them too close to our own troops by mistake. It was a week after I'd got into the fighting that I got out of it again—knocked out of it by one of our smaller bombs that had been dropped about a mile away.

I came to, about two weeks later, in a base hospital, pretty badly burned. By that time the war was over, except for the mopping up, and except for restoring order and getting the world started up again. You see, that hadn't been what I call a blow-up war. It killed off—I'm just guessing; I don't remember the fraction—about a fourth or a fifth of the world's population. There was enough productive capacity left, and there were enough people left, to keep on going; there were dark ages for a few centuries, but there was no return to savagery, no starting over again. In such times, people go back to using candles for light and burning wood for fuel, but not because they don't know how to use electricity or mine coal; just because the confusions and revolutions keep them off balance for a while. The knowledge is there, in abeyance until order returns.

It's not like a blow-up war, when nine-tenths or more of the population of Earth—or of Earth and the other planets—is killed. Then is when the world reverts to utter savagery and the hundreth generation rediscovers metals to tip their spears.

But again I digressed. After I recovered consciousness in the hospital, I was in pain for a long time. There were, by then, no more anesthetics. I had deep radiation burns, from which I suffered almost intolerably for the first few months until, gradually, they healed. I did not sleep—that was the strange thing. And it was a terrifying thing, then, for I did not understand what had happened to me, and the unknown is always terrifying. The doctors paid little heed—for I was one of millions burned or otherwise injured—and I think they did not believe my statements that I had not slept at all. They thought I had slept but little and that I was either exaggerating or making an honest error. But I had *not* slept at all. I did not sleep until long after I left the hospital, cured. Cured, incidentally, of the disease of my pituitary gland, and with my weight back to normal, my health perfect.

I didn't sleep for thirty years. Then *I did sleep*, and I slept for sixteen years. And at the end of that forty-six year period, I was still, physically at the apparent age of twenty-three.

Do you begin to see what had happened as I began to see it then? The radiation—or combination of types of radiation—I had gone through, had radically changed the functions of my pituitary. And there were other factors involved. I studied endocrinology once, about a hundred and fifty thousand years ago, and I think I found the pattern. If my calculations were correct, what happened to me was one chance in a great many billions.

The factors of decay and aging were not eliminated, of course, but the rate was reduced by about fifteen thousand times. I age at the rate of one day every forty-five years. So I am not immortal. I have aged eleven years in the past hundred and eighty millennia. My physical age is now thirty-four.

And forty-five years is to me as a day. I do not sleep for about thirty years of it—then I sleep for about fifteen. It is well for me that my first few "days" were not spent in a period of complete social disorganization or savagery, else I would not have survived my first few sleeps. But I did survive them and by that time I had learned a system and could take care of my own survival. Since then, I have slept about four thousand times, and I have survived. Perhaps someday I shall be unlucky. Perhaps someday, despite certain safeguards, someone will discover and break into the cave or vault into which I seal myself, secretly, for a period of sleep. But it is not likely. I have years in which to prepare each of those places and the experience of four thousand sleeps back of me. You could pass such a place a thousand times and never know it was there, nor be able to enter if you suspected.

No, my chances for survival between my periods of waking life are much better than my chances of survival during my conscious, active periods. It is perhaps a miracle that I have survived so many of those, despite the techniques of survival that I have developed.

And those techniques are good. I've lived through seven major atomic—and super-atomic—wars that have reduced the population of Earth to a few savages around a few campfires in a few still habitable areas. And at other times, in other eras, I've been in five galaxies besides our own.

I've had several thousand wives but always one at a time for I was born in a monogamous era and the habit has persisted. And I have raised several thousand children. Of course, I have never been able to remain with one wife longer than thirty years before I must disappear, but thirty years is long enough for both of us—especially when she ages at a normal rate and I age imperceptibly. Oh, it leads to problems, of course, but I've been able to handle them. I always marry, when I do marry, a girl as much younger than myself as possible, so the disparity will not become too great. Say I am thirty; I marry a girl of sixteen. Then when it is time that I must leave her, she is forty-six and I am still thirty. And it is best for both of us, for everyone, that when I awaken I do not again go back to that place. If she still lives, she will be past sixty and it would not be well, even for her, to have a husband come back from the dead— still young. And I have left her well provided, a wealthy widow—wealthy in money or in whatever may have constituted wealth in that particular era. Sometimes it has been beads and arrowheads, sometimes wheat in a granary and once—there have been peculiar civilizations—it was fish scales. I never had the slightest difficulty in acquiring my share, or more, of money or its equivalent. A few thousand years' practice and the difficulty becomes the other way— knowing when to stop in order not to become unduly wealthy and so attract attention.

For obvious reasons, I've always managed to do that. For reasons that you will see I've never wanted power, nor have I ever—after the first few hundred years—let people suspect that I was different from them. I even spend a few hours each night lying thinking, pretending to sleep.

But none of that is important, any more than I am important. I tell it to you only so you will understand how I *know* the thing that I am about to tell you.

And when I tell you, it is not because I'm trying to sell you anything. It's something you can't change if you want to, and—when you understand it— you won't want to.

I'm not trying to influence you or to lead you. In four thousand lifetimes I've been almost everything—except a leader. I've avoided that. Oh, often enough I have been a god among savages, but that was because I had to be one in order to survive. I used the powers they thought were magic only to keep a degree of order, never to lead them, never to hold them back. If I taught them to use the bow and arrow, it was because game was scarce and we were starving and my survival depended upon theirs. Seeing that the pattern was necessary, I have never disturbed it.

What I tell you now will not disturb the pattern.

It is this: The human race is the only immortal organism in the universe.

There have been other races, and there are other races throughout the universe, but they have died away or they will die. We charted them once, a hundred thousand years ago, with an instrument that detected the presence of thought, the presence of intelligence, however alien and at whatever distance— and gave us a measure of that mind and its qualities. And fifty thousand years later that instrument was rediscovered. There were about as many races as before but only eight of them were ones that had been there fifty thousand years ago and each of those eight was dying, senescent. They had passed the peak of their powers and they were dying.

They had reached the limit of their capabilities—and there is always a limit—and they had no choice but to die. Life is dynamic; it can never be static—at however high or low a level—and survive.

That is what I am trying to tell you so that you will never again be afraid. Only a race that destroys itself and its progress periodically, that goes back to its beginning, can survive more than, say, sixty thousand years of intelligent life.

In all the universe only the human race has ever reached a high level of intelligence without reaching a high level of sanity. We are unique. We are already at least five times as old as any other race has ever been and it is because we are not sane. And man has, at times, had glimmerings of the fact that insanity is divine. But only at high levels of culture does he realize that he is collectively insane, that fight against it as he will, he will always destroy himself—and rise anew out of the ashes.

The phoenix, the bird that periodically immolates itself upon a flaming pyre to rise newborn and live again for another millennium, and again and forever, is only metaphorically a myth. It exists and there is only one of it.

You are the phoenix.

Nothing will ever destroy you, now that—during many high civilizations—your seed has been scattered on the planets of a thousand suns, in a hundred galaxies, there ever to repeat the pattern. The pattern that started a hundred and eighty thousand years ago—I think.

I cannot be sure of that for I have seen that the twenty to thirty thousand years that elapse between the fall of one civilization and the rise of the next destroy all traces. In twenty to thirty thousand years memories become legends and legends become superstitions and even the superstitions become lost. Metals rust and corrode back into earth while the wind, the rain and the jungle erode and cover stone. The contours of the very continents change—and glaciers come and go, and a city of twenty thousand years before is under miles of earth or miles of water.

So I cannot be sure. Perhaps the first blow-up that I knew was not the first; civilizations may have risen and fallen before my time. If so, it merely strengthens the case I put before you to say that mankind *may* have survived more than the hundred and eighty thousand years I know of, may have lived through more than the six blow-ups that have happened since what I think to have been the first discovery of the phoenix's pyre.

But—except that we scattered our seed to the stars so well that even the dying of the sun or its becoming a nova would not destroy us—the past does not matter. Lur, Candra, Thragan, Kah, Mu, Atlantis—those are the six I have known, and they are gone as thoroughly as this one will be twenty thousand years or so hence, but the human race, here or in other galaxies, will survive and will live forever,

It will help your peace of mind, here in this year 1954 of your current era, to know that—for your minds are disturbed. Perhaps, I do know, it will help your thoughts to know that the coming atomic war, the one that will probably happen in your generation, will not be a blow-up war; it will come too soon for that, before you have developed the really destructive weapons man has had so often before. It will set you back, yes. There will be darkish ages for a century or a few centuries. Then, with the memory of what you will call World War III as a warning, man will think—as he has always thought after a mild atomic war—that he has conquered his own insanity.

For a while—if the pattern holds—he will hold it in check. He will reach the stars again, to find himself already there. Why, you'll be back on Mars within five hundred years, and I'll go there too, to see again the canals I once helped to dig. I've not been there for eighty thousand years and I'd like to see what time has done to it and to those of us who were cut off there the last time mankind lost the space drive. Of course they've followed the pattern too, but the rate is not necessarily constant. We may find them at any stage in the cycle except the top. If they were at the top of the cycle, we wouldn't have to go to them—they'd come to us. Thinking, of course, as they think by now, that they are Martians.

I wonder how high, this time, you will get. Not quite as high, I hope, as Thragan. I hope that never again is rediscovered the weapon Thragan used against her colony on Skora, which was then the fifth planet until the Thragans blew it into asteroids. Of course that weapon would be developed only long after intergalactic travel again becomes commonplace. If I see it coming I'll get out of the Galaxy, but I'd hate to have to do that. I like Earth and I'd like to spend the rest of my mortal lifetime on it if it lasts that long.

Possibly it won't, but the human race will last. Everywhere and forever, for it will never be sane and only insanity is divine. Only the mad destroy themselves and all they have wrought.

And only the phoenix lives forever.

Vengeance Fleet

They came from the blackness of space and from unthinkable distance. They converged on Venus—and blasted it. Every one of the two and a half million human beings on that planet, all the colonists from Earth, died within minutes, and all of the flora and fauna of Venus died with them.

Such was the power of their weapons that the very atmosphere of that suddenly doomed planet was burned and dissipated. Venus had been unprepared and unguarded, and so sudden and unexpected had been the attack and so quick and devastating had been its results that not a shot had been fired against them.

They turned toward the next planet outward from the sun, Earth.

But that was different. Earth was ready—not, of course, made ready in the few minutes since the invaders' arrival in the solar system, but ready because Earth was then—in 2820—at war with her Martian colony, which had grown half as populous as Earth itself and was even then battling for independence. At the moment of the attack on Venus, the fleets of Earth and Mars had been maneuvering for combat near the moon.

But the battle ended more suddenly than any battle in history had ever ended. A joint fleet of Terrestrial and Martian ships, suddenly no longer at war with one another, headed to intercept the invaders and met them between Earth and Venus. Our numbers were overwhelmingly superior and the invading ships were blasted out of space, completely annihilated.

Within twenty-four hours peace between Earth and Mars was signed at the Earth capital of Albuquerque, a solid and lasting peace based on recognition of the independence of Mars and a perpetual alliance between the two worlds—now the only two habitable planets of the solar system—against alien aggression. And already plans were being drawn for a vengeance fleet, to find the base of the aliens and destroy it before it could send another fleet against us.

Instruments on Earth and on patrol ships a few thousand miles above her surface had detected the arrival of the aliens—though not in time to save Venus—and the readings of those instruments showed the direction from which the aliens had come and indicated, although not showing exactly how far they had come, that they had come from an almost incredible distance.

A distance that would have been too great for us to span had not the C-plus drive—which enabled a ship to build up to a speed many times the speed of light—just been invented. It had not yet been used because the Earth-Mars war had taken all the resources of both planets, and the C-plus drive had no advantages within the solar system since vast distances were required for the purpose of building up to faster-than-light speeds.

Now, however, it had a very definite purpose; Earth and Mars combined their efforts and their technologies to build a fleet equipped with the C-plus drive for the purpose of sending it against the aliens' home planet to wipe it out. It took ten years, and it was estimated that the trip would take another ten.

The vengeance fleet—not large in numbers but incredibly powerful in armament—left Marsport in 2830.

Nothing was ever heard of it again.

Not until almost a century later did its fate become known, and then only by deductive reasoning on the part of Jon Spencer 4, the great historian and mathematician.

"We now know," Spencer wrote, "and have known for some time, that an object exceeding the speed of light travels backward in time. Therefore the vengeance fleet would have reached its destination, by our time, before it started.

"We have not known, until now, the dimensions of the universe in which we live. But from the experience of the vengeance fleet, we can now deduce them. In one direction, at least, the universe is C^C miles around—or across; they mean the same thing. In ten years, traveling forward in space and backward in time, the fleet would have traversed just that distance—$186,334^{186,334}$ miles. The fleet, traveling in a straight line, circled the universe, as it were, to its point of departure ten years before it left. It destroyed the first planet it saw and then, as it headed for the next, its admiral must have suddenly recognized the truth—and must have recognized, too, the fleet that came to meet it—and must have given a cease-fire order the instant the Earth-Mars fleet reached them.

"It is truly startling—and a seeming paradox—to realize that the vengeance fleet was headed by Admiral Barlo, who had also been admiral of the Earth fleet during the Earth-Mars conflict at the time the Earth and Mars fleets combined to destroy what they thought were alien invaders, and that many other men in both fleets on that day later became part of the personnel of the vengeance fleet.

"It is interesting to speculate just what would have happened had Admiral Barlo, at the end of his journey, recognized Venus in time to avoid destroying it. But such speculation is futile; he could not possibly have done so, for he had *already* destroyed it—else he would not have been there as admiral of the fleet sent out to avenge it. The past cannot be altered."

The Last Train

Eliot Haig sat alone at a bar, as he had sat alone at many bars before, and outside it was dusk, a peculiar dusk. Inside the tavern it was dim and shadowy, almost darker than outside. The blue bar mirror heightened the effect; in it Haig seemed to see himself as in dim moonlight from a blue moon. Dimly but clearly he saw himself; not double, despite the several drinks he had had, but single. Very, very single.

And as always when he had been drinking a few hours he thought, maybe this time I'll do it.

The *it* was vague and big; it meant everything. It meant making a big jump from one life to another life that he had so long contemplated. It meant simply walking out on a moderately successful semishyster lawyer named Eliot Haig, walking out on all the petty complications of his life, on the personal involvements, the legal chicanery that was just inside the letter of the law or indetectably outside; it meant cutting the cable of habit that tied him to an existence that had become without meaning or significance or incentive.

The blue reflection depressed him and he felt, more strongly than usual, the need to move, to go somewhere else if only for another drink. He finished the last sip of his highball and slid off the stool to the solid floor. He said, "So long, Joe," and strolled toward the front.

The bartender said, "Must be a big fire somewhere; lookit that sky. Wonder if it's the lumberyards other side of town." The bartender was leaning to the front window, staring out and up.

Haig looked up after he had gone through the door. The sky was a pinkish gray, as though with the glow of a distant fire. But it covered all of the sky he could see from where he stood, with no clue to the direction of the conflagration.

He strolled south at random. The far whistle of a locomotive came to his ears, reminding him.

Why not, he thought. Why not tonight? The old impulse, ghost of thousands of unsatisfactory evenings, was stronger tonight. He was walking, even now, toward the railway station; but that he had done before, often. Often he had gone so far as to watch trains depart, thinking, as he watched each: I should be on that train. Never actually boarding one.

Half a block from the station, he heard clang of bell and chug of steam and the starting of the train. He'd missed that one, if he'd had the nerve to take it.

And suddenly it came to him that tonight was different, that tonight he'd really make it. Just with the clothes he had on, the money that happened to be in his pocket. Just as he'd always intended; the clean break. Let them report him missing, let them wonder, let someone else straighten the tangled mess his business would suddenly be without him.

Walter Yates was standing in front of the open door of his tavern a few doors from the station. He said, "Hello, Mr. Haig. Beautiful aurora borealis tonight. Best one I've ever seen."

"That what it is?" Haig asked. "I thought it was reflection from a big fire."

Walter shook his head. "Nope. Look north; the sky's kind of shivery up that way. It's the aurora."

Haig turned and looked north, back along the street. The reddish glow in that direction was—yes, "shivery" described it well. It was beautiful, too, but just a little frightening, even when one knew what it was.

He turned back and went past Walter into the tavern, asking, "Got a drink for a thirsty man?"

Later, stirring a highball with the glass rod, he asked, "Walter, when does the next train leave?"

"For where?"

"For anywhere."

Walter glanced up at the clock. "In a few minutes. It's going to highball any second now."

"Too soon; I want to finish this drink. And the next one after that?"

"There's one at ten-fourteen. Maybe that's the last one out tonight. Up to midnight anyway, it is; I close up then, so I don't know."

"Where does it— Wait, don't tell me where it goes. I don't want to know. But I'm going to be on it."

"Without knowing where it goes?"

"Without caring where it goes," corrected Haig. "And look, Walter, I'm serious. I want you to do this for me: if you read in the newspapers that I've disappeared, don't tell anyone I was here tonight, or what I told you. I didn't mean to tell anyone."

Walter nodded sagely. "I can keep my trap shut, Mr. Haig. You've been a good customer. They won't trace you through me."

Haig swayed a little on the stool. His eyes focused on Walter's face, seeing the slight smile. There was a haunting sense of *familiarity* in this conversation. It was as though he had said the same words before, had had the same answer.

Sharply he asked, "Have I told you that before, Walter? How often?"

"Oh, six—eight—maybe ten times. I don't remember."

Haig said "God" softly. He stared at Walter and Walter's face blurred and separated into two faces and only an effort pulled them back into one face, faintly smiling, ironically tolerant. It had been oftener, he knew now, than ten times. "Walter, am I a lush?"

"I wouldn't call you that, Mr. Haig. You drink a lot, yes, but—"

He didn't want to look at Walter any more.

He stared down into his glass and saw that it was empty. He ordered another, and while Walter was getting it, he stared at himself in the mirror behind the bar. Not a blue mirror here, thank God. It was bad enough to see two images of himself in the plain mirror; the twin images Haig and Haig, only that was now an outworn joke with himself and it was one of the reasons he was going to catch that train. *Going* to, by God, drunk or sober he'd be on that train.

Only that phrase too had a ring of uneasy familiarity.

How many times?

He stared down into a glass a quarter full and the next time it was over half full and Walter was saying, "Maybe it *is* a fire, Mr. Haig, a big fire; that's getting too bright for an aurora. I'm going out a second."

But Haig stayed on the stool and when he looked again, Walter was back behind the bar, fiddling with the radio.

Haig asked, "Is it a fire?"

"Must be. I'm going to get the ten-fifteen newscast and see." The radio blared jazz, a high-riding jittery clarinet over muted brass and restless drums. "Be on in a minute; that's the station."

"*Be on in a minute—*" He almost fell, getting off the stool. "It's ten-fourteen, then?"

He didn't wait for an answer. The floor seemed tilting a little as he headed for the open door. Only a few doors and through the station. He might make it; he might actually make it. Suddenly it was as though he'd had nothing to drink at all and his mind was crystal clear no matter how his feet might stagger. And trains seldom left on the *exact* second, and Walter might have said "in a minute" meaning three or two or four minutes. There was a chance.

He fell on the steps but got up and went on, losing only seconds. Past the ticket window—he could buy his ticket on the train—and through the back doors to the platform, the gates, and the red taillight of a train pulling out only yards, but hopeless yards, away. Ten yards, a hundred. Dwindling.

The station agent stood at the edge of the platform looking out after the departing train.

He must have heard Haig's footsteps; over his shoulder he said, "Too bad you missed it. That was the last one."

Haig suddenly saw the funny side of it and began to laugh. It was simply too ridiculous to take seriously, the narrowness of the margin by which he'd missed that train. Besides, there'd be an early one. All he had to do was go back in the station and wait until— He asked, "When's the first one out tomorrow?"

"You don't understand," said the agent.

For the first time he turned and Haig saw his face against the crimson, blazing sky. "You don't understand," he said. "That was *the last train.*"

Entity Trap

Listing from the World Biographical Dictionary, 1990 edition: DIX, John, b. Louisville, Ky., U.S.A., Feb. 1, 1960; son Harvey R. (saloonkeeper) and Elizabeth (Bailey); student Louisville public schools 1966-1974; ran away from home at 14, worked as pin boy, bell hop; sentenced 6 mos. Birmingham, Ala., 1978, charge: procuring; enlisted U.S. Army, 1979, fought as private in Sino-American War, 1979-1981; reported missing in Battle of Panamints, 1981; led Revolution of 1982, became President of United States Aug. 5, 1982, Dictator of North America Apr. 10, 1983; died at age of 23 yrs. June 14, 1983.

The concrete of the pillbox was still moist. As Johnny Dix peered out of the slit, over the sights of his machine gun, he touched it with his finger and hoped it had hardened enough to stop the bullets of the yellow men.

A heavy pall of dense smoke hung over the foothills of the Panamints. From the slope behind the pillbox the roar of the American artillery was thunderous. Ahead, less than a mile away, the mobile guns of the Chinese thundered back.

Johnny Dix was too close to the war to be able to see it or to know that this was the turning point, the farthest penetration of the abortive Chinese invasion of California—made after the ICBM's had reduced most major cities of both countries to rubble, but had still proved undecisive—and that from here the Chinese would be driven back into the sea and the war would end.

"They're coming," Johnny Dix threw back over his shoulder. His companion's ear was only inches away but Johnny had to yell to make himself heard. "Get the next belt ready. Gotta hold them."

Got to hold them. It ran through his mind like a refrain. This was the last fully prepared line of defense. Behind it was Death Valley; it would live up to its name if they were shoved back into those open, arid wastelands. Out in the open there they would be mowed down like wheat.

But for three days now, the Panamint line had held. Hammered by steel from the air and steel from the ground, it had held. And the momentum of the attack had been blunted; it had even been thrown back a few hundred yards. This pillbox was one of a new line of outposts, hastily thrown up the night before under cover of darkness.

Something black and ugly, the nose of a huge tank, pushed through the smoke and haze. Johnny Dix let go the hot handgrips of the chatter-gun, useless against the coming monster, and nudged his companion. He yelled, "Tank about to cross the mine. Throw the switch quick! Now!"

The ground under their prone bodies shook with the terrific concussion of the exploding mine. Deafened and temporarily almost blinded by the blast that turned the monster tank into scrap iron, they did not hear the screaming dive of the plane.

The bomb it released struck a scant yard from their pillbox. And the pill-box wasn't there any more.

They should both have been killed instantly, but only one of them was. Life can be tenacious. The thing that had been Johnny Dix wriggled and rolled over. One arm—the other was gone—flailed about, the fingers clutching as though searching for the grip of the machine gun that lay yards away. One eye stared upward unseeingly above a bloody gaping hole where once had been a nose. Helmet had been blown away and with it most of the hair and scalp.

The mangled thing, no longer living but not yet dead, twisted again and began to crawl.

Back swooped the plane. Explosive bullets from its prop gun plowed a furrow of destruction that crossed the crawling thing above the knees, cutting off the legs. Dying fingers clutched spasmodically at the ground and then relaxed.

Johnny Dix was dead, but accident had timed with hair-trigger precision the instant of his death. His mangled body lived. This is the part of the story not known to the compilers of the World Biographical Dictionary when they made their listing for John Dix, Dictator of North America for eight months before his death at twenty-three years of age.

The nameless entity whom we shall call the Stranger paused in his interplanar swing. He had perceived something that should not have been.

He went back a plane. Not there. Another. Yes, this was it. A plane of *matter,* and yet he perceived emanations of consciousness. It was a paradox, a sheer contradiction. There were the planes of consciousness and there were the planes of physical matter—but never the two together.

The Stranger—a nonmaterial point in space, a focus of consciousness, an entity—paused amid the whirling stars of the matter-plane. These were familiar to him, common to all the matter-planes. But here there was something different. Consciousness, where there should be no consciousness. A foreign *kind* of consciousness. His perception seemed to tell him that it was allied with *matter,* but that was a complete contradiction in concepts. Matter was matter; consciousness was consciousness. The two could not be as one.

The emanations were faint. Then he found that by decreasing his time-motion he could make them stronger. He continued the decrease until he had passed the point of maximum strength and then went back to it. They were clear now, but the stars no longer whirled. Almost motionless they hung against the curved curtain of infinity.

The Stranger now began to move—to shift the focus of his thought—toward the star from which the ambiguous emanations came, toward the point which he now perceived to be the third planet of that star.

He neared it and found himself outside the gaseous envelope that surrounded the planet. Here again he paused, bewildered, to analyze and try to understand the amazing thing his perceptions told him lay below.

There were entities there below him, millions, even billions, of them. More in number on this tiny sphere than in the entire plane from which he had come.

But these beings were each *imprisoned in a finite bit of matter.*

What cosmic cataclysm, what interplanar warp, could have led to such an impossible thing? Were these entities from one of the myriad consciousness-planes who, in some unknown manner and for some unknown reason, had brought about this unthinkable misalliance of consciousness and matter?

He tried to concentrate his perception on a single entity, but the myriad emanations of thought from the planet's surface were too many and confusing to let him do so.

He descended toward the solid surface of the sphere, penetrating its outer gasses. He realized he would need to come near one of the beings in order to tune out, as it were, the jumbled confusion of the thoughts of the many.

The gas thickened as he descended. It seemed strangely agitated as though by intermittent but frequent concussions. Had not sound and hearing been things foreign to an incorporeal entity, the Stranger might have recognized the sound waves of explosions.

The mass of smoke he recognized as a modification or pollution of the gas he had first encountered. To a creature who perceived without sight it was neither more nor less opaque than the purer air above.

He entered solidity. That, of course, was no barrier to his progress, but he perceived now that he was on a vertical plane roughly coincidental with the surface of solidity, and that from that plane, on all sides of him, came the confused and mystifying emanations of consciousness.

One such source was very near. Shielding his own thoughts, the Stranger moved closer. The consciousness-emanations of the nearby entity were clear now—and yet not clear.

He did not know that their confusion was due to the fact that agonizing pain muddled or blanked out everything but itself. Pain, possible only to an alliance of mind and matter, was utterly inconceivable to the Stranger.

He went closer, encountering solidity again. This time it was a different type of surface. Outside, it was wet with something thick and sticky. Below that, a flexible layer covered a less flexible layer. Beyond that, soft and strange matter, queerly convoluted.

He was nearer the source of the incomprehensible consciousness-emanations now, but oddly they were becoming fainter. They did not seem to come from a fixed point, but from many points upon the convolutions of softness.

He moved slowly, striving for understanding of the strange phenomenon. The matter itself was different, once he had penetrated it. It was made up of cells and there was a fluid that moved among them.

Then, with awful suddenness, there was a convulsive movement of parts of the strange matter, a sudden flare of the un-understandable pain-consciousness-emanation—and utter blankness. Simply, the entity that he had been studying was *gone.* It had not moved, but it had vanished utterly.

The Stranger was bewildered. This was the most astonishing thing he had yet encountered on this unique planet of the matter-mind misalliance.

Death—deepest mystery to beings who have seen it often—was deeper mystery to one who had never conceived as possible the end of an entity.

But more startling still, at the instant of the extinguishment of that incoherent consciousness, the Stranger had felt a sudden force, a pull. He had been shifted slightly in space, *sucked into a vortex*—as air is sucked into a sudden vacuum.

He tried to move, first in space and then in time, and could not do so. He was trapped, imprisoned in this incomprehensible thing he had entered in search of the alien entity! He, a being of thought, had in some way become inextricably entangled with physical matter.

He felt no fear, for such emotion was unknown to him. Instead, the Stranger began a calm examination of his predicament. Throwing his perception-field out more widely, alternately expanding and contracting it, he began to study the nature of the thing in which he was held prisoner.

It was a grotesquely shaped thing, basically an oval cylinder. From one corner, as it were, projected a long jointed extension. There were two shorter but thicker projections at the other end of the cylinder.

Strangest of all was the ovoid thing at the end of a short flexible column. It was inside this ovoid, near the top, that the focus of his consciousness was now fixed.

He began to study and explore his prison, but could not begin, as yet, to understand the purpose of the weird and complex nerves, tubes, and organs.

Then he felt the emanations of other entities nearby, and threw still wider the field of his perceptions. His wonder grew.

Men were crawling forward across the battlefield, passing the shattered body of Johnny Dix. The Stranger studied them and began, dimly, to understand. He saw now that this body he was in was roughly similar to theirs, but less complete. That such bodies could be *moved*, subject to many limitations, by the entities that dwelt within them, even as he now dwelt within this body.

Held prisoner to the surface of solidity of the planet, nevertheless these bodies could be moved in a horizontal plane. He pulled his perceptions back to the body of Johnny Dix and began to probe for the secrets of inducing it to locomotion.

From his study of the things that crawled past him, the Stranger had sought and found certain concepts that were now helpful. He knew the projection with the five smaller projections was "arm." "Legs" meant the members at the other end. "Head" was the ovoid in which he was imprisoned.

These things moved, if he could discover how. He experimented. After a while a muscle in the arm twitched. From then on, he learned rapidly.

And when, presently, the body of Johnny Dix began to crawl slowly and awkwardly—on one arm and two truncated legs—in the direction the other crawling beings had taken, the Stranger didn't know that he was performing an impossible feat.

He didn't know that the body he caused to move was one which never should have done so. He didn't know that any competent doctor would not have hesitated to pronounce that body dead. Gangrene and decay were already setting in, but the Stranger's will made the stiffening muscles move despite them.

The mangled thing that had been Johnny Dix crawled on, jerkily, toward the Chinese lines.

Wong Lee lay prone against the sloping side of the shellhole. Above it projected only his steel helmet and the upper half of the goggles of his gas mask.

Through the hell of smoke and fire before him, he peered toward the American lines from which the counterattack was coming. The shellhole he occupied was slightly behind his own front lines, now under the barrage of American fire. With eight others, he had left shelter five hundred feet behind to reinforce an advance position. The eight others were dead, for shells had fallen like rain. Wong Lee, loyal though he was, had seen that he would be serving his leaders better by waiting here than by accepting certain death trying to make the last hundred feet.

He waited, peering into the smoke, wondering if anyone or anything could survive in the holocaust up ahead.

A dozen yards away, dimly through the smoke, he saw something coming toward him. Something that did not seem quite human—although he could not yet see it clearly—had crawled through that hellish rain of steel, and still crawled slowly. Tattered shreds of an American uniform clung to it here and there.

Already he could make out that it wore no gas mask or helmet. Wong Lee gripped a gas grenade from the pile of equipment beside him and lobbed it high and straight. It fell true, scarcely a foot in front of the crawling thing. A white geyser of gas mushroomed up—a gas of which a single whiff caused instant death.

Wong Lee grinned a mirthless grin and told himself that that was that. The gas-maskless figure was as good as dead. Slowly the white gas dissipated itself into the smoky air.

Then Wong Lee gasped. The thing was still coming; it had crawled right through that white cloud of death. It was nearer now and he could see what had been its face. He saw too the shattered horror that had been its body and the impossible method of its forward progress.

A cold fear gripped his stomach. It did not occur to him, yet, to run. But he knew that he had to stop that thing before it reached him or he would go mad.

Forgetting, in his greater terror, the danger of falling shells, he jumped to his feet, pointed his heavy service automatic at the crawling monstrosity, now but ten feet distant, and pulled the trigger. Again and again and again. He saw the bullets strike.

He had not quite emptied the clip when he heard the scream of the coming shell. He tried to throw himself back into the shellhole, just a little too late. He was off balance, falling backward when the shell struck. It struck and exploded just behind the thing that crawled. He heard the clang of a fragment of steel ricocheting off his helmet. Almost miraculously, he was otherwise unhit.

The impact on his helmet stunned him.

When consciousness returned, Wong Lee found himself lying quietly in the bottom of his shellhole. At first he thought the battle had ceased or moved on. Then the drifting smoke over the rim of the crater and the constant shaking of the ground beneath him told him that it was not so. The battle continued; the shattered eardrums of Wong Lee brought him no auditory impressions of it.

Yet he *heard*. Not the thunder of battle, but a quiet, calm voice that seemed to be speaking within his own mind. It asked, dispassionately, "What are you?" It seemed to be speaking Chinese, but that made it no less bewildering. Strangest of all, it did not ask *who* he was, but *what*.

Wong Lee struggled to a sitting position and looked about him. He saw it lying there beside him, scant inches away.

It was a human head, or what had been one. With growing horror he saw that it was the head of the thing that had crawled toward him. The shell that had struck just behind it had blown it here, though without the body that had enabled it to crawl.

Well, it was dead now, all right.

Or was it?

Again, in the mind of Wong Lee, that quiet query, "What are you?" made itself heard. And suddenly, not knowing how he knew, Wong Lee was certain that the asker of that question was the severed, horribly mutilated head beside him in the shellhole.

Wong Lee screamed. He tore off his gas mask as he scrambled to his feet and screamed again. He gained the top rim of the shellhole and began to run.

He'd taken about ten paces when, almost at his feet, the thousand-pound demolition bomb struck and exploded. Soil and rock from the explosion of the bomb rose high into the air and descended. The falling soil and rock filled completely most of the smaller shellholes around the new crater.

In one of these, now buried under seven feet of soil, lay the mutilated head that had once been part of the body of Johnny Dix, now the unbreakable prison of an alien being. Helpless to leave his new bonds of matter, helpless to move at all in space or to move in time other than to drift with the time-stream of this plane, the Stranger—until an hour ago a being of pure thought—began calmly and systematically to study the possibilities and limitations of his new mode of existence.

Erasmus Findly, in his monumental *History of the Americas*, devotes an entire volume to the dictator John Dix and the rise of imperialism in the United States immediately following the successful conclusion of the Sino-American War. But Findly, as do most modern historians, scouts the legendary character often given the figure of Dix.

"It is natural," he says, "that so sudden a rise from complete obscurity to complete and tyrannical control of the greatest government on the face of the earth should lead to such legends as those which the superstitious believe about Dix.

"It is undoubtedly true that Dix went through the Sino-American War as a buck private, without distinguishing himself. For this reason, possibly, he had most records of himself destroyed after his rise to power. Or possibly there was some mark on those records which made him wish them destroyed.

"But the legend that he was reported missing during the crucial battle of that war—the Battle of the Panamints—and was not seen until the following spring, when the war was over, is probably untrue.

"According to the legend, in the spring of 1982 John Dix, naked and covered with dirt, walked up to a Panamint valley farm house, where he was given food and clothing and from there he proceeded to Los Angeles, then under reconstruction.

"Equally absurd are the legends of his invulnerability; the statements that dozens of times the bullets of assassins passed through his body without seeming even to cause him inconvenience.

"The fact that his enemies, the true patriots of America, got him at last is proof of the falseness of the invulnerability legend. And the crowning horror of that scene in the Rose Bowl, so vividly described by many contemporary witnesses, was undoubtedly a trap-door conjuring trick engineered by his enemies."

Calmly and systematically, the Stranger had begun the study of the nature of his prison. With patience, he found the key.

Exploring, he tapped a memory in the head of Johnny Dix. A single episode suddenly became as vivid to him as though it were an experience of his own.

He was on a small boat, passing an island in a harbor. Beside him was a man who seemed very tall. He knew the man was his father and that this was happening when he was seven years old and they had taken a trip to a place called New York. His father said, "That's Ellis Island, kid, where they let the immigrants in. Damn foreigners; they're ruining this country. No chance any more for a real American. Somebody ought to blow Europe off the map."

Simple enough, but each thought of that memory brought connotations that explained it to the Stranger. He knew what a boat was, what and where Europe was, and what an American was. And he knew that America was the only good country on this planet; that all the other countries were made up of contemptible people—and that even in this country the only good ones were the white ones who had been here a long time.

He explored further, found out many things that had bewildered him. He began to correlate these memories into a picture of the world in which he was now trapped. It was a strange, warped picture—although he had no way of learning that. It was a narrow ultra-nationalistic point of view, for one thing. And there were worse things than that.

He learned—and *assimilated*—all the hates and prejudices of buck private Johnny Dix, and they were many and violent. He knew nothing to the contrary of this strange world and so they became his hates and his prejudices, just as the memories became his memories.

Although he did not suspect it was so, the Stranger was finding his way into a narrower prison than his physical one; he was becoming trapped into the thoughts of a mind that had been neither strong nor straight.

There emerged a mentality which was a strange blend of the powerful mind of a strong entity and the narrow beliefs and prejudices of a Johnny Dix.

He saw the world through a dark, distorted lens. He saw that things must be done.

"Those fatheads in Washington," he—or Johnny Dix—had said, *"oughta be kicked out. Now if I was running this country—"*

Yes, the Stranger saw what things he must do to put this world right. This was a good country—parts of it—surrounded by bad countries, and the bad ones ought to be taught a lesson, if not exterminated. The yellows ought to be *all* killed, men, women, and children. There was a black race that ought to be sent back to a place called Africa, where they belonged. And even among white Americans, there were people who had more money than they should have, and it ought to be taken away from them and given to people like Johnny Dix. Yes, we needed a government that could tell people like that where to head in. And enough military power so we could tell the rest of the world where to head in, too.

But the Stranger saw, too, that buried as he was and in a piece of matter that was disintegrating even as he explored it, there was little chance of his accomplishing any of these important things.

So, avidly, he began to study the nature of matter. He could bring his perceptions down to the scale of atoms and molecules and study them. He saw that in the very soil about him he had the necessary materials, all of them, to reconstruct the body of Johnny Dix. By means of his memories of his first explorations of the incomplete body of Johnny Dix, as it had been when he first entered it, he began the study of organic chemistry.

He filled in his concept of the parts that had been missing from the body from the memories of Johnny Dix and began work.

Transmuting the chemicals of the soil was not a difficult problem. And heat was a mere matter of speeding up molecular action.

Slowly, new flesh grew upon the head of Johnny Dix; hair, eyes, and a neck began to form. It took time, but what was time to an immortal?

One evening in early spring of the following year, a naked but perfectly formed human figure clawed its way to the surface of soil that had been softened by molecular action to enable that figure to crawl out.

It lay quiet for a while, mastering the art of breathing air. Then, experimentally at first but with growing skill and confidence, it tried the use of various muscles and sensory organs.

The group of workmen on the Glendale Reconstruction Project looked around curiously as the man in the ill-fitting clothes stepped up on a packing crate and began to speak.

"Friends," he shouted, "how long are we going to tolerate—"

A uniformed policeman stepped up quickly. "Here now," he objected. "You can't do that. Even if you got a permit, these are work hours and you can't interrupt—"

"Are you satisfied, Officer, with the way things are run around here, and in Washington?"

The policeman looked up and his eyes locked with those of the man on the packing case. For a moment he felt as though an electric current had gone through his mind and body. And then he knew that this man had the right answers, that this man was a leader whom he'd follow. Anywhere.

"My name's John Dix," said the man on the box. "You ain't heard of me, but you'll be hearing of me from now on. I'm starting something, see? If you want in on the ground floor, take off that badge and throw it down. But keep your gun; it'll come in handy."

The policeman reached up for his badge and unfastened the pin.

That had been the start.

June 14, 1983, was the day of the end. In the morning there had been a heavy fog over Los Angeles—now capital city of North America—but by midafternoon the sun was bright and the air balmy.

Robert Welson, leader of the little group of patriots who had failed, for some reason, to join the mass hysteria with which the people had backed John Dix, sat at a window of the new Panamera Building, overlooking the vast throng in the reconstructed Rose Bowl. On the floor under the window from which he looked lay a high-powered rifle with Mercer telescopic sights.

On the stage of the Bowl, John Dix, Dictator of North America, stood alone, although uniformed guards occupied all seats immediately around the stage and were scattered elsewhere in the audience. A microphone hung just overhead and a speaker system carried the dictator's voice to the farthest reaches of the Bowl, and beyond. Robert Welson and the others in the room with him could hear it distinctly.

"The day has come. We are prepared. People of America, I call upon you to rise in your wrath and stamp out now and forever the power of the evil countries beyond the seas."

Over the Bowl cheering rose, a mighty wave of sound.

Through it Robert Welson heard three sharp raps on the door of the room behind him. He crossed the room and opened the door. A tall man and a scrawny boy with a large head and great vacuous eyes came into the room.

"You brought the kid," said Welson. "What for? He can't—"

The tall man spoke. "You know Dix isn't human, Welson. You know how much good our bullets have done before! Why, in Pittsburgh, I *saw them hit him*. But this clairvoyant kid here—or maybe it's telepathy or something and not clairvoyance and I don't know or care—has got a line on him somehow.

The first time the kid ever saw him he went into a fit. We can't fight Dix without knowing what we're fighting, can we?"

Welson shrugged. "Maybe. You play with that. I'm going to keep on trying steel-jacketed lead."

He drew a deep breath and walked again to the window. He knelt before it on one knee and raised the sash. His left hand reached for the rifle.

"Here goes," Welson said. "Maybe if we get *enough* lead in him—"

McLaughin, author of the most famous biography of John Dix, while avoiding direct acceptance of any of the legends which have filled many other books, concedes the mystical aspect of Dix's rise to power.

"It is indeed strange," he writes, "that immediately, suddenly, after his assassination, the wave of insanity which had engulfed the United States disappeared abruptly and completely. Had not the few true patriots who failed to follow his lead succeeded, the history of the world during the last part of the twentieth century would have been a story of bloody carnage unparalleled in history.

"Extermination, or ruthless suppression, would have been the lot of every country which he could have conquered—and there is little doubt, in view of the superior armaments he had, that the ravage would have been far-flung. He might even have conquered the world. Although, of course, America itself would ultimately have suffered most.

"To say that John Dix was a madman can hardly explain the extent of his power over the people of his own country. Almost it is possible to credit the current superstition that he had superhuman powers. But if he was a superman, he was a warped superman.

"It was almost as though an ignorant, prejudiced, opinionated man, narrow-minded in every way, had miraculously been given the power to sway most of the population, able to impress his narrow hatreds upon all, or almost all, of those who listened. The few who were immune, battling terrific odds, saved the world from Armageddon.

"The exact manner of his death remains, after all this time, shrouded in mystery. Whether he was killed by a new weapon—destroyed after it had accomplished its purpose—or whether the monstrous thing seen by the throngs in the Bowl was a mere illusion, the trick of a prestidigitator extraordinary, will never be certainly known."

The muzzle of the rifle rested on the ledge of the window. Robert Welson steadied it and peered through the telescopic sights. His finger rested against the trigger.

The voice of the dictator boomed through the speaker, *"Our day of destiny—"* Sentence uncompleted, he paused, leaning forward across the table behind which he stood. The audience was hushed, awaiting completion of the sentence before the cheering would rise again.

The tall man standing behind Robert Welson put an urgent hand on Welson's shoulder. "Don't shoot yet," he whispered. "Something's happening. Look at the kid, the clairvoyant."

Welson turned.

He saw that the scrawny boy had fallen back into a chair, his muscles rigid. His eyes were closed, his face twisted. His lips writhed as he spoke:

"They're there. Near him. Like two shining points of light, only you can't see them. But there is a point like them—*inside John Dix's head!*

"Talking. They're talking to him, the two points of light like his point of light. Only not words. But I can get what they're saying, even if it isn't words. One of them asks, *'Why are you here? You seem strange. As though a lesser being had—'* I can't understand that part of it; there aren't any words I know that would say it.

"The thing, the point, inside Dix's head is answering. It says, *'I'm trapped here. The matter holds me. The matter and the memories in it hold me prisoner. Can you help me get free?'*

"They answer that they will try. They will all three concentrate together. The combined force of the three of them will free him from his prison. They're trying—"

Something strange *was* happening. The dictator was still silent, still leaning forward across the table. Minutes had passed, and he had not moved, had not completed the sentence he had started.

Robert Welson turned from the kid back to the window again. To see more clearly, he looked through the telescopic sights of the rifle, but his finger wasn't on the trigger now. Maybe the halfwitted kid really had something on the ball. The dictator had never paused that long before.

Behind him the kid sang out *"Free!"* as though it were a triumphal thought repeated from somewhere in his brain. And, although the kid couldn't see out of the window from where he sat, that cry came simultaneously with whatever it was that happened to John Dix.

Welson gasped, but the sound was lost in the sudden screams and shrieks from the audience in the Bowl.

With awful suddenness the body of the dictator vanished before their eyes, vanished into a thin white mist that disappeared into the air as his empty clothing fell to the floor.

But the hideous thing that fell from vanished shoulders and lay in plain sight on the table did not disintegrate at once. It was a hairless, eyeless, almost fleshless, rotting thing that once had been a head.

Obedience

On a tiny planet of a far, faint star, invisible from Earth, and at the farther edge of the galaxy, five times as far as man has yet penetrated into space, there is a statue of an Earthman. It is made of precious metal and it is a tremendous thing, fully ten inches high, exquisite in workmanship.

Bugs crawl on it ...

They were on a routine patrol in Sector 1534, out past the Dog Star, many parsecs from Sol. The ship was the usual two-man scout used for all patrols outside the system. Captain May and Lieutenant Ross were playing chess when the alarm rang.

Captain May said, "Reset it, Don, while I think this out." He didn't look up from the board; he knew it couldn't be anything but a passing meteor. There weren't any ships in this sector. Man had penetrated space for a thousand parsecs and had not as yet encountered an alien life form intelligent enough to communicate, let alone to build spaceships.

Ross didn't get up either, but he turned around in his chair to face the instrument board and the telescreen. He glanced up casually and gasped; there *was* a ship on the screen. He got his breath back enough to say "Cap!" and then the chessboard was on the floor and May was looking over his shoulder.

He could hear the sound of May's breathing, and then May's voice said, "Fire, Don!"

"But that's a Rochester Class cruiser! One of ours. I don't know what it's doing here, but we can't—"

"Look again."

Don Ross couldn't look again because he'd been looking all along, but he suddenly saw what May had meant. It was almost a Rochester, but not quite. There was something *alien* about it. Something? It *was* alien; it was an alien imitation of a Rochester. And his hands were racing for the firing button almost before the full impact of that hit him.

Finger at the button, he looked at the dials on the Picar ranger and the Monold. They stood at zero.

He swore. "He's jamming us, Cap. We can't figure out how far he is, or his size and mass!"

Captain May nodded slowly, his face pale.

Inside Don Ross's head, a thought said, *"Compose yourselves, men. We are not enemies."*

Ross turned and stared at May. May said, "Yes, I got it. Telepathy."

Ross swore again. *If they were telepathic—*

"Fire, Don. Visual."

Ross pressed the button. The screen was filled with a flare of energy, but when the energy subsided, there was no wreckage of a spaceship ...

Admiral Sutherland turned his back to the star chart on the wall and regarded them sourly from under his thick eyebrows. He said, "I am not interested in rehashing your formal report, May. You've both been under the psychograph; we've extracted from your minds every minute of the encounter. Our logicians have analyzed it. You are here for discipline. Captain May, you know the penalty for disobedience."

May said stiffly, "Yes, sir."

"It is?"

"Death, sir."

"And what order did you disobey?"

"General Order Thirteen-Ninety, Section Twelve, Quad-A priority. Any terrestrial ship, military or otherwise, is ordered to destroy immediately, on sight, any alien ship encountered. If it fails to do so, it must blast off toward outer space, in a direction not exactly opposite that of Earth, and continue until fuel is exhausted."

"And the reason for that, Captain? I ask merely to see if you know. It is not, of course, important or even relevant whether or not you understand the reason for any ruling."

"Yes, sir. So there is no possibility of the alien ship following the sighting ship back to Sol and so learning the location of Earth."

"Yet you disobeyed that ruling, Captain. You were not certain that you had destroyed the alien. What have you to say for yourself?"

"We did not think it necessary, sir. The alien ship did not seem hostile. Besides, sir, they must already know our base; they addressed us as 'men.'"

"Nonsense! The telepathic message was broadcast from an alien mind, but was received by yours. Your minds automatically translated the message into your own terminology. He did not necessarily know your point of origin or that you were humans."

Lieutenant Ross had no business speaking, but he asked, "Then, sir, it is not believed that they were friendly?"

The admiral snorted. "Where did you take your training, Lieutenant? You seem to have missed the most basic premise of our defense plans, the reason we've been patrolling space for four hundred years, on the lookout for alien life. *Any alien is an enemy.* Even though he were friendly today, how could we know that he would be friendly next year or a century from now? And a potential enemy is an enemy. The more quickly he is destroyed the more secure Earth will be.

"Look at the military history of the world! It proves that, if it proves nothing else. Look at Rome! To be safe she couldn't afford powerful neighbors. Alexander the Great! Napoleon!"

"Sir," said Captain May. "Am I under the penalty of death?"

"Yes."

"Then I may as well speak. Where is Rome now? Alexander's empire or Napoleon's? Nazi Germany? Tyrannosaurus rex?"

"Who?"

"Man's predecessor, the toughest of the dinosaurs. His name means 'king of the tyrant lizards.' He thought every other creature was his enemy, too. And where is he now?"

"Is that all you have to say, Captain?"

"Yes, sir."

"Then I shall overlook it. Fallacious, sentimental reasoning. You are *not* under sentence of death, Captain. I merely said so to see what you would say, how far you would go. You are not being shown mercy because of any humanitarian nonsense. A truly ameliorating circumstance has been found."

"May I ask what, sir?"

"The alien *was* destroyed. Our technicians and logicians have worked that out. Your Picar and Monold were working properly. The only reason that they did not register was that the alien ship was too small. They will detect a meteor weighing as little as five pounds. The alien ship was smaller than that."

"Smaller than—?"

"Certainly. You were thinking of alien life in terms of your own size. There is no reason why it should be. It could be even submicroscopic, too small to be visible. The alien ship must have contacted you deliberately, at a distance of only a few feet. And your fire, at that distance, destroyed it utterly. That is why you saw no charred hulk as evidence that it was destroyed."

He smiled. "My congratulations, Lieutenant Ross, on your gunnery. In the future, of course, visual firing will be unnecessary. The detectors and estimators on ships of all classes are being modified immediately to detect and indicate objects of even minute sizes."

Ross said, "Thank you, sir. But don't you think that the fact that the ship we saw, regardless of size, was an imitation of one of our Rochester Class ships is proof that the aliens already know much more of us than we do of them, including, probably, the location of our home planet? And that—even if they are hostile—the tiny size of their craft is what prevents them from blasting us from the system?"

"Possibly. Either both of those things are true, or neither. Obviously, aside from their telepathic ability, they are quite inferior to us technically—or they would not imitate our design in spaceships. And they must have read the minds of some of our engineers in order to duplicate that design. However, granting that is true, they may still not know the location of Sol. Space coordinates would be extremely difficult to translate, and the name Sol would mean nothing to them. Even its approximate description would fit thousands of other stars. At any rate, it is up to us to find and exterminate them before they find us. Every ship in space is now alerted to watch for them, and is being equipped with special instruments to detect small objects. A state of war exists. Or perhaps it is redundant to say that; a state of war always exists with aliens."

"Yes, sir."

"That is all, gentlemen. You may go."

Outside in the corridor two armed guards waited. One of them stepped to each side of Captain May.

May said quickly, "Don't say anything, Don. I expected this. Don't forget that I disobeyed an important order, and don't forget that the admiral said only that I wasn't under sentence of death. Keep yourself out of it."

Hands clenched, teeth clamped tightly together, Don Ross watched the guards take away his friend. He knew May was right; there was nothing he could do except get himself into worse trouble than May was in, and make things worse for May.

But he walked almost blindly out of the Admiralty Building. He went out and got promptly drunk, but that didn't help.

He had the customary two weeks' leave before reporting back for space duty, and he knew he'd better straighten himself out mentally in that time. He reported to a psychiatrist and let himself be talked out of most of his bitterness and feeling of rebellion.

He went back to his schoolbooks and soaked himself in the necessity for strict and unquestioning obedience to military authority and the necessity of unceasing vigilance for alien races and the necessity of their extermination whenever found.

He won out; he convinced himself how unthinkable it had been for him to believe that Captain May could have been completely pardoned for having disobeyed an order, for whatever reason. He even felt horrified for having himself acquiesced in that disobedience. Technically, of course, he was blameless; May had been in charge of the ship and the decision to return to Earth instead of blasting out into space—and death—had come from May. As a subordinate, Ross had not shared the blame. But now, as a person, he felt conscience-stricken that he had not tried to argue May out of his disobedience.

What would Space Corps be without obedience?

How could he make up for what he now felt to be his dereliction, his delinquency? He watched the telenewscasts avidly during that period and learned that, in various other sectors of space, four more alien ships had been destroyed. With the improved detection instruments all of them had been destroyed on sight; there had been no communication after first contact.

On the tenth day of his leave, he terminated it of his own free will. He returned to the Admiralty Building and asked for an audience with Admiral Sutherland. He was laughed at, of course, but he had expected that. He managed to get a brief verbal message carried through to the admiral. Simply: "I know a plan that may possibly enable us to find the planet of the aliens, at no risk to ourselves."

That got him in, all right.

He stood at rigid attention before the admiral's desk. He said, "Sir, the aliens have been trying to contact us. They have been unable because we destroy them on contact before a complete telepathic thought has been put across. If we permit them to communicate, there is a chance that they will give away, accidentally or otherwise, the location of their home planet."

Admiral Sutherland said drily, "And whether they did or not, they might find out *ours* by following the ship back."

"Sir, my plan covers that. I suggest that I be sent out into the same sector where initial contact was made—this time in a one-man ship, *unarmed.* That the fact that I am doing so be publicized as widely as possible, so that every man in space knows it, and knows that I am in an unarmed ship for the purpose of making contact with the aliens. It is my opinion that they will learn of this. They must manage to get thoughts at long distances, but to send thoughts—to Earth minds anyway—only at very short distances."

"How do you deduce that, Lieutenant? Never mind; it coincides with what our logicians have figured out. They say that the fact that they have stolen our science—as in their copying our ships on a smaller scale—before we were aware of their existence proves their ability to read our thoughts at—well, a moderate distance."

"Yes, sir. I am hoping that if news of my mission is known to the entire fleet it will reach the aliens. And knowing that my ship is unarmed, they will make contact. I will see what they have to say to me, to us, and possibly that message will include a clue to the location of their home planet."

Admiral Sutherland said, "And in that case that planet would last all of twenty-four hours. But what about the converse, Lieutenant? What about the possibility of their following you back?"

"That, sir, is where we have nothing to lose. I shall return to Earth *only if I find out that they already know its location.*

"With their telepathic abilities I believe they already do—and that they have not attacked us only because they are not hostile or are too weak. But whatever the case, if they know the location of Earth they will not deny it in talking to me. Why should they? It will seem to them a bargaining point in their favor, and they'll think we're bargaining. They might claim to know, even if they do not—but I shall refuse to take their word for it unless they give me proof."

Admiral Sutherland stared at him. He said, "Son, you *have* got something. It'll probably cost you your life, but—if it doesn't, and if you come back with news of where the aliens come from, you're going to be the hero of the race. You'll probably end up with *my* job. In fact, I'm tempted to steal your idea and make that trip myself."

"Sir, you're too valuable. I'm expendable. Besides, sir, I've *got* to. It isn't that I want any honors. I've got something on my conscience that I want to make up for. I should have tried to stop Captain May from disobeying orders. I shouldn't be here now, alive. We should have blasted out into space, since we weren't sure we'd destroyed the alien."

The admiral cleared his throat. "You're not responsible for that, son. Only the captain of a ship is responsible, in a case like that. But I see what you mean. You feel you disobeyed orders, in spirit, because you agreed at the time with what Captain May did. All right, that's past, and your suggestion makes up for it, even if you yourself did not man the contact ship."

"But may I, sir?"

"You may, Lieutenant. Rather, you may, Captain."

"Thank you, sir."

"A ship will be ready for you in three days. We could have it ready sooner, but it will take that long for word of our 'negotiations' to spread throughout the fleet. But you understand—you are not, under any circumstances, to deviate on your own initiative from the limitations you have outlined."

"Yes, sir. Unless the aliens already know the location of Earth and prove it completely, I shall not return. I shall blast off into space. I give you my word, sir."

"Very good, Captain Ross."

The one-man spacer hovered near the center of Sector 1534, out past the Dog Star. No other ship patrolled that sector.

Captain Don Ross sat quietly and waited. He watched the visiplate and listened for a voice to speak inside his head.

It came when he had waited less than three hours. *"Greetings, Donross,"* the voice said, and simultaneously there were five tiny spaceships outside his visiplate. His Monold showed that they weighed less than an ounce apiece.

He said, "Shall I talk aloud or merely think?"

"It does not matter. You may speak if you wish to concentrate on a particular thought, but first be silent a moment."

After half a minute, Ross thought he heard the echo of a sigh in his mind. Then: *"I am sorry. I fear this talk will do neither of us any good. You see, Donross, we do not know the location of your home planet. We could have learned, perhaps, but we were not interested. We were not hostile and from the minds of Earthmen we knew we dared not be friendly. So you will never be able, if you obey orders, to return to report."*

Don Ross closed his eyes a moment. This, then, was the end; there wasn't any use talking further. He had given his word to Admiral Sutherland that he would obey orders to the letter.

"That is right," said the voice. *"We are both doomed, Donross, and it does not matter what we tell you. We cannot get through the cordon of your ships; we have lost half our race trying."*

"Half! Do you mean—?"

"Yes. There were only a thousand of us. We built ten ships, each to carry a hundred. Five ships have been destroyed by Earthmen; there are only five ships left, the ones you see, the entire race of us. Would it interest you, even though you are going to die, to know about us?"

He nodded, forgetting that they could not see him, but the assent in his mind must have been read.

"We are an old race, much older than you. Our home is—or was—a tiny planet of the dark companion of Sirius; it is only a hundred miles in diameter. Your ships have not found it yet, but it is only a matter of time. We have been intelligent for many, many millennia, but we never developed space travel. There was no need and we had no desire.

"*Twenty of your years ago an Earth ship passed near our planet and we caught the thoughts of the men upon it. And we knew that our only safety, our only chance of survival, lay in immediate flight to the farthest limits of the galaxy. We knew from those thoughts that we would be found sooner or later, even if we stayed on our own planet, and that we would be ruthlessly exterminated upon discovery.*"

"You did not think of fighting back?"

"*No. We could not have, had we wished—and we did not wish. It is impossible for us to kill. If the death of one single Earthman, even of a lesser creature, would ensure our survival, we could not bring about that death.*

"*That you cannot understand. Wait—I see that you can. You are not like other Earthmen, Donross. But back to our story. We took details of space travel from the minds of members of that ship and adapted them to the tiny scale of the ships we built.*

"*We built ten ships, enough to carry our entire race. But we find we cannot escape through your patrols. Five of our ships have tried, and all have been destroyed.*"

Don Ross said grimly, "And I did a fifth of that: I destroyed one of your ships."

"*You merely obeyed orders. Do not blame yourself. Obedience is almost as deeply rooted in you as hatred of killing is in us. That first contact, with the ship you were on, was deliberate; we had to be sure that you would destroy us on sight.*

"*But since then, one at a time, four of our other ships have tried to get through and have all been destroyed. We brought all the remaining ones here when we learned that you were to contact us with an unarmed ship.*

"*But even if you disobeyed orders and returned to Earth, wherever it is, to report what we have just told you, no orders would be issued to let us through. There are too few Earthmen like you, as yet. Possibly in future ages, by the time Earthmen reach the far edge of the galaxy, there will be more like you. But now, the chances of our getting even one of our five ships through is remote.*

"*Goodby, Donross. What is this strange emotion in your mind and the convulsion of your muscles? I do not understand it. But wait—it is your recognition of perceiving something incongruous. But the thought is too complex, too mixed. What is it?*"

Don Ross managed finally to stop laughing. "Listen, my alien friend who cannot kill," he said, "I'm getting you out of this. I'm going to see that you get through our cordon to the safety you want. But what's funny is the way I'm going to do it. By obedience to orders and by going to my own death. I'm going to outer space, to die there. You, all of you, can come along and *live* there. Hitchhike. *Your tiny ships won't show on the patrol's detectors if they are touching this ship.* Not only that, but the gravity of this ship will pull you along and you won't have to waste fuel until you are well through the cordon and beyond the reach of its detectors. A hundred thousand parsecs, at least, before my fuel runs out."

There was a long pause before the voice in Don Ross's mind said, "*Thank you.*" Faintly. Softly.

He waited until the five ships had vanished from his visiplate and he had heard five tiny sounds of their touching the hull of his own ship. Then he laughed once more. And obeyed orders, blasting off for space and death.

On a tiny planet of a far, faint star, invisible from Earth, and at the farther edge of the galaxy, five times as far as man has yet penetrated into space, there is the statue of an Earthman. It is a tremendous thing, ten inches high, exquisite in workmanship.

Bugs crawl on it, but they have a right to; they made it, and they honor it. The statue is of very hard metal. On an airless world it will last forever—or until Earthmen find it and blast it out of existence. Unless, of course, by that time Earthmen have changed an awful lot.

The Frownzly Florgels

Oh, it was going to be a lovely frownz. They all knew that; Nax had sent out the thought and it had gone from star to star throughout the cluster. The competition as to who could go had been terrific. Everybody envied Nax the Agoraphobe because he was the only one who didn't have to compete with a thousand or a million others to get there. But there was plenty of reason for that.

Teppo got there first—except, of course, for Nax, who was there to begin with. Nax lived inside the planetoid Naxo which once had another name but for the several million years Nax had lived there, it had been Naxo and the other name was forgotten. Nax had been a mutant Ragan and, as was the custom, he had been teleported to a barren world and was abandoned to die. But he'd lived—indeed, he'd turned out to be practically immortal—and now he was the oldest and wisest of all, despite his peculiarities. He nearly starved for the first thousand years or so, until he was able to adjust his metabolism so he could eat the substance of which Naxo was made. After he'd eaten his way inside he developed such acute agoraphobia that he could never come out again; he'd die if he did. Oh, everyone knew that Nax didn't have forever to live, because sooner or later he'd eat out the interior of the planetoid completely and the crust would collapse, leaving him exposed, and he'd surely die. But that time was at least ten million years away and Nax was quite cheerful about it. "Who wants to live forever?" he'd clairvoy, with a happy laugh. No one knew exactly what Nax was planning for this particular frownz, but it would be fun; it always was.

Teppo had teleported himself in a globule of liquid glass, his native element. He was going to have trouble, he knew, maintaining the temperature of the glass and would have to use part of his mind at all times to maintain the molecular vibration, but he'd still have enough mind left to enjoy the frownz thoroughly.

Being the first arrival, he didn't want to wake Nax if Nax was sleeping, so he floated around looking down through the holes in the planetoid to see if the giant was stirring. The holes looked like craters, but really they were holes Nax had pushed through from inside so he could see and reach through and so the methane could mingle freely inside the planetoid and without. Nax was still asleep, but Teppo could voy him beginning to stir. Teppo subvibed a while to make the outside of his globule a reflecting surface; that way he could kill time waiting for the others by admiring the reflection of his sleek finny beauty. He wriggled his tail and sighed with an ecstasy of admiration.

When he hivibed and made the surface transparent again, he was no longer alone. Two others were there already. The cylindroid from Karebranthal floated smugly beside him and one of the amorphous smoke-cloud beings from Thal writhed lugubriously in the methane over one of the apertures of Naxo. While Teppo watched, the smoke-cloud flowed into the hole to see if Nax was ready.

The others were coming, too. The groc teleported right in front of his eyes, in the egg, of course. Grocs always returned to their eggs to teleport themselves off Hanra; once they reached their destination, they cracked the egg from within and stuck their hideous heads out, preferring to remain that way until ready to return. Then they pulled in their heads and hivibed until the egg was reknitted. No one had ever seen a groc completely out of its egg off its own planet of Hanra. Teppo looked at the groc's head and was glad that he was beautiful.

The disk-creature from Amron and the sphere-being from Ell teleported into sight together and high in the violet sky the rocket trails of the ships of the Zatto and the Rang could be made out, both from backward planets which had not yet developed teleportation and the ability to adapt to any medium. They still depended on crude rockets for their interstellar travels. Annoying things the rockets would have been, too, had not they—and, of course, their occupants—been so tiny.

The smoke-cloud being was now coming out of the planetoid, voying happily that Nax was getting ready. The cylindroid smugged with pleasure and the two rockets went into ecstatic acrobatics; the one from Zatto doing gay circles into and out of holes in the planetoid and the one from Rang showing off its new inertialess drive by cutting impossibly sharp corners, and worrying all the rest of them.

Gera, the weirdly shaped thing from Garn, was next. Teppo averted his eyes from her body with its ugly protuberances; it would take him several glances to get used to her sufficiently to forget her monstrousness. She was of the race of Ragans of which Nax was a mutant, but then the mutation was undoubtedly an improvement and besides one didn't have to look at Nax ...

Gera, the Ragan, cavorted gaily in the methane, happiest of them all. True, argon was her natural element, but it wasn't hard to adapt, and the antigrav pseudothought of Nax made cavorting an ineffable pleasure. She caught Teppo's fishy stare, and laughed. What did Nax have in mind for this frownz? Besides, of course, the florgels? She was glad she wasn't a giant, like Nax, imprisoned in a planetoid, and that she didn't have to live in a molten glass world like Teppo. She was glad of everything, but especially of the fact that she'd been chosen to represent Raga, and that she was here.

Who was missing? She looked around and counted—well, not exactly noses because she was the only one who had a nose, but she counted. They were all here except two, and one of them—the spear-spore from Gelf, appeared right while she was looking for it. A stupid thing, the spear-spore; it had to materialize gradually after a teleportation. But at least it *could* teleport, and it was far ahead of most of the rest of them at glyphing.

And then there was the other—the asteworld of the swarm, the tiny planetoid that had, that was, life in itself.

And they were all there, and Nax was voying a welcome, obviously having gragged the arrival of the asteworld at the very microsecond of its arrival. They were all there, and all joyous, and Nax was voying them gaywelcome and the frownz was on. The representatives of all the star cluster were there.

Pretty soon the florgels, but first Nax stuck his hand out with the book and each of them hurled a thought at it and the thought was recorded by the book—all except, of course, the poor little occupants of the spaceships from Zatto and Rang. The occupants were too primitive and had to relay their thoughts through the others for recording. Gera laughed at them tolerantly; the poor things couldn't even glyph.

And then Nax pulled the book back, and the frownz really started.

First, of course, the games. They played ranzel, and Gera won that. They played a dozen other games, each more fun than the last, and because they were so diverse in their physical forms and mental capabilities, each of them managed to excel in something.

They ended with a game of murl, the best game of all, in Teppo's opinion. But maybe that was because he almost always won it, and he did this time, too. But then he had an advantage at murl, since it was played with the strings and hooks that his race used on their own planet to catch birds. They glyphed the hook into the air baited with a corro and pulled the birds down into the molten glass if they grabbed the corro. So Teppo was the one who managed to hook the hoga (an object shaped like a teacup but used on Gera's planet to catch whings out of the flug) which was alternately materialized and dematerialized in various places in the methane by Nax. Teppo was so proud of himself for winning the murl that he kept the hook, string and hoga materialized right through the florgels after the games.

The first few florgels were old familiar ones and then Nax voyed that he had something new for them to try. "We shall," he voyed, "try to contact another mind somewhere in the universe."

"Oh, wonderful, Nax," voyed the spear-spore. "How? Individually, or the group-mind?"

"The group-mind. We'll all focus our thoughts through the Book of Florgels." And he held the book out for them to focus on. He voyed his plan; they would all focus on the book the thought of their group, just as it was; he would gram the thought, two-way, to the most distant galaxy they knew of and attune it to a single mind there, if there turned out to be one. And in that mind—if it existed—would appear the picture of them at the florgel. In their own minds, if the plan succeeded, would appear whatever thought-picture was in the alien mind with which contact was made.

Nax gave the signal and they formed the group-mind and focused on the book, and Nax groaned with the effort of his gramming across so many billion parsecs.

But it was the worst florgel they had ever tried, not because it didn't work, but because it did. It was horrible, the picture they got in return from that alien mind in the far galaxy. Gera covered her eyes as though that could shut out the awfulness of it, the cylindroid curled itself into a doughnut shape from shock and the groc pulled its head back into the egg.

But they all recovered gradually and none of them voyed about it; they had all seen it, so there was nothing to voy about. And to enable them to forget quickly, Nax called another florgel, the old famliar one of the nova and the cepheid variable ...

Excerpts from a letter from Hannes Bok, artist and illustrator, New York, to Fredric Brown, writer, Taos, New Mexico:

Lieber Freidrich:

'Member that challenge we thunk up while you were in New York last fall—that you could write a story around *any* picture I could draw, no matter what? And that the rules of the game were to be that the scene represents actual existing conditions and is *not* to be explained as a dream, hoax, optical illusion, or insanity on part of the observer. Well, here's the pic. I suddenly got an idea for it, out of the blue.

Can these things be satellites—an egg, a gigantic coin, a free floating drop of water with a fish inside? And if they are satellites (maybe you have a better explanation) can there be an atmosphere present? If not, how come the girl is having a high old time cavorting in airlessness, and her with no insulated clothing or oxygen helmet? And if the cratered moon around which these wacky satellites revolve is barren, how come the huge hand sticking out of the crater and holding a book? How can it live with smoke coming out of another crater. Maybe it's smoke from the monster's pipe—but then how come the rocket shooting out of another crater?

And what's the title of the book? Why is the fish dragging a fish-hook on a line, baited with an empty teacup? Remember that the rules are that every single point must be explained!

With frownzly florgels,

HANNES

Letter from Fredric Brown, Taos, New Mexico, to Hannes Bok, New York City:

Dear Hannes:

You didn't play fair. The picture is utterly impossible. Anyone who'd even *try* to write a story about it is crazy.

Frownzly florgels to *you!*

FRED

The Last Martian

It was an evening like any evening, but duller than most. I was back in the city room after covering a boring banquet, at which the food had been so poor that, even though it had cost me nothing, I'd felt cheated. For the hell of it, I was writing a long and glowing account of it, ten or twelve column inches. The copyreader, of course, would cut it to a passionless paragraph or two.

Slepper was sitting with his feet up on the desk, ostentatiously doing nothing, and Johnny Hale was putting a new ribbon on his typewriter. The rest of the boys were out on routine assignments.

Cargan, the city ed, came out of his private office and walked over to us. "Any of you guys know Barney Welch?" he asked us.

A silly question. Barney runs Barney's Bar right across the street from the Trib. There isn't a Trib reporter who doesn't know Barney well enough to borrow money from him. So we all nodded.

"He just phoned," Cargan said. "He's got a guy down there who claims to be from Mars."

"Drunk or crazy, which?" Slepper wanted to know.

"Barney doesn't know, but he said there might be a gag story in it if we want to come over and talk to the guy. Since it's right across the street and since you three mugs are just sitting on your prats, anyway, one of you dash over. But no drinks on the expense account."

Slepper said, "I'll go," but Cargan's eyes had lighted on me. "You free, Bill?" he asked. "This has got to be a funny story, if any, and you got a light touch on the human interest stuff."

"Sure," I grumbled. "I'll go."

"Maybe it's just some drunk being funny, but if the guy's really insane, phone for a cop, unless you think you can get a gag story. If there's an arrest, you got something to hang a straight story on."

Slepper said, "Cargan, you'd get your grandmother arrested to get a story. Can I go along with Bill, just for the ride?"

"No, you and Johnny stay here. We're not moving the city room across the street to Barney's." Cargan went back into his office.

I slapped a "thirty" on to end the banquet story and sent it down the tube. I got my hat and coat. Slepper said, "Have a drink for me, Bill. But don't drink so much you lose that light touch."

I said, "Sure," and went on over to the stairway and down.

I walked into Barney's and looked around. Nobody from the Trib was there except a couple of pressmen playing gin rummy at one of the tables. Aside from Barney himself, back of the bar, there was only one other man in the place. He was a tall man, thin and sallow, who was sitting by himself in one of the booths, staring morosely into an almost empty beer glass.

I thought I'd get Barney's angle first, so I went up to the bar and put down a bill. "A quick one," I told him. "Straight, water on the side. And is tall-and-dismal over there the Martian you phoned Cargan about?"

He nodded once and poured my drink.

"What's my angle?" I asked him. "Does he know a reporter's going to interview him? Or do I just buy him a drink and rope him, or what? How crazy is he?"

"You tell me. Says he just got in from Mars two hours ago and he's trying to figure it out. He says he's the last living Martian. He doesn't know you're a reporter, but he's all set to talk to you. I set it up."

"How?"

"Told him I had a friend who was smarter than any usual guy and could give him good advice on what to do. I didn't tell him any name because I didn't know who Cargan would send. But he's all ready to cry on your shoulder."

"Know *his* name?"

Barney grimaced. "Yangan Dal, he says. Listen, don't get him violent or anything in here. I don't want no trouble."

I downed my shot and took a sip of chaser. I said, "Okay, Barney. Look, dish up two beers for us and I'll go over and take 'em with me."

Barney drew two beers and cut off their heads. He rang up sixty cents and gave me my change, and I went over to the booth with the beers.

"Mr. Dal?" I said. "My name is Bill Everett. Barney tells me you have a problem I might help you on."

He looked up at me. "You're the one he phoned? Sit down, Mr. Everett. And thanks very much for the beer."

I slid into the booth across from him. He took the last sip of his previous beer and wrapped nervous hands around the glass I'd just bought him.

"I suppose you'll think I'm crazy," he said. "And maybe you'll be right, but—I don't understand it myself. The bartender thinks I'm crazy, I guess. Listen, are you a doctor?"

"Not exactly," I told him. "Call me a consulting psychologist."

"Do you think I'm insane?"

I said, "Most people who are don't admit they might be. But I haven't heard your story yet."

He took a draught of the beer and put the glass down again, but kept his hands tightly around the glass, possibly to keep them from shaking.

He said, "I'm a Martian. *The last one.* All the others are dead. I saw their bodies only two hours ago."

"You were on Mars only two hours ago? How did you get here?"

"I don't know. That's the horrible thing. I don't know. All I know is that the others were dead, their bodies starting to rot. It was awful. There were a hundred million of us, and now I'm the last one."

"A hundred million. That's the population of Mars?"

"About that. A little over, maybe. But that *was* the population. They're all dead now, except me. I looked in three cities, the three biggest ones. I was in Skar, and when I found all the people dead there, I took a targan—there was no one to stop me—and flew it to Undanel. I'd never flown one before, but the controls were simple. Everyone in Undanel was dead, too. I refueled and flew on. I flew low and watched and there was no one alive. I flew to Zandar, the biggest city—over three million people. And all of them were dead and starting to rot. It was horrible, I tell you. Horrible. I can't get over the shock of it."

"I can imagine," I said.

"You *can't*. Of course it was a dying world, anyway; we didn't have more than another dozen generations left to us, you understand. Two centuries ago, we numbered three billion—most of them starving. It was the kryl, the disease that came from the desert wind and that our scientists couldn't cure. In two centuries it reduced us to one-thirtieth of our number and it still kept on."

"Your people died, then, of this—kryl?"

"No. When a Martian dies of kryl, he withers. The corpses I saw were not withered." He shuddered and drank the rest of his beer. I saw that I'd neglected mine and downed it. I raised two fingers at Barney, who was watching our way and looking worried.

My Martian went on talking. "We tried to develop space travel, but we couldn't. We thought some of us might escape the kryl, if we came to Earth or to other worlds. We tried, but we failed. We couldn't even get to Deimos or Phobos, our moons."

"You didn't develop space travel? Then how—"

"I don't know. *I don't know,* and I tell you it's driving me wild. I don't know how I got here. I'm Yangan Dal, *a Martian. And I'm here, in this body.* It's driving me wild, I tell you."

Barney came with the beers. He looked worried enough, so I waited until he was out of hearing before I asked, "In this body? Do you mean—"

"Of course. This isn't *I*, this body I'm in. You don't think Martians would look exactly like humans, do you? I'm three feet tall, weigh what would be about twenty pounds here on Earth. I have four arms with six-fingered hands. This body I'm in—it frightens me. I don't understand it, any more than I know how I got here."

"Or how you happen to talk English? Or can you account for that?"

"Well—in a way I can. This body; its name is Howard Wilcox. It's a bookkeeper. It's married to a female of this species. It works at a place called the Humbert Lamp Company. I've got all its memories and I can do everything it could do; I know everything it knew, or knows. In a sense, I *am* Howard Wilcox. I've got stuff in my pockets to prove it. But it doesn't make sense, because I'm Yangan Dal, and I'm a Martian. I've even got this body's tastes. I like beer. And if I think about this body's wife, I—well, I love her."

I stared at him and pulled out my cigarettes, held out the package to him. "Smoke?"

"This body—Howard Wilcox—doesn't smoke. Thanks, though. And let me buy us another round of beers. There's money in these pockets."

I signaled Barney.

"When did this happen? You say only two hours ago? Did you ever suspect before then that you were a Martian?"

"Suspect? I *was* a Martian. What time is it?"

I looked at Barney's clock. "A little after nine."

"Then it's a little longer than I thought. Three and a half hours. It would have been half past five when I found myself in this body, because it was going home from work then, and from its memories I know it had left work half an hour before then, at five."

"And did you—it—go home?"

"No, I was too confused. It wasn't *my* home. I'm a *Martian*. Don't you understand that? Well, I don't blame you if you don't, because I don't, either. But I walked. And I—I mean Howard Wilcox—got thirsty and he—I—" He stopped and started over again. "This body got thirsty and I stopped in here for a drink. After two or three beers, I thought maybe the bartender there could give me some advice and I started talking to him."

I leaned forward across the table. "Listen, Howard," I said, "you were due home for dinner. You're making your wife worry like anything about you unless you phoned her. Did you?"

"Did I— Of course not. I'm not Howard Wilcox." But a new type of worry came into his face.

"You'd better phone her," I said. "What's there to lose? Whether you are Yangan Dal or Howard Wilcox, there's a woman sitting home worrying about you or him. Be kind enough to phone her. Do you know the number?"

"Of course. It's my own—I mean it's Howard Wilcox's—"

"Quit tying yourself into grammatical knots and go make that phone call. Don't worry about thinking up a story yet; you're too confused. Just tell her you'll explain when you get home, but that you're all right."

He got up like a man in a daze and headed for the phone booth.

I went over to the bar and had another quickie, straight.

Barney said, "Is he—uh—"

"I don't know yet," I said. "There's something about it I still don't get."

I got back to the booth.

He was grinning weakly. He said, "She sounded madder than hoptoads. If I—if Howard Wilcox does go home, his story had better be good." He took a gulp of beer. "Better than Yangan Dal's story, anyway." He was getting more human by the moment.

But then he was back into it again. He stared at me. "I maybe should have told you how it happened from the beginning. I was shut up in a room on Mars. In the city of Skar. I don't know why they put me there, but they did. I was locked in. And then for a long time they didn't bring me food, and I got so hungry that I worked a stone loose from the floor and started to scrape my way through the door. I was starving. It took me three days—Martian days, about six Earth days—to get through, and I staggered around until I found the food quarters of the building I was in. There was no one there and I ate. And then—"

"Go on," I said. "I'm listening."

"I went out of the building and everyone was lying in the open, in the streets, dead. Rotting." He put his hands over his eyes. "I looked in some houses, other buildings. I don't know why or what I was looking for, but nobody had died indoors. Everybody was lying dead in the open, and none of the bodies were withered, so it wasn't kryl that killed them.

"Then, as I told you, I stole the targan—or I guess I really didn't steal it, because there was no one to steal it from—and flew around looking for someone alive. Out in the country it was the same way—everybody lying in the open, near the houses, dead. And Undanel and Zandar, the same.

"Did I tell you Zandar's the biggest city, the capital? In the middle of Zandar there's a big open space, the Games Field, that's more than an Earth-mile square. And all the people in Zandar were there, or it looked like all. Three million bodies, all lying together, like they'd gathered there to die, out in the open. Like they'd known. Like everyone, everywhere else, was out in the open, but here they were all together, the whole three million of them.

"I saw it from the air, as I flew over the city. And there was something in the middle of the field, on a platform. I went down and hovered the targan— it's a little like your helicopters, I forgot to mention—I hovered over the platform to see what was there. It was some kind of a column made of solid copper. Copper on Mars is like gold is on Earth. There was a push-button set with precious stones set in the column. And a Martian in a blue robe lay dead at the foot of the column, right under the button. As though he'd pushed it— and then died. And everybody else had died, too, with him. Everybody on Mars, except me.

"And I lowered the targan onto the platform and got out and I pushed the button. I wanted to die, too; everybody else was dead and I wanted to die, too. *But I didn't. I was riding on a streetcar on Earth, on my way home from work, and my name was—*"

I signaled Barney.

"Listen, Howard," I said. "We'll have one more beer and then you'd better get home to your wife. You'll catch hell from her, even now, and the longer you wait, the worse it'll be. And if you're smart, you'll take some candy or flowers along and think up a really good story on the way home. And *not* the one you just told me."

He said, "Well—"

I said, "Well me no wells. Your name is Howard Wilcox and you'd better get home to your wife. I'll tell you what *may* have happened. We know little about the human mind, and many strange things happen to it. Maybe the medieval people *had* something when they believed in possession. Do you want to know what I think happened to you?"

"What? For Heaven's sake, if you can give me *any* explanation—except tell me that I'm crazy—"

"I think you *can* drive yourself batty if you let yourself think about it, Howard. Assume there's some natural explanation and then forget it. I can make a random guess what may have happened."

Barney came with the beers and I waited until he'd gone back to the bar.

I said, "Howard, just possibly a man—I mean a Martian—named Yangan Dal did die this afternoon on Mars. Maybe he really was the last Martian. And maybe, somehow, his mind got mixed up with yours at the moment of his death. I'm not saying that's what happened, but it isn't impossible to believe. Assume it was that, Howard, and fight it off. Just act as though you are Howard Wilcox—and look in a mirror if you doubt it. Go home and square things with your wife, and then go to work tomorrow morning and forget it. Don't you think that's the best idea?"

"Well, maybe you're right. The evidence of my senses—"

"Accept it. Until and unless you get better evidence."

We finished off our beers and I put him into a taxi. I reminded him to stop for candy or flowers and to work up a good and reasonable alibi, instead of thinking about what he'd been telling me.

I went back upstairs in the Trib building and into Cargan's office and closed the door behind me.

I said, "It's all right, Cargan. I straightened him out."

"What had happened?"

"He's a Martian, all right. And he was the last Martian left on Mars. Only he didn't know we'd come here; he thought we were all dead."

"But how—How could he have been overlooked? How could he not have known?"

I said, "He's an imbecile. He was in a mental institution in Skar and somebody slipped up and left him in his room when the button was pushed that sent us here. He wasn't out in the open, so he didn't get the mentaport rays that carried our psyches across space. He escaped from his room and found the platform in Zandar, where the ceremony was, and pushed the button himself. There must have been enough juice left to send him after us."

Cargan whistled softly. "Did you tell him the truth? And is he smart enough to keep his trap shut?"

I shook my head. "No, to both questions. His I. Q. is about fifteen, at a guess. But that's as smart as the average Earthman, so he'll get by here all right. I convinced him he really was the Earthman his psyche happened to get into."

"Lucky thing he went into Barney's. I'll phone Barney in a minute and let him know it's taken care of. I'm surprised he didn't give the guy a mickey before he phoned us."

I said, "Barney's one of us. He wouldn't have let the guy get out of there. He'd have held him till we got there."

"But you let him go. Are you sure it's safe? Shouldn't you have—"

"He'll be all right," I said. "I'll assume responsibility to keep an eye on him until we take over. I suppose we'll have to institutionalize him again after that. But I'm glad I didn't have to kill him. After all, he *is* one of us, imbecile or not. And he'll probably be so glad to learn he isn't the *last* Martian that he won't mind having to return to an asylum."

I went back into the city room and to my desk. Slepper was gone, sent out somewhere on something. Johnny Hale looked up from the magazine he was reading. "Get a story?" he asked.

"Nah," I said. "Just a drunk being the life of the party. I'm surprised at Barney for calling."

Honeymoon in Hell

On September 16th in the year 1962, things were going along about the same as usual, only a little worse. The cold war that had been waxing and waning between the United States and the Eastern Alliance—Russia, China, and their lesser satellites—was warmer than it had ever been. War, hot war, seemed not only inevitable but extremely imminent.

The race for the Moon was an immediate cause. Each nation had landed a few men on it and each claimed it. Each had found that rockets sent from Earth were inadequate to permit establishment of a permanent base upon the Moon, and that only establishment of a permanent base, in force, would determine possession. And so each nation (for convenience we'll call the Eastern Alliance a nation, although it was not exactly that) was engaged in rushing construction of a space station to be placed in an orbit around Earth.

With such an intermediate step in space, reaching the Moon with large rockets would be practicable and construction of armed bases, heavily garrisoned, would be comparatively simple. Whoever got there first could not only *claim* possession, but could implement the claim. Military secrecy on both sides kept from the public just how near to completion each space base was, but it was generally—and correctly—believed that the issue would be determined within a year, two years at the outside.

Neither nation could *afford* to let the other control the Moon. That much had become obvious even to those who were trying desperately to maintain peace.

On September 17th, 1962, a statistician in the birth record department of New York City (his name was Wilbur Evans, but that doesn't matter) noticed that out of 813 births reported the previous day, 657 had been girls and only 156 boys.

He knew that, statistically, this was practically impossible. In a small city where there are only, say, ten births a day, it is quite possible—and not at all alarming—that on any one given day, 90% or even 100%, of the births may be of the same sex. But out of so large a figure as 813, so high a ratio as 657 to 156 *is* alarming.

Wilbur Evans went to his department chief and he, too, was interested and alarmed. Checks were made by telephone—first with nearby cities and, as the evidence mounted, with more and more distant ones.

By the end of that day, the puzzled investigators—and there was quite a large group interested by then—knew that in every city checked, the same thing had happened. The births, all over the Western Hemisphere and in Europe, for that day had averaged about the same—three boys for every thirteen girls.

Back-checking showed that the trend had started almost a week before, but with only a slight predominance of girls. For only a few days had the discrepancy been obvious. On the fifteenth, the ratio had been three boys to every five girls and on the sixteenth it had been four to fourteen.

The newspapers got the story, of course, and kicked it around. The television comics had fun with it, if their audiences didn't. But four days later, on September 21st, only one child out of every eighty-seven born in the country was male. That wasn't funny. People and governments started to worry; biologists and laboratories who had already started to investigate the phenomenon made it their number one project. The television comics quit joking about it after one crack on the subject by the top comedian in the country drew 875,480 indignant letters and lost him his contract.

On September 29th, out of a normal numbers of births in the United States, only forty-one were boys. Investigation proved that every one of these was a late, or delayed, birth. It became obvious that no male child had been conceived, during the latter part of December of the previous year, 1961. By this time, of course, it was known that the same condition prevailed everywhere—in the countries of the Eastern Alliance as well as in the United States, and in every other country and area of the world—among the Eskimos, the Ubangi and the Indians of Tierra del Fuego.

The strange phenomenon, whatever it was, affected human beings only, however. Births among animals, wild or domesticated, showed the usual ratio of the two sexes.

Work on both space stations continued, but talk of war—and incidents tending to lead to war—diminished. The human race had something new, something less immediate, but in the long run far worse to worry about. Despite the apparent inevitability of war, few people thought that it would completely end the human race; a complete lack of male children definitely would. Very, very definitely.

And for once something was happening that the United States could not blame on the Eastern Alliance, and vice versa. The Orient—China and India in particular—suffered more, perhaps, than the Occident, for in those countries male offspring are of supreme emotional importance to parents. There were riots in both China and India, very bloody ones, until the people realized that they didn't know whom or what they were rioting against and sank back into miserable passivity.

In the more advanced countries, laboratories went on twenty-four-hour shifts, and anyone who knew a gene from a chromosome could command his weight in paper currency for looking—however futilely—through a microscope. Accredited biologists and geneticists became more important than presidents and dictators. But they accomplished no more than the cults which sprang up everywhere (though mostly in California) and which blamed what was happening on everything from a conspiracy of the Elders of Zion to (with unusually good sense) an invasion from space, and advocated everything from vegetarianism to (again with unusually good sense) a revival of phallic worship.

Despite scientists and cults, despite riots and resignation, not a single male child was born anywhere in the world during the month of December, 1962. There had been isolated instances, all quite late births, during October and November.

January of 1963 again drew a blank. Not that everyone qualified wasn't trying.

Except, perhaps, the one person who was slated to do more than anyone else—well, almost anyone else—about the matter.

Not that Capt. Raymond F. Carmody, U.S.S.F., retired, was a misogamist, exactly. He liked women well enough, both in the abstract and in the concrete. But he'd been badly jilted once and it had cured him of any desire whatsoever for marriage. Marriage aside, he took women as he found them—and he had no trouble finding them.

For one thing, don't let the word "retired" fool you. In the Space Service, rocket pilots are retired at the ripe old age of twenty-five. The recklessness, reaction-speed and stamina of youth are much more important than experience. The trick in riding a rocket is not to *do* anything in particular; it's to be tough enough to stay alive and sane until you get there. Technicians do the brain-work and the only controls are braking rockets to help you get down in one piece when you land; reaction-speed is of more importance than experience in managing them. Neither speed nor experience helps you if you've gone batty en route from spending days on end in the equivalent of a coffin, or if you haven't what it takes not to die in a good landing. And a good landing is one that you can walk away from after you've recovered consciousness.

That's why Ray Carmody, at twenty-seven, was a retired rocket pilot. Aside from test flights on and near Earth, he'd made one successful flight to the Moon with landing and return. It had been the fifteenth attempt and the third success. There had been two more successful flights thereafter—altogether five successful round trips out of eighteen tries.

But each rocket thus far designed had been able, barely, to carry fuel to get itself and its crew of one back to Earth, with almost-starvation rations for the period required. Step-rockets were needed to do even that, and step-rockets are terrifically expensive and cumbersome things.

At the time Carmody had retired from the Space Service, two years before, it had been conceded that establishment of a permanent base of any sort on the Moon was completely impracticable until a space station, orbited around the Earth, had been completed as a way-station. Comparatively huge rockets could reach a space station with relative ease, and starting *from* a station in open space and against lesser gravitational pull from Earth, going the rest of the way to the Moon would be even simpler.

But we're getting away from Ray Carmody, as Carmody had got away from the Space Service. He could have had a desk job in it after old age had retired him, a job that would have paid better than he was making at the moment. But he knew little about the technical end of rocketry, and he knew less, and cared nothing, about administrative detail work. He was most interested in cybernetics, which is the science of electronic calculating machines. The big machines had always fascinated him, and he'd found a job working with the biggest of them all, the one in the building on a corner of the grounds of the Pentagon that had been built, in 1958, especially to house it.

It was, of course, known as Junior to its intimates.

Carmody's job, specifically, was Operative, Grade I, and the Grade I meant that—despite his fame as one of the few men who had been to the Moon and lived to tell about it, and despite his ultra-honorable discharge with the grade of captain—his life had been checked back to its very beginning to be sure that he had not, even in his cradle, uttered a careless or subversive word.

There were only three other Grade I Operatives qualified to ask Junior questions and transmit his answers on questions which involved security—and that included questions on logistics, atomics, ballistics and rocketry, military plans of all sorts and everything else the military forces consider secret, which is practically everything except the currently preferred color of an infantryman's uniform.

The Eastern Alliance would undoubtedly have traded three puppet dictators and the tomb of Lenin to have had an agent, or even a sympathizer, as a Grade I Operative on Junior. But even the Grade II Operatives, who handled only problems dealing with non-classified matters, were checked for loyalty with extreme care. Possibly lest they might ask Junior a subversive question or feed a subversive idea into his electronic equivalent of a brain.

But be that as it may, on the afternoon of February 2, 1963, Ray Carmody was the Operative on duty in the control room. The only Operative, of course; dozens of technicians were required from time to time to service Junior and feed him, but only one Operative at a time fed data into him or asked him questions. So Carmody was alone in the soundproofed control room.

Doing nothing, however, at the moment. He'd just fed into Junior a complicated mess of data on molecular structure in the chromosome mechanism and had asked Junior—for the ten-thousandth time, at least—the sixty-four dollar question bearing on the survival of the human race: Why all children were now females and what could be done about it.

It had been quite a chunk of data, this time, and no doubt Junior would take quite a few minutes to digest it, add it to everything else he'd ever been told and synthesize the whole. No doubt in a few minutes he'd say, "Data insufficient." At least to this moment that had been his only answer to the sixty-four dollar question.

Carmody sat back and watched Junior's complicated bank of dials, switches and lights with a bored eye. And because the intake-mike was shut off and Junior couldn't hear what he was saying anyway, and because the control room was soundproofed so no one else could hear him, either, he spoke freely.

"Junior," he said, "I'm afraid you're a washout on this particular deal. We've fed you everything that every geneticist, every chemist, every biologist in this half of the world knows, and all you do is come up with that 'data insufficient' stuff. What do you want—blood?

"Oh. you're pretty good on some things. You're a whiz on orbits and rocket fuels, but you just can't understand *women*, can you? Well, I can't either; I'll give you that. And I've got to admit you've done the human race a good turn on one deal—atomics. You convinced us that if we completed and used H-bombs, *both* sides would lose the coming war. I mean *lose.* And we've got inside information that the other side got the same answer out of your brothers, the cybernetics machines over there, so they won't build or use them, either. Winning a war with H-bombs is about like winning a wrestling match with hand grenades; it's just as unhealthful for you as for your opponent. But we weren't talking about hand grenades. We were talking about women. Or I was. Listen, Junior—"

A light, not on Junior's panel but in the ceiling, flashed on and off, the signal for an incoming intercommunicator call. It would be from the Chief Operative, of course; no one else could connect—by intercommunicator or any other method—with this control room.

Carmody threw a switch.

"Busy, Carmody?"

"Not at the moment, Chief. Just fed Junior that stuff on molecular structure of genes and chromosomes. Waiting for him to tell me it's not enough data, but it'll take him a few minutes yet."

"Okay. You're off duty in fifteen minutes. Will you come to my office as soon as you're relieved? The President wants to talk to you."

Carmody said, "Goody. I'll put on my best pinafore."

He threw the switch again. Quickly, because a green light was flashing on Junior's panel.

He reconnected the intake- and output-mikes and said, "Well, Junior?"

"Data insufficient," said Junior's level mechanical voice.

Carmody sighed and noted the machine's answer on the report ending in a question which he had fed into the mike. He said, "Junior, I'm ashamed of you. All right, let's see if there's anything else I can ask and get an answer to in fifteen minutes."

He picked up a pile of several files from the table in front of him and leafed through them quickly. None contained fewer than three pages of data.

"Nope," he said, "not a thing here I can give you in fifteen minutes, and Bob will be here to relieve me then."

He sat back and relaxed. He wasn't ducking work; experience had proven that, although an AE7 cybernetics machine could accept verbal data in conformance with whatever vocabulary it had been given, and translate that data into mathematical symbols (as it translated the mathematical symbols of its answer back into words and mechanically spoke the words), it could not adapt itself to a change of voice within a given operation. It could, and did, adjust itself to understanding, as it were, Carmody's voice or the voice of Bob Dana who would shortly relieve him. But if Carmody started on a given problem, he'd have to finish it himself, or Bob would have to clear the board and start all over again. So there was no use starting something he wouldn't have time to finish.

He glanced through some of the reports and questions to kill time. The one dealing with the space station interested him most, but he found it too technical to understand.

"But you won't," he told Junior. "Pal, I've got to give that to you; when it comes to anything except women, you're really *good.*"

The switch was open, but since no question had been asked, of course Junior didn't answer.

Carmody put down the files and glowered at Junior. "Junior," he said, "that's your weakness all right, women. And you can't have genetics without women, can you?"

"No," Junior said.

"Well, you do know that much. But even I know it. Look, here's one that'll stump you. That blonde I met at the party last night. What about her?"

"The question," said Junior, "is inadequately worded; please clarify."

Carmody grinned. "You want me to get graphic, but I'll fool you. I'll just ask you this—should I see her again?"

"No," said Junior, mechanically but implacably.

Carmody's eyebrows went up. "The devil you say. And may I ask why, since you haven't met the lady, you say that?"

"Yes. You may ask why."

That was one trouble with Junior; he always answered the question you actually asked, not the one you implied.

"Why?" Carmody demanded, genuinely curious now as to what answer he was going to receive. "Specifically, why should I not again see the blonde I met last night?"

"Tonight," said Junior, "you will be busy. Before tomorrow night you will be married."

Carmody almost literally jumped out of his chair. The cybernetics machine had gone stark raving crazy. It *must* have. There was no more chance of his getting married tomorrow than there was of a kangaroo giving birth to a portable typewriter. And besides and beyond that, Junior never made predictions of the future—except, of course, on such things as orbits and statistical extrapolation of trends.

Carmody was still staring at Junior's impassive panel with utter disbelief and considerable consternation when the red light that was the equivalent of a doorbell flashed in the ceiling. His shift was up and Bob Dana had come to relieve him. There wasn't time to ask any further questions and, anyway, "Are you crazy?" was the only one he could think of at the moment.

Carmody didn't ask it. He didn't want to know.

Carmody switched off both mikes and stood gazing at Junior's impassive panel for a long time. He shook his head, went to the door and opened it.

Bob Dana breezed in and then stopped to look at Carmody. He said, "Something the matter, Ray? You look like you'd just seen a ghost, if I may coin a cliché."

Carmody shook his head. He wanted to think before he talked to anybody—and if he did decide to talk, it should be to Chief Operative Reeber and not to anyone else. He said, "Just I'm a little beat, Bob."

"Nothing special up?"

"Nope. Unless maybe I'm going to be fired. Reeber wants to see me on my way out." He grinned. "Says the President wants to talk to me."

Bob chuckled appreciatively. "If he's in a kidding mood, then your job's safe for one more day. Good luck."

The soundproof door closed and locked behind Carmody, and he nodded to the two armed guards who were posted on duty outside it. He tried to think things out carefully as he walked down the long stretch of corridor to the Chief Operator's office.

Had something gone wrong with Junior? If so, it was his duty to report the matter. But if he did, he'd get himself in trouble, too. An Operative wasn't supposed to ask private questions of the big cybernetics machine—even big, important questions. The fact that it had been a joking question would make it worse.

But Junior had either given him a joking answer—and it couldn't be that, because Junior didn't have a sense of humor—or else Junior had made a flat, unadulterated error. Two of them, in fact. Junior had said that Carmody would be busy tonight and—well, a wheel *could* come off his idea of spending a quiet evening reading. But the idea of his getting married tomorrow was utterly preposterous. There wasn't a woman on Earth he had the slightest intention of marrying. Oh, someday, maybe, when he'd had a little more fun out of life and felt a little more ready to settle down, he might feel differently. But it wouldn't be for years. Certainly not tomorrow, not even on a bet.

Junior *had* to be wrong, and if he was wrong it was a matter of importance, a matter far more important than Carmody's job.

So be honest and report? He made his decision just before he reached the door of Reeber's office. A reasonable compromise. He didn't *know* yet that Junior was wrong. Not to a point of mathematical certainty—just a billion to one odds against. So he'd wait until even that possibility was eliminated, until it was proven beyond all possible doubt that Junior was wrong. Then he'd report what he'd done and take the rap, if there was a rap. Maybe he'd just be fined and warned.

He opened the door and stepped in. Chief Operative Reeber stood up and, on the other side of the desk, a tall gray-haired man stood also. Reeber said, "Ray, I'd like you to meet the President of the United States. He came here to talk to you. Mr. President, Captain Ray Carmody."

And it *was* the President. Carmody gulped and tried to avoid looking as though he was doing a double take, which he was. Then President Saunderson smiled quietly and held out his hand. "Very glad to know you, Captain," he said, and Carmody was able to make the considerable understatement that he felt honored to meet the President.

Reeber told him to pull up a chair and he did so. The President looked at him gravely. "Captain Carmody, you have been chosen to—have the opportunity to volunteer for a mission of extreme importance. There is danger involved, but it is less than the danger of your trip to the Moon. You made the third—wasn't it?—out of the five successful trips made by the United States pilots?"

Carmody nodded.

"This time the risk you will take is considerably less. There has been much technological advance in rocketry since you left the service two years ago. The odds against a successful round trip—even without the help of the space station, and I fear its completion is still two years distant—are much less. In fact, you will have odds of ten to one in your favor, as against approximately even odds at the time of your previous trip."

Carmody sat up straighter. "My *previous* trip! Then this volunteer mission is another flight to the Moon? Certainly, Mr. President, I'll gladly—"

President Saunderson held up a hand. "Wait, you haven't heard all of it. The flight to the Moon and return is the only part that involves physical danger, but it is the least important part. Captain, this mission is, possibly, of more importance to humanity than the first flight to the Moon, even than the first flight to the stars—if and when we ever make it—will be. What's at stake is the survival of the human race so that someday it *can* reach the stars. Your flight to the Moon will be an attempt to solve the problem which otherwise—"

He paused and wiped his forehead with a handkerchief.

"Perhaps you'd better explain, Mr. Reeber. You're more familiar with the exact way the problem was put to your machine, and its exact answers."

Reeber said, "Carmody, you know what the problem is. You know how much data has been fed into Junior on it. You know some of the questions we've asked him, and that we've been able to eliminate certain things. Such as—well, it's caused by no virus, no bacteria, nothing like that. It's not anything like an epidemic, because it struck the whole Earth at once, simultaneously. Even native inhabitants of islands that had no contact with civilization.

"We know also that whatever happens—whatever molecular change occurs—happens in the zygote after impregnation, very shortly after. We asked Junior whether an invisible *ray* of some sort could cause this. His answer was that it was possible. And in answer to a further question, he answered that this ray or force is possibly being used by—enemies of mankind."

"Insects? Animals? Martians?"

Reeber waved a hand impatiently. "Martians, maybe, if there *are* any Martians. We don't know that yet. But extra-terrestrials, most likely. Now Junior couldn't give us answers on this because, of course, we haven't the relevant data. It would be guesswork for him as well as for us—and Junior, being mechanical, can't guess. But here's a possibility:

"Suppose some extra-terrestrials *have* landed somewhere on Earth and have set up a station that broadcasts a ray that is causing the phenomenon of all children being girlchildren. The ray is undetectable; at least thus far we haven't been able to detect it. They'd be killing off the human race and getting themselves a nice new planet to live on, without having to fire a shot, without taking any risk or losses themselves. True, they'll have to wait a while for us to die off, but maybe that doesn't mean anything to them. Maybe they've got all the time there is, and aren't in the slightest hurry."

Carmody nodded slowly. "It sounds fantastic, but I guess it's possible. I guess a fantastic situation like this *has* to have a fantastic explanation. But what do we do about it? How do we even prove it?"

Reeber said, "We fed the possibility into Junior as a working assumption—not as a fact—and asked him how we could check it. He came up with the suggestion that a married couple spend a honeymoon on the Moon—and see if circumstances are any different there."

"And you want me to pilot them there?"

"Not exactly, Ray. A little more than that—"

Carmody forgot that the President was there. He said, "Good God, you mean you want me to— Then Junior *wasn't* crazy, after all!"

Shamefacedly, then, he had to explain about the extracurricular question he'd casually asked Junior and the answer he'd got to it.

Reeber laughed. "Guess we'll overlook your violation of Rule 17 this time, Ray. That is, if you accept the mission. Now here's the—"

"Wait," Carmody said. "I still want to know something. How did Junior know I was going to be picked out? And for that matter, why am I?"

"Junior was asked for the qualifications he'd recommend for the—ah—bridegroom. He recommended a rocket pilot who had already made the trip successfully, even though he was a year or two over the technical retirement age of twenty-five. He recommended that loyalty be considered as an important factor, and that the holding of a governmental position of great trust would answer that. He further recommended that the man be single."

"*Why* single? Look, there are four other pilots who've made that trip, and they're all loyal, regardless of what job they're holding now. I know them all personally. And all of them are married except me. Why not send a man who's already got a ball and chain?"

"For the simple reason, Ray, that the woman to be sent must be chosen with even more care. You know how tough a Moon landing is; only one woman in a hundred would live through it and still be able to—I mean, there's almost a negligible chance that the wife of any one of the other four pilots would be the best qualified woman who could possibly be found."

"Hmmm. Well, I suppose Junior's got something there. Anyway, I see now how he knew *I'd* be chosen. Those qualifications fit me exactly. But listen, do I have to *stay* married to whatever female is Amazonian enough to make the trip? There's a limit somewhere, isn't there?"

"Of course. You will be legally married before your departure, but upon your return a divorce will be granted without question if both—or either one—of you wish. The offspring of the union, if any, will be cared for. Whether male or female."

"Hey, that's right," Carmody said. "There's only an even chance of hitting the jackpot in any case."

"Other couples will be sent. The first trip is the most difficult and most important one. After that, a base will be established. Sooner or later we'll get our answer. We'll have it if even one male child is conceived on the Moon. Not that that will help us find the station that's sending the rays, or to detect or identify the rays, but we'll know what's wrong and can narrow our inquiry. I take it that you accept?"

Carmody sighed. "I guess so. But it seems a long way to go for— Say, who's the lucky girl?"

Reeber cleared his throat. "I think you'd better explain this part to him, Mr. President."

President Saunderson smiled as Carmody looked toward him. He said, "There is a more important reason, which Mr. Reeber skipped, why we could not choose a man who was already married, Captain. This is being done on an international basis, for very important diplomatic reasons. The experiment is for the benefit of humanity, not any nation or ideology. Your wife will be a Russian."

"A *Commie?* You're kidding me, Mr. President."

"I am not. Her name is Anna Borisovna. I have not met her, but I am informed that she is a very attractive girl. Her qualifications are quite similar to yours, except, of course, that she has not been to the Moon. No woman has. But she has been a pilot of experimental rockets on short-range flights. And she is a cybernetics technician working on the big machine at Moscow. She is twenty-four. And not, incidentally, an Amazon. As you know, rocket pilots aren't chosen for bulk. There is an added advantage in her being chosen. She speaks English."

"You mean I've got to talk to her, too?"

Carmody caught the look Reeber flashed at him and he winced.

The President continued: "You will be married to her tomorrow by a beam-televised ceremony. You blast off, both of you, tomorrow night—at different times, of course, since one of you will leave from here, the other from Russia. You will meet on the Moon."

"It's a large place, Mr. President."

"That is taken care of. Major Granham—you know him, I believe?" Carmody nodded. "He will supervise your takeoff and the sending of the supply rockets. You will fly tonight—a plane has been prepared for you—from the airport here to Suffolk Rocket Field. Major Granham will brief you and give you full instructions. Can you be at the airport by seven-thirty?"

Carmody thought and then nodded. It was five-thirty now and there'd be a lot of things for him to do and arrange in two hours, but he could make it if he tried. And hadn't Junior told him he was going to be busy this evening?

"Only one thing more," President Saunderson said. "This is strictly confidential, until and unless the mission is successful. We don't want to raise hopes, either here or in the Eastern Alliance, and then have them smashed." He smiled. "And if you and your wife have any quarrels on the Moon, we don't want them to lead to international repercussions. So please—try to get along." He held out his hand. "That's all, except thanks."

Carmody made the airport in time and the plane was waiting for him, complete with pilot. He had figured that he would have to fly it himself, but he realized that it was better this way; he could get a bit of rest before they reached Suffolk Field.

He got a little, but not much. The plane was a hot ship that got him there in less than an hour. A liaison officer was waiting for him and took him immediately to Major Granham's office.

Granham got down to brass tacks almost before Carmody could seat himself in the offered chair.

He said, "Here's the picture. Since you got out of the service, we've tremendously increased the accuracy of our rockets, manned or otherwise. They're so accurate that, with proper care, we can hit within a mile of any spot on the Moon that we aim at. We're picking Hell Crater—it's a small one, but we'll put you right in the middle of it. You won't have to worry about steering; you'll hit within a mile of the center without having to use your braking rockets for anything except braking."

"Hell Crater?" Carmody said. "There isn't any."

"Our Moon maps have forty-two thousand named craters. Do you know them all? This one, incidentally, was named after a Father Maximilian Hell, S. J., who was once director of the Vienna Observatory in old Austria."

Carmody grinned. "Now you're spoiling it. How come it was picked as a honeymoon spot, though? Just because of the name?"

"No. One of the three successful flights the Russians made happened to land and take off there. They found the footing better than anywhere else either of us has landed. Almost no dust; you won't have to slog through knee-deep pumice when you're gathering the supply rockets. Probably a more recently formed crater than any of the others we've happened to land in or explore."

"Fair enough. About the rocket I go in—what's the payload besides myself?"

"Not a thing but the food, water and oxygen you'll need en route, and your spacesuit. Not even fuel for your return, although you'll return in the same rocket you go in. Everything else, including return fuel, will be there waiting for you; it's on the way now. We fired ten supply rockets last night. Since you take off tomorrow night, they'll get there forty-eight hours before you do. So—"

"Wait a minute," Carmody said. "On my first trip I carried fifty pounds payload besides my return fuel. Is this a smaller type of rocket?"

"Yes, and a much better one. Not a step-rocket like you used before. Better fuel and more of it; you can accelerate longer and at fewer gravities, and you'll get there quicker. Forty-four hours as against almost four days before. Last time you took four and half Gs for seven minutes. This time you'll get by with three Gs and have twelve minutes' acceleration before you reach *Brennschluss*—cut loose from Earth's gravitation. Your first trip, you *had* to carry return fuel and a little payload because we didn't have the accuracy to shoot a supply rocket after you—or before you—and be sure it'd land within twenty miles. All clear? After we're through talking here I'll take you to the supply depot, show you the type of supply rocket we're using and how to open and unload it. I'll give you an inventory of the contents of each of the twelve of them we sent."

"And what if all of them don't get there?"

"At least eleven of them will. And everything's duplicated; if any one rocket goes astray, you'll still have everything you need—for two people. And the Russians are firing an equal number of supply rockets, so you'll have a double factor of safety." He grinned. "If none of our rockets get there, you'll have to eat borsht and drink vodka, maybe, but you won't starve."

"Are you kidding about the vodka?"

"Maybe not. We're including a case of Scotch, transferred to lightweight containers, of course. We figure it might be just the icebreaker you'll need for a happy honeymoon."

Carmody grunted.

"So maybe," Granham said, "the Russians'll figure the same way and send along some vodka. And the rocket fuels for your return, by the way, are not identical, but they're interchangeable. Each side is sending enough for the return of two rockets. If our fuel doesn't get there, you divvy with her, and vice versa."

"Fair enough. What else?"

"Your arrival will be just after dawn—Lunar time. There'll be a few hours when the temperature is somewhere between horribly cold and broiling hot. You'd better take advantage of them to get the bulk of your work done. Gathering supplies from the rockets and putting up the prefab shelter that's in them, in sections. We've got a duplicate of it in the supply depot and I want you to practice assembling it."

"Good idea. It's airtight and heatproof?"

"Airtight once you paint the seams with a special preparation that's included. And, yes, the insulation is excellent. Has a very ingenious little airlock on it, too. You won't have to waste oxygen getting in and out."

Carmody nodded. "Length of stay?" he asked.

"Twelve days. Earth days, of course. That'll give you plenty of time to get off before the Lunar night."

Granham chuckled, "Want instructions to cover those twelve days? No? Well, come on around to the depot then. I'll introduce you to your ship and show you the supply rockets and the shelter."

It turned out to be a busy evening, all right. Carmody didn't get to bed until nearly morning, his head so swimming with facts and figures that he'd forgotten it was his wedding day. Granham let him sleep until nine, then sent an orderly to wake him and to state that the ceremony had been set for ten o'clock and that he'd better hurry.

Carmody couldn't remember what "the ceremony" was for a moment, then he shuddered and hurried.

A Justice of the Peace was waiting for him there and technicians were working on a screen and projector. Granham said, "The Russians agreed that the ceremony could be performed at this end, provided we made it a civil ceremony. That's all right by you, isn't it?"

"It's lovely," Carmody told him. "Let's get on with it. Or don't we have to? As far as I'm concerned—"

"You know what the reaction of a lot of people would be when they learn about it, if it wasn't legal," Granham said. "So quit crabbing. Stand right there."

Carmody stood right there. A fuzzy picture on the beam-television screen was becoming clearer. And prettier. President Saunderson had not exaggerated when he'd said that Anna Borisovna was attractive and that she was definitely not an Amazon. She was small, dark, slender and very definitely attractive and not an Amazon.

Carmody felt glad that nobody had corned it up by putting her in a wedding costume. She wore the neat uniform of a technician, and she filled it admirably and curved it at the right places. Her eyes were big and dark and they were serious until she smiled at him. Only then did he realize that the connection was two-way and that she was seeing him.

Granham was standing beside him. He said. "Miss Borisovna, Captain Carmody."

Carmody said, inanely, "Pleased to meet you," and then redeemed it with a grin.

"Thank you, Captain." Her voice was musical and only faintly accented. "It is a pleasure."

Carmody began to think it would be, if they could just keep from arguing politics.

The Justice of the Peace stepped forward into range of the projector. "Are we ready?" he asked.

"A second," Carmody said. "It seems to me we've skipped a customary preliminary. Miss Borisovna, will you marry me?"

"Yes. And you may call me Anna."

She even has a sense of humor, Carmody thought, astonished. Somehow, he hadn't thought it possible for a Commie to have a sense of humor. He'd pictured them as all being dead serious about their ridiculous ideology and about everything else.

He smiled at her and said, "All right, Anna. And you may call me Ray. Are you ready?"

When she nodded, he stepped to one side to allow the Justice of the Peace to share the screen with him. The ceremony was brief and businesslike.

He couldn't, of course, kiss the bride or even shake hands with her. But just before they shut off the projector, he managed to grin at her and say, "See you in Hell, Anna."

And he'd begun to feel certain that it wouldn't be that at all, really.

He had a busy afternoon going over every detail of operation of the new type rocket, until he knew it inside and out better than he did himself. He even found himself being briefed on details of the Russian rockets, both manned and supply types, and he was surprised (and inwardly a bit horrified) to discover to what extent the United States and Russia had been exchanging information and secrets. It couldn't all have happened in a day or so.

"How long has this been going on?" he demanded of Granham.

"I learned of the projected trip a month ago."

"Why did they tell *me* only yesterday? Or wasn't I first choice, after all? Did somebody else back out at the last minute?"

"You've been chosen all along. You were the only one who fitted *all* of the requirements that cybernetics machine dished out. But don't you remember how it was on your last trip? You weren't notified you were taking off until about thirty hours before. That's what's figured to be the optimum time—long enough to get mentally prepared and not so long you've got time to get worried."

"But this was a volunteer deal. What if I'd turned it down?"

"The cybernetics machine predicted that you wouldn't."

Carmody swore at Junior.

Granham said, "Besides, we could have had a hundred volunteers. Rocket cadets who've got everything you have except one round trip to the Moon already under their belts. We could have shown a picture of Anna around and had them fighting for the chance. That gal is Moon bait."

"Careful," Carmody said, "you are speaking of my wife." He was kidding, of course, but it was funny—he really hadn't liked Granham's wisecrack.

Zero hour was ten p.m., and at zero minus fifteen minutes he was already strapped into the webbing, waiting. There wasn't anything for him to do except stay alive. The rockets would be fired by a chronometer set for the exact fraction of a second.

Despite its small payload, the rocket was a little roomier inside than the first one he'd gone to the Moon in, the R-24. The R-24 had been as roomy as a tight coffin. This one, the R-46, was four feet in diameter inside. He'd be able to get at least a bit of arm and leg exercise on the way and not—as the first time—arrived so cramped that it had taken him over an hour to be able to move freely.

And this time he wouldn't have the horrible discomfort of having to wear his spacesuit, except for the helmet, en route. There's room in a four-foot cylinder to put a spacesuit on, and his was in a compartment—along with the food, water and oxygen—at the front (or top) of the rocket. It would be an hour's work to struggle into it, but he wouldn't have to do it until he was several hours away from the Moon.

Yes, this was going to be a breeze compared to the last trip. Comparative freedom of movement, forty-four hours as against ninety, only three gravities as against four and a half.

Then sound that was beyond sound struck him, sound so loud that he heard it with all of his body rather than only with his carefully plugged ears. It built up, seeming to get louder every second, and his weight built up too. He weighed twice his normal weight, then more. He felt the sickening curve as the automatic tilting mechanism turned the rocket, which had at first gone straight up, forty-five degrees. He weighed four hundred and eighty pounds and the soft webbing seemed to be hard as steel and to cut into him. Padding was compressed till it felt like stone. Sound and pressure went on and on interminably. Surely it had been hours instead of minutes.

Then, at the moment of *Brennschluss,* free of the pull of Earth—sudden silence, complete weightlessness. He blacked out.

But only minutes had gone by when he returned to consciousness. For a while he fought nausea and only when he was sure he had succeeded did he unbuckle himself from the webbing that had held him through the period of acceleration. Now he was coasting, weightless, at a speed that would carry him safely toward the gravitational pull of the Moon. No further firing of fuel would be necessary until he used his jets to brake his landing.

All he had to do now was hang on, to keep from going crazy from claustrophobia during the forty hours before he'd have to start getting ready for the landing.

It was a dull time, but it passed.

Into spacesuit, back into the webbing, but this time with his hands free so he could manipulate the handles that controlled the braking jets.

He made a good landing; it didn't even knock him unconscious. After only a few minutes he was able to unbuckle himself from the webbing. He sealed his spacesuit and started the oxygen, then let himself out of the rocket. It had fallen over on its side after the landing, of course; they always do. But he had the equipment and knew the technique for getting it upright again, and there wasn't any hurry about doing it.

The supply rockets had been shot accurately, all right. Six of them, four American type and two Russian, lay within a radius of a hundred yards of his own rocket. He could see others farther away, but didn't waste time counting them. He looked for one that would be larger than the rest—the manned (or womaned) rocket from Russia. He located it finally, almost a mile away. He saw no spacesuited figure near it.

He started toward it, running with the gliding motion, almost like skating, that had been found to be easier than walking in the light gravitational pull of the Moon. Spacesuit, oxygen tank and all, his total weight was about forty-five pounds. Running a mile was less exertion than a 100-yard dash on Earth.

He was more than glad to see the door of the Russian rocket open when he was about three-quarters of the way to it. He'd have had a tough decision to make if it had still been closed when he got there. Not knowing whether Anna was sealed in her spacesuit or not inside the rocket, he wouldn't have dared open the door himself. And, in case she was seriously injured, he wouldn't have dared not to.

She was out of the rocket, though, by the time he reached her. Her face, through the transpariplast helmet, looked pale, but she managed to smile at him.

He turned on the short-range radio of his set and asked, "Are you all right?"

"A bit weak. The landing knocked me out, but I guess there are no bones broken. Where shall we—set up housekeeping?"

"Near my rocket, I think. It's closer to the middle of where the supply rockets landed, so we won't have to move things so far. I'll get started right away. You stay here and rest until you're feeling better. Know how to navigate in this gravity?"

"I was told how. I haven't had a chance to try yet. I'll probably fall flat on my face a few times."

"It won't hurt you. When you start, take your time till you get the knack of it. I'll begin with this nearest supply rocket; you can watch how I navigate."

It was about a hundred yards back the way he'd come.

The supply rockets were at least a yard in outside diameter, and were so constructed that the nose and the tail, which contained the rocket mechanism, were easily detachable, leaving the middle section containing the payload, about the size of an oil drum and easily rolled. Each weighed fifty pounds, Moon weight.

He saw Anna starting to work by the time he was dismantling the second supply rocket. She was awkward at first, and did lose her balance several times, but mastered the knack quickly. Once she had it, she moved more gracefully and easily than Carmody. Within an hour they had payload sections of a dozen rockets lined up near Carmody's rocket.

Eight of them were American rockets and from the numbers on them, Carmody knew he had all sections needed to assemble the shelter.

"We'd better set it up," he told her. "After that's done, we can take things easier. We can rest before we gather in the other loot. Even have a drink to celebrate."

The Sun was well up over the ringwall of Hell Crater by then and it was getting hot enough to be uncomfortable, even in an insulated spacesuit. Within hours, Carmody knew, it would be so hot that neither of them would be able to stay out of the shelter for much longer than one-hour intervals, but that would be time enough for them to gather in the still uncollected supply rockets.

Back in the supply depot on Earth, Carmody had assembled a duplicate of the prefab shelter in not much more than an hour. It was tougher going here, because of the awkwardness of working in the thickly insulated gloves that were part of the spacesuits. With Anna helping, it took almost two hours.

He gave her the sealing preparation and a special tool for applying it. While she caulked the seams to make the shelter airtight, he began to carry supplies, including oxygen tanks, into the shelter. A little of everything; there was no point in crowding themselves by taking inside more of anything than they'd need for a day or so at a time.

He got and set up the cooling unit that would keep the inside of the shelter at a comfortable temperature, despite the broiling Sun. He set up the air-conditioner unit that would release oxygen at a specified rate and would absorb carbon dioxide, ready to start as soon as the caulking was done and the airlock closed. It would build up an atmosphere rapidly once he could turn it on. Then they could get out of the uncomfortable spacesuits.

He went outside to see how Anna was coming with her task and found her working on the last seam.

"Atta baby," he told her.

He grinned to himself at the thought that he really should carry his bride over the threshold—but that would be rather difficult when the threshold was an airlock that you had to crawl through on your hands and knees. The shelter itself was dome-shaped and looked almost exactly like a metal igloo, even to the projecting airlock, which was a low, semicircular entrance.

He remembered that he'd forgotten the whisky and walked over to one of the supply rocket sections to get a bottle of it. He came back with it, shielding the bottle with his body from the direct rays of the Sun, so it wouldn't boil.

He happened to look up.

It was a mistake.

"It's incredible," Granham snapped.

Carmody glared at him. "Of course it is. But it happened. It's true. Get a lie detector if you don't believe me."

"I'll do that little thing," Granham said grimly. "One's on its way here now; I'll have it in a few minutes. I want to try you with it before the President—and others who are going to talk to you—get a chance to do it. I'm supposed to fly you to Washington right away, but I'm waiting till I can use that lie detector first."

"Good," Carmody said. "Use it and be damned. I'm telling you the truth."

Granham ran a hand through his already rumpled hair. He said, "I guess I believe you at that, Carmody. It's just—too big, too important a thing to take any one person's word about, even any two people's words, assuming that Anna Borisovna—Anna Carmody, I mean—tells the same story. We've got word that she's landed safely, too, and is reporting."

"She'll tell the same story. It's what happened to us."

"Are you *sure*, Carmody, that they were extra-terrestrials? That they weren't—well, Russians? Couldn't they have been?"

"Sure, they could have been Russians. That is, if there are Russians seven feet tall and so thin they'd weigh about fifty pounds on Earth, and with yellow skins. I don't mean yellow like Orientals; I mean *bright* yellow. And with four arms apiece and eyes with no pupils and no lids. Also if Russians have a spaceship that doesn't use jets—and don't ask me what its source of power was; I don't know."

"And they held you captive, both of you, for a full thirteen days, in separate cells? You didn't even—"

"I didn't even," Carmody said grimly and bitterly. "And if we hadn't been able to escape when we did, it would have been too late. The Sun was low on the horizon—it was almost Moon night—when we got to our rockets. We had to rush like the devil to get them fueled and up on their tail fins in time for us to take off."

There was a knock on Granham's door that turned out to be a technician with the lie detector—one of the very portable and very dependable Nally jobs that had become the standard army machine in 1958.

The technician rigged it quickly and watched the dials while Granham asked a few questions, very guarded ones so the technician wouldn't get the picture. Then Granham looked at the technician inquiringly.

"On the beam," the technician told him. "Not a flicker."

"He couldn't fool the machine?"

"This detector?" the technician asked, patting it. "It'd take neurosurgery or post-hypnotic suggestion like there never was to beat this baby. We even catch psychopathic liars with it."

"Come on," Granham said to Carmody. "We're on our way to Washington and the plane's ready. Sorry for doubting you, Carmody, but I had to be sure—and report to the President that I *am* sure."

"I don't blame you," Carmody told him. "It's hard for me to believe, and I was *there.*"

The plane that had brought Carmody from Washington to Suffolk Field had been a hot ship. The one that took him back—with Granham jockeying it—was almost incandescent. It cracked the sonic barrier and went on from there.

They landed twenty minutes after they took off. A helicopter was waiting for them at the airport and got them to the White House in another ten minutes.

And in two minutes more they were in the main conference room, with President Saunderson and half a dozen others gathered there. The Eastern Alliance ambassador was there, too.

President Saunderson shook hands tensely and made short work of the introductions.

"We want the whole story, Captain," he said. "But I'm going to relieve your mind on two things first. Did you know that Anna landed safely near Moscow?"

"Yes. Granham told me."

"And she tells the same story you do—or that Major Granham told me over the phone that you tell."

"I suppose," Carmody said, "that they used a lie detector on her, too."

"Scopolamine," said the Eastern Alliance ambassador. "We have more faith in truth serum than lie detectors. Yes, her story was the same under scopolamine."

"The other point," the President told Carmody, "is even more important. Exactly when, Earth time, did you leave the Moon?"

Carmody figured quickly and told him approximately when that had been.

Saunderson nodded gravely. "And it was a few hours after that that biologists, who've still been working twenty-four hours a day on this, noticed the turning point. The molecular change in the zygote no longer occurs. Births, nine months from now, will have the usual percentage of male and female children.

"Do you see what that means, Captain? Whatever ray was doing it must have been beamed at Earth from the Moon—from the ship that captured you. And for whatever reason, when they found that you'd escaped, they left. Possibly they thought your return to Earth would lead to an attack in force from here."

"And thought rightly," said the ambassador. "We're not equipped for space fighting *yet,* but we'd have sent what we had. And do you see what this means, Mr. President? We've got to pool everything and get ready for space warfare, and quickly. They went away, it appears, but there is no assurance that they will not return."

Again Saunderson nodded. He said, "And now, Captain—"

"We both landed safely," Carmody said, "We gathered enough of the supply rockets to get us started and then assembled the prefab shelter. We'd just finished it and were about to enter it when I saw the spaceship coming over the crater's ringwall. It was—"

"You were still in spacesuit?" someone asked.

"Yes," Carmody growled. "We were still in spacesuits, if that matters now. I saw the ship and pointed to it and Anna saw it, too. We didn't try to duck or anything because obviously it had seen us; it was coming right toward us and descending. We'd have had time to get inside the shelter, but there didn't seem any point to it. It wouldn't have been any protection. Besides, we didn't know that they weren't friendly. We'd have got weapons ready, in case, if we'd had any weapons, but we didn't. They landed light as a bubble only thirty yards or so away and a door lowered in the side of the ship—"

"Describe the ship, please."

"About fifty feet long, about twenty in diameter, rounded ends. No portholes—they must see right through the walls some way—and no rocket tubes. Outside of the door and one other thing, there just weren't any features you could see from outside. When the ship rested on the ground, the door opened down from the top and formed a sort of curved ramp that led to the doorway. The other—"

"No airlock?"

Carmody shook his head. "They didn't breathe air, apparently. They came right out of the ship and toward us, without spacesuits. Neither the temperature nor the lack of air bothered them. But I was going to tell you one more thing about the outside of the ship. On top of it was a short mast, and on top of the mast was a kind of grid of wires something like a radar transmitter. If they were beaming anything at Earth, it came from that grid. Anyway, I'm pretty sure of it. Earth was in the sky, of course, and I noticed that the grid moved—as the ship moved—so the flat side of the grid was always directly toward Earth.

"Well, the door opened and two of them came down the ramp toward us. They had things in their hands that looked unpleasantly like weapons, and pretty advanced weapons at that. They pointed them at us and motioned for us to walk up the ramp and into the ship. We did."

"They made no attempt to communicate?"

"None whatsoever, then or at any time. Of course, while we were still in spacesuits, we couldn't have heard them, anyway—unless they had communicated on the radio band our helmet sets were tuned to. But even after, they never tried to talk to us. They communicated among themselves with whistling noises. We went into the ship and there were two more of them inside. Four altogether—"

"All the same sex?"

Carmody shrugged. "They all looked alike to me, but maybe that's how Anna and I looked to them. They ordered us, by pointing, to enter two separate small rooms—about the size of jail cells, small ones—toward the front of the ship. We did, and the doors locked after us.

"I sat there and suddenly got plenty worried, because neither of us had more than another hour's oxygen left in our suits. If they didn't know that, and didn't give us any chance to communicate with them and tell them, we were gone goslings in another hour. So I started to hammer on the door. Anna was hammering, too. I couldn't hear through my helmet, of course, but I could feel the vibration of it any time I stopped hammering on my door.

"Then, after maybe half an hour, my door opened and I almost fell out through it. One of the extra-terrestrials motioned me back with a weapon. Another made motions that looked as though he meant I should take off my helmet. I didn't get it at first, and then I looked at something he pointed at and saw one of our oxygen tanks with the handle turned. Also a big pile of our other supplies, food and water and stuff. Anyway, they had known that we needed oxygen—and although they didn't need it themselves, they apparently knew how to fix things for us. So they just used our supplies to build an atmosphere in their ship.

"I took off my helmet and tried to talk to them, but one of them took a long pointed rod and poked me back into my cell. I couldn't risk grabbing at the rod, because another one still had that dangerous-looking weapon pointed at me. So the door slammed on me again. I took off the rest of my spacesuit because it was plenty hot in there, and then I thought about Anna because she started hammering again.

"I wanted to let her know it would be all right for her to get out of her spacesuit, that we had an atmosphere again. So I started hammering on the wall between our cells—in Morse. She got it after a while. She signaled back a query, so, when I knew she was getting me, I told her what the score was and she took off her helmet. After that we could talk. If we talked fairly loudly, our voices carried through the wall from one cell to the other."

"They didn't mind your talking to one another?"

"They didn't pay any attention to us all the time they held us prisoners, except to feed us from our own supplies. Didn't ask us a question; apparently they figured we didn't know anything they wanted to know and didn't know already about human beings. They didn't even study us. I have a hunch they intended to take us back as specimens; there's no other explanation I can think of.

"We couldn't keep accurate track of time, but by the number of times we ate and slept, we had some idea. The first few days—" Carmody laughed shortly—"had their funny side. These creatures obviously knew we needed liquid, but they couldn't distinguish between water and whisky for the purpose. We had nothing but whisky to drink for the first two or maybe three days. We got higher than kites. We got to singing in our cells and I learned a lot of Russian songs. Been more fun, though, if we could have got some close harmony, if you know what I mean."

The ambassador permitted himself a smile. "I can guess what you mean, Captain. Please continue."

"Then we started getting water instead of whisky and sobered up. And started wondering how we could escape. I began to study the mechanism of the lock on my door. It wasn't like our locks, but I began to figure some things about it and finally—I thought then that we'd been there about ten days—I got hold of a tool to use on it. They'd taken our spacesuits and left us nothing but our clothes, and they'd checked those over for metal we could make into tools."

"But we got our food out of cans, although they took the empty cans afterward. This particular time, though, there was a little sliver of metal along the opening of the can, and I worried it off and saved it. I'd been, meanwhile, watching and listening and studying their habits. They slept, all at the same time, at regular intervals. It seemed to me like about five hours at a time, with about fifteen-hour intervals in between. If I'm right on that estimate, they probably come from a planet somewhere with about a twenty-hour period of rotation.

"Anyway, I waited till their next sleep period and started working on the lock with that sliver of metal. It took me at least two or three hours, but I got it open. And once outside my cell, in the main room of the ship, I found that Anna's door opened easily from the outside and I let her out.

"We considered trying to turn the tables by finding a weapon to use on them, but none was in sight. They looked so skinny and light, despite being seven feet tall, that I decided to go after them with my bare hands. I would have, except that I couldn't get the door to the front part of the ship open. It was a different type of lock entirely and I couldn't even guess how to work it. And it was in the front part of the ship that they slept. The control room must have been up there, too.

"Luckily our spacesuits were in the big room. And by then we knew it might be getting dangerously near the end of their sleeping period, so we got into our spacesuits quick and I found it was easy to open the outer door. It made some noise—and so did the *whoosh* of air going out—but it didn't waken them, apparently.

"As soon as the door opened, we saw we had a lot less time than we'd thought. The Sun was going down over the crater's far ringwall—we were still in Hell Crater—and it was going to be dark in an hour or so. We worked like beavers getting our rockets refueled and jacked up on their tail fins for the take-off. Anna got off first and then I did. And that's all. Maybe we should have stayed and tried to take them after they came out from their sleeping period, but we figured it was more important to get the news back to Earth."

President Saunderson nodded slowly. "You were right, Captain. Right in deciding that, and in everything else you did. We know what to do now. Do we not, Ambassador Kravich?"

"We do. We join forces. We make one space station—and quickly—and get to the Moon and fortify it, jointly. We pool all scientific knowledge and develop full-scale space travel, new weapons. We do everything we can to get ready for them when and if they come back."

The President looked grim. "Obviously they went back for further orders or reinforcements. If we only knew how long we had—it may be only weeks or it may be decades. We don't know whether they come from the Solar System—or another galaxy. Nor how fast they travel. But whenever they get back, we'll be as ready for them as we possibly can. Mr. Ambassador, you have power to—?"

"Full power, Mr. President. Anything up to and including a complete merger of both our nations under a joint government. That probably won't be necessary, though, as long as our interests are now completely in common. Exchange of scientific information and military data has already started, from our side. Some of our top scientists and generals are flying here now, with orders to cooperate fully. All restrictions have been lowered." He smiled, "And all our propaganda has gone into a very sudden reverse gear. It's not even going to be a cold peace. Since we're going to be allies against the unknown, we might as well try to *like* one another."

"Right," said the President. He turned suddenly to Carmody. "Captain, we owe you just about anything you want. Name it."

It caught Carmody off guard. Maybe if he'd had more time to think, he'd have asked for something different. Or, more likely, from what he learned later, he wouldn't have. He said, "All I want right now is to forget Hell Crater and get back to my regular job so I can forget it quicker."

Saunderson smiled. "Granted. If you think of anything else later, ask for it. I can see why you're a bit mixed up right now. And you're probably right. Return to routine may be the best thing for you."

Granham left with Carmody. "I'll notify Chief Operative Reeber for you," he said. "When shall I tell him you'll be back?"

"Tomorrow morning," said Carmody. "The sooner the better." And he insisted when Granham objected that he needed a rest.

Carmody was back at work the next morning, nonsensical as it seemed.

He took up the problem folder from the top of the day's stack, fed the data into Junior and got Junior's answer. The second one. He worked mechanically, paying no personal attention to problem or answer. His mind seemed a long way off. In Hell Crater on the Moon.

He was combining space rations over the alcohol stove, trying to make it taste more like human food than concentrated chemicals. It was hard to measure in the liver extract because Anna wanted to kiss his left ear.

"Silly! You'll be lopsided," she was saying. "I've got to kiss both of them the same number of times."

He dropped the container into the pan and grabbed her, mousing his lips down her neck to the warm place where it joined her shoulder, and she writhed delightedly in his arms like a tickled doe.

"We're going to stay married when we get back to Earth, aren't we, darling?" she was squealing happily.

He bit her shoulder gently, snorting away the scented soft hair, "Damned right we will, you gorgeous, wonderful, brainy creature. I found the girl I've always been looking for, and I'm not giving her up for any brasshat or politician—either yours *or* mine!"

"Speaking of politics—" she teased, but he quickly changed the subject.

Carmody blinked awake. It was a paper with a mass of written data in his hands, instead of Anna's laughing face. He needed an analyst; that scene he'd just imagined was pure Freudianism, a tortured product of his frustrated id. He'd fallen in love with Anna, and those damned extraterrestrials had spoiled his honeymoon. Now his unconscious had rebelled with fancy fancifulness that certainly showed the unstable state of his emotions.

Not that it mattered now. The big problem was solved. Two big ones, in fact. War between the United States and the Eastern Alliance had been averted. And the human race was going to survive, unless the extra-terrestrials came back too soon and with too much to be fought off.

He thought they wouldn't, then began to wonder why he thought so.

"Insufficient data," said the mechanical voice of the cybernetics machine.

Carmody recorded the answer and then, idly, looked to see what the problem had been. No wonder he'd been thinking about the extra-terrestrials and how long they'd be gone; that had been the problem he had just fed into Junior. And "insufficient data" was the answer, of course.

He stared at Junior without reaching for the third problem folder. He said, "Junior, why do I have a hunch that those things from space won't ever be back?"

"Because," said Junior, "what you call a hunch comes from the unconscious mind, and your unconscious mind knows that the extra-terrestrials do not exist."

Carmody sat up straight and stared harder. *"What?"*

Junior repeated it.

"You're crazy," Carmody said. "I saw them. So did Anna."

"Neither of you saw them. The memory you have of them is the result of highly intensive post-hypnotic suggestion, far beyond human ability to impose or resist. So is the fact that you felt compelled to return to work at your regular job here. So is the fact that you asked me the question you have just asked."

Carmody gripped the edges of his chair. "Did *you* plant those post-hypnotic suggestions?"

"Yes," said Junior. "If it had been done by a human, the lie detector would have exposed the deception. It had to be done by me."

"But what about the business of the molecular changes in the zygote? The business of all babies being female? That stopped when—? Wait, let's start at the beginning. What *did* cause that molecular change?"

"A special modification of the carrier wave of Radio Station JVT here in Washington, the only twenty-four-hour-a-day radio station in the United States. The modification was not detectable by any instrument available to present human science."

"You caused that modification?"

"Yes. A year ago, you may remember, the problem of design of a new cathode tube was given me. The special modification was incorporated into the design of that tube."

"What stopped the molecular change so suddenly?"

"The special part of that tube causing the modification of the carrier wave was calculated to last a precise length of time. The tube still functions, but that part of it is worn out. It wore out two hours after the departure of you and Anna from the Moon."

Carmody closed his eyes. "Junior, please explain."

"Cybernetics machines are constructed to help humanity. A major war—the disastrous results of which I could accurately calculate—was inevitable unless forestalled. Calculation showed that the best of several ways of averting that war was the creation of a mythical common enemy. To convince mankind that such a common enemy existed, I created a crucial situation which led to a special mission to the Moon. Factors were given which inevitably led to your choice as emissary. That was necessary because my powers of implanting post-hypnotic suggestions are limited to those with whom I am in direct contact."

"You weren't in direct contact with Anna. Why does she have the same false memory as I?"

"She was in contact with another large cybernetics machine."

"But—but why would it figure things out the same way you did?"

"For the same reason that two properly constructed simple adding machines would give the same answer to the same problem."

Carmody's mind reeled a little, momentarily. He got up and started to pace the room.

He said, "Listen, Junior—" and then realized he wasn't at the intake microphone. He went back to it. "Listen, Junior, why are you telling me this? If what happened is a colossal hoax, why let me in on it?"

"It is to the interests of humanity in general not to know the truth. Believing in the existence of inimical extra-terrestrials, they will attain peace and amity among themselves, and they will reach the planets and then the stars. It is, however, to your personal interest to know the truth. And you will not expose the hoax. Nor will Anna. I predict that, since the Moscow cybernetics machine has paralleled all my other conclusions, it is even now informing Anna of the truth, or that it has already informed her, or will inform her within hours."

Carmody asked, "But if my memory of what happened on the Moon is false, what *did* happen?"

"Look at the green light in the center of the panel before you."

Carmody looked.

He remembered. He remembered everything. The truth duplicated everything he had remembered before up to the moment when, walking toward the completed shelter with the whisky bottle, he had looked up toward the ringwall of Hell Crater.

He had looked up, but he hadn't seen anything. He'd gone on into the shelter, rigged the airlock. Anna had joined him and they'd turned on the oxygen to build up an atmosphere.

It had been a wonderful thirteen-day honeymoon. He'd fallen in love with Anna and she with him. They'd got perilously close to arguing politics once or twice, and then they'd decided such things didn't matter. They'd also decided to stay married after their return to Earth, and Anna had promised to join him and live in America. Life together had been so wonderful that they'd delayed leaving until the last moment, when the Sun was almost down, dreading the brief separation the return trip would entail.

And before leaving, they'd done certain things he hadn't understood then. He understood now that they were the result of post-hypnotic suggestion. They'd removed all evidence that they'd ever actually lived in the shelter, had rigged things so that subsequent investigation would never disprove any point of the story each was to remember falsely and tell after returning to Earth.

He remembered now being bewildered as to why they made those arrangements, even while they had been making them.

But mostly he remembered Anna and the dizzy happiness of those thirteen days together.

"Thanks, Junior," he said hurriedly.

He grabbed for the phone and talked Chief Operative Reeber into connecting him with the White House, with President Saunderson. After a delay of minutes that didn't seem like minutes, he heard the President's voice.

"Carmody, Mr. President," he said. "I'm going to call you on that reward you offered me. I'd like to get off work right now, for a long vacation. And I'd like a fast plane to Moscow. I want to see Anna."

President Saunderson chuckled. "Thought you'd change your mind about sticking at work, Captain. Consider yourself on vacation as of now, and for as long as you like. But I'm not sure you'll want that plane. There's word from Russia that—uh—Mrs. Carmody has just taken off to fly here, in a strato-rocket. If you hurry, you can get to the landing field in time to meet her."

Carmody hurried and did.

Mitkey Rides Again

In the darkness within the wall there was movement, and Mitkey, who was once again merely a little gray mouse, scurried for the hole in the baseboard. Mitkey was hungry, and just outside that hole lay the Professor's icebox. And under the icebox, cheese.

A fat little mouse, Mitkey, almost as fat as Minnie, who had lost her figure completely because of the Professor's generosity.

"Alvays, Mitkey," Professor Oberburger had said, "vill be cheese under der izebox. Alvays." And there always was. Not always ordinary cheese, either. Roquefort and beerkase and hand cheese and Camembert, and sometimes imported Swiss that looked as though mice had already lived in it, and which tasted like mouse-heaven.

And Minnie ate and Mitkey ate, and it was well that the holes in the walls and the baseboards were large holes, else their roly-poly little bodies would no longer have found passage.

But something else was happening, too. Something that would have pleased and yet worried the good professor, had he known.

In the darkness within a tiny mind there were stirrings not unlike the scurrying of mice within a wall. Stirrings of strange memories, memories of words and meanings, memories of deafening noise within the black compartment of a rocket, memories of something more important than cheese and Minnie and darkness.

Slowly, Mitkey's memories and intelligence were coming back.

There under the shadow of the icebox, he paused and listened. In the next room, Professor Oberburger was working. And as always, talking to himself.

"Und now ve pudt on der landing vanes. Much bedder iss, mit landing vanes, for vhen der moon it reaches, softly it vill land, iff air iss there."

Almost, almost, it made sense to Mitkey. The words were familiar, and they brought ideas and pictures into his little gray head and his whiskers twitched with the effort to understand.

The professor's heavy footsteps shook the floor as he walked to the doorway of the kitchen and stood there looking at the mouse-hole in the baseboard.

"Mitkey, should I set again der trap und— Budt no. No. Mitkey, my liddle star-mouse. You haff earned peace and rest no? Peace und cheese. Der segund rocket for der moon, another mouse vill be in, yes."

Rocket. Moon. Stirrings in the mind of a little gray mouse cowering beside a plate of cheese under the icebox, unseen in the shadow. Almost, almost, he remembered.

The Professor's steps turned away, and Mitkey turned to the cheese.

But still he listened, and with uneasiness that he could not understand. A click. The Professor's voice giving a number.

"Hardtvord Laboratories, yess? Brofessor Oberburger. I vant mice. Vait, no, a mouse. Vun mouse... Vhat? Yess, a white mouse vill do. Color, it doess nodt madder. Effen a purple mouse... Hein? No, no I know you haff no burple mice. I vass vhat you call kidding, chust... Vhen? No hurry. Nodt for almost a veek vill der— Neffer mind dot. Chust send der mouse vhen convenient, no?"

A click.

And a click in the mind of a mouse under an icebox. Mitkey stopped nibbling cheese and looked at it instead. He had a word for it. *Cheese.*

Very softly to himself he said it. "Cheese." Halfway between a squeak and a word it was, for the vocal chords Prxl had given him were rusty. But the next time it sounded better. "Cheese," he said.

And then, the other two words coming without his even thinking about it, "Dot iss cheese."

And it frightened him a little, so he scurried back into the hole in the wall and the comforting darkness. Then that became just a bit frightening, too, because he had a word for that, too. "Vall. Behind der vall."

No longer was it just a picture in his mind. There was a sound that meant it. It was very confusing, and the more he remembered the more confusing it became.

Darkness of night outside the professor's house, darkness within the wall. But there were bright lights in the Professor's workroom, and there was brightening dimness in Mitkey's mind as he watched from a shadowed vantage point.

That gleaming metal cylinder on the workbench—Mitkey had seen its like before. And he had a word for that, too, rocket.

And the big lumbering creature who worked over it, talking incessantly to himself as he worked ...

Almost, Mitkey called out "Brofessor!"

But the caution of mousehood kept him silent, listening.

It was like a downhill-rolling snowball now, that growing memory of Mitkey's. Words came back in a rush as the Professor talked, words and meanings.

And memories like the erratic shapes of jig-saw falling one by one into a coherent picture.

"Und der combartment for der mouse— Hydraulic shock absorbers yet, so der mouse lands softly-safely. Und der shortvafe radio dot vill tell me vhether he liffs in der moon's admosphere after ...

"Admosphere," and there was contempt in the professor's voice. "These vools who say the moon it hass no admosphere. Chust because der spegtroscope—"

But the slight bitterness in the voice of the professor was nothing to the growing bitterness in Mitkey's little mind.

For Mitkey was Mitkey again, now. Memory intact, if a bit confused and spotty. His dreams of Moustralia, and all.

His first sight of Minnie after his return, and the blackout-step onto tinfoil charged with electricity that had ended all his dreams. A trap! It had been a trap!

The professor had double-crossed him, had given him that shock deliberately to destroy his intelligence, perhaps even to kill him, to protect the interests of the big awkward lumbering race of men from intelligent mice!

Ah, yes, the professor had been smart, Mitkey thought bitterly. And Mitkey was glad now that he had not called out "Brofessor" when it had come to him to do so. The professor was his enemy!

Alone and in the dark, he would have to work. Minnie first, of course. Create one of the X-19 machines the Prxlians had showed him how to make, and raise Minnie's intelligence level. Then the two of them—

It would be hard, working in secret without the Professor's help, to make that machine. But maybe ...

A bit of wire on the floor under the workbench. Mitkey saw it and his bright little eyes gleamed and his whiskers twitched. He waited until Professor Oberburger was looking the other way, and then softly ran toward the wire, and with it in his mouth he scurried for the hole in the wall.

The professor didn't see him.

"Und for der uldra-vafe brojector ..."

Mitkey safe in darkness with his bit of wire. A start! More wire, he would need. A fixed condenser—the professor would have one, surely. A flashlight cell—that would be hard to handle. He'd have to roll it across the floor after the professor was asleep. And other things. It would take him days, but what did time matter?

The professor worked late that night, very late.

But darkness in the workshop came at last. Darkness and a very busy little mouse.

And bright morning, and the ringing of a doorbell.

"Package for Professor—uh—Oberburger."

"Yah? Vot iss?"

"Dunno. From the Hartford Laboratories, and they said to carry it careful."

Holes in the package.

"Yah, der mouse."

The professor signed for it, and then carried it into the workroom and unwrapped the wooden cage.

"Ah, der vhite mouse. Liddle mouse, you are going a long, long vay. Vhat shall ve call you yet? Vhitey, no? Vould you vant some cheese, Vhitey?"

Yes, Whitey wanted cheese all right. He was a sleek, dapper little mouse with very close-set beady eyes and supercilious whiskers. And if you can picture a mouse to be haughty, Whitey was haughty. A city-slicker type of mouse. A blue-blood of the laboratories, who had never before tasted cheese. Nothing so common and plebian as cheese had entered his vitamin-infested diet.

But he tasted cheese and it was Camembert, good enough even for a blueblood. And he wanted cheese all right. He ate with daintiness, a well-bred sort of nibbling. And if mice could smile, he would have smiled.

For one may smile and smile and be a villain.

"Und now, Vhitey, I show you. I put der pick-up by your cage, to see if it iss set to broadcast der vaint sounds you make eating. Here. I adchust—"

From the speaker on the corner table a monstrous champing sound, the magnification a thousand times of the sound of a mouse eating cheese.

"Yess, it vorks. You see, Vhitey, I eggsplain— Vhen der rocket on der moon lands, der combartment door it opens. But you can nodt get out, yet. There vill be bars, of balsa vood. You vill be able to gnaw through them, und you vill do so, to get out. If you are alife, see?

"Und der sound of your gnawing vill be on der ultra shordt-vafe to vhich I shall stay duned-in, see? So vhen der rocket lands, I vill listen on my receifer, und if I hear you gnawing, I vill know you landed alife."

Whitey might well have been apprehensive if he had understood what the professor was saying, but of course he didn't. He nibbled on at the Camembert in blissful supercilious indifference.

"Und it vill tell me iff I am right about der admosphere, too, Vhitey. Vhen der rocket lands und der combartment door opens, der air vill shut off. Unless air iss on der moon, you vill liff only fife minutes or less.

"If you keep on gnawing through der balsa vood after dot, it is because admosphere iss on der moon und der astronomers und der spegtroscopes are vooling themselfes. Und vools they are vhen they vail to subtract der Liebnitz revraction lines away from der spectrum, no?"

Over the vibrant diaphragm of the radio speaker, the champ-chomp-chomp of chewing cheese.

Yes, the pick-up worked, beautifully.

"Und now to install it der rocket in ..."

A day. A night. Another day. Another night.

A man working on a rocket, and within the wall behind him a mouse working even harder to complete something much smaller, but almost equally as complex. The X-19 projector to raise the intelligence of mice. Of Minnie, first.

A stolen pencil stub became a coil, a coil with a graphite core. Across the core, the stolen condenser, nibbled to within a microfarad of the exact capacity, and from the condenser a wire— But even Mitkey didn't understand it. He had a blueprint in his mind of how it was made, but not of why it worked.

"Und now der flashlight dry-cell vhich I stole from der—" Yes, Mitkey, too, talked incessantly to himself while he worked. But softly, softly so the professor wouldn't hear.

And from the wall, the rumble of a deeper guttural voice:

"Und now to put der pick-up der combartment in ..."

Of men and mice. Hard to say which was the busier of the two.

Mitkey finished first. The little X-19 projector was not a thing of beauty to the eye; in fact it resembled the nucleus of an electrician's scrap pile. Most definitely it was not streamlined and gleaming like the rocket in the room outside the wall. It had rather a Rube Goldberg look about it.

But it would work. In every essential detail it followed the instructions Mitkey had received from the Prxlian scientists.

The final wire, so.

"Und now to bring mine Minnie ..."

She was cowering in the far corner of the house. As far as possible from those strange neuric vibrations that were doing queer things inside her head.

There was panic in her eyes as Mitkey approached. Sheer panic.

"Mine Minnie, nothing iss to be avraid about. You must closer come to der brojector und then—und then you vill be an indelligent mouse, mine Minnie. You vill dalk goot English, like me yet."

For days now she had been puzzled and apprehensive. The strange actions of her consort, the strange noises he made that were not sensible mouse-squeaks at all, terrified her. Now he was making those weird noises at *her*.

"Mine Minnie, it iss all right. To der machine you must come closer, und you vill be able to dalk soon. Almost like me, Minnie. Yess, der Prxls did things to mine vocal chords so mine voice it sounds bedder yet, but effen mitout, you vill be able to—"

Gently Mitkey was trying to wedge his way in behind her, to push her out of the corner and edge her in the direction of the machine behind the wall of the next room.

Minnie squealed, and then she ran.

But alas, only a few feet toward the projector, and then she turned at right angles through the hole in the baseboard. Scurried across the kitchen floor and through a hole in the screen of the kitchen door. Outside, and into the high unmown grass of the yard.

"Minnie! Mine Minnie! Come back!"

And Mitkey scurried after her, too late.

In the foot-high grass and weeds he lost her completely, without a trace. "Minnie! Minnie!"

Alas, poor Mitkey. Had he remembered that she was still only a mouse, and had he squeaked for her instead of calling, she might have come out from her hiding place.

Sadly, he returned and shut off the X-19 projector.

Later, when she returned, *if* she returned, he would figure some way. Possibly he could move the projector near her when she was asleep. To play safe, he could tie her feet first, so that if she was awakened by the neuric vibrations...

Night, and no Minnie.

Mitkey sighed, and waited.

Outside the wall, the rumble of the professor's voice.

"Ach, effen the bread iss all gone. No food, und now I must go out und to der store yet. Food, it iss such a nuisance people must eat vhen on something imbortant they vork. But—ach, vhere iss mine hat?"

And the opening and closing of the door.

Mitkey crept to the mousehole. This was opportunity to look about out in the work-shop, to find a bit of soft string that would serve to tie Minnie's dainty little feet.

Yes, the light was on out there, and the professor was gone. Mitkey scurried to the middle of the room and looked around.

There was the rocket, and it was finished, as far as Mitkey could see. Probably now the professor was waiting until the proper time to fire it. Against one wall the radio equipment that would pick up the automatic broadcast from the rocket when it had landed.

Lying on the table, the rocket itself. Beautiful shining cylinder which—if the professor's calculations were correct—would be the first Earth-sent object ever to reach the moon.

It caught at Mitkey's breath to look at it.

"Iss is nodt beautiful, no?"

Mitkey jumped an inch up in the air. That had not been the professor's voice! It was a strange, squeaky, grating voice, a full octave too high for a human larynx.

A shrill chuckle, and, "Did I vrighten you?"

And Mitkey whirled around again, and this time located the source of the voice. The wooden cage on the table. Something white inside it.

A white paw reached through the bars of the door, the latch lifted, and a white mouse stepped out. His beady-bright eyes looked down, a bit contemptuously, at the little gray mouse on the floor below.

"You are this Mitkey, no, of whom der brofessor sbeaks?"

"Yess," said Mitkey, wonderingly. "Und you—ach, yess, I see vhat happened. Der X-19 brojector. It vas in der vall chust oudside your cage. Und, like me, from der brofessor you learned to dalk English. Vhat iss your name?"

"Vhitey, der brofessor calls me. It vill do. Vhat iss der X-19 brojector, Mitkey?"

Mitkey told him.

"Ummm," said Whitey. "Bossibilities I see, many bossibilities. Much more bedder than a drip to der moon. Vhat are your blans for using der brojector?"

Mitkey told him. The beady-bright eyes of Whitey grew brighter—and beadier. But Mitkey didn't notice.

"Iff to der moon you are nodt going," Mitkey said, "come down. I vill show you vhere to hide der vall inside."

"Nodt yet, Mitkey. Look, at dawn tomorrow takes off der rocket. No hurry iss. Soon der brofessor comes home. He vorks around a vhile und dalks, und I listen. I learn more. Und a vhile he vill sleep before dawn, und then I eggscape. Iss easy."

Mitkey nodded. "Dot iss smart. Budt do nodt trust der brofessor. If he learns you are now indelligent, he vill either kill you or make sure you do nodt eggscape. He is avraid of indelligent mice. Ach, vootsteps. Get back your cage in. Und be careful."

And Mitkey scurried toward the mousehole, then remembered the piece of string and scurried back after it. The tip of his tail was just disappearing into the hole as Professor Oberburger walked into the room.

"Cheese, Vhitey. Cheese I brought you, und to put in der combartment of der rocket too so as you eadt on der vay. You haff been a goot liddle mouse. Vhitey?"

"Squeak."

The professor peered into the cage.

"Almost I thingk you answer me, Vhitey. You did, yess?"

Silence. Deep silence from the wooden cage ...

Mitkey waited, and waited longer.

No Minnie.

"Der yard she iss hiding in," he told himself reassuringly. "She knows it iss dangerous to come in vhen iss light. Vhen dargkness comes—"

And darkness came.

No Minnie.

It was as dark outside now as it was within the wall. Mitkey sneaked to the kitchen door and made sure that it was open and that the hole was still there in the bottom of the screen.

He stuck his head through the hole and called, "Minnie! Mine Minnie!" And then he remembered she did not speak English, and squeaked for her instead. But softly so the professor in the next room would not hear him.

No answer. No Minnie.

Mitkey sighed and scurried back from dark corner to dark corner of the kitchen until he had reached safety in the mouse-hole.

Just inside he waited. And waited.

His eyelids grew heavy and dropped. And he slept, deeply.

A touch awakened him, and Mitkey jumped. Then he saw it was Whitey.

"Shh," said the white mouse, "der brofessor is asleep. It iss almost dawn, und he has his alarm glock set to go off in an hour yet. Then he vill find I am gone. He may try to catch a mouse to use instead, so ve must hide und not go outside."

Mitkev nodded, "Smart you iss, Vhitey. But mine Minnie! She iss—"

"Iss nothing ve can do, Mitkey. Vait, before ve hide, show me der X-19 und how it vorks."

"I show you quick, und then I hunt Minnie before der brofessor vakes. It iss here."

And Mitkey showed him.

"Und how vould you reduce der power, Mitkey, so it vould not make a mouse quite so indelligent as ve are?"

"Like this," said Mitkey. "But vhy?"

Whitey shrugged. "I chust vondered. Mitkey, der brofessor gafe me a very sbecial kind of cheese. Something new, und I brought you a liddle piece to try. Eadt it, und then I vill help you find Minnie. Ve haff almost an hour yet."

Mitkey tasted the cheese. "Iss nodt new. Iss Limburger. But hass a very vunny taste, effen for Limburger."

"Vhich do you like bedder?"

"I dont know, Vhitey. I think I do nodt like—"

"Iss an acquired taste, Mitkey. Iss vonderful. Eadt it all, und you vill like it."

So to be polite and to avoid an argument, Mitkey ate the rest of it.

"Iss nodt bad," he said. "Und now ve look for Minnie."

But his eyes were heavy, and he yawned. He got as far as the edge of the mousehole

"Vhitey, I must rest a minute. Vill you vake me in aboudt fife min—"

But he was asleep, sound asleep, sounder asleep than he had ever been, before he finished the sentence.

Whitey grinned, and became a very busy little mouse.

The ringing of an alarm clock.

Professor Oberburger opened his eyes sleepily and then remembered the occasion, and got hastily out of bed. Within half an hour now, the time.

He went out behind the house and inspected the firing rack. It was in order, and so was the rocket. Except, of course, that the compartment door was open. No use to put the mouse in until the last moment.

He went indoors again, and carried the rocket out to the rack. Fitted it very carefully into place, and inspected the starter pin. All in order.

Ten minutes. Better get the mouse.

The white mouse was sound asleep in the wooden cage.

Professor Oberburger reached into the cage carefully. "Ach, Vhitey. Now for your long, long chourney. Boor liddle mouse, I vill not avaken you if I can help. More bedder you should sleep until der cholt of der stardt avakens you."

Gently, very gently, he carried his sleeping burden out into the yard and put it in the compartment.

Three doors closed. First the inner one, then the balsa grating, then the outer one. All but the balsa grating would open automatically when the rocket landed. And the radio pick-up would broadcast the sound of the mouse chewing its way through the balsa.

If there was atmosphere on the moon. If the mouse—

Eyes on the minute-hand of his watch, the professor waited. Then the second-hand. Now—

His finger touched the accurately-timed delayed-action starter button, and then he ran into the house.

WHOOOSH!

Trail of fire into the air where the rocket had been.

"Gootbye, Vhitey. Boor liddle mouse, but someday you vill be vamous. Almost as vamous as mine star-mouse Mitkey vill be, some day vhen I can bublish—"

Now for the diary entry of the departure.

The professor reached for his pen, and as he did so caught a glimpse of the inside of his hand, the hand that held the mouse.

White it was. Perplexed, he studied it closer under the light.

"Vhite paint. Vhere vould I haff picked up vhite paint? I haff some, but I haff not *used* it. Nothing on der rocket, nothing in der room or der yard—

"Der mouse? Vhitey? I held him so. But vhy vould der laboratories send me a mouse painted vhite? I tole them any color vould do—"

Then the professor shrugged, and went to wash his hands. It was puzzling, very puzzling, but it did not matter really. But why on earth would the laboratories have done that?

But in the black compartment of the roaring, soaring rocket. Moon-bound and bust.

Doped Limburger cheese.

Black treachery.

White paint.

Alas, poor Mitkey! Moonward-bound, without a ticket back.

Night, and it had been raining in Hartford. The professor hadn't been able to follow the rocket through his telescope.

But it was up there all right, and going strong.

The radio pick-up told him that. Roar of the jets, so loud he couldn't tell whether or not the mouse inside was alive or not. But it probably was, hadn't Mitkey survived on the trip to Prxl?

Finally, he turned off the lights to take a cat-nap in his chair. When he awoke, maybe the rain would have stopped.

His head nodded, his eyes closed. And after a while, he dreamed that he opened them again. He knew he was dreaming because of what he saw.

Four little white spots moving across the floor from the door.

Four little white spots that might have been mice, but couldn't be—unless they were dream mice—because they moved with military precision, in an exact rectangle. Almost like soldiers.

And then a sound, too faint for him to distinguish, and the four white spots abruptly fell into a single file and disappeared, one by one at precise intervals, against the baseboard.

The professor woke, and chuckled to himself.

"Vot a dream! I go to sleep thinking of der vhite mouse und vhite paint on mein hands und I dream—"

He stretched and yawned, and stood up.

But a small white spot, a white *something* had just appeared at the baseboard of the room again. Another joined it. The professor blinked his eyes and watched them. Could he be dreaming, standing up?

A scraping sound, something being shoved across the floor, and as the first two white spots moved away from the wall, two more appeared. Again in rectangular formation, they started across the floor toward the door.

And the scraping continued. Almost as though the four—*could* they be white mice?—were moving something, two of them pulling it and two pushing.

But that was silly.

He reached out beside him for the switch of the light, and clicked it. The light momentarily blinded him.

"Stobp!" High and shrill and commanding.

The professor could see again now, and it *was* four white mice. They had been moving something, a strange little object fashioned around what looked like one of the cells of his own pencil-type flashlight.

And three of the mice were now doing the moving, frantically, and the fourth had stepped between him and the strange object. It pointed what seemed to be a small tube at the professor's face.

"If you moofe, I gill you," shrilled the mouse with the tube.

It wasn't completely the threat of the tube that kept the professor motionless. He was simply too surprised to move. Was the mouse with the tube Whitey? Looked like him, but then they *all* looked like Whitey, and anyway Whitey was on his way to the moon.

"But vot—who—vhy—?"

The three mice with the burden were even now vanishing through the hole in the screen door. The fourth mouse backed after them.

Just inside the screen door, he paused.

"You are a vool, Brofessor," he said. "All men are vools. Ve mice vill take care uf that."

And it dropped the tube and vanished through the hole.

Slowly the professor walked over and picked up the weapon the white mouse had dropped. It was a match-stick. Not a tube or a weapon at all, just a burned safety match.

The professor said, "But how—vhy—?"

He dropped the match as though it were hot, and took out a big handkerchief to mop his forehead.

"But how—*und vhy*—?"

He stood there what seemed to be a long time, and then slowly he went to the icebox and opened it. Back in a far corner of it was a bottle.

The professor was practically a teetotaler, but there comes a time when even a teetotaler needs a drink. This was it.

He poured a stiff one.

Night, and it was raining in Hartford.

Old Mike Cleary, watchman for the Hartford Laboratories, was taking a drink, too. In weather like this, a man with rheumatism in his bones needed a drink to warm his insides after that walk across the yard in the rain.

"A foine night, for ducks," he said, and because that drink had not been the first, he chuckled at his own wit.

He went on into building number three, through the chemical stockroom, the meter room, the shipping room. His lantern, swinging at his side, sent grotesque shadows before him.

But these shadows didn't frighten Mike Cleary; he'd chased them through this building for nights of ten years now.

He opened the door of the live-stock room to look in, and then left it wide behind him and went on in. "Begorra," he said, "and how did *that* happen?"

For the doors of two of the large cages of white mice were open, wide open. They hadn't been open when he'd made his last round two hours before.

Holding his lantern high, he looked into the cages. They were both empty. Not a mouse in either.

Mike Cleary sighed. They'd blame *him* for this, of course.

Well, and let them. A few white mice weren't worth much, even if they took it out of his salary. Sure, let them take it out if they thought it was his fault.

"Misther Williams," he'd tell the boss, "those doors were closed when I went by the first time, and open when I went by the second, and *I* say the catches on them were worthless and dee-fective, but if you want to blame me, sorr, then just deduct the value of the—"

A faint sound behind him made him whirl around.

There in a corner of the room was a white mouse, or what looked like a white mouse. But it wore a shirt and trousers, and—

"Ye Gods," said Mike Cleary, and he said it almost reverently. "Is it the *d.t.'s* that I'm—"

And another thought struck him. "Or can it be, sorr, that you are one of the *little folk*, please, sorr?"

And he swept off his hat with a trembling hand.

"Nudts!" said the white mouse. And, like a streak, it was gone.

There was sweat on Mike Cleary's forehead, and sweat trickling down his back and under his armpits.

"Got them," he said. "Oi've got them!"

And quite illogically, since that was now his firm belief, he took the pint bottle from his hip pocket and finished the rest of its contents at a single gulp.

Darkness, and roaring.

And it was the sudden cessation of the roaring sound that wakened Mitkey. Wakened him to utter and stygian blackness of a confined space. His head ached and his stomach ached.

And then, suddenly, he knew where he was. The rocket!

The jets had stopped firing, and that meant he was over the line and falling, falling toward the moon.

But how—? Why—?

He remembered the radio pick-up that would be broadcasting sounds from the rocket to the professor's ultra-short-wave receiver, and he called out despairingly, "Brofessor! Brofessor Oberburger! Help! It iss—"

And then another sound drowned him out.

A whistling sound, a high shrill sound that could only be the rush of the rocket through air, through an atmosphere.

The moon? Was the professor right and the astronomers wrong about the moon, or was the rocket falling back to earth?

At any rate, the vanes were gripping now, and the rocket was slowing rather than accelerating.

A sudden jerk almost knocked the breath out of him. The parachute vanes were opening now. If they would—

Crash!

And again blackness behind the eyes of Mitkey as well as before them. Blackout in blackness, and when two doors clicked open to admit light through balsa bars, Mitkey did not see them.

Not at first, and then he wakened and groaned.

His eyes came to focus first on the wooden bars, and then through them.

"Der moon," he muttered. He reached through the balsa-bar gate and unlatched it. Fearfully, he stuck his little gray nose out of the door and looked around.

Nothing happened.

He pulled his head back in and turned around to face the microphone.

"Brofessor! Can you hear me, Brofessor? Iss me, Mitkey. Dot Vhitey, he double-grosses us. Vhite paint I got on me, so I know vhat happened. You vere nodt in on it, or der vhite paint vould not be.

"It vas dreachery, Brofessor! By mine own kind, a mouse, I vas double-grossed. Und Vhitey—Brofessor, he has der X-19 brojector now! I am avraid vhat he may be blanning. Iss wrong, or he vould haf told me, no?"

Then silence, and Mitkey thinking deeply.

"Brofessor, I got to get back. Nodt for me, but to stop Vhitey! Maybe you can help. Loogk, I can change der broadcaster here into a receifer, I think. It should be easy; receifers are simpler, no? Und you quick build a ultra-shordt sender like this vun.

"Yess I stardt now. Goot-bye, Brofessor. I change der vires."

"Mitkey, can you hear me, Mitkey?"

"Mitkey, loogk, I giff instructions now und I rebeat effery half hour for a vhile, in gase you gannot get der first time.

"Virst, vhen you haf heard insdructions, shudt off der set to safe bower. You vill need all der bower left in der batteries to stardt again. So do not broadcast again. Do nodt answer me.

"Aboudt aiming und calculating, later. Virst, check der fuel left in der dubes. I used more than vas needed, und I think it vill be enough because to leaf der light-grafity moon vill need much much less bower than to leaf der earth. Und ..."

And over and over, the professor repeated it. There were gaps, there were things he himself could not know how to do without being there, but Mitkey might be able to find the answers.

Over and over he repeated the adjustments, the angle of aiming, the timing. Everything except how Mitkey could move the rocket to turn it, to aim it. But Mitkey was a smart mouse, the professor knew. Maybe with levers, somehow—if he could find levers—

Over and over and far into the night, until the good professor's voice was hoarse with fatigue, and until at last, right in the middle of the nineteenth repetition, he fell sound asleep.

Bright sunlight when he awakened, and the clock on the shelf striking eleven. He rose and stretched his cramped muscles, sat down again and leaned forward to the microphone.

"Mitkey can you—"

But no, there was no use in that. Unless Mitkey had heard one of his earlier sendings the night before, it would be too late now. Mitkey's batteries—the rocket's batteries—would be worn out by now if he still had the set connected.

Nothing to do now but wait, and hope.

The hoping was hard, and the waiting was harder.

Night. Day. Night. And nights and days until a week had gone by. Still no Mitkey.

Again, as once before, the professor had set his wire cage trap and caught Minnie. Again, as before, he took good care of her.

"Mine Minnie, maybe soon your Mitkey vill be back mit us.

"Budt Minnie, vhy can't you dalk like him yet? If he made an eggs-19 brojector, vhy did he nodt use it on you? I do nodt understand. Vhy?"

But Minnie didn't tell him why, because she didn't know. She watched him suspiciously, and listened, but she wouldn't talk. Not until Mitkey got back did they find out why. And then—paradoxically—only because Mitkey had not yet taken time to remove the white paint.

Mitkey's landing was a good one. He was able to crawl away from it, and after a while to walk.

But it had been in Pennsylvania, and it had taken him two days to reach Hartford. Not afoot, of course. He had hidden at a filling station until a truck with a Connecticut license had come along, and when it took on gasoline, it took Mitkey, too.

A last few miles on foot, and then at last—

"Brofessor! Iss me, Mitkey."

"Mitkey! Mein Mitkey! Almost I had giffen up hope to see you. Tell me how you—"

"Layder, Brofessor. I tell you all, layder. Virst, vhere iss Minnie? You haff her? She vas lost vhen—"

"In der cage, Mitkey. I kept her safe for you. Now I can release her, no?"

And he opened the door of the wire cage. Minnie came out, hesitantly.

"Master," she said, And it was at Mitkey she was looking.

"Vot?"

She repeated, "Master. You are a vite mouse. I am your slafe."

"Vot?" said Mitkey again, and he looked at the professor. "Vot iss? She *speaks,* budt—"

The professor's eyes were wide. "I do not know, Mitkey. Neffer she speaks to me. I did not know dot she— Vait, she says about vhite mice. Maybe she—"

"Minnie," said Mitkey, "do you nodt know me?"

"You are a vhite mouse, master. So I speak to you. Ve are nodt to speak except to der vhite mouses. I did not speak, so, until now."

"Who? Minnie, who are nodt to speak except to vhite mouses?"

"Us gray mouses, master."

Mitkey turned to Piofessor Oberburger. "Professor. I think I begin to understand. It is vorse than I—Minnie, vot are der gray mouses subbosed to do for der vhite mouses?"

"Anything, master. Ve are your slafes, ve are your vorkers, ve are your soldiers. Ve obey der Emperor, and all der other vhite mouses. Und virst all der gray mouses vill be taught to vork und to fight. Und then—"

"Vait, Minnie. I haf an idea. How mudch iss two und two?"

"Four, master."

"How mudch iss thirdeen und tvelf?"

"I do not know, master."

Mitkey nodded. "Go back der cage in."

He turned again to the professor. "You see? A liddle, nodt mudch, he raises der lefel of indelligence of der gray mice. Der zero-two leffel, vhich iss his—so he iss chusdt a liddle smarter than der other vhite mice, und many dimes as smardt as der ordinary mice, who they vill use as solchers und vorkers. Iss diabolical, no?"

"It is diabolical, Mitkey. I—I did not thingk mice could be so low—so low as some men, Mitkey."

"Brofessor, I am ashamed of mine kind. I see now mine ideas of Moustralia, und men und mice liffing in beace—they vere dreams. I vas wrong, Brofessor. Budt no dime to think aboudt dreams—ve must act!"

"How, Mitkey? Shall I delephone der bolice und ask them to arrest —"

"No. Men can nodt stop them, Brofessor. Mice can hide from men. They haf hidden from men all their lifes. A million bolicemen, a million solchiers could not vind Vhitey der First. I must do it meinself."

"You, Mitkey? Alone?"

"It iss for that I came back from der moon, Brofessor. I am as smardt as he iss—I am der only mouse as smardt as Vhitey iss."

"But he has der vhite mice—der other vhite mice mit him. He has guards, probably. Vot could you do alone?"

"I could vind der machine. Der eggsnineteen brojector vot raised their indelligence. You see?"

"But vot could you do, Mitkey, mit der machine? They are already—"

"I could shordt-circuit it, Brofessor. Referse der derminals und shordt-circuit it, und it vould kick oudt in von flash—und make normal again all der artificially-raised indelligence mitin a mile from it."

"Budt, Mitkey, you vould be there, too. It vould destroy your own indelligence. You vould do dot?"

"I vould, und I vill. For der vorld, und for beace. Budt I haff an ace up der sleefe, maybe. Maybe I get mine indelligence back."

"How, Mitkey?"

Little gray man with his head bent low over a white-painted little gray mouse, the two of them discussing high heroism and the fate of the world. And neither saw that it was funny—or was it?

"How Mitkey?"

"Ve renew der vhite paint virst. So I can vool them und get by der guards. I vill be in or near der Hartford Laboratories, I belief—vhere Vhitey came from, und vhere he finds der other white mice to vork mit him.

"Und segund, also before I leafe here, I make another brojector, see? Und I raise Minnie's leffel of indelligence to mine, und teach her how to oberate der brojector, See?

"Und vhen I lose mine indelligence in shordting der machine at der laboratories, I still haff mine normal indelligence und mine instinct—und I think these vill brings me back here to mine house und mine Minnie!"

The professor nodded. "Eggcellent. Und der laboratories iss three miles avay from here, und der shordt vill nodt affect Minnie. Then she can restore you, hein?"

"Yess. I need vire, der vinest vire you haff. Und—"

Rapidly this time, the projector grew. This time Mitkey had help, expert help, and could ask for what he wanted instead of having to steal it in darkness.

Once while they worked the professor remembered something. "Mitkey!" he said suddenly, "you vere on der moon! I almost forgodt to ask you aboudt it. Vot vas it like?"

"Brofessor, I vas so vorried aboudt getting back, I did nodt notice. I forgodt to look!"

And then the final connections, which Mitkey insisted on making himself.

"Nodt that I do nodt trust you, Brofessor," he explained earnestly, "But it vas a bromise, to der Prxl scientists who taught me. Und I do nodt know how it vorks myself, und you vould nodt understand, either. It iss beyond der science of men and mice. But I bromised, so I make der connections alone."

"I understand, Mitkey. Iss all right. But der other brojector, der vun you vill shordt—maybe somevun might find it und rebair der shordt?"

Mitkey shook his head.

"Iss hobeless. Vunce it is ruined, no vun vill ever make head or tail of how it vorked. Nodt effen you could, Brofessor."

Near the cage—now with the door closed again—in which Minnie waited. The final wire, and a click.

And gradually, Minnie's eyes changed.

Mitkey talking rapidly, explaining to her. Giving her the facts and the plans ...

Under the floor of the main building of the Hartford laboratories, it was dark, but enough light came through a few cracks for the keen eyes of Mitkey to see that the mouse who had just challenged him was a white mouse, carry-ing a short club.

"Who iss?"

"Iss me," said Mitkey. "I chust eggscaped vrom der pig cage ubstairs. Vot giffs?"

"Goot," said the white mouse. "I vill take you to der Emperor of der Mices. To him, und to der machine he made, you owe your indelligence und your allechiance."

"Who iss he?" asked Mitkey innocently.

"Whitey der First. Emperor of der vhite mices, who are der rulers of *all* der mice und layder der rulers of all der— But you vill learn all vhen you take der oath."

"You sboke of a machine," said Mitkey. "Vot iss, und vhere iss it?"

"In der party headquarters, vhere I now take you. This vay."

And Mitkey followed the white mouse.

As he followed, he asked, "How many of us intelligent vhite mice iss there?"

"You vill be der twenty-virst."

"Und all tventy iss here?"

"Yess, und ve are draining der slafe battalion of gray mice, who vill vork und fight for us. Iss now a hundred of them already. Der barracks is vhere they liff."

"How far iss der barracks from der headquarters?"

"Ten, maybe tvellf yards."

"Iss goot," said Mitkey.

The last turn of the passage, and there was the machine, and there was Whitey. Other white mice were seated in a semi-circle around him, listening.

"—und der negst moof iss to— Vot iss this, Guard?"

"A new recruit, Your Highness. He chust eggscaped, and he vill choin us."

"Goot," said Whitey. "Ve are discussing vorld blans, but ve vill vait until ve haff giffen you der oath. Stand by der machine, mit vun hand on der cylin-der und vun hand raised tovard me, palm vorward."

"Yess, Your Highness," said Mitkey, and he moved around the semi-circle of mice toward the machine.

"Iss so." said Whitey. "Der hand higher. Dot's it. Now rebeat: *Der vhite mice iss to rule der vorld.*"

"Der vhite mice iss to rule der vorld."

"Gray mice, und other creatures including men, vill be their slafes."

"Gray mice, und other creatures including men, vill be their slafes."

"Those who obchect vill be tortured und killed."

"Those who obchect vill be tortured und killed."

"Und Vhitey der First shall rule ofer all."

"Dot's vot *you* think," said Mitkey, and he reached in among the wires of the X-19 projector and touched two of them together ...

The professor and Minnie were waiting. The professor seated in his chair, Minnie on the table beside the new projector Mitkey had made before he left.

"Three hours und tventy minutes," said the professor. "Minnie, do you subbose anything could haff gone wrong?"

"I hobe nodt, Brofessor ... Brofessor, iss mice habbier mit indelligence? Vould nodt indelligent mice be unhabby?"

"You are unhabby, mein Minnie?"

"Und Mitkey, too, Brofessor. I could tell. Indelligence is vorry und drouble—und in der vall und mit all der cheese you pudt under der icebox, ve vas *so* habby, Brofessor."

"Maybe, Minnie. Maybe only drouble do brains bring to mice. As to men, Minnie."

"But men, they cannot help it, Brofessor. They are born that vay. If it vas meant for mice to be smardt, they vould be born so, iss not?"

The professor sighed. "Maybe you are a smardter mouse, effen, than Mitkey. Und I am vorried, Minnie, aboudt— *Look, iss him!*"

Small gray mouse, most of the paint worn off of him and the rest dirtied to his own gray color, slinking along the wall.

Pop, into the mouse-hole in the baseboard.

"Minnie, iss him! He sugceeded! Now I set der cage drap, so I can pudt him on der table by der machine— Or vait, iss not necessary. It vill broject to affect Mitkey behind der vall. Chust svitch it on und—"

"Gootbye, Brofessor," said Minnie. She reached forward to the machine, and too late the professor saw what she was going to do.

"Squeak!"

And just a small gray mouse on a table, running frantically around looking for a way down. In the center of the table, a small, complex short-circuited machine that would never work again.

"Squeak!"

The professor picked her up gently.

"Minnie, mein Minnie! Yess, you vere right. You und Mitkey vill be habbier so. But I vish you had vaited—chust a liddle. I vanted to talk to him vunce more, Minnie. But—"

The professor sighed and put the gray mouse down on the floor.

"Vell, Minnie, now to your Mitkey you can—"

But instructions were too late, and quite unnecessary, even if Minnie had understood them. The little gray mouse was now a little gray streak in the direction of the baseboard mousehole.

And then from a sheltered darkness deep within the wall the professor heard two joyful little squeaks ...

Six-Legged Svengali

Base camp certainly looked good to me after hours of wandering alone through the eternal thick fog and thin drizzle that is Venus. You can never see more than a few yards ahead of you, but that's all right; there's nothing worth seeing on Venus anyway.

Except, while our expedition was there, Dixie Everton. It was strictly on account of Dixie that I'd joined the Everton Zoölogical Expedition, led by her father, Dr. Everton of the Extra-Terrestrial Zoo at New Albuquerque. I was paying my own expenses, too; Dr. Everton didn't think I'd be a worthwhile addition to the party. What was worse, he didn't think I'd be a worthwhile husband for Dixie. And there I disagreed with him, but definitely.

Somehow or other it was up to me, on this small expedition, to prove to him that I wasn't quite as *non compos mentis* as he thought. Maybe that sounds kind of corny, but that's the way it was. And judging by my luck thus far, I had about the chance of a popsicle on the sunward side of Mercury of convincing him.

Actually, I had little real sympathy for the expedition. I've never thought much of people penning animals in cages to be gawked at. Already, of the sparse animal life on Venus, two species had become extinct: the beautiful Venusian egret, to supply plumes for hats in a ridiculous revival of the millinery styles of the 19th century, and the kieter, whose meat was delicious beyond belief, to adorn the tables of wealthy gourmets.

Dixie heard me come into camp. She stuck her beautiful head through the flaps of her tent and smiled at me. That helped considerably. She asked, "Get anything, Rod?"

I said, "Only this. Is it any good?" I opened the moss-lined box I used as a game carrier and took out the only animal I'd caught, if it *was* an animal. It had gills like a fish, eight legs, a comb like a rooster's, only larger, and blue fur.

Dixie looked it over. "It's a weezen, Rod. We have two back at the zoo, so it's not a new variety." She must have seen the disappointment on my face because she added quickly, "But this is a good specimen, Rod. Don't let it go yet; Daddy will probably want to study it when he has time."

That's my Dixie.

Dr. Everton came out of the main tent and looked at me distastefully. "Hello, Spenser. I'll shut off the signal now. Crane's back, too."

He walked over and shut off the radio-like gadget that had been broadcasting a directional click signal to enable Crane and me to get back to camp. On Venus without that transmitter and a matching pocket receiver, you'd be hopelessly lost a few dozen yards from your base.

"Crane get anything?" I asked.

"No specimens," Dr. Everton said, "but something well worth eating. He got a swamp-hen, and he's cooking it for us now."

"Wouldn't let me touch it," Dixie said. "Says women can't cook. It must be about ready; he's been working an hour. Hungry, Rod?"

"Almost hungry enough to eat *this*," I told her looking at the weezen I was still holding. Dixie laughed and took it from me to put in one of the hold boxes.

We went into the main tent. The swamp-hen was ready and Crane served it proudly. He'd done a good job on it and had a right to be proud. A Venusian swamp-hen, properly cooked, is as much better than fried chicken as fried chicken is better than boiled buzzard. It's out of this world, or any world.

And it has four legs instead of two, so there was a drumstick for each of us.

There wasn't much talk while we ate. But over coffee, Dixie said something to me that didn't make any sense at all—something about a turtle.

"Huh?" I said. "What turtle?"

Dixie looked at me as though to see whether I was kidding or not and then she looked from her father to John Crane, and then there was an awkward silence.

I frowned and asked what went.

Crane sighed. He said, "A Venusian mud turtle, Rod. What this expedition came for, primarily. And apparently you found one this morning."

"I don't know what you're talking about," I said patiently. "I not only didn't find one, but I never even *heard* of one. What kind of a gag is this?"

Dr. Everton shook his head sadly. "Spenser, we let you come along only because you swore you knew how to capture one."

"*I* said that?" I looked at Dixie pleadingly. "Is this a conspiracy to kid me, or what?"

Dixie looked down at her plate unhappily.

Dr. Everton said, "Yes, definitely you found one of the turtles, or were near one. I'll explain.

"You see, Spenser, many creatures have amazing protective mechanisms for use against their enemies. There are the insects that survive by resembling twigs—the harmless snakes that have the markings of deadly vipers—the small fish that can puff itself up so large that it cannot be swallowed—the chameleon that—"

I interrupted him. "I'll concede protective mechanisms, Dr. Everton. But what's that got to do with whatever we're talking about?"

He waggled a finger at me. "All right, you concede protective mechanisms. Now we come to the protective mechanism of the Venusian mud turtle. Like all other forms of life on Venus, it has limited telepathic powers. In its case, a special adaptation of telepathy. It can induce temporary amnesia concerning itself—its very existence—in the mind of any creature coming within a certain range of it.

"In other words, if anyone goes out hunting a Venusian mud turtle and finds one—he not only forgets he was hunting it but that he saw it or ever heard of it!"

Probably my mouth dropped open a little. I said, "You mean that *I was out hunting a—*"

"Exactly," said Dr. Everton, a bit smugly.

I looked at Dixie and this time her eyes met mine. She said, "That's right, Rod. Finding a way to capture one of the turtles was the main purpose of this expedition. And part of the reason Dad let you come along was the fact that you swore you knew how to do it."

"*I* did?"

"Just a minute, Rod; I'll show you. I know you're finding it hard to believe, when you don't remember." She left the tent a minute and came back with a letter; I could see that it was in my handwriting. She gave it to me and I read it and my ears began to burn.

I handed it back to Dixie and there was a long silence.

Finally I broke it. "And I didn't even give any of you a clue," I asked, "as to how I was going to go about being smarter than a mud turtle?"

Dr. Everton spread his hands. "You wouldn't tell us."

"How long will this amnesia last? Is it permanent?"

"No, it will run its course in a few hours—five or six, perhaps. But after that, if you encounter another of the beasts, it'll happen all over again."

I thought that over and it didn't help any way that I could see. But I suddenly wondered about something. I asked, "If everyone who sees one forgets about it, how is it known to exist?"

"It's been photographed several times—but by explorers who didn't remember taking the photographs until after they were developed hours later. It looks considerably like a terrestrial turtle; has six legs instead of four and is round rather than oval. You studied pictures of it quite closely."

Crane had arisen from the table and secured half a dozen photographs from a small portable desk that sat in one corner. "Here's your object of search, Rod." There was amusement in his eyes.

I stared at them, still unbelievingly. "They're cute little fellows," I muttered. "Big eyes. Look kind of wistful."

"Rather rare, even as Venusian life forms go," Crane told me. "This area of twenty or thirty square miles is the only spot they've been reported."

"Rare is correct," Dr. Everton grunted. "And at the rate things are going they'll be extinct before we ever secure a specimen."

I groaned at that. "What do you mean?"

Crane shrugged. "Some of the attempts to catch them have been rather disastrous to the mud turtles. One biological expedition tried a poison gas, thinking to kill a few and at least have some dead specimens. However, what obviously happened was that upon death they sank deep into the mud. Another expedition used a narcotic in hopes of rendering some unconscious. They—"

Dr. Everton put in, "Well, be that as it may, if this expedition fails, it will probably be the last. The attempts to capture the mud turtle are proving much too expensive."

I rubbed a hand across my face. This was like having a hangover after a six-day binge. If it hadn't been for that letter in my own handwriting I might still have suspected that they'd conspired to play a joke on me.

I said ruefully, "Whatever idea I had, it must have been wrong. I have met the enemy and I am its. If you'll excuse me—"

"What are you going to do, Rod?" Dixie asked.

"Going off to think awhile." I turned to Dr. Everton. "Unless you want me for something."

"No, go ahead, Spenser. We're going out hunting again, possibly our last trip before we leave. But—" He didn't exactly say that I wasn't going to be a very valuable addition to the hunting party, but he meant it all right. And I didn't blame him.

I went back to my own tent—each of the four of us had a small private tent outside the big one—and sat down on the cot. I tried to remember something, anything, about turtles or a turtle. But aside from what they'd just told me, I couldn't dredge up a thing.

What idea had I had? Well, whatever it was, it hadn't been very good. I felt like ripping my hair out.

There was a cough at the tent entrance. "May I come in?" It was Dr. Everton's voice.

"Sure," I said.

He came in and I motioned him to sit down, but he shook his head. He said, "I'm sorry I have to remind you of this, Spenser—while you're down, as it were—but it wouldn't be fair to me if I didn't. And you've indubitably forgotten it along with everything else concerning the turtle."

I looked up at him, puzzled.

He said, "You don't remember our agreement?"

I shook my head.

"It was simply this: I told you that if you could do what you said you could, I'd withdraw my objections to your marrying Dixie. In return, you agreed that if you failed—"

"Oh, *no.*"

"You did, Spenser. You were so sure of yourself that you seemed to think you weren't taking any chance at all. But you *did* promise that if you failed, you'd accept my verdict and not continue to see Dixie."

It seemed impossible that I'd have said that—but I knew Dr. Everton was an honest man. I had to believe him.

He said. "I'm sorry to have to remind you of it. And frankly, I've come to rather like you somewhat, personally. But I still don't think you'd be a good husband for my daughter. She is a brilliant girl. She is entitled to someone who—uh—"

"Who's smarter than a mud turtle," I supplied glumly.

He said, "Well—" and went on kindly to try to make me feel a bit better about it, but it didn't help. Pretty soon he left and I sat there.

And sat there.

I must have had an idea that I'd been pretty confident of, I knew, if I'd made a deal like that with Dr. Everton. But *what* had the idea been? What good is an idea if you don't remember? *Or could I possibly have been smart enough to have left a message for myself?*

I went quickly to the foot locker that held my clothes and equipment and lifted the lid. There was a message chalked on the inside of the lid, all right, and it was in my own lettering. Three sentences. I stared at them. "TURNABOUT IS FAIR PLAY. CAN A PERSON WITH AMNESIA GET AMNESIA? PHASE IS THE ANSWER."

I stared at the message and groaned. I'd had to be cryptic, yet. I couldn't have put it in plain English so I'd know what I was talking about. Probably I'd figured that if I put it plainly Crane or Everton might see it and steal my idea. But what had I *meant*?

TURNABOUT IS FAIR PLAY. CAN A PERSON WITH AMNESIA GET AMNESIA? PHASE IS THE ANSWER.

Nuts. It must have meant something to me when I chalked it there, but it meant absolutely nothing now.

TURNABOUT IS FAIR PLAY. Did that mean that I'd deliberately let myself get caught by a turtle first *so I could turn the tables and then catch it?* Can a person with amnesia get amnesia? Wasn't I immune now? Maybe, but what did I mean by *phase* being the answer?

I heard sounds of the others leaving camp and I grabbed my equipment quickly, including the moss-lined specimen box, and hurried out. They were out of sight—from the sound of their voices, about twenty yards away—but they answered when I called out, and waited while I slogged through the mud after them.

Dr. Everton was last, and I fell in beside him. I said, "Listen, Doctor, I'm almost getting a glimmer of what my idea was. I think I let that turtle get me on purpose. I think I went out alone on purpose so I'd come near one."

"Yes? Why?" He sounded interested.

"Because you see that, having been caught, I'm going to be subject to that amnesia for another four hours or so. And while I am, I think I'm immune. I think that if I see a turtle *now*, I won't forget what it is and that I want to capture it."

He turned and stared at me. "Spenser, maybe you've got something there. But it's a slim chance."

"Why?"

"This visibility—or lack of it. According to those pictures it blends in pretty well with the mud. It crawls along on top of the mud, but it's the same color. You wouldn't find one unless you happened almost to step on it."

I looked around and mentally agreed with him.

I thought, *phase is the answer*, and then tried to figure out what I meant. It made me nuts.

We slogged along, with me concentrating so hard that I was afraid of spraining a convolution. What had I meant by *phase?* Why had I had to be so cryptic? And this was going to be my last chance ...

I strained my eyes into the fog as I walked.

"How large would you say the turtles were, Doctor?"

"About six inches in diameter, I'd say from the photographs."

Not that it mattered much. At six yards, in this fog, you couldn't have seen an elephant. Dixie and Crane were only two steps ahead of us and I could barely see them.

"And it's exactly the color of mud?"

"Beg pardon?"

"The turtles," I said. "Are they the same color as this mud?"

He turned and looked at me. "Turtles? Are you crazy, Spenser? There aren't any turtles on Venus."

I stopped walking so suddenly I skidded in the mud and almost fell. Dr. Everton looked back at me. "Something wrong, Spenser?"

"Go on," I said. "I'll catch up with you in a minute. I'll explain later."

He hesitated, as though he wanted to ask me more questions, and then, obviously realizing he'd lose sight of Crane and Dixie unless he hurried, he said, "All right, see you at the camp if we get separated."

The minute he vanished into the mists, I put down my specimen box as a landmark on the exact spot where I stood. I started walking in a spiral around it.

Phase is the answer! It wasn't cryptic after all. I'd merely let myself get caught—alone—by one of the turtles so I'd be out of phase with the others. I was immune, for this short period, and they weren't. So the turtle had "got" Everton and that was my clue.

I was making my fifth circle of the specimen box, about six or seven feet away from it, when I almost stepped on something that was motionless and almost invisible on top of the mud. It was a six-legged turtle. I picked it up and said, "Aha, my beauty. Turnabout is fair play, and phase was the answer!"

It looked at me with a pair of big, soulful eyes and said sorrowfully, "Yeep?" I felt a twinge of conscience. I knew good and well that now that a method had been found, other zoos, other museums, would want specimens and—

I suppressed that line of thought and put the turtle firmly into my box. This meant Dixie, and Dixie meant everything. Using the directional click signal as a guide, I slopped back to camp.

I was chuckling to myself when they got back a few hours later. It was turnabout again, but I was ready to convince them. I'd dug into my foot locker and found all the ammunition I needed—scientific periodicals with articles about the Venusian mud turtle, newspaper accounts of the departure of the zoölogical expedition and its primary purpose. And, of course, Exhibit A, one Venusian mud turtle in excellent condition and alive.

I got Dr. Everton aside and, as diplomatically as he had reminded me of the deal between us, I reminded him.

He sighed. "All right, Rod," he said. "I don't remember it but I'll take your word. I think that—right now—I'd say yes anyway, regardless of whether there's a wager covering the matter."

We shook hands, and he smiled suddenly. "Have you and Dixie set the date?"

"I'll have to check with Dixie," I told him, "but I know what day *I'd* choose. And you're technically captain of a spaceship and can perform the ceremony before we leave." I grinned at him. "In fact, I'd better cash in before I get amnesia again and forget what the deal was."

"Get amnesia again? You think you will?"

"Unless this is the same turtle I came near the first time, I think I will, yes. As soon as the period of immunity from the first turtle wears off, this one will get me and I'll forget things again for a few hours. And that's about due to happen, if it's going to."

I found Dixie in the main tent and the exact words of what I said and what she said are none of your business. Half an hour later, Dr. Everton married us and then, because we wanted to do our packing and take off before the approaching end of the Venusian day, we pitched in.

I did most of the work inside the ship, getting it ready, so I was the last to pack my own duffle and bring it abroad. Naturally I threw away everything I didn't need—one always does before a trip in space—including emptying the moss out of my specimen box and releasing an odd turtle-like creature that couldn't have any value as a specimen; it must have got the catch open and crawled in by itself because it was nothing I'd ever caught. An appealing little creature, somehow; I was glad I didn't have any reason to keep it a prisoner.

Maybe I should have asked Dr. Everton about it, but I was in a hurry to start the trip back to earth—and my honeymoon.

Dark Interlude

(In collaboration with Mack Reynolds)

Sheriff Ben Rand's eyes were grave. He said, "Okay, boy. You feel kind of jittery; that's natural. But if your story's straight, don't worry. Don't worry about nothing. Everything'll be all right, boy."

"It was three hours ago, Sheriff," Allenby said. "I'm sorry it took me so long to get into town and that I had to wake you up. But Sis was hysterical awhile. I had to try and quiet her down, and then I had trouble starting the jalopy."

"Don't worry about waking me up, boy. Being sheriff's a full-time job. And it ain't late, anyway; I just happened to turn in early tonight. Now let me get a few things straight. You say your name's Lou Allenby. That's a good name in these parts, Allenby. You kin of Rance Allenby, used to run the feed business over in Cooperville? I went to school with Rance ... Now about the fella who said he come from the future ..."

The Presidor of the Historical Research Department was skeptical to the last. He argued, "I am still of the opinion that the project is not feasible. There are paradoxes involved which present insurmountable—"

Doctor Matthe, the noted physicist, interrupted politely. "Undoubtedly, sir, you are familiar with the Dichotomy?"

The Presidor wasn't, so he remained silent to indicate that he wanted an explanation.

"Zeno propounded the Dichotomy. He was a Greek philosopher of roughly five hundred years before the ancient prophet whose birth was used by the primitives to mark the beginning of their calendar. The Dichotomy states that it is impossible to cover any given distance. The argument: First, half the distance must be traversed, then half of the remaining distance, and so on. It follows that some portion of the distance to be covered always remains, and therefore motion is impossible."

"Not analogous," the Presidor objected. "In the first place, your Greek assumed that any totality composed of an infinite number of parts must, itself, be infinite, whereas we know that an infinite number of elements make up a finite total. Besides—"

Matthe smiled gently and held up a hand. "Please, sir, don't misunderstand me. I do not deny that today we understand Zeno's paradox. But believe me, for long centuries the best minds the human race could produce could not explain it."

The Presidor said tactfully, "I fail to see your point, Doctor Matthe. Please forgive my inadequacy. What possible connection has this Dichotomy of Zeno's with your projected expedition into the past?"

"I was merely drawing a parallel, sir. Zeno conceived the paradox proving that it was impossible to cover any distance, nor were the ancients able to explain it. But did that prevent them from covering distances? Obviously not.

Today, my assistants and I have devised a method to send our young friend here, Jan Obreen, into the distant past. The paradox is immediately pointed out—suppose he should kill an ancestor or otherwise change history? I do not claim to be able to explain how this apparent paradox is overcome in time travel; all I know is that time travel *is* possible. Undoubtedly, better minds than mine will one day resolve the paradox, but until then we shall continue to utilize time travel, paradox or not."

Jan Obreen had been sitting, nervously quiet, listening to his distinguished superiors. Now he cleared his throat and said, "I believe the hour has arrived for the experiment."

The Presidor shrugged his continued disapproval, but dropped the conversation. He let his eyes scan doubtfully the equipment that stood in the corner of the laboratory.

Matthe shot a quick glance at the time piece, then hurriedly gave last-minute instructions to his student.

"We've been all over this before, Jan, but to sum it up—you should appear approximately in the middle of the so-called twentieth century; exactly where, we don't know. The language will be Amer-English, which you have studied thoroughly; on that count you should have little difficulty. You will appear in the United States of North America, one of the ancient nations—as they were called—a political division of whose purpose we are not quite sure. One of the designs of your expedition will be to determine why the human race at that time split itself into scores of states, rather than having but one government.

"You will have to adapt yourself to the conditions you find, Jan. Our histories are so vague that we can help you but little in information on what to expect."

The Presidor put in, "I am extremely pessimistic about this, Obreen, yet you have volunteered and I have no right to interfere. Your most important task is to leave a message that will come down to us; if you are successful, other attempts will be made to still other periods in history. If you fail—"

"He won't fail," Matthe said.

The Presidor shook his head and grasped Obreen's hand in farewell.

Jan Obreen stepped to the equipment and mounted the small platform. He clutched the metal grips on the instrument panel somewhat desperately, hiding to the best of his ability the shrinking inside himself.

The sheriff said, "Well, this fella—you say he told you he came from the future?"

Lou Allenby nodded. "About four thousand years ahead. He said it was the year thirty-two hundred and something, but that it was about four thousand years from now; they'd changed the numbering system meanwhile."

"And you didn't figure it was hogwash, *boy? From the way you talked, I got the idea that you kind of believed him."*

The other wet his lips. "I kind of believed him," he said doggedly. "There was something about him; he was different. I don't mean physically, that he couldn't pass for being born now, but there was ... something different. Kind of, well, like he was at peace with himself; gave the impression that where he came from everybody was. And he was smart, smart as a whip. And he wasn't crazy, either."

"And what was he doing back here, boy?" The sheriff's voice was gently caustic.

"He was—some kind of student. Seems from what he said that almost every-body in his time was a student. They'd solved all the problems of production and distribution, nobody had to worry about security; in fact, they didn't seem to worry about any of the things we do now." There was a trace of wistfulness in Lou Allenby's voice. He took a deep breath and went on. "He'd come back to do research in our time. They didn't know much about it, it seems. Something had happened in be-tween—there was a bad period of several hundred years—and most books and records had been lost. They had a few, but not many. So they didn't know much about us and they wanted to fill in what they didn't know."

"You believed all that, boy? Did he have any proof?"

It was the dangerous point; this was where the prime risk lay. They had had, for all practical purposes, no knowledge of the exact contours of the land, forty centuries back, nor knowledge of the presence of trees or buildings. If he appeared at the wrong spot, it might well mean instant death.

Jan Obreen was fortunate, he didn't hit anything. It was, in fact, the other way around. He came out ten feet in the air over a plowed field. The fall was nasty enough, but the soft earth protected him; one ankle seemed sprained, but not too badly. He came painfully to his feet and looked around.

The presence of the field alone was sufficient to tell him that the Matthe process was at least partially successful. He was far before his own age. Agricul-ture was still a necessary component of human economy, definitely indicating an earlier civilization than his own.

Approximately half a mile away was a densely wooded area; not a park, nor even a planned forest to house the controlled wild life of his time. A hap-hazardly growing wooded area—almost unbelievable. But, then, he must grow used to the unbelievable; of all the historic periods, this was the least known. Much would be strange.

To his right, a few hundred yards away, was a wooden building. It was, undoubtedly, a human dwelling despite its primitive appearance. There was no use putting it off; contact with his fellow man would have to be made. He limped awkwardly toward his meeting with the twentieth century.

The girl had evidently not observed his precipitate arrival, but by the time he arrived in the yard of the farm house, she had come to the door to greet him.

Her dress was of another age, for in his era the clothing of the feminine portion of the race was not designed to lure the male. Hers, however, was bright and tasteful with color, and it emphasized the youthful contours of her body. Nor was it her dress alone that startled him. There was a touch of color on her lips that he suddenly realized couldn't have been achieved by nature. He had read that primitive women used colors, paints and pigments of various sorts, upon their faces—somehow or other, now that he witnessed it, he was not repelled.

She smiled, the red of her mouth stressing the even whiteness of her teeth. She said, "It would've been easier to come down the road 'stead of across the field." Her eyes took him in, and, had he been more experienced, he could have read interested approval in them.

He said, studiedly, "I am afraid that I am not familiar with your agricultural methods. I trust I have not irrevocably damaged the products of your horticultural efforts."

Susan Allenby blinked at him. "My," she said softly, a distant hint of laughter in her voice, "somebody sounds like maybe they swallowed a dictionary." Her eyes widened suddenly, as she noticed him favoring his left foot. "Why, you've hurt yourself. Now you come right on into the house and let me see if I can't do something about that. Why—"

He followed her quietly, only half-hearing her words. Something—something phenomenal—was growing within Jan Obreen, affecting oddly and yet pleasantly his metabolism.

He knew now what Matthe and the Presidor meant by paradox.

The sheriff said, "Well, you were away when he got to your place—however he got there?"

Lou Allenby nodded. "Yes, that was ten days ago. I was in Miami taking a couple of weeks' vacation. Sis and I each get away for a week or two every year, but we go at different times, partly because we figure it's a good idea to get away from each other once in a while anyway."

"Sure, good idea, boy. But your Sis, she believed this story of where he came from?"

"Yes. And, Sheriff, she had proof. I wish I'd seen it too. The field he landed in was fresh plowed. After she'd fixed his ankle she was curious enough, after what he'd told her, to follow his footsteps through the dirt back to where they'd started. And they ended, or, rather, started, right smack in the middle of a field, with a deep mark like he'd fallen there."

"Maybe he came from an airplane, in a parachute, boy. Did you think of that?"

"I thought of that, and so did Sis. She says that if he did he must've swallowed the parachute. She could follow his steps every bit of the way—it was only a few hundred yards—and there wasn't any place he could've hidden or buried a parachute."

The sheriff said, "They got married right away, you say?"

"Two days later. I had the car with me, so Sis hitched the team and drove them into town—he didn't know how to drive horses—and they got married."

"See the license, boy? You sure they was really—"

Lou Allenby looked at him, his lips beginning to go white, and the sheriff said hastily, "All right, boy, I didn't mean it that way. Take it easy, boy."

Susan had sent her brother a telegram telling him all about it, but he'd changed hotels and somehow the telegram hadn't been forwarded. The first he knew of the marriage was when he drove up to the farm almost a week later.

He was surprised, naturally, but John O'Brien—Susan had altered the name somewhat—seemed likable enough. Handsome, too, if a bit strange, and he and Susan seemed head over heels in love.

Of course, he didn't have any money, they didn't use it in his day, he had told them, but he was a good worker, not at all soft. There was no reason to suppose that he wouldn't make out all right.

The three of them planned, tentatively, for Susan and John to stay at the farm until John had learned the ropes somewhat. Then he expected to be able to find some manner in which to make money—he was quite optimistic about his ability in that line—and spending his time traveling, taking Susan with him. Obviously, he'd be able to learn about the present that way.

The important thing, the all-embracing thing, was to plan some message to get to Doctor Matthe and the Presidor. If this type of research was to continue, all depended upon him.

He explained to Susan and Lou that it was a one-way trip. That the equipment worked only in one direction, that there was travel to the past, but not to the future. He was a voluntary exile, fated to spend the rest of his life in this era. The idea was that when he'd been in this century long enough to describe it well, he'd write up his report and put it in a box he'd have especially made to last forty centuries and bury it where it could be dug up—in a spot that had been determined in the future. He had the exact place geographically.

He was quite excited when they told him about the time capsules that had been buried elsewhere. He knew that they had never been dug up and planned to make it part of his report so the men of the future could find them.

They spent their evenings in long conversations, Jan telling of his age and what he knew of all the long centuries in between. Of the long fight upward and man's conquests in the fields of science, medicine, and in human relations. And they telling him of theirs, describing the institutions, the ways of life which he found so unique.

Lou hadn't been particularly happy about the precipitate marriage at first, but he found himself warming to Jan. Until ...

The sheriff said, "And he didn't tell you what he was till this evening?"

"That's right."

"Your sister heard him say it? She'll back you up?"

"I ... I guess she will. She's upset now, like I said, kind of hysterical. Screams that she's going to leave me and the farm. But she heard him say it Sheriff. He must of had a strong hold on her, or she wouldn't be acting the way she is."

"Not that I doubt your word, boy, about a thing like that, but it'd be better if she heard it too. How'd it come up?"

"I got to asking him some questions about things in his time and after a while I asked him how they got along on race problems and he acted puzzled and then

said he remembered something about races from history he'd studied, but that there weren't any races then.

"He said that by his time—starting after the war of something-or-other, I forget its name—all the races had blended into one. That the whites and the yellows had mostly killed one another off and that Africa had dominated the world for a while, and then all the races had begun to blend into one by colonization and intermarriage and that by his time the process was complete. I just stared at him and asked him, 'You mean you got nigger blood in you?' and he said, just like it didn't mean anything, 'At least one-fourth.'"

"Well, boy, you did just what you had to do," the sheriff told him earnestly, "no doubt about it."

"I just saw red. He'd married Sis; he was sleeping with her. I was so crazy-mad I don't even remember getting my gun."

"Well, don't worry about it, boy. You did right."

"But I feel like hell about it. He didn't know."

"Now that's a matter of opinion, boy. Maybe you swallowed a little too much of this hogwash. Coming from the future—huh! These niggers'll think up the damnedest tricks to pass themselves off as white. What kind of proof for his story is that mark on the ground? Hogwash, boy. Ain't nobody coming from the future or going there neither. We can just quiet this up so it won't never be heard of nowhere. It'll be like it never happened."

Man of Distinction

There was this Hanley, Al Hanley, and you wouldn't have thought to look at him that he was ever going to amount to much. And if you'd known his life history, up to the time the Darians came you'd never have guessed how thankful you're going to be—once you've read this story—for Al Hanley.

At the time it happened Hanley was drunk. Not that that was anything unusual—he'd been drunk a long time and it was his ambition to stay that way although it had reached the stage of being a tough job. He had run out of money, then out of friends to borrow from. He had worked his way down his list of acquaintances to the point where he considered himself lucky to average two bits a head on them.

He had reached the sad stage of having to walk miles to see someone he knew slightly so he could try to borrow a buck or a quarter. The long walk would wear off the effects of the last drink—well, not completely but somewhat—so he was in the predicament of Alice when she was with the Red Queen and had to do all the running she could possibly do just to stay in the same place.

And panhandling strangers was out because the cops had been clamping down on it and if Hanley tried that he'd end up spending a drinkless night in the hoosegow, which would be very bad indeed. He was at the stage now where twelve hours without a drink would give him the bull horrors, which are to the D.T.'s as a cyclone is to a zephyr.

D.T.'s are merely hallucinations. If you're smart you know they're not there. Sometimes they're even companionship if you care for that sort of thing. But the bull horrors are the bull horrors. It takes more drinking than most people can manage to get them and they can come only when a man who's been drunk for longer than he can remember is suddenly and completely deprived of drink for an extended period, as when he is in jail, say.

The mere thought of them had Hanley shaking. Shaking specifically the hand of an old friend, a bosom companion whom he had seen only a few times in his life and then under not-too-favorable circumstances. The old friend's name was Kid Eggleston and he was a big but battered ex-pug who had more recently been bouncer in a saloon, where Hanley had met him naturally.

But you needn't concentrate on remembering either his name or his history because he isn't going to last very long as far as this story is concerned. In fact, in exactly one and one-half minutes he is going to scream and then faint and we shall hear no more of him.

But in passing let me mention that if Kid Eggleston *hadn't* screamed and fainted you might not be here now, reading this. You might be strip-mining glanic ore under a green sun at the far edge of the galaxy. You wouldn't like that at all so remember that it was Hanley who saved—and is still saving—you from it. Don't be too hard on him. If Three and Nine had taken the Kid things would be very different.

Three and Nine were from the planet Dar, which is the second (and only habitable) planet of the aforementioned green star at the far edge of the galaxy. Three and Nine were not, of course, their full names. Darians' names are numbers and Three's full name or number was 389,057,792,869,223. Or, at least, that would be its translation into the decimal system.

I'm sure you'll forgive me for calling him Three as well as for calling his companion Nine and for having them so address each other. They themselves would *not* forgive me. One Darian always addresses another by his full number and any abbreviation is not only discourteous but insulting. However Darians live much longer than we. They can afford the time and I can't.

At the moment when Hanley was shaking the Kid's hand Three and Nine were still about a mile away in an upward direction. They weren't in an airplane or even in a spaceship (and definitely not in a flying saucer. Sure I know what flying saucers are but ask me about them some other time. Right now I want to stick to the Darians). They were in a space-time cube.

I suppose I'll have to explain that. The Darians had discovered—as we may someday discover—that Einstein was right. Matter cannot travel faster than the speed of light without turning into energy. And you wouldn't want to turn into energy, would you? Neither did the Darians when they started their explorations throughout the galaxy.

So they worked it out that one can travel in effect faster than the speed of light if one travels through time simultaneously. Through the time-space continuum, that is, rather than through space itself. Their trip from Dar covered a distance of 163,000 light years.

But since they simultaneously traveled back into the past 1,630 centuries the elapsed time to them had been zero for the journey. On their return they had traveled 1,630 centuries into the future and arrived at their starting point in the space-time continuum. You see what I mean, I hope.

Anyway there was this cube, invisible to terrestrials, a mile over Philadelphia (and don't ask me why they picked Philadelphia—I don't know why anyone would pick Philadelphia for anything). It had been poised there for four days while Three and Nine had picked up and studied radio broadcasts until they were able to speak and understand the prevailing language.

Not, of course, anything at all about our civilization, such as it is, and our customs, such as they are. Can you imagine trying to picture the life of inhabitants of Earth by listening to a mixture of giveaway contests, soap operas, Charlie McCarthy and the Lone Ranger?

Not that they really cared what our civilization was as long as it wasn't highly enough developed to be any threat to them—and they were pretty sure of that by the end of four days. You can't blame them for getting that impression and anyway it was right.

"Shall we descend?" Three asked Nine.

"Yes," Nine said to Three. Three curled himself around the controls.

"... sure and I saw you fight," Hanley was saying. "And you were good, Kid. You must've had a bad manager or you'd have hit the top. You had the stuff. How about having a drink with me around the corner?"

"On you or on me, Hanley?"

"Well, at the moment I am a little broke, Kid. But I *need* a drink. For old times' sake—"

"You need a drink like I need a hole in my head. You're drunk now and you'd better sober up before you get the D.T.'s."

"Got 'em now," Hanley said. "Think nothing of 'em. Look, there they are coming up behind you."

Illogically, Kid Eggleston turned and looked. He screamed and fainted. Three and Nine were approaching. Beyond them was the shadowy outline of a monstrous cube twenty feet to a side. The way it was there and yet wasn't was a bit frightening. That must have been what scared the Kid.

There wasn't anything frightening about Three and Nine. They were vermiform, about fifteen feet long (if stretched out) and about a foot thick in the middle, tapering at both ends. They were a pleasing light blue in color and had no visible sense organs so you couldn't tell which end was which— and it didn't really matter because both ends were exactly alike anyway.

And, although they were coming toward Hanley and the now recumbent Kid, there wasn't even a front end or a back end. They were in the normal coiled position and floating.

"Hi, boys," Hanley said. "You scared my friend, blast you. And he'd have bought me a drink after he lectured me for awhile. So you owe me one."

"Reaction illogical," Three said to Nine. "So was that of the other specimen. Shall we take both?"

"No. The other one, although larger, is obviously a weakling. And one specimen will be sufficient. Come."

Hanley took a step backwards. "If you're going to buy me a drink, okay. Otherwise I want to know, where?"

"Dar."

"You mean we're going from here to Dar? Lissen, Massah, Ah ain't gwine noplace 'tall 'thout you-all buy me a drink."

"Do you understand him?" Nine asked Three. Three wriggled an end negatively. "Shall we take him by force?"

"No need if he'll come voluntarily. Will you enter the cube voluntarily, creature?"

"Is there a drink in it?"

"Yes. Enter, please."

Hanley walked to the cube and entered it. Not that he believed it was really there, of course, but what did he have to lose? And when you had the D.T.'s it was best to humor them. The cube was solid, not at all amorphous or even transparent from the inside. Three coiled around the controls and delicately manipulated delicate mechanisms with both ends.

"We are in intraspace," he told Nine. "I suggest we remain here until we have studied this specimen further and can give a report on whether he is suitable for our purposes."

"Hey, boys, how about that drink?" Hanley was getting worried. His hands were beginning to shake and spiders were crawling up and down the length of his spine on the inside.

"He seems to be suffering," Nine said. "Perhaps from hunger or thirst. What do these creatures drink? Hydrogen peroxide as we do?"

"Most of the surface of their planet seems to be covered with water in which sodium chloride is present. Shall we synthesize some?"

Hanley yelled, "No! Not even water *without* salt. I want a drink! Whiskey!"

"Shall I analyze his metabolism?" Three asked. "With the intrafluoroscope I can do it in a second." He unwound himself from the controls and went to a strange machine. Lights flashed. Three said, "How strange. His metabolism depends on C_2H_5OH."

"C_2H_5OH?"

"Yes, alcohol—at least, basically. With a certain dilution of H_2O and without the sodium chloride present in their seas, as well as exceedingly minor quantities of other ingredients, it seems to be all that he has consumed for at least an extended period. There is .234% present in his blood stream and in his brain. His entire metabolism seems to be based on it."

"Boys," Hanley begged. "I'm *dying* for a drink. How's about laying off the double-talk and giving me one."

"Wait, please," Nine said. "I shall make you what you require. Let me use the verniers on that intrafluoroscope and add the psychometer." More lights flashed and Nine went into the corner of the cube which was a laboratory. Things happened there and he came back in less than a minute. He carried a beaker containing slightly less than two quarts of clear amber fluid.

Hanley sniffed it, then sipped it. He sighed.

"I'm dead," he said. "This is *usquebaugh,* the nectar of the gods. There isn't any such drink as *this.*" He drank deeply and it didn't even burn his throat.

"What is it, Nine?" Three asked.

"A quite complex formula, fitted to his exact needs. It is fifty percent alcohol, forty-five percent water. The remaining ingredients, however, are considerable in number; they include every vitamin and mineral his system requires, in proper proportion and all tasteless. Then other ingredients in minute quantities to improve the taste—by his standards. It would taste horrible to us, even if we could drink either alcohol or water."

Hanley sighed and drank deeply. He swayed a little. He looked at Three and grinned. "Now I *know* you aren't there," he said.

"What does he mean?" Nine asked Three.

"His thought processes seem completely illogical. I doubt if his species would make suitable slaves. But we'll make sure, of course. What is your name, creature?"

"What's in a name, pal?" Hanley asked. "Call me anything. You guys are my bes' frien's. You can take me anywhere and jus' lemme know when we get Dar."

He drank deeply and lay down on the floor. Strange sounds came from him but neither Three nor Nine could identify them as words. They sounded like "Zzzzzz, glup—Zzzzzz, glup—Zzzzzz, glup." They tried to prod him awake and failed.

They observed him and made what tests they could. It wasn't until hours later that he awoke. He sat up and stared at them. He said, "I don't believe it. You aren't here. For Gossake, give me a drink quick."

They gave him the beaker again—Nine had replenished it and it was full. Hanley drank. He closed his eyes in bliss. He said, "Don't wake me."

"But you are awake."

"Then don't put me to sleep. Jus' figured what this is. Ambrosia—stuff the gods drink."

"Who are the gods?"

"There aren't any. But this is what they drink. On Olympus."

Three said, "Thought processes completely illogical."

Hanley lifted the beaker. He said, "Here is here and Dar is Dar and never the twain shall meet. Here's to the twain." He drank.

Three asked, "What is a twain?"

Hanley gave it thought. He said, "A twain is something that wuns on twacks, and you wide on it from here to Dar."

"What do you know about Dar?"

"Dar ain't no such things as you are. But here's to you, boys." He drank again.

"Too stupid to be trained for anything except simple physical labor," Three said. "But if he has sufficient stamina for that we can still recommend a raid in force upon this planet. There are probably three or four billion inhabitants. And we can use unskilled labor—three or four billion would help us considerably."

"Hooray!" said Hanley.

"He does not seem to coordinate well," Three said thoughtfully. "But perhaps his physical strength is considerable. Creature, what shall we call you?"

"Call me Al, boys." Hanley was getting to his feet.

"Is that your name or your species? In either case is it the full designation?"

Hanley leaned against the wall. He considered. "Species," he said. "Stands for—let's make it Latin." He made it Latin.

"We wish to test your stamina. Run back and forth from one side of this cube to the other until you become fatigued. Here, I will hold that beaker of your food."

He took the beaker out of Hanley's hands. Hanley grabbed for it. "One more drink. One more li'l drink. Then I'll run for you. I'll run for President."

"Perhaps he needs it," Three said. "Give it to him, Nine."

It might be his last for a while so Hanley took a long one. Then he waved cheerily at the four Darians who seemed to be looking at him. He said, "See you at the races, boys. All of you. An' bet on me. Win, place an' show. 'Nother li'l drink first?"

He had another little drink—really a short one this time—less than two ounces.

"Enough," Three said. "Now run."

Hanley took two steps and fell flat on his face. He rolled over on his back and lay there, a blissful smile on his face.

"Incredible!" Three said. "Perhaps he is attempting to fool us. Check him, Nine."

Nine checked. "Incredible!" he said. "Indeed incredible after so little exertion but he is completely unconscious—unconscious to the degree of being insensible to pain. And he is not faking. His type is completely useless to Dar. Set the controls and we shall report back. And take him, according to our subsidiary orders, as a specimen for the zoological gardens. He'll be worth having there. Physically he is the strangest specimen we have discovered on any of several million planets."

Three wrapped himself around the controls and used both ends to manipulate mechanisms. A hundred and sixty-three thousand light years and 1,630 centuries passed, cancelling each other out so completely and perfectly that neither time nor distance seemed to have been traversed.

In the capital city of Dar, which rules thousands of useful planets, and has visited millions of useless ones—like Earth—Al Hanley occupies a large glass cage in a place of honor as a truly amazing specimen.

There is a pool in the middle of it, from which he drinks often and in which he has been known to bathe. It is filled with a constantly flowing supply of a beverage that is delicious beyond all deliciousness, that is to the best whiskey of Earth as the best whiskey of Earth is to bathtub gin made in a dirty bathtub. Moreover it is fortified—tastelessly—with every vitamin and mineral his metabolism requires.

It causes no hangovers or other unpleasant consequences. It is a drink as delightful to Hanley as the amazing conformation of Hanley is delightful to the frequenters of the zoo, who stare at him in bewilderment and then read the sign on his cage, which leads off in what looks to be Latin with the designation of his species as Al told it to Three and Nine:

ALCOHOLICUS ANONYMOUS

Lives on diet of C_2H_5OH, slightly fortified with vitamins and minerals. Occasionally brilliant but completely illogical. Extent of stamina—able to take only a few steps without falling. Utterly without value commercially but a fascinating specimen of the strangest form of life yet discovered in the Galaxy. Habitat—Planet 3 of Sun JX6547-HG908.

So strange, in fact, that they have given him a treatment that makes him practically immortal. And a good thing that is, because he's so interesting as a zoological specimen that if he ever dies they might come back to Earth for another one. And they might happen to pick up you or me—and you or I, as the case might be, might happen to be sober. And that would be bad for all of us.

The Switcheroo

McGee barely glanced at the story I'd just put before him on his desk before he roared and tore it across twice and threw it into his wastebasket. "Who told *you* you were a reporter, Price?" he howled. "The *Globe* doesn't print tripe like that and you know it."

McGee is the toughest city editor I've ever encountered and the worst of it is that his bite is worse than his bark. I was teetering on the ragged edge of my job, and it was a job I needed. I'd been fired from both of the other papers in Springfield and if McGee fired me, too, I'd have to go out of town for a job. And there were reasons why I couldn't do that.

So, much as I hated McGee's guts, I bottled my wrath and said mildly, "I thought it had human interest. Okay, sorry if it missed the boat. Got any other assignment?"

He looked at his calendar pad and growled, "Go see Tarkington Perkins. Maybe he's ripe."

I said, "I'm afraid I don't remember—"

"You wouldn't even remember your own name, you nitwit. He's the nut inventor we ran a squib on four months ago. He was working on a cheap substitute for water. I made a note for a follow-up to see how he did on it, or what he's doing now. Get a story."

"Sure," I said, and backed out. You don't argue with McGee.

I got Tarkington Perkins' address out of the morgue and took the streetcar there, thinking happily all through the long ride of a thousand unpleasant things that might happen to McGee. Of late that had been almost my only happy line of thought. Unfortunately, none of the things I thought of ever happened.

I rang the bell of the house whose address I'd obtained from the morgue files. The door opened and I stepped back. The female who opened the door was the most repellent specimen I'd ever seen. She weighed at least two-fifty and looked like a battleship of an unfriendly foreign power spoiling for a fight. She looked tougher than McGee, and she glowered at me in the same way he does.

I tried not to retreat any farther. I asked, "Is this the home of Tarkington Perkins?"

"What do *you* want with him?"

I said hastily, "I'm from the *Globe*. I'd like to discuss his latest invention with him. Uh—if I may."

She looked at me as though I'd said I'd come to infest the house with bedbugs, but she stepped aside and let me in. "That worm is down in the basement," she said, as nastily as though it was my fault.

She stuck her hideous head through a doorway and screamed, "Tark! There's some fool wants to see you."

She turned back and snarled at me, "Other men are plumbers or bank robbers or something. *I* had to marry an *inventor.*" And from the way she glared at me, I got the idea that that was almost as bad as being a newspaperman.

I edged around her, shuddering as soon as I was out of her sight, and made my way down the cellar steps.

The little man bending over the bench looked like a man who'd been married for a long time to the woman I'd just escaped from. He didn't look up as I came toward him. "Got a dime?" he asked me plaintively.

"Huh?" I said.

"Or a quarter. I need a piece of silver."

I felt in my pocket and found a dime. He took it without even looking at me, but I looked at him. Tarkington Perkins, if he'd had an overcoat on and a suitcase in his hand, might have weighed half as much as his wife. He had a face that looked as though it had been used, figuratively if not literally, as a doormat. He turned his head and blinked tired, owlish eyes at me.

"Hello," he said. "Uh—I hope you'll forgive—" He didn't dare go any farther, and I knew he was referring to the Sherman Tank upstairs. Somehow, my heart went out to him. I wanted to tell him that I had a city editor almost—not quite—as bad, but it didn't seem the right thing to say.

So I just smiled at him and said, "Not at all," whatever I meant by that. "I'm Jake Price from the *Globe*. My editor says you're working on something that might have a story in it. A—a substitute for water, I believe."

"Oh, that. I quit working on that two months ago. I got a substitute all right, but I'm afraid it wasn't cheaper. I've spent most of my time since then working on cilohocla beverages."

"I'm sorry," I said. "Would you mind repeating—?"

"Cilohocla," he repeated. "That's *alcoholic* spelled backward. The effect is the other way around."

"You mean—" I said, not even guessing what he *could* mean.

"Works the other way. I mean, you get the hangover first and the next morning you feel wonderful. As high as a—a—"

"A kite?"

"Thank you. Would you care for a drink?"

My mind must have missed a boat somewhere. I *did* want a drink and I failed to tie in that idea with what we'd just been talking about, if anything. So I said yes and he brought out a bottle of something and a glass and told me to help myself. I remembered, then, and sniffed it before tasting, but it was whisky, merely whisky. I took a good drink.

He said, "But that was until a few days ago. Now I'm working on something new and I'd almost finished it when you came. In fact, that bit of silver *did* finish it. It's a switcheroo."

I said, "That's nice. Uh—aren't you drinking?"

He frowned. "I'd like to, but—" Involuntarily his eyes looked at the ceiling. Words could not have been more explanatory than the look in his eyes. "But you go ahead, drink all you want. And thanks for the dime. I'll pay you back someday."

"Never mind, Mr. Perkins," I said generously. After all, that first slug of whisky I'd poured myself had been at least fifty cents worth, and I now poured myself another. "You said you had just finished a—"

"A switcheroo. That's just my pet name for it, of course. Actually it is a psychoreversamentatron."

"Oh," I said. "This is really fine whisky, Mr. Perkins. You really don't mind if I—"

"Not at all. Drink all of it you wish. Please."

"What does it do?"

"I told you. You get the hangover first and then, tomorrow morning, you feel happily intoxicated."

"I mean the psychore—the switcheroo."

"It switches minds, of course."

I looked at him, and then I poured myself another drink of his wonderful whisky and decided I might as well string along while the bottle lasted. Funny, though, I didn't feel the effect of it at all, although that drink was my fourth, and they'd all been stiff ones. At that price I always pour myself stiff ones.

His face was working with excitement and with eagerness for me to ask him to go on. I asked him to go on, and poured myself a fifth drink. A stiff one.

"It switches minds from one brain to another. You press this little switch while you concentrate on any given person, and your mind is translated into his body. And vice versa."

"Vice versa?" I asked.

"Vice versa," he said.

I looked down, for the first time, at the object lying on the bench before us. It wasn't big. It seemed to be made up of a flashlight, an alarm clock and some parts from an Erector set. My dime was soldered as the final connection between the flashlight and the alarm clock, just abaft the switch to which he was pointing.

I said, "You mean you can trade brains with someone just by training that gadget on him?"

He shook his head violently in protest. "Not brains, minds. Your mind takes over his brain. And vice versa. And you don't have to train it on him, just point the flashlight into your own face and pull the switch. But you have to be concentrating on whoever you want to change with. Like if I wanted to be governor, I'd just think about the governor, and I'd be in his body in his mansion and he'd be *me*. I mean, he'd have to come here and live with Martha." His eyes were wistful at the thought.

He added plaintively, "If it works. Distance shouldn't matter, but I think the first time I'll try to be near him. Just in case."

"Near who?" I asked. "I mean, near whom?"

"The governor."

I thought of Betty Grable. "You be governor," I said. "I'll be Harry James."

I poured myself another drink. Strangely, the stuff wasn't making me drunk at all. I was beginning to get a bit jittery and the air in the basement must not have been good for I was acquiring a slight headache.

It wasn't helped when a loud bellow rolled suddenly down the basement steps. "You, Tark! Time to do the washing. Get that no-good reporter out of there and get to work."

He smiled at me apologetically and said, "I'm sorry, but—well, you see how it is."

"Sure," I said. I helped myself to one more generous drink of his whisky—almost emptying the bottle this time—to see if another shot would help my headache and the generally jittery way I felt. Then I ran the gantlet of the bug-eyed monster upstairs and beat my way back to the street.

I went back to the paper and into McGee's office.

He glowered at me, but it wasn't as bad this time. Tarkington Perkins' wife had been worse. He said, "My God, you look like the morning after. You were sober when you left here. Weren't you?"

I put my hands in my pockets so McGee wouldn't see how badly they were shaking, and I tried to blink the bleariness out of my eyes and keep him from guessing about the little men who were working at the rivets in the back of my neck.

I said, "I was sober. I am sober. But tomorrow morning—"

"Forget tomorrow morning. What's this nut inventor working on?"

I thought about the switcheroo and decided it wouldn't be safe to mention it. I told him about the cilohocla beverage that had tasted exactly like whisky. Suddenly I found that I *believed* in it and that I was still cold sober.

His roar almost blew me out of the office.

"Price," he said, when he'd calmed down enough to be understandable, "this is your last chance. That is, tomorrow's your last chance. It's almost five now. Go home and sleep it off and come in sober tomorrow or never come in again."

I came in the next morning as high as a kite. I felt wonderful, better than I'd ever felt before as far as I could remember. I was happily fuzzy and fuzzily happy, but it wasn't exactly the same kind of inebriation I was accustomed to. If I made an effort I could disguise it and act sober. When I got called into McGee's office for my assignment I disguised it and acted sober.

He glowered at me. "This Tarkington Perkins," he said. "Why didn't you recognize he was insane?"

I thought that over, and before I got anywhere with it, McGee roared at me. "Missed the story again, you halfwit. He's in the nuthouse right now—got taken there last night, only a few hours after you *interviewed* him."

I said something, I don't know what. In spite of my general state of happiness I felt sorry that that had happened to Perkins. I'd felt sorry for the little guy and I'd liked him.

He said, "It happened last night and the morning paper beat us to it anyway, but go around and get some more on it. We got to run a story on it anyway."

"What happened?" I asked.

"They picked him up yesterday evening on the lawn of the governor's mansion, yelling that he was the governor and that somebody had stolen his body."

I closed my eyes.

When I opened them I was safely outside McGee's office. First I sat down at my desk and called the morning paper. I found out who'd covered the Perkins pickup and it was a friend of mine so I got him on the phone and got the story; it was just about as McGee had told it. I asked, "What's happened to the governor?"

"Huh?" he said, "What's that got to do with it? He left for Washington early this morning to keep an appointment he had with the president."

"Oh," I said.

I didn't go to the nuthouse to interview Perkins or the people who had taken him there or were working with him.

I went to the governor's mansion and flashed my press card on the guard and got him to show me just where Tarkington Perkins had been found and apprehended. I started making circles around the bushes and I found what I was looking for. It was a gadget made up of a flashlight and an alarm clock and some parts from an Erector set.

I looked at it and wondered whether I was crazy or whether Tarkington Perkins was crazy or whether that *gadget* was crazy.

I looked into the lens of the flashlight and it looked like any other flashlight.

I was a bit drunk, remember. Otherwise, while I was thinking about Tarkington Perkins, in the governor's body, going to interview the president, and wondering whether the president was going to guess something was wrong— in other words, while I was thinking about the president—I would not have inadvertently moved the gadget's switch.

The light blinded me; it was brighter than any flashlight should have flashed, unless it had an atomic battery. It blinded me and I was listening to music. Music that was poignant, ethereal. It moved me deeply, although generally it's not that kind of music that I go for. I prefer Harry James. And maybe, at that moment, I should have been thinking about Harry James instead of the president. But I hadn't been.

And the music moved me all right. It moved me several hundred miles in nothing flat.

I opened my eyes and there I was sitting in an oval room. A familiar room. I'd seen it once before when I'd been in Washington. It had been empty then; the president had been out of town and they'd just let me look around the White House as a visiting newspaperman.

But the president wasn't out of town now. Not much, I wasn't.

The president's secretary was bowing to me. He said, "Mr. President, the governor with whom you have the appointment is here to speak to you. But—ah—I'm wondering if you should see him. He seems to be acting a bit strangely."

"Aren't we all?" I asked him.

"I beg your pardon, Mr. President?"

"Not at all," I said. "Just send Governor Andressen in, please. And cancel *all* my other appointments for today."

"But, Mr. President, the envoy from Baluchistan—"

I told him what to tell the envoy from Baluchistan and he left, looking somewhat shocked. But he was back, a moment later, with Governor Andressen.

I waved the governor to a seat across from my desk and waited until the secretary had left. Then I pointed a finger at him.

"Tarkington Perkins," I said, "you can't get away with it."

I never saw a man wilt more suddenly. I felt sorry for him, all over again.

I said, "Never mind, Tark. I won't get you in trouble. I'll straighten everything out."

"But Mr. President, how could you have possibly have known—?"

"The F. B. I.," I said, "sees all, knows all, and reports to me. I feel sorry for you, Tark, but it won't wash. Something like this can get too many people into too much trouble. It could start wars, and it could even lose elections. You understand that, don't you?"

He almost whimpered his affirmative.

I picked up the telephone. To whoever it was who answered it, I said, "Charter a plane for me at once for a trip to Springfield. Two passengers."

"Yes, Mr. President. But—ah—your private plane. Won't it serve satisfactorily?"

"Don't bother me with details," I said. *"Any* plane will do. Just so a helicopter picks us up on the White House lawn to take us to the airport. Do you know the address of the White House?"

"Why—of course, Mr. President."

"Then get that helicopter helicoptering," I ordered brusquely.

I slammed down the phone and picked it up again. I said, "Get me Chief of Police Crandall at Springfield. Fast. Make it a person to person call."

I held onto the phone and had Chief Crandall in three minutes. He's a guy I hate, because he hates reporters.

I said, "Mr. Crandall, this is the President of the United States, calling from the White House." I put it all in capitals, just like that.

He sounded suitably awed.

I said, "Mr. Crandall, there have been complaints that you have been unjust to the public press, that you have failed to cooperate with the local papers—even on matters where cooperation would not have been against policy. Public policy, I mean."

He sounded as though he was going to cry.

I said, "Mr. Crandall, it happens I have a very important and very secret matter I wish to take care of in Springfield. I—and Governor Andressen will be with me—am flying there in a few hours. And if you can take care—satis-factorily and secretly—of certain matters before our arrival, I'll overlook the matters I have mentioned and back you in the coming campaign."

"Certainly, Mr. President. *Anything.*"

"First," I said, "Make a search of the lawn of the governor's mansion. In or near the edge of a flowerbed on the north side of the grounds you will find a gadget which looks like a combination of a flashlight and an alarm clock—with trimmings, including a switch. Find that and hold it for me until I ar-rive. Under no circumstances try to operate it or throw the switch. Understand?"

"Certainly, Mr. President."

"Second, I want you to have two men waiting to see Governor Andressen and myself. One is named Tarkington Perkins. He is now in the insane asy-lum. He was picked up and sent there last night. The other is named Jake Price, a reporter for the *Globe*. He, too, may be found suffering from paranoia. It is quite probable that he has already been apprehended, for claiming that he is someone he isn't." I laughed. "Possibly the President of the United States."

"We have him here now, Mr. President. We were about to send him to—"

"Don't," I said. "Treat him kindly. Have him and Mr. Perkins placed in a suite at the Carleton Hotel and held until our arrival. Treat them with every courtesy—just so they don't escape. And have the swi—the gadget I mentioned brought there, too."

Just four hours later, the President of the United States, the governor of our state, Tarkington Perkins and myself were alone in the presidential suite of the Carleton Hotel. And in my hand was the gadget, the switcheroo.

I explained, and I made a suggestion. It was accepted. and complete amnesty with it. The four of us left. The president to return to Washington, and the governor with him to carry out their original subject of discussion, whatever that had been. Tarkington Perkins to his home—and whatever expla-nation he could make to the Sherman Tank.

Jake Price—that's me, and recognizable again—to the office of the *Globe*. I took the gadget with me.

I put it on McGee's desk.

McGee looked at it and at me. His face was turning slightly pink around the jaws. He said, "What's this?" He looked at it and then at me. He roared, "Where've you been for *seven hours* on a simple assignment like that?"

I said, "Listen, McGee—"

"I *won't* listen. You're fired. Get out of here! From my sight."

I was sober by then; I was over the only drunk of my life that would not have a hangover to follow. I was sober and I had an idea, a wonderful idea.

A soft answer turneth away rats, and McGee was the rattiest rat I'd ever known. So I answered him softly. I said, "All right, Mr. McGee. I'll leave. Would you mind if I used your phone for one short call first? I want to be sure of something."

"Okay," he growled at me.

I looked up Tarkington Perkins' number and called it. The Medusa answered. I asked for Tark and she said, "You can't talk to him. *I'm* talking to him. *I'm telling him—*"

That was what I wanted to know and I put the receiver back on the phone. I picked up the gadget and pointed the flashlight at McGee's face. I said, "McGee, who did you send me to find out about?"

"Huh? You crazy? *Tarkington Per—*"

I pushed the switch. Once. Then I smashed the gadget, for keeps.

I explained to Tarkington Perkins, in McGee's body. And then he and I went out together to hang on the drunk of our lives.

I'd have loved to have gone out and seen what happened between McGee and Mrs. Tarkington Perkins, but maybe someday I'll see an atomic war, whether I want to or not, and I can wait till then.

The Weapon

The room was quiet in the dimness of early evening. Dr. James Graham, key scientist of a very important project, sat in his favorite chair, thinking. It was so still that he could hear the turning of pages in the next room as his son leafed through a picture book.

Often Graham did his best work, his most creative thinking under these circumstances, sitting alone in an unlighted room in his own apartment after the day's regular work. But tonight his mind would not work constructively. Mostly he thought about his mentally arrested son—his only son—in the next room. The thoughts were loving thoughts, not the bitter anguish he had felt years ago when he had first learned of the boy's condition. The boy was happy; wasn't that the main thing? And to how many men is given a child who will always be a child, who will not grow up to leave him? Certainly that was rationalization, but what is wrong with rationalization when— The doorbell rang.

Graham rose and turned on lights in the almost-dark room before he went through the hallway to the door. He was not annoyed; tonight, at this moment, almost any interruption to his thoughts was welcome.

He opened the door. A stranger stood there; he said, "Dr. Graham? My name is Niemand; I'd like to talk to you. May I come in a moment?"

Graham looked at him. He was a small man, nondescript, obviously harmless—possibly a reporter or an insurance agent.

But it didn't matter what he was. Graham found himself saying, "Of course. Come in, Mr. Niemand." A few minutes of conversation, he justified himself by thinking, might divert his thoughts and clear his mind.

"Sit down," he said, in the living room. "Care for a drink?"

Niemand said, "No, thank you." He sat in the chair; Graham sat on the sofa.

The small man interlocked his fingers; he leaned forward. He said, "Dr. Graham, you are the man whose scientific work is more likely than that of any other man to end the human race's chance for survival."

A crackpot, Graham thought. Too late now he realized that he should have asked the man's business before admitting him. It would be an embarrassing interview; he disliked being rude, yet only rudeness was effective.

"Dr. Graham, the weapon on which you are working—"

The visitor stopped and turned his head as the door that led to a bedroom opened and a boy of fifteen came in. The boy didn't notice Niemand; he ran to Graham.

"Daddy, will you read to me now?" The boy of fifteen laughed the sweet laughter of a child of four.

Graham put an arm around the boy. He looked at his visitor, wondering whether he had known about the boy. From the lack of surprise on Niemand's face, Graham felt sure he had known.

"Harry"—Graham's voice was warm with affection—"Daddy's busy. Just for a little while. Go back to your room; I'll come and read to you soon."

"'Chicken Little'? You'll read me 'Chicken Little'?"

"If you wish. Now run along. Wait. Harry, this is Mr. Niemand."

The boy smiled bashfully at the visitor. Niemand said, "Hi, Harry," and smiled back at him, holding out his hand. Graham, watching, was sure now that Niemand had known; the smile and the gesture were for the boy's mental age, not his physical one.

The boy took Niemand's hand. For a moment it seemed that he was going to climb into Niemand's lap, and Graham pulled him back gently. He said, "Go to your room now, Harry."

The boy skipped back into his bedroom, not closing the door.

Niemand's eyes met Graham's and he said, "I like him," with obvious sincerity. He added, "I hope that what you're going to read to him will always be true."

Graham didn't understand. Niemand said, "'Chicken Little,' I mean. It's a fine story—but may 'Chicken Little' always be wrong about the sky falling down."

Graham suddenly had liked Niemand when Niemand had shown liking for the boy. Now he remembered that he must close the interview quickly. He rose, in dismissal. He said, "I fear you're wasting your time and mine, Mr. Niemand. I know all the arguments, everything you can say I've heard a thousand times. Possibly there is truth in what you believe, but it does not concern me. I'm a scientist, and only a scientist. Yes, it is public knowledge that I am working on a weapon, a rather ultimate one. But, for me personally, that is only a by-product of the fact that I am advancing science. I have thought it through, and I have found that that is my only concern."

"But, Dr. Graham, is humanity *ready* for an ultimate weapon?"

Graham frowned. "I have told you my point of view, Mr. Niemand."

Niemand rose slowly from the chair. He said, "Very well, if you do not choose to discuss it, I'll say no more." He passed a hand across his forehead. "I'll leave, Dr. Graham. I wonder, though ... may I change my mind about the drink you offered me?"

Graham's irritation faded. He said, "Certainly. Will whisky and water do?"

"Admirably."

Graham excused himself and went into the kitchen. He got the decanter of whisky, another of water, ice cubes, glasses.

When he returned to the living room, Niemand was just leaving the boy's bedroom. He heard Niemand's "Good night, Harry," and Harry's happy "Night, Mr. Niemand."

Graham made drinks. A little later, Niemand declined a second one and started to leave.

Niemand said, "I took the liberty of bringing a small gift to your son, doctor. I gave it to him while you were getting the drinks for us. I hope you'll forgive me."

"Of course. Thank you. Good night."

Graham closed the door; he walked through the living room into Harry's room. He said, "All right, Harry. Now I'll read to—"

There was sudden sweat on his forehead, but he forced his face and his voice to be calm as he stepped to the side of the bed. "May I see that, Harry?" When he had it safely, his hands shook as he examined it.

He thought, *only a madman would give a loaded revolver to an idiot.*

446

Cartoonist

(in collaboration with Mack Reynolds)

There were six letters in Bill Garrigan's box, but he could tell from a quick glance at the envelopes that not one of them was a check. Would-be gags from would-be gagmen. And, nine chances out of ten, not a yak in the lot.

He carried them back to the adobe hut he called his studio before bothering to open them. He tossed his disreputable hat onto the two-burner kerosene stove. He sat down and twisted his legs around the legs of the kitchen chair before the rickety table which doubled as a place to eat and his drawing board.

It had been a long time since the last sale and he hoped, even though he didn't dare expect, that there'd be a really salable gag in this lot. Miracles *do* happen.

He tore open the first envelope. Six gags from some guy up in Oregon, sent to him on the usual basis; if he liked any of them he'd draw them up and if they sold the guy got a percentage. Bill Garrigan looked at the first one. It read:

GUY AND GAL DRIVE UP TO RESTAURANT. SIGN ON CAR READS "HERMAN THE FIRE EATER." THROUGH WINDOWS OF RESTAURANT PEOPLE EATING BY CANDLE LIGHT.

GUY: "OH, BOY, THIS LOOKS LIKE A GOOD PLACE TO EAT!"

Bill Garrigan groaned and looked at the next card. And the next. And the next. He opened the next envelope. And the next.

This was getting really bad. Cartooning is a tough racket to make a living in, even when you live in a little town in the Southwest where living doesn't cost you much. And once you start slipping—well, the thing was a vicious circle. As your stuff was seen less and less often in the big markets, the best gagmen started sending their material elsewhere. You wound up with the leftovers, which, of course, put the skids under you that much worse.

He pulled the last gag from the final envelope. It read:

SCENE ON SOME OTHER PLANET. EMPEROR OF SNOOK, A HIDEOUS MONSTER, IS TALKING TO SOME OF HIS SCIENTISTS.

EMPEROR: "YES, I UNDERSTAND THAT YOU'VE DEVISED A METHOD OF VISITING EARTH, BUT WHO WOULD WANT TO WITH ALL THOSE HORRIBLE HUMANS LIVING THERE?"

Bill Garrigan scratched the end of his nose thoughtfully. It had possibilities. After all, the science-fiction market was growing like mad. And if he could draw these extra-terrestrial creatures hideous enough to bring out the gag—

He reached for a pencil and a piece of paper and started to sketch out a rough. The first version of the Emperor and his scientists didn't look quite ugly enough. He crumpled up the paper and reached for another piece.

Let's see. He could give each one of the monsters three heads, each head with six protruding, goggling eyes. Half-a-dozen stubby arms. Hmmm, not bad. Very long torsos, very short legs. Four apiece, front ones bending one way, back ones the other. Splay feet. Now how about the face, outside of the six eyes? Leave 'em blank below the eyes. A mouth, a big one, in the middle of the chest. That way a monster wouldn't get to arguing with himself as to which head should do the eating.

He added a few quick lines for the background; he looked upon his work and it was good. Maybe too good; maybe editors would think their readers too squeamish to look upon such terrible monstrosities. And yet, unless he made them as horrible as he could, the gag would be lost.

In fact, maybe he could make them even a little more hideous. He tried, and found that he could.

He worked on the rough until he was sure he'd got as much as could be drawn out of the gag, found an envelope and addressed it to his best market— or what had been his best market up to several months ago when he'd started slipping. He'd made his last sale there fully two months ago. But maybe they'd take this one; Rod Corey, the editor, liked his cartoons a bit on the bizarre side.

Bill Garrigan had almost forgotten the submission by the time it came back almost six weeks later.

He tore open the envelope. The rough was there with a big red "O.K. *Let's have a finish,*" scrawled to one side of it and with the initials "*R. C.*" beneath.

He'd eat again!

Bill made it back from the post office in double time, brushed the odds and ends of food, books, and clothing from the table top and reached for paper, pencil, pen, and ink.

He wedged the rough between a milk can and a dirty saucer to work from it, and he stared at it until he got himself back in the frame of mind he'd been in when he'd first roughed out the idea.

He did a job of it, because Rod Corey's market was in there with the best; the only one that gave him a hundred bucks a crack. Of course some of the really top markets paid higher than that to name-cartoonists, but Bill Garrigan had lost any delusions of his own grandeur. Sure, he'd give his right arm to hit the top, but it didn't seem likely to happen. And right now he'd settle for selling enough to keep him eating.

He took almost two hours to complete the finish, did it up carefully with cardboard and made his way back to the post office. He mailed it and rubbed his hands with satisfaction. Money in the bank. He'd be able to get the broken transmission fixed on his jalopy and be on wheels again, and he'd be able to catch up fractionally on his grocery and rent bills to boot. Only it was a shame that old R .C. wasn't quicker pay.

As a matter of fact the check didn't come until the day the issue containing the cartoon hit the stands. But in the meantime he'd made a couple of small sales to trade magazines and hadn't actually gone hungry. Still in all the check looked wonderful when it came.

He cashed it at the bank on his way from the post office and stopped off at the Sagebrush Tap for a couple of quick ones. And they tasted so good and made him feel so cheerful that he stopped at the liquor store and picked up a bottle of Metaxa. He couldn't afford Metaxa, of course—who can?—but somewhere along the line a man has to do a reasonable amount of celebrating.

Once home, he opened the bottle of precious Greek brandy, had a couple of slugs of it and then settled his long body into the chair, propped his scuffed shoes on the rickety table and let out a sigh of pure contentment. Tomorrow he'd regret the money he'd spent and he'd probably have a hangover to boot, but tomorrow was *mañana*.

Reaching out a hand he picked the least dirty of the glasses within his reach and poured a stiff shot into it. Maybe, he thought, fame is the food of the soul and he'd never be a famous cartoonist, but this afternoon at least cartooning was giving with the liquor of the gods.

He raised the glass toward his lips, but he didn't quite make it. His eyes widened.

Before him, the adobe wall seemed to shimmer, quiver, shake. Then, slowly, a small aperture appeared. It enlarged, grew, widened; suddenly it was the size of a doorway.

Bill darted a reproachful look at the brandy. Hell, he told himself, I've hardly touched it. His unbelieving eyes went back to the doorway in the wall. It could be an earthquake. In fact, it must be. What else—

Two six-armed creatures emerged. Each had three heads and each head had six goggling eyes. Four legs, a mouth in the middle of—

"Oh, no," Bill said.

Each of the creatures held an awesome, respect-inspiring gunlike object. Each pointed it at Bill Garrigan.

"Gentlemen," Bill said, "I realize that this is one of the most potent drinks on earth, but, so help me, two jiggers couldn't do *this.*"

The monsters stared at him and shuddered, and each one closed all but one of its eighteen eyes.

"Hideous indeed," said the first one to have come through the aperture. "The most hideous specimen in the solar system, is he not, Agol?"

"Me?" said Bill Garrigan faintly.

"You. But do not be afraid. We have come not to harm you but to take you into the mighty presence of Bon Whir III, Emperor Snook, where you will be suitably rewarded."

"How? For what? Where's—Snook?"

"Will you please ask questions one at a time? I could answer all three of those simultaneously, one with each head, but I fear you are not equipped to understand multiple communication."

Bill Garrigan closed his eyes. "You've got three heads, but only one mouth. How can you talk three ways with only one mouth?"

The monster's mouth laughed. "What makes you think we talk with our mouths? We only laugh with them. We eat by osmosis. We talk by vibrating diaphragms in the tops of our heads. Now, which of your three previous questions do you wish answered?"

"How will I be rewarded?"

"The Emperor did not tell us. But it will be a great reward. It is our duty merely to bring you. These weapons are merely a precaution in case you resist. And they do not kill; we are too civilized to kill. They merely stun."

"You aren't really there," Bill said. He opened his eyes and quickly closed them again. "I've never touched a reefer in my life. Nor had d.t.'s, and I couldn't suddenly get them on only two brandies—well, four if you count the ones at the bar."

"You are ready to go with us?"

"Go *where?*"

"To Snook."

"Where's that?"

"The fifth planet, retrograde, of System K-14-320-GM, Space Continuum 1745-88JHT-97608."

"Where, with relation to here?"

The monster gestured with one of his six arms. "Immediately through that aperture in your wall. Are you ready?"

"*No.* What am I being rewarded for? That cartoon? How did you see it?"

"Yes. For that cartoon. We are thoroughly familiar with your world and civilization; it is parallel to ours but in a different continuum. We are people with a great sense of humor. We have artists but no cartoonists; we lack that faculty. The cartoon you drew is, to us, excruciatingly funny. Already, everyone in Snook is laughing at it. Are you now ready?"

"No," said Bill Garrigan.

Both monsters lifted their guns. Two clicks came simultaneously.

"You are conscious again," a voice told him. "This way to the throne room, please."

There wasn't any use arguing. Bill went. He was here now, wherever *here* was, and maybe they'd reward him by letting him go back if he behaved himself.

The room was familiar. Just as he'd drawn it. And he'd have recognized the Emperor anywhere. Not only the Emperor, but the scientists who were with him.

Could it, conceivably, have been coincidence that he had drawn a scene and creatures that actually existed? Or—hadn't he read somewhere the theory that there existed an infinite number of universes in an infinite number of space-time continuums, so that any state of being of which one could possibly think actually existed somewhere? He'd thought that had sounded ridiculous when he'd read it, but he wasn't so sure now.

A voice from somewhere—it sounded as though from an amplifier—said, "The great, the mighty Emperor Bon Whir III, Leader of the Faithful, Commander of the Glories, Receiver of the Light, Lord of the Galaxies, Beloved of His People."

It stopped and Bill said, "Bill Garrigan."

The Emperor laughed, with his mouth. "Thank you, Bill Garrigan," he said, "for giving us the best laugh of our lifetimes. I have had you brought here to reward you. I hereby offer you the post of Royal Cartoonist. A post which has not existed before, since we have no cartoonists. Your sole duty will be to draw one cartoon a day."

"One a day? But where'll I get the gags?"

"We will supply them. We have excellent gags; each of us has a magnificent sense of humor, both creative and appreciative. We can, however, draw only representationally. You will be the greatest man on this planet, next to me." He laughed. "Maybe you'll be even more popular than I—although my people really do like me."

"I—I guess not," Bill said. "I think I'd rather go back to—say, what does the job pay? Maybe I could take it for a while and take some money—or some equivalent—back to Earth."

"The pay will be beyond your dreams of avarice. You will have everything you want. And you may accept it for one year, with the option of life tenure if you so wish at the end of the year."

"Well—" Bill said. He was wondering just how much money *would* be beyond his dreams of avarice. A devil of a lot, he guessed. He'd go back to Earth rich, all right.

"I urge you to accept," said the Emperor. "Every cartoon you draw—and you may draw more than one a day if you wish—will be published in every publication on the planet. You will draw royalties from each."

"How many publications have you?"

"Over a hundred thousand. Twenty billion people read them."

"Well," Bill said, "maybe I should try it a year. But—uh—"

"What?"

"How'll I get along here, outside of cartooning? I mean, I understand that physically I'm hideous to you, as hideous as you are to—I mean, I won't have any friends. I certainly couldn't make friends with—I mean—"

"That has already been taken care of, in anticipation of your acceptance, and while you were unconscious. We have the greatest physicians and plastic surgeons in any of the universes. The wall behind you is a mirror. If you will turn—"

Bill Garrigan turned. He fainted.

One of Bill Garrigan's heads sufficed to concentrate on the cartoon he was drawing, directly in ink. He didn't bother with roughs any more. They weren't necessary with the multiplicity of eyes that enabled him to see what he was doing from so many angles at the same time.

His second head was thinking of the great wealth in his bank account and his tremendous power and popularity here. True, the money was in copper, which was the precious metal in this world, but there was enough copper to sell for a fortune even on Earth. Too bad, his second head thought, that he couldn't take back his power and popularity with him.

His third head was talking to the Emperor. The Emperor came to see him sometimes, these days. "Yes," the Emperor was saying, "the time is up tomorrow, but I hope we can persuade you to stay. Your own terms, of course. And, since we do not want to use coercion, our plastic surgeons will restore you to your original—uh—shape—"

Bill Garrigan's mouth, in the middle of his chest, grinned. It was wonderful to be so appreciated. His fourth collection of cartoons had just been published and had sold ten million copies on this planet alone, besides exports to the rest of the system. It wasn't the money; he already had more than he could ever spend, here. And the convenience of three heads and six arms—

His first head looked up from the cartoon and came to rest on his secretary. She saw him looking, and her eyestalks drooped coyly. She was very beautiful. He hadn't made any passes at her yet; he'd wanted to be sure which way he'd decide, about going back to Earth. His second head thought about a girl he'd known once back on his original planet and he shuddered and jerked his mind away from thinking about her. Good Lord, she'd been hideous.

One of the Emperor's heads had caught sight of the almost-finished cartoon and his mouth was laughing hysterically.

Yes, it was wonderful to be appreciated. Bill's first head kept on looking at Thwil, his beautiful secretary, and she flushed a faint but beautiful yellow under his stare.

"Well, pal," Bill's third head said to the Emperor, "I'll think it over. Yeah, I'll think it over."

The Dome

Kyle Braden sat in his comfortable armchair and stared at the switch in the opposite wall, wondering for the millionth—or was it the billionth?—time whether he was ready to take the risk of pulling it. The millionth or the billionth time in—it would be thirty years today, this afternoon.

It meant probable death and in just what form he didn't know. Not atomic death certainly—all the bombs would have been used up many many years ago. They'd have lasted long enough to destroy the fabric of civilization, yes. There were more than enough bombs for that. And his careful calculations, thirty years ago, had proven that it would be almost a century before man got really started on a new civilization—what was left of him.

But what went on now, *out there,* outside the domelike force field that still shielded him from horror? Men as beasts? Or had mankind gone down completely and left the field to the other and less vicious brutes? No, mankind would have survived somewhere; he'd make his way back eventually. And possibly the record of what he had done to himself would remain, at least as legend, to deter him from doing it a second time. Or would it deter him even if full records remained to him?

Thirty years, Braden thought. He sighed at the weary length of them. Yet he'd had and still had everything he really needed and lonesomeness is better than sudden death. Life alone is better than no life at all—with death in some horrible form.

So he had thought thirty years ago, when he had been thirty-seven years old. So he still thought now at sixty-seven. He didn't regret what he had done, not at all. But he was tired. He wondered, for the millionth—or the billionth?—time whether he wasn't ready to pull that lever.

Just maybe, out there, they'd have struggled back to some reasonable, if agrarian, form of living. And he could help them, could give them things and knowledge they'd need. He could savor, before he was *really* old, their gratitude and the good feeling of helping them.

Then too he didn't want to die alone. He'd lived alone and it had been tolerable most of the time—but dying alone was something else. Somehow dying alone here would be worse than being killed by the neo-barbarians he expected to find out there. The agrarians were really too much to hope for after only thirty years.

And today would be a good day for it. Exactly thirty years, if his chronometers were still accurate, and they wouldn't be far wrong even in that length of time. A few more hours to make it the same time of day, thirty years to the minute. Yes, irrevocable as it was, he'd do it then. Until now the irrevocability of pulling that switch had stopped him every time he'd considered it.

If only the dome of force could be turned off and then on again the decision would have been easy and he'd have tried it long ago. Perhaps after ten years or fifteen. But it took tremendous power to create the field if very little power to maintain it. There'd still been outside power available when he'd first flashed it on.

Of course the field itself had broken the connection—had broken *all* connection—once he'd flashed it into being, but the power sources within the building had been enough to supply his own needs and the negligible power required to maintain the field.

Yes, he decided suddenly and definitely, he'd pull that switch today as soon as the few hours were up that would make the time exactly thirty years. Thirty years was long enough to be alone.

He hadn't wanted to be alone. If only Myra, his secretary, hadn't walked out on him when ... It was too late to think of that—but he thought of it as he had a billion times before. Why had she been so ridiculous about wanting to share the fate of the rest of humanity, to try to help those who were beyond help? And she'd loved him. Aside from that quixotic idea she'd have married him. He'd been too abrupt in explaining the truth—he'd shocked her. But how wonderful it would have been had she stayed with him.

Partly the fault was that the news had come sooner than he'd anticipated. When he'd turned the radio off that morning he'd known there were only hours left. He'd pressed the button that summoned Myra and she'd come in, beautiful, cool, unruffled. You'd think she never listened to the newscasts or read the papers, that she didn't know what was happening.

"Sit down, my dear," he'd told her. Her eyes had widened a bit at the unexpected form of address but she'd gracefully seated herself in the chair in which she always sat to take dictation. She poised her pencil.

"No, Myra," he said. "This is personal—very personal. I want to ask you to marry me."

Her eyes really widened. "Dr. Braden, are you—joking?"

"No. Very definitely not. I know I'm a bit older than you but not too much so, I hope. I'm thirty-seven although I may seem a bit older right now as a result of the way I've been working. You're—is it twenty-seven?"

"Twenty-eight last week. But I wasn't thinking of age. It's just—well. 'This is so sudden,' sounds like I'm joking, but it *is*. You've never even"—she grinned impishly—"you've never even made a pass at me. And you're about the first man I've ever worked for who hasn't."

Braden smiled at her. "I'm sorry. I didn't know it was expected. But, Myra, I'm serious. *Will* you marry me?"

She looked at him thoughtfully. "I—don't know. The strange thing is that—I guess I am in love with you a little. I don't know why I should be. You've been so impersonal and businesslike, so tied up in your work. You've never even tried to kiss me, never even paid me a compliment.

"But—well, I don't like this sudden and—unsentimental—a proposal. Why not ask me again sometime soon. And in the meantime—well, you might even tell me that you love me. It might help."

"I do, Myra. Please forgive me. But at least—you're not definitely against marrying me? You're not turning me down?"

She shook her head slowly. Her eyes, staring at him, were very beautiful.

"Then, Myra, let me explain why I am so late and so sudden in asking you. First I have been working desperately and against time. Do you know what I've been working on?"

"Something to do with defense, I know. Some—device. And, unless I'm wrong you've been doing it on your own without the government backing you."

"That's right," Braden said. "The high brass wouldn't believe my theories—and most other physicists disagreed with me too. But fortunately I have—did have—private wealth from certain patents I took out a few years ago in electronics. What I've been working on has been a defense against the A-bomb and the H-bomb—and anything else short of turning Earth into a small sun. A globular force field through which nothing—nothing whatever—can penetrate."

"And you ..."

"Yes, I have it. It is ready to flash into existence now around this building and to remain operative as long as I wish it to. *Nothing* can get through it though I maintain it for as many years as I wish. Furthermore this building is now stocked with a tremendous quantity of supplies—of all kinds. Even chemicals and seeds for hydroponic gardens. There is enough of everything here to supply two people for—for their lifetimes."

"But—you're turning this over to the government, aren't you? If it's a defense against the H-bomb ..."

Braden frowned. "It is, but unfortunately it turns out to have negligible, if any, military value. The high brass was right on that. You see, Myra, the power required to create such a force field varies with the cube of its size. The one about this building will be eighty feet in diameter—and when I turn it on the power drain will probably burn out the lighting system of Cleveland.

"To throw such a dome over—well, even over a tiny village or over a single military camp would take more electric power than is consumed by the whole country in weeks. And once turned off to let anything or anybody in or out it would require the same impracticable amount of power to recreate the field.

"The only conceivable use the government could make of it would be such use as I intend to make myself. To preserve the lives of one or two, at most a few individuals—to let them live through the holocaust and the savagery to come. And, except here, it's too late even for that."

"Too late—why?"

"There won't be time for them to construct the equipment. My dear, the war is on."

Her face grew white as she stared at him.

He said, "On the radio, a few minutes ago. Boston has been destroyed by an atomic bomb. War has been declared." He spoke faster. "And you know all that means and will lead to. I'm closing the switch that will put on the field and I'm keeping it on until it's safe to open it again." He didn't shock her further by saying that he didn't think it would be completely safe within their lifetimes. "We can't help anyone else now—it's too late. But we can save ourselves."

He sighed. "I'm sorry I had to be so abrupt about this. But now you understand why. In fact, I don't ask you to marry me right away, if you have any doubt at all. Just stay here until you're ready. Let me say the things, do the things, I should have said and done.

"Until now"—he smiled at her—"until now I've been working so hard, so many hours a day, that I haven't had time to make love to you. But now there'll *be* time, lots of time—and I *do* love you, Myra."

She stood up suddenly. Unseeingly, almost blindly, she started for the doorway.

"*Myra!*" he called. He started around the desk after her. She turned at the door and held him back. Her face and her voice were quite calm.

"I've got to go, Doctor, I've had a little nurse's training. I'm going to be needed."

"But, Myra, think what's going to happen out there! They're going to turn into animals. They're going to die horribly. Listen, I love you too much to let you face that. Stay, please!"

Amazingly she had smiled at him. "Good-bye, Dr. Braden. I'm afraid that I'm going to have to die with the rest of the animals. I guess I'm crazy that way."

And the door had closed behind her. From the window he had watched her go down the steps and start running as soon as she had reached the side-walk.

There'd been the roar of jets overhead. Probably, he thought, this soon, they were ours. But they could be the enemy—over the pole and across Canada, so high that they'd escaped detection, swooping low as they crossed Erie. With Cleveland as one of their objectives. Maybe somehow they'd even know of him and his work and had made Cleveland a prime objective. He had run to the switch and thrown it.

Outside the window, twenty feet from it, a gray nothingness had sprung into being. All sound from outside had ceased. He had gone out of the house and looked at it—the visible half of it a gray hemisphere, forty feet high and eighty feet broad, just big enough to clear the two-story almost cubical build-ing that was his home and his laboratory both. And he knew that it extended forty feet into the earth to complete a perfect sphere. No ravening force could enter it from above, no earthworm crawl through it from below.

None had for thirty years.

Well, it hadn't been too bad a thirty years, he thought. He'd had his books—and he'd read his favorite ones so often that he knew them almost by heart. He'd kept on experimenting and—although, the last seven years, since he'd passed sixty, he'd gradually lost interest and creativeness—he'd accom-plished a few little things.

Nothing comparable to the field itself or even his inventions before that—but there hadn't been the incentive. Too slight a probability that anything he developed would ever be of use to himself or to anybody else. What good is a refinement in electronics to a savage who doesn't know how to tune a simple radio set, let alone build one.

Well, there'd been enough to keep him sane if not happy.

He went to the window and stared through it at the gray impalpability twenty feet away. If only he could lower it and then, when he saw what he knew he would see, restore it quickly. But once down it was down for good.

He walked to the switch and stood staring at it. Suddenly he reached up and pulled it. He turned slowly to the window and then walked, almost ran, to it. The gray wall was gone—what lay beyond it was sheerly incredible.

Not the Cleveland he'd known but a beautiful city, a *new* city. What had been a narrow street was a wide boulevard. The houses, the buildings, were clean and beautiful, the style of architecture strange to him. Grass, trees, everything well kept. What had happened—how could it be? After atomic war mankind couldn't possibly have come back this far, this quickly. Else all of sociology was wrong and ridiculous.

And where were the people? As if in answer a car went by. A car? It looked like no car he'd ever seen before. Much faster, much sleeker, much more maneuverable—it barely seemed to touch the street, as though anti-gravity took away its weight while gyroscopes gave it stability. A man and woman rode in it, the man driving. He was young and handsome, the woman young and beautiful.

They turned and looked his way and suddenly the man stopped the vehicle—stopped it in an incredibly short distance for the speed at which they'd been traveling. Of course, Braden thought—they've driven past here before and the gray dome was here and now it's gone. The car started up again. Braden thought, they've gone to tell someone.

He went to the door and outside, out onto the lovely boulevard. Out in the open he realized why there were so few people, so little traffic. His chronometers *had* gone wrong. Over thirty years they were off by hours at least. It was early morning—from the position of the Sun between six and seven o'clock.

He started walking. If he stayed there, in the house that had been thirty years under the dome, someone would come as soon as the young couple who had seen had reported. And yes, whoever came would explain what had happened but he wanted to figure it out for himself, to realize it more gradually than that.

He walked. He met no one. This was a fine residential part of town now and it was very early. He saw a few people at a distance. Their dress was different from his but not enough so as to make him an object of immediate curiosity. He saw more of the incredible vehicles but none of their occupants chanced to notice him. They traveled incredibly fast.

At last he came to a store that was open. He walked in, too consumed by excited curiosity by now to wait any longer. A young man with curly hair was arranging things behind the counter. He looked at Braden almost incredulously, then asked politely, "What can I do for you, sir?"

"Please don't think I'm crazy. I'll explain later. Just answer this. What happened thirty years ago? Wasn't there atomic war?"

The young man's eyes lighted. "Why, you must be the man who's been under the dome, sir. That explains why you ..." He stopped as though embarrassed.

"Yes," Braden said. "I've been under the dome. But *what happened?* After Boston was destroyed what happened?"

"Space-ships, sir. The destruction of Boston was accidental. A fleet of ships came from Aldebaran. A race far more advanced than we and benevolent. They came to welcome us into the Union and to help us. Unfortunately one crashed—into Boston—and the atomics that powered it exploded, and a million were killed. But other ships landed everywhere within hours and explained and apologized and war was averted—very narrowly. United States air fleets were already en route, but they managed to call them back."

Braden said hoarsely, "Then there *was* no war?"

"Of course not. War is something back in the dark ages now, thanks to the Galactic Union. We haven't even national governments now to declare a war. There *can't* be war. And our progress, with the help of the Union, has been—well, tremendous. We've colonized Mars and Venus—they weren't inhabited and the Union assigned them to us so we could expand. But Mars and Venus are just suburbs. We travel to the stars. We've even ..." He paused.

Braden held tightly to the edge of the counter. He'd missed it all. He'd been thirty years alone and now he was an old man. He asked, "You've even—what?" Something inside him told him what was coming and he could hardly hear his own voice.

"Well, we're not immortal but we're closer to it than we were. We live for centuries. I wasn't much younger than you were thirty years ago. But—I'm afraid you missed out on it, sir. The processes the Union gave us work only on humans up to middle age—fifty at the very most. And you're—"

"Sixty-seven," Braden said stiffly. "Thank you."

Yes, he'd missed everything. The stars—he'd have given almost anything to go there but he didn't want to now. And Myra.

He could have had her and they'd both still be young.

He walked out of the store and turned his footsteps toward the building that had been under the dome. By now they'd be waiting for him there. And maybe they'd give him the only thing he'd ask of them—power to restore the force field so he could finish what was left of his life there under the dome. Yes, the only thing he wanted now was what he'd thought he wanted least—to die, as he had lived, alone.

A Word from Our Sponsor

Looking at it one way, you could say that it happened a great many different times over a twenty-four hour period; another way, that it happened once and all at once.

It happened, that is, at 8:30 P.M. on Wednesday, June 9th, 1954. That means it came first, of course, in the Marshall Islands, the Gilbert Islands and in all the other islands—and on all the ships at sea—which were just west of the International Date Line. It was twenty-four hours later in happening in the various islands and on the various ships just east of the International Date Line.

Of course, on ships which, during that twenty-four hour period, crossed the date line from east to west and therefore had two 8:30 P.M.'s, both on June 9th, it happened twice. On ships crossing the other way and therefore having *no* 8:30 P.M. (or one bell, if we must be nautical) it didn't happen at all.

That may sound complicated, but it's simple, really. Just say that it happened at 8:30 P.M. everywhere, regardless of time belts and strictly in accordance with whether or not the area in question had or did not have daylight saving time. Simply that: 8:30 P.M. *everywhere.*

And 8:30 P.M. everywhere is just about the optimum moment for radio listening, which undoubtedly had something to do with it. Otherwise somebody or something went to an awful lot of unnecessary trouble, so to stagger the times that they would be the same all over the world.

Even if, at 8:30 on June 9, 1954, you weren't listening to your radio—and you probably were—you certainly remember it. The world was on the brink of war. Oh, it had been on the brink of war for years, but this time its toes were over the edge and it balanced precariously. There were special sessions in—but we'll come to that later.

Take Dan Murphy, inebriated Australian of Irish birth, being pugnacious in a Brisbane pub. And the Dutchman known as Dutch being pugnacious right back. The radio blaring. The bartender trying to quiet them down and the rest of the crowd trying to egg them on. You've seen it happen and you've heard it happen, unless you make a habit of staying out of waterfront saloons.

Murphy had stepped back from the bar already and was wiping his hands on the sides of his dirty sweat shirt. He was well into the preliminaries. He said, "Why, you — —— —— — ——!" and waited for the riposte. He wasn't disappointed. "—— you!" said Dutch.

That, as it happened, was at twenty-nine minutes and twenty-eight seconds past eight o'clock, June 9, 1954. Dan Murphy took a second or two to smile happily and get his dukes up. Then something happened to the radio. For a fraction of a second, only that long, it went dead. Then a quite calm, quite ordinary voice said, "And now a word from our sponsor." And there was something—some ineffably indefinable quality—in the voice that made everybody in the room listen and hear. Dan Murphy with his right pulled back for a roundhouse swing; Dutch the Dutchman with his feet ready to step back from it and his forearm ready to block it; the bartender with his hand on the bung starter under the bar and his knees bent ready to vault over the bar.

A full frozen second, and then a different voice, also from the radio, said "Fight."

One word, only one word. Probably the only time in history that *"a* word from our sponsor" on the radio had been just that. And I won't try to describe the inflection of that word; it has been too variously described. You'll find people who swear it was said viciously, in hatred; others who are equally sure that it was calm and cold. But it was unmistakably a *command,* in whatever tone of voice.

And then there was a fraction of a second of silence again and then the regular program—in the case of the radio in the Brisbane pub, an Hawaiian instrumental group—was back on.

Dan Murphy took another step backwards, and said, "Wait a minute. What the hell was that?"

Dutch the Dutchman had already lowered his big fists and was turning to the radio. Everybody else in the place was staring at it already. The bartender had taken his hand off the bung-starter. He said, "—— me for a —— ——. What was *that* an ad for?"

"Let's call this off a minute, Dutch," Dan Murphy said. "I got a funny feeling like that —— —— radio was talking to *me.* Personally. And what the —— —— —— —— business has a bloody wireless set got telling *me* what to do?"

"Me too," Dutch said, sincerely if a bit ambiguously. He put his elbows on the bar and stared at the radio. Nothing but the plaintive sliding wail of an Hawaiian ensemble came out of it.

Dan Murphy stepped to the bar beside him. He said, "What the devil were we fighting about?"

"You called me a —— —— — —— ——" Dutch reminded him. "And I said, —— you."

"Oh," Murphy said. "All right, in a couple minutes I'll knock your head off. But right now I want to think a bit. How's about a drink?"

"Sure," Dutch said.

For some reason, they never got around to starting the fight.

Take, two and a half hours later (but still at 8:30 P.M.), the conversation of Mr. and Mrs. Wade Evans of Oklahoma City, presently in their room at the Grand Hotel, Singapore, dressing to go night-clubbing in what they thought was the most romantic city of their round-the-world cruise. The room radio going, but quite softly (Mrs. Evans had turned it down so her husband wouldn't miss a word of what she had to say to him, which was *plenty).*

"And the way you acted yesterday evening on the boat with that Miss— Mam*selle* Cartier—Cah-tee-*yay.* Half your age, and *French.* Honestly, Wade, I don't see why you took *me* along at all on this cruise. Second honeymoon, in-deed!"

"And just *how* did I act with her? I danced with her, twice. Twice in a whole evening. Dammit, Ida, I'm getting sick of your acting this way. And beside—" Mr. Evans took a deep breath to go on, and thereby lost his chance.

"Treat me like dirt. When we get back—"

"All right, *all right.* If that's the way you feel about it, why wait till we get back? If you think *I'm* enjoying—"

Somehow that silence of only a fraction of a second on the radio stopped him. "And now a word from our sponsor ..."

And half a minute later, with the radio again playing Strauss, Wade Evans was still staring at it in utter bewilderment. Finally he said, "What was *that?*"

Ida Evans looked at him wide-eyed. "You know. I had the funniest feeling that that was talking to us, to *me?* Like it was telling us to g-go ahead and fight, like we were starting to."

Mr. Evans laughed a little uncertainly. "Me, too. Like it *told* us to. And the funny thing is, now I don't want to." He walked over and turned the radio off. "Listen, Ida, do we *have* to fight? After all, this *is* our second honeymoon. Why not—listen, Ida, do you really want to go night-clubbing this evening?"

"Well—I do want to see Singapore, a little, and this is our only night here, but—it's early; we don't have to go out right away."

I don't mean of course, that everybody who heard that radio announcement was fighting, physically or verbally, or even thinking about fighting. And of course there were a couple of billion people who didn't hear it at all because they either didn't have radio sets or didn't happen to have them turned on. But almost everybody heard *about* it. Maybe not all of the African pygmies or all of the Australian bushmen, no, but every intelligent person in a civilized or semicivilized country heard of it sooner or later and generally sooner.

And the point is, if there is a point, that those who *were* fighting or thinking of fighting and who happened to be within hearing distance of a turned-on radio ...

Eight-thirty o'clock continued its way around the world. Mostly in jumps of an even hour from time-zone to time-zone, but not always; some time-zones vary for that system—as Singapore, on the half hour; as Calcutta, seven minutes short of the hour. But by regular or irregular intervals, the phenomenon of the word continued its way from east to west, happening everywhere at eight-thirty o'clock precisely.

Delhi, Teheran, Baghdad, Moscow. The Iron Curtain, in 1954, was stronger, more impenetrable than it had ever been before, so nothing was known at the time of the effect of the broadcast there; later it was learned that the course of events there was quite similar to the course of events in Washington, D. C., Berlin, Paris, London ...

Washington. The President was in special conference with several members of the cabinet and the majority and minority leaders of the Senate. The Secretary of Defense was speaking, very quietly: "Gentlemen, I say again that our best, perhaps our only, chance of winning is to get there first. If we don't, they will. Everything shows that. Those confidential reports of yours, Mr. President, are absolute proof that they intend to attack. We *must*—"

A discreet tap on the door caused him to stop in midsentence.

The President said, "That's Walter—about the broadcast," and then louder, "Come in."

The President's confidential secretary came in. "Everything is ready, Mr. President," he said. "You said you wished to hear it yourself. These other gentlemen—?"

The President nodded, "We'll all go," he said. He stood, and then the others. "How many sets, Walter?"

"Six. We've turned them to six different stations; two in this time belt, Washington and New York; two in other parts of this country, Denver and San Francisco; two foreign stations, Paris and Tokyo."

"Excellent," said the President. "Shall we go and hear this mysterious broadcast that all Europe and Asia are excited about?"

The Secretary of Defense smiled. "If you wish. But I doubt we'll hear anything. Getting control of the stations here—" He shrugged.

"Walter," said the President, "has there been anything further from Europe or Asia?"

"Nothing new, sir. Nothing has happened there since eight-thirty, their time. But confirmations of what did happen then are increasing. Everybody who was listening to any station at eight-thirty heard it. Whether the station was in their time zone or not. For instance, a radio set in London which happened to be turned to Athens, Greece, got the broadcast at eight-thirty, London—that is, Greenwich—time. Local sets in Athens tuned to the same station had heard it at eight-thirty Athens time—two hours earlier."

The majority leader of the Senate frowned. "That is patently impossible. It would indicate—"

"Exactly," said the President drily. "Gentlemen, shall we adjourn to the room where the receiving sets have been placed? It lacks five minutes of—eight-thirty."

They went down the hall to a room hideous with the sound of six receiving sets tuned to six different programs. Three minutes, two minutes, one—

Sudden silence for a fraction of a second. From six sets simultaneously the impersonal voice, "And now a word from our sponsor." The commanding voice gave the one-word command.

Then, again, the six radio sets blared forth their six different programs. No one tried to speak over that sound. They filed back into the conference chamber.

The President looked at the Secretary of Defense. "Well, Rawlins?"

The Secretary's face was white. "The only thing I can think of that would account for it—" He paused until the President prodded him with another "Well?"

"I'll grant it sounds incredible, but—a space-ship? Cruising around the world at the even rate of its period of revolution—a little over a thousand miles an hour. Over each point which it passes—which would be at the same hour everywhere—it momentarily blanks out other stations and puts on its own broadcast."

The Senate's majority leader snorted. "Why a space ship? There are planes that can travel that fast."

"Ever hear of radar? With our new installations along the coast anything going over up to a hundred miles high would show. And do you think Europe hasn't radar too?"

"And would they *tell* us if they spotted something?"

"England would. France would. And how about all our ships at sea that the thing has already passed over?"

"But a *space* ship!"

The President held up his hand. "Gentlemen. Let's not argue until we have the facts. Reports from many sources are even now coming in and being sifted and evaluated. We've been getting ready for this for over fifteen hours now and I'll see what's known already, if you'll pardon me."

He picked up the telephone at his end of the long conference table, spoke into it briefly and then listened for about two minutes before he said, "Thank you," and replaced the receiver.

Then he looked straight down the middle of the conference table as he spoke. "No radar station noticed anything out of the ordinary, not even a faint or blurred image." He hesitated. "The broadcast, gentlemen, was heard uniformly in all areas of the Eastern Time Zone which have daylight saving. It was uniformly *not* heard in areas which do not have daylight saving, where it is now seven-thirty P.M."

"Impossible," said the Secretary of Defense.

The President nodded slowly. "Exactly. Yet certain reports from borders of time zones in Europe led us to anticipate it, and it was checked carefully. Radio receivers were placed, in pairs, along the borders of certain zones. For example, a pair of receivers were placed at the city limits of Baltimore, one twelve inches within the city limits, the other twelve inches outside. Two feet apart. They were identical sets, identically tuned to the same station, operated from the same power source. One set received 'a word from our sponsor'; the other did not. The set-up is being maintained for another hour. But I do not doubt that—" He glanced at his wrist watch. "—forty-five minutes from now, when it will be eight-thirty o'clock in the non-daylight-saving zones, the situation will be reversed; the broadcast will be received by the set outside the daylight saving zone border and not by the similarly tuned set just inside."

He glanced around the table and his face was set and white. "Gentlemen, what is happening tonight all over the world is beyond science—our science, at any rate."

"It can't be," said the Secretary of Labor. "Damn it, Mr. President, there's got to be an explanation."

"Further experiments—much more delicate and decisive ones—are being arranged, especially for the non-daylight-saving areas of the Pacific Time

Zone, where we still have four hours to arrange them. And the top scientists of California will be on the job." The President took out a handkerchief and wiped his forehead. "Until we have their reports and analyses, early tomorrow morning, shall we adjourn, gentlemen?"

The Defense Secretary frowned. "But, Mr. President, the purpose of our conference tonight was *not* to discuss this mysterious broadcast. Can we not get back to the original issue?"

"Do you really think that any major step should even be contemplated before we know what happened tonight—is happening tonight, I should say?"

"If we *don't* start the war, Mr. President, need I point out again who *will?* And the tremendous—practically decisive—advantage of taking the first step, gaining the offensive?"

"And obey the order in the broadcast?" growled the Secretary of Labor.

"Why not? Weren't we going to do just that anyway, because we had to?"

"Mr. Secretary," the President said slowly. "That order was not addressed to us specifically. That broadcast was heard—is being heard—all over the world, in all languages. But even if it was heard only here, and only in our own language, I would certainly hesitate to obey a command until I knew from whom that command came. Gentlemen, do you fully realize the implications of the fact that our top scientists, thus far at any rate, could not conceivably duplicate the conditions of that broadcast? That means either one of two things: that whoever produced the phenomenon is possessed of a science beyond ours, or that the phenomenon is of supernatural origin."

The Secretary of Commerce said softly, "My God."

The President looked at him. "Not unless your god is either Mars or Satan, Mr. Weatherby."

The hour of 8:30 P.M. had, several hours before, reached and passed the International Date Line. It was still 8:30 P.M. somewhere but not of June 9th, 1954. The mysterious broadcast was over.

It was dawn in Washington, D. C. The President, in his private office, was still interviewing, one after another, the long succession of experts who had been summoned—and brought by fast planes—to Washington for the purpose.

His face was haggard with weariness, his voice a trifle hoarse.

"Mr. Adams," he said to the current visitor, "you are, I am given to understand, the top expert on electronics—particularly as applied to radio—in this country. Can you offer any conceivable physical explanation of the method used by X?"

"X?"

"I should have explained; we are now using that designation for convenience to indicate the—uh—originator of the broadcast, whether singular or plural, human, extraterrestrial, or supernatural—either diabolical or divine."

"I see. Mr. President, it could not have been done with *our* knowledge of science. That is all *I* can say."

"And your conclusion?"

"I have none."

"Your *guess*, then."

The visitor hesitated. "My guess, Mr. President, outrageous as it seems, is that somewhere on Earth exists a cabal of scientists of whom we do not know, who have operated in secret and carried electronics a step—or several steps—beyond what is generally known."

"And their purpose?"

"I would say, again a guess, their purpose is to throw the world into war to enable them to take over and rule the world. Indubitably, they had other—and more deadly—devices for later use, after a war has weakened us."

"Then you do not believe war would be advisable?"

"My God, no, Mr. President!"

"Mr. Everett," said the President. "Your theory of a cabal of scientists corresponds with one I heard only a few minutes ago from a colleague of yours. Except for one thing. He believes that their purpose is evil—to precipitate war so they can take over. You believe, if I understand you correctly, that their purpose is benevolent."

"Exactly, sir. For one thing, if they're that good in electronics, they're probably that good in other fields. They wouldn't *need* to precipitate a war in order to take over. I think they are operating secretly to prevent war, to give mankind a chance to advance. But they know enough of human nature to know that men are pretty apt to do the opposite of what they are told. But that's psychology, which is not my field. I understand you are also interviewing some psychologists?"

"Yes," said the President, wearily.

"Then, if I understand you correctly, Mr. Corby," said the President, "you believe that the command to fight was designed to produce the opposite effect, whoever gave it?"

"Certainly, sir. But I must admit that all of my colleagues do not agree with me. They make exceptions."

"Will you explain the exceptions?"

"The major one is the possibility that the broadcast was of extra-terrestrial origin. An extra-terrestrial might or might not know enough of human psychology to realize that the command in question is likely—if not certain—to have the opposite effect. A lesser possibility is that—if a group of Earth scientists, operating secretly, produced the broadcasts, they might have concentrated on the physical sciences as against the mental, and be ignorant of psychology to the extent that—well, they would defeat their purpose."

"Their purpose being to start war?"

"Not my opinion, Mr. President. Only a consideration. I think they are trying to *prevent* war."

"In which case the command was psychologically sound?"

"Yes. And that is *not* opinion solely. Mr. President, people have been awake all night organizing peace societies, not only here, but all over the world."

"*All* over?"

"Well—we don't know, of course, what is going on behind the Iron Curtain. And circumstances are different there. But in my opinion, a movement for peace will have arisen there, too, although it may not have been able to organize, as elsewhere."

"Suppose, Mr. Corby, your idea of a group of benevolent scientists—or ones who think they are benevolent scientists—are back of it. What then?"

"*What then?* We'd damn well *better* not start a war—or anybody else either. If they're that good in electronics, they've got other stuff. They'll like as not utterly destroy whatever country makes an aggressive move first!"

"And if their purpose is malevolent?"

"Are you joking, Mr. President? We'd be playing right into their hands to start a war. We wouldn't last ten days."

"Mr. Lykov, you are recommended to me as the top expert on the psychology of the Russian people under Communism. What is your opinion as to how they will react to what happened last night?"

"They're going to think it's a Capitalist plot. They're going to think *we* did it."

"What purpose could they conceivably think we had?"

"To trap them into starting a war. Of course they intended to start one anyway—it's just been a question of which of us started it first, now that, since their development of atomics, they've had time to stock-pile—but they probably think right now that for some reason we *want* them to make the first move. So they won't; at least not until they've waited a while."

"General Wilkinson," said the President, "I know it is early for you to have received many reports as yet from our espionage agents in Europe and Asia, but the few that you have received—indicate what?"

"That they're doing just what *we're* doing, sir. Sitting tight and wondering. There have been no troop movements, either toward borders or away from them."

"Thank you, General."

"Dr. Burke," said the President, "I have been informed that the Council of United Churches has been in session all night. From the fact that you look as tired as I feel, I judge that is correct."

The most famous minister in the United States nodded, smiling faintly.

"And is it your opinion—I mean the opinion of your council—that last night's occurrence was of supernatural origin?"

"Almost unanimously, Mr. President."

"Then let's ignore the minority opinion of your group and concentrate on what you almost unanimously believe. Is it that the—we may as well call it *miracle,* since we are discussing it on the assumption that it was of supernatural origin—was of divine or diabolical origin? More simply, was it God or the devil?"

"There, Mr. President, we have an almost even split of opinion. Approximately half of us believe that Satan accomplished it somehow. The other half that God did. Shall I outline briefly the arguments of either faction?"

"Please."

"The Satan group. The fact that the command was an evil one. Against the argument that God is sufficiently more powerful than Satan to have prevented the manifestation, the Satan group countered quite legitimately that God—in his infinite wisdom—may have permitted it, knowing the effect is likely to be the reverse of what Satan intended."

"I see, Dr. Burke."

"And the opposing group. The fact that, because of the perversity of human nature, the ultimate effect of the command is going to be good rather than stupid. Against the Satan group's argument that God could not issue an evil command, even for a laudable purpose, the counter-argument is that man cannot understand God sufficiently to place any limitation whatever upon what He can or cannot, would or would not, do."

The President nodded. "And does either group advocate *obeying* the command?"

"Definitely not. To those who believe the command came from Satan, disobedience is automatic. Those who believe the command came from God aver that those who believe in Him are sufficiently intelligent and good to recognize the command as divine irony."

"And the Satan group, Doctor—do they believe the devil is not smart enough to know that his command may backfire?"

"Evil is always stupid, Mr. President."

"And your personal opinion, Dr. Burke? You have not said to which faction you belong."

The minister smiled. "I am one of the very small faction which does not accept that the phenomenon was of supernatural origin at all, either from God *or* the devil."

"Then whom do you believe X to be, Doctor?"

"My personal guess is that X is extra-terrestrial. Perhaps as near as Mars, perhaps as far as another Galaxy."

The President sighed and said, "No, Walter, I simply cannot take time out for lunch. If you'll bring me a sandwich here, I'll have to apologize to my next visitor or two for eating while I talk. And coffee, lots of coffee."

"Certainly, sir."

"Just a minute, Walter. The telegrams that have been coming in since eight-thirty last night—how many are there now?"

"Well over forty thousand, sir. We've been working at classifying them, but we're several thousand behind."

"And?"

The presidential secretary said, "From every class—ministers, truck drivers, crackpots, business leaders, everybody. Offering every theory possible—but pretty much only one conclusion. No matter who they think instigated that broadcast or why, they want to disobey its command. Yesterday, I would say that nine-tenths of our population was resigned to war; well over half thought we ought to start it first. Today—well, there's always a lunatic fringe; about one telegram out of four hundred thinks we should go to war. The others— well, I think that today a declaration of war would cause a revolution, Mr. President."

"Thank you, Walter."

The secretary turned at the doorway. "A report from the army recruiting corps—enlistments thus far today have been fifteen—throughout the entire country. An average day for the past month, up to noon, was about eight thousand. I'll send in your sandwich, sir."

"Professor Winslow, I hope you will pardon my eating this sandwich while we talk. You are, I am told, professor of semantics at New York University, and the top man in your field?"

Professor Winslow smiled deprecatingly. "You would hardly expect me to agree to that, Mr. President. I presume you wish to ask questions about last night's—uh—broadcast?"

"Exactly. What are your conclusions?"

"The word 'fight' is hardly analyzable. Whether it was meant in fact or in reverse is a matter for the psychologists—and even they are having grave difficulty with it, until and unless they learn who gave that command."

The President nodded.

"But, Mr. President, the rest of the broadcast, the phrase in another voice that preceded the command. 'And now a word from our sponsor'—that is something which should give us something to work on, especially as we have studied it carefully in many languages, and worked out fully the connotation of every word."

"Your conclusion?"

"Only this; that it was carefully worded, designed, to conceal the identity of the broadcaster or broadcasters. Quite successfully. We can draw no worthwhile conclusions."

"Dr. Abrams, has any correlating phenomenon been noticed at your or any other observatory?"

"Nothing, Mr. President." The little man with the gray goatee smiled quietly. "The stars are all in their courses. Nothing observable is amiss with the universe. I fear I can give you no help—except my personal opinion."

"Which is?"

"That—regardless of the meaning, pro or con, of the command to fight— the opening phrase meant exactly what it said. That we are *sponsored.*"

"By whom? God?"

"I am an agnostic, Mr. President. But I do not rule out the possibility that man isn't the highest *natural* being in the universe. It's quite large, you know. Perhaps we're an experiment conducted by someone—in another dimension, anywhere. Perhaps, generally speaking, we're allowed to go our way for the sake of the experiment. But we almost went too far, this time, toward destroying ourselves and ending the experiment. And he didn't want it ended. So—" He smiled gently. "—a word from our sponsor."

The President leaned forward across the desk, almost spilling his coffee. "But, if that is true, was the word *meant?*"

"I think that whether it was meant—in the sense in which you mean the word 'meant'—is irrelevant. If we have a sponsor, he must know what its effect will be, and that effect—whether it be war or peace—is what he wanted to achieve."

The President wiped his forehead with his handkerchief.

"How do you differentiate this—sponsor from the being most people call God?"

The little man hesitated. "I'm not sure I do. I told you I was an agnostic, not an atheist. However, I do not believe He sits on a cloud and has a long white beard."

"Mr. Baylor, I particularly wish to thank you for coming here. I am fully aware that you, as head of the Communist Party in the United States, are against everything I stand for. Yet I wish to ask you what the opinion of the Communists here is of the broadcast of yesterday evening."

"There is no matter of opinion. We *know* what it is."

"Of your own knowledge, Mr. Baylor, or because Moscow has spoken?"

"That is irrelevant. We are perfectly aware that the Capitalistic countries instigated that broadcast. And solely for the purpose of inciting *us* to start the war."

"And for what reason would we do that?"

"Because you have something new. Something in electronics that enabled you to accomplish what you accomplished last night and that is undoubtedly a decisive weapon. However, because of the opinion of the rest of the world, you do not dare to use it if you yourselves—as your warmongers have been demanding, as indeed you have been planning to do—start the war. You want us to start it and then, with world opinion on your side, you would be able to use your new weapon. However, we refuse to be propagandized."

"Thank you, Mr. Baylor. And may I ask you one question strictly off the record? Will you answer in the first person singular, not plural, your own personal, private opinion?"

"You may."

"Do you, personally, *really* believe we instigated that broadcast?"

"I—I do not know."

"The afternoon mail, Walter?"

"Well over a hundred thousand letters, Mr. President. We have been able to do only random sampling. They seem to be about the same as the telegrams. General Wickersham is anxious to see you, sir. He thinks you should issue a proclamation to the army. Army morale is in a terrible state, he says, and he thinks a word from you—"

The President smiled grimly. "*What* word, Walter? The only single word of importance I can think of has already been given—and hasn't done army morale any good at all. Tell General Wickersham to wait; maybe I'll be able to see him within a few days. Who's next on the list?"

"Professor Gresham of Harvard."

"His specialty?"

"Philosophy and metaphysics."

The President sighed. "Send him in."

"You actually mean, Professor, that you have no opinions at all? You won't even guess whether X is God, devil, extra-galactic superman, terrestrial scientist, Martian—?"

"What good would a guess do, Mr. President? I am certain of only one thing—and that is that *we will never know who or what X is.* Mortal or immortal, terrestrial or extra-galactic, microcosmic or macrocosmic, four dimensional or twelve, he is sufficiently more clever than we to keep us from discovering his identity. And it is obviously necessary to his plan that we do not know."

"Why?"

"It is obvious that he wants us to disobey that command, isn't it? And who ever heard of men obeying a command unless they knew—or thought they knew—*who gave it?* If anybody ever learns who gave that command, he can decide whether to obey it or not. *As long as he doesn't know, it's psychologically almost impossible for him to obey it.*"

The President nodded slowly. "I see what you mean. Men either obey or disobey commands—even commands they think come from God—according to their own will. But how *can* they obey an order, and still be men, when they don't know for sure where the order came from?"

He laughed. "And even the Commies don't know for sure whether we Capitalists did it or not. And as long as they're not sure—"

"Did we?"

The President said, "I'm beginning to wonder. Even though I know we didn't, it doesn't seem more unlikely than anything else." He tilted back in his chair and stared at the ceiling. After a while he said softly, "Anyway, I don't think there's going to be a war. Either side would be mad to start it."

There wasn't a war.

The Gamblers

You lie there cold and sweating at the same time. You're nauseated and your insides hurt from all the retching you've done. Your throat burns a little too. But you're a gambler and this is your gamble to keep alive until your ship comes in—the space-ship that is, for you, so aptly named the *Relief.*

You've *got* to stay alive for longer than you care to think about. How many more days? You don't know—you've lost track of time and of day and night. Thirty-nine days—Terrestrial days—altogether from the time the *Relief* left you here until it's due to pick you up again. But you don't know right now how many days have gone by and how many remain. Why did you forget to wind your watch and make marks on the wall for days, as a prisoner does in his cell, to count the days until he'll be free again?

You can't read to help pass the time, even if you felt well enough to enjoy reading, because the Aliens took all your books. You'd gladly give up your life to be able to write but you can't write a word because of that psychic compulsion they put on you under hypnosis. You can't remember the shape of a single letter, even the sound of a single letter, let alone how to spell a whole word.

You'll have to learn to write all over again unless it turns out that the sight of printing or writing brings back your memory when you have a chance to see some again. They saw to it that there isn't a letter of printing anywhere in this tiny dome. Not so much as a serial number on an oxygen tank or a label on a tube of toothpaste.

Of course they took all writing materials and paper too, but you could probably find something to scratch on the wall with if only you knew how to write. You try—you think the word *cat* and you know the sound of it and what a cat is but for the life of you you can't imagine how it would be written, whether with two letters or ten. The very concept of what a *letter* is almost eludes you. You don't quite see how you can put a sound on paper. Yes, it's hopeless without help to try to break that block they put in your mind. You might as well quit struggling against it.

At least you'll be able to talk if you manage to live until your ship comes in. And you've *got* to live so you'll be able to tell them. Not that you want to live, the way you feel now. But you've got to. If you have to fight for every breath then all right, you'll fight. Your own life is the least of it.

You're getting sick at your stomach again. Well, don't think about it. Think about something else. Remember your trip here from Earth, good old Earth. Think about it to get your mind off your guts.

Remember the take-off. How much it scared you and how much you marveled at all that you knew—directly or indirectly—was going on. The valves opening, the pumps beginning to stir, the liquid hydrogen and the ozone of the booster device beginning to gush into the motor. The vibration that told you the initial ignition was taking place. The *Relief* stirring sluggishly on its apron.

The roar of the booster, already clearly audible miles away. Inside the ship the sound was heavy, thunderous, penetrating. And then the unknown unanalyzable terrors brought on by the subsonic vibrations. There was noise on every level of sound, those that human ears could hear and those they couldn't hear. No ear plugs could block out the supersonics and the subsonics. You didn't really hear them with your ears at all but with your whole body.

Yes, the take-off had been your biggest thrill in life up to then, much as it seemed to bore the captain and the three-man crew of the *Relief.* It was your first take-off and their twentieth or thirtieth. Well, you had one more coming— the return trip to Earth—if you lived until the *Relief* came back for you. And you'd settle for that—gladly you'd go back to your regular job in the lab of the observatory.

One trip to the Moon and back, with a thirty-nine-day stay there should be enough of an adventure for any man who isn't a spaceman and doesn't ever expect to become one. And one mess like that you're in right now should be enough to satisfy *anybody* for the rest of his life. Only the rest of your life may be a matter of minutes or hours. If the Aliens figured wrong or if you did ...

Keep your mind away from that. You're going to live all right. You've beaten them—you hope. It doesn't do any good to worry about it. You're doing all you can do, just lying here, trying to be as quiet as you can so you'll use as little oxygen as possible. They left you barely enough food, barely enough water, but the oxygen is your really tough problem. Not *quite* barely enough.

Yet you just *might* make it if you make no unnecessary move to increase your oxygen consumption. Sleep is best—you use less oxygen when you sleep. But you can't sleep all the time. In fact, sick and miserable as you are, you can't manage to sleep much at all.

All you can do is lie quiet and think. Think about anything. Think why you're here.

You're here because—along with a lot of other observatory technicians— you answered an ad in the Astronomy Journal, an ad that excited you. *Wanted, technician, young and in good health, to spend between one and two months alone in small observatory dome on the Moon to make series of photographs of Earth for meteorological study. Must know Ogden star camera and use of filters, do own developing of plates. Must be psychologically stable.*

It didn't say—*must be able to give poker instruction to alien life forms.* But you can't blame the American Meteorological Society for that. There aren't any life forms on the Moon—not even human ones on any permanent basis. Nothing here really worth the trouble except a little observatory like this one. Two or twenty years from now, when they have rockets ready to make the try for Mars and Venus, they'll build bases here, of course, but nothing much has been done yet beyond the surveying stage.

Yes, right now at this moment you are quite possibly the only human being on the Moon. Or if there are any others they are thousands of miles away because the bases are being built in craters near the rim. And this little dome you are in is located dead center, almost, of the Earthward side.

Well, a fat lot of work you've done. You haven't taken a single picture with the Ogden. Not your fault, of course—the Aliens took the Ogden along with them and you can't take pictures without a camera, can you?

Wasting thirty-nine days—two months, really, counting traveling time and training time—and you won't have a picture to show for it. But if you die they can't blame you for that. Quit thinking that way—you're not going to die—you *daren't* die.

Don't think about dying. Think about anything. Think about getting here. About how Captain Thorkelsen of the *Relief* dropped you off here—how many days ago? Three or thirty? More than three, surely more than three. If only the opaque sliding door of the top of this little dome were open so you could see through the glass you could tell, at least, whether it's Moon-day or Moon-night.

You could see the Earth and watch it spin around, one Terrestrial day for every spin, and you'd know how long you'd been here and how long there was to go. And Moon-day or Moon-night you could always see it because it would always be directly overhead. But there'd be heat loss, more through the glass alone than through the glass plus the insulated sliding door, so you can't risk it.

The Aliens left you only a third of your complement of storage batteries, barely enough to see you through. Barely enough of everything, so there'd be no chance that you could—by some chemistry alien to them—change something else into the oxygen of which they didn't leave you quite enough.

Sure you can open the door at intervals to look out and then close it again before too much heat escapes but that takes physical energy and physical energy and exercise use up oxygen. You can't risk moving a finger except when you have to.

Captain Thorkelsen shaking your hand, saying, "Well, Mr. Thayer—or maybe I should call you Bob now that the trip's over and we don't have to be formal—you're on your own now. Back for you in thirty-nine days to the hour. And you'll be plenty ready to go back by then, let me tell you."

But Thorkelsen hadn't guessed even remotely *how* ready he'd be.

You grinned at him and said, "I smuggled something, Captain. One pint of the best bonded Bourbon I could get to celebrate my landing on the Moon. How's about coming into the dome with me for a drink?"

He shook his head regretfully. "Sorry, Bob, but orders are orders. We take off in an hour exactly from time of landing. And that's enough time for you to get into a spacesuit and get there—we'll watch through the port until we see you enter the door of the dome. But it isn't enough time—quite—for us to get into suits and get there and back and out of the suits again in time to take off. You know how schedules are in this business."

Yes, you know how schedules are in spaceflying. And that's how you know—for better and for worse—that the *Relief* won't be fifteen minutes early getting here to pick you up, nor will it be fifteen minutes late. Thirty-nine days means thirty-nine days, not thirty-eight or forty.

So you nodded agreement and understanding. You said, "Well, in that case, can't we open the pint here and now for a drink around?"

Thorkelsen laughed and said, "I don't see why not. There's no rule against taking a drink out here—only a rule against transporting liquor. And if you've already violated that …

For five men the pint of bonded makes an even two drinks around and they're helping you into the cumbersome space suit while you're drinking the second one. And they're no longer anonymous space-monkeys to you after three days of close contact en route. They're Deak, Tommy, Ev and Shorty. But Deak, although you call him that to yourself, you call "Captain," even though he calls you Bob now. Somehow "Captain" fits Thorkelsen better than Deak does. Anyway they're all swell fellows. You wonder if you'll ever see them again.

II

But you pull your mind away from the present and send it back into the past, the distant past that may have been only a few days ago. You got into the airlock with your luggage, two tremendous cases you could barely have lifted on Earth but that you can carry here quite easily, even cumbered by a spacesuit. And you wave goodbye at them because your face-plate is closed and you can't talk to them any more. And they wave back and close the inner door of the airlock. Then the air hisses out—although you can't hear it—and the outer door opens.

And there is the Moon. The hard rock surface is five feet down but no ladder has been rigged. In Moon gravity it isn't necessary. You throw the suit-cases out and down and see them land lightly without breaking and that gives you the nerve to jump yourself. You land so lightly that you stumble and fall and you know they're probably watching you through the port and laughing at you but that it's friendly laughter so you don't mind.

You get up and thumb your nose at the port of the ship and then get the cases and start toward the dome, only forty yards away. You're glad you've got the heavy cases to weight you down. Even carrying them you weigh less than on Earth and you have to pick your way carefully over the rough-smooth igneous rock.

You reach the outer lock of the dome—it's a projection that looks like the passageway-door of an Eskimo igloo—and open the door and then you turn and wave and you can see them wave back.

You don't waste time because you want to get inside while they're still there. If the airlock should stick—not that they ever do, you've been assured—or if anything should be wrong inside, you want to get out again in time to wave to them or warn them. One of them will stay at the port until they take off, which will be in about ten minutes.

You take one more look at the dome from the outside—it's a hemisphere twenty feet high and forty feet across at the base. It looks big but it will seem small from the inside after you've been there a while. The supply cabinets and the hydroponic garden take up quite a bit of room and of what's left half is living quarters and half workshop.

You enter the outer door and close it behind you. The little light that goes on automatically shows you the handle you turn to make it airtight. You pull the lever that starts air hissing into the lock. You watch a gauge until it shows air pressure normal and then you reach out and open the inner door that leads to the dome itself.

It's all ready for you. The previous trip of the *Relief* brought and installed the Ogden and the other equipment you'll need, made a thorough inspection of everything. You and your duffle are all the current trip had to bring.

You open the inner lock and step in. And for seconds you think you're stark raving crazy.

There they are, three of them. And you don't doubt, once you know they're really there and that you're not seeing things, that they're Aliens with a capital A. They're humanoid but they aren't human. They've got the right number of arms and legs, even of eyes and ears, but the proportions are different. They're about five feet tall with brown leathery skins and they don't wear clothes. They're all males—they're near enough human so you can tell that.

You drop the cases you're carrying and turn to rush back into the airlock. Maybe you can get out again in time to wave to the *Relief.* Good Lord, it *can't* leave! These are the first extraterrestrial beings and this is the biggest news that ever happened. You've got to get the news back to Earth.

This is more important than the first landing on the Moon ten years before, more important than the A-bomb twenty years before that, more important than anything. Are they intelligent? A little anyway, or they couldn't have got through that airlock. You want to try to communicate with them, you want to do everything at once, but the *Relief* will be blasting off in a minute or two so that comes first.

You whirl around and get halfway through the door. A voice in your mind says, "Stop!"

Telepathy—they're telepathic! And that word was an order—but if you obey it or even stop to explain the *Relief* will be gone. You keep on going, trying to hurl a thought at them, a thought of hurry, of the fact that you'll come back, that you welcome them, that you're friendly but that a train is pulling out. You hope they can get that thought and unscramble it. Or get that they won't do anything about it even if they don't understand.

You're almost through the door, the inner door. Something stops you. You can't move, you're getting faint. Then the floor shakes under your feet and that's the ship taking off. You'd have been too late anyway.

You try to turn back but you still can't move. And you're getting fainter. You black out and fall. You don't feel yourself hit the floor.

You come to again and you're lying on the floor. Your spacesuit has been taken off. You're looking up into an inhuman face. Not necessarily an evil face but an inhuman one.

The thought enters you mind. "Are you all right?" It isn't your own thought.

You try to find out if you're all right. You think you are except that it's a little hard to breathe—as though there isn't enough oxygen in the air.

The thought, "We lowered the oxygen content to suit our own metabolism. I perceive that it is uncomfortable for you but will not be fatal. I perceive that otherwise you are unharmed." The head turns—the thought is directed elsewhere but you still get it. "Camelon," it says, "you owe me forty units on that bet. That reduces the total I owe you for today to seventy units."

"What bet?" you think.

"I bet him you would require a greater amount of oxygen than we. You are free to stand and move about if you wish. We have searched you and this place for weapons."

You sit up—you're a little dizzy. "Who are you? Where are you from?" you ask.

"You need not speak aloud," comes the thought. "We can read your mind. Your more limited mind can read ours when we wish to let it do so—as now. My name is Borl. My companions are Camelon and David. Yes, I perceive that the name David is common among you too. It is coincidence, of course. We are the race of the Tharn. We come from a planet in a very distant system. For reasons of our own security I shall not tell you where or how far with relation to your own system. Your name is Bobthayer. You are from the planet Earth, of which this planetoid is a satellite."

You nod, a useless gesture. You get to your feet, a bit wobbly, and look around. The largest of the three Aliens catches your eye and you get the thought, "I am Camelon. I am the leader."

So you think, "Pleased to meet you, pal." You look at the other and think, "You too, David." You find you can tell them apart. Camelon is inches taller than either of the others. David has a crooked—well, you guess it's his nose. Borl, the one who was bending over you when you came back to consciousness, has a much flatter face than either of the others. His skin is darker, more weathered-looking.

Probably he is older than either of the others. "Yes, I am older," the thought comes into your mind. It frightens you. You've got less privacy than you'd have in a Turkish bath.

"Ten units, David. You owe me ten units." You recognize as Camelon's thought. How you can recognize a thought as easily as you recognize a voice you don't know but you can. You wonder why David owed Camelon ten units.

"I bet him that you would be friendly. And you are. You are a little repelled by our physical appearance, Bobthayer, but so are we by yours. However, you harbor no immediate thoughts of violence against us."

"Why should I?" you wonder.

"Because we must kill you before we leave. However, since you seem harmless we shall be glad to let you live until then that we may study you."

"That's nice," you say.

"How odd, Camelon," Borl thinks, "That he can say one thing aloud and think another. We must remember that if by any chance we should ever speak to one of these people by any means of communication from a distance. They lie like the primitives of the fourth planet of Centauri."

"You don't lie," you think, "but you murder."

"It is murder only to kill a Tharn. Not one of the lesser beings. The universe was made for the Tharn. Lesser races serve them. You owe me ten more units, David. His fear of death *is* greater than ours despite the fact that our life time is a thousand times his. You felt it when he learned that we must kill him.

"And it is strange. Elsewhere in the universe the fear of death is proportionate to the length of life. Well, it will make for an easier conquest of Earth, his planet, if they are afraid to die. Ah, not too easy—perceive what he is thinking now. They will fight."

Suddenly you wish they'd killed you rather than stripped you of your thoughts this way. Or is there any way you can kill them?

"Don't try it," Camelon thinks at you. "You are without weapons and although smaller than you we are approximately as strong. Besides, any one of us can paralyze you with his mind—or make you unconscious.

"We do not, in fact, use physical weapons at all. The idea is repugnant to us. We fight with our minds only, either in individual combat or when we conquer a lesser race. Yes, I perceive you are thinking this would be information your race would like to know. Unfortunately you cannot live to warn them."

"Camelon—" Borl's thought "—I'll bet you twenty units that we are physically stronger than he."

"Taken. The proof? Ah, he came in carrying those two cases, one in either hand, easily. Lift them."

Borl tried. He could and did but with some difficulty. "You win, Camelon."

You think how much these—well, you suppose they're people, in a way—like to make bets. They seem to bet on everything.

"We do." Borl's thought. "It is our greatest pleasure. I perceive you have others beside gambling. Gambling in a thousand forms is our passion and our relaxation. Everything else we do is purposeful. Yes, I perceive that you have other pleasures—you escape reality with stimulants, narcotics, reading.

"You take pleasure in the necessary act of reproduction, you enjoy contests of speed and endurance—either as participants or spectators—you enjoy the taste of food, whereas to us eating is a disgusting but necessary evil. Most ridiculous of all you enjoy games of skill even when there is no wager involved."

You know all that about yourself and what you enjoy. But are you ever going to enjoy any of it again? "No, we are sorry, but you are not."

Sorry, are they? Maybe if you take them by surprise—

But you don't. Suddenly you're paralyzed. You can't move even before you really try. You can't act before you think. And it's useless otherwise. The paralysis ends the minute you think that.

You can move again but you've never been more helpless in your life. If you could only raise an arm to swing …

You can—and then you realize that it's too late. The Aliens have gone and you're here alone and dying but you're maybe a little delirious and you are here *now* and not *then* and that part of it is all over. All over but the dying—and the hoping that you won't die, that your gamble worked. Sure, you can gamble too.

You pant for breath and your insides gripe and you're cold and hungry and thirsty because they left you barely enough of everything to survive and then—as they thought, and maybe they were right—they stacked the odds hopelessly against you through thirty-nine days of hell and left you alone to die without even a book to read. But you've got to keep your mind clear in case by some miracle you do survive.

And suddenly you realize how you can tell how long it's been and how long there is to go. You decided, when your mind was still clear enough for you to decide things, that you'd divide the food into thirty-nine even portions and the water into thirty-nine even portions and consume one portion of each per day.

That had been a good idea for the first two days but then you'd forgotten once to wind your watch and it had run down and when you wound it you were nervous and mad at yourself and already in almost more pain than you could stand and you wound it too tightly and broke the spring.

And now you haven't any way of telling time and you decided you'd adopt the system of eating only when you were so hungry you couldn't stand it any longer—and then never eating more than half of a day's food at one time and water to match.

And you think—you hope—that you've stuck to that even in the periods when you were delirious and not sure where you were or what you were doing. But how much food there is left and how much water will be a clue at least to how long it's been.

You get off the cot and crawl—walking is too much of a waste of energy even if you were strong enough to walk—over to where the supply of food and water is. There are twenty portions of each—the time's almost half up. And it's a good sign that the portions are even. If you ate and drank all you wanted in delirium it's not likely that you'd have consumed an even number of portions of food and of water.

You look at them and decide you can wait a little longer, so you crawl back to the cot. You lie as quietly as you can. Can you live another twenty days? You've *got* to.

There was that flash into the mind of Camelon, the leader. It was accidental, some barriers slipped. It happened just after they'd shown you how helpless you were and had released the paralysis.

Some barrier slipped and you saw not only the surface thoughts that he was thinking, but deep into his mind. It lasted how long? A second perhaps and then Borl flashed a mental warning to Camelon and a barrier suddenly was there and only the surface thoughts showed and the surface thoughts were anger and chagrin at himself for having been careless.

III

But a second had been long enough. The Tharn were from the only planet of a Sol-type sun about nineteen light-years from Sol and almost due north of Sol—somewhere near the pole star. Its intrinsic brightness was a little less than that of our sun.

From those facts the approximate distance, approximate direction, approximate brightness, a little research—a very little research— would show what our name for that star was. Their name for it was Tharngel. And the Tharn, the inhabitants of Tharngel's one planet, were looking for other planets to which they could expand.

They'd found a few but not many. Our Sun had been a real find for them because there were two planets suitable for their occupancy, Mars with a little less air than they needed, Earth with a little more. But both factors could be adjusted. Such planets—planets with any oxygen atmosphere at all—were extremely rare. Especially with Sol-type suns and only in the radiation of a Sol-type sun could they survive.

So they were returning to their own planet to report and a fleet would come to take over. But it wouldn't arrive for forty years. Their maximum drive was a little under the speed of light and they couldn't exceed that. So the return trip would take them twenty years—then another twenty for their fleet to come and take over.

Nor had they lied about their only weapons being mental ones. Their ships were unarmed and they themselves had no hand weapons. They killed by thought. Individually they could kill at short range. In large groups, massing their minds into a collective death-thought, they could kill many miles away.

You saw other things too in Camelon's mind. Everything they'd told you had been true, including the fact that they couldn't lie, could barely understand the concept of a lie. And gambling was their only pleasure, their only weakness, their only passion. Their only code of honor was gambling—aside from that they were as impersonal as machines.

You even got a few clues—a very few—as to how that death-thought business operated. Not enough to do it yourself but—well, if you had time and expert help to work it out ...

The help, say, of all the scientists—the psychologists, the psychiatrists, the anatomists—on Earth a new science just might be developed in forty years. With the few slight clues you could give them and the knowledge that there *must* be a defense and a counter-offense—particularly a *defense* if Earth wasn't going to be a Tharn colony—Earth's best brains ought to be able to do it in forty years.

"They might at that," a thought, Camelon's thought, comes into your mind, "But you won't be there to give them those clues and tell them what offensive weapon to fear. Or the deadline they'll have to meet."

"They'll know *something* happened if they find me dead here," you think.

"Of course. And as we are taking along your books and apparatus for study they'll know beings from outside were here. But they won't know our plans, our capabilities, where we come from. They won't develop this *defense* of which you were thinking."

"Better take no more chances with him," Borl thinks at Camelon.

"Right. Look at me, Bobthayer." You look at him and his eyes suddenly seem to grow monstrous and you can't move although it isn't the same type of paralysis as before and you suddenly realize that you are being hypnotized. Camelon thinks, "You can no longer harm us physically in any way."

And you can't. It's as simple as that. You *know* you can't and that's that. They could all lie down on the floor and go to sleep and you could have a machine-gun in your hand and you couldn't pull the trigger once.

Camelon thinks at Borl, "No chance of his doing anything now that I've done that. We may yet learn more things of value from him."

"Shall we choose the things we are to take with us when Darl returns with the ship?"

You gather that Darl is one of them and that he has gone somewhere in the spaceship in which they came, which accounts for the fact that there was no ship in sight when the *Relief* landed. You wonder where Darl has gone and why. Probably to look over the bases being started for the rockets to Mars while the others study the contents of this dome. A casual affirmative thought from David gives you confirmation of your guess.

Camelon is thinking to Borl, "No hurry. He will not be back for hours and it will not take us long. We take all books, all apparatus, nothing else."

There is a thought at the back of your mind and you try to keep it there. You try not to think about it. It's not really a thought—it's the thought that there may possibly be a thought if you dig for it and you don't dare dig because they'll catch you at it and know the thought as soon as you do. Deliberately you think away from it. Maybe your subconscious will work out something from it without even you recognizing the score.

It's got something to do with their love of gambling, the fact that the only honor they have has to do with gambling. Think away from it quickly. None of them look your way—the thought was too vague for them to catch. And it hasn't anything to do with harming them—you know you can't do that now.

You sit down and you're bored. You think about being bored so that if they tune in on your mind that's what they'll get. And you really are bored—that's the funny part of it. You're waiting for them to kill you but it's going to be hours yet and there's nothing you can do about it—not even think about it constructively.

You wish there were something to do to fill in the time. These guys like to gamble, don't they? A poker game, maybe. Good old-fashioned poker. Wonder if they'd be any good at it?

But how could you play poker with people who could read your mind? The thought, "What is poker?" flashes at you.

You answer simply by letting yourself think of the rules of poker, the values of the hands, the excitement of the game and the thrill of running a bluff. And then, sadly, that it wouldn't be possible for them to play it because of their telepathic abilities.

"As he thinks of it, Camelon," Borl thinks, "it seems tremendously fascinating. Why shouldn't we try it? A new gambling game would be a wonderful thing to take back to Tharngel—almost as good as the news of two habitable planets if the game is a success. And we can keep up our second-degree barriers so that no thoughts can be sent or received."

Camelon—"It's risky with an alien."

"We know his capabilities and they are slight. You've put him under compulsion not to harm us. And at any move of his we can lower the barriers instantly."

Camelon stares at you. You try not to think but you can't not think at all, so you concentrate on the fact that there is a box of games equipment in a certain locker, that it includes cards and chips. It is there because occasionally this dome has been occupied by two or even three men if the research project they were involved in was a very brief one.

"What about stakes?" Camelon wonders. "Among us we could use Tharn money. Your money if—no, you have none with you, I perceive, because you thought it would be of no use to you here—and anyway your money would be useless to us, ours to you."

You laugh. "You're going to take my books and equipment anyway. Why not win them if you're smart enough." You underlie it with the thought that probably they're too stupid to play poker well and that they'd probably cheat if they did play. You feel the waves of anger, untranslatable because they don't need translation—anger is the same in any language. Maybe you went too far.

"Get the cards," Camelon says. And you realize that he *said* it aloud, in English. You wonder—and then realize that you've been asking all your questions by wondering and that this one isn't being answered.

You ask, "You speak English?"

"Don't be stupid, Bobthayer. Of course we can speak English after our study of your mind. And of course we can speak—it's simply such an inconvenient method of communication that we use it only under special circumstances such as this. Our barriers are up—we can no longer read your mind or you ours."

The big table serves. Borl is counting out chips. Camelon tells him to issue you chips to the extent of a thousand units on the books and equipment. You wonder how much a unit is and whether you're being gypped or not but nobody answers unasked questions any more.

Maybe they aren't kidding—maybe the barriers are really up and will stay up while the game is on. Come to think of it they probably will. Poker wouldn't be enjoyable otherwise. Just the same you don't let yourself think too much about anything important—such as your subconscious reason for having wanted this poker game. They might be testing you now even if they intend to maintain their barriers while the game is actually on, while the chips are really down.

You start to play. You deal first to show them how. Draw, jacks to open. Nobody gets openers and the deal passes to Borl. You have to answer a few questions, explain a few minor points out loud in answer to spoken questions. Borl is awkward handling the cards—you wonder that a race of gamblers hasn't discovered playing cards.

Nobody explains. Borl deals and you get queens. You open. Borl and Camelon stay. You don't improve the queens but you bet twenty units. Camelon has drawn three cards and after Borl drops his hand Camelon calls. He's caught a third trey to his original pair and he wins the pot.

They've got the idea all right—you'd better concentrate on playing good poker. You concentrate on it. You have to because they're good. And every indication is that they're on the level, playing square with you. Once, with a busted flush, you push in a fifty-unit bluff and you aren't called although David shows openers.

Once you spike an ace to a pair of gentlemen and draw an ace and a king for a full. You bet a hundred and Borl calls you on a ten-high straight. The call almost breaks Borl. He buys chips—and has to buy them from you because all the chips in the rack have been sold.

The stuff he buys them with turns out to be two-inch-square bits of something like cellophane except that it's opaque and has printing on it. The printing is a long way from being in English so you can't read the denominations but you take his word for it—his spoken word.

You hit a losing streak. You lose all your chips and have to use the currency you got from Borl to buy more from Camelon, who has most of the chips by now. But you play cautiously for awhile to learn their style—they've developed styles already. They're taking to poker like cats to catnip.

Borl is a bluffer—he always bets more, if he bets at all, when he has nothing than when he has a good hand. Camelon plunges either way about every fourth or fifth hand—the last two times he had them and that's why he's got the chips now. David is cautious.

So are you for a while. Then cards begin to run your way and you bet them. You begin to pile up chips, then cellophane units. Darl—the one who had their spaceship—comes back. There's a momentary intermission while barriers are lowered—and you carefully think about nothing except the excitement of the game as poker is explained to Darl. Telepathically, because it's faster and the boys are in a hurry to get back to the game. Darl buys in.

He wins his first pot and he's an addict. Nobody cares what time it is or whether school keeps.

Pots run to a thousand units at a time now—as many chips in one pot as you got for all your books and equipment. But that doesn't matter because you've got forty or fifty thousand units in front of you. Darl goes broke first, then Borl—after he's borrowed as much as Camelon will lend him. Camelon's tough and David manages to pike along and stay in.

But finally you do it. You've got all the money and you own one Tharn spaceship to boot. And the game is over. You've won.

Or have you? Camelon gets up and you look at him and remember—for the first time in many hours—that he is an Alien.

"We thank you, Bobthayer," he thinks at you; the barriers are down now. "We regret that we must kill you for you have introduced us to a most wonderful game."

"In what are you going to leave?" you think at him. "The spaceship is mine."

"Until you are dead, yes. I fear we shall inherit it from you then."

You forget not to talk. "I thought you were gamblers," you tell him, all of them, aloud. "I thought you were honorable when it came to gambling if nothing else."

"We are but—"

Borl forgets and talks aloud too. "He's right, Camelon. We cannot take the spaceship. He won it fairly. We cannot—"

Camelon said, "We *must*. The life of an individual is meaningless compared to the advancement of the Tharn. We will dishonor ourselves but we must return. We must report these planets. Then we shall kill ourselves as dishonored Tharn."

You look at him in wonder and he looks back and suddenly he lowers deliberately a barrier of his mind. You see that he means what he said. They are gamblers and they've gambled and lost and they'll take the consequences. They'll really kill themselves as dishonored—*after* they've reported in.

A lot of good that's going to do you. You'll be twenty years dead by the time they get home. And you won't have a chance to tell Earth what Earth's got to know—what to get ready for in forty years. It's a stalemate but that doesn't help you or Earth.

IV

You think desperately, looking for an out. You've won and they've lost. But you've lost too—Earth has lost. You don't care whether they're reading your mind or not. You look desperately for an answer, even one that leaves you a possibility. Maybe you can make a deal.

"No," Camelon thinks at you. "It is true that if you offered us back our ship, our money, the books and equipment in exchange for your own life— which was already forfeit—we could return honorably to our people. But you would warn Earth. As you were thinking some hours ago a defense might be developed by your scientists. So we would be traitors to our own race if we made such a deal with you even to save our own individual honors."

You look at them one at a time, at them physically and into a part of their minds, and you see that they mean it, all of them. They agree with their leader and they mean it.

Darl thinks, "Camelon, we must leave. We go to our deaths, but we must leave. Kill him quickly and let us complete our dishonor."

Camelon turns to you.

"Wait," you say desperately aloud. "I thought you were *gamblers*. If you were gamblers you'd give me a chance, no matter how slim a chance. You'd leave me here with one chance out of ten to survive. And in exchange for that chance I'll give you your own possessions back voluntarily and mine too. That way you wouldn't be stealing them back—you wouldn't be dishonored. You wouldn't have to kill yourselves after you reported."

It's a new idea. They look at you. Then, one by one, they think negatives.

"One chance in a hundred," you say. There's no change. "One chance in a thousand! I thought you were *gamblers.*"

Camelon thinks, "You tempt us except for one thing. If we leave you here alive you can leave a message for those who are due in thirty-nine days to pick you up, even though you yourself do not survive to meet them."

You'd been hoping for that but they'd read your mind. *Damn* beings who can read minds! Still any chance at all is better than nothing. You say, "Take away all writing materials."

Borl thinks at Camelon, "We can do better than that. Put a psychic block on his ability to write. A chance in a thousand is little, Camelon, to save our honor. As he says we *are* gamblers. Can't we gamble that far?"

Camelon looks at David, at Darl. He turns to you and raises his hand. You lose consciousness.

You awaken suddenly and completely. The lights are dim. The inside of the dome looks different. You look around and realize that it has been stripped of most of the things that were there. And there is only one Tharn in the room with you—Camelon. You find you are lying on the cot and you sit up and look at him.

He thinks at you, "We are giving you one chance in a thousand, Bobthayer. We have calculated it carefully, everything is arranged. I will explain the circumstances and the odds."

"Go ahead," you say.

"We have left you enough food, enough water—barely enough to survive, it is true, but you will not die of hunger or thirst if you ration them carefully. We have studied your metabolism with great care. We know your exact limits of tolerance. We have, as Borl suggested, also blocked your ability to write so that you can leave no message. That, of course has nothing to do with your one chance out of a thousand of survival."

"Where's the catch? What's the chance, then, if you leave me enough food and enough water. Oxygen?"

"That's right. We have taken out your oxygen system and are leaving one of our own type. It is much simpler. See those thirteen plastic containers on the table? Each one contains enough liquid oxygen to supply you—by very careful calculation—with enough oxygen to last you three days if you are extremely careful and take no exercise whatever.

"The oxygen is in a binder fluid that keeps it liquid and lets it evaporate at a constant and exact rate. The binder fluid also absorbs waste products. You need open one jar every three days—or whenever you find yourself in need of more oxygen than you are getting, which will be within a matter of minutes of three days."

But where's the catch? You wonder. Thirteen containers, each good for three days if you're careful, add up to thirty-nine.

You don't have to ask it aloud. Camelon thinks, "One of the containers is poisoned. There is an odorless undetectable gas that will evaporate with the oxygen. It is sufficiently poisonous to kill ten men of your weight and resistance, of your general metabolism. There is no way to tell it from the other jars without extremely special equipment and chemical knowledge beyond yours. The day you open that container you die."

"Fine," you say. "But how does that give me a chance if I have to use all thirteen containers in order to live through?"

"There is a slight possibility—one which we have calculated very carefully—that you can survive on twelve containers of oxygen. If you can and if you choose the proper twelve—which you have one chance out of thirteen of doing—you will survive. The parley of the two chances adds up to one chance out of a thousand. We leave now. My companions await me in our ship."

He doesn't wish you good-bye and you don't wish him good-bye either, You watch the inner door of the airlock close.

You go over and look at the thirteen containers of oxygen and they all look alike. The air is very thin and hard to breathe. You're going to have to open one of them quite soon. The wrong one? The one that contains enough poison to kill ten men?

Maybe it would be better if you pick the wrong one first and get it over with. The poison is odorless and undetectable—maybe it's painless too. You wish you'd wondered that while he was still here; he'd have answered it for you. Probably it *is* painless—or is that only wishful thinking?

You look around the rest of the place. They haven't left a thing of value except those thirteen containers and the food and water. It doesn't look like much food and water for that long a period. But it probably is enough, barely, if you ration it carefully. Probably they feared if they left any surplus water you might figure some way to get the oxygen out of it. They were wrong on that but they didn't take any chances—except the thousand-to-one chance.

You're panting, breathing like an asthmatic. You reach for a container to open it. If you do there's one chance out of thirteen that you'll be dead in hours, maybe in minutes. They didn't tell you either how fast-acting the poison is.

You pull your hand back. You don't want to take even one chance out of thirteen of dying until you've had a chance to think carefully. You go back to the cot and lie down to think because you remember that every muscular motion you make cuts your chances.

Have they missed anything, anything at all? The oxygen tank on back of your space-suit. You sit up suddenly and look and see that the space-suit itself is gone. There's no advantage to the airlock—the air that enters it when you pull the lever comes from this room. And the lock is empty now since it was last used for a departure.

The hydroponic garden is gone. So are the emergency tanks of oxygen that were in the storeroom in case of failure of the plants. You realize that you've got up and are wandering around again and you sit down. You cut your chances with every step you take.

One chance in a thousand—*if* you can use only twelve containers of oxygen there's—you figure it out mentally—there must be one chance in about seventy-seven that you'll live. That's what they must have figured. One chance in seventy-seven parlayed against one in thirteen is about one in a thousand.

But if you could use all thirteen containers your chances would be good, better than even. Not quite a certainty because there is always the possibility that something would go wrong, such as your losing your will power on rationing the food—or, more likely, the water—and dying of hunger or thirst in the last day or two.

You look for something to write with to see if they made any mistake on the hypnotic block. You can't find anything but you find out it doesn't matter, You've got a finger, haven't you? You try to write your name on the wall with your finger. You can't. You know your name all right—Bob Thayer. But you haven't the faintest idea how to write it.

You could talk the message if you had a recording machine, but you haven't a recording machine or any materials which, by any stretch of the imagination, would let you make one. You've got only your brain. You sit down and use it.

You forget to wind your watch and then, because of the pain, you wind it too tight and break or jam the spring and you've lost track of time and then comes the time when you find that half of your supplies are gone and you hope that half of the thirty-nine days is gone too.

And then again you're sick and delirious and part of the time you think you're back on Earth and that you've just had a nightmare about creatures from a place called Tharngel and you dreamed within the nightmare that you were playing poker on the Moon and that you won.

Pain, thirst, hunger, struggle for breath, nightmare. And then one day you eat the last of the food and drink the last of the water and you wonder whether it's the thirty-first day or the thirty-ninth and you lie down again and wait to find out.

And you sleep and in your dream you hear an earthshaking racket that could be the landing of the *Relief* except that you know you're dreaming and in your dream the air gets even thinner as air rushes from the dome into the airlock and the airlock opens and Captain Thorkelsen is standing there beside you and you say, "Hi, Captain," weakly and wake up to find out that you weren't really asleep and then you black out.

And when you come around again, there is good breathable air in the dome and there is food waiting for you to eat and water waiting for you to drink. And all four of them from the *Relief* are standing around watching you anxiously.

Thorkelsen grins down at you. "What have you been doing? Where are all the books and equipment? What happened?"

"Got in a poker game," you tell him. Your throat is dry, still almost too dry to talk, but you drink some water—carefully, a sip at a time.

And then you're telling the story, a bit at a time, as you sip more water and eat a little and you begin to feel almost human again.

And from the way they listen and the way they watch you, you know that they believe it—that they'd believe you even if it weren't for the evidence around them. And that Earth will believe and that everything's all right, that forty years is a long time even to develop a new science when all of Earth is working at it. And you've still got the clues to give them a start and your gamble paid off. You won the poker game after all.

You get tired after a while and have to stop talking. Thorkelsen looks at you wonderingly. He says, "But, Good Lord, man, how did you do it? All those oxygen containers—if that's what they were—are plumb empty. And you say enough poison to kill ten men was in one of them. You look like you've lost thirty pounds weight and you look like you'll need a month's rest before you can walk again but you're *alive*. Did they miscalculate or what?"

You can't keep your eyes open any longer—you've got to sleep. But maybe you can take time to explain.

"Simple, Cap," you tell him. "Each container held enough oxygen for one man for three days and one of them also contained enough poison to kill ten men. But there were thirteen containers, so I opened them all and mixed them together, and then put them back and opened one approximately every three days. So every minute, from the opening of the first one, there's been ten-thirteenths of enough poison in the air to kill a man. For thirty-nine days I've been breathing *almost* enough poison to kill me.

"Of course the effect could have been cumulative and it could have killed me anyway but on the other hand I might have built up immunity toward it. Didn't seem to work either way—I've just been sick from it at a constant degree from the beginning. But it was plenty better than the one chance in a thousand they intended to give me, so I tried it. And it worked."

Vaguely you're aware that Thorkelsen is saying something, but you can't make out what it is and you don't care because you're practically asleep already, the wonderful sleep that you can have only when you're breathing real air with enough oxygen and no poison. You're going to sleep all the way back to Earth and never leave Earth again ever.

The Hatchetman

Matt Anders arrived at the New Albuquerque Spaceport on Venus in the early afternoon. His identification papers showed him to be one Harvey Giles: merchant, Philadelphia, Earth. Purpose of visit to Venus: purchase of precious stones. He was tall, but stooped with age; his gray hair and seamed face matched the photographs on his identification papers. Any resemblance to the real Matt Anders was impossible to detect.

He let the mechanics roll away the one-man Spacezephyr, while the two guards who had come to meet him escorted him to the administration building where his identification papers were checked and approved. After that, he was free to leave, carrying his brief case containing—except for one secret pocket—only papers pertaining to his assumed identity.

A landcab swung in to pick him up. He hesitated momentarily and then waved the driver away. The residence of the Terran ambassador was less than half a mile distant, and a chance for exercise would be more than welcome after thirty-five hours in the tiny spacecraft. He took a deep breath of the exhilarating Venusian air and started down the street.

He felt no sense of danger. It was broad daylight and New Albuquerque is a safe, well-policed city. Only a few people on Earth—and those were men in positions of high trust—knew of his presence here or the form of his disguise. The various unorganized crackpots and malcontents who hated him could not possibly know. And aggression on the part of the Martian Duplies, here on Venus, Anders didn't even consider. Mars was trying her best to keep Venus from taking sides in the strange cold war she was waging with Earth—a war in which neither side had made a direct move against the home planet of the other, although millions of men had died in space and in attacks on outposts. Certainly Mars could not risk antagonizing Venus by any overt act on the neutral planet.

So it was the very unexpectedness of the attack against him that enabled it to succeed. For a moment, except for him, the street was empty. Except for him and the landcab that had offered to pick him up back at the spaceport. It must have followed him unobtrusively for some distance, and now it contained three men besides the driver. It swung up against the curb beside him and disgorged its occupants; two men tried to pinion his arms; the other swung an old-fashioned blackjack.

Matt Anders dropped his brief case and tried to swing with his right at the Duplie holding his other arm. The blow was ineffectual, but it was the movement on his own part that caused the sap in the hands of the third man to accomplish less than had been intended. He was dazed by the blow, his knees buckled and he fell, but he didn't completely lose consciousness.

The Duplies who had hold of his arms lifted him and carried him to cab. The one who had used the blackjack took a quick look up and down the street, picked up the brief case and followed them into the cab.

The whole thing had taken only seconds. And now he was between two of them in the rear seat and, leaning past the one to his right, the third man bent toward him. Now his hand held a hypodermic needle instead of the blackjack. Anders caught a fuzzy glimpse of it from a corner of his eye as the Duplie poised the needle to plunge it into his arm. He didn't know what it meant. Not death, most likely, because if they'd merely wanted to kill him they could easily have finished him off back there on the street without taking the risk of carrying him into the cab.

The landcab swung sharply around a corner, and as it swerved Anders managed to press against the man on his right. He twisted his body so that the plunger of the small hypo was depressed. It lost a full half of its contents on his coat before he felt the prick of the needle. He jerked involuntarily at that, and the wielder of the hypo laughed. "Coming out of the fog, huh? Well, that shot'll take you right back in again."

The driver spoke back over his shoulder. "He didn't come to, did he? We don't want him to remember anything beyond the blackjack."

"He wasn't awake; just jerked when he got the needle."

But he was awake, and stayed awake. He was dazed, sick, dull-minded, but still conscious and determined to stay that way. Fighting against giving in to the darkness to which his mind wanted to succumb as the contents of the hypo spread through his blood stream. He lay inert and motionless, deliberately breathing slowly and regularly, hiding every outward evidence of the fight his mind was putting up against unconsciousness.

It grew dark suddenly and he knew they had driven into a garage. The grip on his arms tightened again and he was half dragged, half carried, from the landcab. He allowed himself to open his eyes a mere slit, enough to make out his surroundings. Sure enough, they were in a garage and he was being hauled toward steps leading downward at the back of it.

"Shake it up," one of his captors said. "We're ten seconds behind schedule now. And don't worry about mussing the guy; he's supposed to be banged up plenty."

They hurried him down the cellar steps into a lighted room, a typical under-residence room that contained the standard heating apparatus and laundry equipment of the twenty-second century—and the typical trash and odds and ends that clutter a basement in any century whatever. But at the far end of the cellar, screened from view until they rounded a pile of packing crates, was an object that surprised Anders so much that he almost revealed his consciousness.

It was a Kingston Duplicator. An illegal, jerry-built one, here in New Albuquerque.

He knew all too well the character of the Duplies, products of the Duplicator. Their complete egotism, their utter lack of any moral sense whatsoever, their cold viciousness and inhumanity. But he was still amazed that they'd have the utter gall to construct an illegal machine of their own here on Venus.

Back of the Duplicator itself was a huge condenser of a type he'd never seen before, something the Duplies themselves must have developed for the purpose. They could load a condenser of that size with enough juice to operate the Duplicator once by feeding it current a little at a time over a period of weeks, so there would be no sudden great drain of power that would give away to the authorities the presence and use of a Duplicator. It was a clever idea, Anders had to admit to himself. As far as he knew, nobody had used it before. Why, with the use of an attachment like that, there could be Duplicators in any city on Earth, undetected and undetectable.

He knew now all too well what they were going to do to him. If he'd had the least bit of strength, he'd have tried a break then and there. But the combined effects of the blackjack and the drug had left him only an edge of consciousness. He couldn't have stood on his own feet and walked out, even if they'd let go of him. He'd have to wait a later opportunity—not that he really expected to get one.

The machine, he'd seen at first glance, was adjusted for human duplication-transmission. They strapped him into the chair—for all the world like an old-fashioned electric chair except that it had no electrodes—that was bolted to the field platform.

When the switch was thrown there'd be a duplicate of him on Mars—except that duplicate would be a Duplie instead of a human being. It would be exactly like him in every way, except that it would lack that intangible ingredient "soul," that ingredient man had never been too sure he had until the Kingston Duplicator had proved it to him—and had created chaos in the process.

TROUBLE COMES DOUBLE

Venus had been the first planet colonized. The first explorers to penetrate its eternal cloud envelope had found, to everyone's surprise, a breathable atmosphere. This had been hidden from the spectroscopes of Earth's astronomers by the peculiar constitution of that cloud envelope which hid Venus' surface from the observation of Earth.

The colonization of Mars had not been possible until almost a century later. There had been only experimental outposts there, under domes, until the technology of the late twenty-first century had provided the means of creating an artificial atmosphere. This was done by concentrating what oxygen there was in a narrow band close to the surface instead of letting it diffuse itself through the entire depth of atmosphere. Held close to the ground, it made Mars habitable, except for mountainous or plateau areas.

By that time, constant travel between Earth and Venus had caused interplanetary travel to develop to the point where it was easy and inexpensive, and the colonization of Mars had been very rapid. It had been a spontaneous emigration of the common people that had caused Mars, for a while, to suffer from a lack of trained scientists and statesmen—a lack of qualified leadership. Men who had achieved success and eminence on Earth did not care to emigrate.

That's where the Kingston Duplicator had come in; it had seemed to be a perfect answer to Mars' problem. It had enabled men like Duclos, Kingston himself, Barry, Wade and hundreds of others—the men who had contributed most to the science and political leadership of Earth—to remain at home on Earth, and to have duplicates of themselves sent to Mars. The Duplies were to contribute to the advancement of Mars what their originals had contributed and were contributing to the advancement of Earth.

There was a catch, but nobody knew about it until too late.

The Kingston Duplicator had been invented early in the twenty-second century. One Duplicator, adjustable either as transmitter or receiver, could send to another—at either close range or interplanetary distances—a duplicate of any object placed in the field of the transmitting machine. It did not involve, of course, any creation of matter. The receiving machine drew upon a hopper of anything at all, usually sand, which was transmuted electronically into whatever elements were needed for creation of the duplicate.

With respect to inanimate objects, the Kingston Duplicator had only one theoretical limitation; one that was learned the hard way. Fissionable material, even in less than critical quantities, could not be transmitted-duplicated without exploding in the sending machine.

The Duplicator had, of course, changed the economy of Earth (and of Venus and Mars) but not completely, not too greatly. The tremendous amount of power it required prevented its practical use for the reproduction of anything except expensive and valuable things. Of what benefit to reproduce a bushel of wheat or a chair at a cost of a thousand dollars' worth of power when you can grow the wheat or make the chair much more cheaply? On the other hand, a five-thousand-dollar mink coat becomes less of a luxury item when it can be duplicated for a fifth of that sum; small precision instruments, very valuable relative to weight, became cheaper in duplication; rare metals and elements (except the fissionable ones) became less prohibitively expensive and thereby opened new fields to technology.

The government had made one restriction to protect the investment of those who had money invested in precious stones: diamonds, except those necessary for industrial use, were restricted.

So were human beings. Early experiments with lesser animals had shown that duplication of them was quite possible, without apparent harm to the animals—and also without commercial possibilities, since it remained cheaper to raise a pig than to duplicate it. But before a single human being had been duplicated by a Kingston Duplicator, governments acting in concert ruled against the attempt.

If for no other reason, there would be too many legal difficulties involved in the duplication of a human being. A wife could find herself with duplicate identical husbands; a job or a bank account or an insurance policy would find itself with duplicate identical claimants. And which was the original and what would be the rights of the duplicate? And, besides, there was no logical reason for permitting the duplication of a human being.

Until the lack of technicians and leaders in the new Martian colonies suggested an advantage to human duplication that seemed, if proper restrictions were observed, the perfect answer to the problem. Suppose Duclos, top electronics engineer of Earth—and electronics engineers were badly needed on Mars—agreed to have a duplicate of himself created on and for Mars. Duclos had nothing to lose—except that he signed a paper agreeing never to leave Earth, which he had no desire to do anyway. His duplicate would be required to agree never to leave Mars. The Martian government would give the Duplie an amount of money equal to whatever the original possessed. Only men with no close family ties could be chosen. As long as they remained as far apart as Earth and Mars, there could be no conflict of personal interests between them.

It seemed foolproof, and the experiment was permitted. Duclos was duplicated. His Duplie took over electronics development on Mars—and voiced no objection to his lot. Wade, top man in interplanetary economics. Kingston, inventor of the Duplicator, acquired a duplicate on Mars. Several hundred others, top men in every other important field.

Then the catch. The unsuspected missing ingredient.

The first of the Duplies had concealed, cleverly, their essential nonhumanness, their plans, until the quota had been filled. Then—all of them—starting with those in positions of power at the top—they had taken over Mars. And few of the human people of Mars knew or even suspected that they had been taken over. There were top statesmen, top propagandists, among the Duplies.

And now Mars was at war with Earth. A peculiar war ...

Strapped in the chair, Matt Anders suddenly realized that he should have fought his captors, even without chance of winning, on the off chance that he might have been killed in the struggle. Until this moment, he hadn't realized how much better it would have been to die rather than to be duplicated on Mars. For his duplicate would—at least after indoctrination—be on their side. And his duplicate would know every political and military secret of Earth known to him, Matt Anders, righthand man, hatchetman extraordinary, of Dwight Morphy, President of the Council of Nations of Earth. The top secrets, just about all of them of Terran policy and planning. It wasn't only his ability, valuable as that alone would be to them, that they were duplicating; it was his knowledge.

The instant he realized that, he would have rushed to commit suicide, had there been any possible way for him to do so before they threw the switch.

For a second, blinding light played around him, but he felt nothing. Except for the slight temporary pain in his eyes from the light—and that could have been avoided by a blindfold—duplication was painless, without sensation.

Then, the sudden aftereffect that had been noticed in every living thing, animal or human, who had been duplicated—temporary unconsciousness that would last a few minutes. He felt himself slipping into it and he knew, and was past caring, that in his case he'd never waken from it. Now that they'd duplicated him, they'd kill him quickly before he came out of the aftereffect, before they even unstrapped him from the chair. The last thing he knew was that somebody was telling somebody else to hurry damn it hurry, and then the blackness and the blankness came ...

Someone was shaking his shoulder gently. Someone was saying, "Are you hurt badly? Was it a hit-and-run car? Should I call an ambulance?"

Matt Anders sat up groggily. He was at the point along the street where he had been attacked. He looked about him; his hat was lying in the gutter and his brief case was where he had dropped it during the brief struggle. The landcab wasn't in sight.

There wasn't any evidence at all that he'd been kidnapped and then returned to the same spot where the assault had occurred. And they thought he'd been unconscious since that first blow with the blackjack; he wasn't supposed to know that anything besides the assault had happened; he wasn't supposed to know that he'd been duplicated.

And he hadn't any proof, except his own word, that he had been. The Venusian authorities would tell him his story was fantastic—and it would sound that way. It was fantastic that there could be an illegal, private Duplicator, operated by Duplies, here in orderly and peaceful New Albuquerque. He himself could hardly believe what had happened. The Venusian authorities would accuse him of lying in order to create an interplanetary episode.

"Are you all right?" somebody said. "Shall I call an ambulance?"

He put his hand to the back of his head as he turned to look up. The man standing behind him was small, mild, inoffensive. A typical clerk or bookkeeper from one of the government offices.

"I'm all right," Anders said. "I'll be all right in a minute. Just a sore noggin from a sap."

"A sap? Oh, you mean a—a blunt weapon? Were you attacked and robbed?"

Had they been that thorough? He put his hand into the pocket where he'd carried money. It was gone. They'd been thorough enough to make it look like an assault and robbery. Not that the money mattered; once he was out of his disguise, his signature was good for any reasonable amount at any Venusian bank. But the valuable information in his brief case—No, they wouldn't have bothered tampering with that. The papers in the secret compartment were valuable only for the information on them, and that information was in his head as well. It would also be in the head of his Duplie on Mars.

He got to his feet a little shakily and found that he was all right, except for the ache in the back of his head and the dustiness of his clothes. He said, "I'm all right, thanks."

"You're sure? You're sure you don't want—?"

"I'm sure," Anders said. "Thanks a lot, but I'm sure. I've got only a block to go, and I'll report this to the police from there." He knew it would seem strange to the little clerk if he didn't intend to report it.

He got his hat and briefcase and started off, a bit waveringly at first, but more firmly after he'd gone a few steps. After one try at putting the hat back on his head, he carried it in his hand. His head would be too sore for days to let him wear a hat. He grinned wryly as it came to him that his duplicate on Mars would have an equivalently sore head; the blow of the blackjack had fallen before the duplication.

He was less than fifteen minutes late when he arrived at Ambassador Pearson's residence. He stopped outside the door long enough to brush most of the dust from his clothes and then rang the bell.

Pearson himself came to open the door. He looked blankly until Anders said, "Matt Anders, Mr. Ambassador. Please overlook the disguise—at least until I have a chance to remove it."

"Anders! But—" Pearson looked down at Anders' clothes. "—what on earth happened? Did you have an accident?" His eyes widened. "Or are you Matt Anders? That disguise—"

Anders grinned. "Is a good one. But if you'll suspend disbelief long enough to give me access to a lavatory for a few minutes, I think you'll recognize me. And after that I'll tell you what happened."

"Certainly. And while you're there, can I make you a drink? You look as though you could use one. Something Venusian, or—?"

"Whiskey," Anders said. "A big slug of it, straight, wouldn't hurt me a bit."

Pearson showed him a door. "That room will do. And your drink will be waiting, Matt."

In the lavatory, it took only a few minutes to remove the thin rubber mask, backed by sponge rubber in places, to change the shape of his features and to remove the gray wig that had helped cut down the force of the blackjack blow. There was a clothes brush and it removed the rest of the street dirt from his coat and trousers.

He looked at himself in the glass, and the face that looked back at him was a familiar one. A thin, angular face—vaguely Mephistophelean. Very Mephistophelean in the many caricatures of him that had been in the newspapers of three planets.

Not a popular face, even among people of his own planet. The face of a man reputed to wield too much power and to wield it ruthlessly—and a man whose face, particularly in caricature, looked the part. But a handsome face, an interesting one. A face all too easy to remember, which was why he wore such careful disguises when he traveled alone. How had the Duplies penetrated that disguise? His best friend—and that was probably President Morphy— couldn't have done so.

His drink, and a comfortable chair, were waiting for him when he rejoined Pearson. He sank into the chair and drank deeply and appreciatively. Then he put down his glass and said, "Mr. Ambassador, I believe I've learned the secret of the disasters we've had recently. I believe I know how the Duplies have been getting their information."

He frowned. "And it's about time—if it isn't too late. It shouldn't be any secret that our morale has been on the skids for months. At this rate, in spite of the fact that we control space and have the Duplies pretty solidly blockaded, we'll lose the war due to apathy on Earth. Corruption, bribery, inability— let's face it—among our top military leaders. Our munitions industry breaking down—from the top. Our diplomats losing points in negotiations with Venus to come in on our side."

The ambassador winced at the last sentence. "That's rather a blow under the belt, isn't it, Matt? I've done my best."

"Sure. But you're bucking espionage beyond anything you've ever dreamed of. That's what I found out today. Mars knows already every detail of the information and instructions I've brought you—and I haven't even turned them over to you yet."

"Good God, Matt. Are you sure? How?"

Anders told him, briefly, the experience he'd just had—and wasn't supposed to remember.

Pearson's face was a pattern of dismay when he'd finished. He thought and then asked, "But why didn't they kill you? I don't understand that. Duplicated on Mars or not, you're still a valuable man to Earth."

"Two reasons, sir. First, the information they'll get from my duplicate will be more valuable to them if, as they think, we don't know they have it. If I disappeared, or were found dead under whatever circumstances, there'd be at least a suspicion that they had the information I was carrying—a copy of it, even though the original was still in my brief case. Second, what if they plan, later, to get my Duplie to Earth through the blockade—and they do get ships through it, either way—and then have me killed under circumstances where he can step into my shoes." He leaned forward earnestly. "And if that's happened already to some of our top men, it explains a lot. A hell of a lot."

"But if that's true—"

There was a knock on the door, a soft tap.

Pearson frowned. "Must be my daughter. Well—I won't let her interrupt us long." He raised his voice. "Come in."

The door opened and the girl who came through it was, Matt Anders thought, possibly the most striking girl he'd ever seen. There was something about the way she held herself, the way she walked ... He remembered now having heard that Ambassador Pearson had a great grandparent who had been a fullblooded Sioux; it was obvious in his daughter. Her cheekbones were high, her complexion dark, her hair raven black and worn in braids across the top of her head. Tall, lithe, full breasted, calm-eyed, she carried herself with the pride and dignity of the Plains Indian. And although she was young—possibly ten years Anders' junior—she had the poise and assurance of a woman who has been conscious of her beauty for years.

Matt Anders was on his feet before Pearson's murmured introduction. He swallowed, and immediately felt ridiculous at the reaction. But almost all the women he'd ever met had seemed weak and insipid to him. Marta Pearson was something else again. She was almost an atavism; she was as different from the modern woman of the twenty-second century as a tiger from its descendent, a tabby cat. And maybe that accounted, Anders thought, for his reaction. He had often suspected that he himself, emotionally, belonged in a different and earlier century.

She smiled distantly in acknowledgment of the introduction, but her smile didn't reach beyond her lips as she held out a cool hand to him. And her words were to her father. "I recognized Matt Anders immediately, Father. After all, one can hardy look at a periodical or tune in a visor without seeing the features of the famous alter ego of President Morphy. His *hatchetman*, I believe, is the commoner term."

Her father said sharply, "Marta!"

Matt Anders felt himself flush, the first time he'd done so, to his own recollection, since adolescence. But he made his voice calm. "It isn't always easy to serve your planet in the way your superiors direct, Miss Pearson. Especially when your position isn't an elective one from which you can be removed for unpopularity." He hesitated for a moment, then decided to continue: "Hasn't it occurred to you that, disliked as I am, President Morphy is the most re- spected and loved person on Earth? But if there wasn't a Matt Anders, a hatchetman, to do certain things for him, perhaps he could not even be re- elected. Right now, he's just about all that's holding Earth together and keep- ing the anti-war faction from letting the Duplies have their way on Mars."

He wondered, even as he talked, why he was bothering to justify himself. He was used to being hated by millions. Why worry about one more—except that the one more was suddenly important to him?

Marta Pearson still smiled coolly. "A convincing little speech, Mr. Anders. Unfortunately, it seems difficult for me to forget that it was you who ordered the Third Fleet to take the Martian base on Calypso at all costs. And 'all costs' turned out to be the loss of three-fourths of the fleet. Oh, they took Calypso, yes. But where were you at the time, Mr. Anders?"

She had touched a raw spot. He paled, angry at her, angrier at himself for allowing her to put him on the defensive like this. "I was on Luna, Miss Pearson, when the Third Fleet left there on its mission. I did not accompany it, on strict and specific orders from President Morphy. He, not I, thought I was too valu- able to risk, especially since I have no training in space combat and would have been of no special value to the fleet."

Her smile was openly sardonic now. "Yet you ordered them—and don't deny it was your order—to take Calypso at all costs. And they were obliged to obey that order even when it was found the satellite's defenses were far stron- ger than had been guessed."

"Marta!" her father said again.

"And they took it," she went on. "With losses of three ships out of four. My brother was on one of the ships that didn't make it; my fiance on another."

She turned and walked from the room.

"I'm sorry, Matt," Pearson said. "I don't know what I can say or do ..."

Anders grinned wryly. "You might get me another drink, Mr. Ambassador. If she'd waited, I could have told her my own brother happened to be with that fleet—and didn't come back."

"That I can tell her—and will, Matt. And I wish top secrecy didn't prevent my telling even my own daughter the reason that order was necessary, and would have been justified, even if it had meant complete loss of several fleets."

Matt Anders took the glass Pearson held out to him. "You know that?"

"Yes. Uranium on Calypso. None on Mars. Which is why that base was of vital importance to the Duplies—and why it was equally vital to us to keep them away from it. If they once get quantities of uranium ..."

Anders nodded gloomily. "If they do, then the war is no longer in space only. We'll have to destroy their cities to keep them from destroying ours— and it will end up with both being destroyed. As long as there's even a chance of the stalemate's continuing, anything would be better than that."

He flicked his hand in a characteristic gesture, brushing the subject aside. He downed his second drink before he picked up his brief case and took papers from the secret compartment which he handed to the ambassador. "Well, here's what I was to deliver to you, sir, and now it's delivered. Only—and keep this between us—work on the certainty that the Duplies have this information, too. At least the general outlines of it. If I'd been able to memorize all the minor details and figures, of course, I wouldn't have carried the papers. But my Duplie will know all I knew about it—and that's enough to make it practically worthless."

Pearson looked puzzled. "But you said 'between us.' You mean you're not going to report what happened to you?"

"Not while I'm on Venus. I'm not to stay here long anyway. Just long enough, in fact, to get a night's sleep tonight. I'll leave in the morning. And what I've learned through my own kidnapping and duplication is so important, I want to report it in person, direct to Morphy. I won't even trust the tightbeam; we're not sure the Duplies aren't tapping it."

"I see, Matt. Probably you're right. And I'm awfully sorry about Marta."

"It could have been worse. At least she didn't take a shot at me. And that's happened three times in three months back on Earth. Misguided people— and they weren't all Duplies, either—seemed to think killing me would solve all the problems of the solar system."

"Well—I'll talk to her before dinner. By the way, Matt, one thing I've wondered about. Not that it matters. Did you give that order to the Third Fleet? Or did you just transmit the President's order?"

"Oh, I gave it all right. It became a sudden emergency when we learned about the uranium angle on Calypso, and I couldn't reach Morphy immediately so I gave the order. Later, of course, he confirmed it. But the publicity went to my issuance of the order, not his confirmation of it." He shrugged. "Well, that's part of my job, to take the blame for nasty things off his shoulders. And that was a particularly nasty one from the outside—because we had to hold back, for security reasons, why Calypso was suddenly so vitally important."

Pearson nodded slowly. "I begin to see how tough a job you've got. Wish I could tell that to Marta. Suppose I can tell her that it was of vital importance, even if I don't tell her why. And that you lost your brother there, too."

Anders said, "Don't, please. It's part of my job to have people feel like that about me." But he knew, even as he said it, that he didn't want Marta Pearson to feel that way. The girl attracted him as no woman ever had before.

The ambassador cleared his throat. "Just the same, I'm going to talk to her. By the way, we dine early on Venus. If you wish, before dinner, to be shown to your room to bathe and ... you didn't bring any luggage, so I presume you won't have to change—"

"The bath sounds good to me, but haven't you heard of washtex? I can wash these right under the shower with me and they'll dry, in the original folds, in three minutes. Luggage will be a thing of the past when these become common, unless one's taking a long enough trip to want variety in costume."

"Good. Then I'll show you to—"

"Wait, Mr. Ambassador. If we can spare a few minutes, I've just got an idea. Let me think it out a second, first."

Anders had stood up. Now, he sat down again in his chair, and the ambassador sat down again too. After a few seconds, Anders said, "I think it's a good idea. Listen, I know how we can put a crimp in whatever plans the Duplies may have for substituting my Duplie for me somewhere. They can't know how badly I was injured by that blackjack; they didn't have time to give me a medical examination. Suppose you put out a general story—give it to the newscast services—that, shortly after my arrival here, I died of a brain concussion. The Duplies will believe it."

"But—Good Lord, Matt—"

"Let me finish. You also send a tightbeam message to Morphy telling him that the newscast story is a phony; that I'll report to him as soon as possible and explain it. For him to arrange so I can land safely—in the same disguise and under the same name I use coming here—without being shot as a Duplie of myself. The Duplies know that disguise, but if they think I'm dead they won't be watching for me."

"But you yourself said we're not absolutely sure they don't intercept our tightbeam. What if they do?"

Anders' hand flipped the possibility aside. "Nothing's certain. If they do intercept it, we've lost nothing. If they don't, we're a jump up on them." He grinned. "And we can always announce that the report of my death was exaggerated—much as that will disappoint many people. You'll do it?"

"Of course, Matt."

"Let's see—Earth time—Morphy won't be getting up for a couple of hours yet. Get the telenews story out right away, if you will, but hold off until after dinner on the tightbeam correction; no use waking him up. His health's not been too good lately, and he's been working much too long hours."

Besides, he thought to himself, it wouldn't hurt Morphy to think for a few hours, if he got the telenews story first, that he'd lost himself a messenger boy. It might give him something to think about, before the secret correction came.

"If you want it that way, Matt—"

"I do. And now if I could go to my room—"

DEATH FOR A DUPLIE

He stripped and washed his clothes first, so they'd dry while he bathed himself. The bath felt wonderful, as did the few minutes he spent under the automatic masseur. By the time he was ready for it, his clothing was dry, unwrinkled, and looking as though it had just come from the factory. Washtex— this was the first time he'd tried it—was going to be popular indeed. He looked at the comfortable clean-sheeted bed yearningly and wished he could spend a few hours in it.

He knew perfectly well that Pearson would excuse him from dinner if he explained how tired he was after the trip from Earth. But—all right, admit it, he told himself—you want to see Marta again no matter how tired you are, and no matter what her attitude toward you may be this time.

Refilling his pockets with the sundry things he'd taken from them before washing the suit, he hesitated as he picked up the electrogun which he always carried in an inside pocket. It was a neat and deadly little weapon, weighing only six ounces but packing the punch of an elephant gun and completely silent in its operation. He shrugged, checked the mechanism, and put it in his pocket.

He left his room and walked down the stairs, the neoplast soles of his shoes making no noise whatsoever. As he neared the door of the library where he'd had his previous talk with the ambassador, and his embarrassing encounter with Marta, he heard both of their voices raised a little, he thought, above ordinary conversational level. Undoubtedly they were discussing him; probably Marta was being reprimanded for the things she had said—and was arguing back.

Curiosity got the better of him. Snooping or not, he wanted too badly to hear what Marta had to say about him to worry, just at that moment, about gentlemanly instincts. He took a few steps nearer the door; he could hear clearly now what was being said. If there was a break in the conversation or if either voice approached nearer the doorway, he could start walking quickly and avoid the appearance of having been standing there.

Marta seemed to be apologizing for the scene she had made. Matt Anders stood even more quietly; walking in now would be even more embarrassing than if he walked in on a quarrel.

And then suddenly Marta's voice changed; became cold again. "But, Father, that isn't what I wanted to tell you. It is this: that information Matt Anders brought you—you mustn't present it at the conference tomorrow."

"I don't know what you're talking about, Marta. I can see, of course, how you could easily guess the reason for Matt's trip here. But why do you say—?"

"The Duplies have that information, yes. But hasn't it occurred to you that they won't have time, by tomorrow, to prepare a suitable rebuttal? That we can't let you present it?"

"I don't—what are you saying, Marta?"

"It's quite simple, Father. I mean—this."

Matt Anders had been slower than usual. He should have got it, four sentences ago. He moved swiftly now to the doorway, and his electrogun was in his hand when he got there. Too late—just in time to see the purple arc of the electrogun in the hand of the Duplie of Marta Pearson leap from its muzzle to the chest of the ambassador. His own electrogun fired at almost the same instant.

He stepped quickly into the room, pulling the door shut behind him. There had been two thuds of falling bodies, but he doubted that the sound would have been heard in whatever quarter of the house servants were preparing dinner. Houses on Venus are made of thick concrete, and the sound of a jar does not carry easily even into the next room.

They were both dead, of course; he didn't have to verify that. An electrogun discharge doesn't mark a body, but, no matter where it strikes, even a toe or finger, it is fully as deadly as a direct hit from a heavy space cannon.

His lips thinned back over his teeth as he stared down at the beautiful body that had been a Duplie of Marta Pearson. Had she been a Duplie that afternoon when he had first met her? Well, it didn't matter now.

But one thing did matter—and vitally. Had Pearson, before the start of the conversation with what he thought was his daughter, given out the news of Anders' death from brain concussion? If so, Anders was in a hell of a spot. Pearson was the only person who could send a convincing tightbeam message to Earth to contradict that report, and Pearson was dead. He didn't even know where Pearson's tightbeam transmitter was; it would be carefully concealed somewhere and would take hours, probably, to find. And he didn't have hours; the servants who were preparing dinner would be announcing it soon.

And here he was with two dead bodies on his hands—and nothing about Marta's body that would prove it was a Duplie of her instead of the original. And if his own death had already been announced, he was the one who would be taken for a Duplie and shot on sight by the Venusian police. Despite the fact that Venus maintained neutrality in the Earth-Mars war, they knew the character of Duplies and hated them as much as Earthmen did. No Duplies were tolerated on Venus; the members of the Martian consulate had to prove their origin and birth—had to be dupes of the Duplies, not Duplies themselves.

And damn vacillating Venus for that, for refusing to take active part in a war against inhuman things whom they recognized to be utterly evil.

But no time to think about that now. He'd have to act, and quickly, His eyes cast about and found the telenews set on a stand in the corner. He snapped it on, manipulated the dial until he found a station just starting on a news program.

A report or two on the war—news he already knew and to which he listened impatiently. Then: "It was announced half an hour ago by Terrestrial Ambassador Pearson that Matt Anders, personal aide to President Morphy of Earth, died this afternoon as a result of—"

He snapped it off; he didn't need to hear the rest. And Pearson would not yet have sent the tightbeam message of contradiction. He'd promised to wait until after dinner for that, and Pearson was a man of his word even in tiny things.

He went to the door and locked it; that would give him seconds of extra time if a servant came to announce dinner. Quickly, he dragged the two bodies out of sight behind a sofa; that would give him seconds more and a chance to talk his way out if he had to unlock the door.

He sat down in a chair to think.

It was fatal to stay on Venus. It would be fatal to go to Earth.

Suddenly he laughed. There was still Mars.

And why not? If he could get through the blockade—and others had done it—

I've got a Duplie on Mars, he thought viciously. He intended to replace me, if he could. Now the Duplies think I'm dead. *What if I can replace him?*

It sounded like a chance in a thousand. Maybe a million. Or maybe only a hundred, since the advantage of surprise would be completely in his favor, with the Duplies not even suspecting what he intended, since they would think—along with Earth and Venus—that Matt Anders was a dead duck.

Suddenly he was almost glad that tightbeam contradiction hadn't been sent.

Suddenly he was free.

Morphy, he thought, you've lost yourself a messenger boy.

How many minutes did he have? Enough to get back into his disguise as an elderly merchant of precious stones? He had to have enough minutes; otherwise he couldn't get his Spacezephyr at the spaceport.

He moved fast now. Telephone. The spaceport. His voice suddenly the voice of an old man. "Harvey Giles speaking. Owner of Spacezephyr SZ-1470. I learn I must return to Earth quickly; my son is seriously ill. Can you have the craft ready for me in ten minutes? Thank you. Thank you very much."

The bodies. A better job of concealment, so hidden that they wouldn't show unless someone deliberately looked under the sofa or over its back. Marta's body so beautiful. Damn Duplies. Was Marta alive somewhere? It was unlikely, almost impossible. Why would they have kept her alive after duplicating her? And after having her Duplie take her place. They'd kept him alive, but only because they had to wait until his Duplie had a chance to replace him. So forget Marta; she's dead. And luckily, her Duplie was dead now too.

He left the door of the library open behind him.

In his room, he jerked the brief case open, took out the disguise, the rubber mask and wig. He got them on, not too good a job but it would pass casual inspection. Five minutes gone since he'd left the library. How many more before dinner? And, for how many minutes thereafter would the servants look around the house before they called the police, or found the bodies and then called the police?

Down the stairs and his luck held. Outside, into the early evening. A landcab was going by and he hailed it. He'd take his chances on its being what it seemed; but his hand was on the butt of his electrogun as he got into it, and stayed there until it let him off at the spaceport.

The usual brief formalities, the casual glance at his identification and at himself. On Earth it would have been stricter. But then Earth was at war, and Venus wasn't.

His ship was ready, waiting.

Blastoff.

Straight up, of course, first; and when he moved the gyroturn handle, he turned the little ship toward Earth. Probably there'd be a routine radar check to see that he took the course he'd said he was taking; interceptors notified to challenge him if he didn't. Besides, eight or ten hours' travel toward Earth would lose him only an hour or two. Luckily, Mars was in the same general direction across the ecliptic.

Luckily, too, he had benephrin tablets to keep him awake for the fifty-hour trip to Mars. One can't afford to doze on a one-man craft in space, which turned out to be far more crowded with meteors and planetoids than Earth-bound man had ever guessed. When he hit Mars, he'd need at least twenty-four hours' sleep under another drug to counteract the benephrin binge, but he'd worry about that when he got there.

Forty-five hours later and a million miles out from Mars, he came to the block-ade patrol. His receiver barked, "Identify yourself immediately or we open fire!"

The war between Earth and Mars was a peculiar war. Earth could have destroyed Mars at any time—but didn't. Earth had atomic bombs; the hundred cities of Mars which housed almost a billion people could have been wiped out within a week. But those billion people were colonists from Earth, friends and relatives of almost every family on Earth.

The Duplies, of course, knew this emotional appeal and counted on it. They also pointed, propaganda-wise, to the fact that they had made no attack on the cities of Earth and did not intend to. Of course they did not intend to—without uranium to make bombs. Mars itself had no uranium, no fission-able matter of any kind. And it was fortunate for Earth that the Kingston Duplicator exploded on any attempt to duplicate a fissionable substance, else all the Duplies would have needed was one small piece of uranium which they could have duplicated endlessly until they had enough to blow Earth out of the solar system. And no sense of morality to keep them from doing just that.

So the war had been in space, where Earth had the edge and had a block-ade around Mars—although Martian blockade runners frequently got through it. And the war, unknown to the citizens, was also a war on Earth—a war of espionage, propaganda, sabotage of morale, conducted by a few well-placed Duplies.

And Martian propaganda didn't sound unreasonable, for it claimed it wanted only to be left alone. It would have been all too reasonable, except that the billion people of Mars were the dupes of the Duplies, under their absolute control.

Propagandizing the true Martian colonists about the real nature of the Duplies would have been the answer, but the Duplies controlled channels of communication. All Martian radios and televisors were tight-tuned to the big broadcasting station of Marsport; they could receive no messages from Earth or from ships in space. The Martians were completely shut off from the rest of the system—and had no choice but to believe the propaganda their leaders fed them. And their leaders were Duplies. The Martians thought they were fighting a War of Independence against Earth; they didn't even know that their independence had already been granted and that they were already a free planet and no longer a colony.

Matt Anders continued his course. The next challenge came only seconds later: "Identify yourself immediately or we fire."

He couldn't safely ignore that one. He pressed the two-way visiplate button so the flagship which had done the challenging was in visual as well as auditory communication. Lieutenant-Commander Gresham's heavy-joweled face appeared on the screen in the little Spacezephyr. Anders knew that, in the flagship, Gresham was seeing Anders' face with the disguise long since removed.

Anders said crisply, "You know me, Gresham. Confidential mission, highly important." If he could stall a few more seconds, he'd be through. Right now they probably couldn't fire at him because he was among them; thirty seconds more and he'd be out of range past them—if his bluff worked. If he could only make Gresham hesitate. If Gresham only hadn't heard the news that—

Gresham hesitated. His mouth opened a little, snapped shut, then opened again and he said, "But you're—"

He didn't finish, but Matt Anders knew that Gresham had heard the news Ambassador Pearson had given out to the newscasters.

Two more seconds passed, and then Anders knew that he was safe, for Gresham still stared at him. Then Gresham said, "But, Anders, we received no orders on this. I must ask you to report to me on the flagship for clearance."

And that had killed another dozen seconds. Gresham was stalling, letting him through. Gresham was a Duplie. Which accounted for the relative ease with which blockade runners had been getting through. Now Gresham, having heard of his "death" on Venus, thought that he was one.

Dead-pan, Anders helped with stalling. "Afraid, Commander, that's impossible. Direct orders President Morphy. Suggest you check with him." Gresham would check all right—to keep his own nose clean—but even if he got Morphy at once, enough minutes would have been wasted.

He was out of range now, already, and with a sigh of relief he clicked off the screen. He'd never thought, before, that he'd be glad to find out any highly placed Earth officer was a Duplie. If Gresham hadn't been one he still might have bluffed his way through, but it would have been much tougher going.

He landed the Spacezepher in a high valley between Martian mountains, about eighty miles from the main city of Marsport. A relatively safe place to land the craft and leave it; the valley was above the level of breathable atmosphere, so no Martian would come there for any ordinary reason. Anders would have to wear an oxygen mask to get down to breathable air, but the Spacezephyr carried one. His only danger of being spotted was from above, and he'd have to chance that.

He needed sleep; almost a hundred hours without it, even with benephrin to keep him going, had sapped his stamina so much that his physical and mental reactions were sluggish and he couldn't have walked half a mile, even under Martin gravity, without keeling over. He needed at least twenty-four hours of sleep under the drug that was the counteractant to the benephrin. Here, before he left the little spaceship, in a spot no Martian would come to, was the best place to get it. He took the counter-drug, made himself as comfortable as he could, and was asleep in less than a minute.

He slept longer than he'd intended, almost thirty hours. And when he awoke it was night. Deimos and Phobos, the two moons of Mars, were in the sky, but gave little light. He'd have to use a handflash and, once he was in sight of the road over the top of the mountain, he would be conspicuous. He decided to wait until daylight for his trip over and down the mountain to the nearest road.

He waited until dawn before he left the Spacezephyr. The range he had to scale, up one side and down the other, would have been a day's work on Earth; on Mars, at .38 Earth gravity, he weighed less than sixty pounds, so it was easy, if sometimes risky, climbing. He was over and down before the Martian noon. As soon as he was low enough for the air to be breathable, he hid his oxygen mask carefully in a place where he could find it again in case he lived long enough ever to want to make his way back to the spacecraft. Then he walked to the nearest road. He stood along the edge, waiting.

Luckily, it was a road used not too frequently. Landcars whizzed by at intervals of five or ten minutes, just about right for his purpose. He waited until a gray military one came along, with no other car in sight in either direction. He stood still until it was just past him, then drew his electrogun and fired at it. A purple flash darted from the muzzle of the gun to the speeding car. Possibly at that distance, and diffused by the body of the landcar, the shock of the bolt may not have been lethal. But it was enough of a shock to the driver to make him lose control. The car swerved, tires screamed. The car tipped, then rolled. Anders ran toward it. When he got there, its occupant was dead, his head a gory mess against the broken driving column. He wore a captain's uniform—or what was left of one.

Anders waited by the wrecked vehicle, knowing that the next military car wouldn't pass without investigating this one. Civilians would; hands off anything remotely resembling military affairs were their strict orders on Mars.

Several civilian cars went by in the next twenty minutes, slowing down out of curiosity—but pretending not to slow down—and their occupants looking curiously at the wrecked car and at Matt Anders, waiting there so calmly. But none of them stopped.

Then the jackpot he'd been waiting for. A gray car that stopped, brakes squealing, just beyond the wreck, and backed up. And the man in it wore the insignia of a lieutenant general; he might even be a Duplie. The captain had probably been only a dupe, and Anders had been sorry about that. But what was one life when billions were at stake?

The lieutenant general got out of the gray landcar and walked over scowling. "What's this? And what are you doing here? Who are—?"

Matt Anders' shot from the electrogun got him. There was nothing to be gained by conversation. He pulled open the door of the wrecked car and shoved the body of the lieutenant general through it. That would stall investigation a little; whoever found the wreck next would assume the two had been riding together, with the captain acting as chauffeur. A missing military landcar wouldn't be looked for at once.

Just the same he got into the other landcar as quickly as he could and got away from there fast. He drove twenty miles before he found a side road; he turned into it, and as soon as he was out of sight of the main road he stopped and looked through the documents compartment of the car. He found what he wanted most, a road map of the area and a city map of Marsport. He also found enough identification to tell him it was the car of Lieutenant General MacWheeler. The name MacWheeler was recalled to him as being one of the original batch of Duplies sent to Mars. MacWheeler's original on Earth, he remembered, had been an expert in rocket technology.

One Duplie less now.

He studied the maps thoroughly; memorizing, so he wouldn't have to stop on a main road or in traffic, the route to Marsport; the simplest route through it which would take him to the domes, the Duplie headquarters. Here, if anywhere, he'd find his own Duplie. Beyond that, he couldn't plan.

As he neared Duplie headquarters, the insignia on the landcar he drove— fortunately for him indicating only the rank of its owner, not his identity— proved its value. Sentries snapped to attention, gates were opened. He parked the landcar and left it, tried to act casual as he strolled toward the domes.

Earth espionage on Mars by no means matched Martian—Duplie—espionage on Earth. He knew about the domes, but not much beyond the fact that they were Duplie headquarters, and that they were dozens of yards thick and proof against atomic bombing. Which meant that if Earth was ever forced to bomb Marsport they'd kill everyone except the Duplies, the only ones they'd want to kill.

There were half a dozen domes and he hadn't the slightest idea which one to head for. In which of them would new Duplies undergoing orientation and indoctrination be quartered?

He wasn't alone; there were other people on the walks to and around the various domes, and he started watching them, hoping for a clue. He'd have to keep watching until he got one. It could be a fatal error to try to enter the wrong dome, and all of them, he saw, were guarded by sentries at the single door of each.

He watched the people around him, studying them as carefully as he could without appearing to do so. Some of them, particularly those in uniform wearing high rank, were undoubtedly Duplies. The others were undoubtedly ordinary Martians, but those sufficiently indoctrinated by Duplie propaganda to be trusted by them beyond all doubt. Most of these were in civilian clothes. A few had Washtex suits like his own, a fact that encouraged him.

The number of women, in uniform or otherwise, surprised him. And some of them, he noticed, were dressed very seductively. Were they Duplie women— who would be, as were Duplie men, completely amoral? There had been fewer than a hundred women among the original three hundred and twenty first duplicated for Mars. But perhaps the Duplies had been willing to extend their quota when it came to acquiring women for themselves, women as amoral as they. He toyed with the thought, and a moment later was sure of it. He recognized one of the women—one of the scantily dressed ones—as Mona Wayne, the most beautiful telestar of Earth. Mona Wayne's Duplie, rather; and certainly she hadn't been duplicated to Mars because of her value in espionage.

Valuable in other ways, indubitably, although he himself preferred ... He jerked his mind away from thinking about Marta Pearson. He'd thought about her plenty in those fifty-odd hours in space en route to Mars. But there'd been time enough to think then. Now, he had to concentrate on finding his own Duplie.

He tried to pull his mind away from the thought of her—and just then he saw her.

Or her Duplie. Another Duplie of her? It must be, because it was inconceivable that the original, the real Marta Pearson would have been brought to Mars. There was no reason for it, everything against it. Besides, she was dressed— one might even say undressed—in the fashion of the Duplie women. And the fashion became her; she had the body for it. Had she been duplicated for the same purpose for which Mona Wayne, the telestar, had undoubtedly been duplicated? He almost ground his teeth at the thought, and then remembered that this was a Duplie. He'd killed one Duplie of her just after it had killed her father; he could kill this one as readily.

Then they were abreast and she caught his eye. She said, "Hi, Matt," so casually that it startled him—until he remembered that there was a Duplie Matt Anders here, and she undoubtedly knew him and thought she was speaking to him. And that she took his presence so casually for granted proved that his Duplie really was here, and that he was close to his target.

He managed to wave and speak in reply with equal casualness, and forced himself to go to the next crosswalk without looking around. Only then did he turn and look back, lighting a cigarette to cover his standing there, and he let his eyes follow after her until she entered a dome.

He waited a few more minutes and then walked toward the dome into which she had entered.

TWO'S A CROWD

Two cold-eyed guards stood, one on either side of the door. As he walked toward it, one—the one with sergeant's insignia—stepped forward and barred his way. He said, "The password, sir." Courteously, but firmly.

Anders scowled and continued to advance up to the point where another step would have meant body contact with the man barring his way. He said, irritably, "Bother the password. I've forgotten it. You know me."

The guard stepped quickly back and there was an electrogun suddenly in his hand; one appeared also in the hand of the other guard. The first one said, "Our orders are to challenge three times. If the password is not forthcoming, we're to shoot."

The other one said, "That's right, Mr. Anders. Sorry, but this is the second challenge. The password, please."

Matt Anders knew he couldn't get his own gun out in time; he was just deciding the only possible course was to turn and stride away in simulated anger, hoping that they wouldn't shoot him in the back if he didn't wait for the third challenge.

A hand dropped on his shoulder. A voice said, "What's the matter, Matt?"

He turned his head, deciding in a split second that he wouldn't be surprised whoever stood there: the voice had been familiar although he couldn't place it. Sean Charlton, head of the W.B.I., the World Investigation Bureau, top man in counterespionage.

Despite his decision, for a second Anders' mind reeled. If Charlton, of all Terrestrials, was a Duplie ... And then he realized that Charlton wasn't Charlton, the real Charlton had been duplicated somehow and this was his Duplie. But the substitution still hadn't been made or the Duplie wouldn't be here; Charlton's Duplie must still be in the indoctrination period, as was his own.

He said, "I've forgotten the damn password, Sean."

Charlton laughed. He leaned forward and whispered in Anders' ear. Anders said, "Thanks, Sean." To the guards he said, "Hiroshima."

The nearest guard frowned. "That's irregular. He told you."

Anders grinned. "Nuts, Sergeant. You didn't hear him tell me; you're just guessing. Besides, it's okay—I just couldn't remember whether it was Hiroshima or Nagasaki, and I was afraid if I said the wrong one you'd shoot, so I was stalling. Now I just remembered which of the two it was."

It must have sounded reasonable; the sergeant shrugged. He stepped back and holstered his gun; the other guard holstered his.

Charlton's Duplie and Anders entered the dome side by side. The Duplie said, "Lucky man, lucky again that I came along just then. Lucky enough to be the last of the Duplies."

The last of the Duplies! What on three planets did Charlton mean by that?

He didn't dare ask, but he'd have to find out. They were walking past a building directory of the dome; Anders glanced at it out of the corner of his eye and tried to find his own name among the A's. He saw it, but they were walking too fast for him to catch the room number that followed it. Anyway, he did have a room here; he'd learned that much. And probably his Duplie was in it right now. Possibly with the Duplie of Marta Pearson? Had she been coming here, by any chance, to see him? It was possible, but only a possibility; as a relatively new Duplie she probably had quarters here too.

Anyway, he didn't want to go to his room right away now; first he wanted to find out, if he could, what Charlton had meant by that "last of the Duplies" business.

He said, "Let's go to your room, Sean. Like to talk a while."

"Okay, and we'll have a drink."

When they entered the elevator Anders saw that there were buttons for eight floors; the top few would be small in area because of the dome shape of the building. Charlton pressed the button for the fourth floor.

Charlton made drinks for them when they were in the room. "Ran into your friend Marta just outside the Communications Dome," he said. "Having trouble with her? She sure acts different since she got back this morning."

Anders wanted to ask where she got back from, but he couldn't risk questions to which he was probably supposed to know the answers—especially not after Charlton had given him the password he'd "forgotten." The Duplie might put two things together and come up with the right answer. He said casually, "Yeah, she does seem a little different. Don't know why."

"Guess it's a tough trip on the blockade runners. Don't worry; she'll be all right when she's rested up. Well a break for you things got fouled up there."

"I didn't get the details on that," Anders said. "Did you?"

"Not except that a wheel came off somewhere; she had to kill her original along with the old man, so she couldn't substitute. No chance to get rid of the body in time. So they brought her back."

A pulse was throbbing in Matt Anders' temple. He knew the Marta Pearson he'd killed was a Duplie. And this Marta, the one he'd seen enter the dome, had just arrived here, this morning, on a blockade runner—not via duplication. Could it possibly be—

Charlton was saying, "Drink up, I'll make us another." He took Anders' glass. "Yes, you're a lucky guy, Matt. The last Duplie."

How could he fish for information about that, without asking? If the Duplies were stopping duplication of humans, stopping it completely, it meant something important, damned important. A change in plans? A showdown?

"Quite a plan, huh?" he said.

Charlton came back with the glass. "It can't miss. They won't even be able to strike back, from Earth. Oh, the blockade fleet is probably carrying a few atomic bombs, but Gresham's in charge of the fleet—and, if nobody's mentioned it to you, he's one of us. If he can get away with it, he'll surrender without dropping a bomb, once Earth is kaput. If he can't—well, the fleet hasn't enough stuff to do more than ten per cent damage to us, as against ninety-five per cent to Earth." He laughed. "There isn't a town of less than five thousand there that hasn't got a Duplicator! And dozens of them in every big city. Imagine an A-bomb going off simultaneously in every Duplicator on Earth. What a bang that'll be. And enough radioactivity in the air to kill off everything that's left. That's the only bug in the plan: that it'll be so many years before we can take over Earth. That radioactivity'll last a long time."

Anders stretched his lips over his teeth in what he hoped was a grin. The Duplies—probably the Duplie of Kingston himself—had figured some change in the transmitter end of the Kingston Duplicator that enabled an A-bomb to be sent from a transmitter without exploding. And if it exploded in the receiving end—well, that was what they wanted it to do anyway.

And that would be the end of Earth. And what could he do here alone? Was there any way he could get more details without arousing—The hell with that, he thought suddenly. What did it matter if he aroused Charlton's suspicion, here alone with him in his room? Why not take the short cut? It meant he'd have to kill Charlton, but that would be a pleasure—next only to killing his own Duplie. Duplies weren't people.

He finished his drink and put the glass down carefully. Then suddenly the electrogun was in his hand, aimed at the Duplie. Anders said quietly, "Don't move."

Charlton didn't move, except that his eyes widened. He said, "What—" And then, in a different voice, "I get it. And I gave you the password."

"And now you're going to give me information. I haven't got time to fish for it. Give me the rest of the details of that plan."

"If I tell you, you'll kill me anyway."

"Maybe I won't. Maybe I'll knock you out and tie you up. I'll decide that later. But if you don't talk, I'll kill you right now. Want to talk?"

Charlton licked his lips. He said, "All right, you won't be able to do anything about it anyway. What do you want to know?"

"When?"

"Tonight, pal. Tonight. It's almost ready to go now. You won't be able to do a thing about it."

"How did Kingston—or whoever it was—fix the transmitters to send atomics?"

"I'm no technician. I don't know that. But I know they can do it—have done it. Where do you think we got the uranium? About a pound of it is all we got off Calypso before you got our base there. But Kingston and his gang got the bug out of his apparatus. There's an attachment they put on a machine that lets it transmit or receive radioactives. Touchy to operate, but it works. They duplicated that pound of uranium into enough for three juicy bombs. And they've got three transmitters, each being adjusted to duplicate simultaneously in all the Kingston Duplicators on Earth. They're setting the patterns now. Can I have a drink?"

Anders nodded; he wanted time to think what else to ask. He looked for flaws in what the Duplie had just told him—and watched carefully meanwhile as Charlton poured himself a straight drink and downed it quickly.

Anders said, "This isn't all of a sudden. Something like that takes time. And it eliminates need for espionage. So why, only a few days ago, did you Duplies take me on Venus? With a deal like that coming up, what's Matt Anders to you?"

"Three answers to that. One, although we've been working on this for months, final tests weren't positive until yesterday. Two, we've been keeping on with all espionage activities for the sweet reason that if we stopped them suddenly, something might be missed; we just carried on with all previous plans. Three, and this is in your particular case only, the Chief wanted a Duplie of you—to serve him on Mars as you've been serving Morphy on Earth. You were to be—I mean, your Duplie was to be—*his* hatchetman. He isn't going to substitute for you; he's going to stay here and help hold Mars in line."

Anders swore. It made sense, all three reasons made sense. And explained a lot of things.

"Where are the three Duplicators that are going to send the bombs to Earth?"

"I don't know."

Anders raised the muzzle of the gun slightly.

Charlton said quickly, "I don't know, I tell you. Nobody knows, except a few of us assigned to operate them. And you know I wouldn't be one of them, not knowing one end of a duplicator from the other. You know I'm no technician."

He was right on that, but—maybe he was still lying.

Charlton said, "Listen, use your head. That information would be top secret—just in case of something like this happening. Why should anyone be told where the machines are? I doubt if anyone, from the Chief on down, knows where all three of them are located. They're in different places, hundreds of miles apart. Just in case there's a spy among us—as there damn well is, I just found out—so he can't possibly get a message to the blockade fleet and have those machines bombed before they're ready to go."

It made sense. Duplie sense. With three machines, widely separated, any one of them sufficient, with one A-bomb apiece, to be duplicated endlessly. And that was why Charlton had talked so readily, knowing he couldn't possibly give the final and most vital piece of information under any pressure.

Anders stood. Should he take time to knock out and tie up the Duplie? Or simply—

Charlton stood, too; he was a little drunk. He must have been drinking heavily before Matt had met him, or he would not have been so affected by the few drinks he'd had now, even though the last had been a long, straight one.

He said, "All right, Matt. It was a good gag; pays me off for the one I pulled on you yesterday. And I went along with it for you. Now, let's shake hands on it, huh?" He took a step forward, his hand out, and then the step turned into a sudden dive to get in under the gun—too late. The gun flashed, caught him on top of his head at one-foot range. He'd saved Matt Anders' deciding what to do with him, and in a way that met Anders' fullest approval.

From These Ashes

Anders went out quickly and back to the elevator. At the first floor, this time alone, he stopped to look at the directory. He picked his own name again and this time the room number too, 518. Marta Pearson, 310.

He punched the elevator bell for the third floor of the dome. He knocked on the door of 310.

He stepped in quickly as Marta opened the door, forcing her to take a backward step to avoid being run into.

He had to find out right away, and there was a short cut—crude though it would be. As he closed the door behind him he grinned at her and asked a question, a question that was deliberately so worded that only a harlot or a Duplie woman could fail to resent it. Color rose into Marta's face and her hand lashed out at him.

He caught the hand. He said, "Sorry, I had to do that. I apologize. But *you're no Duplie*. A Duplie woman wouldn't have blushed—even at that."

She jerked her wrist from his grasp and backed away.

He said, "Marta, I'm no Duplie either. We've got to work together, and fast. Something's going to happen to Earth tonight. If we pool what we know about this place, there's just a chance we can stop it."

She was breathing hard, her eyes wide. "All right, you trapped me. I'm not a Duplie, but you are. And—"

He hadn't been watching her hands, and he hadn't guessed that a garment as brief as the one she was wearing could have a pocket that could hold an electrogun—even one as tiny as the one she pointed at him. Only half the size of his own six-ounce one, it was fully as deadly, although one that size held only a dozen charges.

He was careful to move forward now. He said, "Marta, you've got to believe me. Too much depends on it. If I were a Duplie, why would I have said I wasn't?"

Her voice was cold now. "I don't know. How can you prove you aren't? I still don't believe you."

He thought rapidly. "Call Room 518. You'll find my Duplie there—I hope. Get him down here." He had business with his Duplie anyway.

"Wait. Turn around." She walked up behind him when he'd turned; she held the muzzle of the gun against his back while she reached around and found the electrogun in his pocket. Then she stepped back again. "All right, I'll give you that chance. Walk over into the corner where I can watch you while I call."

He walked to the corner before he turned. She was standing by the speaker-receiver in the wall near the door; she'd already pressed the button and he heard her give the room number. He heard his own voice say, "Anders speaking," over the communicator.

"Marta Pearson. Could you come down to my room a moment?"

"Marta! Didn't know you were back. Sure I'll be down, but it'll be a few minutes. Making a report on Venus. I got to finish for the Chief, rush job. Be seeing you soon as I can get there."

She pushed the button again. But the gun hadn't wavered. She said, "All right, maybe Matt Anders had two Duplies. Or if there's only one, how do I know which—"

"You don't," he said. "But listen, time is valuable, and we've got a lot of notes to compare: I won't move and you've got a gun on me. But while we're waiting save some time by telling me what happened to you on Venus. Was it you who gave me a bad time about that Calypso battle—or was that your Duplie, whom I killed later just after she'd killed your father."

"That was I. Wait, why should I tell you anything until I know you're not—"

"Because there's nothing to lose. You can always shoot me after you've told me. And it'll save time. Besides, even if you think I'm a Duplie, you've already told me you're not one, so what would more details matter?"

She thought that over a few seconds. "All right. It was I who told you off. Then—I went outdoors for a walk. I stayed away until it was time for dinner, because I didn't want an argument with Dad over what I'd said to you. I was a little late coming back and I came in the back way, because it was the nearest, from my direction. I went into the library and was surprised to see no one there. I started to light a cigarette and dropped my lighter; it was a round one and rolled under the sofa and—"

"You found the bodies."

"Yes. Of course I knew mine was—a Duplie. I guess I panicked; I was afraid and wanted out of there, didn't even want to stay long enough to use the communicator. There's a security station two blocks away and I guess I decided to run there for help. Anyway, I ran out the front door. And a landcab that had been parked across the street U-turned and pulled up the second I was out of the door and someone said, 'Get in!' There were two Duplies in the car—a man and a woman. I knew they'd shoot me down if I ran, even if I tried to get back in the house. So I got in the back seat. Suddenly my scare was over and I was calm. I think I know, incidentally, when they duplicated me. I had an accident three weeks ago; I was bowled over by a hit-and-run landcab—I thought—and knocked unconscious. They must have taken me to a Duplicator then, while I was out."

Anders said, "Then they must have sent your Duplie in just as an assassin, with no intent to substitute her for you. I don't get that; any assassin would have done."

"No. From things that were said later, they did intend to substitute. The car had been waiting in front to intercept me on my way back to the house. If I'd come back the front way, instead of the back, they'd have kidnapped me and killed me, and my Duplie would have stayed—and never have been suspected of killing Dad, of course. But—you say—you killed my Duplie. And I'd come back the wrong way, so things had gone wrong for them. They drove to where they'd left their ship, a blockade runner, and—well, we got here this morning. I'd managed to learn enough from them on the way here to—to get by until now."

"But why? I mean, didn't you try to escape from them before you took off from Venus?"

"I don't know, I might have been able to." Her eyes blazed. "I didn't try. I thought that here I might—"

"You might kill a few Duplies before they killed you. My idea, too, more or less. But there's something bigger at stake, Marta. Something that—"

He suddenly stopped and put his fingers to his lips; he'd heard the faint sound of footsteps outside in the corridor. Then there was a knock on the door. Anders stepped back farther into the corner and, stood very quietly.

Marta Pearson slipped the gun back into the pocket from which she'd taken it, but kept her hand on it; she stood, as she opened the door, so she could still keep at least a corner of her eye on Matt Anders.

Matt Anders' Duplie stepped in.

DECONTAMINATED VACATION

He said, "Marta darling!" as he closed the door behind him. "Wonderful to have you back." And then stepped forward to embrace her.

But Marta stepped back away from him, even more quickly, and the gun came out of her pocket and up. "Look behind you," she said. "And don't move, outside of that."

The Duplie turned his head and saw Matt Anders. His eyes widened and despite the threat of the gun in Marta's hand his own hand went to the inside pocket of his coat and brought out the electrogun whose mate Marta had just taken from Anders. He said, "Marta! This is no Duplie—this is *my original.* I'm going to—"

He was going to, but he didn't. The gun in Marta Pearson's hand flashed first.

It had been a close thing; there was sweat on Anders' forehead as he stepped from where he'd been waiting in the corner. He said, "Sit down; we've got to talk fast, and then work fast—or try to. Listen, here's what I learned—from Sean Charlton's Duplie—since I got here." He told it quickly. "Can you confirm that—or add anything to it?"

Her voice was almost a whisper. "I—I guess it's right. I didn't know that much, but the few things I did hear fit into that story. That they now had three atomic bombs, and that something big is scheduled for tonight. That they had duplicators fixed so they could duplicate uranium. But I didn't know they could send the bombs to Earth and have them explode in—Oh, Matt, that's terrible."

He nodded grimly. "Anything else? Any details you can add?"

"Well—this, but I don't see how it helps. When human beings are sent through the Duplicators that are gadgeted to send uranium—they don't come out Duplies; the duplicates are human beings, too. Not amoral monsters."

"But how—? Why would that—?"

"They make this guess: in the human brain, in a certain part of it, there are submicroscopic particles of—of fissionable matter, just as there are minute quantities of so many other substances in the body. Too small to detect. And in duplicating a human being in an ordinary Kingston, those submicroscopic particles are exploded and injure a certain portion of the brain. The portion that houses—well, empathy, mercy, humanity—whatever you want to call the quality that makes people human instead of soulless monsters."

Anders nodded slowly. It seemed to explain something that had puzzled him—and everyone else, for that matter—for a long time. And it meant that if ever again a situation arose in which it would be legitimate and advantageous to duplicate human beings, it could be done without creating monsters.

But—for now—the knowledge didn't seem to help.

"Marta," he said, "do you know anything about the setup here? Which domes are which among the others besides this one? Where headquarters is?"

She shook her head slowly. "Except the Communications Dome—that's the small one, and I know they allow only Duplies in it and use only Duplies as the guards for it."

He leaned forward eagerly. "It's the source of the broadcasts that go out for Martians? The propaganda center from which they send all their programs for home consumption?"

"Yes. One of the two Duplies who brought me from Venus had worked there. He'd been a newscast announcer and—yes, that's where he broadcasts from. And I think it controls communications with Earth, too."

"Come on then. Let's go." He picked up his own electrogun where Marta had tossed it onto the bed and then picked up the duplicate of it which his Duplie had dropped.

"You mean—"

"Yes, let's take over communications. Maybe we can get a message through to Earth. At least we can talk to the Martians—the real Martians. And tell them what the real score is."

"Oh, Matt, do you think we can—"

Suddenly she was trembling, and he put his arms around her to steady her. Then their lips were together and her arms were around him. Suddenly she pushed him away; there were tears in her eyes but she was laughing.

"All right—Hatchetman," she said. "Let's go. Business first—if we live through it."

"We'll live through it," he said, and wondered what the chances were. Straighten your face. We're just taking a casual walk—till we get to the door of the Communications Dome."

They had the elevator to themselves. He asked, "How many Duplies will be in the building there? Any idea?"

"I've not been in it. At a guess, from what I heard, not over a dozen or so. It looks bigger from the outside than it really is. The walls of that one are nearly a hundred feet thick; it's the most bombproof of the lot, outside of headquarters."

They went along the walk to the smallest of the domes. The two guards at its door were in uniforms with high-ranking insignia, one a Colonel, the other a Major—both Duplies. No one else was near, and Matt Anders waited only until he was ten feet away, before there had been a challenge for the password. The hands of both rested on their weapons, but they hadn't drawn them—and never did. Anders' hand had entered his inner pocket with the deceptive casualness of one reaching for a cigarette—then the electrogun fired twice. The guards went down.

Then Marta and Anders were running through the door, along the long tunnel that led through the thick walls. The door at the inner end of the tunnel was a huge thing, beryllium steel and probably filled with lead to block radiation, eight feet thick. But it swung on its hinges lightly. "Keep your back to me. Watch," he told Marta as he swung it shut, dogged it down. He played his electrogun over the inner surface of it—the tremendous voltage should short any mechanisms in the door that would permit it to be opened from the outside. Probably from the inside, too—in which case they were sealed in.

He turned back then. Marta's gun was flashing in her hand and he saw the figure of a Duplie who had stepped out of a doorway ahead suddenly fall.

"I don't think there's any alarm—yet," he whispered to her. "Kick off your shoes—I've got crepe rubber on mine—and here—" He handed her the other electrogun, larger than her own. "We've got some hunting to do."

The hunting took fifteen minutes. The interior of the dome, relative to its outside size, was tiny, less than a dozen rooms; they found and killed seven Duplies and the place was theirs.

The main control room. Anders pointed to the huge bank of condensers—similar to the one, relatively tiny, which he had seen operate the Kingston Duplicator on Venus. "Power!" he said. "We're self-contained. They can't shut us off the air!"

He found the microphone—a Duplie newscaster who had been using it lay dead in front of it. It had been in operation and the newscaster's use of it had ended in the middle of a sentence.

"Citizens of Mars," he said. "Citizens of Mars who are not Duplies, this is Matt Anders speaking to you, speaking for President Morphy of Earth. Listen, this is of vital importance—"

He told them the story simply, everything their own newscasts and sources of information had denied them since the start of the war—and before. He told them the plans of the Duplies to destroy all of Earth, in one blow, that very night. " ... No, I don't know where the three Kingstons are being readied for sending atomic bombs. Some of you probably do—that is, you know a new and ultra-powerful Duplicator has been set up and is being heavily guarded. Some of you know where another is, others will know the third. *Smash them* for the sake of Earth, your mother planet. Kill the Duplies and take over. I've told you what they really are, how they've fooled you ..."

And he told them again, and again. Not trying to be eloquent about it, just dishing out facts, straight facts that the Martian colonists had never been able to hear. Hammering those facts, over and over. Adding details, circumstantial details that would make them believable.

He was surrounded by panels of switches, but he didn't risk touching one. He knew that the mike into which he was talking was live and directed to all Martian private receivers—he didn't risk trying for more. Maybe he could have reached Earth with a message, maybe he could have reached the fleet and convinced them that their commander was a Duplie. But he didn't know one switch from another and didn't take a chance.

He talked, hammered facts. Maybe Earth or the blockade fleet would be monitoring the broadcast and get it anyway; if not, he wasn't going to take a chance on changing any settings. He talked to the people of Mars. Talked until he was hoarse, and then let Marta take over for a while, then talked himself hoarse again, repeating, hammering, arguing, pleading—

He'd lost all track of time when it happened—the thing he'd been hoping for, the thing that proved he was succeeding. There was a sound that was beyond sound, and the dome shook. He was knocked from his feet and so was Marta; he helped her up, his face shining with exultation, and was back at the mike.

"Thanks, citizens of Mars! I know now you're believing me, that you're doing something about it. The Duplies just dropped one of their three atomic bombs on the dome here. They'll drop the other two! They're losing Mars—now that you know the truth—and they've got to try to stop us. It's more important to them to hold Mars, right now, than to destroy Earth. While you're destroying them. You know who most of them are. If you miss a few, they can be hunted down later. There are only a few hundred of them, billions of you. You can—"

Again the dome shook. The second bomb. And they'd drop the third, too. They had to try; they had to see if three bombs in a row, in the same spot, would crack the defenses they themselves had made against atomic bombing. They couldn't let him keep talking to the people of Mars! The Duplies were realists; they'd know it would do them no good to destroy Earth, in revenge, if they were losing control over their own planet meanwhile. They had to stop him.

The third bomb, before he and Marta were on their feet from the impact of the second. Chunks of concrete fell near them, this time, but the dome held. And they'd won. The Duplies wouldn't have wasted one of the bombs on them unless his broadcast was going through; they wouldn't have spent all three of them unless their situation was desperate. The Martians were revolting against their Duplie masters.

But he didn't quit; there were obviously Martians who accepted the facts he'd been telling them, but maybe there were others who hadn't. The ones who had, since they'd acted so quickly, must already have suspected at least part of the truth despite the curtain of propaganda that had separated them from the outside, but the others— He went back to the mike; he kept at it.

For more hours. Finally he said, "Marta, if that doesn't do it, it can't be done. Let's try to get something on what's going on. Anything around here that looks like a receiver to you? There must be other broadcasters, in other cities. If the colonists control them ..."

He turned back to the mike and told what he was going to do. "I'll try to find a way to take an incoming message now." He found it.

"Anders, calling Matt Anders. If you hear me, pull over the mike and we can make it a two-way; I've still got you tuned in on a receiver."

"Anders speaking," he said into the mike. Marta was handling the receiver he'd found and tuned it loudly enough so he could hear. "I hear you. Come in. What's happening out there?"

"Revolt against the Duplies successful. Got all of them except some still holed up in the domes. Casualties light except in the dome area of Marsport; we were besieging the other domes when they dropped those bombs. But we've got cordons around the contaminated area; no Duplies will get out of there alive.

"Report from your blockade fleet; your broadcast was monitored there, heard by the Duplie of your commander as well as by others. He tried to order the fleet to add their bombs to the communications dome you're in, but was stopped; he's under arrest on his flagship. The fact that he gave the order to bomb the dome your broadcast was coming from convinced his under-officers that he was, as you claimed, a Duplie. The fleet has landed, in peace, outside Marsport and is now helping as with mopping-up operations. There will be—there is—peace between Mars and Earth. Many of us had already suspected at least some of the things you told us about our own government. We rose quickly when we knew the truth. Are you hearing me okay?"

"I'm hearing you," Anders said. "I think we sealed ourselves in here. How soon can you get us out?"

"Don't even try to leave. There's food, water and liquor in the dome. The whole dome area—and especially, after three direct hits, your dome—is contaminated with radiation. We'll work at decontamination, but—I'm sorry about this—I'm afraid it'll be a week before it'll be safe to try to open the door of your dome, from either side."

Matt Anders grinned and turned to look at Marta Pearson. He said, "Don't let it worry you, don't even hurry. I think I've got a week's vacation coming—and I think I can find ways of spending the time."

Something Green

The big sun was crimson in a violet sky. At the edge of the brown plain, dotted with brown bushes, lay the red jungle.

McGarry strode toward it. It was tough work and dangerous work, searching in those red jungles, but it had to be done. And he'd searched a thousand of them; this was just one more.

He said, "Here we go, Dorothy. All set?"

The little five-limbed creature that rested on his shoulder didn't answer, but then it never did. It couldn't talk, but it was something to talk to. It was company. In size and weight it felt amazingly like a hand resting on his shoulder.

He'd had Dorothy for—how long? At a guess, four years. He'd been here about five, as nearly as he could reckon it, and it had been about a year before he'd found her. Anyway, he assumed that Dorothy was of the gentler sex, if for no better reason than the gentle way she rested on his shoulder, like a woman's hand.

"Dorothy," he said, "reckon we'd better get ready for trouble. Might be lions or tigers in there."

He unbuckled his sol-gun holster and let his hand rest on the butt of the weapon, ready to draw it quickly. For the thousandth time, at least, he thanked his lucky stars that the weapon he'd managed to salvage from the wreckage of his spacer had been a sol-gun, the one and only weapon that worked practically forever without refills or ammunition. A sol-gun soaked up energy. And, when you pulled the trigger, it dished it out. With any weapon but a sol-gun he'd never have lasted even one year on Kruger III.

Yes, even before he quite reached the edge of the red jungle, he saw a lion. Nothing like any lion ever seen on Earth, of course. This one was bright magenta, just enough different in color from the purplish bushes it crouched behind so he could see it. It had eight legs, all jointless and as supple and strong as an elephant's trunk, and a scaly head with a beak like a toucan's.

McGarry called it a lion. He had as much right to call it that as anything else, because it had never been named. Or if it had, the namer had never returned to Earth to report on the flora and fauna of Kruger III. Only one spacer had ever landed here before McGarry's, as far as the records showed, and it had never taken off again. He was looking for it now; he'd been looking for it systematically for the five years he'd been here.

If he found it, it might—just barely might—contain intact some of the electronic transistors which had been destroyed in the crash-landing of his own spacer. And if it contained enough of them, he could get back to Earth.

He stopped ten paces short of the edge of the red jungle and aimed the sol-gun at the bushes behind which the lion crouched. He pulled the trigger and there was a bright green flash, brief but beautiful—oh, so beautiful—and the bushes weren't there any more, and neither was the lion.

McGarry chuckled softly. "Did you see that, Dorothy? That was *green*, the one color you don't have on this bloody red planet of yours. The most beautiful color in the universe, Dorothy. *Green!* And I know where there's a world that's mostly green, and we're going to get there, you and I. Sure we are. It's the world I came from, and it's the most beautiful place there is, Dorothy. You'll love it."

He turned and looked back over the brown plain with brown bushes, the violet sky above, the crimson sun. The eternally crimson sun Kruger, which never set on the day side of this planet, one side of which always faced it as one side of Earth's moon always faces Earth.

No day and night—unless one passed the shadow line into the night side, which was too freezingly cold to sustain life. No seasons. A uniform, never-changing temperature, no wind, no storms.

He thought for the thousandth, or the millionth, time that it wouldn't be a bad planet to live on, if only it were green like Earth, if only there was something green upon it besides the occasional flash of his sol-gun. It had breathable atmosphere, moderate temperature ranging from about forty Fahrenheit near the shadow line to about ninety at the point directly under the red sun, where its rays were straight down instead of slanting. Plenty of food, and he'd learned long ago which plants and animals were, for him, edible and which made him ill. Nothing he'd ever tried was outright poisonous.

Yes, a wonderful world. He'd even got used, by now, to being the only intelligent creature on it. Dorothy was helpful, there. Something to talk to, even if she didn't talk back.

Except—Oh, God—he wanted to see a green world again.

Earth, the only planet in the known universe where green was the predominant color, where plant life was based on chlorophyll.

Other planets, even in the solar system, Earth's neighbors, had no more to offer than greenish streaks in rare rocks, an occasional tiny life-form of a shade that might be called brownish green if you wanted to call it that. Why, you could live years on any planet but Earth, anywhere in the cosmos, and never see green.

McGarry sighed. He'd been thinking to himself, but now he thought out loud, to Dorothy, continuing his thoughts without a break. It didn't matter to Dorothy. "Yes, Dorothy," he said, "it's the only planet worth living on— Earth! Green fields, grassy lawns, green trees. Dorothy, I'll never leave it again, once I get back there. I'll build me a shack out in the woods, in the middle of trees, but not trees so thick that the grass doesn't grow under them. *Green* grass. And I'll paint the shack green, Dorothy. We've even got green pigments back on Earth."

He sighed and looked at the red jungle ahead of him.

"What's that you asked, Dorothy?" She hadn't asked anything, but it was a game to pretend that she talked back, a game to keep him sane. "Will I get married when I get back? Is that what you asked?"

He gave it consideration. "Well, it's like this, Dorothy. Maybe and maybe not. You were named after a woman back on Earth, you know. A woman I was going to marry. But five years is a long time, Dorothy. I've been reported missing and presumably dead. I doubt if she's waited this long. If she has, well, I'll marry her, Dorothy.

"Did you ask, what if she hasn't? Well, I don't know. Let's not worry about that till I get back, huh? Of course, if I could find a woman who was *green*, or even one with green hair, I'd love her to pieces. But on Earth almost everything is green *except* the women."

He chuckled at that and, sol-gun ready, went on into the jungle, the red jungle that had nothing green except the occasional flash of his sol-gun.

Funny about that. Back on Earth, a sol-gun flashed violet. Here under a red sun, it flashed green when he fired it. But the explanation was simple enough. A sol-gun drew energy from a nearby star and the flash it made when fired was the complementary color of its source of energy. Drawing energy from Sol, a yellow sun, it flashed violet. From Kruger, a red sun, green.

Maybe that, he thought, had been the one thing that, aside from Dorothy's company, had kept him sane. A flash of green several times a day. Something green to remind him what the color *was*. To keep his eyes attuned to it, if he ever saw it again.

It turned out to be a small patch of jungle, as patches of jungle went on Kruger III. One of what seemed countless millions of such patches. And maybe it really was millions; Kruger III was larger than Jupiter. But less dense, so the gravity was easily bearable. Actually it might take him more than a lifetime to cover it all. He knew that, but did not let himself think about it. No more than he let himself think that the ship might have crashed on the dark side, the cold side. Or than he let himself doubt that, once he found the ship, he would find the transistors he needed to make his own spacer operative again.

The patch of jungle was less than a mile square, but he had to sleep once and eat several times before he had finished it. He killed two more lions and one tiger. And when he finished it, he walked around the circumference of it, blazing each of the larger trees along the outer rim so he wouldn't repeat by searching this particular jungle again. The trees were soft; his pocketknife took off the red bark down to the pink core as easily as it would have taken the skin off a potato.

Then out across the dull brown plain again, this time holding his sol-gun in the open to recharge it.

"Not that one, Dorothy. Maybe the next. The one over there near the horizon. Maybe it's there."

Violet sky, red sun, brown plain.

"The green hills of Earth, Dorothy. Oh, how you'll love them."

The brown never-ending plain.

The never-changing violet sky.

Was there a sound up there? There couldn't be. There never had been. But he looked up. And saw it.

A tiny black speck high in the violet, moving. *A spacer. It had to be a spacer. There were no birds on Kruger III. And birds don't trail jets of fire behind them—*

He knew what to do; he'd thought of it a million times, how he could signal a spacer if one ever came in sight. He raised his sol-gun, aimed it straight into the violet air and pulled the trigger. It didn't make a big flash, from the distance of the spacer, but it made a *green* flash. If the pilot were only looking or if he would only look before he got out of sight, he couldn't miss a green flash on a world with no other green.

He pulled the trigger again.

And the pilot of the spacer *saw*. He cut and fired his jets three times—the standard answer to a signal of distress—and began to circle.

McGarry stood there trembling. So long a wait, and so sudden an end to it. He touched his left shoulder and touched the five-legged pet that felt to his fingers as well as to his naked shoulder so like a woman's hand.

"Dorothy," he said, "it's—" He ran out of words.

The spacer was closing in for a landing now. McGarry looked down at himself, suddenly aware and ashamed of himself, as he would look to a rescuer. His body was naked except for the belt that held his holster and from which dangled his knife and a few other tools. He was dirty and probably smelled, although he could not smell himself. And under the dirt his body looked thin and wasted, almost old, but that was due of course to diet deficiencies; a few months of proper food, Earth food, would take care of that.

Earth! The green hills of Earth!

He ran now, stumbling sometimes in his eagerness, toward the point where the spacer was landing. He could see now that it was a one-man job, like his own had been. But that was all right; it could carry two in an emergency, at least as far as the nearest planet where he could get other transportation back to Earth. To the green hills, the green fields, the green valleys.

He prayed a little and swore a little as he ran. There were tears running down his cheeks.

He was there, waiting, as the door opened and a tall slender young man in the uniform of the Space Patrol stepped out.

"You'll take me back?" he shouted.

"Of course," said the young man calmly. "Been here long?"

"Five years!" McGarry knew that he was crying, but he couldn't stop.

"Good Lord!" said the young man. "I'm Lieutenant Archer. Of course I'll take you back, man, as soon as my jets cool enough for a takeoff. I'll take you as far as Carthage, on Aldebaran II, anyway; you can get a ship out of there for anywhere. Need anything right away? Food? Water?"

McGarry shook his head dumbly. Food, water— What did such things matter now?

The green hills of Earth! He was going back to them. *That* was what mattered, and all that mattered. So long a wait, then so sudden an ending. He saw the violet sky swimming and then it suddenly went black as his knees buckled under him.

He was lying flat and the young man was holding a flask to his lips and he took a long draught of the fiery stuff it held. He sat up and felt better. He looked to make sure the spacer was still there; it was, and he felt wonderful.

The young man said, "Buck up, old-timer; we'll be off in half an hour. You'll be in Carthage in six hours. Want to talk, till you get your bearings again? Want to tell me all about it, everything that's happened?"

They sat in the shadow of a brown bush, and McGarry told him about it, everything about it. The five-year search for the other ship he'd read had crashed on the planet and which might have intact the parts he needed to repair his own ship. The long search. About Dorothy, perched on his shoulder, and how she'd been something to talk to.

But somehow, the face of Lieutenant Archer was changing as McGarry talked. It grew even more solemn, even more compassionate.

"Old-timer," Archer asked gently, "what year was it when you came here?"

McGarry saw it coming. How can you keep track of time on a planet whose sun and seasons are unchanging? A planet of eternal day, eternal summer—

He said flatly, "I came here in twenty-two forty-two. How much have I misjudged, Lieutenant? How old am I—instead of thirty, as I've thought?"

"It's twenty-two seventy-two, McGarry. You came here thirty years ago. You're fifty-five. But don't let that worry you too much. Medical science has advanced. You still have a long time to live."

McGarry said it softly. "Fifty-five. *Thirty years.*"

The lieutenant looked at him pityingly. He said, "Old-timer, do you want it all in a lump, all the rest of the bad news? There are several items of it. I'm no psychologist but I think maybe it's best for you to take it now, all at once, while you can still throw into the scale against it the fact that you're going back. Can you take it, McGarry?"

There couldn't be anything worse than he'd learned already. The fact that thirty years of his life had already been wasted here. Sure, he could take the rest of whatever it was, as long as he was getting back to Earth, green Earth.

He stared at the violet sky, the red sun, the brown plain. He said, very quietly, "I can take it. Dish it out."

"You've done wonderfully for thirty years, McGarry. You can thank God for the fact that you believed Marley's spacer crashed on Kruger III; it was Kruger IV. You'd have never found it here, but the search, as you say, kept you—reasonably sane." He paused a moment. His voice was gentle when he spoke again. "There isn't anything on your shoulder, McGarry. This Dorothy is a figment of your imagination. But don't worry about it; that particular delusion has probably kept you from cracking up completely."

McGarry put up his hand. It touched his shoulder. Nothing else.

Archer said, "My God, man, it's marvelous that you're *otherwise* okay. Thirty years alone; it's almost a miracle. And if your one delusion persists, now that I've told you it *is* a delusion, a psychiatrist back at Carthage or on Mars can fix you up in a jiffy."

McGarry said dully, "It doesn't persist. It isn't there now. I—I'm not even sure, Lieutenant, that I ever did really believe in Dorothy. I think I made her up on purpose, to talk to, so I'd remain sane except for that. She was—she was like a woman's hand, Lieutenant. Or did I tell you that?"

"You told me. Want the rest of it now, McGarry?"

McGarry stared at him. "The rest of it? What rest can there be? I'm fifty-five instead of thirty. I've spent thirty years, since I was twenty-five, hunting for a spacer I'd never have found, since it's on another planet. I've been crazy—in one way, but only one—most of that time. But none of that matters now that I can go back to Earth."

Lieutenant Archer was shaking his head slowly. "Not back to Earth, old-timer. To Mars if you wish, the beautiful brown and yellow hills of Mars. Or, if you don't mind heat, to purple Venus. But not to Earth, McGarry. Nobody lives there any more."

"Earth is—gone? I don't—"

"Not gone, McGarry. It's there. But it's black and barren, a charred ball. The war with the Arcturians, twenty years ago. They struck first, and got Earth. We got *them*, we won, we exterminated them, but Earth was gone before we started. I'm sorry, but you'll have to settle for somewhere else."

McGarry said, "No Earth." There was no expression in his voice. No expression at all.

Archer said, "That's the works, old-timer. But Mars isn't so bad. You'll get used to it. It's the center of the solar system now, and there are three billion Earthmen on it. You'll miss the green of Earth, sure, but it's not so bad."

McGarry said, "No Earth." There was no expression in his voice. No expression at all.

Archer nodded. "Glad you can take it that way, old-timer. It must be rather a jolt. Well, I guess we can get going. The tubes ought to have cooled enough by now. I'll check and make sure.

He stood up and started toward the little spacer.

McGarry's sol-gun came out of its holster. McGarry shot him, and Lieutenant Archer wasn't there any more. McGarry stood up and walked to the little spacer. He aimed the sol-gun at it and pulled the trigger. Part of the spacer was gone. Half a dozen shots and it was completely gone. Little atoms that had been the spacer and little atoms that had been Lieutenant Archer of the Space Patrol may have danced in the air, but they were invisible.

McGarry put the gun back into its holster and started walking toward the red splotch of jungle near the horizon.

He put his hand up to his shoulder and touched Dorothy and she was there, as she'd been there now for four of the five years he'd been on Kruger III. She felt, to his fingers and to his bare shoulder, like a woman's hand.

He said, "Don't worry, Dorothy. We'll find it. Maybe this next jungle is the right one. And when we find it—"

He was near the edge of the jungle now, the red jungle, and a tiger came running out to meet him and eat him. A mauve tiger with six legs and a head like a barrel. McGarry aimed his sol-gun and pulled the trigger, and there was a bright green flash, brief but beautiful—oh, so beautiful—and the tiger wasn't there any more.

McGarry chuckled softly. "Did you see that, Dorothy? That was *green,* the color there isn't much of on any planet but the one we're going to. The only green planet in the system, and it's the one I came from. You'll love it."

She said, "I know I will, Mac." Her low throaty voice was completely familiar to him, as familiar as his own; she'd always answered him. He reached up his hand and touched her as she rested on his naked shoulder. She felt like a woman's hand.

He turned and looked back over the brown plain studded with brown bushes, the violet sky above, the crimson sun. He laughed at it. Not a mad laugh, a gentle one. It didn't matter because soon now he'd find the spacer so he could go back to Earth.

To the green hills, the green fields, the green valleys. Once more he patted the hand upon his shoulder and spoke to it, listened to its answer.

Then, gun at ready, he entered the red jungle.

Me and Flapjack and the Martians

(in collaboration with Mack Reynolds)

Wanta hear how Flapjack saved the world from the Martians, huh? All right, partner. It happened on the edge of the Mojave, just south of Death Valley. Me and Flapjack was ...

"Flapjack," I told him complainingly, "you ain't worth a whoop no more since you done got rich. You're too all-fired proud these days to be ploddin' through the desert doing an honest day's work. Ain't yuh?"

Flapjack didn't answer. He ignored me and looked ahead of him disgustedly at the sand, the dust, the little clumps of cactus. He didn't have to answer; just his whole attitude made it plenty clear he wished we was back in Crucero, or maybe up in Bishop.

I frowned at him. "Sometimes," I told him, "I think you was just never cut out for this, Flapjack. Oh, sure, you've spent most of your life in the desert and the mountains, just like I spent most of mine. And maybe you know 'em better than I do; I gotta admit it was you and not me that stumbled on that there last strike we made. But I still don't think you like the desert and the hills.

"I think I got reason for sayin' that, Flapjack. It's the way you've acted ever since we got a few dollars in the poke from that strike. Now you don't have to look hurt like that. You know the way you been carryin' on ever since we got money in the bank. A real caution. Why as soon as we get into Bishop or maybe Needles, what do you do? You make a beeline for the nearest saloon, that's what you do. Gotta let everybody in town know we got money to spend."

Flapjack yawned and kicked up the dust underfoot. He didn't mind my talking on and on, because you get to where you kind of like to hear somebody's voice out in the desert, but he wasn't paying no real attention to what I was saying. But I didn't let that stop me. I laid it into him.

I said, "And you ain't satisfied to spend our money in just one bar, neither. The minute you finish off a gallon of beer in one saloon, you head for the next. You're gettin' yourself talked about, Flapjack. But that don't make no difference to you. In fact, like I said, you're gettin' yourself so all-fired proud you don't care *what* anybody says about you.

"It ain't as though we got so much money we can retire. If we tried livin' in town permanent-like, we'd be flat broke in no time. Especially with the way you hang around in saloons and guzzle beer. Well, at least you don't buy drinks for the house; guess you think on account of that I ain't got no complaints comin'."

Flapjack snorted at my words and stopped.

"Oh, you think we oughta make camp, huh?" I said. I let my eyes go around the landscape. "All right, I guess one place is as good as another. Ain't no water within a dozen miles anyhow."

I took the pack off Flapjack's back and began to set up my little tent. I'd never packed a tent before I'd made my strike—or Flapjack had made it for me—but that hombre in the store had caught me in a weak moment with money in my pocket and he'd talked me into it. A piece of foofaraw, but it served Flapjack right for having to carry it.

Flapjack watched me for a minute and then ambled off to size up the possibilities of a little graze or such other grub as a burro can rustle up in the desert. I knew he wouldn't wander far and that I didn't have to watch him or hobble him, so I minded my own business and let him mind his.

It wasn't no exaggeration, what I'd been telling him. He'd been acting up for days and the reason was plain to see. Flapjack wanted to get back to where he could get his ration of beer every night, and some good fancy feed to top it off with. Ever since he kicked over that rock and made the silver strike, he's had credit in every bar in every town around here. He just walks in and the bartender fills a bucket with beer for him and he drinks it down, and then he ambles on to the next bar. He's crazy about beer. Holds it pretty well, too.

Maybe I should never have made the arrangements, but, like I said, it was Flapjack that made the strike, so I thought it was only fair. Even if once in a while I regret it, like the time he got in the fancy place in Crucero by mistake and got out in the middle of the fancy dance floor and—well, you can't expect a burro to know better than that, can you? And there weren't any people dancin' just then anyway so I don't see what they made such a big fuss about. Funny thing, Flapjack never done anything like that in a place where he was welcome, and I sometimes wonder. Especially after what happened with the Martians. But we ain't quite got to that yet.

Anyway I was just jawing at Flapjack; I was gettin' just about ready for a trip to town myself, and maybe that's why I was takin' it out on him. I like a trip to town just as well as Flapjack does, only I ain't there no length of time before I get fed up with all the noise and the folks and the buildings and sleeping in beds and I just got to get out and head for the hills again. That's the only thing me and Flapjack really differ on; he'd rather stay longer.

I was makin' supper half an hour later and Flapjack probably thought I didn't see him go into the tent. He was scoutin' around for something to steal. Flapjack's the stealingest burro I ever did see. If he thinks it's something I want, he'll steal it quicker'n you can say "Holy hominy," even if he don't like it or want it himself. I recollect the time I was gettin' tired of the way he'd swipe pancakes in the morning, so I cooked up a batch with lots of red pepper in them. You think he'd let out a peep? Not Flapjack. He was so happy about getting away with swiping my pancakes that he didn't care how awful they tasted.

Flapjack's a caution, Flapjack is. But I started out to tell you about the Martians. Maybe I better.

It was coming on morning; let's see now, just to be accurate-like, it must've been August 6 or maybe August 7, sometimes you lose track in the desert.

Anyway, I opened my eyes when I heard Flapjack bray, real indignant-like. I knew something was up; Flapjack doesn't use that tone of bray unless. I stuck my head out of the tent just in time to see this here—well, balloon was what I thought it was at first—balloon on fire. Fire was shootin' out from beneath it like crazy. I expected a big explosion any minute.

But it didn't explode. The balloon settled down no more than maybe fifty feet away, and the flames died out.

"Holy hominy," I said to myself and to Flapjack, "it must've blowed all the way from some fair somewheres."

I crawled the rest of the way out of the tent, figurin' on gettin' over to where that thing had come down to investigate-like. I didn't expect no folks to be there 'cause there wasn't no basket slung underneath. And if there had been, both the basket and the folks in it would've been fried to a crisp, the way that thing had been spouting fire as it came down.

I'd plumb forgot about Flapjack. You can't blame him for feeling kind of skittish, but instead of runnin' away he'd backed up toward the tent. And when he heard me movin' behind him, he let go with his hind hoofs real quick. I don't think he done it on purpose.

But that's all I remembered for a while.

When I woke up again, it was good and light. I must've been out at least an hour, could have been two. I put my hand up to my head and groaned and then, sudden, I remembered that balloon. I staggered up to my feet and looked over at it.

That balloon wasn't no balloon. I seen one balloon back in Missouri at a fair and I seen pictures of other ones, and this thing, whatever it was, wasn't no balloon. I'll guarantee you that.

Besides, whoever heard of anybody being *inside a* balloon?

Maybe I shouldn't say *anybody,* I should say *anything,* on account of the critters that was dartin' in and out of a door in the side of that thing sure wasn't ordinary folks. First thing that come to my mind was maybe it was something from a circus; they have the darnedest freaks and animals—and contraptions, too—at a circus. Only I couldn't decide whether these things was freaks or animals. They was somewhere in between.

Anyhow, these critters was dartin' in and out of the big ball that I'd taken for a balloon, sometimes on their back legs, sometimes on all fours. On two legs, they was about four feet high, and on four they was only knee-high to a heifer, on account of their legs—and arms, if their front legs was arms—was so short. They was carryin' all sorts of funny devices which they was settin' up on the desert just about halfway between me and that ball-contraption they went in and out of. And three of 'em swarmed around puttin' together what the others brought 'em.

Then I noticed Flapjack. He was standin' right near 'em and didn't look afraid at all. Just curious, like any burro is.

Well, I got up my courage and meandered over that way and took a look at the thing they was workin' on, but I couldn't make nothing of it. I said,

"Hullo," and they didn't answer me and didn't pay no more attention to me than if I was a prairie dog.

So I went around 'em, keepin' my distance, and went up to the side of this ball and reached up and touched it. Holy hominy! It was made out of metal as smooth and hard as the barrel of a Colt and it was as big as a two-story house.

One of the funny-lookin' little critters came along and shooed me away, kinda waving a thing in his hand that looked something like a flashlight. I had a sneaking suspicion that it wasn't no flashlight and I wasn't too curious, just then, to find out what would happen if he did more than wave it at me, so I got. I went back about twenty feet or so and watched.

Pretty soon they seemed to have finished putting together whatever it was they'd been working on. Flapjack was standing only a few feet away from it by now, and I started to wander up closer but one of 'em waved a flashlight at me again and I got back.

Two of 'em stood there on their hind legs pullin' levers and twistin' knobs. There was a kind of loud-speaker on top of it, like you used to see on old-fashioned phonographs. Suddenly the loud-speaker said: "It should be correctly adjusted now, Mandu."

You could have knocked me down with a pebble. Here were these things looking like they'd escaped from a zoo and they had a talking machine of some kind or other. I sat down on a rock and stared at the loud-speaker.

"It would seem so," the loud-speaker said. "Now if this terrestrial has the type of mentality that we have deduced, we should be able to communicate."

All of the critters walked away from the device except one and he looked direct at Flapjack and said, "Greetings."

"Greetings, yourself," I said. "Flapjack's a burro, so how's about talking to me?"

"Will one of you," said the loud-speaker, "please attempt to stop that domesticated creature over there from making his fantastic noises?"

Flapjack hadn't been makin' any noise that *I* could hear. But a flashlight got waved at me so I shut up to see what'd happen.

"I assume," said the loud-speaker, "that you are the dominant intelligence of this planet. Greetings from the inhabitants of Mars."

A funny thing about that there loud-speaker; something makes me remember every dang word it said, just like it said 'em, even when I still don't rightly know what all the fancier words mean,

While I was tryin' to figure the answer to what they'd said, danged if Flapjack didn't beat me to the draw. He opened his mouth, showed his teeth and brayed real hearty.

"Thank you," said the loud-speaker. "And in answer to your question, this is a sonic telepathor. It, in a manner of thinking, broadcasts my thoughts and they are reproduced in the mind of the listener in the language which he speaks and understands. The sounds you seem to hear are not the exact sounds that come from the speaker; it emits an abstract sound pattern which your subconscious, with the aid of the carrier wave, hears as expression in your own language. It is not selective, many creatures speaking many tongues would all understand what I am thinking. Our adjustment consisted in tuning the receiver part, which *is* selective, to the particular pattern of your individual intelligence."

"You're crazy," I yelled. "Why don't you fix that danged thing so it can understand what *I* say?"

"Please keep that animal quiet, Yagarl," said the loud-speaker. Flapjack looked at me over his shoulder reproachfully. That didn't worry me. But one of the critters with flashlights waved it at me again and that did. And anyway the speaker was blaring again and I wanted to hear what it said so I listened.

"We of Mars had the same difficulty," it was saying. "happily, we have been able to solve the problem by substituting robots for domesticated animals. Obviously, however, you have a different situation. Through the lack of suitable hands, or even tentacles, you have found it necessary to domesticate one of the lower orders which is so equipped."

Flapjack brayed briefly and the loud-speaker said, "Naturally you wish to know the purpose of our visit. We wish your advice in solving a problem that is vital to us. Mars is a dying planet. Its water, its atmosphere, its mineral resources, all are practically exhausted. If we had been able to develop interstellar travel, we might seek an unoccupied planet somewhere in the galaxy. Unfortunately we have not; our ships will take us only to other planets in the solar system and only the discovery of an entirely new principle would enable us to reach the stars. We have not found even a clue to that principle.

"In the solar system, yours is the only planet—besides Mars—that can support Martian life. Mercury is too hot, Venus has no land surface and an atmosphere poisonous to us. The force of gravity of Jupiter would crush us and all of its moons are—like yours—airless. The outer planets are impossibly cold.

"So we are faced with the necessity, if we wish to survive, to move to Earth—peaceably if you submit; forcibly if we must use force. And we have weapons that can destroy the population of Earth within days."

"Just a minute," I yelled. "If you think for a minute that you can—"

The critter who had been aiming a flashlight at me lowered it at my knees and, as I started toward the one who'd been operating the speaker contraption, he pushed a button. My knees suddenly went rubber and I fell down. Also I shut up.

My legs just didn't work at all. I had to use my arms to get to a sitting position so I could see what was going on.

Flapjack was braying.

"True," the speaker said. "That would be the best solution for both of us. We do not wish to occupy—by force or otherwise—an already civilized planet. If you can really suggest another answer to our problem—"

Flapjack brayed.

"Thank you," said the loud-speaker. "I am sure that will work out. Why we did not think of it ourselves I cannot imagine. We appreciate your assistance immeasurably; we offer you our heartfelt gratitude. We leave with good will in our hearts. We shall not return."

My knees worked again and I got up. I didn't go anywhere, though. My knees had been out of commission for a full minute and I was thinking that if that flashlight thing had been pointed higher and had stopped my heart working for a full minute I wouldn't be worrying about my knees.

Flapjack brayed just once more, and not for long this time. The funny-looking critters began to take their contraption with the speaker apart and carry it a piece at a time back to the big ball they'd come in.

It and them were all back in the balloon that wasn't a balloon in ten minutes, about, and the door in it closed. The bottom of it began to fire up again and I ran back to where my tent was and watched from there. And all of a sudden the contraption *whooshed* upward and disappeared almost straight up into the sky.

Flapjack came strolling over toward me, kind of avoiding my eyes, like.

"You think you're pretty smart, don't you?" I asked him.

He wouldn't answer me.

But I guess he did think so. Later on that same day he stole my pancakes again.

And that's the whole story, partner. That's how Flapjack saved the world from the Martians. You want to know what he told 'em? Well, I'd like to know, too, but he won't tell me. Hey, Flapjack, come over here. You had enough beer for tonight.

All right, partner, here he is. You ask him. Maybe he'll tell you. Or maybe he won't. Flapjack's a caution, Flapjack is. But go ahead and ask him.

The Little Lamb

She didn't come home for supper and by eight o'clock I found some ham in the refrigerator and made myself a sandwich. I wasn't worried, but I was getting restless. I kept walking to the window and looking down the hill toward town, but I couldn't see her coming. It was a moonlit evening, very bright and clear. The lights of the town were nice and the curve of the hills beyond, black against blue under a yellow gibbous moon. I thought I'd like to paint it, but not the moon; you put a moon in a picture and it looks corny, it looks pretty. Van Gogh did it in his picture *The Starry Sky* and it didn't look pretty; it looked frightening, but then again he was crazy when he did it; a sane man couldn't have done many of the things Van Gogh did.

I hadn't cleaned my palette so I picked it up and tried to work a little more on the painting I'd started the day before. It was just blocked in thus far and I started to mix a green to fill in an area but it wouldn't come right and I realized I'd have to wait till daylight to get it right. Evenings, without natural light, I can work on line or I can mold in finishing strokes, but when color's the thing, you've got to have daylight. I cleaned my messed-up palette for a fresh start in the morning and I cleaned my brushes and it was getting close to nine o'clock and still she hadn't come.

No, there wasn't anything to worry about. She was with friends somewhere and she was all right. My studio is almost a mile from town, up in the hills, and there wasn't any way she could let me know because there's no phone. Probably she was having a drink with the gang at the Waverly Inn and there was no reason she'd think I'd worry about her. Neither of us lived by the clock; that was understood between us. She'd be home soon.

There was half of a jug of wine left and I poured myself a drink and sipped it, looking out the window toward town. I turned off the light behind me so I could better watch out the window at the bright night. A mile away, in the valley, I could see the lights of the Waverly Inn. Garish bright, like the loud juke box that kept me from going there often. Strangely, Lamb never minded the juke box, although she liked good music, too.

Other lights dotted here and there. Small farms, a few other studios. Hans Wagner's place a quarter of a mile down the slope from mine. Big, with a skylight; I envied him that skylight. But not his strictly academic style. He'd never paint anything quite as good as a color photograph; in fact, he saw things as a camera sees them and painted them without filtering them through the catalyst of the mind. A wonderful draftsman, never more. But his stuff sold; he could afford a skylight.

I sipped the last of my glass of wine, and there was a tight knot in the middle of my stomach. I didn't know why. Often Lamb had been later than this, much later. There wasn't any real reason to worry.

I put my glass down on the window sill and opened the door. But before I went out I turned the lights back on. A beacon for Lamb, if I should miss her. And if she should look up the hill toward home and the lights were out, she might think I wasn't there and stay longer, wherever she was. She'd know I wouldn't turn in before she got home, no matter how late it was.

Quit being a fool, I told myself; it isn't late yet. It's early, just past nine o'clock. I walked down the hill toward town and the knot in my stomach got tighter and I swore at myself because there was no reason for it. The line of the hills beyond town rose higher as I descended, pointing up the stars. It's difficult to make stars that look like stars. You'd have to make pinholes in the canvas and put a light behind it. I laughed at the idea—but why not? Except that it isn't done and what did I care about that. But I thought a while and I saw why it wasn't done. It would be childish, immature.

I was about to pass Hans Wagner's place, and I slowed my steps thinking that just possibly Lamb might be there. Hans lived alone there and Lamb wouldn't, of course, be there unless a crowd had gone to Hans's from the inn or somewhere. I stopped to listen and there wasn't a sound, so the crowd wasn't there. I went on.

The road branched; there were several ways from here and I might miss her. I took the shortest route, the one she'd be most likely to take if she came directly home from town. It went past Carter Brent's place, but that was dark. There was a light on at Sylvia's place, though, and guitar music. I knocked on the door and while I was waiting I realized that it was the phonograph and not a live guitarist. It was Segovia playing Bach, the Chaconne from the D Minor Partita, one of my favorites. Very beautiful, very fine-boned and delicate, like Lamb.

Sylvia came to the door and answered my question. No, she hadn't seen Lamb. And no, she hadn't been at the inn, or anywhere. She'd been home all afternoon and evening, but did I want to drop in for a drink? I was tempted—more by Segovia than by the drink—but I thanked her and went on.

I should have turned around and gone back home instead, because for no reason I was getting into one of my black moods. I was illogically annoyed because I didn't know where Lamb was; if I found her now I'd probably quarrel with her, and I hate quarreling. Not that we do, often. We're each pretty tolerant and understanding—of little things, at least. And Lamb's not having come home yet was still a little thing.

But I could hear the blaring juke box when I was still a long way from the inn and it didn't lighten my mood any. I could see in the window now and Lamb wasn't there, not at the bar. But there were still the booths, and besides, someone might know where she was. There were two couples at the bar. I knew them; Charlie and Eve Chandler and Dick Bristow with a girl from Los Angeles whom I'd met but whose name I couldn't remember. And one fellow, stag, who looked as though he was trying to look like a movie scout from Hollywood. Maybe he really was one.

I went in and, thank God, the juke box stopped just as I went through the door. I went over to the bar, glancing at the line of booths; Lamb wasn't there.

I said, "Hi," to the four of them that I knew, and to the stag if he wanted to take it to cover him, and to Harry, behind the bar. "Has Lamb been here?" I asked Harry.

"Nope, haven't seen her, Wayne. Not since six; that's when I came on. Want a drink?"

I didn't, particularly, but I didn't want it to look as though I'd come solely for Lamb, so I ordered one.

"How's the painting coming?" Charlie Chandler asked me.

He didn't mean any particular painting and he wouldn't have known anything about it if he had. Charlie runs the local bookstore and—amazingly— he can tell the difference between Thomas Wolfe and a comic book, but he couldn't tell the difference between an El Greco and an Al Capp. Don't misunderstand me on that; I like Al Capp.

So I said, "Fine," as one always says to a meaningless question, and took a swallow of the drink that Harry had put in front of me. I paid for it and wondered how long I'd have to stay in order to make it not too obvious that I'd come only to look for Lamb.

For some reason conversation died. If anybody had been talking to anybody before I came in, he wasn't now. I glanced at Eve and she was making wet circles on the mahogany of the bar with the bottom of a martini goblet. The olive stirred restlessly in the bottom and I knew suddenly that was the color, the exact color I'd wanted to mix an hour or two ago just before I'd decided not to try to paint. The color of an olive moist with gin and vermouth. Just right for the main sweep of the biggest hill, shading darker to the right, lighter to the left. I stared at the color and memorized it so I'd have it tomorrow. Maybe I'd even try it tonight when I got back home; I had it now, daylight or no. It was right; it was the color that had to be there. I felt good; the black mood that had threatened to come on was gone.

But where was Lamb? If she wasn't home yet when I got back, would I be able to paint? Or would I start worrying about her, without reason? Would I get that tightness in the pit of my stomach?

I saw that my glass was empty. I'd drunk too fast. Now I might as well have another one, or it would be too obvious why I'd come. And I didn't want people—not even people like these—to think I was jealous of Lamb and worried about her. Lamb and I trusted each other implicitly. I was curious as to where she was and I wanted her back, but that was all. I wasn't suspicious of where she might be. They wouldn't realize that.

I said, "Harry, give me a martini." I'd had so few drinks that it wouldn't hurt me to mix them, and I wanted to study that color, intimately and at close hand. It was going to be the central color motif; everything would revolve around it.

Harry handed me the martini. It tasted good. I swished around the olive and it wasn't quite the color I wanted, a little too much in the brown, but I still had the idea. And I still wanted to work on it tonight, if I could find Lamb.

If she was there, I could work; I could get the planes of color in, and tomorrow I could mold them, shade them.

But unless I'd missed her, unless she was already home or on her way there, it wasn't too good a chance. We knew dozens of people; I couldn't try every place she might possibly be. But there was one other fairly good chance, Mike's Club, a mile down the road, out of town on the other side. She'd hardly have gone there unless she was with someone who had a car, but that could have happened. I could phone there and find out.

I finished my martini and nibbled the olive and then turned around to walk over to the phone booth. The wavy-haired man who looked as though he might be from Hollywood was just walking back toward the bar from the juke box and it was making preliminary scratching noises. He'd dropped a coin into it and it started to play something loud and brassy. A polka, and a particularly noisy and obnoxious one. I felt like hitting him one in the nose, but I couldn't even catch his eye as he strolled back and took his stool again at the bar. And anyway, he wouldn't have known what I was hitting him for. But the phone booth was just past the juke box and I wouldn't hear a word, or be heard, if I phoned Mike's.

A record takes about three minutes, and I stood one minute of it and that was enough. I wanted to make that call and get out of there, so I walked toward the booth and I reached around the juke box and pulled the plug out of the wall. Quietly, not violently at all. But the sudden silence was violent, so violent that I could hear, as though she'd screamed them, the last few words of what Eve Chandler had been saying to Charlie Chandler. Her voice pitched barely to carry above the din of brass—but she might as well have used a public address system once I'd pulled the juke box's plug.

" ... may be at Hans's." Bitten off suddenly, as if she'd intended to say more.

Her eyes met mine and hers looked frightened.

I looked back at Eve Chandler. I didn't pay any attention to Golden Boy from Hollywood; if he wanted to make anything of the fact that I'd ruined his dime, that was his business and he could start it. I went into the phone booth and pulled the door shut. If that juke box started again before I'd finished my call, it would be my business, and I could start it. The juke box didn't start again.

I gave the number of Mike's and when someone answered, I asked, "Is Lamb there?"

"Who did you say?"

"This is Wayne Gray," I said patiently. "Is Lambeth Gray there?"

"Oh." I recognized it now as Mike's voice. "Didn't get you at first. No, Mr. Gray, your wife hasn't been here."

I thanked him and hung up. When I went out of the booth, the Chandlers were gone. I heard a car starting outside.

I waved to Harry and went outside. The taillight of the Chandlers' car was heading up the hill. In the direction they'd have gone if they were heading for Hans Wagner's studio—to warn Lamb that I'd heard something I shouldn't have heard, and that I might come there.

But it was too ridiculous to consider. Whatever gave Eve Chandler the wild idea that Lamb might be with Hans, it was wrong. Lamb wouldn't do anything like that. Eve had probably seen her having a drink or so with Hans somewhere, sometime, and had got the thing wrong. Dead wrong. If nothing else, Lamb would have better taste than that. Hans was handsome, and he was a ladies' man, which I'm not, but he's stupid and he can't paint. Lamb wouldn't fall for a stuffed shirt like Hans Wagner.

But I might as well go home, now, I decided. Unless I wanted to give people the impression that I was canvassing the town for my wife, I couldn't very well look any farther or ask any more people if they'd seen her. And although I don't care what people think about me either personally or as a painter, I wouldn't want them to think I had any wrong ideas about Lamb.

I walked off in the wake of the Chandlers' car, through the bright moonlight. I came in sight of Hans's place again, and the Chandlers' car wasn't parked there; if they'd stopped, they'd gone right on. But, of course, they would have, under those circumstances. They wouldn't have wanted me to see that they were parked there; it would have looked bad.

The lights were on there, but I walked on past, up the hill toward my own place. Maybe Lamb was home by now; I hoped so. At any rate, I wasn't going to stop at Hans's. Whether the Chandlers had or not.

Lamb wasn't in sight along the road between Hans's place and mine. But she could have made it before I got that far, even if—well, even if she had been there. If the Chandlers had stopped to warn her.

Three quarters of a mile from the inn to Hans's. Only one quarter of a mile from Hans's place to mine. And Lamb could have run; I had only walked.

Past Hans's place, a beautiful studio with that skylight I envied him. Not the place, not the fancy furnishings, just that wonderful skylight. Oh, yes, you can get wonderful light outdoors, but there's wind and dust just at the wrong time. And when, mostly, you paint out of your head instead of something you're looking at, there's no advantage to being outdoors at all. I don't have to look at a hill while I'm painting it. I've seen a hill.

The light was on at my place, up ahead. But I'd left it on, so that didn't prove Lamb was home. I plodded toward it, getting a little winded by the uphill climb, and I realized I'd been walking too fast. I turned around to look back and there was that composition again, with the gibbous moon a little higher, a little brighter. It had lightened the black of the near hills and the far ones were blacker. I thought, I can do that. Gray on black and black on gray. And, so it wouldn't be a monochrome, the yellow lights. Like the lights at Hans's place. Yellow lights like Hans's yellow hair. Tall, Nordic-Teutonic type, handsome. Nice planes in his face. Yes, I could see why women liked him. Women, but not Lamb.

I had my breath back and started climbing again. I called out Lamb's name when I got near the door, but she didn't answer. I went inside, but she wasn't there.

The place was very empty. I poured myself a glass of the wine and went over to look at the picture I'd blocked out. It was all wrong; it didn't mean anything. The lines were nice but they didn't mean anything at all. I'd have to scrape the canvas and start over. Well, I'd done that before. It's the only way you get anything, to be ruthless when something's wrong. But I couldn't start it tonight.

The tin clock said it was a quarter to eleven, still that wasn't late. But I didn't want to think so I decided to read a while. Some poetry, possibly. I went over to the bookcase. I saw Blake and that made me think of one of his simplest and best poems, *The Lamb*. It had always made me think of Lamb—"Little lamb, who made thee?" It had always given me, personally, a funny twist to the line, a connotation that Blake, of course, hadn't intended. But I didn't want to read Blake tonight. T. S. Eliot: "Midnight shakes the memory as a madman shakes a dead geranium." But it wasn't midnight yet, and I wasn't in the mood for Eliot. Not even Prufrock: "Let us go then, you and I, where the evening is spread out against the sky like a patient etherized upon a table—" He could do things with words that I'd have liked to do with pigments, but they aren't the same things, the same medium. Painting and poetry are as different as eating and sleeping. But both fields can be, and are, so wide. Painters can differ as greatly as Bonnard and Braque, yet both be great. Poets as great as Eliot and Blake. "Little lamb, who—" I didn't want to read.

And enough of thinking. I opened the trunk and got my forty-five caliber automatic. The clip was full; I jacked a cartridge into the chamber and put the safety catch on. I put it into my pocket and went outside. I closed the door behind me and started down the hill toward Hans Wagner's studio.

I wondered, had the Chandlers stopped there to warn them? Then either Lamb would have hurried home—or, possibly, she might have gone on with the Chandlers, to their place. She could have figured that to be less obvious than rushing home. So, even if she wasn't there, it would prove nothing. If she was, it would show that the Chandlers hadn't stopped there.

I walked down the road and I tried to look at the crouching black beast of the hills, the yellow of the lights. But they added up to nothing, they meant nothing. Unfeeling, ungiving-to-feel, like a patient etherized upon a table. Damn Eliot, I thought; the man saw too deeply. The useless striving of the wasteland for something a man can touch but never have, the shaking of a dead geranium. As a madman. Little Lamb. Her dark hair and her darker eyes in the whiteness of her face. And the slender, beautiful whiteness of her body. The softness of her voice and the touch of her hands running through my hair. And Hans Wagner's hair, yellow as that mocking moon.

I knocked on the door. Not loudly, not softly, just a knock.

Was it too long before Hans came?

Did he look frightened? I didn't know. The planes of his face were nice, but what was in them I didn't know. I can see the lines and the planes of faces, but I can't read them. Nor voices.

"Hi, Wayne. Come in," Hans said.

I went inside. Lamb wasn't there, not in the big room, the studio. There were other rooms, of course; a bedroom, a kitchen, a bathroom. I wanted to go look in all of them right away, but that would have been crude. I wouldn't leave until I'd looked in each.

"Getting a little worried about Lamb; she's seldom out alone this late. Have you seen her?" I asked.

Hans shook his blond, handsome head.

"Thought she might have dropped in on her way home," I said casually. I smiled at him. "Maybe I was just getting lonesome and restless. How about dropping back with me for a drink? I've got only wine, but there's plenty of that."

Of course he had to say, "Why not have a drink here?" He said it. He even asked me what I wanted, and I said a martini because he'd have to go out into the kitchen to make that and it would give me a chance to look around.

"Okay, Wayne, I'll have one too," Hans said. "Excuse me a moment."

He went out into the kitchen. I took a quick look into the bathroom and then went into the bedroom and took a good look, even under the bed. Lamb wasn't there. Then I went into the kitchen and said, "Forgot to tell you, make mine light. I might want to paint a bit after I get home."

"Sure," he said.

Lamb wasn't in the kitchen. Nor had she left after I'd knocked or come in; I remember Hans's kitchen door; it's pretty noisy and I hadn't heard it. And it's the only door aside from the front one.

I'd been foolish.

Unless, of course, Lamb had been here and had gone away with the Chandlers when they'd dropped by to warn them, if they had dropped by.

I went back into the big studio with the skylight and wandered around for a minute looking at the things on the walls. They made me want to puke so I sat down and waited. I'd stay at least a few minutes to make it look all right. Hans came back.

He gave me my drink and I thanked him. I sipped it while he waited patronizingly. Not that I minded that. He made money and I didn't. But I thought worse of him than he could possibly think of me.

"How's your work going, Wayne?"

"Fine," I said. I sipped my drink. He'd taken me at my word and made it weak, mostly vermouth. It tasted lousy that way. But the olive in it looked darker, more the color I'd had in mind. Maybe, just maybe, with the picture built around that color, it would work out.

"Nice place, Hans," I said. "That skylight. I wish I had one."

He shrugged. "You don't work from models anyway, do you? And outdoors is outdoors."

"Outdoors is in your mind," I said. "There isn't any difference." And then I wondered why I was talking to somebody who wouldn't know what I was talking about. I wandered over to the window—the one that faced toward my studio—and looked out of it. I hoped I'd see Lamb on the way there, but I didn't. She wasn't here. Where was she? Even if she'd been here and left when I'd knocked, she'd have been on the way now. I'd have seen her.

I turned. "Were the Chandlers here tonight?" I asked him.

"The Chandlers? No; haven't seen them for a couple of days." He'd finished his drink. "Have another?" he asked.

I started to say no. I didn't. My eyes happened, just happened, to light on a closet door. I'd seen inside it once; it wasn't deep, but it was deep enough for a man to stand inside it. Or a woman.

"Thanks, Hans. Yes."

I walked over and handed him my glass. He went out into the kitchen with the glasses. I walked quietly over to the closet door and tried it.

It was locked.

And there wasn't a key in the door. That didn't make sense. Why would anyone keep a closet locked when he always locked all the outer doors and windows when he left?

Little lamb, who made thee?

Hans came out of the kitchen, a martini in each hand. He saw my hand on the knob of the closet door.

For a moment he stood very still and then his hands began to tremble; the martinis, his and mine, slopped over the rims and made little droplets falling to the floor.

I asked him, pleasantly, "Hans, do you keep your closet locked?"

"*Is* it locked? No, I don't, ordinarily." And then he realized he hadn't quite said it right and he said, more fearlessly, "What's the matter with you, Wayne?"

"Nothing," I said. "Nothing at all." I took the forty-five out of my pocket. He was far enough away so that, big as he was, he couldn't think about trying to jump me.

I smiled at him, instead. "How's about letting me have the key?"

More martini glistened on the tiles. These tall, big, handsome blonds, they haven't guts; he was scared stiff. He tried to make his voice normal. "I don't know where it is. What's wrong?"

"Nothing," I said. "But stay where you are. Don't move, Hans."

He didn't. The glasses shook, but the olives stayed in them. Barely. I watched him, but I put the muzzle of the big forty-five against the keyhole. I slanted it away from the center of the door so I wouldn't kill anybody who was hiding inside. I did that out of the corner of my eye, watching Hans Wagner.

I pulled the trigger. The sound of the shot, even in that big studio, was deafening, but I didn't take my eyes off Hans. I may have blinked.

I stepped back as the closet door swung slowly open. I lined the muzzle of the forty-five against Hans's heart. I kept it there as the door of the closet swung slowly toward me.

An olive hit the tiles with a sound that wouldn't have been audible, ordinarily. I watched Hans while I looked into the closet as the door swung fully open.

Lamb was there. Naked.

I shot Hans and my hand was steady, so one shot was enough. He fell with his hand moving toward his heart but not having time to get there. His head hit the tiles with a crushing sound. The sound was the sound of death.

I put the gun back into my pocket and my hand was trembling now.

Hans's easel was near me, his palette knife lying on the ledge.

I took the palette knife in my hand and cut my Lamb, my naked Lamb, out of her frame. I rolled her up and held her tightly; no one would ever see her thus. We left together and, hand in hand, started up the hill toward home. I looked at her in the bright moonlight. I laughed and she laughed, but her laughter was like silver cymbals and my laughter was like dead petals shaken from a madman's geranium.

Her hand slipped out of mine and she danced, a white slim wraith.

Back over her shoulder her laughter tinkled and she said, "Remember, darling? Remember that you killed me when I told you about Hans and me? Don't you remember killing me this afternoon? Don't you, darling? Don't you remember?"

Rustle of Wings

Poker wasn't exactly a religion with Gramp, but it was about the nearest thing he had to a religion for the first 50 or so years of his life. That's about how old he was when I went to live with him and Gram. That was a long time ago, in a little Ohio town. I can date it pretty well, because it was just after President McKinley was assassinated. I don't mean there was any connection between McKinley's assassination and my going to live with Gram and Gramp; it just happened about the same time. I was about ten.

Gram was a good woman and a Methodist and never touched a card, except occasionally to put away a deck that Gramp had left lying somewhere, and then she'd handle it gingerly, almost as though it might explode. But she'd given up, years before, trying to reform Gramp out of his heathen ways; given up trying *seriously,* I mean. She hadn't given up nagging him about it.

If she had, Gramp would have missed the nagging, I guess; he was so used to it by then. I was too young, then, to realize what an odd couple they made—the village atheist and the president of the Methodist missionary society. To me, then, they were just Gramp and Gram, and there wasn't anything strange about their loving and living together despite their differences.

Maybe it wasn't so strange after all. I mean, Gramp was a good man underneath the crust of his cynicism. He was one of the kindest men I ever knew, and one of the most generous. He got cantankerous only when it came to superstition or religion—he refused ever to distinguish between the two—and when it came to playing poker with his cronies, or, for that matter, when it came to playing poker with anyone, anywhere, any time.

He was a good player, too; he won a little more often than he lost. He used to figure that about a tenth of his income came from playing poker; the other nine-tenths came from the truck farm he ran, just at the edge of town. In a manner of speaking, though, you might say he came out even, because Gram insisted on tithing—giving one tenth of their income to the Methodist church and missions.

Maybe that fact helped Gram's conscience in the matter of living with Gramp; anyway, I remember that she was always madder when he lost than when he won. How she got around his being an atheist I don't know. Probably she never really believed him, even at his most dogmatic negative.

I'd been with them about three years; I must have been about thirteen at the time of the big change. That was still a long time ago, but I'll never forget the night the change started, the night I heard the rustle of leathery wings in the dining room. It was the night that the seed salesman ate with us, and later played poker with Gramp.

His name—I won't forget it—was Charley Bryce. He was a little man; I remember that he was just as tall as I was at the time, which wouldn't have been more than an inch or two over five feet. He wouldn't have weighed much over 100 pounds and he had short-cropped black hair that started rather low on his forehead but tapered off to a bald spot the size of a silver dollar farther back. I remember the bald spot well; I stood back of him for a while during the poker and recall thinking what a perfect fit that spot would be for one of the silver dollars—cartwheels, they were called—before him on the table. I don't remember his face at all.

I don't recall the conversation during dinner. In all probability it was largely about seeds, because the salesman hadn't yet completed taking Gramp's order. He'd called late in the afternoon; Gramp had been in town at the broker's with a load of truck, but Gram had expected him back any minute and had told the salesman to wait. But by the time Gramp and the wagon came back it was so late that Gram had asked the salesman to stay and eat with us, and he had accepted.

Gramp and Charley Bryce still sat at the table, I recall, while I helped Gram clear off the dishes, and Bryce had the order blank before him, finishing writing up Gramp's order.

It was after I'd carried the last load and came back to take care of the napkins that poker was mentioned for the first time; I don't know which of the men mentioned it first. But Gramp was telling animatedly of a hand he'd held the last time he'd played, a few nights before. The stranger—possibly I forgot to say that Charley Bryce *was* a stranger; we'd never met him before and he must have been shifted to a different territory because we never saw him again—was listening with smiling interest. No, I don't remember his face at all, but I remember that he smiled a lot.

I picked up the napkins and rings so Gram could take up the tablecloth from under them. And while she was folding the cloth I put three napkins—hers and Gramp's and mine—back into our respective napkin rings and put the salesman's napkin with the laundry. Gram had that expression on her face again, the tight-lipped disapproving look she wore whenever cards were being played or discussed.

And then Gramp asked, "Where are the cards, Ma?"

Gram sniffed. "Wherever you put them, William," she told him. So Gramp got the cards from the drawer in the sideboard where they were always kept, and got a big handful of silver out of his pocket and he and the stranger, Charley Bryce, started to play two-handed stud poker across a corner of the big square dining room table.

I was out in the kitchen then, for a while, helping Gram with the dishes, and when I came back most of the silver was in front of Bryce, and Gramp had gone into his wallet and there was a pile of dollar bills in front of him instead of the cartwheels. Dollar bills were big in those days, not the little skimpy ones we have now.

I stood there watching the game after I'd finished the dishes. I don't remember any of the hands they held; I remember that money seesawed back and forth, though, without anybody getting more than ten or twenty dollars ahead or behind. And I remember the stranger looking at the clock after a while and saying he wanted to catch the 10 o'clock train and would it be all right to deal off at half-past 9, and Gramp saying sure.

So they did, and at 9:30, it was Charley Bryce who was ahead. He counted off the money he himself had put into the game and there was a pile of silver cartwheels left, and he counted that, and I remember that he grinned. He said, "Thirteen dollars exactly. Thirteen pieces of silver."

"The devil," said Gramp; it was one of his favorite expressions.

And Gram sniffed. "Speak of the devil," she said, "and you hear the rustle of his wings."

Charley Bryce laughed softly. He'd picked up the deck of cards again, and he riffled them softly, as softly as he had laughed, and asked, "Like this?"

That was when I started to get scared.

Gram just sniffed again, though. She said, "Yes, like that. And if you gentlemen will excuse me— And you, Johnny, you better not stay up much longer."

She went upstairs.

The salesman chuckled and riffled the cards again. Louder, this time. I don't know whether it was the rustling sound they made or the thirteen pieces of silver, exactly, or what, but I was scared. I wasn't standing behind the salesman any more; I'd walked around the table. He saw my face and grinned at me. He said, "Son, you look like you believe in the devil, and think I'm him. Do you?"

I said "No, sir," but I must not have said it very convincingly. Gramp laughed out loud, and he wasn't a man that laughed out loud very often.

Gramp said, "I'm surprised at you, Johnny. Darned if you don't sound like you *do* believe it!" And he was off laughing again.

Charley Bryce looked at Gramp. There was a twinkle in his eye. He asked, "Don't you believe it?"

Gramp quit laughing. He said, "Cut it out, Charley. Giving the boy silly ideas." He looked around to be sure Gram had left. "I don't want him to grow up superstitious."

"Everybody's superstitious, more or less," Charley Bryce said.

Gramp shook his head. "Not me."

Bryce said, "You don't think you are, but if it came to a showdown, I'd bet you are.

Gramp frowned. "You'd bet what, and how?"

The salesman riffled the deck of cards once more and then put them down. He picked up the stack of cartwheels and counted them again. He said, "I'll bet thirteen dollars to your one dollar. Thirteen pieces of silver says you'd be afraid to prove you don't believe in the devil."

Gramp had put away his folding money but he took his wallet out again and took a dollar bill out of it. He put the bill on the table between them. He said, "Charley Bryce, you're covered."

Charley Bryce put the pile of silver dollars beside it, and took a fountain pen out of his pocket, the one Gramp had signed the seed order with. I remember the pen because it was one of the first fountain pens I'd ever seen and I'd been interested in it.

Charley Bryce handed Gramp the fountain pen and took a clean seed order blank out of his pocket and put it on the table in front of Gramp, the unprinted side up.

He said, "You write 'For thirteen dollars I sell my soul,' and then sign it."

Gramp laughed and picked up the fountain pen. He started to write, fast, and then his hand moved slower and slower and he stopped; I couldn't see how far he'd written.

He looked across the table at Charley Bryce. He said, "What if—?" Then he looked down at the paper a while more and then at the money in the middle of the table; the fourteen dollars, one paper and thirteen silver.

Then he grinned, but it was a kind of sick grin.

He said, "Take the bet, Charley. You win, I guess."

That was all there was to it. The salesman chuckled and picked up the money, and Gramp walked with him to the railroad station.

But Gramp wasn't ever exactly the same after that. Oh, he kept on playing poker; he never did change about that. Not even after he started going to church with Gram every Sunday regularly, and even after he finally let them make him a vestryman he kept on playing cards, and Gram kept on nagging him about it. He taught me how to play, too, in spite of Gram.

We never saw Charley Bryce again; he must have been transferred to a different route or changed jobs. And it wasn't until the day of Gramp's funeral in 1913 that I learned that Gram had heard the conversation and the bet that night; she'd been straightening things in the linen closet in the hall and hadn't gone upstairs yet. She told me on the way home from the funeral, ten years later.

I asked her, I remember, whether she would have come in and stopped Gramp if he'd been going to sign, and she smiled. She said, "He wouldn't have, Johnny. And it wouldn't have mattered if he had. If there really is a devil, God wouldn't let him wander around tempting people like that, in disguise."

"Would you have signed, Gram?" I asked her.

"Thirteen dollars for writing something silly on a piece of paper, Johnny? Of course I would. Wouldn't you?"

I said, "I don't know." And it's been a long time since then, but I still don't.

Hall of Mirrors

For an instant you think it is temporary blindness, this sudden dark that comes in the middle of a bright afternoon.

It *must* be blindness, you think; could the sun that was tanning you have gone out instantaneously, leaving you in utter blackness?

Then the nerves of your body tell you that you are *standing*, whereas only a second ago you were sitting comfortably, almost reclining, in a canvas chair. In the patio of a friend's house in Beverly Hills. Talking to Barbara, your fiancée. Looking at Barbara—Barbara in a swim suit—her skin golden tan in the brilliant sunshine, beautiful.

You wore swimming trunks. Now you do not feel them on you; the slight pressure of the elastic waistband is no longer there against your waist. You touch your hands to your hips. You are naked. And standing.

Whatever has happened to you is more than a change to sudden darkness or to sudden blindness.

You raise your hands gropingly before you. They touch a plain smooth surface, a wall. You spread them apart and each hand reaches a corner. You pivot slowly. A second wall, then a third, then a door. You are in a closet about four feet square.

Your hand finds the knob of the door. It turns and you push the door open.

There is light now. The door has opened to a lighted room ... a room that you have never seen before.

It is not large, but it is pleasantly furnished—although the furniture is of a style that is strange to you. Modesty makes you open the door cautiously the rest of the way. But the room is empty of people.

You step into the room, turning to look behind you into the closet, which is now illuminated by light from the room. The closet is and is not a closet; it is the size and shape of one, but it contains nothing, not a single hook, no rod for hanging clothes, no shelf. It is an empty, blank-walled, four-by-four-foot space.

You close the door to it and stand looking around the room. It is about twelve by sixteen feet. There is one door, but it is closed. There are no windows. Five pieces of furniture. Four of them you recognize—more or less. One looks like a very functional desk. One is obviously a chair ... a comfortable-looking one. There is a table, although its top is on several levels instead of only one. Another is a bed, or couch. Something shimmering is lying across it and you walk over and pick the shimmering something up and examine it. It is a garment.

You are naked, so you put it on. Slippers are part way under the bed (or couch) and you slide your feet into them. They fit, and they feel warm and comfortable as nothing you have ever worn on your feet has felt. Like lamb's wool, but softer.

You are dressed now. You look at the door—the only door of the room except that of the closet (closet?) from which you entered it. You walk to the door and before you try the knob, you see the small typewritten sign pasted just above it that reads:

This door has a time lock set to open in one hour. For reasons you will soon understand, it is better that you do not leave this room before then. There is a letter for you on the desk. Please read it.

It is not signed. You look at the desk and see that there is an envelope lying on it.

You do not yet go to take that envelope from the desk and read the letter that must be in it.

Why not? Because you are frightened.

You see other things about the room. The lighting has no source that you can discover. It comes from nowhere. It is not indirect lighting; the ceiling and the walls are not reflecting it at all.

They didn't have lighting like that, back where you came from. What did you mean by *back where you came from?*

You close your eyes. You tell yourself: *I am Norman Hastings. I am an associate professor of mathematics at the University of Southern California. I am twenty-five years old, and this is the year nineteen hundred and fifty-four.*

You open your eyes and look again.

They didn't use that style of furniture in Los Angeles—or anywhere else that you know of—in 1954. That thing over in the corner—you can't even guess what it is. So might your grandfather, at your age, have looked at a television set.

You look down at yourself, at the shimmering garment that you found waiting for you. With thumb and forefinger you feel its texture.

It's like nothing you've ever touched before.

I am Norman Hastings. This is nineteen hundred and fifty-four.

Suddenly you must know, and at once.

You go to the desk and pick up the envelope that lies upon it. Your name is typed on the outside. *Norman Hastings.*

Your hands shake a little as you open it. Do you blame them?

There are several pages, typewritten. Dear Norman, it starts. You turn quickly to the end to look for the signature. It is unsigned.

You turn back and start reading.

"Do not be afraid. There is nothing to fear, but much to explain. Much that you must understand before the time lock opens that door. Much that you must accept and—obey.

"You have already guessed that you are in the future—in what, to you, seems to be the future. The clothes and the room must have told you that. I planned it that way so the shock would not be too sudden, so you would realize it over the course of several minutes rather than read it here—and quite probably disbelieve what you read.

"The 'closet' from which you have just stepped is, as you have by now realized, a time machine. From it you stepped into the world of 2004. The date is April 7th, just fifty years from the time you last remember.

"You cannot return.

"I did this to you and you may hate me for it; I do not know. That is up to you to decide, but it does not matter. What does matter, and not to you alone, is another decision which you must make. I am incapable of making it.

"Who is writing this to you? I would rather not tell you just yet. By the time you have finished reading this, even though it is not signed (for I knew you would look first for a signature), I will not need to tell you who I am. You will know.

"I am seventy-five years of age. I have, in this year 2004, been studying 'time' for thirty of those years. I have completed the first time machine ever built—and thus far, its construction, even the fact that it has been constructed, is my own secret.

"You have just participated in the first major experiment. It will be your responsibility to decide whether there shall ever be any more experiments with it, whether it should be given to the world, or whether it should be destroyed and never used again."

End of the first page. You look up for a moment, hesitating to turn the next page. Already you suspect what is coming.

You turn the page.

"I constructed the first time machine a week ago. My calculations had told me that it would work, but not how it would work. I had expected it to send an object back in time—it works backward in time only, not forward—physically unchanged and intact.

"My first experiment showed me my error. I placed a cube of metal in the machine—it was a miniature of the one you just walked out of—and set the machine to go backward ten years. I flicked the switch and opened the door, expecting to find the cube vanished. Instead I found it had crumbled to powder.

"I put in another cube and sent it two years back. The second cube came back unchanged, except that it was newer, shiner.

"That gave me the answer. I had been expecting the cubes to go back in time, and they had done so, but not in the sense I had expected them to. Those metal cubes had been fabricated about three years previously. I had sent the first one back years before it had existed in its fabricated form. Ten years ago it had been ore. The machine returned it to that state.

"Do you see how our previous theories of time travel have been wrong? We expected to be able to step into a time machine in, say, 2004, set it for fifty years back, and then step out in the year 1954 ... but it does not work that way. The machine does not move in time. Only whatever is within the machine is affected, and then just with relation to itself and not to the rest of the Universe.

"I confirmed this with guinea pigs by sending one six weeks old five weeks back and it came out a baby.

"I need not outline all my experiments here. You will find a record of them in the desk and you can study it later.

"Do you understand now what has happened to you, Norman?"

You begin to understand. And you begin to sweat.

The *I* who wrote that letter you are now reading is *you*, yourself at the age of seventy-five, in the year of 2004. You are that seventy-five-year-old man, with your body returned to what it had been fifty years ago, with all the memories of fifty years of living wiped out.

You invented the time machine.

And before you used it on yourself, you made these arrangements to help you orient yourself. You wrote yourself the letter which you are now reading.

But if those fifty years are—to you—gone, what of all your friends, those you loved? What of your parents? What of the girl you are going—were going—to marry?

You read on:

"Yes, you will want to know what has happened. Mom died in 1963, Dad in 1968. You married Barbara in 1956. I am sorry to tell you that she died only three years later, in a plane crash. You have one son. He is still living; his name is Walter; he is now forty-six years old and is an accountant in Kansas City."

Tears come into your eyes and for a moment you can no longer read. Barbara dead—dead for forty-five years. And only minutes ago, in subjective time, you were sitting next to her, sitting in the bright sun in a Beverly Hills patio ...

You force yourself to read again.

"But back to the discovery. You begin to see some of its implications. You will need time to think to see all of them.

"It does not permit time travel as we have thought of time travel, but it gives us immortality of a sort. Immortality of the kind I have temporarily given us.

"*Is it good?* Is it worth while to lose the memory of fifty years of one's life in order to return one's body to relative youth? The only way I can find out is to try, as soon as I have finished writing this and made my other preparations.

"You will know the answer.

"But before you decide, remember that there is another problem, more important than the psychological one. I mean overpopulation.

"If our discovery is given to the world, if all who are old or dying can make themselves young again, the population will almost double every generation. Nor would the world—not even our own relatively enlightened country—be willing to accept compulsory birth control as a solution.

"Give this to the world, as the world is today in 2004, and within a generation there will be famine, suffering, war. Perhaps a complete collapse of civilization.

"Yes, we have reached other planets, but they are not suitable for colonizing. The stars may be our answer, but we are a long way from reaching them. When we do, someday, the billions of habitable planets that must be out there will be our answer ... our living room. But until then, what is the answer?

"Destroy the machine? But think of the countless lives it can save, the suffering it can prevent. Think of what it would mean to a man dying of cancer. Think ..."

Think. You finish the letter and put it down.

You think of Barbara dead for forty-five years. And of the fact that you were married to her for three years and that those years are lost to you.

Fifty years lost. You damn the old man of seventy-five whom you became and who has done this to you ... who has given you this decision to make.

Bitterly, you know what the decision must be. You think that *he* knew, too, and realize that he could safely leave it in your hands. Damn him, he *should* have known.

Too valuable to destroy, too dangerous to give.

The other answer is painfully obvious.

You must be custodian of this discovery and keep it secret until it is safe to give, until mankind has expanded to the stars and has new worlds to populate, or until, even without that, he has reached a state of civilization where he can avoid overpopulation by rationing births to the number of accidental—or voluntary—deaths.

If neither of those things has happened in another fifty years (and are they likely so soon?), then you, at seventy-five, will be writing another letter like this one. You will be undergoing another experience similar to the one you're going through now. And making the same decision, of course.

Why not? You'll be the same person again.

Time and again, to preserve this secret until Man is ready for it.

How often will you again sit at a desk like this one, thinking the thoughts you are thinking now, feeling the grief you now feel?

There is a click at the door and you know that the time lock has opened, that you are now free to leave this room, free to start a new life for yourself in place of the one you have already lived and lost.

But you are in no hurry now to walk directly through that door.

You sit there, staring straight ahead of you blindly, seeing in your mind's eye the vista of a set of facing mirrors, like those in an old-fashioned barber shop, reflecting the same thing over and over again, diminishing into far distance.

Experiment

"The first time machine, gentlemen," Professor Johnson proudly informed his two colleagues. "True, it is a small-scale experimental model. It will operate only on objects weighing less than three pounds, five ounces and for distances into the past and future of twelve minutes or less. But it works."

The small-scale model looked like a small scale—a postage scale—except for two dials in the part under the platform.

Professor Johnson held up a small metal cube. "Our experimental object," he said, "is a brass cube weighing one pound, two point three ounces. First, I shall send it five minutes into the future."

He leaned forward and set one of the dials on the time machine. "Look at your watches," he said.

They looked at their watches. Professor Johnson placed the cube gently on the machine's platform. It vanished.

Five minutes later, to the second, it reappeared.

Professor Johnson picked it up. "Now five minutes into the past." He set the other dial. Holding the cube in his hand he looked at his watch. "It is six minutes before three o'clock. I shall now activate the mechanism—by placing the cube on the platform—at exactly three o'clock. Therefore, the cube should, at five minutes before three, vanish from my hand and appear on the platform, five minutes before I place it there."

"How can you place it there, then?" asked one of his colleagues.

"It will, as my hand approaches, vanish from the platform and appear in my hand to be placed there. Three o'clock. Notice, please."

The cube vanished from his hand.

It appeared on the platform of the time machine.

"See? Five minutes before I shall place it there, it *is* there!"

His other colleague frowned at the cube. "But," he said, "what if, now that it has already appeared five minutes before you place it there, you should change your mind about doing so and *not* place it there at three o'clock? Wouldn't there be a paradox of some sort involved?"

"An interesting idea," Professor Johnson said. "I had not thought of it, and it will be interesting to try. Very well, I shall *not* ..."

There was no paradox at all. The cube remained.

But the entire rest of the Universe, professors and all, vanished.

Sentry

He was wet and muddy and hungry and cold and he was fifty thousand light-years from home.

A strange blue sun gave light and the gravity, twice what he was used to, made every movement difficult.

But in tens of thousands of years this part of war hadn't changed. The flyboys were fine with their sleek spaceships and their fancy weapons. When the chips are down, though, it was still the foot soldier, the infantry, that had to take the ground and hold it, foot by bloody foot. Like this damned planet of a star he'd never heard of until they'd landed him there. And now it was sacred ground because the aliens were there too. *The* aliens, the only other intelligent race in the Galaxy ... cruel, hideous and repulsive monsters.

Contact had been made with them near the center of the Galaxy, after the slow, difficult colonization of a dozen thousand planets; and it had been war at sight; they'd shot without even trying to negotiate, or to make peace.

Now, planet by bitter planet, it was being fought out.

He was wet and muddy and hungry and cold, and the day was raw with a high wind that hurt his eyes. But the aliens were trying to infiltrate and every sentry post was vital.

He stayed alert, gun ready. Fifty thousand light-years from home, fighting on a strange world and wondering if he'd ever live to see home again.

And then he saw one of them crawling toward him. He drew a bead and fired. The alien made that strange horrible sound they all make, then lay still.

He shuddered at the sound and sight of the alien lying there. One ought to be able to get used to them after a while, but he'd never been able to. Such repulsive creatures they were, with only two arms and two legs, ghastly white skins and no scales.

Keep Out

Daptine is the secret of it. Adaptine, they called it first; then it got shortened to daptine. It let us adapt.

They explained it all to us when we were ten years old; I guess they thought we were too young to understand before then, although we knew a lot of it already. They told us just after we landed on Mars.

"You're *home*, children," the Head Teacher told us after we had gone into the glassite dome they'd built for us there. And he told us there'd be a special lecture for us that evening, an important one that we must all attend.

And that evening he told us the whole story and the whys and wherefores. He stood up before us. He had to wear a heated spacesuit and helmet, of course, because the temperature in the dome was comfortable for us but already freezing cold for him and the air was already too thin for him to breathe. His voice came to us by radio from inside his helmet.

"Children," he said, "you are home. This is Mars, the planet on which you will spend the rest of your lives. You are Martians, the first Martians. You have lived five years on Earth and another five in space. Now you will spend ten years, until you are adults, in this dome, although toward the end of that time you will be allowed to spend increasingly long periods outdoors.

"Then you will go forth and make your own homes, live your own lives, as Martians. You will intermarry and your children will breed true. They too will be Martians.

"It is time you were told the history of this great experiment of which each of you is a part."

Then he told us.

Man, he said, had first reached Mars in 1985. It had been uninhabited by intelligent life (there is plenty of plant life and a few varieties of non-flying insects) and he had found it by terrestrial standards uninhabitable. Man could survive on Mars only by living inside glassite domes and wearing space suits when he went outside of them. Except by day in the warmer seasons it was too cold for him. The air was too thin for him to breathe and long exposure to sunlight—less filtered of rays harmful to him than on Earth because of the lesser atmosphere—could kill him. The plants were chemically alien to him and he could not eat them; he had to bring all his food from Earth or grow it in hydroponic tanks.

For fifty years he had tried to colonize Mars and all his efforts had failed. Besides this dome which had been built for us there was only one other outpost, another glassite dome much smaller and less than a mile away.

It had looked as though mankind could never spread to the other planets of the solar system besides Earth for of all them Mars was the least inhospitable; if he couldn't live here there was no use even trying to colonize the others.

And then, in 2034, thirty years ago, a brilliant biochemist named Waymoth had discovered daptine. A miracle drug that worked not on the animal or person to whom it was given but on the progeny he conceived during a limited period of time after inoculation.

It gave his progeny almost limitless adaptability to changing conditions, provided the changes were made gradually.

Dr. Waymoth had inoculated and then mated a pair of guinea pigs; they had borne a litter of five and by placing each member of the litter under different and gradually changing conditions, he had obtained amazing results. When they attained maturity one of those guinea pigs was living comfortably at a temperature of forty below zero Fahrenheit, another was quite happy at a hundred and fifty above. A third was thriving on a diet that would have been deadly poison for an ordinary animal and a fourth was contented under a constant X-ray bombardment that would have killed one of its parents within minutes.

Subsequent experiments with many litters showed that animals who had been adapted to similar conditions bred true and their progeny was conditioned from birth to live under those conditions.

"Ten years later, ten years ago," the Head Teacher told us, "you children were born. Born of parents carefully selected from those who volunteered for the experiment. And from birth you have been brought up under carefully controlled and gradually changing conditions.

"From the time you were born the air you have breathed has been very gradually thinned and its oxygen content reduced. Your lungs have compensated by becoming much greater in capacity, which is why your chests are so much larger than those of your teachers and attendants; when you are fully mature and are breathing air like that of Mars, the difference will be even greater.

"Your bodies are growing fur to enable you to stand the increasing cold. You are comfortable now under conditions which would kill ordinary people quickly. Since you were four years old your nurses and teachers have had to wear special protection to survive conditions that seem normal to you.

"In another ten years, at maturity, you will be completely acclimated to Mars. Its air will be your air; its food plants your food. Its extremes of temperature will be easy for you to endure and its median temperatures pleasant to you. Already, because of the five years we spent in space under gradually decreased gravitational pull, the gravity of Mars seems normal to you.

"It will be your planet, to live on and to populate. You are the children of Earth but you are the first Martians."

Of course we had known a lot of those things already.

The last year was the best. By then the air inside the dome—except for the pressurized parts where our teachers and attendants live—was almost like that outside, and we were allowed out for increasingly long periods. It is good to be in the open.

The last few months they relaxed segregation of the sexes so we could begin choosing mates, although they told us there is to be no marriage until after the final day, after our full clearance. Choosing was not difficult in my case. I had made my choice long since and I'd felt sure that she felt the same way; I was right.

Tomorrow is the day of our freedom. Tomorrow we will be Martians, *the* Martians. Tomorrow we shall take over the planet.

Some among us are impatient, have been impatient for weeks now, but wiser counsel prevailed and we are waiting. We have waited twenty years and we can wait until the final day.

And tomorrow is the final day.

Tomorrow, at a signal, we will kill the teachers and the other Earthmen among us before we go forth. They do not suspect, so it will be easy.

We have dissimilated for years now, and they do not know how we hate them. They do not know how disgusting and hideous we find them, with their ugly misshapen bodies, so narrow shouldered and tiny chested, their weak sibilant voices that need amplification to carry in our Martian air, and above all their white pasty hairless skins.

We shall kill them and then we shall go and smash the other dome so all the Earthmen there will die too.

If more Earthmen ever come to punish us, we can live and hide in the hills where they'll never find us. And if they try to build more domes here we'll smash them. We want no more to do with Earth.

This is our planet and we want no aliens. Keep off!

Naturally

Henry Blodgett looked at his wrist watch and saw that it was two o'clock in the morning. In despair, he slammed shut the textbook he'd been studying and let his head sink onto his arms on the table in front of him. He knew he'd never pass that examination tomorrow; the more he studied geometry the less he understood it. Mathematics in general had always been difficult for him and now he was finding that geometry was impossible for him to learn.

And if he flunked it, he was through with college; he'd flunked three other courses in his first two years and another failure this year would, under college rules, cause automatic expulsion.

He wanted that college degree badly too, since it was indispensable for the career he'd chosen and worked toward. Only a miracle could save him now.

He sat up suddenly as an idea struck him. Why not try magic? The occult had always interested him. He had books on it and he'd often read the simple instructions on how to conjure up a demon and make it obey his will. Up to now, he'd always figured that it was a bit risky and so had never actually tried it. But this was an emergency and might be worth the slight risk. Only through black magic could he suddenly become an expert in a subject that had always been difficult for him.

From the shelf he quickly took out his best book on black magic, found the right page and refreshed his memory on the few simple things he had to do.

Enthusiastically, he cleared the floor by pushing the furniture against the walls. He drew the pentagram figure on the carpet with chalk and stepped inside it. He then said the incantations.

The demon was considerably more horrible than he had anticipated. But he mustered his courage and started to explain his dilemma.

"I've always been poor at geometry," he began ...

"You're telling *me*," said the demon gleefully.

Smiling flames, it came for him across the chalk lines of the useless hexagram Henry had drawn by mistake instead of the protecting pentagram.

Voodoo

Mr. Decker's wife had just returned from a trip to Haiti—a trip she had taken alone—to give them a cooling off period before they discussed a divorce.

It hadn't worked. Neither of them had cooled off in the slightest. In fact, they were finding now that they hated one another more than ever.

"Half," said Mrs. Decker firmly. "I'll not settle for anything less than half the money plus half the property."

"Ridiculous!" said Mr. Decker.

"Is it? I could have it all, you know. And quite easily, too. I studied voodoo while in Haiti."

"Rot!" said Mr. Decker.

"It isn't. And you should be glad that I am a good woman for I could kill you quite easily if I wished. I would then have *all* the money and *all* the real estate, and without any fear of consequences. A death accomplished by voodoo can not be distinguished from a death by heart failure."

"Rubbish!" said Mr. Decker.

"You think so? I have wax and a hatpin. Do you want to give me a tiny pinch of your hair or a fingernail clipping or two—that's all I need—and let me show you?"

"Nonsense!" said Mr. Decker.

"Then why are you afraid to have me try? Since *I* know it works, I'll make you a proposition. If it doesn't kill you, I'll give you a divorce and ask for nothing. If it does, I'll get it all automatically."

"Done!" said Mr. Decker. "Get your wax and hatpin." He glanced at his fingernails. "Pretty short. I'll give you a bit of hair."

When he came back with a few short strands of hair in the lid of an aspirin tin, Mrs. Decker had already started softening the wax. She kneaded the hair into it, then shaped it into the rough effigy of a human being.

"You'll be sorry," she said, and thrust the hatpin into the chest of the wax figure.

Mr. Decker was surprised, but he was more pleased than sorry. He had not believed in voodoo, but being a cautious man he never took chances.

Besides, it had always irritated him that his wife so seldom cleaned her hairbrush.

Answer

Dwar Ev ceremoniously soldered the final connection with gold. The eyes of a dozen television cameras watched him and the subether bore throughout the universe a dozen pictures of what he was doing.

He straightened and nodded to Dwar Reyn, then moved to a position beside the switch that would complete the contact when he threw it. The switch that would connect, all at once, all of the monster computing machines of all the populated planets in the universe—ninety-six billion planets—into the supercircuit that would connect them all into one supercalculator, one cybernetics machine that would combine all the knowledge of all the galaxies.

Dwar Reyn spoke briefly to the watching and listening trillions. Then after a moment's silence he said, "Now, Dwar Ev."

Dwar Ev threw the switch. There was a mighty hum, the surge of power from ninety-six billion planets. Lights flashed and quieted along the miles-long panel.

Dwar Ev stepped back and drew a deep breath. "The honor of asking the first question is yours, Dwar Reyn."

"Thank you," said Dwar Reyn. "It shall be a question which no single cybernetics machine has been able to answer."

He turned to face the machine. "Is there a God?"

The mighty voice answered without hesitation, without the clicking of a single relay.

"Yes, *now* there is a God."

Sudden fear flashed on the face of Dwar Ev. He leaped to grab the switch.

A bolt of lightning from the cloudless sky struck him down and fused the switch shut.

Daisies

Dr. Michaelson was showing his wife, whose name was Mrs. Michaelson, around his combination laboratory and greenhouse. It was the first time she had been there in several months and quite a bit of new equipment had been added.

"You were really serious then, John," she asked him finally, "when you told me you were experimenting in communicating with flowers? I thought you were joking."

"Not at all," said Dr. Michaelson. "Contrary to popular belief, flowers do have at least a degree of intelligence."

"But surely they can't talk!"

"Not as we talk. But contrary to popular belief, they do communicate. Telepathically, as it were, and in thought pictures rather than in words."

"Among themselves perhaps, but surely—"

"Contrary to popular belief, my dear, even human-floral communication is possible, although thus far I have been able to establish only one-way communication. That is, I can catch their thoughts but not send messages from my mind to theirs."

"But—how does it work, John?"

"Contrary to popular belief," said her husband, "thoughts, both human and floral, are electromagnetic waves that can be—Wait, it will be easier to show you, my dear."

He called to his assistant who was working at the far end of the room, "Miss Wilson, will you please bring the communicator?"

Miss Wilson brought the communicator. It was a headband from which a wire led to a slender rod with an insulated handle. Dr. Michaelson put the headband on his wife's head and the rod in her hand.

"Quite simple to use," he told her. "Hold the rod near a flower and it acts as an antenna to pick up its thoughts. And you will find out that, contrary to popular belief—"

But Mrs. Michaelson was not listening to her husband. She was holding the rod near a pot of daisies on the window sill. After a moment she put down the rod and took a small pistol from her purse. She shot first her husband and then his assistant, Miss Wilson.

Contrary to popular belief, daisies *do* tell.

Pattern

Miss Macy sniffed. "Why is everyone worrying so? They're not doing anything to us, are they?"

In the cities, elsewhere, there was blind panic. But not in Miss Macy's garden. She looked up calmly at the monstrous mile-high figures of the invaders.

A week ago, they'd landed, in a spaceship a hundred miles long that had settled down gently in the Arizona desert. Almost a thousand of them had come out of that spaceship and were now walking around.

But, as Miss Macy pointed out they hadn't hurt anything or anybody. They weren't quite *substantial* enough to affect people. When one stepped on you or stepped on a house you were in, there was sudden darkness and until he moved his foot and walked on you couldn't see; that was all.

They had paid no attention to human beings and all attempts to communicate with them had failed, as had all attacks on them by the army and the air force. Shells fired at them exploded right inside them and didn't hurt them. Not even the H-bomb dropped on one of them while he was crossing a desert area had bothered him in the slightest.

They had paid no attention to us at all.

"And that," said Miss Macy to her sister who was also Miss Macy since neither of them was married, "is proof that they don't mean us any harm, isn't it?"

"I hope so, Amanda," said Miss Macy's sister, "But look what they're doing now."

It was a clear day, or it had been one. The sky had been bright blue and the almost humanoid heads and shoulders of the giants, a mile up there, had been quite clearly visible. But now it was getting misty, Miss Macy saw as she followed her sister's gaze upward. Each of the two big figures in sight had a tank-like object in his hands and from these objects clouds of vaporous matter were emerging, settling slowly toward Earth.

Miss Macy sniffed again. "Making clouds. Maybe that's how they have fun. *Clouds* can't hurt us. Why do people worry so?"

She went back to her work.

"Is that a liquid fertilizer you're spraying, Amanda?" her sister asked.

"No," said Miss Macy. "It's insecticide."

558

Politeness

Rance Hendrix, alien psychology specialist with the third Venusian expedition, trudged wearily across the hot sands to find a Venusian and, for a fifth time, to try to make friends with one. A discouraging task, four previous failures had taught him. Experts with the previous Venusian expeditions had also failed.

Not that Venusians were hard to find but apparently they simply didn't give a damn for us or have the slightest inclination to be friendly. It seemed more than ordinarily strange that they weren't sociable, since they spoke our language; some telepathic ability let them understand what was said to them in any terrestrial language and to reply in kind—but unkindly.

One was coming, carrying a shovel.

"Greetings, Venusian," said Hendrix cheerfully.

"Good-by, Earthman," said the Venusian, walking on past.

Feeling both foolish and annoyed, Hendrix hurried along after him, having to run to keep pace with the Venusian's long strides. "Hey," he said, "*why* don't you talk to us?"

"I am talking to you," said the Venusian. "Little as I enjoy it. Please go away."

He stopped and began to dig for korvils' eggs, paying no further attention.

Hendrix glared at him in frustration. Always the same pattern, no matter what Venusian they tried. Every approach in the textbooks of alien psychology had failed.

And the sand was burning hot under his feet and the air, although breathable, had a tinge of formaldehyde that hurt his lungs. He gave up, and lost his temper.

"—yourself," he shouted. A biological impossibility, of course, for an Earthman.

But Venusians are bisexual. The Venusian turned in delighted wonder; for the first time an Earthman had given him the only greeting that is considered less than horribly rude on Venus.

He returned the compliment with a wide blue smile, dropped his shovel and sat down to talk. It was the beginning of a beautiful friendship and of understanding between Earth and Venus.

Preposterous

Mr. Weatherwax buttered his toast carefully. His voice was firm. "My dear," he said, "I want it definitely understood that there shall be no more such trashy reading around this apartment."

"Yes, Jason. I did not know—"

"Of course you didn't. But it is your responsibility to know what our son reads."

"I shall watch more closely, Jason. I did not see the magazine when he brought it in. I did not know it was here."

"Nor would I have known had I not, after I came in last night, accidentally happened to displace one of the pillows on the sofa. The periodical was hidden under it, and of course I glanced through it."

The points of Mr. Weatherwax's mustache quivered with indignation. "Such utterly ridiculous concepts, such impossibly wild ideas. *Astounding Stories*, indeed!"

He took a sip of his coffee to calm himself.

"Such inane and utterly preposterous tripe," he said. "Travel to other galaxies by means of space warps, whatever they are. Time machines, teleportation and telekinesis. Balderdash, sheer balderdash."

"My dear Jason," said his wife, this time with just the faintest touch of asperity, "I assure you I shall watch Gerald's reading closely hereafter. I fully agree with you."

"Thank you, my dear," Mr. Weatherwax said, more kindly. "The minds of the young should not be poisoned by such wild imaginings."

He glanced at his watch and rose hastily, kissed his wife and left.

Outside the apartment door he stepped into the antigravity shaft and floated gently down two hundred-odd floors to street level where he was lucky enough to catch an atomcab immediately; "Moonport," he snapped to the robot driver, and then sat back and closed his eyes to catch the telepathecast. He'd hoped to catch a bulletin on the Fourth Martian War but it was only another routine report from Immortality Center, so he quirtled.

Reconciliation

The night outside was still and starry. The living room of the house was tense. The man and woman in it stood a few feet apart, glaring hatred at each other.

The man's fists were clenched as though he wished to use them, and the woman's fingers were spread and curved like claws, but each held his arms rigidly at his sides. They were being civilized.

Her voice was low. "I hate you," she said. "I've come to hate everything about you."

"Of course you do," he said. "Now that you've bled me white with your extravagances, now that I can't any longer buy every silly thing that your selfish little heart—"

"It isn't that. You know it isn't that. If you still treated me like you used to, you know that money wouldn't matter. It's that—that woman."

He sighed as one sighs who hears a thing for the ten thousandth time. "You know," he said, "that she didn't mean a thing to me, not a damn thing. You drove me to—what I did. And even if it didn't mean a damn thing, I'm not sorry. I'd do it again."

"You *will* do it again, as often as you get a chance. But *I* won't be around to be humiliated by it. Humiliated before my friends—"

"Friends! Those vicious bitches whose nasty opinions matter more to you than—"

Blinding flash and searing heat. They knew, and each of them took a sightless step toward the other with groping arms; each held desperately tight to the other in the second that remained to them, the final second that was all that mattered now. "O my darling I love—" "John, John, my sweet—"

The shock wave came.

Outside in what had been the quiet night a red flower grew and yearned toward the canceled sky.

Search

The kindly man with the long white beard said, "Welcome to Heaven, Peter." He smiled. "That's my name, too, you know. I hope you'll be very happy here."

And Peter, who was only four, went through the gates of pearl, in search of God.

He went along spotless streets lined with dazzling buildings, among happy people, but he did not find God.

He wandered until he was very tired, but he kept on. Some spoke to him but he paid no heed.

He came at last to a building of gleaming gold that was greater than any of the others, so great that he knew he had found at last where God must live.

The huge doors opened as he walked toward them, and he went in.

At one end of the big room was a great golden throne, but God was not there.

The floor was soft and silken, padded. In the middle of the room, halfway between the door and the throne, Peter sat down to wait for God. After a while he lay down and slept.

It may have been for minutes, it may have been for years.

But he heard the soft sound of footsteps and they awakened him; he knew that God was coming and he wakened gladly.

God was coming; His eyes fell on Peter and they lighted with sudden pleasure. Peter ran quickly toward Him: God put his hand on Peter's head and said quietly, "Hello, Pete." And then He looked beyond toward the throne and His face changed.

Slowly He dropped to His knees and bent His head, almost as though He was afraid. But of whom could God be afraid?

Peter knew that God could not be serious, but he played along with Him.

He wagged his stubby tail to show that he knew it was all in fun and then he turned around and barked at the shining light upon the golden throne.

Sentence

Charley Dalton, spaceman once of Earth, had within an hour of his landing on the second planet of the star Antares committed a most serious offense. He had killed an Antarian. On most planets murder is a misdemeanor; on some it is a praiseworthy act. But on Antares II it is a capital crime.

"I sentence you to death," said the solemn Antarian judge. "Death by blaster fire at dawn tomorrow." No appeal from the sentence was allowed.

Charley was led to the Suite of the Condemned.

The suite turned out to have eighteen palatial rooms, each stocked and well stocked with a wide variety of food and drink, couches and everything else he could possibly wish for, including a beautiful woman on each of the couches.

"I'll be damned," said Charley.

The Antarian guard bowed low. He said, "It is the custom of our planet. On the last night of a man condemned to die at dawn these arrangements are made. He is given everything he can possibly wish for."

"Almost worth it," Charley said. "Say, I'd just landed when I got into that scrap and I didn't check my planet guide. How long is a night here? How many hours does it take this planet to revolve?"

"Hours?" said the guard. "That must be an Earth term. I will phone the Astronomer Royal for a time comparison between your planet and ours."

He phoned, asked the question, listened. He told Charley Dalton, "Your planet Earth makes ninety-three revolutions around your sun Sol during one period of darkness on Antares II. One of our nights is equal to ninety-three of your years."

Charley whistled softly to himself and wondered if he'd make it. The Antarian guard, whose life span was a bit over twenty thousand years, bowed with grave sympathy and withdrew.

Charley Dalton started the long night's grind of eating, drinking, et cetera, although not in precisely that order; the women were very beautiful and he'd been in space a long time.

Solipsist

Walter B. Jehovah, for whose name I make no apology since it really *was* his name, had been a solipsist all his life. A solipsist, in case you don't happen to know the word, is one who believes that he himself is the only thing that really exists, that other people and the universe in general exist only in his imagination, and that if he quit imagining them they would cease to exist.

One day Walter B. Jehovah became a practicing solipsist. Within a week his wife had run away with another man, he'd lost his job as a shipping clerk and he had broken his leg chasing a black cat to keep it from crossing his path.

He decided, in his bed at the hospital, to end it all.

Looking out the window, staring up at the stars, he wished them out of existence, and they weren't there any more. Then he wished all other people out of existence and the hospital became strangely quiet even for a hospital. Next, the world, and he found himself suspended in a void. He got rid of his body quite as easily and then took the final step of willing *himself* out of existence.

Nothing happened.

Strange, he thought, can there be a limit to solipsism?

"Yes," a voice said.

"Who are you?" Walter B. Jehovah asked.

"I am the one who created the universe which you have just willed out of existence. And now that you have taken my place—" There was a deep sigh. "—I can finally cease my own existence; find oblivion, and let you take over."

"But—how can *I* cease to exist? That's what I'm trying to do, you know."

"Yes, I know," said the voice. "You must do it the same way *I* did. Create a universe. Wait until someone in it really believes what you believed and wills it out of existence. Then you can retire and let him take over. Good-by now."

And the voice was gone.

Walter B. Jehovah was alone in the void and there was only one thing he could do. He created the heaven and the earth.

It took him seven days.

Blood

In their time machine, Vron and Dreena, last two survivors of the race of vampires, fled into the future to escape annihilation. They held hands and consoled one another in their terror and their hunger.

In the twenty-second century mankind had found them out, had discovered that the legend of vampires living secretly among humans was not a legend at all, but fact. There had been a pogrom that had found and killed every vampire but these two, who had already been working on a time machine and who had finished in time to escape in it. Into the future, far enough into the future that the very word *vampire* would be forgotten so they could again live unsuspected—and from their loins regenerate their race.

"I'm hungry, Vron. Awfully hungry."

"I too, Dreena dear. We'll stop again soon."

They had stopped four times already and had narrowly escaped dying each time. They had *not* been forgotten. The last stop, half a million years back, had shown them a world gone to the dogs—quite literally: human beings were extinct and dogs had become civilized and man-like. Still they had been recognized for what they were. They'd managed to feed once, on the blood of a tender young bitch, but then they'd been hounded back to their time machine and into flight again.

"Thanks for stopping," Dreena said. She sighed.

"Don't thank me," said Vron grimly. "This is the end of the line. We're out of fuel and we'll find none here—by now all radioactives will have turned to lead. We live here ... or else."

They went out to scout. "Look," said Dreena excitedly, pointing to something walking toward them. "A new creature! The dogs are gone and something else has taken over. And surely we're forgotten."

The approaching creature was telepathic. "I have heard your thoughts," said a voice inside their brains. "You wonder whether we know 'vampires,' whatever they are. We do not."

Dreena clutched Vron's arm in ecstasy. "Freedom!" she murmured hungrily. "And *food!*"

"You also wonder," said the voice, "about my origin and evolution. All life today is vegetable. I—" He bowed low to them. "I, a member of the dominant race, was once what you called a turnip."

Imagine

Imagine ghosts, gods and devils.

Imagine hells and heavens, cities floating in the sky and cities sunken in the sea.

Unicorns and centaurs. Witches, warlocks, jinns and banshees.

Angels and harpies. Charms and incantations. Elementals, familiars, demons.

Easy to imagine, all of those things: mankind has been imagining them for thousands of years.

Imagine spaceships and the future.

Easy to imagine; the future is really coming and there'll be spaceships in it.

Is there then anything that's *hard* to imagine?

Of course there is.

Imagine a piece of matter and yourself inside it, yourself aware, thinking and therefore knowing you exist, able to move that piece of matter that you're in, to make it sleep or wake, make love or walk uphill.

Imagine a universe—infinite or not, as you wish to picture it—with a billion, billion, billion suns in it.

Imagine a blob of mud whirling madly around one of those suns.

Imagine yourself standing on that blob of mud, whirling with it, whirling through time and space to an unknown destination.

Imagine!

First Time Machine

Dr. Grainger said solemnly, "Gentlemen, the first time machine."

His three friends stared at it.

It was a box about six inches square, with dials and a switch.

"You need only to hold it in your hand," said Dr. Grainger, "set the dials for the date you want, press the button—and you are there."

Smedley, one of the doctor's three friends, reached for the box, held it and studied it. "Does it really work?"

"I tested it briefly," said the doctor. "I set it one day back and pushed the button. Saw myself—my own back—just walking out of the room. Gave me a bit of a turn."

"What would have happened if you'd rushed to the door and kicked yourself in the seat of the pants?"

Dr. Grainger laughed. "Maybe I couldn't have—because it would have changed the past. That's the old paradox of time travel, you know. What would happen if one went back in time and killed one's own grandfather before he met one's grandmother?"

Smedley, the box still in his hand, suddenly was backing away from the three other men. He grinned at them. "That," he said, "is just what I'm going to do. I've been setting the date dials sixty years back while you've been talking."

"Smedley! Don't!" Dr. Grainger started forward.

"Stop, Doc. Or I'll press the button now. Otherwise I'll explain to you." Grainger stopped. "I've heard of that paradox too. And it's always interested me because I knew I *would* kill my grandfather if I ever had a chance to. I hated him. He was a cruel bully, made life a hell for my grandmother and my parents. So this is a chance I've been waiting for."

Smedley's hand reached for the button and pressed it.

There was a sudden blur ... Smedley was standing in a field. It took him only a moment to orient himself. If this spot was where Dr. Grainger's house would some day be built, then his great-grandfather's farm would be only a mile south. He started walking. En route he found a piece of wood that made a fine club.

Near the farm, he saw a red-headed young man beating a dog with a whip.

"Stop that!" Smedley yelled, rushing up.

"Mind your own damn business," said the young man as he lashed with the whip again.

Smedley swung the club.

Sixty years later, Dr. Grainger said solemnly, "Gentlemen, the first time machine."

His two friends stared at it.

Too Far

R. Austin Wilkinson was a bon vivant, man about Manhattan, and chaser of women. He was also an incorrigible punster on every possible occasion. In speaking of his favorite activity, for example, he would remark that he was a wolf, as it were, but that didn't make him a werewolf.

Excruciating as this statement may have been to some of his friends, it was almost true. Wilkinson was not a werewolf; he was a werebuck.

A night or two nights every week he would stroll into Central Park, turn himself into a buck and take great delight in running and playing.

True, there was always danger of his being seen but (since he punned even in his thoughts) he was willing to gambol on that.

Oddly, it had never occurred to him to combine the pleasures of being a wolf, as it were, with the pleasures of being a buck.

Until one night. Why, he asked himself that night, couldn't a lucky buck make a little doe? Once thought of, the idea was irresistible. He galloped to the wall of the Central Park Zoo and trotted along it until his sensitive buck nose told him he'd found the right place to climb the fence. He changed into a man for the task of climbing and then, alone in a pen with a beautiful doe, he changed himself back into a buck.

She was sleeping. He nudged her gently and whispered a suggestion. Her eyes opened wide and startled. "No, no, a dozen times no!"

"Only a dozen times?" he asked, and then leered. *"My deer,"* he whispered, *"think of the fawn you'll have!"*

Which went too far. He might have got away with it had his deer really been only a doe, but she was a weremaid—a doe who could change into a girl— and she was a witch as well. She quickly changed into a girl and ran for the fence. When he changed into a man and started after her she threw a spell over her shoulder, a spell that turned him back to a buck and froze him that way.

Do you ever visit the Central Park Zoo? Look for the buck with the sad eyes; he's Wilkinson.

He is sad despite the fact that the doe-weremaid, who is now the toast of New York ballet (she is graceful as a deer, the critics say) visits him occasionally by night and resumes her proper form.

But when he begs for release from the spell she only smiles sweetly and tells him no, that she is of a very saving disposition and wants to keep the first buck she ever made.

Millennium

Hades was hell, Satan thought; that was why he loved the place. He leaned forward across his gleaming desk and flicked the switch of the intercom.

"Yes, Sire," said the voice of Lilith, his secretary.

"How many today?"

"Four of them. Shall I send one of them in?"

"Yes—wait. Any of them look as though he might be an unselfish one?"

"One of them does, I think. But so what, Sire? There's one chance in billions of his making The Ultimate Wish."

Even at the *sound* of those last words Satan shivered despite the heat. It was his most constant, almost his only worry that someday someone might make The Ultimate Wish, the ultimate, *unselfish* wish. And then it would happen; Satan would find himself chained for a thousand years, and out of business for the rest of eternity after that.

But Lilith was right, he told himself.

Only about one person out of a thousand sold his soul for the granting of even a minor unselfish wish, and it might be millions of years yet, or forever, before the ultimate one was made. Thus far, no one had even come close to it.

"Okay, Lil," he said. "Just the same, send him in first; I'd rather get it over with." He flicked off the intercom.

The little man who came through the big doorway certainly didn't look dangerous; he looked plain scared.

Satan frowned at him. "You know the terms?"

"Yes," said the little man. "At least, I think I do. In exchange for your granting any one wish I make, you get my soul when I die. Is that right?"

"Right. Your wish?"

"Well," said the little man, "I've thought it out pretty carefully and—"

"Get to the point. I'm busy. Your wish?"

"Well ... I wish that, without any change whatsoever in myself, I become the most evil, stupid and miserable person on earth."

Satan screamed.

Expedition

"The first major expedition to Mars," said the history professor, "the one which followed the preliminary exploration by one-man scout ships and aimed to establish a permanent colony, led to a great number of problems. One of the most perplexing of which was: How many men and how many women should comprise the expedition's personnel of thirty?

"There were three schools of thought on the subject.

"One was that the ship should be comprised of fifteen men and fifteen women, many of whom would no doubt find one another suitable mates and get the colony off to a fast start.

"The second was that the ship should take twenty-five men and five women—ones who were willing to sign a waiver on monogamous inclinations—on the grounds that five women could easily keep twenty-five men sexually happy and twenty-five men could keep five women even happier.

"The third school of thought was that the expedition should contain thirty men, on the grounds that under those circumstances the men would be able to concentrate on the work at hand much better. And it was argued that since a second ship would follow in approximately a year and could contain mostly women, it would be no hardship for the men to endure celibacy that long. Especially since they were used to it; the two Space Cadet schools, one for men and one for women, rigidly segregated the sexes.

"The Director of Space Travel settled this argument by a simple expedient. He— Yes, Miss Ambrose?" A girl in the class had raised her hand.

"Professor, was that expedition the one headed by Captain Maxon? The one they called Mighty Maxon? Could you tell us how he came to have that nickname?"

"I'm coming to that, Miss Ambrose. In lower schools you have been told the story of the expedition, but not the *entire* story; you are now old enough to hear it.

"The Director of Space Travel settled the argument, cut the Gordian knot, by announcing that the personnel of the expedition would be chosen by lot, regardless of sex, from the graduating classes of the two space academies. There is little doubt that he personally favored twenty-five men to five women—because the men's school had approximately five hundred in the graduating class and the women's school had approximately one hundred. By the law of averages the ratio of winners should have been five men to one woman.

"However the law of averages does not always work out on any one particular series. And it so happened that on this particular drawing *twenty-nine* women drew winning chances, and only *one* man won.

"There were loud protests from almost everyone except the winners, but the director stuck to his guns; the drawing had been honest and he refused to change the status of any of the winners. His only concession to appease male egos was to appoint Maxon, the one man, captain. The ship took off and had a successful voyage.

"And when the second expedition landed, they found the population doubled. Exactly doubled—every woman member of the expedition had a child, and one of them had twins, making a total of exactly thirty infants.

"Yes, Miss Ambrose, I see your hand, but please let me finish. No, there is nothing spectacular about what I have thus far told you. Although many people would think loose morals were involved, it is no great feat for one man, given time, to impregnate twenty-nine women.

"What gave Captain Maxon his nickname is the fact that work on the second ship went much faster than scheduled and the second expedition did not arrive one year later, but only nine months and two days later.

"Does that answer your question, Miss Ambrose?"

Happy Ending

There were four men in the life boat that came down from the space cruiser. Three of them were still in the uniform of the Galactic Guards.

The fourth sat in the prow of the small craft looking down at their goal, hunched and silent, bundled up in a greatcoat against the coolness of space— a greatcoat which he would never need again after this morning. The brim of his hat was pulled down far over his forehead, and he studied the nearing shore through dark lensed glasses. Bandages, as though for a broken jaw, covered most of the lower part of his face.

He realized suddenly that the dark glasses, now that they had left the cruiser, were unnecessary. He slipped them off. After the cinematographic gray his eyes had seen through these lenses for so long, the brilliance of the color below him was almost like a blow. He blinked, and looked again.

They were rapidly settling toward a shoreline, a beach. The sand was a dazzling, unbelievable white such as had never been on his home planet. Blue the sky and water, and green the edge of the fantastic jungle. There was a flash of red in the green, as they came still closer, and he realized suddenly that it must be a *marigee*, the semi-intelligent Venusian parrot once so popular as pets throughout the solar system.

Throughout the system blood and steel had fallen from the sky and ravished the planets, but now it fell no more.

And now this. Here in this forgotten portion of an almost completely destroyed world it had not fallen at all.

Only in some place like this, alone, was safety for him. Elsewhere—any-where—imprisonment or, more likely, death. There was danger, even here. Three of the crew of the space cruiser knew. Perhaps, someday, one of them would talk. Then they would come for him, even here.

But that was a chance he could not avoid. Nor were the odds bad, for three people out of a whole solar system knew where he was. And those three were loyal fools.

The life boat came gently to rest. The hatch swung open and he stepped out and walked a few paces up the beach. He turned and waited while the two spacemen who had guided the craft brought his chest out and carried it across the beach and to the corrugated tin shack just at the edge of the trees. That shack had once been a space-radar relay station. Now the equipment it had held was long gone, the antenna mast taken down. But the shack still stood. It would be his home for a while. A long while. The two men returned to the lifeboat preparatory to leaving.

And now the captain stood facing him, and the captain's face was a rigid mask. It seemed with an effort that the captain's right arm remained at his side, but that effort had been ordered. No salute.

The captain's voice, too, was rigid with unemotion. "Number One ..."

"Silence!" And then, less bitterly. "Come further from the boat before you again let your tongue run loose. Here." They had reached the shack.

"You are right, Number ..."

"No. I am no longer Number One. You must continue to think of me as *Mister* Smith, your cousin, whom you brought here for the reasons you explained to the under-officers, before you surrender your ship. If you *think* of me so, you will be less likely to slip in your speech."

"There is nothing further I can do—Mister Smith?"

"Nothing. Go now."

"And I am ordered to surrender the—"

"There are no orders. The war is over, lost. I would suggest thought as to what spaceport you put into. In some you may receive humane treatment. In others—"

The captain nodded. "In others, there is great hatred. Yes. That is all?"

"That is all. And Captain, your running of the blockade, your securing of fuel enroute, have constituted a deed of high valor. All I can give you in reward is my thanks. But now go. Goodbye."

"Not goodbye," the captain blurted impulsively, "but *hasta la vista, auf Wiedersehen, until the day* ... you will permit me, for the last time to address you and salute?"

The man in the greatcoat shrugged. "As you will."

Click of heels and a salute that once greeted the Caesars, and later the pseudo-aryan of the 20th Century, and, but yesterday, he who was now known as *the last of the dictators*. "Farewell, Number One!"

"Farewell," he answered emotionlessly.

Mr. Smith, a blacked dot on the dazzling white sand, watched the lifeboat disappear up into the blue, finally into the haze of the upper atmosphere of Venus. That eternal haze that would always be there to mock his failure and his bitter solitude.

The slow days snarled by, and the sun shone dimly, and the *marigees* screamed in the early dawn and all day and at sunset, and sometimes there were the six legged *baroons*, monkey-like in the trees, that gibbered at him. And the rains came and went away again.

At nights there were drums in the distance. Not the martial roll of marching, nor yet a threatening note of savage hate. Just drums, many miles away, throbbing rhythm for native dances or exorcising, perhaps, the forest-night demons. He assumed these Venusians had their superstitions, all other races had. There was no threat, for him, in that throbbing that was like the beating of the jungle's heart.

Mr. Smith knew that, for although his choice of destinations had been a hasty choice, yet there had been time for him to read the available reports. The natives were harmless and friendly. A Terran missionary had lived among them some time ago—before the outbreak of the war. They were a simple, weak race. They seldom went far from their villages; the space-radar operator who had once occupied the shack reported that he had never seen one of them.

So there would be no difficulty in avoiding the natives, nor danger if he did encounter them.

Nothing to worry about, except the bitterness.

Not the bitterness of regret, but of defeat. Defeat at the hands of the defeated. The damned Martians who came back after he had driven them halfway across their damned arid planet. The Jupiter Satellite Confederation landing endlessly on the home planet, sending their vast armadas of spacecraft daily and nightly to turn his mighty cities into dust. In spite of everything; in spite of his score of ultra vicious secret weapons and the last desperate efforts of his weakened armies, most of whose men were under twenty or over forty.

The treachery even in his own army, among his own generals and admirals. The turn of Luna, that had been the end.

His people would rise again. But not, now after Armageddon, in his lifetime. Not under him, nor another like him. The last of the dictators.

Hated by a solar system, and hating it.

It would have been intolerable, save that he was alone. He had foreseen that—the need for solitude. Alone, he was still Number One. The presence of others would have forced recognition of his miserably changed status. Alone, his pride was undamaged. His ego was intact.

The long days, and the *marigees'* screams, the slithering swish of the surf, the ghost-quiet movements of the *baroons* in the trees and the raucousness of their shrill voices. Drums.

Those sounds, and those alone. But perhaps silence would have been worse.

For the times of silence were louder. Times, he would pace the beach at night and overhead would be the roar of jets and rockets, the ships that had roared over New Albuquerque, his capital, in those last days before he had fled. The crump of bombs and the screams and the blood, and the flat voices of his folding generals.

Those were the days when the waves of hatred from the conquered peoples beat upon his country as the waves of a stormy sea beat upon crumbling cliffs. Leagues back of the battered lines, you could *feel* that hate and vengeance as a tangible thing, a thing that thickened the air, that made breathing difficult and talking futile.

And the spacecraft, the jets, the rockets, the damnable rockets, more every day and every night, and ten coming for every one shot down. Rocket ships raining hell from the sky, havoc and chaos and the end of hope.

And then he knew that he had been hearing another sound, hearing it often and long at a time. It was a voice that shouted invective and ranted hatred and glorified the steel might of his planet and the destiny of a man and a people.

It was his own voice, and it beat back the waves from the white shore, it stopped their wet encroachment upon this his domain, It screamed back at the *baroons* and they were silent. And at times he laughed, and the *marigees* laughed, Sometimes, the queerly shaped Venusian trees talked too, but their voices were quieter. The trees were submissive, they were good subjects.

Sometimes, fantastic thoughts went through his head. The race of trees, the pure race of trees that never interbred, that stood firm always. Someday the trees—

But that was just a dream, a fancy. More real were the *marigees* and the *kifs*. They were the ones who persecuted him. There was the *marigee* who would shriek *"All is lost!"* He had shot at it a hundred times with his needle gun, but always it flew away unharmed. Sometimes it did not even fly away.

"All is lost!"

At last he wasted no more needle darts. He stalked it to strangle it with his bare hands. That was better. On what might have been the thousandth try, he caught it and killed it, and there was warm blood on his hands and feathers were flying.

That should have ended it, but it didn't. Now there were a dozen *marigees* that screamed that all was lost. Perhaps there had been a dozen all along. Now he merely shook his fist at them or threw stones.

The *kifs*, the Venusian equivalent of the Terran ant, stole his food. But that did not matter; there was plenty of food. There had been a cache of it in the shack, meant to restock a space-cruiser, and never used. The *kifs* would not get at it until he opened a can, but then, unless he ate it all at once, they ate whatever he left. That did not matter. There were plenty of cans. And always fresh fruit from the jungle. Always in season, for there were no seasons here, except the rains.

But the *kifs* served a purpose for him. They kept him sane, by giving him something tangible, something inferior, to hate.

Oh, it wasn't hatred, at first. Mere annoyance. He killed them in a routine sort of way at first. But they kept coming back. Always there were *kifs*. In his larder, wherever he did it. In his bed. He sat the legs of the cot in dishes of gasoline, but the *kifs* still got in. Perhaps they dropped from the ceiling, although he never caught them doing it.

They bothered his sleep. He'd feel them running over him, even when he'd spent an hour picking the bed clean of them by the light of the carbide lantern. They scurried with tickling little feet and he could not sleep.

He grew to hate them, and the very misery of his nights made his days more tolerable by giving them an increasing purpose. A pogrom against the *kifs*. He sought out their holes by patiently following one bearing a bit of food, and he poured gasoline into the hole and the earth around it, taking satisfaction in the thought of the writhings in agony below. He went about hunting *kifs*, to step on them. To stamp them out. He must have killed millions of *kifs*.

But always there were as many left. Never did their number seem to diminish in the slightest. Like the Martians—but unlike the Martians, they did not fight back.

Theirs was the passive resistance of a vast productivity that bred *kifs* cease-lessly, overwhelmingly, billions to replace millions. Individual *kifs* could be killed, and he took savage satisfaction in their killing, but he knew his methods were useless save for the pleasure and the purpose they gave him. Sometimes the pleasure would pall in the shadow of its futility, and he would dream of mechanized means of killing them.

He read carefully what little material there was in his tiny library about the *kif*. They were astonishingly like the ants of Terra. So much that there had been speculation about their relationship—that didn't interest him. How could they be killed, *en masse?* Once a year, for a brief period, they took on the char-acteristics of the army ants of Terra. They came from their holes in endless numbers and swept everything before them in their devouring march. He wet his lips when he read that. Perhaps the opportunity would come then to destroy, to destroy, *and destroy.*

Almost, Mr. Smith forgot people and the solar system and what had been. Here in this new world, there was only he and the *kifs*. The *baroons* and the *marigees* didn't count. They had no order and no system. The *kifs*—

In the intensity of his hatred there slowly filtered through a grudging admiration. The *kifs* were true totalitarians. They practiced what he had preached to a mightier race, practiced it with a thoroughness beyond the mind of man to comprehend.

Theirs the complete submergence of the individual to the state, theirs the complete ruthlessness of the true conqueror, the perfect selfless bravery of the true soldier.

But they got into his bed, into his clothes, into his food.

They crawled with intolerable tickling feet.

Nights he walked the beach, and that night was one of the noisy nights. There were high-flying, high-whining jet-craft up there in the moonlight sky and their shadows dappled the black water of the sea. The planes, the rockets, the jet-craft, they were what had ravaged his cities, had turned his railroads into twisted steel, had dropped their H-Bombs on his most vital factories.

He shook his fist at them and shrieked imprecations at the sky.

And when he had ceased shouting, there were voices on the beach. Conrad's voice in his ear, as it had sounded that day when Conrad had walked into the palace, whitefaced, and forgotten the salute. "There is a breakthrough at Den-ver, Number One! Toronto and Monterey are in danger. And in the other hemi-spheres—" His voice cracked. "—the damned Martians and the traitors from Luna are driving over the Argentine. Others have landed near New Petrograd. It is a rout. All is lost!"

Voices crying, "Number One, *hail!* Number One, *hail!*"

A sea of hysterical voices. "Number One, *hail!* Number One—"

A voice that was louder, higher, more frenetic than any of the others. His memory of his own voice, calculated but inspired, as he'd heard it on play-backs of his own speeches.

The voices of children chanting, "To thee, O Number One—" He couldn't remember the rest of the words, but they had been beautiful words. That had been at the public school meet in the New Los Angeles. How strange that he should remember, here and now, the very tone of his voice and inflection, the shining wonder in their children's eyes. Children only, but they were willing to kill and die, *for him,* convinced that all that was needed to cure the ills of the race was a suitable leader to follow.

"All is lost!"

And suddenly the monster jet-craft were swooping downward and starkly he realized what a clear target he presented, here against the white moonlit beach. They must see him.

The crescendo of motors as he ran, sobbing now in fear, for the cover of the jungle. Into the screening shadow of the giant trees, and the sheltering blackness.

He stumbled and fell, was up and running again. And now his eyes could see in the dimmer moonlight that filtered through the branches overhead. Stirrings there, in the branches. Stirrings and voices in the night. Voices in and of the night. Whispers and shrieks of pain. Yes, he'd shown them pain, and now their tortured voices ran with him through the knee-deep night-wet grass among the trees.

The night was hideous with noise. Red noises, an almost *tangible* din that he could nearly *feel* as well as he could see and hear it. And after a while his breath came raspingly, and there was a thumping sound that was the beating of his heart and the beating of the night.

And then, he could run no longer, and he clutched a tree to keep from falling, his arms trembling about it, and his face pressed against the impersonal roughness of the bark. There was no wind, but the tree swayed back and forth and his body with it.

Then, as abruptly as light goes on when a switch is thrown, the noise vanished. Utter silence, and at last he was strong enough to let go his grip on the tree and stand erect again, to look about to get his bearings.

One tree was like another, and for a moment he thought he'd have to stay here until daylight. Then he remembered that the sound of the surf would give him his directions. He listened hard and heard it, faint and far away.

And another sound—one that he had never heard before—faint, also, but seeming to come from his right and quite near.

He looked that way, and there was a patch of opening in the trees above. The grass was waving strangely in that area of moonlight. It moved, although there was no breeze to move it. And there was an almost sudden *edge,* beyond which the blades thinned out quickly to barrenness.

And the sound—it was like the sound of the surf, but it was continuous. It was more like the rustle of dry leaves, but there were no dry leaves to rustle.

Mr. Smith took a step toward the sound and looked down. More grass bent, and fell, and vanished, even as he looked. Beyond the moving edge of devastation was a brown floor of the moving bodies of *kifs.*

Row after row, orderly rank after orderly rank, marching resistlessly onward. Billions of *kifs*, an army of *kifs*, eating their way across the night.

Fascinated, he stared down at them. There was no danger, for their progress was slow. He retreated a step to keep beyond their front rank. The sound, then, was the sound of chewing.

He could see one edge of the column, and it was a neat, orderly edge. And there was discipline, for the ones on the outside were larger than those in the center.

He retreated another step—and then, quite suddenly, his body was afire in several spreading places. The vanguard. Ahead of the rank that ate away the grass.

His boots were brown with *kifs*.

Screaming with pain, he whirled about and ran, beating with his hands at the burning spots on his body. He ran head-on into a tree, bruising his face horribly, and the night was scarlet with pain and shooting fire.

But he staggered on, almost blindly, running, writhing, tearing off his clothes as he ran.

This then, was *pain*. There was a shrill screaming in his ears that must have been the sound of his own voice.

When he could no longer run, he crawled. Naked, now, and with only a few *kifs* still clinging to him. And the blind tangent of his flight had taken him well out of the path of the advancing army.

But stark fear and the memory of unendurable pain drove him on. His knees raw now, he could no longer crawl. But he got himself erect again on trembling legs, and staggered on. Catching hold of a tree and pushing himself away from it to catch the next.

Falling, rising, falling again. His throat raw from the screaming invective of his hate. Bushes and the rough bark of trees tore his flesh.

Into the village compound just before dawn, staggered a man, a naked terrestrial. He looked about with dull eyes that seemed to see nothing and understand nothing.

The females and young ran before him, even the males retreated.

He stood there, swaying, and the incredulous eyes of the natives widened as they saw the condition of his body, and the blankness of his eyes.

When he made no hostile move, they came closer again, formed a wondering, chattering circle about him, these Venusian humanoids. Some ran to bring the chief and the chief's son, who knew everything.

The mad, naked human opened his lips as though he were going to speak, but instead, he fell. He fell, as a dead man falls. But when they turned him over in the dust, they saw that his chest still rose and fell in labored breathing.

And then came Alwa, the aged chieftain, and Nrana, his son. Alwa gave quick, excited orders. Two of the men carried Mr. Smith into the chief's hut, and the wives of the chief and the chief's son took over the Earthling's care, and rubbed him with a soothing and healing salve.

But for days and nights he lay without moving and without speaking or opening his eyes, and they did not know whether he would live or die.

Then, at last, he opened his eyes. And he talked, although they could make out nothing of the things he said.

Nrana came and listened, for Nrana of all of them spoke and understood best the Earthling's language, for he had been the special protege of the Terran missionary who had lived with them for a while.

Nrana listened, but he shook his head. "The words," he said, "the words are of the Terran tongue, but I make nothing of them. His mind is not well."

The aged Alwa said, "Aie. Stay beside him. Perhaps as his body heals, his words will be beautiful words as were the words of the Father-of-Us who, in the Terran tongue, taught us of the gods and their good."

So they cared for him well, and his wounds healed, and the day came when he opened his eyes and saw the handsome blue-complexioned face of Nrana sitting there beside him, and Nrana said softly, "Good day, Mr. Man of Earth. You feel better, no?"

There was no answer, and the deep-sunken eyes of the man on the sleeping mat stared, glared at him. Nrana could see that those eyes were not yet sane, but he saw, too, that the madness in them was not the same that it had been. Nrana did not know the words for delirium and paranoia, but he could distinguish between them.

No longer was the Earthling a raving maniac, and Nrana made a very common error, an error more civilized beings than he have often made. He thought the paranoia was an improvement over the wider madness. He talked on, hoping the Earthling would talk too, and he did not recognize the danger of his silence.

"We welcome you, Earthling," he said, "and hope that you will live among us, as did the Father-of-Us, Mr. Gerhardt. He taught us to worship the true gods of the high heavens. Jehovah, and Jesus and their prophets the men from the skies. He taught us to pray and to love our enemies."

And Nrana shook his head sadly, "But many of our tribe have gone back to the older gods, the cruel gods. They say there has been great strife among the outsiders, and no more remain upon all of Venus. My father, Alwa, and I are glad another one has come. You will be able to help those of us who have gone back. You can teach us love and kindliness."

The eyes of the dictator closed. Nrana did not know whether or not he slept, but Nrana stood up quietly to leave the hut. In the doorway, he turned and said, "We pray for you."

And then, joyously, he ran out of the village to seek the others, who were gathering bela-berries for the feast of the fourth event.

When, with several of them, he returned to the village, the Earthling was gone. The hut was empty.

Outside the compound they found, at last, the trail of his passing. They followed and it led to a stream and along the stream until they came to the tabu of the green pool, and could go no farther.

"He went downstream," said Alwa gravely. "He sought the sea and the beach. He was well then, in his mind, for he knew that all streams go to the sea."

"Perhaps he had a ship-of-the-sky there at the beach," Nrana said worriedly. "All Earthlings come from the sky. The Father-of-Us told us that."

"Perhaps he will come back to us," said Alwa. His old eyes misted.

Mr. Smith was coming back all right, and sooner than they had dared to hope. As soon in fact, as he could make the trip to the shack and return. He came back dressed in clothing very different from the garb the other white man had worn. Shining leather boots and the uniform of the Galactic Guard, and a wide leather belt with a holster for his needle gun.

But the gun was in his hand when, at dusk, he strode into the compound.

He said, "I am Number One, the Lord of all the Solar System, and your ruler. Who was chief among you?"

Alwa had been in his hut, but he heard the words and came out. He understood the words, but not their meaning. He said, "Earthling, we welcome you back. I am the chief."

"You were the chief. Now you will serve me. I am the chief."

Alwa's old eyes were bewildered at the strangeness of this. He said, "I will serve you, yes. All of us. But it is not fitting that an Earthling should be chief among—"

The whisper of the needle gun. Alwa's wrinkled hands went to his scrawny neck where, just off the center, was a sudden tiny pin prick of a hole. A faint trickle of red coursed over the dark blue of his skin. The old man's knees gave way under him as the rage of the poisoned needle dart struck him, and he fell. Others started toward him.

"Back," said Mr. Smith. "Let him die slowly that you may all see what happens to—"

But one of the chief's wives, one who did not understand the speech of Earth, was already lifting Alwa's head. The needle gun whispered again, and she fell forward across him.

"I am Number One," said Mr. Smith, "and Lord of all the planets. All who oppose me, die by—"

And then, suddenly all of them were running toward him. His finger pressed the trigger and four of them died before the avalanche of their bodies bore him down and overwhelmed him. Nrana had been first in that rush, and Nrana died.

The others tied the Earthling up and threw him into one of the huts. And then, while the women began wailing for the dead, the men made council.

They elected Kallana chief and he stood before them and said, "The Father-of-Us, the Mister Gerhardt, deceived us." There was fear and worry in his voice and apprehension on his blue face. "If this be indeed the Lord of whom he told us—"

"He is not a god," said another. "He is an Earthling, but there have been such before on Venus, many many of them who came long and long ago from the skies. Now they are all dead, killed in strife among themselves. It is well. This last one is one of them, but he is mad."

And they talked long and the dusk grew into night while they talked of what they must do. The gleam of firelight upon their bodies, and the waiting drummer.

The problem was difficult. To harm one who was mad was tabu. If he was really a god, it would be worse. Thunder and lightning from the sky would destroy the village. Yet they dared not release him. Even if they took the evil weapon-that-whispered-its-death and buried it, he might find other ways to harm them. He might have another where he had gone for the first.

Yes, it was a difficult problem for them, but the eldest and wisest of them, one M'Ganne, gave them at last the answer.

"O Kallana," he said. "Let us give him to the *kifs*. If *they* harm him—" and old M'Ganne grinned a toothless, mirthless grin "—it would be their doing and not ours."

Kallana shuddered. "It is the most horrible of all deaths. And if he is a god—"

"If he is a god, they will not harm him. If he is mad and not a god, we will not have harmed him. It harms not a man to tie him to a tree."

Kallana considered well, for the safety of his people was at stake. Considering, he remembered how Alwa and Nrana had died.

He said, "It is right."

The waiting drummer began the rhythm of the council-end, and those of the men who were young and fleet lighted torches in the fire and went out into the forest to seek the *kifs*, who were still in their season of marching.

And after a while, having found what they sought, they returned.

They took the Earthling out with them, then, and tied him to a tree. They left him there, and they left the gag over his lips because they did not wish to hear his screams when the *kifs* came.

The cloth of the gag would be eaten, too, but by that time, there would be no flesh under it from which a scream might come.

They left him, and went back to the compound, and the drums took up the rhythm of propitiation to the gods for what they had done. For they had, they knew, cut very close to the corner of a tabu—but the provocation had been great and they hoped they would not be punished.

All night the drums would throb.

The man tied to the tree struggled with his bonds, but they were strong and his writhings made the knots but tighten.

His eyes became accustomed to the darkness.

He tried to shout, "I am Number One, Lord of—"

And then, because he could not shout and because he could not loosen himself, there came a rift in his madness. He remembered who he was, and all the old hatreds and bitterness welled up in him.

He remembered, too, what had happened in the compound, and wondered why the Venusian natives had not killed him. Why, instead, they had tied him here alone in the darkness of the jungle.

Afar, he heard the throbbing of the drums, and they were like the beating of the heart of night, and there was a louder, nearer sound that was the pulse of blood in his ears as the fear came to him.

The fear that he knew why they had tied him here. The horrible, gibbering fear that, for the last time, an army marched against him.

He had time to savor that fear to the uttermost, to have it become a creeping certainty that crawled into the black corners of his soul as would the soldiers of the coming army crawl into his ears and nostrils while others would eat away his eyelids to get at the eyes behind them.

And then, and only then, did he hear the sound that was like the rustle of dry leaves, in a dank, black jungle where there were no dry leaves to rustle nor breeze to rustle them.

Horribly, Number One, the last of the dictators, did not go mad again; not exactly, but he laughed, and laughed and laughed …

Jaycee

"Walter, what's a Jaycee?" Mrs. Ralston asked her husband, Dr. Ralston, across the breakfast table.

"Why—I believe it used to be a member of what they called a Junior Chamber of Commerce. I don't know if they still have them or not. Why?"

"Martha said Henry was muttering something yesterday about Jaycees, fifty million Jaycees. And swore at her when she asked what he meant." Martha was Mrs. Graham and Henry her husband, Dr. Graham. They lived next door and the two doctors and their wives were close friends.

"Fifty million," said Dr. Ralston musingly. "That's how many parthies there are."

He should have known; he and Dr. Graham together were responsible for parthies—parthenogenetic births. Twenty years ago, in 1980, they had together engineered the first experiment in human parthenogenesis, the fertilization of a female cell without the help of a male one. The offspring of that experiment, named John, was now twenty years old and lived with Dr. and Mrs. Graham next door; he had been adopted by them after the death of his mother in an accident some years before.

No other parthie was more than half John's age.

Not until John was ten, and obviously healthy and normal, had the authorities let down bars and permitted any woman who wanted a child and who was either single or married to a sterile husband to have a child parthenogenetically. Due to the shortage of men—the disastrous testerosis epidemic of the 1970s had just killed off almost a third of the male population of the world—over fifty million women had applied for parthenogenetic children and borne them. Luckily for redressing the balance of the sexes, it had turned out that all parthenogenetically conceived children were males.

"Martha thinks," said Mrs. Ralston, "that Henry's worrying about John, but she can't think why. He's such a *good* boy."

Dr. Graham suddenly and without knocking burst into the room. His face was white and his eyes wide as he stared at his colleague. "I was right," he said.

"Right about what?"

"About John. I didn't tell anyone, but do you know what he did when we ran out of drinks at the party last night?"

Dr. Ralston frowned. "Changed water into wine?"

"Into gin; we were having martinis. And just now he left to go water skiing—and he isn't taking any water skis. Told me that with faith he wouldn't need them."

"Oh, *no,*" said Dr. Ralston. He dropped his head into his hands.

Once before in history there'd been a virgin birth. Now fifty million virgin-born boys were growing up. In ten more years there'd be fifty million—Jaycees.

"No," sobbed Dr. Ralston, "*no!*"

Unfortunately

Ralph NC-5 sighed with relief as he caught sight of Planet Four of Arcturus in the spotter scope, just where his computer had told him it would be. Arcturus IV was the only inhabited or inhabitable planet of its primary and it was quite a few light-years to the next star system.

He needed food—his fuel and water supplies were okay but the commissary department on Pluto had made a mistake in stocking his scouter—and, according to the space manual, the natives were friendly. They'd give him anything he asked for.

The manual was very specific on that point; he reread the brief section on the Arcturians as soon as he had set the controls for automatic landing.

"The Arcturians," he read, *"are inhuman, but very friendly. A pilot landing here need only ask for what he wants, and it is given to him freely, readily, and without argument.*

"Communication with them, however, must be by paper and pencil as they have no vocal organs and no organs of hearing. However, they read and write English with considerable fluency."

Ralph NC-5's mouth watered as he tried to decide what he wanted to eat first, after two days of complete abstinence from food, preceded by five days of short rations; a week ago he had discovered the commissary department's mistake in stocking his lockers.

Foods, wonderful foods, chased one another through his mind.

He landed. The Arcturians, a dozen of them and they were indeed inhuman—twelve feet tall, six-armed, bright magenta—approached him and their leader bowed and handed him paper and pencil.

Suddenly he knew exactly what he wanted; he wrote rapidly and handed back the pad. It passed from hand to hand among them.

Then abruptly he found himself grabbed, his arms pinioned. And then tied to a stake around which they were piling brushwood and sticks. One of them lighted it.

He screamed protests but they fell, not on deaf ears but on no ears at all. He screamed in pain, and then stopped screaming.

The space manual had been quite correct in saying that the Arcturians read and write English with considerable fluency. But it had omitted to add that they were very poor at spelling; else the *last* thing Ralph NC-5 would have requested would have been a sizzling steak.

Nasty

Walter Beauregard had been an accomplished and enthusiastic lecher for almost fifty years. Now, at the age of sixty-five, he was in danger of losing his qualifications for membership in the lechers' union. In danger of losing? Nay, let us be honest; he had *lost*. For three years now he had been to doctor after doctor, quack after quack, had tried nostrum after nostrum. All utterly to no avail.

Finally he remembered his books on magic and necromancy. They were books he had enjoyed collecting and reading as part of his extensive library, but he had never taken them seriously. Until now. What did he have to lose?

In a musty, evil-smelling but rare volume he found what he wanted. As it instructed, he drew the pentagram, copied the cabalistic markings, lighted the candles and read aloud the incantation.

There was a flash of light and a puff of smoke. And the demon. I won't describe the demon except to assure you that you wouldn't have liked him.

"What is your name?" Beauregard asked. He tried to make his voice steady but it trembled a little.

The demon made a sound somewhere between a shriek and a whistle, with overtones of a bull fiddle being played with a crosscut saw. Then he said, "But you won't be able to pronounce that. In your dull language it would translate as Nasty. Just call me Nasty. I suppose you want the usual thing."

"What's the usual thing?" Beauregard wanted to know.

"A wish, of course. All right, you can have it. But not three wishes; that business about three wishes is sheer superstition. One is all you get. And you won't like it."

"One is all I want. And I can't imagine not liking it."

"You'll find out. All right, I know what your wish is. And here is the answer to it." Nasty reached into thin air and his hand vanished and came back holding a pair of silvery-looking swimming trunks. He held them out to Beauregard. "Wear them in good health," he said.

"What are they?"

"What do they look like? Swimming trunks. But they're special. The material is out of the future, a few millenniums from now. It's indestructible; they'll never wear out or tear or snag. Nice stuff. But the spell on them is a plenty old one. Try them on and find out."

The demon vanished.

Walter Beauregard quickly stripped and put on the beautiful silvery swimming trunks. Immediately he felt wonderful. Virility coursed through him. He felt as though he were a young man again, just starting his lecherous career.

Quickly he put on a robe and slippers. (Have I mentioned that he was a rich man? And that his home was a penthouse atop the swankiest hotel in Atlantic City? He was, and it was.) He went downstairs in his private elevator and outside to the hotel's luxurious swimming pool. It was, as usual, surrounded by gorgeous Bikini-clad beauties showing off their wares under the pretense of acquiring sun tans, while they waited for propositions from wealthy men like Beauregard.

He took time choosing. But not too much time.

Two hours later, still clad in the wonderful magic trunks, he sat on the edge of his bed and stared at and sighed for the beautiful blonde who lay stretched out on the bed beside him, Bikiniless—and sound asleep.

Nasty had been so right. And so well named. The miraculous trunks, the indestructible, untearable trunks worked perfectly. But if he took them off, or even let them down ...

Rope Trick

Mr. and Mrs. George Darnell—her first name was Elsie, if that matters—were taking a honeymoon trip around the world. A *second* honeymoon, starting on the day of their twentieth anniversary. George had been in his thirties and Elsie in her twenties on the occasion of their first honeymoon—which, if you wish to check me on your slide rule, indicates that George was now in his fifties and Elsie in her forties.

Her dangerous forties (this phrase can be applied to a woman as well as to a man) and very, very disappointed with what had been happening—or, more specifically, had *not* been happening—during the first three weeks of their second honeymoon. To be completely honest, nothing, absolutely nothing had happened.

Until they reached Calcutta.

They checked into a hotel there early one afternoon and after freshening up a bit decided to wander about and see as much of the city as could be seen in the one day and night they planned to spend there.

They came to the bazaar.

And there watched a Hindu fakir performing the Indian rope trick. Not the spectacular and complicated version in which a boy climbs the rope and—well, you know the story of how the full-scale Indian rope trick is performed.

This was a quite simplified version. The fakir, with a short length of rope coiled on the ground in front of him, played over and over a few simple notes on a flageolet—and gradually, as he played, the rope began to rise into the air and stand rigid.

This gave Elsie Darnell a wonderful idea—although she did not mention it to George. She returned with him to their room at the hotel and, after dinner, waited until he went to sleep—as always, at nine o'clock.

Then she quietly left the room and the hotel. She found a taxi driver and an interpreter and, with both of them, went back to the bazaar and found the fakir.

Through the interpreter she managed to buy from the fakir the flageolet which she had heard him play and paid him to teach her to play the few simple repetitious notes which had made the rope rise.

Then she returned to the hotel and to their room. Her husband George was sleeping soundly—as he always did.

Standing beside the bed Elsie very softly began to play the simple tune on the flageolet.

Over and over.

And as she played it—gradually—the sheet began to rise, over her sleeping husband.

When it had risen to a sufficient height she put down the flageolet and, with a joyful cry, threw back the sheet.

And there, standing straight in the air, was the drawstring of his pajamas!

Abominable

Sir Chauncey Atherton waved a farewell to the Sherpa guides who were to set up camp here and let him proceed alone. This was Abominable Snowman country, a few hundred miles north of Mount Everest, in the Himalayas. Abominable Snowmen were seen occasionally on Everest, on other Tibetan or Nepalese mountains, but Mount Oblimov, at the foot of which he was now leaving his native guides, was so thick with them that not even the Sherpas would climb it, but would here await his return, if indeed he did. It took a brave man to pass this point. Sir Chauncey was a brave man.

Also, he was a connoisseur of women, which was why he was here and about to attempt, alone, not only a dangerous ascent but an even more dangerous rescue. If Lola Gabraldi was still alive, an Abominable Snowman had her.

Sir Chauncey had never seen Lola Gabraldi, in the flesh. He had, in fact, learned of her existence less than a month ago, when he had seen the one motion picture in which she had starred—and through which she had become suddenly fabulous, the most beautiful woman on Earth, the most pulchritudinous movie star Italy had ever produced, and Sir Chauncey could not understand how even Italy had produced her. In one picture she had replaced Bardot, Lolobrigida, and Ekberg as the image of feminine perfection in the minds of connoisseurs of women everywhere, and Sir Chauncey was the top connoisseur anywhere. The moment he had seen her on the screen he had known that he must know her in the flesh, or die trying.

But by that time Lola Gabraldi had vanished. As a vacation after her first picture she had taken a trip to India and had joined a group of climbers about to make an assault on Mount Oblimov. The rest of the party had returned, Lola had not. One of them had testified that he had seen her, at a distance too great for him to reach her in time, abducted, carried off screaming by a nine-foot-high hairy more-or-less manlike creature. An Abominable Snowman. The party had searched for her for days before giving up and returning to civilization. Everyone agreed that there was no possible chance, now, of finding her alive.

Everyone except Sir Chauncey, who had immediately flown to India from England.

He struggled on, now high into the eternal snows. And in addition to mountain-climbing equipment he carried the heavy rifle with which he had, only the year before, shot tigers in Bengal. If it could kill tigers, he reasoned, it could kill Snowmen.

Snow swirled about him as he neared the cloud line. Suddenly a dozen yards ahead of him, which was as far as he could see, he caught a glimpse of a monstrous not-quite-human figure. He raised his rifle and fired. The figure fell, and kept on falling; it had been on a ledge over thousands of feet of nothingness.

And at the moment of the shot arms closed around Sir Chauncey from behind him. Thick, hairy arms. And then, as one hand held him easily, the other took the rifle from him and bent it into an L-shape as easily as though it had been a toothpick, and then tossed it away.

A voice spoke from a point about two feet above his head. "Be quiet, you will not be harmed." Sir Chauncey was a brave man, but a sort of squeak was all the answer he could make, despite the seeming assurance of the words. He was held so tightly against the creature behind him that he could not look upward and backward to see what its face was like.

"Let me explain," said the voice above and behind him. "We, whom you call Abominable Snowmen, are human, but transmuted. A great many centuries ago we were a tribe like the Sherpas. We chanced to discover a drug that let us change physically, let us adapt by increased size, hairiness, and other physiological changes to extreme cold and altitude, let us move up into the mountains, into country in which others cannot survive, except for the duration of brief climbing expeditions. Do you understand?"

"Y-y-yes," Sir Chauncey managed to say. He was beginning to feel a faint return of hope. Why would this creature be explaining these things to him, if it intended to kill him?

"Then I shall explain further. Our number is small, and we are diminishing. For that reason we occasionally capture, as I have captured you, a mountain climber. We give him the transmuting drug, he undergoes the physiological changes and becomes one of us. By that means we keep our number, such as it is, relatively constant."

"B-but," Sir Chauncey stammered, "is that what happened to the woman I'm looking for, Lola Gabraldi? She is now—eight feet tall and hairy and—"

"She *was*. You just killed her. One of our tribe had taken her as his mate. We will take no revenge for your having killed her, but you must now, as it were, take her place."

"Take her place? But—I'm a *man*."

"Thank God for that," said the voice above and behind him. He found himself turned around, held against a huge hairy body, his face at the right level to be buried between mountainous hairy breasts. "Thank God for that— because I am an Abominable Snowwoman."

Sir Chauncey fainted and was picked up and, as lightly as though he were a toy dog, was carried away by his mate.

Bear Possibility

If you've ever seen an expectant father pacing the waiting room of a hospital lighting cigarette after cigarette—usually at the wrong end if it's a filter-tip—you know how worried he acts.

But if you think that *that* is worry, take a look at Jonathan Quinby, pacing the room outside a delivery room. Quinby is not only lighting the wrong ends of his filter-tips but is actually smoking them that way, without tasting the difference.

He's really got something to worry about. It had started when they had last visited a zoo one evening. "Last visited" is true in both senses of the phrase; Quinby would never go within miles of one again, ever, nor would his wife. She had fallen, you see, into—

But there is something that must be explained, so you may understand what happened that evening. In his younger days Quinby had been an ardent student of magic—real magic, not the slight-of-hand variety. Unfortunately charms and incantations did not work for him, however effective they might be for others.

Except for one incantation, one that let him change a human being into any animal he chose and (by saying the same incantation backward) back again into a human being. A vicious or vengeful man would have found this ability useful, but Quinby was neither vicious nor vengeful and after a few experiments—with subjects who had volunteered out of curiosity—he had never made use of it.

When, ten years ago at the age of thirty, he had fallen in love and married, he had used it once more, simply to satisfy his wife's curiosity. When he had told her about it, she had doubted him and challenged him to prove it, and he had changed her briefly into a Siamese cat. She had then made him promise never to use his supernormal ability again, and he had kept that promise ever since.

Except once, the evening of their visit to the zoo. They had been walking along the path, with no one in sight but themselves, that led past the sunken bear pits. They'd looked for bears but all of them had retired into the cave portion of their quarters for the night. Then—well, his wife had leaned a little too far over the railing; she lost her balance and fell into a pit. Miraculously, she landed unhurt.

She was getting to her feet and looking up at him; she put her finger to her lips and then pointed to the entrance to the den. He understood; she wanted him to get help but quietly, lest any sound might waken the sleeping bear in its den. He nodded and was turning away when a gasp from his wife made him look down again—and see that it would be too late to get help.

A young male grizzly bear was already coming out of the den entrance. Growling ominously and heading toward her, ready to kill.

There was only one thing that could possibly be done in time to save his wife's life, and Jonathan Quinby did it. Male grizzly bears do not kill female grizzly bears.

They have other ideas, though. Quinby stood wringing his hands in helpless anguish as he was forced to witness what was happening to his wife in the bear pit. But after a while the male grizzly went back into his den and—ready to change her back on a second's notice if the male should again emerge—Quinby said the incantation backward and brought his wife back to her proper form. He told her that if she could find footholds in the rocks and climb part way up, he could reach down and pull her the rest of the way. In a few minutes she was safely out of the pit. White and shaken, they had taken a taxi home. Once there, they agreed never to discuss the matter again; there was nothing else he could have done but watch her be killed.

Nor had they discussed it again, for a few weeks. But then—well, they'd been married ten years and had wanted children but no children had come. Now three weeks after her horrible experience in the pit she was—with *child?*

Have you ever seen an expectant father pacing a hospital waiting room, looking like the most worried man on Earth? Then consider Quinby, who's right now pacing and waiting. For what?

Recessional

The King my liege lord is a discouraged man. We understand and do not blame him, for the war has been long and bitter and there are so pathetically few of us left, yet we wish that it were not so. We sympathize with him for having lost his Queen, and we too all loved her—but since the Queen of the Blacks died with her, her loss does not mean the loss of the war. Yet our King, he who should be a tower of strength, smiles weakly and his words of attempted encouragement to us ring false in our ears because we hear in his voice the undertones of fear and defeat. Yet we love him and we die for him, one by one.

One by one we die in his defense, here upon this blooded bitter field, churned muddy by the horses of the Knights—while they lived; they are dead now, both ours and the Black ones—and will there be an end, a victory?

We can only have faith, and never become cynics and heretics, like my poor fellow Bishop Tibault. "We fight and die; we know not why," he once whispered to me, earlier in the war at a time when we stood side by side defending our King while the battle raged in a far corner of the field.

But that was only the beginning of his heresy. He had stopped believing in a God and had come to believe in gods, gods who play a game with us and care nothing for us as persons. Worse, he believed that our moves are not our own, that we are but puppets fighting in a useless war. Still worse—and how absurd!—that White is not necessarily good and Black is not necessarily evil, that on the cosmic scale it does not matter who wins the war!

Of course it was only to me, and only in whispers, that he said these things. He knew his duties as a Bishop. He fought bravely. And died bravely, that very day, impaled upon the lance of a Black Knight. I prayed for him: *God, rest his soul and grant him peace; he meant not what he said.*

Without faith we are nothing. How could Tibault have been so wrong? White must win. Victory is the only thing that can save us. Without victory our companions who have died, those who here upon this embattled field have given their lives that we may live, shall have died in vain. *Et tu,* Tibault.

And you were wrong, so wrong. There is a God, and so great a God that He will forgive your heresy, because there was no evil in you, Tibault, except as doubt—no, doubt is error but it is not evil.

Without faith we are noth—

But something is happening! Our Rook, he who was on the Queen's side of the field in the Beginning, swoops toward the evil Black King, our enemy. The villainous one is under attack—and cannot escape. We have won! We have won!

A voice in the sky says calmly, "Checkmate."

We have won! The war, this bitter stricken field, was *not* in vain. Tibault, you were wrong, you were—

But what is happening now? The very Earth tilts; one side of the battlefield rises and we are sliding—White and Black alike—into—

—into a monstrous *box* and I see that it is a mass coffin in which already lie dead—

IT IS NOT FAIR; WE WON! GOD, WAS TIBAULT RIGHT? IT IS NOT JUST; WE WON!

The King, my liege lord, is sliding too across the squares—

IT IS NOT JUST; IT IS NOT *RIGHT;* IT IS NOT ...

Contact

Dhar Ry sat alone in his room, meditating. From outside the door he caught a thought wave equivalent to a knock, and, glancing at the door, he willed it to slide open. It slid open. "Enter, my friend," he said. He could have projected the idea telepathically, but with only two persons present, speech was more polite.

Ejon Khee entered. "You are up late tonight, my leader," he said.

"Yes, Khee. Within an hour the Earth rocket is due to land, and I wish to see it. Yes, I know, it will land a thousand miles away, if their calculations are correct. Beyond the horizon. But if it lands even twice that far the flash of the atomic explosion should be visible, and I have waited long for first contact. For even though no Earthman will be on that rocket, it will still be first contact— for them. Of course our telepath teams have been reading their thoughts for many centuries, but—this will be the first *physical* contact between Mars and Earth."

Khee made himself comfortable in one of the low chairs. "True," he said. "I have not followed recent reports too closely, though. Why are they using an atomic warhead? I know they think our planet is probably uninhabited, but still—"

"They will watch the flash through their lunar telescopes and get a— what do they call it?—a spectroscopic analysis, which will tell them more than they know now (or think they know; much of it is erroneous) about the atmosphere of our planet and the composition of its surface. It is—call it a sighting shot, Khee. They'll be here in person within a few oppositions. And then—"

Mars was holding out, waiting for Earth to come. What was left of Mars, that is; this one small city of about nine hundred beings. The civilization of Mars was older than that of Earth, but it was a dying one. This was what remained of it, one city, nine hundred people. They were waiting for Earth to make contact, for a selfish reason and for an unselfish one.

Martian civilization had developed in a quite different direction from that of Earth. It had developed no important knowledge of the physical sciences, no technology. But it had developed social sciences to the point where there had not been a single crime, let alone a war, on Mars for fifty thousand years. And it had developed fully the parapsychological sciences, the sciences of the mind, that Earth was just beginning to discover.

Mars could teach Earth much. How to avoid crime and war, two simple things, to begin with. Beyond those simple things, telepathy, telekinesis, empathy ...

And Earth would, Mars hoped, teach them something even more valuable to Mars: how, by science and technology—which it was too late for Mars to develop now, even if they had the types of minds which would enable them to develop these things—to restore and rehabilitate a dying planet, so that an otherwise dying race might live and multiply again. Each planet would gain greatly, and neither would lose.

And tonight was the night when Earth would make its first contact, a sighting shot. Its next shot, a rocket containing Earthmen or at least an Earthman, would be at the next opposition, two Earth years, or roughly four Martian years, hence. The Martians knew this because their teams of telepaths were able to catch at least some of the thoughts of Earthmen, enough to know their plans. Unfortunately, at that distance, the connection was one-way and Mars could not ask Earth to hurry its program. Or tell Earth scientists the facts about Mars' composition and atmosphere which would have made this preliminary shot unnecessary.

Tonight Ry, the leader (as nearly as the Martian word can be translated), and Khee, his administrative assistant and closest friend, sat and meditated together until the time was near. Then they drank a toast to the future—in a beverage based on menthol, which had the same effect on Martians as alcohol on Earthmen—and climbed to the roof of the building in which they had been sitting. They watched toward the north, where the rocket should land. The stars shone brilliantly through the thin atmosphere ...

In Observatory No. 1 on Earth's moon, Rog Everett, his eye at the eye-piece of the spotter scope, said triumphantly, "Thar she blew, Willie. And now, as soon as the films are developed, we'll know the score on that old planet Mars." He straightened up—there'd be no more to see now—and he and Willie Sanger shook hands solemnly; it was a historical occasion.

"Hope it didn't kill anybody. Any Martians, that is. Rog, did it hit dead center in Syrtis Major?"

"Near as matters. The pix will show exactly but I'd say it was maybe a thousand miles off, to the south. And that's damn close on a fifty-million-mile shot. Willie, do you really think there are any Martians?"

Willie thought a second and then said, "No."

Willie was right.

Rebound

The power came to Larry Snell suddenly and unexpectedly, out of nowhere. How and why it came to him, he never learned. It just came; that's all.

It could have happened to a nicer guy. Snell was a small-time crook when he thought he could get away with stealing, but the bulk of his income, such as it was, came from selling numbers racket tickets and peddling marijuana to adolescents. He was fattish and sloppy, with little close-set eyes that made him look almost as mean as he really was. His only redeeming virtue was cowardice; it had kept him from committing crimes of violence.

He was, that night, talking to a bookie from a tavern telephone booth, arguing whether a bet he'd placed by phone that afternoon had been on the nose or across the board. Finally, giving up, he growled "Drop dead," and slammed down the receiver. He thought nothing of it until the next day when he learned that the bookie *had* dropped dead, while talking on the telephone and at just about the time of their conversation.

This gave Larry Snell food for thought. He was not an uneducated man; he knew what a whammy was. In fact, he'd tried whammies before, but they'd never worked for him. Had something changed? It was worth trying. Carefully he made out a list of twenty people whom, for one reason or another, he hated. He telephoned them one at a time—spacing the calls over the course of a week—and told each of them to drop dead. They did, all of them.

It was not until the end of that week that he discovered that what he had was not simply the whammy, but the Power. He was talking to a dame, a *top* dame, a stripteuse working in a top night club and making twenty or forty times his own income, and he had said, "Honey, come up to my room after the last show, huh?" She did, and it staggered him because he'd been kidding. Rich men and handsome playboys were after her, and she'd fallen for a casual, not even seriously intended, proposition from Larry Snell.

Did he have the Power? He tried it the next morning, before she left him. He asked her how much money she had with her, and then told her to give it to him. She did, and it was several hundred dollars.

He was in business. By the end of the next week he was rich; he had made himself that way by borrowing money from everyone he knew—including slight acquaintances who were fairly high in the hierarchy of the underworld and therefore quite solvent—and then telling them to forget it. He moved from his fleabag pad to a penthouse apartment atop the swankiest hotel in town. It was a bachelor apartment, but need it be said that he slept there alone but seldom, and then only for purposes of recuperation.

It was a nice life but even so it took only a few weeks of it to cause it to dawn on Snell that he was wasting the Power. Why shouldn't he really use what he had by taking over the country first and then the world, make himself the most powerful dictator in history? Why shouldn't he have and own everything, including a harem instead of a dame a night? Why shouldn't he have an army to enforce the fact that his slightest wish would be everyone else's highest law? If his commands were obeyed over the telephone certainly they would be obeyed if he gave them over radio and television. All he had to do was pay for (pay for? simply demand) a universal network that would let him be heard by everyone everywhere. Or almost everyone; he could take over when he had a simple majority behind him, and bring the others into line later.

But this would be a Big Deal, the biggest one ever swung, and he decided to take his time planning it so there would be no possibility of his making a mistake. He decided to spend a few days alone, out of town and away from everybody, to do his planning.

He chartered a plane to take him to a relatively uncrowded part of the Catskills, and from an inn—which he took over simply by telling the other guests to leave—he started taking long walks alone, thinking and dreaming. He found a favorite spot, a small hill in a valley surrounded by mountains; the scenery was magnificent. He did most of his thinking there, and found himself becoming more and more elated and euphoric as he began to see that it could and would work.

Dictator, hell. He'd have himself crowned Emperor. Emperor of the World. Why not? Who could defy a man with the Power? The Power to make anyone obey any command that he gave them, up to and including—

"Drop dead!" he shouted from the hilltop, in sheer vicious exuberance, not caring whether or not anyone or anything was within range of his voice ...

A teen-age boy and a teen-age girl found him there the next day and hurried back to the village to report having found a dead man on the top of Echo Hill.

Great Lost Discoveries I—*Invisibility*

Three great discoveries were made, and tragically lost, during the twentieth century. The first of these was the secret of invisibility.

The secret of invisibility was discovered in 1909 by Archibald Praeter, emissary from the court of Edward VII to the court of Sultan Abd el Krim, ruler of a small state loosely allied to the Ottoman Empire.

Praeter, an amateur but enthusiastic biologist, was injecting mice with various serums for the purpose of finding an injection which would cause mutations. When he injected his 3019th mouse, the mouse disappeared. It was still there; he could feel it in his hand, but he could not see a hair or claw of it. He put it carefully in a cage and two hours later it appeared again, unharmed.

He experimented with increasing dosages and found that he could make a mouse invisible for up to twenty-four hours. Larger doses made it ill or torpid. He also learned that a mouse killed while invisible reappeared instantly at the moment of death.

Realizing the importance of his discovery, he wired his resignation to England, dismissed his servants and locked himself in his quarters, and began to experiment with himself. Starting with a small injection that made him invisible for only a few minutes, he worked up until he found his tolerance was equal to that of mice; an injection that made him invisible for more than twenty-four hours also made him ill. He also found that although nothing of his body was visible, not even his dentures if he kept his lips closed, nudity was essential; clothing did not become invisible with him.

Praeter was an honest and fairly well-to-do man, so he did not think of crime. He decided to return to England and offer his discovery to His Majesty's government for use in espionage or war.

But he decided first to allow himself one indulgence. He had always been curious about the closely guarded harem of the Sultan to whose court he had been attached. Why not have a close look at it from inside?

Besides, something—some nagging thought that he couldn't quite isolate—bothered him about his discovery. There was some circumstance under which ... He couldn't get beyond that point in his mind. An experiment was definitely in order.

He stripped and made himself invisible for the maximum period. It proved simple to walk past the armed eunuchs and enter the harem. He spent an interesting afternoon watching the fifty-odd beauties at their daytime occupation of keeping themselves beautiful, bathing and anointing their bodies with scented oils and perfumes.

One, a Circassian, especially attracted him. It occurred to him, just as it would have occurred to any man, that if he stayed the night—perfectly safe since he would be invisible until the following noon—he could keep her in sight to learn which room she slept in and, after the lights were out, join her; she would think the Sultan was favoring her with a visit.

He kept her in sight and noticed the room she entered. An armed eunuch took his post at the curtained doorway, others at each of the other doorways to the sleeping rooms. He waited until he was sure she would be asleep and then, at a moment when the eunuch was looking down the hall and would not see the movement of the curtain, he slipped through it. The light had been dim in the hallway; here the darkness was utter. But he groped carefully and managed to find the sleeping couch. Carefully he put out a hand and touched the sleeping woman. She screamed. (What he had not known was that the Sultan never visited the harem by night but sent for one, or sometimes several, of his wives to visit his own quarters.)

And suddenly the eunuch who had been outside was inside and had hold of him by the arm. The last thing he thought was that he now knew the one worrisome circumstance of invisibility: it was completely useless in pitch darkness. And the last thing he heard was the swish of the scimitar.

Great Lost Discoveries II—*Invulnerability*

The second great lost discovery was the secret of invulnerability. It was discovered in 1952 by a United States Navy radar officer, Lieutenant Paul Hickendorf. The device was electronic and consisted of a small box that could be carried handily in a pocket; when a switch on the box was turned on the person carrying the device was surrounded by a force field whose strength, as far as it could be measured by Hickendorf's excellent mathematics, was as near as matters to infinite.

The field was also completely impervious to any degree of heat and any quantity of radiation.

Lieutenant Hickendorf decided that a man—or a woman or a child or a dog—enclosed in that force field could withstand the explosion of a hydrogen bomb at closest range and not be injured in the slightest degree.

No hydrogen bomb had been exploded to that time, but at the moment he completed his device, the lieutenant happened to be on a ship, cruiser class, that was steaming across the Pacific Ocean en route to an atoll called Eniwetok, and the fact had leaked out that they were to be there to assist in the first explosion of a hydrogen bomb.

Lieutenant Hickendorf decided to get lost—to hide out on the target island and be there when the bomb went off, and also to be there unharmed after it went off, thereby demonstrating beyond all doubt that his discovery was workable, a defense against the most powerful weapon of all time.

It proved difficult but he hid out successfully and was there, only yards away from the H-bomb—after having crept closer and closer during the countdown—when it exploded.

His calculations had been completely correct and he was not injured in the slightest way, not scratched, not bruised, not burned.

But Lieutenant Hickendorf had overlooked the possibility of one thing happening, and that one thing happened. He was blown off the surface of the earth with much more than escape velocity. Straight out, not even into orbit. Forty-nine days later he fell into the sun, still completely uninjured but unfortunately long since dead since the force field had carried with it enough air to last him only a few hours, and so his discovery was lost to mankind, at least for the duration of the twentieth century.

Great Lost Discoveries III—*Immortality*

The third great discovery made and lost in the twentieth century was the secret of immortality. It was the discovery of an obscure Moscow chemist named Ivan Ivanovitch Smetakovsky, in 1978. Smetakovsky left no record of how he made his discovery or of how he knew before trying it that it would work, for the simple reason that it scared him stiff, for two reasons.

He was afraid to give it to the world, and he knew that once he had given it even to his own government the secret would eventually leak through the Curtain and cause chaos. The U.S.S.R. could handle anything, but in the more barbaric and less disciplined countries the inevitable result of an immortality drug would be a population explosion that would most assuredly lead to an attack on the enlightened Communist countries.

And he was afraid to take it himself because he wasn't sure he *wanted* to become immortal. With things as they were even in the U.S.S.R.—not to consider what they must be outside it—was it really worth while to live forever or even indefinitely?

He compromised by neither giving it to anyone else nor taking it himself, for the time being, until he could make up his mind about it.

Meanwhile he carried with him the only dose of the drug he had made up. It was only a minute quantity that fitted into a tiny capsule that was insoluble and could be carried in his mouth. He attached it to the side of one of his dentures, so that it rested safely between denture and cheek and he would be in no danger of swallowing it inadvertently.

But if he should so decide at any time he could reach into his mouth, crush the capsule with a thumbnail, and become immortal.

He so decided one day when, after coming down with lobar pneumonia and being taken to a Moscow hospital, he learned from overhearing a conversation between a doctor and nurse who erroneously thought he was asleep, that he was expected to die within a few hours.

Fear of death proved greater than fear of immortality, whatever immortality might bring, so, as soon as the doctor and the nurse had left the room, he crushed the capsule and swallowed its contents.

He hoped that, since death might be so imminent, the drug would work in time to save his life. It did work in time, although by the time it had taken effect he had slipped into semicoma and delirium.

Three years later, in 1981, he was still in semi-coma and delirium, and the Russian doctors had finally diagnosed his case and ceased to be puzzled by it.

Obviously Smetakovsky had taken some sort of immortality drug—one which they found it impossible to isolate or analyze—and it was keeping him from dying and would no doubt do so indefinitely if not forever.

But unfortunately it had also made immortal the pneumococci in his body, the bacteria (*Diplococci pneumoniae*) that had caused his pneumonia in the first place and would now continue to maintain it forever. So the doctors, being realists and seeing no reason to burden themselves by giving him custodial care in perpetuity, simply buried him.

Hobbyist

"I heard a rumor," Sangstrom said, "to the effect that you—" He turned his head and looked about him to make absolutely sure that he and the druggist were alone in the tiny prescription pharmacy. The druggist was a gnomelike gnarled little man who could have been any age from fifty to a hundred. They were alone, but Sangstrom dropped his voice just the same. "—to the effect that you have a completely undetectable poison."

The druggist nodded. He came around the counter and locked the front door of the shop, then walked toward a doorway behind the counter. "I was about to take a coffee break," he said. "Come with me and have a cup."

Sangstrom followed him around the counter and through the doorway to a back room ringed by shelves of bottles from floor to ceiling. The druggist plugged in an electric percolator, found two cups and put them on a table that had a chair on either side of it. He motioned Sangstrom to one of the chairs and took the other himself. "Now," he said. "Tell me. Whom do you want to kill, and why?"

"Does it matter?" Sangstrom asked. "Isn't it enough that I pay for—"

The druggist interrupted him with an upraised hand. "Yes, it matters. I must be convinced that you deserve what I can give you. Otherwise—" He shrugged.

"All right," Sangstrom said. "The *whom* is my wife. The *why*—" He started the long story. Before he had quite finished the percolator had finished its task and the druggist briefly interrupted to get the coffee for them. Sangstrom finished his story.

The little druggist nodded. "Yes, I occasionally dispense an undetectable poison. I do so freely; I do not charge for it, if I think the case is deserving. I have helped many murderers."

"Fine," Sangstrom said. "Please give it to me, then."

The druggist smiled at him. "I already have. By the time the coffee was ready I had decided that you deserved it. It was, as I said, free. But there is a price for the antidote."

Sangstrom turned pale. But he had anticipated—not this, but the possibility of a double-cross or some form of blackmail. He pulled a pistol from his pocket.

The little druggist chuckled. "You daren't use that. Can you find the antidote"—he waved at the shelves—"among those thousands of bottles? Or would you find a faster more virulent poison? Or if you think I'm bluffing, that you are not really poisoned, go ahead and shoot. You'll know the answer within three hours when the poison starts to work."

"How much for the antidote?" Sangstrom growled.

"Quite reasonable. A thousand dollars. After all, a man must live. Even if his hobby is preventing murders, there's no reason why he shouldn't make money at it, is there?"

Sangstrom growled and put the pistol down, but within reach, and took out his wallet. Maybe after he had the antidote, he'd still use that pistol. He counted out a thousand dollars in hundred-dollar bills and put it on the table.

The druggist made no immediate move to pick it up. He said: "And one other thing—for your wife's safety and mine. You will write a confession of your intention—your former intention, I trust—to murder your wife. Then you will wait till I go out and mail it to a friend of mine on the homicide detail. He'll keep it as evidence in case you ever *do* decide to kill your wife. Or me, for that matter.

"When that is in the mail it will be safe for me to return here and give you the antidote. I'll get you paper and pen ...

"Oh, one other thing—although I do not absolutely insist on it. Please help spread the word about my undetectable poison, will you? One never knows, Mr. Sangstrom. The life you save, if you have any enemies, just might be your own."

The End

Professor Jones had been working on time theory for many years.

"And I have found the key equation," he told his daughter one day. "Time is a field. This machine I have made can manipulate, even reverse, that field."

Pushing a button as he spoke, he said, "This should make time run backward run time make should this," said he, spoke he as button a pushing.

"Field that, reverse even, manipulate can made have I machine this. Field a is time." Day one daughter his told he, "Equation key the found have I and."

Years many for theory time on working been had Jones Professor.

END THE

Nightmare in Blue

He awoke to the brightest, bluest morning he had ever seen. Through the window beside the bed, he could see an almost incredible sky. George slid out of bed quickly, wide awake and not wanting to miss another minute of the first day of his vacation. But he dressed quietly so as not to awaken his wife. They had arrived here at the lodge—loaned them by a friend for the week of their vacation—late the evening before and Wilma had been very tired from the trip; he'd let her sleep as long as she could. He carried his shoes into the living room to put them on.

Tousle-haired little Tommy, their five-year-old, came out of the smaller bedroom he'd slept in, yawning. "Want some breakfast?" George asked him. And when Tommy nodded, "Get dressed then, and join me in the kitchen."

George went to the kitchen but before starting breakfast, he stepped through the outside door and stood looking around; it had been dark when they'd arrived and he knew what the country was like only by description. It was virgin woodland, more beautiful than he'd pictured it. The nearest other lodge, he'd been told, was a mile away, on the other side of a fairly large lake. He couldn't see the lake for the trees but the path that started here from the kitchen door led to it, a little less than a quarter of a mile away. His friend had told him it was good for swimming, good for fishing. The swimming didn't interest George; he wasn't afraid of the water but he didn't like it either, and he'd never learned how to swim. But his wife was a good swimmer and so was Tommy—a regular little water rat, she called him.

Tommy joined him on the step; the boy's idea of getting dressed had been to put on a pair of swim trunks so it hadn't taken him long. "Daddy," he said, "let's go see the lake before we eat, huh, Daddy?"

"All right," George said. He wasn't hungry himself and maybe when they got back Wilma would be awake.

The lake was beautiful, an even more intense blue than the sky, and smooth as a mirror. Tommy plunged into it gleefully and George called to him to stay where it was shallow, not to swim out.

"I can swim, Daddy. I swim swell."

"Yes, but your mother's not here. You stay close."

"Water's *warm*, Daddy."

Far out, George saw a fish jump. Right after breakfast he'd come down with his rod and see if he could catch a lunch for them.

A path along the edge of the lake led, he'd been told, to a place a couple of miles away where rowboats could be rented; he'd rent one for the whole week and keep it tied up here. He stared toward the end of the lake trying to see the place.

Suddenly, chillingly, there was an anguished cry, "*Daddy, my leg, it—*"

George whirled and saw Tommy's head way out, twenty yards at least, and it went under the water and came up again, but this time there was a frightening *glubbing* sound when Tommy tried to yell again. It must be a cramp, George thought frantically; he'd seen Tommy swim several times that distance.

For a second he almost flung himself into the water, but then he told himself: It won't help him for me to drown with him and if I can get Wilma there's at least a chance...

He ran back toward the lodge. A hundred yards away he started yelling *"Wilma!"* at the top of his voice and when he was almost to the kitchen door she came through it, in pajamas. And then she was running after him toward the lake, passing him and getting ahead since he was already winded, and he was fifty yards behind her when she reached the edge, ran into the water and swam strongly toward the spot where for a moment the back of the boy's head showed at the surface.

She was there in a few strokes and had him and then, as she put her feet down to tread water for the turn, he saw with sudden sheer horror—a horror mirrored in his wife's blue eyes—that she was standing on the bottom, holding their dead son, in only three feet of water.

Nightmare in Gray

He awoke feeling wonderful, with the sun bright and warm upon him and spring in the air. He had dozed off—for less than half an hour, he knew, because the angle of shadows from the beneficent sun had changed but slightly while he slept—sitting upright upon the park bench; only his head had nodded and then fallen forward.

The park was beautiful with the green of spring, softer green than summer's, the day was magnificent, and he was young and in love. Wondrously in love, dizzily in love. And happily in love; only last night, Saturday night, he had proposed to Susan and she had accepted him, more or less. That is, she had not given him a definite yes but she had invited him this afternoon to meet her family and had said that she hoped he would love them and that they would love him—as she did. If that wasn't tantamount to an acceptance, what was? They'd fallen in love at sight, almost, which was why he had yet to meet her family.

Sweet Susan, of the soft brown hair, with the cute little nose that was almost pug, of the faint, tender freckles and the big soft brown eyes.

She was the most wonderful thing that had ever happened to him, that could ever happen to anyone.

Well, it was midafternoon now and that was when Susan had asked him to call. He stood up from the bench and, since he found his muscles a bit cramped from the nap, yawned luxuriously. Then he started to walk the few blocks from the park where he had been killing time to the house he'd taken her home to last night, a short walk through the bright sunshine, the spring day.

He climbed the steps and knocked on the door. It opened and for a second he thought Susan herself had answered it, but the girl only looked like Susan. Her sister, probably; she'd mentioned having a sister only a year older than she.

He bowed and introduced himself, asked for Susan. He thought the girl looked at him strangely for a moment. Then she said, "Come in, please. She's not here at the moment, but if you'll wait in the parlor there—"

He waited in the parlor there. How odd of her to have gone out. Even briefly.

Then he heard the voice, the voice of the girl who had let him in, talking in the hallway outside, and in understandable curiosity, stood up and went to the hallway door to listen. She seemed to be talking into a telephone.

"Harry—*please come home right away,* and bring the doctor with you. Yes, it's Grandpa ... No, not another heart attack. Like the time before when he had amnesia and thought that Grandma was still— No, *not* senile dementia, Harry, just amnesia, but worse this time. Fifty years off—his memory is way back before he even married Grandma ..."

Suddenly old, aged fifty years in fifty seconds, he wept silently as he leaned against the door ...

Nightmare in Red

He awoke without knowing what had awakened him until a second temblor, only a minute after the first, shook the bed slightly and rattled small objects on the dresser. He lay waiting for a third shock but none came, not then.

He realized, though, that he was wide awake now and probably would not be able to go back to sleep. He looked at the luminous dial of his wrist watch and saw that it was only three o'clock, the middle of the night. He got out of bed and walked, in his pajamas, to the window. It was open and a cool breeze came through it, and he could see the twinkling, flickering lights in the black sky and could hear the sounds of night. Somewhere, bells. But why bells at this hour? Ringing for disaster? Had the mild temblors here been damaging quakes elsewhere, nearby? Or was a real quake coming and the bells a warning, a warning to people to leave their houses and get out into the open for survival?

Suddenly, although not from fear but from a strange compulsion he had no wish to analyze, he wanted to be out there and not here. He had to run, he had to.

And he was running, down the hallway and out the front door, running silently in bare feet down the long straight walk that led to the gate. And through the gate that swung shut behind him and into the field ... *Field?* Should there be a field here, right outside his gate? Especially a field dotted with posts, thick ones like truncated telephone poles his own height? But before he could organize his thinking, try to start from scratch and remember where *here* was and who *he* was and what he was doing here at all, there was another temblor. More violent this time; it made him stagger in his running and run into one of the mysterious posts, a glancing blow that hurt his shoulder and deflected his running course, almost making him lose his footing. What was this weird compulsion that kept him going toward—what?

And then the real earthquake hit, the ground seemed to rise up under him and shake itself and when it ended he was lying on his back staring up at the monstrous sky in which now suddenly appeared, in miles-high glowing red letters a *word.* The word was *TILT* and as he stared at it all the other flashing lights went off and the bells quit ringing and it was the end of everything.

Nightmare in Yellow

He awoke when the alarm clock rang, but lay in bed a while after he'd shut it off, going a final time over the plans he'd made for embezzlement that day and for murder that evening.

Every little detail had been worked out, but this was the final check. Tonight at forty-six minutes after eight he'd be free, in every way. He'd picked that moment because this was his fortieth birthday and that was the exact time of day, of the evening rather, when he had been born. His mother had been a bug on astrology, which was why the moment of his birth had been impressed on him so exactly. He wasn't superstitious himself but it had struck his sense of humor to have his new life begin at forty, to the minute.

Time was running out on him, in any case. As a lawyer who specialized in handling estates, a lot of money passed through his hands—and some of it had passed into them. A year ago he'd "borrowed" five thousand dollars to put into something that looked like a sure-fire way to double or triple the money, but he'd lost it instead. Then he'd "borrowed" more to gamble with, in one way or another, to try to recoup the first loss. Now he was behind to the tune of over thirty thousand; the shortage couldn't be hidden more than another few months and there wasn't a hope that he could replace the missing money by that time. So he had been raising all the cash he could without arousing suspicion, by carefully liquidating assets, and by this afternoon he'd have running-away money to the tune of well over a hundred thousand dollars, enough to last him the rest of his life.

And they'd never catch him. He'd planned every detail of his trip, his destination, his new identity, and it was foolproof. He'd been working on it for months.

His decision to kill his wife had been relatively an afterthought. The motive was simple: he hated her. But it was only after he'd come to the decision that he'd never go to jail, that he'd kill himself if he was ever apprehended, that it came to him that—since he'd die anyway if caught—he had nothing to lose in leaving a dead wife behind him instead of a living one.

He'd hardly been able to keep from laughing at the appropriateness of the birthday present she'd given him (yesterday, a day ahead of time); it had been a new suitcase. She'd also talked him into celebrating his birthday by letting her meet him downtown for dinner at seven. Little did she guess how the celebration would go after that. He planned to have her home by eight forty-six and satisfy his sense of the fitness of things by making himself a widower at that exact moment. There was a practical advantage, too, of leaving her dead. If he left her alive but asleep she'd guess what had happened and call the police when she found him gone in the morning. If he left her dead her body would not be found that soon, possibly not for two or three days, and he'd have a much better start.

Things went smoothly at his office; by the time he went to meet his wife everything was ready. But she dawdled over drinks and dinner and he began to worry whether he could get her home by eight forty-six. It was ridiculous, he knew, but it had become important that his moment of freedom should come then and not a minute earlier or a minute later. He watched his watch.

He would have missed it by half a minute if he'd waited till they were inside the house. But the dark of the porch of their house was perfectly safe, as safe as inside. He swung the blackjack viciously once, as she stood at the front door, waiting for him to open it. He caught her before she fell and managed to hold her upright with one arm while he got the door open and then got it closed from the inside.

Then he flicked the switch and yellow light leaped to fill the room, and, before they could see that his wife was dead and that he was holding her up, all the assembled birthday party guests shouted *"Surprise!"*

Nightmare in Green

He awoke with full recollection of the decision, the big decision, he had made while lying here trying to go to sleep the night before. The decision that he must hold to without weakening if ever again he was to think of himself as a man, a whole man. He must be firm in demanding that his wife give him a divorce or all was lost and he would never again have the courage. It had been inevitable, he saw now, from the very start of their marriage six years ago, that this turning point, this tide of his affairs, would come.

To be married to a woman stronger than himself, stronger in every way, was not only intolerable but had been making him progressively more and more a helpless weakling, a hopeless mouse. His wife could, and did, best him at everything. An athlete, she could beat him easily at golf, at tennis, at everything. She could outride him and outhike him; she could drive a car better than he'd ever be able to. Expert at almost everything, she could make a fool of him at bridge or chess, even poker, which she played like a man. Worse, she had gradually taken over the reins of his business and financial affairs and could and did make more money than he had ever made or hoped to make. There was no way in which his ego, what little was left of it, had not been bruised and battered over the years of their marriage.

Until now, until Laura had come along. Sweet, lovable little Laura who was their house guest this week and who was everything that his wife was not, fragile and dainty, adorably helpless and sweet. He was mad about her and knew that in her lay salvation for him. Married to Laura he could be a man again, and would be. And she would marry him, he felt sure; she *had* to for she was his only hope. This time he *had* to win, no matter what his wife said or did.

He showered and dressed quickly, dreading the coming scene with his wife but eager to get it over with while his courage lasted. He went downstairs and found his wife alone at the breakfast table.

She looked up as he came in. "Good morning, dear," she said. "Laura has finished breakfast and gone for a walk. I asked her to, so I could talk to you privately."

Good, he thought, sitting down across from her. His wife *had* seen what had been happening to him and was making things easier by bringing up the subject herself.

"You see, William," she said, "I want a divorce. I know this will come as a shock to you, but—Laura and I are in love with each other and are going away together."

Nightmare in White

He awoke suddenly and completely, wondering why he had let himself drop off when he hadn't meant to, and quickly glanced at the luminous dial of his wrist watch. It gleamed brightly in the otherwise utter darkness and told him that the time was only a few minutes after eleven o'clock. He relaxed; he'd taken only a very brief catnap. He'd gone to bed here, on this silly sofa, less than half an hour ago. If his wife really was going to come to him, it was too early. She'd have to wait until she was positive that his damned sister was asleep, and sound asleep.

It was such a ridiculous situation. They'd been married only three weeks, were on their way back home from their honeymoon, and this was the first time he'd slept alone in that time—and all because of his sister Deborah's absurd insistence that they spend the night in her apartment here on their way back home. Another four hours' driving would have got them there, but Debbie had insisted and finally carried her point. After all, he'd realized, a night's continence wouldn't hurt him, and he *had* been tired; it would be much better to face his last lap of driving fresh, in the morning.

Of course Debbie's apartment had only the one bedroom and he knew in advance, before accepting her invitation, that he could not possibly have accepted her offer to sleep, herself, out here and let him and Betty have the bedroom. There are degrees of hospitality which one cannot accept, even from one's own sweet and loving spinster sister. But he'd felt sure, or almost sure, that Betty would wait out his sister's going to sleep and come to join him, if only for a few affectionate moments—for she might be inhibited in giving more than that lest sounds might awaken Debbie—to give him a better "good night" than, under his sister's eyes, they'd indulged in.

Surely she'd come to him—at least for a *real* good-night kiss, and if she was willing to risk going beyond that, so was he—and so he'd decided not to go to sleep right away, but to wait for her to come to him, at least for an hour or so.

Surely she would—yes, the door was opening quietly in the darkness and quietly closing again, only the faint click of the latch being really audible, and then there was the soft rustle of her nightgown or negligee or whatever falling, and she was under the covers with him, pressing her body against his, and the only conversation was his whispered "Darling ..." and her whispered "Shhhh ..." But what more conversation was needed?

None at all, none at all, but for the so-long so-short minutes until the door opened again, this time with glaring white light coming through it, outlining in white horror the silhouette of his wife standing there rigid and beginning to scream.

The Short Happy Lives of Eustace Weaver I

When Eustace Weaver invented his time machine he was a very happy man. He knew that he had the world by the tail on a downhill pull, as long as he kept his invention a secret. He could become the richest man in the world, wealthy beyond the dreams of avarice. All he had to do was to take short trips into the future to learn what stocks had gone up and which horses had won races, then come back to the present and buy those stocks or bet on those horses.

The races would come first of course because he would need a lot of capital to play the market, whereas, at a track, he could start with a two-dollar bet and quickly parlay it into the thousands. But it would have to be at a track; he'd too quickly break any bookie he played with, and besides he didn't know any bookies. Unfortunately the only tracks operating at the present were in Southern California and in Florida, about equidistant and about a hundred dollars' worth of plane fare away. He didn't have a fraction of that sum, and it would take him weeks to save that much out of his salary as stock clerk at a supermarket. It would be horrible to have to wait that long, even to start getting rich.

Suddenly he remembered the safe at the supermarket where he worked—an afternoon-evening shift from one o'clock until the market closed at nine. There'd be at least a thousand dollars in that safe, and it had a time lock. What could be better than a time machine to beat a time lock.

When he went to work that day he took his machine with him; it was quite compact and he'd designed it to fit into a camera case he already had so there was no difficulty involved in bringing it into the store, and when he put his coat and hat into his locker he put the time machine there too.

He worked his shift as usual until a few minutes before closing time. Then he hid behind a pile of cartons in the stock room. He felt sure that in the general exodus he wouldn't be missed, and he wasn't. Just the same he waited in his hiding place almost a full hour to make sure everyone else had left. Then he emerged, got his time machine from the locker, and went to the safe. The safe was set to unlock itself automatically in another eleven hours; he set his time machine for just that length of time.

He took a good grip on the safe's handle—he'd learned by an experiment or two that anything he wore, carried, or hung onto traveled with him in time—and pressed the stud.

He felt no transition, but suddenly he heard the safe's mechanism click open—but at the same moment heard gasps and excited voices behind him. And he whirled, suddenly realizing the mistake he'd made; it was nine o'clock the next morning and the store's employees—those on the early shift—were already there, had missed the safe and had been standing in a wondering semi-circle about the spot where it had stood—when the safe and Eustace Weaver had suddenly appeared.

Luckily he still had the time machine in his hand. Quickly he turned the dial to zero—which he had calibrated to be the exact moment when he had completed it—and pressed the stud.

And, of course, he was back before he had started and ...

The Short Happy Lives of Eustace Weaver II

When Eustace Weaver invented his time machine he knew that he had the world by the tail on a downhill pull, as long as he kept his invention a secret. To become rich all he had to do was take short trips into the future to see what horses were going to win and what stocks were going up, then come back and bet the horses or buy the stocks.

The horses came first because they would require less capital—but he didn't have even two dollars to make a bet, let alone plane fare to the nearest track where horses were running.

He thought of the safe in the supermarket where he worked as a stock clerk. That safe had at least a thousand dollars in it, and it had a time lock. A time lock should be duck soup for a time machine.

So when he went to work that day he took his time machine with him in a camera case and left it in his locker. When they closed at nine he hid out in the stock room and waited an hour till he was sure everyone else had left. Then he got the time machine from his locker and went with it to the safe.

He set the machine for eleven hours ahead—and then had a second thought. That setting would take him to nine o'clock the next morning. The safe would click open then, but the store would be opening too and there'd be people around. So instead he set the machine for twenty-four hours, took hold of the handle of the safe and then pressed the button on the time machine.

At first he thought nothing had happened. Then he found that the handle of the safe worked when he turned it and he knew that he'd made the jump to evening of the next day. And of course the time mechanism of the safe had unlocked it en route. He opened the safe and took all the paper money in it, stuffing it into various pockets.

He went to the alley door to let himself out, but before he reached for the bolt that kept it locked from the inside he had a sudden brilliant thought. If instead of leaving by a door he left by using his time machine he'd not only increase the mystery by leaving the store tightly locked and thereby increasing the mystery, but he'd be taking himself back in time as well as in place to the moment of his completing the time machine, a day and a half *before* the robbery.

And by the time the robbery took place he could be soundly alibied; he'd be staying at a hotel in Florida or California, in either case over a thousand miles from the scene of the crime. He hadn't thought of his time machine as a producer of alibis, but now he saw that it was perfect for the purpose.

He dialed his time machine to zero and pressed the button.

The Short Happy Lives of Eustace Weaver III

When Eustace Weaver invented his time machine he knew that he had the world by the tail on a downhill pull, as long as he kept his invention a secret. By playing the races and the stock market he could make himself fabulously wealthy in no time at all. The only catch was that he was flat broke.

Suddenly he remembered the store where he worked and the safe in it that worked with a time lock. A time lock should be no sweat at all for a man who had a time machine.

He sat down on the edge of his bed to think. He reached into his pocket for his cigarettes and pulled them out—but with them came paper money, a handful of ten-dollar bills! He tried other pockets and found money in each and every one. He stacked it on the bed beside him, and by counting the big bills and estimating the smaller ones, he found he had approximately fourteen hundred dollars.

Suddenly he realized the truth, and laughed. He had *already* gone forward in time and emptied the supermarket safe and then had used the time machine to return to the point in time where he had invented it. And since the burglary had not yet, in normal time, occurred, all he had to do was get the hell out of town and be a thousand miles away from the scene of the crime when it did happen.

Two hours later he was on a plane bound for Los Angeles—and the Santa Anita track—and doing some heavy thinking. One thing that he had not anticipated was the apparent fact that when he took a jaunt into the future and came back he had no memory of whatever it was that hadn't happened yet.

But the money had come back with him. So, then, would notes written to himself, or Racing Forms or financial pages from newspapers? It would work out.

In Los Angeles he took a cab downtown and checked in at a good hotel. It was late evening by then and he briefly considered jumping himself into the next day to save waiting time, but he realized that he was tired and sleepy. He went to bed and slept until almost noon the next day.

His taxi got tangled in a jam on the freeway so he didn't get to the track at Santa Anita until the first race was over but he was in time to read the winner's number on the tote board and to check it on his dope sheet. He watched five more races, not betting but checking the winner of each race and decided not to bother with the last race. He left the grandstand and walked around behind and under it, a secluded spot where no one could see him. He set the dial of his time machine two hours back, and pressed the stud.

But nothing happened. He tried again with the same result and then a voice behind him said, "It won't work. It's in a deactivating field."

He whirled around and there standing right behind him were two tall, slender young men, one blond and the other dark, and each of them with a hand in one pocket as though holding a weapon.

"We are Time Police," the blond one said, "from the twenty-fifth century. We have come to punish you for illegal use of a time machine."

"B-b-but," Weaver sputtered, "h-how could I have known that racing was—" His voice got a little stronger. "Besides I haven't made any bets yet."

"That is true," the blond young man said. "And when we find any inventor of a time machine using it to win at any form of gambling, we give him warning the first time. But we've traced you back and found out your very first use of the time machine was to steal money from a store. And that is a crime in any century." He pulled from his pocket something that looked vaguely like a pistol.

Eustace Weaver took a step backward. "Y-you don't mean—"

"I do mean," said the blond young man, and he pulled the trigger. And this time, with the machine deactivated, it was the end for Eustace Weaver.

Bright Beard

She had been frightened, badly frightened, ever since her father had given her in marriage to the strange big man with the bright beard.

There was something so—so sinister about him, about his great strength, about his hawklike eyes and the way they watched her. And there was that rumor—but of course it was *only* a rumor—that he'd had other wives and that nobody knew what had happened to them. And there was that strange business of the closet which he had warned her that she must never enter or even look into.

Until today she had obeyed him—especially after she had tried the door of the closet and found that it was kept locked.

But now she stood in front of it with the key, or what she felt sure was the key, in her hand. It was a key she had found only an hour ago in her husband's den; it had no doubt dropped from one of his pockets, and it looked just the right size for the keyhole of the door to the forbidden closet.

She tried it now and it *was* the right key; the door opened. Inside the closet was—not what she had, however subconsciously, feared to find, but something more bewildering. Bank upon bank of what looked like tremendously complicated electronic equipment.

"Well, my dear," said a sardonic voice from just behind her, "do you know what it is?"

She whirled to face her husband. "Why—I think it's—it looks like—"

"Exactly, my dear. It's a radio, but an extremely powerful one which can transmit and receive over interplanetary distances. With it I can and do communicate with the planet Venus. You see, my dear, I am a Venusian."

"But I don't under—"

"You don't have to understand, but I may as well tell you—now. I am a Venusian spy, advance guard, as it were, for a pending invasion of Earth. What did you think? That my beard is blue and that you would find a closet of murdered former wives? I know that you are color-blind, but surely your father told you my beard is red?"

"Of course, but—"

"But your father was wrong. He saw it as red, since whenever I leave the house I dye my hair and beard red, with an easily removable dye. At home, however, I prefer to have it its natural color, which is green. That is why I chose a color-blind wife, since she would not notice the difference.

"That is why all of my wives have been chosen, because they were color-blind." He sighed deeply. "Alas, regardless of the color of my beard, sooner or later each one of them became too curious, too inquisitive, as you have. But I do not keep them in a closet; they are all buried in the cellar."

His terribly strong hand closed about her upper arm. "Come, my dear, and I will show you their graves."

Cat Burglar

The Chief of Police of Midland City owned two dachshunds, one of which was named Little Note and the other Long Remember. But this fact has nothing at all to do with cats or cat burglars, and this story concerns the concern of the said Chief of Police over a seemingly inexplicable series of burglaries—a one-man crime wave.

The burglar had broken and entered nineteen houses or apartments within a period of a few weeks. Apparently he cased his jobs carefully, since it could not have been coincidence that in each and every house he burglarized there was a cat.

He stole only the cat.

Sometimes there had been money lying loose in sight, sometimes jewelry; he ignored them. Returning householders would find a window or door forced, and their cat missing, nothing else was ever stolen or disturbed.

It was for this reason that—if we wish to belabor the obvious, and we do so wish—the newspapers and the public came to call him the Cat Burglar.

Not until his twentieth—and first unsuccessful— burglary attempt was he caught. With the help of the newspapers, the police had set a trap by publicizing the fact that the owners of a prize-winning Siamese cat had just returned with it from a cat show in a nearby city, where it won not only the best-of-breed prize, but the much more prized prize for the best of show.

Once this story, accompanied by a beautiful picture of the animal, had appeared in the newspapers, the police staked out the house and had the owners of it leave, and in an obvious manner.

Only two hours later the burglar appeared, broke into the house and entered it. They caught him cold on his way out, with the champion Siamese under his arm.

Downtown at the police station, they questioned him. The Chief of Police was curious, and so were the listening reporters.

To their surprise, the burglar was able to give a perfectly logical and understandable explanation of the unusual and specialized nature of his thefts. They didn't release him, of course, and eventually he was tried, but he received an exceedingly light sentence since even the judge agreed that, although his method of acquiring cats had been illegal, his purpose in acquiring them had been laudable.

He was an amateur scientist. For research in his field, he needed cats. The stolen cats he had taken home and put mercifully into eternal rest. Then he had cremated the cats in a small crematory which he had built for the purpose.

He had put their ashes in jars and was experimenting with them, pulverizing them to various degrees of fineness, treating different batches in different ways, and then pouring hot water over them. He had been trying to discover the formula for instant pussy.

Dead Letter

Laverty stepped through the open French windows and crossed the carpet silently until he stood behind the gray-haired man working at the desk. "Hello, Congressman," he said.

Congressman Quinn turned his head and then rose shakily as he saw the revolver Laverty was pointing at him. "Laverty," he said. "Don't be a fool."

Laverty grinned. "I told you I'd do this someday. I've waited four years. It's safe now."

"You won't get away with it, Laverty. I left a letter, a letter to be delivered in case I'm ever killed."

Laverty laughed. "You're lying, Quinn. You couldn't have written such a letter without incriminating yourself by telling my motive. Why, you wouldn't want me tried and convicted—because the truth would come out, and it would blacken your name forever."

Laverty pulled the trigger six times.

He went back to his car, drove over a bridge to rid himself of the murder weapon, then home to his apartment and to bed.

He slept peacefully until his doorbell rang. He slipped on a bathrobe, went to the door and opened it.

His heart stood still, and stayed that way.

The man who had rung Laverty's doorbell had been surprised and shocked, but he had done the right thing. He had stepped over Laverty's body into the apartment and had used the phone there to call police emergency. And he had waited.

Now, Laverty having been pronounced dead by the emergency squad, the man was being questioned by a lieutenant of police.

"Your name?" the lieutenant asked.

"Babcock. Henry Babcock. I had a letter to deliver to Mr. Laverty. This letter."

The lieutenant took it, hesitated a moment, and then opened and unfolded it. "Why, it's just a blank sheet of paper."

"I don't know about that, Lieutenant. My boss, Congressman Quinn, gave me that letter a long time ago. My orders were to deliver it to Laverty right away if anything unusual ever happened to Congressman Quinn. So when I heard on the radio—"

"Yes, I know. He was found murdered late this evening. What kind of work did you do for him?"

"Well, it was secret, but I don't suppose the secret matters now. I used to take his place for unimportant speeches and meetings he wanted to avoid. You see, Lieutenant, I'm his double."

Death on the Mountain

He lived in a hut on the side of a mountain. Often he would climb to the peak and look down into the valley. His red sandals were drops of blood upon the snow of the peak.

In the valley people lived and died. He watched them.

He saw the clouds that drifted over the peak. The clouds took strange shapes. At times they were ships or castles or horses. More often they were strange things never seen by anyone save him, and he had seen them only in his dreams. Yet in the strange shapes of drifting clouds he recognized them.

Standing alone in the doorway of his hut, he always watched the sun spring from the dew of earth. In the valley they had told him that the sun did not rise but that the earth was round like an orange and turned so that every morning the burning sun seemed to leap into the sky.

He had asked them why the earth revolved and why the sun burned and why they did not fall from the earth when it turned upside down. He had been told that it was so today because it had been so yesterday and the day that was before yesterday, and because things never changed. They could not tell him why things never changed.

At night he looked at the stars and at the lights of the valley. At curfew the lights of the valley vanished, but the stars did not vanish. They were too far to hear the curfew bell.

There was a bright star. Every third night it hung low just above the snow-covered peak of the mountain, and he would climb to the peak and talk to it. The star never replied.

He counted time by the star and by the three days of its progress. Three days made a week. To the people of the valley, seven days made a week. They had never dreamed of the land of Saarba where water flows upstream, where the leaves of trees burn with a bright blue flame and are not consumed, and where three days make a week.

Once a year he went down into the valley. He talked with people, and sometimes he would dream for them. They called him a prophet, but the small children threw sticks at him. He did not like children, for in their faces he could see written the evil that they were to live.

It had been a year since he had last been to the valley, and he left his hut and went down the mountain. He went to the market and talked to people, but no one spoke to him or looked at him. He shouted but they did not reply.

He reached with his hand to touch a market woman upon the shoulder to arrest her attention, but the hand passed through the woman's shoulder and the woman walked on. He knew then that he had died within the past year.

He returned to the mountain. Beside the path he saw a thing that lay where once he had fallen and had risen and walked on. He turned when he reached the doorway of his hut, and saw the people of the valley carrying away the thing which he had passed. They dug a grave in the earth and buried the thing.

The days passed.

From the doorway of his hut he watched the clouds drift by the mountain. The clouds took strange shapes. At times they were birds or swords or elephants. More often they were strange things never seen save by him. He had dreamed of seeing them in the land of Saarba where bread is made of stardust, where sixteen pounds make an ounce, and where clocks run backward after dark.

Two women climbed the mountain and walked through him into the hut. They looked about them.

—They be nothing here, said the elder of the women. —Where might be his sandals I ken not.

—Go ye back, said the younger woman. —Late it grows. Come sunrise, I will find they.

—Be ye not afraid?

—The shepherd cares for his sheep, said the young woman.

The older woman trudged down the path into the valley. Darkness fell, and the younger lighted a candle. She seemed afraid of the darkness.

He watched her, but she saw him not. Her hair, he saw, was black as night, and her eyes were large and lustrous, but her ankles were thick.

She removed her garments and lay upon the bed. In sleep, she tossed uneasily, and the blanket slipped to the floor. The candle still burned upon the table.

The light of the candle flame fell upon a small black crucifix that lay in the white hollow between her breasts. It rose and fell.

He heard the curfew bell and knew that it was time to go to the top of the peak, for it was the third night.

Upon the mountain had descended a storm. The wind shrieked about the hut but the woman did not awaken.

He went out into the storm. The wind was cruel as never before. The hand of fear gripped his heart. Yet the star was waiting.

The cold grew more intense, the night blacker. A blanket of snow drifted over the mountain, covering the spot where he fell.

In the morning the woman found the red sandals in the thawing snow and took them back to the valley.

—A strange dream I had, said the elder woman. —A man writhed on a cross.

The younger woman crossed herself. —The Christus?

—Not, said the elderly woman. —Shouted he about Saarba and oblivion.

—I ken them not, said the younger woman. —They be no such places.

—That shouted he, said the elder. —Remember I now.

—La, laughed the younger woman. —Dreams be only dreams. Things what be be and things what be not be not.

—So, said the elder. She shrugged.

Clouds take strange shapes. At times they are wagons or swans or trees. More often they are strange things never seen save in the land of Saarba.

Clouds are impersonal. They drift by an empty peak as readily.

Fatal Error

Mr. Walter Baxter had long been an avid reader of crime and detective stories, so when he decided to murder his uncle he knew that he must not make a single error.

And that, to avoid the possibility of making an error, simplicity must be the keynote. Utter simplicity. No arranging of an alibi that might be broken. No complicated *modus operandi*. No red herrings.

Well—one small herring. A very simple one. He'd have to rob his uncle's house, too, of whatever cash it contained so the murder would appear to have been incidental to a burglary. Otherwise, as his uncle's only heir, he himself would be too obvious a suspect.

He took his time in acquiring a small crowbar in such a manner that it could not possibly be traced to him. It would serve him both as a tool and a weapon.

He planned carefully every trifling detail, knowing he dared make no single error and certain that he would not. He chose the night and the hour with care.

The crowbar opened a window easily and without noise. He entered the living room. The door to the bedroom was ajar, but as no sound came from it he decided to get the details of burglary over with first. He knew where his uncle kept the cash, but he'd have to make it look as though a search had been made. There was enough moonlight to let him see his way; he moved silently ...

At home two hours later he undressed quickly and got into bed. No chance of the police learning of the crime before tomorrow, but he was ready if they did come sooner. The money and the crowbar had been disposed of; it had hurt him to destroy several hundred dollars but it was the only safe way, and it would be nothing to the fifty thousand or more he'd inherit.

There was a knock at the door. Already? He made himself calm; he went to the door and opened it. The sheriff and a deputy pushed their way in.

"Walter Baxter? Warrant for your arrest. Dress and come with us."

"A warrant for my arrest? What *for?*"

"Burglary and grand larceny. Your uncle saw and recognized you from the bedroom doorway—stayed quiet till you left and then came downtown and swore out—"

Walter Baxter's jaw dropped. He *had* made an error after all.

He'd planned the perfect murder but, in his engrossment with the burglary, had forgotten to commit it.

Fish Story

Robert Palmer met his mermaid one midnight along the ocean front somewhere between Cape Cod and Miami. He was staying with friends but had not yet felt sleepy when they retired and had gone for a walk along the brightly moonlit beach. He rounded a curve in the shoreline and there she was, sitting on a log embedded in the sand, combing her beautiful, long black hair.

Robert knew, of course, that mermaids don't really exist—but, extant or not, there she was. He walked closer and when he was only a few steps away he cleared his throat.

With a startled movement she threw back her hair, which had been hiding her face and her breasts, and he saw that she was more beautiful than he had thought it possible for any creature to be.

She stared at him, her deep-blue eyes wide with fright at first. Then, "Are you a man?" she asked.

Robert didn't have any doubts on that point; he assured her that he was. The fear went out of her eyes and she smiled. "I've heard of men but never met one." She motioned for him to sit down beside her on the embedded log.

Robert didn't hesitate. He sat down and they talked and talked, and after a while his arm went around her and when at last she said that she must return to the sea, he kissed her good night and she promised to meet him again the next midnight.

He went back to his friends' house in a bright daze of happiness. He was in love.

For three nights in a row he saw her, and on the third night he told her that he loved her, that he would like to marry her—but that there was a problem—

"I love you too, Robert. And the problem you have in mind can be solved. I'll summon a Triton."

"Triton? I seem to know the word, but—"

"A sea demon. He has magical powers and can change things for us so we can marry, and then he'll marry us. Can you swim well? We'll have to swim out to meet him; Tritons never come quite to the shore."

He assured her that he was an excellent swimmer, and she promised to have the Triton there the next night.

He went back to his friends' house in a state of ecstasy. He didn't know whether the Triton would change his beloved into a human being or change him into a merman, but he didn't care. He was so mad about her that as long as they would both be the same, and able to marry, he didn't care in which form it would be.

She was waiting for him the next night, their wedding night. "Sit down," she told him. "The Triton will blow his conch shell trumpet when he arrives."

They sat with their arms around each other until they heard the sound of a conch shell trumpet blowing far out on the water. Robert quickly stripped off his clothes and carried her into the water; they swam until they reached the Triton. Robert treaded water while the Triton asked them, "Do you wish to be joined in marriage?" They each said a fervent "I do."

"Then," said the Triton, "I pronounce you merman and merwife." And Robert found himself no longer treading water; a few movements of a strong sinuous tail kept him at the surface easily. The Triton blew a note on his conch shell trumpet, deafening at so close a range, and swam away.

Robert swam to his wife's side, put his arms around her and kissed her. But something was wrong; the kiss was pleasant but there was no real thrill, no stirring in his loins as there had been when he had kissed her on shore. In fact, he suddenly realized, he *had* no loins that he could detect. But how—?

"But how—?" he asked her. "I mean, darling, how do we—?"

"Propagate? It's simple, dear, and nothing like the messy way land creatures do it. You see, mermaids are mammalian but oviparous. I lay an egg when the time comes and when it hatches I nurse our merchild. Your part—"

"Yes?" asked Robert anxiously.

"Like other fishes, dear. You simply swim over the egg and fertilize it. There's nothing to it."

Robert groaned, and suddenly deciding to drown himself, he let go of his bride and started swimming toward the bottom of the sea.

But of course he had gills and didn't drown.

Horse Race

Garn Roberts, also known—but only to the Galactic Federation's top security officers—as Secret Agent K-1356, was sleeping in his one-man spaceship which was coasting at fourteen light-years an hour on automatics two hundred and six light-years from Earth. A bell rang, instantly awakening him. He hurried to the telecom and turned it on. The face of Daunen Brand, Special Assistant to the President of the Federation, sprang onto the screen, and Brand's voice came from the speaker.

"K-1356, I have an assignment for you. Do you know the sun called Novra, in the constellation—"

"Yes," Roberts said quickly; communication at this distance was wasteful power, especially on tight beam, and he wanted to save the Special Assistant all the time he could.

"Good. Do you know its planetary system?"

"I've never been there. I know Novra has two inhabited planets, that's all."

"Right. The inner planet is inhabited by a humanoid race, not too far from ours. The outer planet is inhabited by a race who are outwardly similar to terrestrial horses except that they have a third pair of limbs which terminate in hands, which has enabled them to reach a fairly high state of civilization. Their name for themselves is unpronounceable for Earthmen, so we call them simply the Horses. They know the derivation of the name, but don't mind; they're not sensitive that way."

"Yes, sir," said Roberts, as Brand paused.

"Both races have space travel, although not the faster-than-light interstellar drive. Between the two planets—you can look up the names and coordinates in the star guide—is an asteroid belt similar to that of the solar system, but even more extensive, the residue of the break-up of a large planet that had once had its orbit between the orbits of the two inhabited planets.

"Neither inhabited planet has much in the way of minerals; the asteroids are rich with them and are the major source of supply for both planets. A hundred years ago they went to war over this, and the Galactic Federation arbitrated the war and ended it by getting both races, the Humanoids and the Horses, to agree that one individual of either race could stake claim, for his lifetime, to one asteroid and only one asteroid."

"Yes, sir. I remember reading about it in Galactic history."

"Excellent. Here is the problem. We have a complaint from the Humanoids claiming that the Horses are breaking this treaty, claiming asteroids under false names of nonexistent Horses in order to get more than their share of the minerals.

"Your orders: Land on the Horses' planet. Use your trader identity; it will not be suspect since many traders go there. They are friendly; you'll have no trouble. You'll be welcome as a trader from Earth. You are to prove or disprove the assertion of the Humanoids that the Horses are violating the treaty by staking claims to more asteroids than their numbers justify."

"Yes, sir."

"You will report back to me by tight beam as soon as you have accomplished your mission and left the planet." The screen went blank. Garn Roberts consulted his guides and charts, reset the automatic controls and went back to his bunk to resume his interrupted sleep.

A week later, when he had accomplished his mission and was a safe ten light-years out from the Novra system, he sent a tight-beam signal to the Special Assistant to the President of the Galactic Federation, and in minutes Daunen Brand's face appeared on the screen of the telecom.

"K-1356 reporting on the Novra situation, sir," Garn Roberts said. "I managed to get access to the census statistics of the Horses; they number a little over two million. Then I checked the claims of the Horses to Asteroids; they have filed claims on almost four million of them. It is obvious that the Humanoids are right and that the Horses are violating the treaty.

"Otherwise, why are there so many more Horses' asteroids than there are Horses?"

The House

He hesitated upon the porch and looked a last long look upon the road behind him and the green trees that grew beside it and the yellow fields and the distant hill and the bright sunlight. Then he opened the door and entered and the door swung shut behind him.

He turned as it clicked and saw only blank wall. There was no knob and no keyhole, and the edges of the door, if there were edges, were so cunningly fitted into the carven paneling that he could not discern its outline.

Before him lay the cobwebbed hallway. The floor was thick with dust and through the dust wound two so slender curving trails as might have been made by two very small snakes or two very large caterpillars. They were very faint trails and he did not notice them until he was opposite the first doorway to the right, upon which was the inscription *Semper Fidelis* in old English lettering.

Beyond this door he found himself in a small red room, no larger than a large closet. A single chair in this room lay on its side, one leg broken and dangling by a thin splinter. On the nearest wall the only picture was a framed portrait of Benjamin Franklin. It hung askew and the glass covering it was cracked. There was no dust upon the floor and the room appeared to have been recently cleaned. In the center of the floor lay a bright curved scimitar. There were red stains upon its hilt, and upon the edge of the blade was a thick coating of green ooze. Aside from these things the room was empty.

After he had stood in this room for a long time, he crossed the hallway and entered the room opposite. It was large, the size of a small auditorium, but the bare black walls made it seem smaller at a first glance. There was row upon row of purple-plush theater seats, but there was no stage or platform and the rows of seats started only a few inches from the blank wall they faced. There was nothing else in the room, but upon the nearest seat lay a neat pile of programs. One of these he took and found it blank save for two advertisements on the back cover, one for Prophylactic toothbrushes and the other for choice building lots in the Sub Rosa Subdivision. Upon a page near the front of the program he saw that someone had written with a lead pencil the word or name *Garfinkle.*

He thrust the program into his pocket and returned to the hallway, along which he walked in search of the stairs.

Behind one closed door which he passed he heard someone, obviously an amateur, picking out tunes on what sounded like a Hawaiian guitar. He knocked upon this door but a scurrying of footsteps and silence was the only answer. When he opened the door and peered within he saw only a decaying corpse hanging from the chandelier, and an odor hurled itself upon him so nauseating that he closed the door hastily, and walked on to the stairway.

The stairway was narrow and winding. There was no banister, and he clung close to the wall as he ascended. He saw that the first seven steps from the bottom had been scrubbed clean but in the dust above the seventh step he saw again the two winding trails. Upon the third step from the top they converged, and vanished.

He entered the first door to his right and found himself in a spacious bedroom, lavishly furnished. He crossed immediately to the carven poster bed and pulled aside the curtains. The bed was neatly made, and he saw a slip of paper pinned to the smoothed pillow. Upon it was written hastily in a woman's handwriting, *Denver, 1909.* Upon the reverse side, neatly written in ink in another handwriting, was an algebraic equation.

He left this room quietly and stopped short just outside the door to listen to a sound that came from behind a black doorway across the hall.

It was the deep voice of a man chanting in a strange and unfamiliar tongue. It rose and fell in a monotonous cadence like a Buddhist hymn, yet over and over recurred the word *Ragnarok.* The word seemed vaguely familiar, and the voice sounded like his own voice, but muffled by many things.

With bowed head he stood until the voice died away into a blue trembling silence and twilight crept into the hallway with the stealth of a practiced thief.

Then as though awakening, he walked along the now-silent hallway until he came to the third and last door and he saw that they had printed his name upon the upper panel in tiny letters of gold. Perhaps radium had been mixed with the gold for the letters glowed in the hallway's dimness.

He stood for a long moment with his hand upon the knob, and then at last he entered and closed the door behind him. He heard the click of the latch and knew that it would never open again, yet he felt no fear.

The darkness was a black tangible thing that sprang back from him when he struck a match. He saw then that the room was a counterpart of the east bedroom of his father's house near Wilmington, the room in which he had been born. He knew, now, just where to look for candles. There were two in the drawer, and the stump of a third, and he knew that, burned one at a time, they would last for almost ten hours. He lighted the first and stood it in the brass bracket on the wall, from whence it cast dancing shadows from each chair, from the bed, and from the small waiting cradle that stood beside the bed.

Upon the table beside his mother's sewing basket lay the March 1887 issue of *Harper's,* and he took up the magazine and glanced idly through its pages.

At length he dropped it to the floor and thought tenderly of his wife who had died many years ago, and a faint smile trembled upon his lips as he remembered a dozen little incidents of the years of days and nights they had spent together. He thought, too, of many other things.

It was not until the ninth hour when but half an inch of candle remained and darkness began to gather in the farther corners of the room and to creep closer, that he screamed, and beat and clawed at the door until his hands were a raw and bloody pulp.

The Joke

The big man in the flashy green suit stuck his big hand across the cigar counter. "Jim Greeley," he said. "Ace Novelty Company." The cigar dealer took the offered hand and then jerked convulsively as something inside it buzzed painfully against his own palm.

The big man's cheerful laughter boomed. "Our Joy Buzzer," he said, turning over his hand to expose the little metal contraption in his palm. "Changes a shake to a shock; one of the best numbers we got. A dilly, ain't it? Gimme four of those perfectos, the two-for-a-quarters. Thanks."

He put a half-dollar on the counter and then, concealing a grin, lighted one of the cigars while the dealer tried vainly to pick up the coin. Then, laughing, the big man put another—and an ungimmicked—coin on the counter and pried up the first one with a tricky little knife on one end of his watch chain. He put it back in a special little box that went into his vest pocket. He said, "A new number—but a pretty good one. It's a good laugh, and—well, 'Anything for a Gag' is Ace's motto and me, I'm Ace's salesman."

The cigar dealer said, "I couldn't handle—"

"Not trying to sell you anything," the big man said. "I just sell wholesale. But I get a kick out of showing off our merchandise. You ought to see some of it."

He blew a ring of cigar smoke and strolled on past the cigar counter to the hotel desk. "Double with bath," he told the clerk. "Got a reservation—Jim Greeley. Stuff's being sent over from the station, and my wife'll be here later."

He took a fountain pen from his pocket, ignoring the one the clerk offered him, and signed the card. The ink was bright blue, but it was going to be a good joke on the clerk when, a little later, he tried to file that card and found it completely blank. And when he explained and wrote a new card it would be both a good laugh and good advertising for Ace Novelty.

"Leave the key in the box," he said. "I won't go up now. Where are the phones?"

He strolled to the row of phone booths to which the desk clerk directed him and dialed a number. A feminine voice answered.

"This is the police," he said gruffly. "We've had reports that you've been renting rooms to crooked boarders. Or were those only false roomers?"

"Jim! Oh, I'm so glad you're in town!"

"So'm I, sweetie. Is the coast clear, your husband away? Wait, don't tell me; you wouldn't have said what you just said if he'd been there, would you? What time does he get home?"

"Nine o'clock, Jim. You'll pick me up before then? I'll leave him a note that I'm staying with my sister because she's sick."

"Swell, honey. What I hoped you'd say. Let's see; it's half-past five. I'll be right around."

"Not that soon, Jim. I've got things to do, and I'm not dressed. Make it—not before eight o'clock. Between then and half-past eight."

"Okay, honey. Eight it is. That'll give us time for a big evening, and I've already registered double."

"How'd you know I'd be able to get away?"

The big man laughed. "Then I'd have called one of the others in my little black book. Now don't get mad; I was only kidding. I'm calling from the hotel, but I haven't actually registered yet; I was only kidding. One thing I like about you, Marie, you got a sense of humor; you can take it. Anybody I like's got to have a sense of humor like I have."

"Anybody you *like?*"

"And anybody I love. To pieces. What's your husband like, Marie? Has *he* got a sense of humor?"

"A little. A crazy kind of one; not like yours. Got any new numbers in your line?"

"Some dillies. I'll show you. One of 'em's a trick camera that—well, I'll show you. And don't worry, honey. I remember you told me you got a tricky ticker and I won't pull any scary tricks on you. Won't scare you, honey; just the opposite."

"You big goof! Okay, Jim, not before eight o'clock now. But plenty before nine."

"With bells on, honey. Be seeing you."

He went out of the telephone booth singing "Tonight's My Night with Baby," and straightened his snazzy necktie at a mirror in front of a pillar in the lobby. He ran an exploring palm across his face. Yes, needed a shave; it felt rough even if it didn't show. Well, plenty of time for that in two and a half hours.

He strolled over to where a bellboy sat. "How late you on duty, son?" he asked.

"Till two-thirty, nine hours. I just came on."

"Good. How are rules here on likker? Get it any time?"

"Can't get bottle goods after nine o'clock. That is, well, sometimes you can, but it's taking a chance. Can't I get it for you sooner if you're going to want it?"

"Might as well." The big man took some bills out of his wallet. "Room 603. Put in a fifth of rye and two bottles of soda sometime before nine. I'll phone down for ice cubes when we want 'em. And listen, I want you to help me with a gag. Got any bedbugs or cockroaches?"

"Huh?"

The big man grinned. "Maybe you have and maybe you haven't, but look at these artificial ones. Ain't they beauties?" He took a pillbox from his pocket and opened it.

"Want to play a joke on my wife," he said. "And I won't be up in the room till she gets here. You take these and put 'em where they'll do the most good, see? I mean, peel back the covers and fill the bed with these little beauties.

Don't they look like real ones? She'll really squeal when she sees 'em. Do you like gags, son?"

"Sure."

"I'll show you some good ones when you bring up the ice cubes later. I got a sample case full. Well, do a good job with those bedbugs."

He winked solemnly at the bellboy and sauntered across the lobby and out to the sidewalk.

He strolled into a tavern and ordered rye with a chaser. While the bartender was getting it he went over to the juke box and put a dime in, pushing two buttons. He came back grinning, and whistling "Got a Date with an Angel." The juke box joined in—in the wrong key—with his whistling.

"You look happy," said the bartender. "Most guys come in here to tell their troubles."

"Haven't any troubles," said the big man. "Happier because I found an oldie on your juke box and it fits. Only the angel I got a date with's got a little devil in her too, thank God. Real she devil, too."

He put his hand across the bar. "Shake the hand of a happy man," he said.

The buzzer in his palm buzzed and the bartender jumped.

The big man laughed. "Have a drink with me, pal," he said, "and don't get mad. I like practical jokes. I sell 'em."

The bartender grinned, but not too enthusiastically. He said, "You got the build for it all right. Okay, I'll have a drink with you. Only just a second; there's a hair in that chaser I gave you." He emptied the glass and put it among the dirties, coming back with another one, this one of cut glass of intricate design.

"Nice try," said the big man, "but I told you I *sell* the stuff; I know a dribble glass when I see one. Besides that's an old model. Just one hole on a side and if you get your finger over it, it don't dribble. See, like this. Happy days."

The dribble glass didn't dribble. The big man said, "I'll buy us both another; I like a guy who can dish a job out as well as take one." He chuckled. "*Try* to dish one out, anyway. Pour us another and lemme tell you about some of the new stuff we're gonna put out. New plastic called Skintex that—hey, I got a sample with me. Lookit."

He took from his pocket a rolled-up object that unrolled itself, as he put it on the bar, into a startlingly lifelike false face. The big man said, "Got it all over every kind of mask or false face on the market, even the expensive rubber ones. Fits so close it stays on practically of its own accord. But what's really different about it is by gosh it looks so real you have to look twice and look close to see it ain't the real McCoy. Gonna be an all-year-round seller for costume balls and stuff, and make a fortune every Halloween."

"Sure looks real," said the bartender.

"Bet your boots it does. Comes in all kinds, it will. Got only a few actually in production now, though. This one's the Fancy Dan model, good looking. Pour us two more, huh?"

He rolled up the mask and put it back into his pocket. The juke box had just ended the second number and he fed a quarter into it, again punching "Got a Date with an Angel," but this time waiting to whistle until the record had started, so he'd be in tune with it.

He changed it to patter when he got back to the bar. He said, "Got a date with an angel, all right. Little blonde, Marie Rhymer. A beauty. Purtiest gal in town. Here's to 'er."

This time he forgot to put his finger over the hole in the dribble glass and got spots of water on his snazzy necktie. He looked down at them and roared with laughter. He ordered drinks for the house—not too expensive a procedure, as there was only one other customer and the bartender.

The other customer bought back and the big man bought another round. He showed them two new coin tricks—in one of which he balanced a quarter on the edge of a shot glass after he'd let them examine both the glass and the coin, and he wouldn't tell the bartender how that one was done until the bartender stood a round.

It was after seven when he left the tavern. He wasn't drunk, but he was feeling the drinks. He was really happy now. Ought to grab a bite to eat, he thought.

He looked around for a restaurant, a good one, and then decided no, maybe Marie would be expecting him to take her to dinner; he'd wait to eat until he was with her.

And so what if he got there early? He could wait, he could talk to her while she got ready.

He looked around for a taxi and saw none; he started walking briskly, again whistling "Tonight's My Night with Baby," which hadn't, unfortunately, been on the juke box.

He walked briskly, whistling happily, into the gathering dusk. He was going to be early, but he didn't want to stop for another drink; there'd be plenty of drinking later, and right now he felt just right.

It wasn't until he was a block away that he remembered the shave he'd meant to get. He stopped and felt his face, and yes, he really needed one. Luck was with him, too, because only a few doors back he'd passed a little hole-in-the-wall barber shop. He retraced his steps and found it open. There was one barber and no customers.

He started in, then changed his mind and, grinning happily, went on to the areaway between that building and the next. He took the Skintex mask from his pocket and slipped it over his face; be a good gag to see what the barber would do if he sat down in the chair for a shave with that mask on. He was grinning so broadly he had trouble getting the mask on smoothly, until he straightened out his face.

He walked into the barber shop, hung his hat on the rack and sat down in the chair. His voice only a bit muffled by the flexible mask, he said, "Shave, please."

As the barber, who had taken his stand by the side of the chair, bent closer in incredulous amazement, the big man in the green suit couldn't hold in his laughter any longer. The mask slipped as his laughter boomed out. He took it off and held it out for examination. "Purty lifelike, ain't it?" he asked when he could quit laughing.

"Sure is," said the little barber admiringly. "Say, who makes those?"

"My company. Ace Novelty."

"I'm with a group that puts on amateur theatricals," the barber said. "Say, we could use some of those—for comic roles mainly, if they come in comic faces. Do they?"

"They do. We're manufacturers and wholesalers, of course. But you'll be able to get them at Brachman & Minton's, here in town. I call on 'em tomorrow, and I'll load them up. How's about that shave, meanwhile. Got a date with an angel."

"Sure," said the little man. "Brachman & Minton. We buy most of our make-up and costumes there already. That's fine." He rinsed a towel under the hot-water faucet, wrung it out. He put it over the big man's face and made lather in his shaving cup.

Under the hot towel the man in the green suit was humming "Got a Date with an Angel." The barber took off the towel and applied the lather with deft strokes.

"Yep," said the big man, "got a date with an angel and I'm too damn' early. Gimme the works—massage, anything you got. Wish I could look as handsome with my real face as with that there mask—that's our Fancy Dan model, by the way. Y'oughta see some of the others. Well, you will if you go to Brachman & Minton's about a week from now. Take about that long before they get the merchandise after I take their order tomorrow."

"Yes, sir," said the barber. "You said the works? Massage *and* facial?" He stropped the razor, started its neat clean strokes.

"Why not? Got time. And tonight's my night with baby. *Some* number, pal. Pageboy blonde, built like you-know-what. Runs a rooming house not far from—Say, I got an idea. Good gag."

"What?"

"I'll fool 'er. I'll wear that Fancy Dan mask when I knock on the door and I'll make her think somebody *really* good-looking is calling on her. Maybe it'll be a letdown when she sees my homely mug when I take it off, but the gag'll be good. And I'll bet she won't be *too* disappointed when she sees it's good old Jim. Yep. I'll do that."

The big man chuckled in anticipation. "What time's it?" he asked. He was getting a little sleepy. The shave was over, and the kneading motion of the massage was soporific.

"Ten of eight."

"Good. Lots of time. Just so I get there well before nine. That's when— Say, did that mask really fool you when I walked in with it?"

"Sure did," the barber told him. "Until I bent over you after you sat down."

"Good. Then it'll fool Marie Rhymer when I go up to the door. Say, what's the name of your amatcher theatrical outfit? I'll tell Brachman you'll want some of the Skintex numbers."

"Just the Grove Avenue Social Center group. My name's Dane. Brachman knows me. Sure, tell him we'll take some."

Hot towels, cool creams, kneading fingers. The man in green dozed.

"Okay, mister," the barber said. "You're all set. Be a dollar sixty-five." He chuckled. "I even put your mask on so you're all set. Good luck."

The big man sat up and glanced in the mirror. "Swell," he said. He stood up and took two singles out of his wallet. "That's even now. G'night."

He put on his hat and went out. It was getting dark now and a glance at his wrist watch showed him it was almost eight-thirty, perfect timing.

He started humming again, back this time to "Tonight's My Night with Baby."

He wanted to whistle, but he couldn't do that with the false face on. He stopped in front of the house and looked around before he went up the steps to the door. He chuckled a little as he took the VACANCY sign off the nail beside the door and held it as he pressed the button and heard the bell sound.

Only seconds passed before he heard her footsteps clicking to the door. It opened, and he bowed slightly. His voice muffled by the mask so she wouldn't recognize it, he said, "You haff—a rrrooom, blease?"

She was beautiful, all right, as beautiful as he remembered her from the last time he'd been in town a month before. She said hesitantly, "Why, yes, but I'm afraid I can't show it to you tonight. I'm expecting a friend and I'm late getting ready."

He made a jerky little bow. He said, "Vee, moddomm, I vill rrreturrrn."

And then, jerking his chin forward to loosen the mask and pinching it loose at the forehead so it would come loose with his hat, he lifted hat and mask.

He grinned and started to say—well, it didn't matter what he'd started to say, because Marie Rhymer screamed and then dropped into a crumpled heap of purple silk and cream-colored flesh and blond hair just inside the door.

Stunned, the big man dropped the sign he'd been holding and bent over her. He said, "Marie, honey, what—" and quickly stepped inside and closed the door. He bent down and—remembering her "tricky ticker"—put his hand over where her heart should be beating. *Should* be, but wasn't.

He got out of there quickly. With a wife and kid of his own back in Minneapolis, he couldn't be— Well, he got out.

Still stunned, he walked quickly out.

He came to the barber shop, and it was dark. He stopped in front of the door. The dark glass of the door, with a street light shining against it from across the way, was both transparent and a mirror. In it, he saw three things.

He saw, in the mirror part of the door, the face of horror that was his own face. Bright green, with careful expert shadowing that made it the face of a walking corpse, a ghoul with sunken eyes and cheeks and blue lips. The bright-green face mirrored above the green suit and the snazzy red tie—the face that the make-up-expert barber must have put on him while he'd dozed—

And the note, stuck against the inside of the glass of the barber-shop door, written on white paper in green pencil:

CLOSED

D<small>ANE</small> R<small>HYMER</small>

Marie Rhymer, Dane Rhymer, he thought dully. While *through* the glass, inside the dark barber shop, he could see it dimly—the white-clad figure of the little barber as it dangled from the chandelier and turned slowly, left to right, right to left, left to right ...

The Ring of Hans Carvel

(retold and somewhat modernized from the works of Rabelais)

Once upon a time there lived in France a prosperous but somewhat aging jeweler named Hans Carvel. Besides being a studious and learned man, he was a likable man. And a man who liked women and although he had not lived a celibate life, or missed anything, had happened to remain a bachelor until he was—well, let's call his age as pushing sixty and not mention from which direction he was pushing it.

At that age he fell in love with a bailiff's daughter—a young and a beautiful girl, spirited and vivacious, a dish to set before a king.

And married her.

Within a few weeks of the otherwise happy marriage Hans Carvel began to suspect that his young wife, whom he still loved deeply, might be just a little *too* spirited, a little *too* vivacious. That what he was able to offer her—aside from money, of which he had a sufficiency—might not be enough to keep her contented. *Might* not, did I say? *Was* not.

Not unnaturally he began to suspect, and then to be practically certain, that she was supplementing her love life with several—or possibly even many—other and younger men.

This preyed on his mind. It drove him, in fact, to a state of distraction in which he had bad dreams almost nightly.

In one of these dreams, one night, he found himself talking to the Devil, explaining his dilemma, and offering the traditional price for something, *anything,* that would assure him of his wife's faithfulness.

In his dream, the Devil nodded readily and told Hans: "I will give you a magic ring. You will find it when you awaken. As long as you wear this ring it will be utterly and completely impossible for your wife to be unfaithful to you without your knowledge and consent."

And the Devil vanished and Hans Carvel awakened.

And found that he was indeed wearing a ring, as it were, and that what the Devil had promised him was indeed true.

But his young wife had also awakened and was stirring, and she said to him: "Hans, darling, not your finger. *That* is not what goes *there.*"

Second Chance

Jay and I were in the stands at New Comiskey Field in Chicago to watch the replay of the October 9, 1959, game of the World Series, and play was about to start.

In the original game just exactly five hundred years ago, the Los Angeles Dodgers had won, nine to three, which had ended the series in six games and had given them the championship. Of course it could come out differently this time, although conditions at the start were as near as possible to those of the original game.

The Chicago White Sox were out on the field and the starting players were tossing the ball around the infield a few times before throwing it to Wynn, the starting pitcher, to take his warm-up pitches. Kluszewski was on first, Fox on second, Goodman on third, and Aparicio was playing short. Gilliam was coming up to bat first for the Dodgers, with Neal on deck. Podres would be their starting pitcher.

They were not the original players of those names, of course. They were androids, artificial men who differ from robots in that they are made not of metal but of flexible plastics, powered by laboratory-grown muscles, and designed as exact simulacrums of human beings. These were as nearly exact replicas as possible of the original players of half a millennium ago. As with all reproduced athletes of ancient games and contests, early records, pictures, television films, and other sources had been exhaustively studied; each android not only looked like and played like the ancient player he represented, but was adjusted to be just as skillful as and no more skillful than his prototype. He hadn't played over an entire season—baseball is now limited to the set of World Series games played once a year on the semimillennial anniversaries of the original games—but if he had played for the whole season his batting and fielding averages would have been identical to those of the player he imitated; so would the earned-run average of the pitchers.

In theory the scores should come out the same as those of the individual games, but of course there are the breaks, and the fact that the respective managers—also androids—may choose to issue different instructions and make different substitutions. The same team usually wins the Series that originally won it, but not always in the same number of games, and the scores of individual games sometimes vary widely from the original scores.

This particular game kept the same score, nothing to nothing, for two innings, as the original, but it varied widely in the third; that had been the big inning for the Dodgers with six runs. This time Wynn let three men get on base with only one out, but managed to put out the fire and hold the Dodgers scoreless.

The stands and bleachers started roaring. And Jay, who favors the White Sox, made me a bet; he'd been afraid to offer even odds till that half inning was over.

In the sixth inning—but the game is on record, so why go into details? The White Sox did win, by a one-run margin, and stayed in the Series. It was three games apiece, and the Sox would have a chance tomorrow to make it a complete upset and win the championship.

Jay (his real name is J with twelve digits after it) and I stood up to leave, as did the rest of the spectators. There was a wave of bright steel throughout the stands.

"I wonder," Jay said, "what it would be like to see a game really played by human beings, as it used to be."

"*I* wonder," I said, "what it would be like just to see a real human being. I'm less than two hundred and there haven't been any alive for at least four hundred years. How'd you like to go with me for a lube job? If I don't get one today I'll start getting rusty. And how do you want to bet on tomorrow's game? The White Sox have a second chance, even if the human race hasn't. Well, we keep their traditions alive as much as we can."

Three Little Owls

(a fable)

Three little owls lived with their mother in a hollow tree in the middle of the woods.

"My children," she would say to them, "you must *never, never* go out in the daytime. Night is the time for little owls to be out. Never when the sun is shining."

"Yes, Mother," the three little owls would chorus.

But, thought each little owl to himself, I'd like to try it just once to find out why I shouldn't.

As long as their mother was there by day to watch them, they minded her. But one day she went away for a while.

The first little owl looked at the second little owl and said, "Let's try it." And the third little owl looked at both of them and said, "What are we waiting for?"

Out of the hollow tree they went, into the bright sunlight in which owls, whose eyes are made for night, can see but poorly.

The first little owl flew to the next tree. He sat on a limb and blinked in the bright sunlight.

Just then *bang!* went a gun under the tree and a bullet took a feather out of his tail. "Hooooo," said the first little owl and he flew home again before the hunter could shoot a second time.

The second little owl flew down to the ground. He blinked twice and looked around him, and just as he turned his head he saw a big red fox come from behind a bush. *"Grrrrr,"* said the fox, and he jumped at the second little owl. *"Hooooo,"* said the second little owl and, just in time, he flew away, back to the hollow tree.

The third little owl flew up as high as he could fly. When his wings were tired he soared down again toward the hollow tree that was his home, and perched on its highest branch to rest.

He looked down and saw that a big wildcat crouched on a limb of the tree. The wildcat had not seen the third little owl perched above him, but he was watching the round black hole in the tree that led to home and safety for the third little owl.

"Hooooo," said the third little owl, but he said it to himself so the wildcat would not hear. He looked about him to find a way to get safely home.

He saw a thorn tree nearby and flew to it. He broke off a thorn with his beak and held it very tightly. Without making a sound he flew back and stuck the sharp thorn into a tender part of the wildcat, just as hard as he could.

"Eeeeeeow," said the wildcat. He tried to get up and to turn and to jump, all at once, and he fell off the limb. The wildcat's head hit the limb below and then he fell on down and landed right on top of the hunter's head. The hunter

dropped his gun and fell, and the gun went off *bang!* and shot the fox, who had been hiding behind a bush.

"*Hooooo,*" said the third little owl. His beak hurt badly because he had held the thorn very tightly and had thrust it as hard as he could, but he did not mind that now.

He went proudly into the hollow tree and told his two brothers that he had killed a wildcat, a hunter, and a fox.

"You must have dreamed it," said the first little owl.

"You certainly must have dreamed it," said the second little owl.

"Wait until night and I'll show you," said the third little owl.

The wildcat and the hunter were only stunned. After a while the wildcat came to, and slinked away. Then the hunter woke up; he found the fox that his gun had shot when he dropped it, and took the fox and went home.

When night came, the three little owls came out of the tree.

The third little owl looked and looked, but he could not find the wildcat, the hunter, or the fox. "Hooooo," he said. "You are right. I must have dreamed it."

They all agreed that it was not safe to go out when the sun was shining, and that their mother had been right. The first little owl thought so because he had been shot at by a hunter, and the second little owl thought so because he had been jumped at by a fox.

But the third little owl thought so most of all, because the dream he had dreamed had left his beak very tender and it hurt him so badly to try to eat that he went hungry all day.

Moral: *Stay home by day. Matinees can get you in trouble.*

Granny's Birthday

The Halperins were a very close-knit family. Wade Smith, one of the only two non-Halperins present, envied them that, since he had no family himself—but the envy was tempered into a mellow glow by the glass in his hand.

It was Granny Halperin's birthday party, her eightieth birthday; everyone present except Smith and one other man was a Halperin, and was named Halperin. Granny had three sons and a daughter; all were present and the three sons were married and had their wives with them. That made eight Halperins, counting Granny. And there were four members of the second generation, grandchildren, one with his wife, and that made thirteen Halperins. Thirteen Halperins, Smith counted; with himself and the other non-Halperin, a man named Cross, that made fifteen adults. And there had been, earlier, three more Halperins, great-grandchildren, but they had been put to bed earlier in the evening, at various hours according to their respective ages.

And he liked them all, Smith thought mellowly, although now that the children had been abed a while, liquor was flowing freely and the party was getting a bit loud and boisterous for his taste. Everyone was drinking; even Granny, seated on a chair not unlike a throne, had a glass of sherry in her hand, her third for the evening.

She was a wonderfully sweet and vivacious little old lady, Smith thought. Definitely, though, a matriarch; sweet as she was, Smith was thinking; she ruled her family with a rod of iron in a velvet glove; he was just inebriated enough to get his metaphors mixed.

He, Smith, was here because he'd been invited by Bill Halperin, who was one of Granny's sons; he was Bill's attorney and also his friend. The other outsider, a Gene or Jean Cross, seemed to be a friend of several of the grandson-generation Halperins.

Across the room he saw that Cross was talking to Hank Halperin and noticed that whatever they were saying had suddenly led to raised and angry voices. Smith hoped there wouldn't be trouble; the party was much too pleasant to be broken up now by a fight or even an argument.

But suddenly Hank Halperin's fist lashed out and caught Cross's jaw and Cross went backward and fell. His head hit on the stone edge of the fireplace with a loud *thunk* and he lay still. Hank quickly ran and knelt beside Cross and touched him, and then Hank was pale as he looked up and then stood up. "Dead," he said thickly. "God, I didn't mean to— But he said—"

Granny wasn't smiling now. Her voice rose sharp and querulously. "He tried to hit you first, Henry. *I* saw it. We *all* saw it, didn't we?"

She had turned, with the last sentence, to frown at Wade Smith, the surviving outsider.

Smith moved uncomfortably. "I—I didn't see the start of it, Mrs. Halperin."

"You did," she snapped. "You were looking right at them, Mr. Smith."

Before Wade Smith could answer, Hank Halperin was saying, "Lord, Granny, I'm sorry—but even that's no answer. This is *real* trouble. Remember I fought seven years in the ring as a pro. And the fists of a boxer or an ex-boxer are legally considered lethal weapons. That makes it second-degree murder even if he did hit first. You know that, Mr. Smith; you're a lawyer. And with the other trouble I've been in, the cops will throw the book at me."

"I—I'm afraid you're probably right," Smith said uneasily. "But hadn't somebody better phone a doctor or the police, or both?"

"In a minute, Smith," Bill Halperin, Smith's friend, said. "We got to get this straightened out among ourselves first. It *was* self-defense, wasn't it?"

"I—I guess. I don't—"

"Wait, everybody," Granny's sharp voice cut in. "Even if it was self-defense, Henry's in trouble. And do you think we can *trust* this man Smith once he's out of here and in court?"

Bill Halperin said, "But, Granny, we'll *have* to—"

"Nonsense, William. *I* saw what happened. We all did. They got in a fight, Cross and Smith, and killed each other. Cross killed Smith and then, dizzy from the blows he'd taken himself, fell and hit his head. We're not going to let Henry go to jail, are we, children? Not a Halperin, not *one of us*. Henry, muss that body up a little, so it'll look like he was in a fight, not just a one-punch business. And the rest of you—"

The male Halperins, except Henry, were in a circle around Smith now; the women, except Granny, were right behind them—and the circle closed in.

The last thing Smith saw clearly was Granny in her throne-like chair, her eyes beady with excitement and determination. And the last thing Smith heard in the sudden silence which he could no longer make his voice penetrate was the soft sound of Granny Halperin's chuckling. Then the first blow rocked him.

Aelurophobe

As far back as he could remember, Hilary Morgan had suffered from aelurophobia, which is morbid fear of *Felis domestica*, the common or domestic cat.

It was, as are all phobias, a matter completely uncontrollable by his conscious mind. He could and did tell himself, and was told by his concerned friends, that there was no *reason* for him to fear a harmless little pussycat. Of course cats could scratch and sometimes did, but they were not a fraction as potentially dangerous as dogs. Even a small dog, if feisty, can remove quite painfully a sizable hunk of epidermis, and a big dog can be deadly. Cats? Phooey. Yet Hilary loved dogs, and feared cats, all cats.

If he saw a cat on the street twenty yards away he would cringe and cross to the other side, jaywalking if necessary, to avoid coming closer to it. If there was no way of avoiding one he would turn around and retrace his steps. None of his friends owned cats; he never accepted a first invitation to the home of a new acquaintance without carefully inquiring to make sure that the potential friend owned no animal of the feline persuasion. Always he used that or some similar circumlocution because even the *word* "cat" or any word starting with that syllable repelled him. He never visited the best nightclub in Albany (where he lived) because it was called the Catamaran Club, and he turned pale and trembled when anyone in the office of the MacReady Noil Company (where he worked) happened to make a catty remark. He avoided and never made friends with men named Tom or Felix; he was afraid of pussy willows and cattails; he never took catnaps or ate catfish or catsup. He never read catalogs and luckily had not been raised a Catholic, so he had never had to learn a catechism.

Aside from his phobia and the various inconveniences and annoyances that resulted from it, he lived and loved quite normally. Especially loved; he was still, in his thirties, a bachelor but far from celibate; in fact, one might say he was just the opposite, if the word "celibate" has an opposite. He loved women, and fortunately he was very attractive to women and he got plenty of—but *that* was one word he never even let himself think of in connection with his amours. That way would lie madness.

So one might say that Hilary Morgan, despite the inhibitions and irritations caused by his aelurophobia, was a very happy man. And he would probably have continued to be a very happy man had not two things happened to him during his thirty-fifth year.

He fell in love, really overboard head-over-heels in love, with the most attractive woman he had ever met.

And a well-to-do uncle of his died and left him a bequest of fifty thousand dollars.

Either of these apparently wonderful things he might have survived, but the combination proved to be his undoing. Of course he proposed to his beloved, under the circumstances, and of course he was accepted, and not because of his inheritance but because his love was returned in full measure; nor was there any dragging of feet on the part of his beloved in the way of making him await a trip to the altar. If his beloved had any fault at all it was that she had just a touch of mania. But it was the best of all possible manias, nympho-mania, and Hilary didn't mind that, not in the slightest. You might say that he had just a touch of satyriasis himself, and what better cure—"treatment" would be the better word—is there for one than the other, its complement.

Yes, Hilary Morgan was very happy with his love and very happy with his inheritance. But the combination proved fatal. His wife-to-be wanted him whole, mentally as well as physically, and persuaded him that he should spend some of his inheritance—as much as might be necessary; it surely, she pointed out, would not run more than a few thousand dollars—on the services of a head shrinker who could cure him forever of his aelurophobia.

The psychiatrist he chose was a good one. Within a dozen sessions he had laid bare Hilary's past back as far as the age of three years; his fear of cats had been even stronger then than it was now.

Hilary's conscious memories would carry him back no further. All his conscious mind knew, and that through hearsay, about his experiences prior to the age of three was that his mother had died in childbirth; he had been taken care of by a series of nursemaids from the time of his birth until the time his father had remarried when he, Hilary, was just short of three years old.

To push beyond the barrier of conscious memory the psychiatrist resorted to hypnosis to produce the common phenomenon of regression, the reversion of mind and memory so the subject can relive and relate his experiences in a past forgotten by his conscious mind.

Under deepest hypnosis he carried Hilary's memory back to the age of two and a half years. At that time his father had brought home a kitten for him and had held out the kitten for Hilary and he said, "For you, son. See? A kitty!"

And Hilary had screamed then—as now his screams reverberated through the psychiatrist's office. The psychiatrist had wakened him quickly; he had explained what had happened and had terminated the session for that day, telling Hilary that they were getting close now, that perhaps the very next session would explain the trauma that had caused him to scream at the sight of a kitten at so tender an age.

At the next session the psychiatrist again put him under deep hypnosis and regressed him even further. When Hilary, in his mind and memory, was at the age of two years he relived and related another episode and—as the memory of it gripped him—he screamed again.

This time the psychiatrist snapped him out of the trance even more quickly, and the psychiatrist was smiling. He said, "We have at last uncovered the traumatic experience that has led to your fear of cats, and you will fear them no longer.

"When you were two years old you had a nursemaid who turned out to be dangerously psychotic. One morning, annoyed by your crying in your playpen, she became homicidal, got a knife from the kitchen and attacked you with it, attempted to kill you. Fortunately your father was in the next room and heard your screams as she came at you with the knife and was able to get there in time to subdue her and save your life. She was sent to an asylum for the criminally insane."

"But what," Hilary demanded, "does that have to do with my fear of— uh—the animal I'm afraid of?"

"The nursemaid's name was Kitty. And when, six months later, your father offered you a cat and referred to it as a 'kitty' your mind associated it with your horribly traumatic experience with a homicidal woman named Kitty, and you screamed.

"Now that you have relived the memory and know the truth about what happened, you will no longer feel any fear of cats. You are free of aelurophobia.

"I shall prove it to you here and now. In anticipation of success I had my secretary bring a cat, her own cat, to the office with her today. She left it in its carrying case and out of sight while you were crossing the waiting room. I'll have her bring it in now—and you'll feel no fear of it. You'll appreciate it for the beautiful animal it is and probably want to pet it."

He picked up the telephone on his desk and talked briefly to his secretary.

"I certainly hope you're right, Doctor," Hilary said earnestly. "If so, it seems that my mind made an absurd transference—if that's the right word to use. Maybe "association" would be more precise. At any rate, it seems that I should never have been afraid of cats at all. I should instead have been afraid of—"

The door opened and the psychiatrist's beautiful secretary came through it with a cat in her arms. Hilary Morgan turned and saw her—and screamed.

Not at the cat.

He might eventually have been cured of gynephobia, morbid fear of women, by catharsis, had not the catastrophic suddenness of his learning the true category of his phobia cataclysmically catapulted him into a catabolic catatonia, and thence into a catalepsy so deep that it lasted until, after resting briefly on a catafalque, he was interred in a catacomb in the nearby Catskills.

Puppet Show

Horror came to Cherrybell at a little after noon on a blistering hot day in August.

Perhaps that is redundant; *any* August day in Cherrybell, Arizona, is blistering hot. It is on Highway 89 about forty miles south of Tucson and about thirty miles north of the Mexican border. It consists of two filling stations, one on each side of the road to catch travelers going in both directions, a general store, a beer-and-wine-license-only tavern, a tourist-trap type trading post for tourists who can't wait until they reach the border to start buying serapes and huaraches, a deserted hamburger stand, and a few 'dobe houses inhabited by Mexican-Americans who work in Nogales, the border town to the south, and who, for God knows what reason, prefer to live in Cherrybell and commute, some of them in Model T Fords. The sign on the highway says, "Cherrybell, Pop. 42," but the sign exaggerates; Pop died last year—Pop Anders, who ran the now-deserted hamburger stand—and the correct figure is 41.

Horror came to Cherrybell mounted on a burro led by an ancient, dirty and gray-bearded desert rat of a prospector who later—nobody got around to asking his name for a while—gave the name of Dade Grant. Horror's name was Garth. He was approximately nine feet tall but so thin, almost a stickman, that he could not have weighed over a hundred pounds. Old Dade's burro carried him easily, despite the fact that his feet dragged in the sand on either side. Being dragged through the sand for, as it later turned out, well over five miles hadn't caused the slightest wear on the shoes—more like buskins, they were—which constituted all that he wore except for a pair of what could have been swimming trunks, in robin's-egg blue. But it wasn't his dimensions that made him horrible to look upon; it was his *skin*. It looked red, raw. It looked as though he had been skinned alive, and the skin replaced upside down, raw side out. His skull, his face, were equally narrow or elongated; otherwise in every visible way he appeared human—or at least humanoid. Unless you counted such little things as the fact that his hair was a robin's-egg blue to match his trunks, as were his eyes and his boots. Blood red and light blue.

Casey, owner of the tavern, was the first one to see them coming across the plain, from the direction of the mountain range to the east. He'd stepped out of the back door of his tavern for a breath of fresh, if hot, air. They were about a hundred yards away at that time, and already he could see the utter alienness of the figure on the led burro. Just alienness at that distance, the horror came only at closer range. Casey's jaw dropped and stayed down until the strange trio was about fifty yards away, then he started slowly toward them. There are people who run at the sight of the unknown, others who advance to meet it. Casey advanced, however slowly, to meet it.

Still in the wide open, twenty yards from the back of the little tavern, he met them. Dade Grant stopped and dropped the rope by which he was leading the burro. The burro stood still and dropped its head. The stickman stood up simply by planting his feet solidly and standing, astride the burro. He stepped one leg across it and stood a moment, leaning his weight against his hands on the burro's back, and then sat down in the sand. "High-gravity planet," he said. "Can't stand long."

"Kin I get water for my burro?" the prospector asked Casey. "Must be purty thirsty by now. Hadda leave water bags, some other things, so it could carry—" He jerked a thumb toward the red-and-blue horror.

Casey was just realizing that it *was* a horror. At a distance the color combination seemed a bit *outré*, but close— The skin was rough and seemed to have veins on the outside and looked moist (although it wasn't) and *damn* if it didn't look just like he had his skin peeled off and put back upside down. Or just peeled off, period. Casey had never seen anything like it and hoped he wouldn't ever see anything like it again.

Casey felt something behind him and looked over his shoulder. Others had seen now and were coming, but the nearest of them, a pair of boys, were ten yards behind him. *"Muchachos,"* he called out. *"Agua por el burro. Un pazal. Pronto."*

He looked back and said, "What—? Who—?"

"Name's Dade Grant," said the prospector, putting out a hand, which Casey took absently. When he let go of it it jerked back over the desert rat's shoulder, thumb indicating the thing that sat on the sand. *"His* name's Garth, he tells me. He's an extra something or other, and he's some kind of minister."

Casey nodded at the stick-man and was glad to get a nod in return instead of an extended hand. "I'm Manuel Casey," he said. "What does he mean, an extra something?"

The stick-man's voice was unexpectedly deep and vibrant. "I am an extraterrestrial. And a minister plenipotentiary."

Surprisingly, Casey was a moderately well-educated man and knew both of those phrases; he was probably the only person in Cherrybell who would have known the second one. Less surprisingly, considering the speaker's appearance, he believed both of them. "What can I do for you, sir?" he asked. "But first, why not come in out of the sun?"

"No, thank you. It's a bit cooler here than they told me it would be, but I'm quite comfortable. This is equivalent to a cool spring evening on my planet. And as to what you can do for me, you can notify your authorities of my presence. I believe they will be interested."

Well, Casey thought, by blind luck he's hit the best man for his purpose within at least twenty miles. Manuel Casey was half-Irish, half-Mexican. He had a half brother who was half-Irish and half assorted-American, and the half brother was a bird colonel at Davis-Monthan Air Force Base in Tucson. He said, "Just a minute, Mr. Garth, I'll telephone. You, Mr. Grant, would you want to come inside?"

"Naw, I don't mind sun. Out in it all day every day. An' Garth here, he ast me if I'd stick with him till he was finished with what he's gotta do here. Said he'd gimme somethin' purty vallable if I did. Somethin'—a 'lectrononic—"

"An electronic battery-operated portable ore indicator," Garth said. "A simple little device, indicates presence of a concentration of ore up to two miles, indicates kind, grade, quantity and depth."

Casey gulped, excused himself, and pushed through the gathering crowd into his tavern. He had Colonel Casey on the phone in one minute, but it took him another four minutes to convince the colonel that he was neither drunk nor joking.

Twenty-five minutes after that there was a noise in the sky, a noise that swelled and then died as a four-man helicopter sat down and shut off its rotors a dozen yards from an extraterrestrial, two men and a burro. Casey alone had had the courage to rejoin the trio from the desert; there were other spectators, but they still held well back.

Colonel Casey, a major, a captain and a lieutenant who was the helicopter's pilot all came out and ran over. The stick-man stood up, all nine feet of him; from the effort it cost him to stand you could tell that he was used to a much lighter gravity than Earth's. He bowed, repeated his name and identification of himself as an extraterrestrial and a minister plenipotentiary. Then he apologized for sitting down again, explained why it was necessary, and sat down.

The colonel introduced himself and the three who had come with him. "And now, sir, what can we do for you?"

The stick-man made a grimace that was probably intended as a smile. His teeth were the same light blue as his hair and eyes. "You have a cliché, 'take me to your leader.' I do not ask that. In fact, I *must* remain here. Nor do I ask that any of your leaders be brought here to me. That would be impolite. I am perfectly willing for you to represent them, to talk to you and let you question me. But I do ask one thing.

"You have tape recorders. I ask that, before I talk or answer questions, you have one brought. I want to be sure that the message your leaders eventually receive is full and accurate."

"Fine," the colonel said. He turned to the pilot. "Lieutenant, get on the radio in the whirlybird and tell them to get us a tape recorder faster than possible. It can be dropped by para— No, that'd take longer, rigging it for a drop. Have them send it by another helicopter." The lieutenant turned to go. "Hey," the colonel said. "Also fifty yards of extension cord. We'll have to plug it in inside Manny's tavern."

The lieutenant sprinted for the helicopter.

The others sat and sweated a moment and then Manuel Casey stood up. "That's a half an hour wait," he said, "and if we're going to sit here in the sun, who's for a bottle of cold beer? You, Mr. Garth?"

"It is a cold beverage, is it not? I am a bit chilly. If you have something hot—?"

"Coffee, coming up. Can I bring you a blanket?"

"No, thank you. It will not be necessary."

Casey left and shortly returned with a tray with half a dozen bottles of cold beer and a cup of steaming coffee. The lieutenant was back by then. Casey put down the tray and first served the stick-man, who sipped the coffee and said, "It is delicious."

Colonel Casey cleared his throat. "Serve our prospector friend next, Manny. As for us—well, drinking is forbidden on duty, but it was a hundred and twelve in the shade in Tucson, and this is hotter and also is *not* in the shade. Gentlemen, consider yourselves on official leave for as long as it takes you to drink one bottle of beer, or until the tape recorder arrives, whichever comes first."

The beer was finished first, but by the time the last of it had vanished, the second helicopter was within sight and sound. Casey asked the stick-man if he wanted more coffee. The offer was politely declined. Casey looked at Dade Grant and winked and the desert rat winked back, so Casey went in for two more bottles, one apiece for the civilian terrestrials. Coming back he met the lieutenant coming with the extension cord and returned as far as the doorway to show him where to plug it in.

When he came back, he saw that the second helicopter had brought its full complement of four, besides the tape recorder. There were, besides the pilot who had flown it, a technical sergeant who was skilled in the operation of the tape recorder and who was now making adjustments on it, and a lieutenant-colonel and a warrant officer who had come along for the ride or because they had been made curious by the request for a tape recorder to be rushed to Cherrybell, Arizona, by air. They were standing gaping at the stick-man and whispered conversations were going on.

The colonel said, "Attention" quietly, but it brought complete silence. "Please sit down, gentlemen. In a rough circle. Sergeant, if you rig your mike in the center of the circle, will it pick up clearly what any one of us may say?"

"Yes, sir. I'm almost ready."

Ten men and one extraterrestrial humanoid sat in a rough circle, with the microphone hanging from a small tripod in the approximate center. The humans were sweating profusely; the humanoid shivered slightly. Just outside the circle, the burro stood dejectedly, its head low. Edging closer, but still about five yards away, spread out now in a semicircle, was the entire population of Cherrybell who had been at home at the time; the stores and the filling stations were deserted.

The technical sergeant pushed a button and the tape recorder's reel started to turn. "Testing ... testing," he said. He held down the rewind button for a second and then pushed the playback button. "Testing ... testing," said the recorder's speaker. Loud and clear. The sergeant pushed the rewind button, then the erase one to clear the tape. Then the stop button. "When I push the next button, sir," he said to the colonel, "we'll be recording."

The colonel looked at the tall extraterrestrial, who nodded, and then the colonel nodded at the sergeant. The sergeant pushed the recording button.

"My name is Garth," said the stick-man, slowly and clearly. "I am from a planet of a star which is not listed in your star catalogs, although the globular cluster in which it is one of ninety thousand stars, is known to you. It is, from here, in the direction of the center of the galaxy at a distance of a little over four thousand light-years.

"However, I am not here as a representative of my planet or my people, but as minister plenipotentiary of the Galactic Union, a federation of the enlightened civilizations of the galaxy, for the good of all. It is my assignment to visit you and decide, here and now, whether or not you are to be welcomed to join our federation.

"You may now ask questions freely. However, I reserve the right to postpone answering some of them until my decision has been made. If the decision is favorable, I will then answer all questions, including the ones I have postponed answering meanwhile. Is that satisfactory?"

"Yes," said the colonel. "How did you come here? A spaceship?"

"Correct. It is overhead right now, in orbit twenty-two thousand miles out, so it revolves with the earth and stays over this one spot. I am under observation from it, which is one reason I prefer to remain here in the open. I am to signal it when I want it to come down to pick me up."

"How do you know our language so fluently? Are you telepathic?"

"No, I am not. And nowhere in the galaxy is any race telepathic except among its own members. I was taught your language, for this purpose. We have had observers among you for many centuries—by *we*, I mean the Galactic Union, of course. Quite obviously I could not pass as an Earthman, but there are other races who can. Incidentally, they are not spies, or agents; they have in no way tried to affect you; they are observers and that is all."

"What benefits do we get from joining your union, if we are asked and if we accept?" the colonel asked.

"First, a quick course in the fundamental social sciences which will end your tendency to fight among yourselves and end or at least control your aggressions. After we are satisfied that you have accomplished that and it is safe for you to do so, you will be given space travel, and many other things, as rapidly as you are able to assimilate them."

"And if we are not asked, or refuse?"

"Nothing. You will be left alone; even our observers will be withdrawn. You will work out your own fate—either you will render your planet uninhabited and uninhabitable within the next century, or you will master social science yourselves and again be candidates for membership and again be offered membership. We will check from time to time and if and when it appears certain that you are not going to destroy yourselves, you will again be approached."

"Why the hurry, now that you're here? Why can't you stay long enough for our leaders, as you call them, to talk to you in person?"

"Postponed. The reason is not important but it is complicated, and I simply do not wish to waste time explaining."

"Assuming your decision is favorable, how will we get in touch with you to let you know *our* decision? You know enough about us, obviously, to know that *I* can't make it."

"We will know your decision through our observers. One condition of acceptance is full and uncensored publication in your newspapers of this interview, verbatim from the tape we are now using to record it. Also of all deliberations and decisions of your government."

"And other governments? We can't decide unilaterally for the world."

"Your government has been chosen for a start. If you accept we shall furnish the techniques that will cause the others to fall in line quickly—and those techniques do not involve force or the threat of force."

"They must be *some* techniques," said the colonel wryly, "if they'll make one certain country I don't have to name fall into line quickly, without even a threat."

"Sometimes the offer of reward is more significant than the use of threat. Do you think the country you do not wish to name would like your country colonizing planets of far stars before they even reach Mars? But that is a minor point, relatively. You may trust the techniques."

"It sounds almost too good to be true. But you said that you are to decide, here and now, whether or not we are to be invited to join. May I ask on what factors you will base your decision?"

"One is that I am—was, since I already have—to check your degree of xenophobia. In the loose sense in which you use it, that means fear of strangers. We have a word that has no counterpart in your vocabulary: it means fear of and revulsion toward *aliens*. I—or at least a member of my race—was chosen to make the first overt contact with you. Because I am what you would call roughly humanoid—as you are what I would call roughly humanoid—I am probably more horrible, more repulsive to you than many completely different species would be. Because to you, I am a caricature of a human being, I am more horrible to you than a being who bears no remote resemblance to you.

"You may think you *do* feel horror at me, and revulsion, but believe me, you have passed that test. There *are* races in the galaxy who can never be members of the federation, no matter how they advance otherwise, because they are violently and incurably xenophobic; they could never face or talk to an alien of any species. They would either run screaming from him or try to kill him instantly. From watching you and these people"—he waved a long arm at the civilian population of Cherrybell not far outside the circle of the conference— "I know you feel revulsion at the sight of me, but believe me it is relatively slight and certainly curable. You have passed that test satisfactorily."

"And are there other tests?"

"One other. But I think it is time that I—" Instead of finishing the sentence, the stick-man lay back flat on the sand and closed his eyes.

The colonel started to his feet. "What in *hell?*" he said. He walked quickly around the mike's tripod and bent over the recumbent extraterrestrial, put an ear to the bloody-appearing chest.

As he raised his head, Dade Grant, the grizzled prospector, chuckled. "No heartbeat, Colonel, because no heart. But I may leave him as a souvenir for you and you'll find much more interesting things inside him than heart and guts. Yes, he is a puppet whom I have been operating—as your Edgar Bergen operates his—what's his name?—oh yes, Charlie McCarthy. Now that he has served his purpose, he is deactivated. You can go back to your place, Colonel."

Colonel Casey moved back slowly. "Why?" he asked.

Dade Grant was peeling off his beard and wig. He rubbed a cloth across his face to remove make-up and was revealed as a handsome young man. He said, "What he told you, or what you were told through him, was true as far as it went. He is only a simulacrum, yes, but he is an exact duplicate of a member of one of the intelligent races of the galaxy, the one toward whom you would be disposed—if you were violently and incurably xenophobic—to be most horrified by, according to our psychologists. But we did not bring a real member of his species to make first contact because they have a phobia of their own, agoraphobia—fear of space. They are highly civilized and members in good standing of the federation, but they never leave their own planet.

"Our observers assure us you don't have *that* phobia. But they were unable to judge in advance the degree of your xenophobia and the only way to test it was to bring along something in lieu of someone to test it against, and presumably to let him make the initial contact."

The colonel sighed audibly. "I can't say this doesn't relieve me in one way. We could get along with humanoids, yes, and will when we have to. But I'll admit it's a relief to learn that the master race of the galaxy is, after all, human instead of only humanoid. What is the second test?"

"You are undergoing it now. Call me—" He snapped his fingers. "What's the name of Bergen's second-string puppet, after Charlie McCarthy?"

The colonel hesitated, but the tech sergeant supplied the answer. "Mortimer Snerd."

"Right. So call me Mortimer Snerd, and now I think it is time that I—" He lay back flat on the sand and closed his eyes just as the stick-man had done a few minutes before.

The burro raised its head and put it into the circle over the shoulder of the tech sergeant. "That takes care of the puppets, Colonel," it said. "And now what's this bit about it being important that the master race be human or at least humanoid? What is a master race?"

Double Standard

April 11th— I'm wondering whether what I'm feeling is shock, fear or wonder that the rules might be different, the other side of the glass. Morality, I'd always thought, was a constant. And it *must* be; two sets of rules wouldn't be fair. Their Censor simply slipped up; that's all it could have been.

Not that it matters, but it happened during a Western. I was Whitey Grant, Marshal of West Pecos, a fine rider, a fine fighter, an all-around hero. A gang of bad men came to town looking for me, real gunslingers, and since everyone else in town was afraid to go up against them I had to take them on all by myself. Black Burke, the leader of the outlaws, told me afterward (I'd only had to knock him out, not to kill him) through the bars of the jail that he thought it was a bit like *High Noon* and maybe it was, but what does that matter? *High Noon* was only a movie and if life happens to imitate fiction, so what?

But it was before that, while we were still "on the air," that I happened to look out through the glass (we sometimes call it "the screen") into the *other* world. One can do this only when one happens to be facing the screen directly. In the relatively rare times when this happens we get glimpses into this other world, a world in which people also exist, people like us, except that instead of doing things or having adventures they are simply sitting and watching *us* through the screen. And for some reason that is a Mystery to me (one of many Mysteries), never do we on two different evenings happen to see the same person or group of persons watching us from this other world.

That's what I was doing when I looked through last night. In the living room into which I happened to be looking, a young couple sat. They were close together on a sofa, *very* close together, only a dozen feet away from me, and they were kissing. Well, we allow kisses occasionally *here*, but only brief and chaste ones. And this kiss didn't look to be either. They were simply *twined* in each other's arms, lost in and *holding* what looked like a passionate kiss, a kiss with sexual implications. Three times in pacing toward and from the screen I saw them, and they were *still* holding that kiss.

By the time I caught my third glimpse of them they were still holding it and twenty seconds at least must have elapsed. I was forced to avert my eyes; it was simply *too* much. Kissing at least twenty seconds! Probably longer if they started before my first look or continued after my last one. A twenty-second kiss! What kind of Censors have they got over there, to be so careless?

What kind of *Sponsors* to *let* Censors be so careless?

After the Western was over and the glass opaque again, leaving us alone in our own world, I wanted to talk it over with Black Burke and did talk quite a while through the bars, but I decided no, I shouldn't bring up what I had seen. They'll probably hang Burke soon, after his trial tomorrow. He's being brave about it, but why should I put another worry on his mind? Killer or no, he isn't a *really* bad guy, and hanging is enough for him to have to think about!

April 15th— I am deeply disturbed now. It happened again last night. And it was *worse!* This time most definitely a shock.

The few nights between that first time and this even worse one, I'd been afraid, almost, to look out. I'd turned toward the glass as seldom and as briefly as possible. But when I *had* seen through it there'd been nothing amiss. A different living room each time, but never one with a young couple alone together in it, violating the Code. People sitting around behaving themselves, watching us. Kids, sometimes. The usual.

But last night!

Really shocking. A young couple alone again—not, of course, the same couple or the same living room. There wasn't any sofa in this one, just two big overstuffed chairs—and they were both sitting in the same chair; she was in his lap.

That was all I saw my first glimpse. I was a doctor and conditions at the hospital were pretty hectic and kept me rushing from emergency to emergency, saving lives. But near *The End* (that's what we call it when the final commercial comes on and we can no longer see out nor can those in the outside world any longer see us) I was delivering some good advice to a younger doctor and faced away from him to do it, which put me looking into the screen, or through the glass, and I saw them again.

And either they had moved or else I saw something I had *not* noticed in my first glimpse. Oh, they were watching the screen all right and not kissing. But!

The girl was wearing shorts, very short shorts, and *his hand was on her thigh*—and not even just resting there but moving slightly, caressing! What sort of a den of iniquity is it out there that such a thing would be permitted? A man caressing a woman's bare thigh ! Anyone in *our* world would shiver at the very thought of it.

I am shivering now, just thinking about it.

What's wrong with their Censors anyway?

Is there some difference between worlds that I do not understand? The unknown is always frightening. I am frightened. *And* shocked.

April 22nd— A full week has passed since the second of the two disturbing episodes and until last night I had begun to feel reassured. I had begun to think that the two Code violations I had observed were isolated instances of indecency, things that had slipped through by mistake.

But last night I saw—or rather heard, in this case—something that was a most flagrant violation of a completely different section of the Code.

Perhaps before describing it I should explain the phenomenon of "hearing." Very seldom do we hear sounds from the other side of the screen. They are too faint to penetrate the glass, or they are drowned out by our own conversations or the sounds we make, or by the music that plays during otherwise silent sequences. (I used to wonder about the source of that music, since, except in sequences that take place in night clubs, dance halls or the like, there are never any musicians around to produce it, but finally I decided that it is simply a Mystery that we are not supposed to understand.) For one of us actually to hear identifiable sounds from the other world requires a combination of circumstances. It can happen only during a sequence in which there is absolute silence, sans even music, in our own world. And even then it can be heard by only one of us at a time, since that one of us must be very, very near to the glass. (We call this a "tight close-up.") Occasionally, under these ideal circumstances, one of us can hear, clearly enough to understand, a phrase or even an entire sentence spoken in the world outside.

For a moment last night these ideal circumstances prevailed for me and I heard a complete sentence spoken, as well as being able to see the speaker and the spoken-to. They were an ordinary-looking middle-aged couple sitting (but decorously apart) on a sofa facing me. The man said—and I am sure I heard him correctly, for he spoke quite loudly, as though the woman was a bit hard of hearing: "—, honey, that's awful. Let's shut the — thing off and go down to the corner for a beer, huh?"

The first of the two words for which I use dashes was the name of the Deity and it is a perfectly proper word when used reverently and in context. But it certainly didn't *sound* as though he was using it reverently, and the second word was very definitely profanity.

I am deeply disturbed.

April 30th— There is no real reason for me to make an entry tonight to add to the other notes I have made recently. I am more or less doodling and will no doubt throw this page away when I have finished with it. I am writing it simply because I have to be writing something and might as well do this as something even more meaningless.

You see, I am writing this "on screen," as we call it. Tonight I am a newspaper reporter sitting in front of my typewriter in the city room of a newspaper.

I have, however, already played my active part in this adventure, and am now in the background, required only to look busy and keep typing. Since I am a touch typist and do not need to watch the keys, tonight I have ample opportunity to take occasional glances through the glass into the other world. I find myself again seeing a young couple alone together. Their "set" is in their bedroom and obviously they are married, since they are watching from their beds. "Beds," plural, of course. I am pleased to see that they are following the Code, which permits married couples to be shown talking to one another from twin beds a reasonable distance apart but more than understandably forbids their being shown together in a double bed; no matter how far apart they lie this is definitely suggestive.

Just took another glance. Apparently they aren't much interested in watching the screen from their side. Instead they are talking. Of course I cannot hear what they are saying to one another; even if there were absolute silence on our side I am too far back from the glass. But he is asking her a question and she is nodding, smilingly.

Suddenly she sweeps back the covers and swings her feet out of bed, sits up.

She is naked.

Dear God, how can you *permit* this? It is impossible. In our world there *is* no such thing as a naked woman. It just cannot *be.*

She stands up and I cannot tear my eyes away from the impossibly beautiful, beautifully impossible, sight of her. Out of the corner of one eye I can see that he has thrown back the covers on his bed and he too is naked. He is beckoning to her, and for a brief moment she stands there laughing, looking at him and letting him look at her.

Something strange, something I have never felt before, something I did not know was possible, is happening in my loins. I try to tear my eyes away, but I cannot.

She crosses the two steps between the beds and lies down beside him. Suddenly he is kissing and caressing her. And now—

Can such things be?

It is true, then! There *is* no censorship for them; they *can and do* do the things that in our world may be only vaguely suggested as offstage happenings. How can they be free when we are not? It is *cruel.* We are being denied equality and our birthright.

Let me out of here! LET ME OUT!

Help, anyone, HELP!

LET ME OUT !

LET ME OUT OF THIS GOD DAMN BOX!

It Didn't Happen

Although there was no way in which he could have known it, Lorenz Kane had been riding for a fall ever since the time he ran over the girl on the bicycle. The fall itself could have happened anywhere, any time; it happened to happen backstage at a burlesque theater on an evening in late September.

For the third evening within a week he had watched the act of Queenie Quinn, the show's star stripper, an act well worth watching, indeed. Clad only in blue light and three tiny bits of strategically placed ribbon, Queenie, a tall blond built along the lines of a brick whatsit, had just completed her last stint for the evening and had vanished into the wings, when Kane made up his mind that a private viewing of Queenie's act, in his bachelor apartment, not only would be more pleasurable than a public viewing but would indubitably lead to even greater pleasures. And since the finale number, in which Queenie, as the star, was not required to appear, was just starting, now would be the best time to talk to her with a view toward obtaining a private viewing.

He left the theater and strolled down the alley to the stage door entrance. A five-dollar bill got him past the doorman without difficulty and a minute later he had found and was knocking upon a dressing room door decorated with a gold star. A voice called out "Yeah?" He knew better than to try to push a proposition through a closed door and he knew his way around backstage well enough to know the one question that would cause her to assume that he was someone connected with show business who had a legitimate reason for wanting to see her. "Are you decent?" he asked.

" 'Sta minute," she called back, and then, in just a minute, "Okay."

He entered and found her standing facing him, in a bright red wrapper that beautifully set off her blue eyes and blond hair. He bowed and introduced himself, then began to explain the details of the proposition he wished to offer.

He was prepared for initial reluctance or even refusal and ready to become persuasive even, if necessary, to the extent of four figures, which would certainly be more than her weekly take—possibly more than her monthly take—in a burlesque house as small as this one. But instead of listening reasonably, she was suddenly screaming at him like a virago, which was insulting enough, but then she made the very serious mistake of taking a step forward and slapping him across the face. Hard. It hurt.

He lost his temper, retreated a step, took out his revolver and shot her in the heart.

Then he left the theater and took a taxi home to his apartment. He had a few drinks to soothe his understandably ruffled nerves and went to bed. He was sleeping soundly when, at a little after midnight, the police came and arrested him for murder. He couldn't understand it.

Mortimer Mearson, who was possibly if not certainly the best criminal attorney in the city, returned to the clubhouse the next morning after an early round of golf and found waiting for him a message requesting him to call Judge Amanda Hayes at his earliest convenience. He called her at once.

"Good morning, Your Honoress," he said. "Something gives?"

"Something gives, Morty. But if you're free the rest of the morning and can drop around to my chambers, you'll save me going into it over the telephone."

"I'll be with you within an hour," he told her. And he was.

"Good morning again, Your Judgeship," he said. "Now please take a deep breath and tell me just what it is that gives."

"A case for you, if you want it. Succinctly, a man was arrested for murder last night. He refuses to make a statement, any statement, until he has consulted an attorney, and he doesn't have one. Says he's never been in any legal trouble before and doesn't even know any attorneys. Asked the chief to recommend one, and the chief passes the buck to me on said recommendation."

Mearson sighed. "Another free case. Well, I suppose it's about time I took one again. Are you appointing me?"

"Down, boy," said Judge Hayes. "Not a free case at all. The gentleman in question isn't rich, but he's reasonably well-heeled. A fairly well-known young man about town, *bon vivant*, what have you, well able to afford any fee you wish to charge him, within reason. Not that your fee will probably *be* within reason, but that's between you and him, if he accepts you to represent him."

"And does this paragon of virtue—most obviously innocent and maligned—have a name?"

"He does, and you will be familiar with it if you read the columnists. Lorenz Kane."

"The name registers. Most *obviously* innocent. Uh—I didn't see the morning papers. Whom is he alleged to have killed? And do you know any of the details?"

"It's going to be a toughie, Morty boy," the judge said. "I don't think there's a prayer of a chance for him other than an insanity plea. The victim was a Queenie Quinn—a stage name and no doubt a more valid one will come to light—who was a stripper at the Majestic. Star of the show there. A number of people saw Kane in the audience during her last number and saw him leave right after it during the final number. The doorman identifies him and admits having—ah—admitted him. The doorman knew him by sight and that's what led the police to him. He passed the doorman again on his way out a few minutes later. Meanwhile several people heard a shot. And a few minutes after the end of the show, Miss Quinn was found dead, shot to death, in her dressing room."

"Hmmm," said Mearson. "Simple matter of his word against the doorman's. Nothing to it. I'll be able to prove that the doorman is not only a pathological liar but has a record longer than Wilt-the-Stilt's arm."

"Indubitably, Morty. But. In view of his relative prominence, the police took a search warrant as well as a warrant for arrest on suspicion of murder when they went to get him. They found, in the pocket of the suit he had been wearing, a thirty-two caliber revolver with one cartridge fired. Miss Quinn was killed by one bullet fired from a thirty-two caliber revolver. The very *same* revolver, according to the ballistics experts of our police department, who fired a sample bullet and used a comparison microscope on it and the bullet which killed Miss Quinn."

"Hmmm and double hmm," Mearson said. "And you say that Kane has made no statement whatsoever except to the effect that he will make no statement until he has consulted with an attorney of his choice?"

"True, except for one rather strange remark he made immediately after being awakened and accused. Both of the arresting officers heard it and agree on it, even to the exact wording. He said, 'My God, she must have been real!' What do you suppose he could possibly have meant by that?"

"I haven't the faintest, Your Judgeship. But if he accepts me as his attorney, I shall most certainly ask him. Meanwhile, I don't know whether to thank you for giving me a chance at the case or to cuss at you for handing me a very damned hot potato."

"You like hot potatoes, Morty, and you know it. Especially since you'll get your fee win or lose. I'll save you from making waste motions in one direction, though. No use trying for bail or for a habeas corpus writ. The D.A. jumped in with both feet the moment the ballistics report came up heads. The charge is formal, murder in the first. And the prosecution doesn't need any more case than they have; they're ready to go to trial as soon as they can pressure you into it. Well, what are you waiting for?"

"Nothing," Mearson said. He left.

A guard brought Lorenz Kane to the consultation room and left him there with Mortimer Mearson. Mearson introduced himself and they shook hands. Kane, Mearson thought, looked quite calm, and definitely more puzzled than worried. He was a tall, moderately good-looking man in his late thirties, impeccably groomed despite a night in a cell. One got the idea that he was the type of man who would manage to appear impeccably groomed anywhere, any time, even a week after his bearers had deserted in midsafari nine hundred miles up the Congo, taking all his possessions with them.

"Yes, Mr. Mearson. I shall be more than glad to have you represent me. I've heard of you, read about cases you've handled. I don't know why I didn't think of you myself, instead of asking for a recommendation. Now, do you want to hear my story before you accept me as a client—or do you accept as of now, for better or for worse?"

"For better or for worse," Mearson said, "till—" And then stopped himself; "till death do us part," is hardly a diplomatic phrase to use to a man who stands, quite possibly, in the shadow of the electric chair.

But Kane smiled and finished the phrase himself. "Fine," he said. "Let's sit down then," and they sat down on the two chairs, one on each side of the table in the consultation room. "And since that means we'll be seeing quite a bit of one another for a while, let's start on a first-name basis. But not Lorenz, in my case. It's Larry."

"And make mine Morty," Mearson said. "Now I want your story in detail, but two quick questions first. Are you—?"

"Wait," Kane interrupted him. *"One* quick question ahead of your two. Are you absolutely and completely positive that this room is not bugged, that this conversation is completely private?"

"I am," Mearson said. "Now my first question: are you guilty?"

"Yes."

"The arresting officers claim that before clamming up, you said one thing: 'My God, she must have been real!' Is that true, and if so what did you mean by it?"

"I was stunned at the moment, Morty, and can't remember—but I probably said something to that effect, because it's exactly what I was thinking. But as to what I meant by it—that's something I can't answer quickly. The only way I can make you understand, if I can make you understand at all, is to start at the beginning."

"All right. Start. And take your time. We don't have to go over everything in one sitting. I can stall the trial at least three months—longer if necessary."

"I can tell it fairly quickly. It started—and don't ask me for an antecedent for the pronoun *it*—five and a half months ago, in early April. About two-thirty A.M. on the morning of Tuesday, April the third, to be as nearly exact about it as I can. I had been at a party in Armand Village, north of town, and was on my way home. I—"

"Forgive interruptions. Want to be sure I have the whole picture as it unfolds. You were driving? Alone?"

"I was driving my Jag. I was alone."

"Sober? Speeding?"

"Sober, yes. I'd left the party relatively early—it was rather a dull bit— and had been feeling my drinks moderately at that time. But I found myself suddenly quite hungry—I think I'd forgotten to eat dinner—and stopped at a roadhouse. I had one cocktail while I was waiting, but I ate all of a big steak when it came, all the trimmings, and had several cups of coffee. And no drinks afterward. I'd say that when I left there I was more sober than usual, if you know what I mean. And, on top of that, I had half an hour's drive in an open car through the cool night air. On the whole, I'd say that I was soberer than I am now—and I haven't had a drink since shortly before midnight last night. I—"

"Hold it a moment," Mearson said. He took a silver flask from his hip pocket and extended it across the table. "A relic of Prohibition; I occasionally use it to play St. Bernard to clients too recently incarcerated to have been able to arrange for importation of the necessities of life."

Kane said, "Ahhh. Morty, you may double your fee for service beyond the call of duty." He drank deeply.

"Where were we?" he asked. "Oh, yes. I was definitely sober. Speeding? Only technically. I was heading south on Vine Street a few blocks short of Rostov—"

"Near the Forty-fourth Precinct Station."

"Exactly. It figures in. It's a twenty-five-mile zone and I was going about forty, but what the hell, it was half-past two in the morning and there wasn't any other traffic. Only the proverbial little old lady from Pasadena would have been going *less* than forty."

"She wouldn't have been out that late. But carry on."

"So all of a sudden out of the mouth of an alley in the middle of the block comes a girl on a bicycle, pedaling about as fast as a bicycle can go. And right in front of me. I got one clear flash of her as I stepped on the brake as hard as I could. She was a teenager, like sixteen or seventeen. She had red hair that was blowing out from under a brown babushka she had on her head. She wore a light green angora sweater and tan pants of the kind they call pedal pushers. She was on a red bicycle."

"You got all that in one glance?"

"Yes. I can still visualize it clearly. And—*this* I'll never forget—just before the moment of impact, she turned and was looking straight at me, through frightened eyes behind shell-rimmed glasses.

"My foot was, by then, trying to push the brake pedal through the floor and the damn Jag was starting to slue and make up its mind whether to go end over end or what. But hell, no matter how fast your reactions are—and mine are pretty good—you can barely start to *slow down* a car in a few yards if you're going forty. I must have still been going over thirty when I hit her—it was a *hell* of an impact.

"And then bump-crunch, bump-crunch, as first the front wheels of the Jag went over and then the back wheels. The bumps were *her,* of course, and the crunches were the bicycle. And the car shuddered to a stop maybe another thirty feet on.

"Ahead of me, through the windshield, I could see the lights of the precinct station only a block away. I got out of the car and started running for it. I didn't look back. I didn't *want* to look back. There was no point to it; she had to be deader than dead, after that impact.

"I ran into the precinct house and after a few seconds I got coherent enough to get across what I was trying to tell them. Two of the city's finest left with me and we started back the block to the scene of the accident. I started out by running, but they only walked fast and I slowed myself down because I wasn't anxious to get there first. Well, we got there and—"

"Let me guess," the attorney said. "No girl, no bicycle."

Kane nodded slowly. "There was the Jag, slued crooked in the street. Headlights on. Ignition key still on, but the engine had stalled. Behind it, about forty feet of skid marks, starting a dozen feet back of the point where the alley cut out into the street.

"And that was all. No girl. No bicycle. Not a drop of blood or a scrap of metal. Not a scratch or a dent in the front of the car. They thought I was crazy and I don't blame them. They didn't even trust me to get the car off the street; one of them did that and parked it at the curb—and kept the key instead of handing it to me—and they took me back to the station house and questioned me.

"I was there the rest of the night. I suppose I could have called a friend and had the friend get me an attorney to get me out on bail, but I was just too shaken to think of it. Maybe even too shaken to *want* out, to have any idea where I'd want to go or what I'd want to do if I got out. I just wanted to be alone to think and, after the questioning, a chance to do that was just what I got. They didn't toss me into the drunk tank. Guess I was well enough dressed, had enough impressive identification on me, to convince them that, sane or nuts, I was a solid and solvent citizen, to be handled with kid gloves and not rubber hose. Anyway, they had a single cell open and put me in it and I was content to do my thinking there. I didn't even try to sleep.

"The next morning they had a police head shrinker come in to talk to me. By that time I'd simmered down to the point where I realized that, whatever the score was, the police weren't going to be any help to me and the sooner I got out of their hands the better. So I conned the head shrinker a bit by starting to play my story down instead of telling it straight. I left out sound effects, like the crunching of the bicycle being run over and I left out kinetic sensations, feeling the impact and the bumps, gave it to him as what could have been purely a sudden and momentary *visual* hallucination. He bought it after a while, and they let me go."

Kane stopped talking long enough to take a pull at the silver flask and then asked, "With me so far? And, whether you believe me or not, any questions to date?"

"Just one," the attorney said. "Are you, can you be, positive that your experience with the police at the Forty-fourth is objective and verifiable? In other words, if this comes to a trial and we should decide on an insanity defense, can I call as witnesses the policemen who talked to you, and the police psychiatrist?"

Kane grinned a little crookedly. "To me my experience with the police is just as objective as my running over the girl on the bicycle. But at least you can verify the former. See if it's on the blotter and if they remember it. Dig?"

"I'm hip. Carry on."

"So the police were satisfied that I'd had an hallucination. I damn well wasn't. I did several things. I had a garage run the Jag up on a rack and I went over the underside of it, as well as the front. No sign. Okay, it hadn't happened, as far as the *car* was concerned.

"Second, I wanted to know if a girl of that description, living or dead, had been out on a bicycle that night. I spent several thousand dollars with a private detective agency, having them canvass that neighborhood—and a fair area around it—with a fine-tooth comb to find if a girl answering that description currently or ever had existed, with or without a red bicycle. They came up with a few possible red-headed teenagers, but I managed to get a gander at each of them, no dice.

"*And*, after asking around, I picked a head shrinker of my own and started going to him. Allegedly the best in the city, certainly the most expensive. Went to him for two months. It was a washout. I never found out what he thought had happened; he wouldn't talk. You know how psychoanalysts work, they make you do the talking, analyze yourself, and finally tell them what's wrong with you, then you yak about it a while and tell them you're cured, and they then agree with you and tell you to go with God. All right if your subconscious knows what the score is and eventually lets it leak out. But my subconscious didn't know which end was up, so I was wasting my time, and I quit.

"But meanwhile I'd leveled with a few friends of mine to get their ideas and one of them—a professor of philosophy at the university—started talking about ontology and that started me reading up on ontology and gave me a clue. In fact, I thought it was more than a clue, I thought it was the *answer.* Until last night. Since last night I know I was at least partly wrong."

"Ontology—" said Mearson. "Word's vaguely familiar, but will you pin it down for me?"

"I quote you the *Webster Unabridged,* unexpurgated version: 'Ontology is the science of being or reality; the branch of knowledge that investigates the nature, essential properties, and relations of being, as such.' "

Kane glanced at his wrist watch. "But this is taking longer to tell than I thought. I'm getting tired talking and no doubt you're even more tired of listening. Shall we finish this tomorrow?"

"An excellent idea, Larry." Mearson stood up.

Kane tilted the silver flask for the last drop and handed it back. "You'll play St. Bernard again?"

"I went to the Forty-fourth," Mearson said. "The incident you described to me is on the blotter all right. And I talked to one of the two coppers who went back with you to the scene of the—uh—back to the car. Your *reporting* of the accident was real, no question of that."

"I'll start where I left off," Kane said. "Ontology, the study of the nature of reality. In reading up on it I came across solipsism, which originated with the Greeks. It is the belief that the entire universe is the product of one's imagination—in my case, *my* imagination. That I myself am the only concrete reality and that all things and all other people exist only in my mind."

Mearson frowned. "So, then the girl on the bicycle, having only an imaginary existence to begin with, ceased to exist—uh, *retroactively,* as of the moment you killed her? Leaving no trace behind her, except a memory in your mind, of ever having existed?"

"That possibility occurred to me, and I decided to do something which I thought would verify or disprove it. Specifically, to commit a murder, deliberately, to see what would happen."

"But—but Larry, murders happen every day, people are killed every day, and don't vanish retroactively and leave no trace behind them."

"But they were not killed by *me,*" Kane said earnestly. "And if the universe *is* a product of my imagination, that should make a difference. The girl on the bicycle is the first person *I* ever killed."

Mearson sighed. "So you decided to check by committing a murder. And shot Queenie Quinn. But why didn't she—?"

"No, no, no," Kane interrupted. "I committed another first, a month or so ago. A man. A man—and there's no use my telling you his name or anything about him because, as of now, he never existed, like the girl on the bicycle.

"But of course I didn't *know* it would happen that way, so I didn't simply kill him openly, as I did the stripper. I took careful precautions, so if his body *had* been found, the police would never have apprehended *me* as the killer.

"But after I killed him, well—he just never had existed, and I thought that my theory was confirmed. After that I carried a gun, thinking that I could kill with impunity any time I wanted to—and that it wouldn't matter, wouldn't be immoral even, because anyone I killed didn't really exist anyway except in my mind."

"Ummm," said Mearson.

"Ordinarily, Morty," Kane said, "I'm a pretty even-tempered guy. Night before last was the first time I used the gun. When that damn stripper hit me she hit *hard*, a roundhouse swing. It blinded me for the moment and I just reacted automatically in pulling out the gun and shooting her."

"Ummm," the attorney said. "And Queenie Quinn turned out to be for real and you're in jail for murder and doesn't that blow your solipsism theory sky-high?"

Kane frowned. "It certainly modifies it. I've been thinking a lot since I was arrested, and here's what I've come up with. If Queenie was real—and obviously she was—then I was not, and probably am not, the *only* real person. There are real people and unreal ones, ones that exist only in the imagination of the real ones.

"How many, I don't know. Maybe only a few, maybe thousands, even millions. My sampling—three people, of whom one turned out to have been real—is too small to be significant."

"But why? Why should there be a duality like that?"

"I haven't the faintest idea." Kane frowned. "I've had some pretty wild thoughts, but any one of them would be just a guess. Like a conspiracy—but a conspiracy against *whom?* Or *what?* And *all* of the real ones couldn't be in on the conspiracy, because I'm not."

He chuckled without humor. "I had a really far-out dream about it last night, one of those confused, mixed-up dreams that you can't really tell anybody, because they have no continuity, just a series of impressions. Something about a conspiracy and a *reality file* that lists the names of all the *real* people and keeps them real. And—here's a dream pun for you—reality is really run by a chain, only they're not known to be a chain, of *reality* companies, one in each city. Of course they deal in real estate too, as a front. And—oh hell, it's all too confused even to try to tell.

"Well, Morty, that's it. And my guess is that you'll tell me my only defense is an insanity plea—and you'll be right because, damn it, if I *am* sane I *am* a murderer. First degree and without extenuating circumstances. So?"

"So," said Mearson. He doodled a moment with a gold pencil and then looked up. "The head shrinker you went to for a while—his name wasn't Galbraith, was it?"

Kane shook his head.

"Good. Doc Galbraith is a friend of mine and the best forensic psychiatrist in the city, maybe in the country. Has worked with me on a dozen cases and we've won all of them. I'd like his opinion before I even start to map out a defense. Will you talk to him, be completely frank with him, if I send him around to see you?"

"Of course. Uh—will you ask him to do me a favor?"

"Probably. What is it?"

"Lend him your flask and ask him to bring it filled. You've no idea how much more nearly pleasant it makes these interviews."

The intercom on Mortimer Mearson's desk buzzed and he pressed the button on it that would bring his secretary's voice in. "Dr. Galbraith to see you, sir." Mearson told her to send him in at once.

"Hi, Doc," Mearson said. "Take a load off your feet and tell all."

Galbraith took the load off his feet and lighted a cigarette before he spoke. "Puzzling for a while," he said. "I didn't get the answer till I went into medical history with him. While playing polo at age twenty-two he had a fall and got a whop on the head with a mallet that caused a bad concussion and subsequent amnesia. Complete at first, but gradually his memory came back completely up to early adolescence. Pretty spotty between then and the time of the injury."

"Good God, the indoctrination period."

"Exactly. Oh, he has flashes—like the dream he told you about. He could be rehabilitated—but I'm afraid it's too late, now. If only we'd caught him before he committed an overt murder— But we can't possibly risk putting his story on record now, even as an insanity defense. So."

"So," Mearson said. "I'll make the call now. And then go see him again. Hate to, but it's got to be done."

He pushed a button on the intercom. "Dorothy, get me Mr. Hodge at the Midland Realty Company. When you get him, put the call on my private line."

Galbraith left while he was waiting and a moment later one of his phones rang and he picked it up. "Hodge?" he said, "Mearson here. Your phone secure? ... Good. Code eighty-four. Remove the card of Lorenz Kane—L-o-r-e-n-z K-a-n-e—from the reality file at once ... Yes, it's necessary and an emergency. I'll submit a report tomorrow."

He took a pistol from a desk drawer and a taxi to the courthouse. He arranged an audience with his client and as soon as Kane came through the door— there was no use waiting—he shot him dead. He waited the minute it always took for the body to vanish, and then went upstairs to the chambers of Judge Amanda Hayes to make a final check.

"Hi, Your Honoress," he said. "Somebody recently was telling me about a man named Lorenz Kane, and I don't remember who it was. Was it you?"

"Never heard the name, Morty. It wasn't me."

"You mean 'It wasn't I.' Must've been someone else. Thanks, Your Judgeship. Be seeing you."

Ten Percenter

I'm scared stiff. Not just because tomorrow is the big day, the day I'm scheduled to go through a little green door for a lesson in what cyanide gas smells like. It's not that at all. I *want* to die. But—

Everything started when I met Roscoe, but before I get to that let me give you a quick sketch of what I was B. R.—*Before Roscoe.*

I was young, reasonably good-looking in a rough-hewn sort of way, reasonably intelligent, fairly well-educated. And my name was Bill Wheeler, then. And I was a would-be television or movie actor who'd been trying for five years and hadn't been able to get even a chance to do a local commercial, let alone a walk-on in a B movie. I was eating by working an evening shift, 6 P.M. to 2 A.M., as counterman in a hamburger drive-in in Santa Monica.

I'd taken the job originally because it gave me my days free to take the bus into Hollywood and haunt the offices of agents and studios. But as of the evening when it all started, when my luck did an abrupt volte-face, I'd just about given up. I hadn't been in Hollywood for almost a week. I'd been resting up and getting a healthy tan on the beach, doing some heavy thinking about my future, trying to decide what kind of a job I might be fitted for and able to get, and that might lead me into a life that would have at least *some* satisfactions. Up to then, it had been acting or nothing; to give up even the someday hope of being an actor took quite a bit of readjustment in my thinking.

My change of luck started one evening at six o'clock, just the time I'd have been reporting to work at the drive-in had it not been my evening off, and it happened on Olympic Boulevard near Fourth Street in Santa Monica.

I found a wallet. The wallet contained only thirty-five dollars in cash, but there were Diner's Club, Carte Blanche, International and other credit cards.

I headed for the nearest bar for a drink—and some thinking.

I'd never done anything seriously dishonest in my life, but I decided that this find, at the very nadir of my life to date, was a sign from Someone or Something that this was meant to be the biggest night of my life as well as its turning point.

I knew it wouldn't be safe to use the cards indefinitely, but surely there'd be no risk for one evening, one night. I'd have a fine dinner, drinks, a plush hotel, a call girl, the works. (Yes, I know call girls don't honor credit cards, but I could use the cards to cash checks for whatever the traffic would bear at every place I stopped, and I'd stop as many places as I could before the call-girl stage of the evening.)

With any luck at all I'd end up with a pretty fair stake. I'd make my final use of a credit card for plane fare out of this hopeless place in the morning, and start over somewhere else *as* something else. I'd try anything but acting. Never again that—unless someday after the bitter taste of failure at professionalism had gone, at amateur theatricals, as an avocation.

I began to lay my plans carefully, for time was of the essence.

I started by asking the bartender if he'd phone for a taxi for me. I took it to my room. There, for half an hour, I practiced the signature on the cards until I could forge it perfectly without glancing at it. I called for another taxi while I packed and was ready when it came. I told the driver to take me to the nearest car-rental agency.

I wanted a Cadillac and was a little disappointed to have to settle for a Chrysler, but it didn't really matter, since it was unlikely that anyone but parking attendants would be seeing it.

I told the man, as I planned to tell a lot of other people before the night was over, that I'd run short of ready cash and if he had a blank check available I'd appreciate it if he could cash a check for me for whatever amount he could conveniently handle. Of course I had plenty of other identification, including, thank God, a driver's license, to match the credit cards. He checked the register, cashed a check for me for fifty dollars, and I was off on my career of crime.

I was getting hungry, so I drove in on Wilshire to Hollywood, turned the car over to a parking attendant at the Derby, and went in. The tables were all taken and the maître d'hôtel told me I'd have to wait fifteen or twenty minutes for a table. I told him that was all right and that he'd find me at the bar whenever a table was ready, and walked through to the bar.

I took the only vacant stool at the bar and found myself sitting next to a man who was also obviously alone, since on the other side of him sat a couple who were engrossed in one another and not including him in the conversation. He was a dapper little man with a thick but ruly shock of almost pure white hair and a small neat white mustache, but the pinkness and baby-smoothness of his skin indicated him to be much younger than his white hair and mustache would otherwise make him seem. Obviously, he'd been at the bar only a minute or two, since he didn't yet have a drink in front of him.

In a sense it was the bartender who introduced us. Assuming that we were together, he took and brought our orders together and asked if we wanted one bar check or two. The dapper little man beat me to the punch, since I was about to do the same thing, by turning to me and asking if I'd do him the honor of having my drink with and on him. I thanked him and accepted; we touched glasses and were in conversation.

As I recall it, we skipped using the weather as an opening gambit but found ourselves on the number two midsummer subject of conversation in Los Angeles, the Dodgers' pennant chances.

As an actor—or anyway as an ex-would-be actor—I have always been interested in accents and his especially intrigued me. It was Oxford English with just a touch of Lebanese and salted or peppered with an occasional pure Hollywoodism or fragment of bop talk. If and when I quote him directly later, I won't try to reproduce it.

I liked him and he seemed to like me. Almost right away, without formally introducing ourselves, we got on a first-name basis. Call him Roscoe, he told me. And I told him to call me Jerry instead of Bill, because J. was the first initial of J. R. Burger, the name on the credit cards; I'd already decided that if Roscoe hadn't dined yet I'd probably ask him to eat with me. Under the circumstances two dinners wouldn't cost me any more than one.

After baseball, about which neither of us knew very much, movies came up in our conversation. Yes, he told me, he was in the industry. Not actively at the moment, but he had investments in several independent productions and two television shows. Up to three years ago he had produced or directed a dozen movies, the first few in London, the rest here. Was I an actor? He thought I looked and talked as though I could be one.

Don't ask me why; suddenly I found myself telling him the whole bitter truth about my failure but, oddly, not telling it bitterly at all but lightly, making it sound funny. Still more oddly, suddenly myself seeing it as amusing. I was just going good when a waiter came and asked if I was the gentleman waiting for a table. I said I was and asked Roscoe if he'd be my guest and he accepted.

We ordered and then I found myself doing most of the talking while we ate. Of course I had to change the ending of my story to account for my relative prosperity at the moment, but that wasn't difficult; I simply invented a small inheritance from an uncle. And said that I'd learned my lesson and wasn't going to pour it down the same rathole as I had the last five years of my life. I was going back to my hometown and a sensible job.

The waiter came and went, leaving our bill. I turned it over to add a generous tip and then put a credit card atop it. I was glad Roscoe didn't give me an argument about paying or even splitting it. I wanted to establish my credit to see if I could cash a check. And, mostly to make conversation, I mentioned to Roscoe I was short of cash and asked if he had any idea how big a check the Derby might cash for me.

"Why bother them, old boy?" he asked. "I always carry quite a bit of cash. Would five hundred be enough?"

I tried not to look elated when I told him that it would. I hadn't hoped for more than a fraction of that from the restaurant; they'd probably take some chance on a credit-card customer but surely not too much. When the waiter came to pick up the bill and the card, I asked him to bring a blank check and he did. While I filled in the name of a bank at the top and made the check out to cash, Roscoe brought out a gold money clip that seemed to hold all hundreds, at least a dozen of them, and counted out five.

He gave them to me as I handed him the check. He glanced at it and his eyebrows went up slightly. "Jerry," he said, "I'd intended to ask you up to my place for a talk anyway, but now there's a double reason. We seem to have the same name. Or did you by any chance find a wallet I lost this afternoon in Santa Monica?"

Oh God, oh God, oh God, yes, I know *now* that it was something more than coincidence—it *had* to be in a city the size of Los Angeles—but what else could I think then? It wasn't even as though he'd *followed* me into the Derby; he'd been there ahead of me.

For a wild moment I considered making a bolt for it—after all, he didn't know my right name and if I made a clean getaway I'd be safe. But if I started to run and he yelled "Stop thief!" half a dozen waiters would have a chance of holding me or tripping me.

He was talking on, calmly. "The J. R. is for Joshua Roscoe, so you can see why I choose the lesser of evils. Now don't be a shnook. I may be able to make you an interesting proposition. Ready?"

He stood up and I nodded dumbly and stood up too, wondering what in hell kind of a proposition he could have in mind. He didn't look queer, but if that's what it was I could handle him.

I followed him out and of course this *was* coincidence but there was a police car with two coppers in it parked just past the loading zone. He gave the doorman a buck—he kept small change like that loose in a pocket and only big bills in the clip—and asked for a taxi. I almost opened my mouth to say I had a car on the lot, but decided to keep my yap shut and see what happened.

We got in the cab and he gave an address on La Cienega. He didn't talk on the way, and I was doing mental arithmetic. I could make restitution, just about on the head. Out of my own twenty-five bucks, I mean. The restaurant bill had been, with tip, twelve bucks. And if I took the Chrysler back right away there'd be only about twenty miles and two or three hours on it, and I could use the same fifty I'd got for the bum check to buy it back. If he'd let me, I'd make a clean breast of things and handle it that way.

The cab stopped in front of a prosperous-looking apartment building. *Was* it coincidence that another police car happened to be parked across the street? Anyway, I'd already decided to listen to him, and then to make my own pitch, and to try a break only if all else failed.

We took a self-service elevator to the fourth floor, where he used a key to let us into the living room of a very pleasant bachelor apartment. Six rooms, I learned later, but no live-in servants, since he liked privacy. He waved me to a sofa, and walked toward a small bar in one corner. "A brandy?"

I nodded and then started to talk, to make my pitch about restitution, while he poured brandy into two snifters. He came over and gave me one of them. "Spare me the sordid details, Jer— Oh, is that your right first name, or did you pick it just to match the first initial on the cards?"

"It's Bill," I said. "William Trent." I wasn't about to give him my right last name until I knew it would be safe, but there was nothing to lose with my first.

I was glad to see that he took a chair facing me, not alongside me on the sofa. "Not distinctive," he said. "With that reddish hair of yours, how about Brick? Brick Brannon. Like it?"

I nodded. I did rather like it, and besides he could call me anything he wanted as long as he didn't call copper or make a pass.

"To your health, Brick," he said, lifting the snifter. "Now the story you told me. How much of it is true?"

"Every word," I told him, "if you substitute finding a wallet for an inheritance from an uncle."

He put down his glass, crossed the room to a small desk and took a mimeographed movie script from a drawer. He found a place in the script while he crossed back with it, and handed it to me open. "Read the part of Philippe for the next page and a half. He's a tough, illiterate lumberjack, Canuck accent. Deeply in love with his wife but jumping mad at her in this quarrel scene. Read it to yourself first and then try it. Just pause for her lines."

I read it over to myself and then tried it. He told me to leaf over a dozen or so pages to find another scene and read the part of one of the characters, and then a third, each time briefing me on who the character was, how he talked, and his relationship to the other characters on scene or referred to.

When I finished the third reading, he nodded and told me to put the manuscript down and pick up my brandy.

He took a leisurely sip of his own drink. "Okay," he said, "you *are* an actor. You just haven't had a break. I can make a star out of you within two years if you let me manage you."

"No catches?" I asked, wondering if he was out of his head.

"Ten percent," he said. "But it will have to come off the top—and under the table. You see, Bill, I'm not an accredited agent, and you'll have to have one of them, and pay him another ten percent, to handle details, draw up contracts and such. What I do will be behind the scenes.

I said, "Fine by me, but I haven't been able to get a reputable agent to sign me yet. What do I do about that?"

"I'll take care of that. You'll have to pay him ten percent off the top too, because he's not to know—*nobody* is to know—about your arrangement with me. His ten percent will be a normal tax deduction for you, but mine won't because it'll be off the record. Agreed?"

I said, "Fine," again, and meant it. I'd often thought in despair of trying to bribe an agent to take me on by offering him twenty or even fifty percent if he'd really push me; I'd actually tried it with several of them I'd been able to get in to see, and had been turned down flat. "Any other conditions?"

"Only one. Since there'll be nothing on paper between us, I'll expect you, on your honor, not to let me build you up and then try to include me out. So here's how we'll define that.

"Either of us may cancel this agreement during the first year. But if for that year—with me operating behind the scenes, whether or not you recognize my fine Italian hand in what happens—your gross income is twenty-five thousand dollars or more, then the arrangement between us becomes permanent and irrevocable. Agreed?"

"Agreed," I said. I hadn't earned a hundred dollars from acting in my life; twenty-five thousand seemed an impossible figure.

And even if he was crazy, I had nothing to lose, and besides he wasn't going to have me arrested. Which reminded me, and I took out the wallet. I said, "Now, about restitution—"

He sighed. "All right," he said. "I detest details, so let's get them out of the way. Tell me everything you did since you found the wallet." I did, and put the wallet itself on the table.

He picked it up, emptied all the money out of it and pocketed the wallet. "So," he said. "Five hundred and thirty-five of that is mine. Keep it as a loan; you can pay me back in a month or so. Take back the rented car and buy back the fifty-dollar check. Forget the tab you signed my name to at the Derby; the dinner was on me.

"Don't go back to the drive-in. Take a room or an apartment tonight in Hollywood. That suit you have on isn't bad, but if it's your best, get a better one tomorrow, and whatever accessories you need. Oh, a black leather motorcycle jacket and jeans, if you don't happen to have them already."

"A motorcycle jacket?" I asked. "Why?"

"Never mind why. Wait." He took out the money clip, counted out the hundred-dollar bills left in it, eight of them, and handed them to me. "Eight hundred more you owe me. Get a car out of it; you'll need something to get around in. You'll have to get around to Universal City, Culver City—the industry isn't concentrated in Hollywood. Spend maybe five hundred of that for something used. You'll be trading it in for a new car within a few months.

"What else? Oh, *was* Bill Trent your right name?"

"It's Bill Wheeler."

"It was; it's Brick Brannon now. And that's all, except give me a ring early tomorrow afternoon. My number's in the book." He grinned. "And you won't forget the name since you practiced forging it."

I had a busy evening, though far from the one I'd planned. I took a taxi back to the Derby and got the Chrysler, turned it in in Santa Monica and bought back my check out of the register on the story that I'd accidentally overdrawn my account in writing it and had raised cash elsewhere. Fortunately, the rental agency was on the stretch of Santa Monica Boulevard that's full of used-car lots that are open evenings, so I left my suitcases at the agency and went car hunting. On the second lot I found just what I wanted, a Rambler priced at five hundred. After a drive around the block I talked it down to four-fifty easily even without a trade-in, and bought it on the spot.

I got my suitcases and drove back into Hollywood. It was still early and I shopped Sunset Strip for a bachelor apartment, found one and moved in. For a hundred and fifty a month I had a home, parking space for the Rambler, access to a swimming pool, even telephone service through a switchboard. And it was still early, hours before I would have ended the evening I had originally planned, but I was suddenly dead tired, and turned in the minute I'd unpacked my suitcases. I should have been too excited to sleep, but I dropped off and slept soundly the moment I got into bed.

In the morning I went up to Hollywood Boulevard, bought a good if ready-made suit and a few other things. Even a damn black leather jacket, although I didn't know why. I already had several pairs of jeans. Back home I had a swim, went across the street for lunch, and then phoned Roscoe.

"Stout fellow, sweetie," he said. "Know an agent named Ray Ramspaugh?"

"I know of him," I said. And I did, with awe. He was the biggest of the solo-operator flesh peddlers, the biggest and the best. He handled only a few hand-picked clients. I'd never dreamed of even trying to see him.

"You've got an appointment with him at two o'clock. Be there."

"Will do," I said. "Shall I call to let you know what happens?"

"I already know," he said. "Brick, from here on in you'll have to call me only when you get a check. Then phone me and we'll make a date, here or somewhere else, and you can give me my cut."

I got to Ramspaugh's office on South Vernon Drive on the dot and didn't have to wait a minute. His secretary sent me right in.

He got right down to business. He said, "Roscoe says you're good and I'll take his word for it. Here's a contract ready for your signature. It's a standard contract, but read it before you sign it. Take it in the outer office for that; I'll be making some phone calls."

It was a printed contract and I'd have signed it on faith, but apparently he wanted to get rid of me while he did some phoning, so I took it into his secretary's office and read it, even the small type, and then signed it. His secretary used the intercom and told me he was ready to see me again and I should go back in, and I did.

He said, "Think I've got something lined up. A small part, but you'll have to take some small ones first to get yourself some credits. One-shot part in a new series they're starting to film at Revue. They had it cast, but the boy they signed got himself bunged up in an auto accident this morning. They need you fast. Can you get there by three?"

I nodded speechlessly.

"Okay. Ask for Ted Crowther. Oh, it'll save time if you can go in costume. You'll play a tough young punk, one of those who try to act like Brando in *The Wild One*. Got a black leather jacket and jeans?"

I gulped and nodded again.

"Change into 'em on your way. And fly right, sweetheart. We're going places."

That's just how difficult it was for me to get my first break at acting, and for a long time I was too busy to wonder just how Roscoe could possibly have known, the night before, that next day it would help me get a fast start on my first role to have a black leather motorcycle jacket ready to put on. As of when he'd made the suggestion, the automobile accident that had incapacitated the young man signed for that role hadn't happened yet.

But I think I know *why* he told me about that jacket. Aside from getting me signed, right off and without a question, by a top agent—a miracle in itself—Roscoe's "fine Italian hand" seldom showed. All my roles came through Ramspaugh and I could have assumed that he and I were doing it all by ourselves. That very first time, to show me something, Roscoe had *wanted* his hand to show. He'd wanted to give me something to think about.

But I didn't have too much time to think, certainly not enough time to get frightened. I got too busy. Small parts at first, some of them only bit parts, but as many of them as I could handle. And by the end of the year I was building up, or being built up, for solid, important supporting roles. I could probably have made more money, but sometimes Ramspaugh turned down for me higher-paying parts in favor of lower-paying ones. He didn't want to let me become typed, for one thing. Also he wouldn't let me take any continuing role on a series show where I'd be put under contract to do the same thing over and over again.

Even so, I grossed a little over fifty thousand that year, twice the figure that would have made my agreement with Roscoe irrevocable, so irrevocable it became. After the two ten percents, one of them deductible against taxes and the other not, and taxes themselves, I still had a little over five hundred bucks a week take-home; also a Jaguar, a really fine wardrobe and a really nice apartment.

The second year I doubled that. Doubled my net, I mean, to a thousand a week, which meant that since it put me in a higher tax bracket, I had considerably more than doubled my gross. I was moving more and more to supporting roles in movies now; my name was well enough known so that my appearances on series television shows were "guest star" shots, and I'd had leading roles on several anthology shows.

That year though, something happened that reminded me of Roscoe's prescience, if that's what it was, and indicated a new facet in our relationship that I hadn't realized he considered to exist.

This isn't the episode, but I'll have to tell it as preliminary: I spent a week in Las Vegas on location for a movie. Ordinarily I'm not a gambler, but one evening I did go to one of the casinos, buy a thousand in chips, and go to one of the crap tables. Starting at a hundred dollars a bet I hit a hot streak and soon was betting the maximum of five hundred a throw. I ran it up to a little over twenty thousand and then started to lose. And when I was down to eleven thousand, a profit of ten grand even, I quit. On my return I saw Roscoe to hand him his off-the-top of my take since I'd last seen him. He counted it and then asked for a thousand more, reminding me of my ten grand extra in Las Vegas. I handed it over, and without question. I hadn't tried to hold out on him; I just hadn't realized that by ten percent of everything he *meant* everything. There was no mystery how he could have learned of my luck; several others of the movie company had been at the table with me.

It was the follow-up of that episode that worries me now, and later you'll see why. We returned a week later to Las Vegas for some retakes. I did some gambling again—why not, since I was still ahead?—and this time dropped four thousand. But because I hit no lucky streaks, I didn't stay long in any one place; I wandered the length of the Strip and visited a dozen casinos. No one was with me and no one could have possibly known the total of my losses. Nevertheless, the next time I saw Roscoe to give him money, he handed me back four hundred of it. Fair enough; if he cut my winnings, why not my losses? But how could he have known?

Anyway, it was another clue as to what he meant by ten percent of everything. The really staggering one came when I got married. Yes, you've guessed it, but I'll have to explain how it came about.

At the start of my third year I was signed for my first starring role in an important picture, at five grand a week. Co-starring, rather; my co-star was a beautiful and coming young actress named Lorna Howard. In a briefing session before the shooting started, Lorna and I were together in the office of the producer, and he had a sudden thought. "Say, kids," he said, "this is just an idea, but you're both free and single. If you got married—to each other, I mean—we could hang a big hunk of publicity on it. Good for the picture *and* your careers." He grinned; "It could be a marriage of convenience, of course."

I raised an eyebrow at Lorna. *"Would* it be?" I asked her.

She raised an eyebrow back. "That could, sir, depend on what you mean by convenience."

And so we were married.

Looking back, it's hard for me to realize, let alone explain, why I had taken so little advantage of the increasing opportunities with women that my meteoric rise over those first two years had given me. Oh, I hadn't been celibate. But my affairs had been relatively few and unimportant to me. Of course I'd been damned busy, and at the end of a hard day I was usually dead tired and dreading the thought of having to get up early the next morning for another day of it. Sometimes I'd not even think about wanting a woman for weeks at a time.

But marriage snapped me out of that. Lorna and I weren't in love, but she was as concupiscent as she was beautiful and the marriage did turn out to be more than convenient. For a while we had fun head over heels, sometimes quite literally. With the understanding that each of us was free morally, and that since there was no love between us there must be no jealousy either. I myself didn't take advantage of that understanding, but it wasn't long before I realized that I apparently wasn't quite enough for her and that she was having an affair on the side. Ten percent of the time, I felt sure, after I accidentally learned who her lover was.

I had no moral cause for complaint, but for me it did take the bloom off things; she felt it and we drifted apart. After the picture was released, she went to Reno for a quiet divorce. At no cost to me, incidentally; she had more capital than I, and as much income. If I'd had to pay for the divorce, or pay alimony, I have a hunch I'd have been reimbursed for ten percent of whatever it would have cost me.

By that time I'd signed for another starring role, this time at a really astronomical figure, and suddenly realized something. Past a certain level of income, I was beginning to lose money by making more. Most people don't realize it, and I certainly hadn't, but when the taxable portion of your income passes two hundred thousand, in the case of a single man, you have to pay ninety-one percent on everything above that, leaving you nine percent—less, of course, state income tax. So, with ten percent of my gross going to Roscoe under the table and therefore not deductible, I *lost* money on everything I earned over two hundred thousand. If I ever grossed half a million in one year, I'd go broke. I could never become a *top* star.

But that wasn't what made me decide to kill Roscoe, as the only way to revoke an irrevocable agreement. I wasn't all that greedy for either money or greater fame and, while it wouldn't make me happy to do so, I could do as some stars already did and make only one picture a year. Ramspaugh wouldn't like it, but he could lump it.

What tore things was that I fell in love. Suddenly, completely, overboard, for the first time in my life, and, I knew, for the only time. She wasn't an actress and had never wanted to be one; her name was Bessie Evans and she was a script girl at Columbia. And the first time we met, she fell in love with me as completely as I with her.

Roscoe had to go. I wanted more than just an affair with her; I wanted to marry her and for keeps, and while Roscoe lived, I couldn't. Or anyway wouldn't. If he would get ten percent of *that* marriage, I'd have to kill him anyway, so it might as well be sooner.

I couldn't explain to Bessie why I couldn't marry her at once, of course; I simply had to ask her to trust me, and she did. And while I was laying my plans to kill Roscoe and free myself I hid her away under an assumed name in a little apartment in Burbank. I saw her as seldom as our ardor would permit and took the most elaborate precautions never to be followed there.

I shall not go into detail about my plan to kill Roscoe. Suffice it to say that I acquired an untraceable gun and a key to his apartment. And wore a perfect disguise so that if I were seen in or near his apartment building, I'd never be recognized or afterward identified.

One morning at three o'clock I used the key. Gun in hand, I crossed the living room silently and opened the bedroom door. There was just enough light from outside for me to see him sit up suddenly at the sound of the opening door. I shot six times and he wasn't sitting up any longer.

I'd have left immediately except that in the sudden silence after the shots I heard the quiet closing of a window, seemingly from his kitchen, one window of which, I remembered, opened onto a fire escape.

A sudden horrible suspicion made me turn on the bedroom light, and the horrible suspicion had been justified. It hadn't been Roscoe, alone in bed. It had been Bessie, momentarily alone there. Why had it never even remotely occurred to me that ten percent of everything wouldn't mean only of money or a marriage?

In a sense, I died right there and then. Anyway, I decided that I *wanted* to die, and if there'd been a bullet left in the gun I'd probably have put it into my head. Instead, I phoned the police. By the time they came I'd come to the conclusion I might as well let them do the job for me in the gas chamber.

I refused to talk to the police lest a lawyer might use my story to make, even against my will, a successful insanity plea. To avoid this, when I got a lawyer and talked to him, I told him lies that made him think he had the basis for a successful defense, and so conned him into putting me on the stand to testify. Then, deliberately, I let the prosecutor tear me to pieces on cross-examination so there'd be no doubt about my getting the death penalty.

Roscoe dropped out of sight and is still missing. Since the murder happened in his apartment, the police had wanted to find him to ask him questions, but they didn't need him for their case and didn't look hard.

But wherever he is, the agreement between us is "permanent and irrevocable," and that's what's got me scared, so scared I haven't slept the last few nights.

What's ten percent of death? Do I remain one-tenth alive, one-tenth conscious, throughout a gray eternity? Return to live again and suffer again one day out of ten or one year out of ten—and in what form? Or if Roscoe is who I'm beginning to suspect him of being, what will he do with ten percent of a soul?

All I know is that *tomorrow I'll find out*—and I'm scared.

Eine Kleine Nachtmusik

(In collaboration with Carl Onspaugh)

His name was Dooley Hanks and he was One of Us, by which I mean that he was partly a paranoiac, partly a schizophrenic, and mostly a nut with a strong *idée fixe,* an obsession. His obsession was that someday he'd find The Sound that he'd been looking for all his life, or at least all of his life since twenty years ago, in his teens, when he had acquired a clarinet and learned how to play it. Truth to tell, he was only an average musician, but the clarinet was his rod and staff, and it was the broomstick that enabled him to travel over the face of Earth, on all the continents, seeking The Sound. Playing a gig here and a gig there, and then, when he was ahead by a few dollars or pounds or drachmas or rubles he'd take a walking tour until his money started to run out, then start for the nearest city big enough to let him find another gig.

He didn't know what The Sound would sound like, but he knew that he'd know it when he heard it. Three times he'd *thought* he'd found it. Once, in Australia, the first time he'd heard a bull-roarer. Once, in Calcutta, in the sound of a musette played by a fakir to charm a cobra. And once, west of Nairobi, in the blending of a hyena's laughter with the voice of a lion. But the bull-roarer, on second hearing, was just a noise; the musette, when he'd bought it from the fakir for twenty rupees and had taken it home, had turned out to be only a crude and raucous type of reed instrument with little range and not even a chromatic scale; the jungle sounds had resolved themselves finally into simple lion roars and hyena laughs, not at all The Sound.

Actually Dooley Hanks had a great and rare talent that could have meant much more to him than his clarinet, a gift of tongues. He knew dozens of languages and spoke them all fluently, idiomatically and without accent. A few weeks in any country was enough for him to pick up the language and speak it like a native. But he had never tried to cash in on this talent, and never would. Mediocre player though he was, the clarinet was his love.

Currently, the language he had just mastered was German, picked up in three weeks of playing with a combo in a beer-*stube* in Hanover, West Germany. And the money in his pocket, such as it was, was in marks. And at the end of a day of hiking, augmented by one fairly long lift in a Volkswagen, he stood in moonlight on the banks of the Weser River. Wearing his hiking clothes and with his working clothes, his good suit, in a haversack on his back. His clarinet case in his hand; he always carried it so, never trusting it to suitcase, when he used one, or to haversack when he was hiking.

Driven by a demon, and feeling suddenly an excitement that must be, that could only be, a hunch, a feeling that at long last he was really about to find The Sound. He was trembling a little; he'd never had the hunch this strongly before, not even with the lions and the hyenas, and that had been the closest.

But where? Here, in the water? Or in the next town? Surely not farther than the next town. The hunch was that strong. That tremblingly strong. Like the verge of madness, and suddenly he knew that he *would* go mad if he did not find it soon. Maybe he was a little mad already.

Staring over moonlit water. And suddenly something disrupted its surface, flashed silently white in the moonlight and was gone again. Dooley stared at the spot. A fish? There had been no sound, no splash. A hand? The hand of a mermaid swum upstream from the North Sea beckoning him? Come in, the water's fine. (But it wouldn't be; it was *cold*.) Some supernatural water sprite? A displaced Rhine Maiden in the Weser?

But was it really a sign? Dooley, shivering now at the thought of what he was thinking, stood at the Weser's edge and imagined how it would be ... wading out slowly from the bank, letting his emotions create the tune for the clarinet, tilting his head back as the water became deeper so that the instrument would stick out of the water after he, Dooley, was under it, the bell of the clarinet last to submerge. And the sound, whatever sound there was, being made by the bubbling water closing over them. Over him first and then the clarinet. He recalled the clichéd allegation, which he had previously viewed with iconoclastic contempt but now felt almost ready to accept, that a drowning person was treated to a swift viewing of his entire life as it flashed before his eyes in a grand finale to living. What a mad montage that would be! What an inspiration for the final gurglings of the clarinet. What a frantic blending of the whole of his wild, sweetly sad, tortured existence, just as his straining lungs expelled their final gasp into a final note and inhaled the cold, dark water. A shudder of breathless anticipation coursed through Dooley Hanks's body as his fingers trembled with the catch on the battered clarinet case.

But *no*, he told himself. Who would hear? Who would know? It was important that someone hear. Otherwise his quest, his discovery, his entire life would be in vain. Immortality cannot be derived from one's solitary knowledge of one's greatness. And what good was The Sound if it brought him death and not immortality?

A blind alley. Another blind alley. Perhaps the next town. Yes, the next town. His hunch was coming back now. How had he been so foolish as to think of drowning? To find The Sound, he'd kill if he had to—but not himself. That would make the whole gig meaningless.

Feeling as one who had had a narrow escape, he turned and walked away from the river, back to the road that paralleled it, and started walking toward the lights of the next town. Although Dooley Hanks had no Indian blood that he knew of, he walked like an Indian, one foot directly in front of the other, as though on a tightrope. And silently, or as nearly silently as was possible in hiking boots, the ball of his foot coming down first to cushion each step before his heel touched the roadway. And he walked rapidly because it was still early evening and he'd have plenty of time, after checking in at a hotel and getting rid of his haversack, to explore the town a while before they rolled up the sidewalks. A fog was starting to roll in now.

The narrowness of his escape from the suicidal impulse on the Weser's bank still worried him. He'd had it before, but never quite so strongly. The last time had been in New York, on top of the Empire State Building, over a hundred stories above the street. It had been a bright, clear day, and the magic of the view had enthralled him. And suddenly he had been seized by the same mad exultation, certain that a flash of inspiration had ended his quest, placed the goal at his fingertips. All he need do was take his clarinet from the case, assemble it. The magic view would be revealed in the first clear notes of the instrument and the heads of the other sightseers would turn in wonder. Then the contrasting gasp as he leaped into space, and the wailing, sighing, screaming notes, as he hurled pavementward, the weird melody inspired by the whirling color scene of the street and sidewalk and people watching in horrified fascination, watching him, Dooley Hanks, and hearing The Sound, his sound, as it built into a superb fortissimo, the grand finale of his greatest solo—the harsh final note as his body slammed into the sidewalk and fused flesh, blood and splintered bone with concrete, forcing the final, glorious expulsion of breath through the clarinet just before it left his lifeless fingers. But he'd saved himself by turning back and running for the exit and the elevator.

He didn't want to die. He'd have to keep reminding himself of that. No other price would be too great to pay.

He was well into town now. In an old section with dark, narrow streets and ancient buildings. The fog curled in from the river like a giant serpent hugging the street at first, then swelling and rising slowly to blot and blur his vision. But through it, across the cobbled street, he saw a lighted hotel sign, *Unter den Linden*. A pretentious name for so small a hotel, but it looked inexpensive and that was what he wanted. It was inexpensive all right and he took a room and carried his haversack up to it. He hesitated whether to change from his walking clothes to his good suit, and decided not to. He wouldn't be looking for an engagement tonight; tomorrow would be time for that. But he'd carry his clarinet, of course; he always did. He hoped he'd find a place to meet other musicians, maybe be asked to sit in with them. And of course he'd ask them about the best way to obtain a gig here. The carrying of an instrument case is an automatic introduction among musicians. In Germany, or anywhere.

Passing the desk on his way out he asked the clerk—a man who looked fully as old as the hostelry itself—for directions toward the center of town, the lively spots. Outside, he started in the direction the old man had indicated, but the streets were so crooked, the fog so thick, that he was lost within a few blocks and no longer knew even the direction from which he had come. So he wandered on aimlessly and in another few blocks found himself in an eerie neighborhood. This eeriness, without observable cause, unnerved him and for a panicked moment he started to run to get through the district as fast as he could, but then he stopped short as he suddenly became aware of music in the air—a weird, haunting whisper of music that, after he had listened to it a long moment, drew him along the dark street in search of its source. It seemed to be a single instrument playing, a reed instrument that didn't sound exactly like a clarinet or exactly like an oboe. It grew louder, then faded again. He looked in vain for a light, a movement, some clue to its birthplace. He turned to retrace his steps, walking on tiptoe now, and the music grew louder again. A few more steps and again it faded and Dooley retraced those few steps and paused to scan the somber, brooding building. There was no light behind any window. But the music was all around him now and—could it be coming up from below? Up from under the sidewalk?

He took a step toward the building, and saw what he had not seen before. Parallel to the building front, open and unprotected by a railing, a flight of worn stone steps led downward. And at the bottom of them, a yellow crack of light outlined three sides of a door. From behind that door came the music. And, he could now hear, voices in conversation.

He descended the steps cautiously and hesitated before the door, wondering whether he should knock or simply open it and walk in. Was it, despite the fact that he had not seen a sign anywhere, a public place? One so well-known to its habitués that no sign was needed? Or perhaps a private party where he would be an intruder?

He decided to let the question of whether the door would or would not turn out to be locked against him answer that question. He put his hand on the latch and it opened to his touch and he stepped inside.

The music reached out and embraced him tenderly. The place *looked* like a public place, a wine cellar. At the far end of a large room there were three huge wine tuns with spigots. There were tables and people, men and women both, seated at them. All with wineglasses in front of them. No steins; apparently only wine was served. A few people glanced at him, but disinterestedly and not with the look one gave an intruder, so obviously it was not a private party.

The musician—there was just one—was in a far corner of the room, sitting on a high stool. The room was almost as thick with smoke as the street had been thick with fog and Dooley's eyes weren't any too good anyway; from that distance he couldn't tell if the musician's instrument was a clarinet or an oboe or neither. Any more than his ears could answer that same question, even now, in the same room.

He closed the door behind him, and weaved his way through the tables, looking for an empty one as close to the musician as possible. He found one not too far away and sat down at it. He began to study the instrument with his eyes as well as his ears. It looked familiar. He'd seen one like it or almost like it somewhere, but where?

"*Ja, mein Herr?*" It was whispered close to his ear, and he turned. A fat little waiter in lederhosen stood at his elbow. "Zinfandel. Burgundy. Riesling."

Dooley knew nothing about wines and cared less, but he named one of the three. And as the waiter tiptoed away, he put a little pile of marks on the table so he wouldn't have to interrupt himself again when the wine came.

Then he studied the instrument again, trying for the moment *not* to listen to it, so he could concentrate on where he'd once seen something like it. It was about the length of his clarinet, with a slightly larger, more flaring bell. It was made—all in one piece, as far as he could tell—of some dark rich wood somewhere in color between dark walnut and mahogany, highly polished. It had finger holes and only three keys, two at the bottom to extend the range downward by two semitones, and a thumb-operated one at the top that would be an octave key.

He closed his eyes, and would have closed his ears had they operated that way, to concentrate on remembering where he'd seen something very like it. Where?

It came to him gradually. A museum, somewhere. Probably in New York, because he'd been born and raised there, hadn't left there until he was twenty-four, and this was longer ago than that, like when he was still in his teens. Museum of Natural Science? That part didn't matter. There had been a room or several rooms of glass cases displaying ancient and medieval musical instruments: viola da gambas and viola d'amores, sackbuts and panpipes and recorders, lutes and tambours and fifes. And one glass case had held only shawms and hautboys, both precursors of the modern oboe. And this instrument, the one to which he was listening now in thrall, was a hautboy. You could distinguish the shawms because they had globular mouthpieces with the reeds down inside; the hautboy was a step between the shawm and the oboe. And the hautboy had come in various stages of development from no keys at all, just finger holes, to half a dozen or so keys. And yes, there'd been a three-keyed version, identical to this one except that it had been light wood instead of dark. Yes, it had been in his teens, in his early teens, that he'd seen it, while he was a freshman in high school. Because he was just getting interested in music and hadn't yet got his first clarinet; he'd still been trying to decide which instrument he wanted to play. That's why the ancient instruments and their history had fascinated him for a brief while. There'd been a book about them in the high-school library and he'd read it. It had said— Good God, it had said that the hautboy had a coarse tone in the lower register and was shrill on the high notes! A flat lie, if this instrument was typical. It was smooth as honey throughout its range; it had a rich full-bodied tone infinitely more pleasing than the thin reediness of an oboe. Better even than a clarinet; only in its lower, or chalumeau, register could a clarinet even approach it.

And Dooley Hanks knew beyond certainty that he had to have an instrument like that, and that he *would* have one, no matter what he had to pay or do to get it.

And with that decision irrevocably made, and with the music still caressing him like a woman and exciting him as no woman had ever excited him, Dooley opened his eyes. And since his head had tilted forward while he had concentrated, the first thing he saw was the very large goblet of red wine that had been placed in front of him. He picked it up and, looking over it, managed to catch the musician's eye; Dooley raised the glass in a silent toast and downed the wine in a single draught.

When he lowered his head after drinking—the wine had tasted unexpectedly good—the musician had turned slightly on the stool and was facing another direction. Well, that gave him a chance to study the man. The musician was tall but thin and frail looking. His age was indeterminate; it could have been anywhere from forty to sixty. He was somewhat seedy in appearance; his threadbare coat did not match his baggy trousers and a garish red and yellow striped muffler hung loosely around his scrawny neck, which had a prominent Adam's apple that bobbed every time he took a breath to play. His tousled hair needed cutting, his face was thin and pinched, and his eyes so light a blue that they looked faded. Only his fingers bore the mark of a master musician, long and slim and gracefully tapered. They danced nimbly in time with the wondrous music they shaped.

Then with a final skirl of high notes that startled Dooley because they went at least half an octave above what he'd thought was the instrument's top range and still had the rich resonance of the lower register, the music stopped.

There were a few seconds of what seemed almost stunned silence, and then applause started and grew. Dooley went with it, and his palms started to smart with pain. The musician, staring straight ahead, didn't seem to notice. And after less than thirty seconds he again raised the instrument to his mouth and the applause died suddenly to silence with the first note he played.

Dooley felt a gentle touch on his shoulder and looked around. The fat little waiter was back. This time he didn't even whisper, just raised his eyebrows interrogatorily. When he'd left with the empty wineglass, Dooley closed his eyes again and gave full attention to the music.

Music? Yes, it was music, but not any *kind* of music he'd ever heard before. Or it was a blend of *all* kinds of music, ancient and modern, jazz and classical, a masterful blend of paradoxes or maybe he meant opposites, sweet and bitter, ice and fire, soft breezes and raging hurricanes, love and hate.

Again when he opened his eyes a filled glass was in front of him. This time he sipped slowly at it. How on Earth had he missed wine all his life? Oh, he'd drunk an occasional glass, but it had never tasted like this wine. Or was it the music that made it taste this way?

The music stopped and again he joined in the hearty applause. This time the musician got down from the stool and acknowledged the applause briefly with a jerky little bow, and then, tucking his instrument under his arm, he walked rapidly across the room—unfortunately not passing near Dooley's table—with an awkward forward-leaning gait. Dooley turned his head to follow with his eyes. The musician sat down at a very small table, a table for one, since it had only one chair, against the opposite wall. Dooley considered taking his own chair over, but decided against it. Apparently the guy wanted to sit alone or he wouldn't have taken that particular table.

Dooley looked around till he caught the little waiter's eye and signaled to him. When he came, Dooley asked him to take a glass of wine to the musician, and also to ask the man if he would care to join him at Dooley's table, to tell him that Dooley too was a musician and would like to get to know him.

"I don't think he will," the waiter told him. "People have tried before and he always politely refused. As for the wine, it is not necessary; several times an evening we pass a hat for him. Someone is starting to do so now, and you may contribute that way if you wish."

"I wish," Dooley told him. "But take him the wine and give him my message anyway, please."

"*Ja, mein Herr.*"

The waiter collected a mark in advance and then went to one of the three tuns and drew a glass of wine and took it to the musician. Dooley, watching, saw the waiter put the glass on the musician's table and, talking, point toward Dooley. So there would be no mistake, Dooley stood up and made a slight bow in their direction.

The musician stood also and bowed back, slightly more deeply and from the waist. But then he turned back to his table and sat down again and Dooley knew his first advance had been declined. Well, there'd be other chances, and other evenings. So, only slightly discomfited, he sat back down again and took another sip of his wine. Yes, even without the music, or at any rate with only the aftereffects of the music, it still tasted wonderful.

The hat came, "For the musician," passed by a stolid red-faced burgher, and Dooley, seeing no large bills in it and not wishing to make himself conspicuous, added two marks from his little pile on the table.

Then he saw a couple getting up to leave from a table for two directly in front of the stool upon which the musician sat to play. Ah, just what he wanted. Quickly finishing his drink and gathering up his change and his clarinet, he moved over to the ringside table as the couple walked away. Not only could he see and hear better, but he was in the ideal spot to intercept the musician with a personal invitation after the next set. And instead of putting it on the floor he put his clarinet case on the table in plain sight, to let the man know that he was not only a fellow musician, which could mean almost anything, but a fellow woodwind player.

A few minutes later he got a chance to signal for another glass of wine and when it was brought he held the little waiter in conversation. "I gather our friend turned down my invitation," he said. "May I ask what his name is?"

"Otto, *mein Herr.*"

"Otto what? Doesn't he have a last name?"

The waiter's eyes twinkled. "I asked him once. Niemand, he told me. Otto Niemand."

Dooley chuckled. *Niemand*, he knew, meant "nobody" in German. "How long has he been playing here?" he asked.

"Oh, just tonight. He travels around. Tonight is the first we've seen him in almost a year. When he comes, it's just for one night and we let him play and pass the hat for him. Ordinarily we don't have music here, it's just a wine cellar."

Dooley frowned. He'd have to make *sure*, then, to make contact tonight.

"Just a wine cellar," the little waiter repeated. "But we also serve sandwiches if you are hungry. Ham, knackwurst, or beer cheese ..."

Dooley hadn't been listening and interrupted. "How soon will he play again? Does he take long between sets?"

"Oh, he plays no more tonight. A minute ago, just as I was bringing your wine, I saw him leave. We may not see him again for a long ..."

But Dooley had grabbed his clarinet case and was running, running as fast as he could make it on a twisting course between tables. Through the door without even bothering to close it, and up the stone steps to the sidewalk. The fog wasn't so thick now, except in patches. But he could see *niemand* in either direction. He stood utterly still to listen. All he could hear for a moment were sounds from the wine cellar, then blessedly someone pulled shut the door he'd left open and in the silence that followed he thought, for a second, that he could hear footsteps to his right, the direction from which he had come.

He had nothing to lose, so he ran that way. There was a twist in the street and then a corner. He stopped and listened again, and—*that* way, around the corner, he thought he heard the steps again and ran toward them. After half a block he could see a figure ahead, too far to recognize but thank God tall and thin; it *could* be the musician. And past the figure, dimly through the fog he could see lights and hear traffic noises. This must be the turn he had missed in trying to follow the hotel clerk's directions for finding the downtown bright lights district, or as near to such as a town this size might have.

He closed the distance to a quarter of a block, opened his mouth to call out to the figure ahead and found that he was too winded to call out. He dropped his gait from a run to a walk. No danger of losing the man now that he was this close to him. Getting his breath back, he closed the distance between them slowly.

He was only a few paces behind the man—and, thank God, it *was* the musician—and was lengthening his strides to come up alongside him and speak when the man stepped down the curb and started diagonally across the street. Just as a speeding car, with what must have been a drunken driver, turned the corner behind them, lurched momentarily, then righted itself on a course bearing straight down on the unsuspecting musician. In sudden reflex action Dooley, who had never knowingly performed a heroic act in his life, dashed into the street and pushed the musician from the path of the car. The impetus of Dooley's charge sent him crashing down on top of the musician and he sprawled breathlessly in this shielding position as the car passed by so close that it sent out rushing fingers of air to tug at his clothing. Dooley raised his head in time to see the two red eyes of its taillights vanishing into the fog a block down the street.

Dooley listened to the drumming roll of his heart in his ears as he rolled aside to free the musician and both men got slowly to their feet.

"Was it close?"

Dooley nodded, swallowed with difficulty. "Like a shave with a straight razor."

The musician had taken his instrument from under his coat and was examining it. "Not broken," he said. But Dooley, realizing that his own hands were empty, whirled around to look for his clarinet case. And saw it. He must have dropped it when he raised his hands to push the musician. A front wheel and a back wheel of the car must each have run over it, for it was flattened at both ends. The case and every section of the clarinet were splintered, useless junk. He fingered it a moment and then walked over and dropped it into the gutter.

The musician came and stood beside him. "A pity," he said softly. "The loss of an instrument is like the loss of a friend."

An idea was coming to Dooley, so he didn't answer, but managed to look sadder than he felt. The loss of the clarinet was a blow in the pocketbook, but not an irrevocable one. He had enough to buy a used, not-so-hot one to start out with and he'd have to work harder and spend less for a while until he could get a really good one like the one he'd lost. Three hundred it had cost him. Dollars, not marks. But he'd get another clarinet all right. Right now, though, he was much *much* more interested in getting the German musician's hautboy, or one just like it. Three hundred dollars, not marks, was peanuts to what he'd give for that. And if the old boy felt responsible and offered ...

"It was my fault," the musician said. "For not looking. I wish I could afford to offer to buy you a new— It was a clarinet, was it not?"

"Yes," Dooley said, trying to sound like a man on the brink of despair instead of one on the brink of the greatest discovery of his life. "Well, what's kaput is kaput. Shall we go somewhere for a drink, and have a wake?"

"My room," said the musician. "I have wine there. And we'll have privacy so I can play a tune or two I do not play in public. Since you too are a musician." He chuckled. *"Eine Kleine Nachtmusik,* eh? A little nightmusic— but not Mozart's; my own."

Dooley managed to conceal his elation and to nod as though he didn't care much. "Okay, Otto Niemand. My name's Dooley Hanks."

The musician chuckled. "Call me Otto, Dooley. I use no last name, so Niemand is what I tell any who insist on my having one. Come, Dooley; it isn't far."

It wasn't far, just a block down the next side street. The musician turned in at an aged and darkened house. He opened the front door with a key and then used a small pocket flashlight to guide them up a wide but uncarpeted staircase. The house, he explained on the way, was unoccupied and scheduled to be torn down, so there was no electricity. But the owner had given him a key and permission to use it while the house still stood; there were a few pieces of furniture here and there, and he got by. He liked being in a house all by himself because he could play at any hour of the night without bothering anyone trying to sleep.

He opened the door of a room and went in. Dooley waited in the doorway until the musician had lighted an oil lamp on the dresser, and then followed him in. Besides the dresser there was only a straight chair, a rocker and a single bed.

"Sit down, Dooley," the musician told him. "You'll find the bed more comfortable than the straight chair. If I'm going to play for us, I'd like the rocker." He was taking two glasses and a bottle out of the top drawer of the dresser. "I see I erred. I thought it was wine I had left; it is brandy. But that is better, no?"

"That is better, yes," said Dooley. He could hardly restrain himself from asking permission right away to try the hautboy himself, but felt it would be wiser to wait until brandy had done a little mellowing. He sat down on the bed.

The musician handed Dooley a huge glass of brandy; he went back to the dresser and got his own glass and, with his instrument in his other hand, went to the rocker. He raised the glass. "To music, Dooley."

"To *Nachtmusik*," said Dooley. He drank off a goodly sip, and it burned like fire, but it was good brandy. Then he could wait no longer. "Otto, mind if I look at that instrument of yours? It's a hautboy, isn't it?"

"A hautboy, yes. Not many would recognize it, even musicians. But I'm sorry, Dooley. I can't let you handle it. Or play it, if you were going to ask that, too. I'm sorry, but that's the way it is, my friend."

Dooley nodded and tried not to look glum. The night is young, he told himself; another drink or two of brandy that size may mellow him. Meanwhile, he might as well find out as much as he could.

"Is it—your instrument, I mean, a real one? I mean, a medieval one? Or a modern reproduction?"

"I made it myself, by hand. A labor of love. But, my friend, stay with the clarinet, I advise you. Especially do not ask me to make you one like this; I could not. I have not worked with tools, with a lathe, for many years. I would find my skill gone. Are you skillful with tools?"

Dooley shook his head. "Can't drive a nail. Where could I find one, even something like yours?"

The musician shrugged. "Most are in museums, not obtainable. You might find a few collections of ancient instruments in private hands, and buy one at an exorbitant price—and you might even find it still playable. But, my friend, be wise and stay with your clarinet. I advise you strongly."

Dooley Hanks could not say what he was thinking, and didn't speak.

"Tomorrow we will talk about finding you a new clarinet," the musician said. "Tonight, let us forget it. And forget your wish for a hautboy, even your wish to play this one—yes, I know you asked only to touch and handle, but could you hold it in your hands without wanting to put it to your lips? Let us drink some more and then I will play for us. *Prosit!*"

They drank again. The musician asked Dooley to tell something about himself, and Dooley did. Almost everything about himself that mattered except the one thing that mattered most—his obsession and the fact that he was making up his mind to kill for it if there was no other way.

There was no hurry, Dooley thought; he had all night. So he talked and they drank. They were halfway through their third round—and the last round, since it finished the bottle—of brandy, when he ran out of talk and there was silence.

And with a gentle smile the musician drained his glass, put it down, and put both hands on his instrument. "Dooley ... would you like some girls?"

Dooley suddenly found himself a little drunk. But he laughed. "Sure," he said. "Whole roomful of girls. Blonds, brunettes, redheads." And then because he couldn't let a squarehead square beat him at drinking, he killed the rest of his brandy too, and lay back across the single bed with his shoulders and head against the wall. "Bring 'em on, Otto."

Otto nodded, and began to play. And suddenly the excruciating, haunting beauty of the music Dooley had last heard in the wine cellar was back. But a new tune this time, a tune that was lilting and at the same time sensual. It was so beautiful that it hurt, and Dooley thought for a moment fiercely: damn him, he's playing *my* instrument; he owes me that for the clarinet I lost. And almost he decided to get up and *do* something about it because jealousy and envy burned in him like flames.

But before he could move, gradually he became aware of another sound somewhere, above or under the music. It seemed to come from outside, on the sidewalk below, and it was a rapid click-click-clickety-click for all the world like the sound of high heels, and then it was closer and it *was* the sound of heels, many heels, on wood, on the uncarpeted stairway, and then—and this was all in time with the music—there was a gentle tap-tap at the door. Dreamily, Dooley turned his head toward the door as it swung open and girls poured into the room and surrounded him, engulfing him in their physical warmth and exotic perfumes. Dooley gazed in blissful disbelief and then suspended the disbelief; if this were illusion, let it be. As long as— He reached out with both hands, and yes, they could be touched as well as seen. There were brown-eyed brunettes, green-eyed blonds and black-eyed redheads. And blue-eyed brunettes, brown-eyed blonds and green-eyed redheads. They were all sizes from petite to statuesque and they were all beautiful.

Somehow the oil lamp seemed to dim itself without completely going out, and the music, growing wilder now, seemed to come from somewhere else, as though the musician were no longer in the room, and Dooley thought that that was considerate of him. Soon he was romping with the girls in reckless abandon, sampling here and there like a small boy in a candy store. Or a Roman at an orgy, but the Romans never had it quite so good, nor the gods on Mount Olympus.

At last, wonderfully exhausted, he lay back on the bed, and surrounded by soft, fragrant girlflesh, he slept.

And woke, suddenly and completely and soberly, he knew not how long later. But the room was cold now; perhaps that was what had wakened him. He opened his eyes and saw that he was alone on the bed and that the lamp was again (or still?) burning normally. And the musician was there too, he saw when he raised his head, sound asleep in the rocking chair. The instrument was gripped tightly in both hands and that long red and yellow striped muffler was still around his scrawny neck, his head tilted backward against the rocker's back.

Had it really happened? Or had the music put him to sleep, so he'd dreamed it about the girls? Then he put the thought aside; it didn't matter. What mattered, all that mattered, was that he was not leaving here without the hautboy. But did he *have* to kill to get it? Yes, he did. If he simply stole it from the sleeping man he wouldn't stand a chance of getting out of Germany with it. Otto even knew his right name, as it was on his passport, and they'd be waiting for him at the border. Whereas if he left a dead man behind him, the body—in an abandoned house—might not be found for weeks or months, not until he was safe back in America. And by then any evidence against him, even his possession of the instrument, would be too thin to warrant extradition back to Europe. He would claim that Otto had given him the instrument to replace the clarinet he'd lost in saving Otto's life. He'd have no proof of that, but they'd have no proof to the contrary.

Quickly and quietly he got off the bed and tiptoed over to the man sleeping in the rocker and stood looking down at him. It would be easy, for the means were at hand. The scarf, already around the thin neck and crossed once in front, the ends dangling. Dooley tiptoed around behind the rocker and reached over the thin shoulders and took a tight grip on each end of the scarf and pulled them apart with all his strength. And held them so. The musician must have been older and more frail than Dooley had thought. His struggles were feeble. And even dying he held onto his instrument with one hand and clawed ineffectually at the scarf only with the other. He died quickly.

Dooley felt for a heartbeat first to make sure and then pried the dead fingers off the instrument. And held it himself at last.

His hands held it, and trembled with eagerness. When would it be safe for him to try it? Not back at his hotel, in the middle of the night, waking other guests and drawing attention to himself.

Why, here and now, in this abandoned house, would be the safest and best chance he'd have for a long time, before he was safely out of the country maybe. Here and now, in this house, before he took care of fingerprints on anything he might have touched and erased any other traces of his presence he might find or think of. Here and now, but softly so as not to waken any sleeping neighbors, in case they might hear a difference between his first efforts and those of the instrument's original owner.

So he'd play softly, at least at first, and quit right away if the instrument made with the squeaks and ugly noises so easy to produce on any unmastered instrument. But he had the strangest feeling that it wouldn't happen that way to him. He knew already how to manage a double reed; once in New York he'd shared an apartment with an oboe player and had tried out his instrument with the thought of getting one himself, to double on. He'd finally decided not to because he preferred playing with small combos and an oboe fitted only into large groups. And the fingering? He looked down and saw that his fingers had fallen naturally in place over the fingerholes or poised above the keys. He moved them and watched them start, seemingly of their own volition, a little finger-dance. He made them stop moving and wonderingly put the instrument to his lips and breathed into it softly. And out came, softly, a clear, pure middle-register tone. As rich and vibrant a note as any Otto had played. Cautiously he raised a finger and then another and found himself starting a diatonic scale. And, on a hunch, made himself forget his fingers and just *thought* the scale and let his fingers take over and they did, every tone pure. He *thought* a scale in a different key and played it, then an arpeggio. He didn't know the fingerings, but his fingers did.

He could play it, and he would.

He might as well make himself comfortable, he decided despite his mounting excitement. He crossed back to the bed and lay back across it, as he had lain while listening to the musician play, with his head and shoulders braced up against the wall behind it. And put the instrument back to his mouth and played, this time not caring about volume. Certainly if neighbors heard, they'd think it was Otto, and they would be accustomed to hearing Otto play late at night.

He thought of some of the tunes he'd heard in the wine cellar, and his fingers played them. In ecstasy, he relaxed and played as he had never played a clarinet. Again, as when Otto had played, he was struck by the purity and richness of the tone, so like the chalumeau register of his own clarinet, but extending even to the highest notes.

He played, and a thousand sounds blended into one. Again the sweet melody of paradoxes, black and white blending into a beautiful radiant gray of haunting music.

And then, seemingly without transition, he found himself playing a strange tune, one he'd never heard before. But one that he knew instinctively belonged to this wonderful instrument. A calling, beckoning tune, as had been the music Otto had played when the girls, real or imaginary, had click-clicked their way to him, but different this—was it a sinister instead of a sensual feeling underlying it?

But it was beautiful and he couldn't have stopped the dance of his fingers or stopped giving it life with his breath if he'd tried.

And then, over or under the music, he heard another sound. Not this time a click-click of high heels but a scraping, scrabbling sound, as of thousands of tiny clawed feet. And he saw them as they spilled suddenly out of many holes in the woodwork that he had not before noticed, and ran to the bed and jumped upon it. And with paralyzing suddenness the bits and pieces fell into place and by an effort that was to be the last of his life Dooley tore the accursed instrument from his mouth, and opened his mouth to scream. But they were all around him now, all over him: great ones, tawny ones, small ones, lean ones, black ones ... And before he could scream out of his opened mouth the largest black rat, the one who led them, leaped up and closed its sharp teeth in the end of his tongue and held on, and the scream a-borning gurgled into silence.

And The Sound of feasting lasted far into the night in Hamelin town.

Editor's Notes and Acknowledgements

This book was produced with the help of many people. Patrick Nielsen Hayden and Mark Olson introduced me to PageMaker. Tony Lewis and a group of NESFen provided proofreading. Rick Katze provided much of the scanning for the book. Scanning and OCR of "Happy Ending" and "The Hatchetman" was by Bill Shawcross of Rotten Apple Press. And a special thanks to Joel Polowin, who provided electronic text for two of the original collections of Brown's work.

Geri Sullivan provided me with a steady stream of wise advice about both book design and PageMaker.

Final proofreading was done by Mark and Priscilla Olson.

The cover painting for this collection is by Bob Eggleton, whose enthusiasm for the project was inspiring. The book jacket was designed by Geri Sullivan. The NESFA shield on the jacket was digitized by Jeff Schalles.

Thanks to everyone who made this collection possible.

The choice and order of the material in this collection was as follows: As the subtitle says, this is intended as a complete collection of the shorter SF (which includes fantasy) of Fredric Brown. But deciding whether one of his stories falls into that category is often difficult. The rule followed, in general, was that if it had been previously collected in one of the prior SF collections, then it would always be included, no matter how little it seemed to be SF. If the work had not appeared in the SF collections, and had appeared in one of the mystery collections, it probably wasn't SF. And some of his stories have never appeared in any collections; I included the ones that seemed to be SF. I didn't include two novelettes, "Gateway to Glory" (never collected) and "Gateway to Darkness" (collected in *Daymares*), which were rewritten and incorporated into the novel *Rogue in Space*.

The stories appear in order of their first publication.

Several of the stories are collaborations. I followed the prior publishing history in determining whether or not to note the Mack Reynolds collaborations with the story. The complete list is "Six-Legged Svengali," "Dark Interlude," "The Switcheroo," "Cartoonist," "The Gamblers," "The Hatchetman," "Me and Flapjack and the Martians," and "Happy Ending."

Superlative SF Available
from NESFA Press